Pindlebryth of Lenland

The Five Artifacts

Christopher D. Ochs

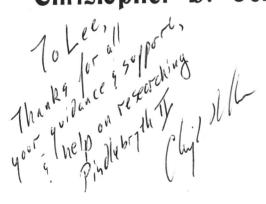

To Lee,
Thanks for all
your guidance & support,
& help on researching
Pindlebryth II

ISBN: 1500257362
ISBN-13: 978-1500257361

EDITORS

Sean Dolbow, Susan Kling Monroe

COVER ART & ILLUSTRATIONS

Elizabeth Dolbow

DEDICATION

Judy Iobst
Cory Clayton
William Hankins
Mark Klee
Gail Ferguson
Mom
the Hon. Gay Elwell
Friends Gone Too Soon

ACKNOWLEDGMENTS

Thanks to the Beta Reader Corps:
Karl Monroe, T. Epstein, S. Wahlberg
for their patience, fortitude, and wit.

Pindlebryth of Lenland
The Five Artifacts

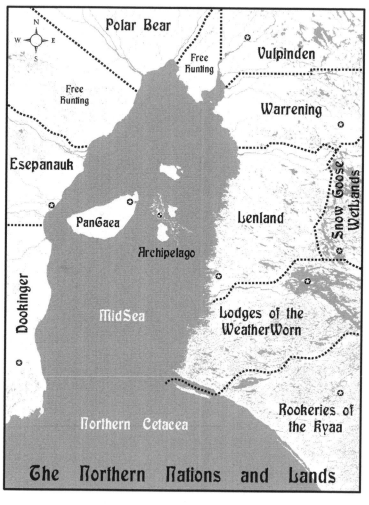

The Northern Nations and Lands

☼ – CityState(s)   ✺ – Vulcanis Major

The Quickening Spirit has bestowed upon the Nation of Lemmings an ability like no other. This shall hereafter be known as the Name of Power. Each Name is foretold by a dream common to the entire Lemming nation the evening before the birth of the recipient. The recipient of the Name of Power also receives several boons commensurate with it: a lifetime extended long beyond the years of a normal Lemming, an immunity to natural disease, and a resistance to lesser magicks. Lastly, any and all recipients may live under the protection in the Royal City as they choose, in order to attain their desired place in the world and possibly their true destiny.

Along with His Gift, the Quickening Spirit has bestowed unto all Lemmings the land of Lenland: East of the Midland Sea, West of the Snow Goose WetLands, South of the Great Warrens of the Arctic Hare, North of the WeatherWorn Lake Lodges, and the Kyaa and his Rookeries.

None may revoke these legacies.

Gazelikus, Wizard to the First Royal Court of Lenland

I - The True Name of Power

Pindlebryth could not recall how he fell asleep at his desk. His stylus fell off the blotter as he picked his head up from between the pages of a textbook. He squinted at the last entry he had made in his thesis notebook – not only did he fall asleep in mid-thought, but his ink stylus had also leaked, obscuring much of the last page. He tried to blot away the ink that stained his right paw, but it had long since dried. As the cobwebs of dreamless sleep fell away, he realized it was not lamplight by which he read his notes. The mid-morning sun beamed slivers of light through the lace curtains framing the east window.

It was most unusual for him to fall asleep during his work, and the fact that he could not even recall being tired last night perplexed him. But such thoughts quickly evaporated when he remembered his University classes and appointments for the coming day.

He collected himself up from the desk, straightening his fur and muzzle with his clean paw. He then closed his evening jacket as he shivered against the morning chill, as none of the apartment fireplaces had been started. He pulled the velvet bell strap near the hallway door to call for TwitchNose to bring breakfast and for BlackEars to prepare his student's robes. He had fully straightened out his workspace and bookshelves, when he realized no one had yet answered his call.

Pindlebryth opened the door from his study and called aloud to his staff. No answer was forthcoming. Muttering to himself while rubbing the sleep from his eyes, he called again up and down both stairwells. Silence replied, except for a strong spring breeze exhaling through the ajar foyer door. He tromped down the stairs and closed the front door, and went through the dining room to the kitchen in a huff.

Those rooms too, were empty and cold. Not even a morning kettle of tea had been started. He glanced outside the kitchen window panes, then continued to search the ground floor. Suddenly feeling quite alone, he climbed the stairs to his private rooms, then the next flight to the servant's quarters. No sign of BlackEars or TwitchNose was to be found. He was about to descend the steps again, when he paused to look over his shoulder, as if something amiss were calling his attention back to their rooms. Examining both their quarters more closely, it was apparent the beds had been slept in, and the covers were thrown open. However, their uniforms and livery were still unused on heavily laden clothing trees.

What happened to the two of them? Did they go outside in the middle of the night with only their bedclothes? Puzzled and concerned for their safety, he proceeded down to the second floor, and began to dress himself for the outside world.

His ears twitched as he heard a carriage approach on the private lane leading from the street. He descended the stairs to the foyer, as frantic pounding came at the front door. He opened it to see his old friend leaning on the door jamb and gasping for breath. A Hooded Crow, the bluish tinge in his black feathers about his head and neck clashed with the red scarf hastily thrown about his neck.

"Hakayaa, your feathers look better than my fur. I don't know about you, but I'm famished. I'd like to invite you in for some breakfast, but I can't receive you properly just now. I can't seem to account for the whereabouts of my staff. Perhaps we can go out for a quick breakfast."

"You're still here!" Hakayaa burst through the doorway as he clasped Pindlebryth's shoulders.

"Whatever do you mean?"

"Then you haven't heard, Pindie? All the Lemmings in PanGaea are either missing, or..." he hesitated. In a slightly quieter voice, he completed his thought, "...or they've been found dead along the Eastern Bay."

"Quickening Spirit! Have you any news of BlackEars or TwitchNose?"

"I'm afraid not." Grabbing Pindlebryth's greatcoat from the rack near the door, he said, "If you wish, I can take you to the local constabulary to report your missing staff, and perchance likewise hear some news about your fellow Lemmings." Pindlebryth bundled up against the strengthening wind. Although a warming spring Sun was rising, dark threatening clouds began to form far off towards the sea to occlude it.

The carriage wended its way through alleys then the main thoroughfare to the police station. Progress was painfully slow, as all the streets were choked with both vehicular and pedestrian traffic. Criers for *The Facade* and other local yellow journals bellowed at each corner, attracting large crowds which clogged every intersection. Buildings were surrounded by throngs of Beaver, Ferret, Arctic Hare, Crow, Arctic Fox and a smattering of Raccoon, Otter and Badger, all of whom were milling about frantically yet aimlessly, like a hive of bees without a queen. There were whose who were visibly upset, and demanding to know where their Lemming friends and neighbors had gone. They contended against small but boisterous knots of folk who were happily gossiping amongst themselves with morbid speculations.

"Lords Below, Haka! You're right! Not a single Lemming to be found. What in the world happened? The whole CityState is thrown into confusion," marveled Pindlebryth.

Hakayaa swiveled his head out the window, looking up and down the press of the crowd.

"Feh! I was hoping to avoid the crowd before it got too bad. It was difficult enough to swim through it on the way to your house in the first place!" He craned his head higher to see as far as he could down the street, then sat back in the carriage to straighten his ruffled plumage. "If the crowd saw you or any other Lemming about, the curious would not leave us alone. So when we arrive at the police station, I suggest you turn your collar up against prying eyes, lest we get mobbed."

Constables were trying to control traffic and maintain the peace at several intersections along the way, but were having a rough go of it.

As they passed one constable, Hakayaa leapt out of his seat. "Wait here!" he said, as he leaned out of the window, and snatched the constable's hat. The furious Beaver immediately launched himself after Hakayaa. He was halfway through the window when Hakayaa offered him back his hat as if he had saved it from an errant gust of wind. "My good fellow, this Lemming needs to get to the nearest police station as quickly as possible. Can you help us?"

The bobby's scornful expression quickly switched to surprise, as he grumbled resentfully and snatched his hat back. The constable then stood on the runner, and blew his whistle with three long blasts, and sliced the air forwards and backwards with his arm. Officers at each intersection snapped around, and began to clear the right of way as best they could. Pindlebryth's ears folded down against the painfully shrill whistle.

When Pindlebryth and Hakayaa finally arrived at the station, Pindlebryth upended his collar and dodged his head as his Crow friend suggested. The two exited the carriage, and climbed the concrete stairs. The Beaver constable opened the heavily hasped doors with barred windows, and ushered them through the main lobby into the duty office. When in the safety of the building's interior, Pindlebryth turned down his collar and searched for someone in authority. The Beaver pointed him with a grunt to a central desk.

A flurry of activity filled the office of uniformed Otter, Raccoon, and a handful of Badger. But the cacophony of hustle and bustle fell precipitously to a deathly silence, as more and more of the officers stopped their work and discussions to stare at the newcomers.

Pindlebryth was warily self-conscious as he stepped forward. "I need to I report two missing persons," he declared as he stood in front of the large desk.

The Raccoon desk sergeant looked past Pindlebryth's shoulder, as a voice behind him cleared his throat.

"Good day, sir," said an Otter. His epaulet of command was conspicuous. "Inspector SwimQuick at your service. Who do you wish to report missing?"

Pindlebryth's professional interest was piqued by the Otter's accent in common tongue, but he knew he desperately needed not to be distracted. "My staff has disappeared overnight."

"I see. Please step inside my office, and you can describe the details." He beckoned a Badger constable to accompany them into his office, after Pindlebryth and Hakayaa entered. The inspector shut behind him the glass door with his name and rank painted in gold, and closed the louvered blinds as he invited the pair to sit. Afterwards he sat behind his desk, and asked, "Before we begin, I'm sure I need not tell you that we are dealing with a bit of an emergency. Although that leaves us stretched a little thin at this moment, we shall help as best we can." He dipped his pen in an inkwell, and began scribbling while talking quite mechanically, "What is your name and occupation, sir?"

"Prince Pindlebryth of Lenland. I'm studying for my doctorate in languages at PanGaea University."

"Indeed." He interrupted his writing, as he regarded Pindlebryth with a raised eyebrow. "You will have to excuse me, then, if I do not observe all the niceties, for time is short.

When did you notice that your staff had disappeared?"

"Of that I'm not exactly sure. I fell asleep late last night, and when I woke up, they were nowhere to be found."

"All right. Please describe your activities the preceding evening. Specifically, where were you before you returned home?"

"My good friend here, Hakayaa, and I were at the Roasted Sesame having a late dinner after we finished our respective classes and duties for the day. We were discussing our plans for the coming year, and eventual matriculation. After coffee and a liqueur, we left the restaurant about an hour before midnight. Hakayaa left me at my apartment, and I went upstairs to my study to complete notes to teach my advisor's class the coming morning. TwitchNose had just finished baking quickbread for breakfast." Pindlebryth momentarily closed his eyes and took a deep breath. A slight smile passed his lips as he recalled the sweet aroma. "She then checked on me in the study, and retired for the night. I switched to work on my thesis, as BlackEars began to close and secure the outside doors for the night. Then he, too, retired."

"TwitchNose and BlackEars," the Otter rambled as he wrote.

"Yes. My housekeeper and butler, amongst other duties."

"Are there any other staff missing?"

"No, they are the only two I require."

Pindlebryth held up his ink-stained paw for a moment or two, trying again to remember how he fell asleep. His whiskers twitched as he grew more puzzled that he still had no memory of feeling tired the night before. He turned his paw to show the inspector.

"The last thing I remember is writing in my notebook. It was mid-morning when I rose from my desk. I was the only one in my apartment, and the front door was wide open. The staff's quarters were slept in, but their uniforms were still hung on their posts. It's as if they both left in the middle of the night in their bedclothes."

Hakayaa was silent during Pindlebryth's description, but he eyed the Badger standing next to them with concern. The formidable constable had his hand on his nightstick and seemed ready for violence. SwimQuick finished recording his notes on his tablet, and focused on Pindlebryth.

"There are others who can corroborate your whereabouts?"

"Yes, sir," interjected Hakayaa. "It is as Prince Pindlebryth has said. The maitre'd at the Roasted Sesame knows both of us well. I can vouch that we went our separate ways after we arrived at his apartments about a quarter before midnight. I then continued to my own residence. My exceedingly observant landlady will no doubt corroborate that."

Inspector SwimQuick took a moment to pull the topmost sheet of paper from his in-box, and read the list written there. Pindlebryth could see that it had several columns of data, followed by a single column of annotations, but for only some entries. SwimQuick sighed and stolidly faced Pindlebryth.

"Sir, I'm very sorry, but there is no easy way to tell you this. Both your staff were found last night, washed up on the boulders of the Eastern Bay's shield wall, along with several other Lemmings."

Pindlebryth was unabashedly saddened. "Lords Above... Are you sure?"

"Quite so. They have been positively identified by the constable that frequents your street. Our coroner has determined the cause of death was drowning."

Hakayaa leaned over to the prince. "Pindlebryth, I would advise that you speak carefully from now on. I think the police are not just taking information, but are also taking your statement." Hakayaa sat back upright and eyed SwimQuick with an emotionless mask.

"Your friend may have a valid concern. But you may put yourself at ease; you are by no means a suspect of any malfeasance at this point. However, we are left with one salient fact – you are the only living Lemming we have seen all day."

"Quickening Spirit! So it's true!" blurted Pindlebryth. "All the Lemmings in PanGaea are affected so?"

"Excepting yourself, I'm afraid so. I am unfortunately required to say that we may have to treat you as a state's witness. In any event, we are at least obligated to provide you protection until we get to the root of this matter. Because of this, I must ask you not to leave the station. We will make every effort to make you as comfortable as possible. Considering the circumstances, I'm sure you'll agree this is a necessary precaution."

Before either Hakayaa or Pindlebryth could protest, the sergeant from the front desk unceremoniously opened the inspector's door. Past him strode a Raccoon in a highly decorated uniform, including a badge identifying him as the Chief of Detectives.

Inspector SwimQuick abruptly stood up from his chair, as his stylus clattered on his desk. Both he and the Badger constable snapped to attention with quick salutes, while the Chief calmly interjected, "Thank you, inspector." He returned the salute with a minimum of energy.

"Apologies for the inconvenience, M'Lord. Chief RingWash at your service," he said with a resigned tiredness to Pindlebryth. "Inspector SwimQuick is essentially correct. Considering the calamity befallen your people, it is wisest that we do everything we can to assure your continued safety, until we better understand exactly what has taken place and what caused this tragedy. However, I believe we can afford you better amenities than we can offer you here at the station." Turning again to his subordinate, he continued, "Inspector SwimQuick, have M'Lord Pindlebryth escorted to his residence. Make the arrangements to have his premises guarded around the clock, until we receive instructions from our government how to proceed."

"I understand, sir," SwimQuick said perfunctorily. The Badger bristled with disdain, though still at attention.

"Sergeant, have Constable QuillBane here and another officer escort M'Lord to his home. Arrange for another pair of officers to relieve them in a couple of hours," ordered the inspector.

"My carriage is at your disposal," added the chief.

Pindlebryth cursorily thanked the chief and the inspector and quickly followed the sergeant and constable out of the office. Hakayaa said nothing, but only nodded to them, still with a look of suspicion in his eye.

The sergeant corralled another uniformed officer, and forged through the main staff room. He was about to escort the group of four out of the main lobby, when he realized he was missing someone. He peered around the room, and froze when he spied Hakayaa still standing near the inspector's closed door.

"Master BlueHood!" he angrily exclaimed. "If you would be so kind to join us, we can be on our way."

Hakayaa complied, and strolled past the glaring sergeant. Before he opened the front doors, Constable QuillBane asked the friends to stay inside, until he was able to requisition the chief's carriage. Almost immediately, he returned and shepherded them into the conveyance emblazoned with a police insignia, already waiting for them. Hakayaa quickly reminded Pindlebryth to turn up his collar again. Once inside, QuillBane sat facing them in the cabin, while the other officer rode outside with the driver. Several blocks passed by without a word from any of the three passengers.

Pindlebryth eventually remarked to Hakayaa, "You seem much more mistrustful of the police than I expected. Why were you dawdling about the inspector's door?"

Constable QuillBane sat quietly fuming at the Crow across the cabin. Hakayaa leaned back and crossed his legs, somewhat pleased with himself. "I thought I might pick up some useful information, while the inspector and chief had their little conclave. And I was right! Didn't you find it curious the inspector wasn't aware of your name, title and station, but the chief was? Almost as curious as the sergeant already knowing my name!"

"I assumed that was because you and the police have had such a close relationship in the past!" Pindlebryth said blithely.

"Quite..." Hakayaa responded slowly, eyeing QuillBane again nervously. "As it turns out, you are not alone in this crisis. There are a few other Lemmings who have survived the night."

"Really! Who?" Pindlebryth exclaimed.

"Your country's ambassador to PanGaea for one. She personally contacted the chief to ensure your safety."

"Quentain, I believe is her name," Pindlebryth said haltingly as he searched his memory.

"Yes, that was it! There were one or two others, but all their names were unfamiliar to me. Their names were that Lemming prattling that makes no sense to me. Now, TwitchNose – there's a *proper* Lemming name!"

"Ah," Pindlebryth said slowly, as he tried to absorb what Hakayaa was saying. "Then it seems that all who survived have Names, like I do. Oh, poor TwitchNose," he sighed, pouting as his shoulders sagged.

Though the constables directing traffic gave priority to their police carriage over the entire distance, it was only a marginally quicker trip back to Pindlebryth's apartments than before. Hakayaa was obviously more fidgety than Pindlebryth, who stared out the window with concern and bewilderment.

What a momentous day it had been, Pindlebryth reflected:

first he fell asleep as if he were drugged; then his staff mysteriously disappeared; next he learned all his fellow Lemmings were taken by some nameless force; then it was confirmed his staff was listed among the dead; lastly, he was to be secluded away for an indeterminate period of time. He started out the day merely being concerned for his own small responsibilities and welfare, but now was faced with several much larger problems.

His mind reeled at the possibilities of what awaited him in Lenland. He sat up with a start.

Names! His parents, the King and Queen!

"I must get back home! I've got to find out what has happened to my family! To all of Lenland!"

Hakayaa's beak clattered together for a moment, as the carriage crossed from smooth paving to cobblestone. "Quite right," he said as his eyes widened with alarm. "We need to get you on your way as soon as possible."

Pindlebryth flopped back against his seat, looking irritated. He crossed his arms, and set his shoulders hunched together. "But I cannot."

"But why? Surely you're not concerned about University! I'm sure they're closed, like almost everything else, considering the state of things!"

"No, of course not!" Pindlebryth berated his friend. "Aside from the fact I do not have any transportation to Lenland, there is still the matter of these gentlemen riding with us," he said, pointing a thumb at QuillBane. "They have their instructions to keep me bottled up on PanGaea."

"But you have diplomatic immunity, correct? Can't you just traipse off to Lenland when you like? As for transport, I'm sure I can whip something up."

After it achieved the cobblestone roads, the carriage made easy progress using its police escort and by avoiding the main thoroughfares. The carriage turned one final corner to Pindlebryth's apartments.

"You heard the inspector and the chief, Hakayaa," Pindlebryth said. "I'm under their protection. My political status doesn't enter into it anymore. I cannot leave until they, or someone from Lenland with authority here in PanGaea, says I may. I don't expect either of those things will happen anytime soon."

Pindlebryth looked wistfully out his window as the carriage

rolled up to his empty home away from home. Observing this, Hakayaa offered, "Shall I see you inside? Perhaps I can keep you company for a while."

Pindlebryth nodded gloomily. The carriage shuddered to a halt, and the two colleagues entered the apartment, while QuillBane and the other officer assumed positions outside the front door.

"Perhaps I can fix something for you to eat. It's long past lunch," suggested Hakayaa, as he closed the outer door and untied his scarf. "Those inconsiderate bumpkins at the constabulary didn't even offer you a cup of tea! I may not know my way about the kitchen, but I'm sure I can find something."

After spending so much time away from his house, the aroma of last night's quickbread still lingered faintly, but still announced itself plainly. Normally, Pindlebryth never passed up the chance for a piece or two of TwitchNose's delicacy, but this day he did not care for any.

"Thank you no, Haka. I've lost my appetite."

But his friend would not be put off. "Then what do you want to do? Tell me how I can help. I am at your command!" he bowed with an exaggerated flourish, trying to raise his friend's spirits.

Pindlebryth stood in the foyer, still wearing his greatcoat. He looked up the stairs, at the door of his study. "You mentioned the University. Maybe I'll just work on my thesis, to take my mind off of things," he said pensively.

Hakayaa sighed with mock exasperation, as he pulled the greatcoat off of Pindlebryth's back and hung it in the foyer. "No, no, no – that just won't do! Listen, are you going to be all right by yourself for a little while?" the Crow said as he hung his scarf next to Pindlebryth's coat. "I'll go see if there is some way I can speed things up, to get you back home. Meanwhile, it's a good idea to keep yourself busy. But not with University nonsense! Instead, get yourself packed and ready to go."

Hakayaa opened the door, and marched past the two officers.

"Speed things up?" Pindlebryth called after his friend. "But you saw the traffic!"

"Oh come now, Pindie!" Hakayaa snorted with disbelief as he spread his wings and preened himself with a quick single pass.

"What about your scarf?"

"I would lose it along the way. This is not my usual flying attire, but I'm sure the society editor of *The Facade* will forgive me!" He flapped once then twice to test the air, then firmly pointed a wing at QuillBane.

"Keep a close eye on M'Lord," he said in hushed tones. "He shouldn't be left entirely alone right now." He saluted the officers on the incorrect side intentionally, then launched himself into the air.

QuillBane growled and ground his teeth at the receding Crow, but he followed his suggestion nonetheless. He ordered his fellow officer to remain outside, as he stepped inside and closed the door. "I'll be here, if M'Lord needs me." He stationed himself beside the door, and kept watch through the foyer window.

Pindlebryth climbed the stairs to his rooms. He looked into his study – everything was as he left it this morning. He stood there quite a while lost in thought, reminiscing about so many memories in this house that had become his second home. He wondered if he could bring himself to stay in this house, or if he should move to a new one.

He took a deep breath, and put such thoughts out of his head – there would be time to mourn and decide later. But now, he had to concentrate on returning to his real home. He went to his bedroom, while he prepared a mental list of what to pack.

Although Pindlebryth preferred to dress himself when away from home, BlackEars still happily had taken charge of the actual contents and organization of the wardrobe. As a result, Pindlebryth consumed a considerable amount of time finding everything he wanted to pack for his return home. Merely finding a small trunk for his belongings also proved to be quite the task.

He had almost finished his packing, when he heard the foyer door open downstairs, and Hakayaa's voice as he taunted QuillBane. The Crow hopped up the stairs, calling Pindlebryth's name excitedly, until they met in the hallway.

"That fool Beaver! I told him to keep an eye on you!"

"As you can see, I'm quite all right," Pindlebryth said, trying to calm his friend. "Any new developments?"

"Yes! I met with this Quentain you mentioned, and she tells me one of your Royal Guard has just arrived at the embassy from Lenland. She's tending to the paperwork for your immediate release. The guard will probably be right behind me. Are you packed?"

"Lords Above! He must have made the trip in record time! That means I'll need my riding gear. I'll be right back!"

Pindlebryth dashed across the hall to the guest bedroom, which he had partly converted to a trophy room. A few awards for sharpshooting and show riding hung on the wall. He reflected that he was seldom in this room, but TwitchNose kept the room immaculate. He gathered his favorite crossbow, a quiver full of quarls, his saddle bag and holster, all hung on pegs under his awards. A chest of drawers and closet that normally would have been for overnight guests, instead was half-filled with riding jerkins, chaps and other gear.

Pindlebryth slung the bag and his riding clothes over his shoulder, and crossed the hallway again to his bedroom. He deposited his gear on the bed, then dove into the trunk, to glean only those absolute necessities that would fit in the saddle bags. Hakayaa had disappeared for a few minutes, but soon returned from the first floor with a small package wrapped in a ragged tablecloth from the staff's eating table.

"Get the ladder to the roof, would you? It's in the hatch above the stairs," requested Pindlebryth, as he changed into his jerkin and chaps.

Hakayaa went to the topmost floor and unfolded the ladder recessed in the ceiling. He climbed up, unlocked the hatchway and surveyed the rooftop. He quickly returned, reporting, "I think I see him coming. He's got another bird in tow." He assisted Pindlebryth in carrying his belongings up to floor above and ultimately the roof.

"Thanks for all your help, Haka. I would be lost today without your assistance and counsel."

"You're more than welcome, Pindie." Hakayaa pulled the ladder up by its guide rope, and closed the rooftop cover. He regarded Pindlebryth with sad introspection. "The next time I see you, I fear it will be long after these days at PanGaea. I might not be able to treat you so familiarly."

"Come now, Haka! You will always be welcome in my house, be it a humble university apartment, or a palatial estate. Next I see you, I expect to address you as Doctor of History. I also expect to see the results after your final molt, and your full abilities as the Quickening Spirit gave your family. I ask one last favor – inform the authorities they are allowed to search these premises to help solve the mystery of my people's demise, and let my University advisor GrayMask know my situation. Tell him I shall return to complete my work as soon as the situation allows."

"Done and done."

A keening cry came from above, as two snow petrels descended. Despite the rising turbulence in the easterly wind, they gently landed on the apartment roof. Pindlebryth and Hakayaa waved as a Lemming in Royal Guard riding gear dismounted his steed and hurried over.

"Captain Decardan, M'Lord," he said, accompanied by a crisp salute.

"Yes, I recall, Captain – one of Colonel Farthun's best riders."

"If you could hurry, M'Lord, there is great need for you in Lenland." He picked up Pindlebryth's saddle bag, and the three of them approached the awaiting birds.

"Captain, can you tell me what is going on back home?" Pindlebryth inquired as they walked. Decardan glanced inquisitively at Hakayaa. "Captain, I can vouch for my friend."

"I'm sorry, M'Lord," Decardan retorted, "but the Prime Minister specifically ordered me not to disclose any details until after we are under way."

Pindlebryth's heart sank at his words. Such secrecy immediately confirmed to him that things were bad in Lenland. But why was it the Prime Minister who issued such an order, and not his father the King? Pindlebryth shivered as he fought off a sudden surge of despondency. He replied sullenly, "I understand."

He turned to Hakayaa one last time, and wordlessly clasped him again about the shoulders. Hakayaa returned the gesture.

Pindlebryth trudged past Decardan and his mount to his own. He unslung his crossbow complement with one paw, and grabbed the tow line with the other.

"Voyager!" exclaimed Pindlebryth. The petrel in tow lowered his head, with his beak firmly holding the bit. He nuzzled his head under Pindlebryth's arm, and cooed with familiarity. After they lovingly greeted each other, Pindlebryth undid the tow line and attached the weapon and quiver to his saddle. With firm familiarity he mounted Voyager, as Decardan mounted his petrel Swifter. They waited momentarily for the wind to lose a sudden and ominous burst of turbulence.

Finally, a strong sustained gust washed over the roof, and the two Lemmings' mounts leapt into the air. Climbing away and towards the bay, Pindlebryth looked back one last time to see Hakayaa likewise take to the air, then dive to land in front of Constable QuillBane, who was engaged in conversation with Inspector SwimQuick and two additional police officers.

The two Lemmings on their petrels continued to climb, and the deep cerulean of the sea came into view over the horizon. Winds and storm clouds continued to brew and grow from the southeast, making Decardan veer slightly northward during their eastern ascent. Once they were on a clear and constant path due east, Pindlebryth brought Voyager alongside Decardan.

"Finally we can talk. What news from Lenland? What has happened to my parents?" he called over the rushing wind.

Decardan faced Pindlebryth so he could be heard, but kept his gaze fixed on the path ahead. Occasionally, his eyes darted in various directions, looking for any approaching danger.

"It is a long story, and I can only tell what I myself have seen, and what I have been told. In summary, the entire nation of Lenland has fallen under the pall of some hypnotic spell. We feared that it may have extended to Lemmings around the globe, and to your own personage. Obviously, the events of PanGaea confirm our worst fears have come to pass.

"Around Spirit's Midnight, all of Lenland fell asleep. Even those of us with Names of Power, which should have protected us from spells, fell under the sway of this unnatural sleep. Police, border guards, even the Royal Guard were stricken down. We all stayed unconscious while the common folk all rose from their slumber. But they were not aware of their surroundings. They all with one mind began a trek towards the western coast of Lenland. The very young and very infirm were left behind, and many died as they nonetheless tried to follow.

"Come the morning, those who were supposed to be awake and on duty, quickly realized the situation, and awoke all the armed forces they could find in their locales. But only those with Names could be found. General Vadarog immediately jumped into action, taking charge of the multiple crises. He sent our fastest flyers to ensure the border patrols were awake and secure. With Admiral Carvolo, he had several teams of sailors pick up dozens of Lemmings lost at sea, all of which were half-asleep yet swimming westward towards the open sea.

Several other teams rescued those who were being dashed against the rocky shores, stirred up by ever-strengthening waves and rip tides. Finally, he had teams build makeshift stockades to hold the spellbound commoners, and shepherd the ever increasing crowds away from the ocean. It pains me to inform you that the death toll is already in the hundreds, and could be much worse by the time we return to Lenland. The General could only spare one Lemming to collect you, or scores more would die. He selected me since you already knew and trusted me."

"But what of my Father, King Hatheron? And what of the Queen Wenteberei who is with child?"

"They have not risen from the spell – they are seemingly well, but they slumber still. But that is not the worst. The week before this cursed spell, Queen Wenteberei gave birth."

"What!? But I did not dream of it! Neither did TwitchNose nor BlackEars."

"And so it was in all of Lenland. His kinship to the Throne, and the Queen's fidelity was unfortunately quickly called into question. King Hatheron was livid. The ghosts of his family's past were forcing their way back into his life."

Pindlebryth knew precisely all that such an event entailed. Hatheron's mother, the first Queen to Enorel III, died in childbirth. While Hatheron was still in his youth, Enorel III selected a new Queen, Garaden, and remarried. When Garaden gave birth to Hatheron's half-brother, there were similarly no dreams amongst the Lemmings to indicate the Name of Power given by the Quickening Spirit to the newborn pup. Gossip led to panic and anger which filled the castle.

It all culminated on that very day during the new Prince's presentation ceremony, the Queen declared with an evil grin that the true Garaden was dead. Though she was the very image of the Queen dreamed of by Lenland so long ago, she named herself as the enchantress Selephylin, and proudly confessed how she had murdered and taken the place of the hapless Garaden.

Witnessed by the entire Royal Court, she declared her scion to be named Selephyrex. Producing a wand seemingly out of thin air, the sorceress mother and her unholy child both disappeared in a thunderclap and a sphere of blinding blue light.

The effect on the land was shattering. Initial panic swept

over the entire country at the deception. After weeks of managing the crisis of confidence, Enorel III regained control of the country, but the initial shock, loss and ensuing struggle left him a mere shadow of his former self.

Only through the efforts of the King's wizard Graymalden was Enorel III's court able to verify the nature of the enchantress' deception: within a week Graymalden had found the shallow grave where poor Garaden lay. Selephylin had murdered her with magick most foul while she was en route to the CityState, and took her place. Once in the castle, she inveigled her way into Enorel III's heart.

The only mystery that still puzzled Graymalden was how Selephylin had a Name of Power that was never dreamed of by anyone in the nation of Lenland.

Pindlebryth found himself breathing rapidly and grinding his teeth, as the events described by Decardan piled one upon another in his mind. "How fares the child?" he panted.

"Now we come to the last of my information: Selephylin has returned, and spirited the queen's newborn BlueEye away with her."

"Selephylin!" Pindlebryth exploded. "What did we ever do to Selephylin to warrant her recurring evil? Lords Below take her!"

"King Hatheron and the Queen entered their bedchambers as Grefdel and I, the two attendant Royal Guards that day, closed the doors and took our positions outside. The Queen's wet-nurse was attending the child. We could hear angry conversation between King Hatheron and Queen Wenteberei over the cries of the infant prince. It was interrupted, however, with a thunderclap that nearly rocked us off our feet, and a bright blue flash that seeped through the gaps and seals of the doors. There was a strangled cry, and regaining our footing, we threw open the doors.

"There was Selephylin, not a day older than so many decades ago. The King and Queen were strewn on the bed, and the wet-nurse was knocked to the floor, on all fours trying to catch her breath. In one hand Selephylin held the infant, and in the other, a long wand the length of her arm. The wand was topped with a pulsating blue gem, and I swear it looked like an eye was carved out of it. We charged the witch with our halberds, but were repelled by an invisible sphere, that crackled to blue life when we tried to breach it. The nurse, who happened to be inside the sphere of mystical energy, picked herself off the floor, and without a second thought threw herself at Selephylin to rescue the child. The sorceress uttered a single word, and there was another blast of thunder and what sounded like a hundred avalanches.

"Grefdel and I lay there the rest of the night, until all those with Names of Power were released by the mystical sleep. They found us unconscious, the metal of our weapons melted and warped, but they saw our Majesties lying peacefully on the bed with hands clasped together and bathed in a dim aura of sapphire. The poor wet-nurse lay in a pool of her own blood, where her chest was blown clean through with a hole the size of a cannonball. Selephylin and the infant are nowhere to be found. The King and Queen still suffer a sleep akin to death. Every magick, medicine and vapour available to us seems to be powerless to rouse them."

Decardan fell silent, and a specter of self-condemnation shadowed his features. Pindlebryth's forehead was plowed deep with furrows. The weight of these events and the ever increasing buffeting of the weather built inside himself a wall of anger, brick upon brick.

Decardan veered again, but this time to the south, heading to the northernmost isles of the MidSea Archipelago. "Our mounts have been in flight since the beginning of the day, and we all can use a rest."

They descended to a small atoll crowned with a few breadfruit trees, and landed on the beach. Decardan dismounted and removed two packages of dried fish for the birds. Pindlebryth and Decardan then sat down amongst a patch of soft reeds several paces away from the trees that swayed gently from a southeastern wind. Pindlebryth undid the tablecloth-wrapped package placed by Hakayaa in his saddlebag. He chuckled and gave thanks, but he was quickly overcome with a sober look.

"What's wrong, M'Lord?" said Decardan returning with a few staples from his saddlebag.

Pindlebryth unwrapped a loaf of quickbread. "This was part of the breakfast TwitchNose made the night before she... she disappeared. She was as sweet and kind as any have been to me, and this was one of her specialties. She was a giving sort. She would want me to share this." He broke the loaf in two, and offered one half to Decardan. Two finished their small meal in silence, both of them periodically looking at the growing thunderclouds from the south. The gentle ocean breeze began to take a more serious turn.

Decardan collected their things, and packed them in his mount's saddlebag. They drank from their canteens, then gave the remaining water to their mounts. They greedily gulped down the water after the salted fish, and the efforts of a full day's flying. "We had best be going, M'Lord. If the wind gets more turbulent with unpredictable gusts, we may have a spot of trouble." Pindlebryth agreed, and unhitched the mounts from the breadfruit trees.

They resumed their journey's heading, turning to the east. For half an hour, they ascended even higher to get a better perspective of the southern storm. Dark pendulous clouds spewed from deep within the center of the Archipelago. Decardan pulled a spy glass out of his other saddlebag.

"The storm seems to be gathering around one of the islands with the tallest volcano." He sniffed the air. "But I smell no brimstone. So the volcano is dead and cannot the origin of the clouds. Yet somehow it is the center of the storm."

"I wonder what old Graymalden would glean from that," pondered Pindlebryth aloud.

"Oh. I'm sorry, M'Lord. I'm afraid he passed away while you were at University."

Pindlebryth bowed his head in silence. How many more of his circle of friends would be missing or dead upon his return? Decardan continued, "The Quickening Spirit had selected an apt apprentice, and Graymalden taught her well while he still could. Darothien is almost as crafty as he was, and she might uncover something we do not see."

"I will miss the old curmudgeon," smirked Pindlebryth, as he remembered the happy times and some of the arguments they had. "But Darothien? That spindly waif is up to the task of the important position of Wizard?"

"No doubt she was a ragamuffin when she first arrived, but her Name of Power was, after all, foretold in dream to us all quite a while back. Now that she is not living in abject poverty, she is proving herself to be quite the equal to Graymalden. She could even have become his better, had the two more time together. The only question left is, did she learn all of Graymalden's secrets before he finally succumbed to the Alchemist's Disease?"

"Consumption?"

"Aye."

"Well, I hope her skills in the craft make up for the experience and wisdom old Gray would bring against this magick waged against the entire Lemming race. She is untried, and certainly has a trial by fire set before her."

They continued their sojourn eastward, but the clouds behind them continued to grow. They seemed to keep pace with their speed, as the clouds never fully disappeared behind the horizon. Pindlebryth spurred Voyager onto higher speeds, and bid Decardan to coax Swifter to keep up. Within an hour the steeds began to labor at their breathing. "We must slacken the pace, if we are to spare the birds," worried Decardan.

"We are almost there, are we not?" Pindlebryth declared. Voyager keened shrilly as Pindlebryth persuaded him even faster. Within minutes, the coastline of dear Lenland crept into view. The flyers finally relinquished their steeds' labors a bit, but quickly regained their speed as they descended and caught an ocean tailwind. But as they neared the shoreline, the flyers once again slowed their birds as they began to observe the unfolding tableau below.

Pindlebryth and Decardan peered ahead, left and right with mouths agape in disbelief. All sizes of groups of Lemmings' bodies, from small knots to large flotillas, bobbed along with the ocean foam. Their bodies were bloated from long exposure to the sun and water. The scavengers of the sea had begun to feed on them. Those few that were still alive flailed westward, tossed to and fro by the waves and currents. A few vessels lumbered back to the shores of Lenland, nearly foundering under the weight of all the people their crews could rescue. Pindlebryth despaired that those left in the water would soon be unconscious from exhaustion, and ultimately dead.

As the flyers continued, they made landfall, and saw hundreds more Lemmings make their slow somnambulistic progress down towards the shore. Some were dressed in clothes customary to the capital city, others were citizens of surrounding counties. Dotted among them were several wearing traditional garb that indicated the nearby cantons of Lenland were also affected, and only recently began to arrive in their slow death march. Another horror of the sleepwalking was realized, when they flew over bodies of Lemmings who fell from boulders, or lost their footing on a rocky descent. Their bodies were broken and bleeding from internal injuries, severed arteries, or compound fractures. Oblivious to the pain and wreckage of their injuries, the crippled continued to limp, hobble, or crawl on to their doom.

"We cannot stop and give aid, M'Lord," trembled Decardan's voice with emotion. "It would be best to see General Vadarog as soon as we get to the CityState castle." The reason soon came apparent – squads of uniformed Lemmings scurried to fell trees and build fences to herd the sleepwalkers to the makeshift stockades Decardan told of during their flight. Those awake were terribly outnumbered, and easily overwhelmed. The army saved hundreds, but scores still slipped past the cordons to the beach and beyond – once in the waves, little help could be afforded them. Decardan and Pindlebryth at last arrived at the castle's central field, and landed. In the setting sun, amidst the purple hues of twilight, a faint blue glow could be seen emanating from the windows of the Royal Quarters. No stable hands greeted them to take their mounts, so Decardan tied the steeds' reins to the iron staves of the West Gate.

Pindlebryth followed Decardan to the Great Audience Hall in the South Wing, where General Vadarog had made a temporary command center. Amidst a constant flurry of orders and activity, Vadarog caught sight of the pair. Decardan exchanged speedy salutes with his superior, who then sighed relief and clasped Pindlebryth's hand in both of his. "M'Lord, I am so very relieved to see you safe! I feared you might suffer the same fate as our King and Queen."

"I too slept in PanGaea, when all others slept here. Obviously, I do not share the sleep akin to death Decardan described. How fare my parents now?"

A young doe dressed in iridescent green stepped forward and reported, "They still lie quietly on their bed, surrounded by a blue glow that repels all attempts to revive them."

"You must be Darothien," observed Pindlebryth.

"Yes, M'Lord," she said as she offered an expedient curtsey. "I have made attempts to defeat the spell that holds the King and Queen – without success. Neither can I find any reference in Graymalden's voluminous notes that match the spell, nor the wand that Decardan saw Selephylin wield."

"Report on your journey, Captain," ordered Vadarog, his hands clasped behind his back.

"Lemmings at PanGaea were glamored to sleepwalk to the

East, not the West as we saw here in Lenland. Those in PanGaea still met the same fate, however, of drowning in PanGaea's CityState's Eastern Bay. A storm started to pick up when I collected the Prince – a storm that grows even now, and covers a large expanse of MidSea. It seems most unnatural, and centered on a large volcanic isle in the MidSea Archipelago."

"Vulcanis Major?" asked Darothien.

"I believe so. However, the volcano remained dormant when I spied it."

Pindlebryth asked, "All of our people sought to die in MidSea?"

"No," retorted Darothien firmly, almost sardonically, putting her finger to her chin. "Rather, I think they are being drawn to a central point. I don't think it's a coincidence that Vulcanis tries to hide behind a storm."

Pindlebryth glared at Darothien for her impudence, but he held his tongue.

The General added, "That seems to agree with what two of our flyers saw. When at first we believed we could save the drowning hordes, we sent spotters over the ocean to direct rescue efforts. Before we realized how fruitless such a task was, they reported a large ark carrying hundreds of our people, and heading northwest. Such a vessel would have trouble crossing the entirety of MidSea, but could make its way as far as the MidSea Archipelago. I believe they are probably being shipped to Vulcanis."

"But for what purpose?" Darothien murmured, still staring off far away.

"We will only find out by investigating," declared Pindlebryth. "General, assign a guard for Darothien and an additional steed for them. Decardan on Swifter will accompany me on Voyager. The four of us will take off at the crack of dawn tomorrow for the MidSea Archipelago."

"M'Lord, I do not think you should take such a dangerous journey. Rather, I would recommend..."

"General, if I could assist in saving our people by remaining here, I would. But linguistics and diplomacy, or a single additional crossbow are not what this situation calls for.

"This witch has attacked the King and Queen. My *parents*! I must go face this thing directly. Decardan and Darothien, we leave at dawn." Pindlebryth turned his back on them all and left through Henejer Hall.

The General bowed and with some sadness closed, "As you wish M'Lord." Facing the others, he came to a decision. "Captain Decardan, take Captain Pendenar from the south fence with you. His patrol of the castle perimeter will be done soon, after which he and his squad will be resting in their quarters for a few hours. I'll have Colonel Farthun assign another Royal Guard to command his squad. Go and prepare what you need." He dismissed the others with a salute, then attended to continuing his efforts of directing the construction of fences and holding pens, and movements of available troops to build them, in an attempt to protect as much of the populace as he could manage.

The hours of fitful sleep passed and dawn was soon upon them, but Decardan could not find Pindlebryth in his quarters. After a quick inquiry, he knocked and entered the quarters of the King and Queen. Pindlebryth was sitting in a chair placed near their bed. He looked quietly at his mother and father, as the restless winds made the windows rattle occasionally.

Pindlebryth was wrestling with a sadness he had never truly experienced before – an anguish that teetered on the edge of a bottomless despair. He had always had the guidance of his father and the patience of his mother to rely on. But now he was separated from those pillars of strength on which he depended, by a wall of mysterious blue energy.

After a period measured in several breaths, he looked up at Decardan. "I could not sleep. I feared if I did, I would suffer the sleep of death that has enthralled my parents, and might never wake again." He sighed as he got up. He wanted to hail his parents a farewell, but he dared not touch them through the cyan glow that undulated about them.

"Let us be off." He returned to his quarters, his footsteps echoing along the halls with purpose. He threw on his travel gear from yesterday, then followed Decardan down to the courtyard. One could barely tell that morning had broken, as the storm clouds from the west had thickened so much that they hid the eastern sunrise. Pindlebryth called to the rest of the party already mounted, Decardan again on Swifter, and Pendenar and Darothien paired on an albatross named Keen. "We are off to the MidSea Archipelago. Unless we see anything to indicate different, we shall head to Vulcanis to rescue our people." He signaled, and they all took off.

Turbulence in the wind immediately began to fight them, as

soon as they climbed over the shielding of the walls and the castle roof. They wheeled westward and began to climb steeply higher in hopes of topping the storm. But they could not. Even though they achieved an altitude that made the most experienced flyer's head spin, they still could not gain a position above the thunderheads. The thin air made breathing difficult, and their steeds labored against both it and the growing turbulence.

Darothien asked Pendenar to hold Keen as stable as possible, then pulled her wand hidden under her thick green coat of jute and uttered a handful of words that Pendenar could not make out. Gripping the wand firmly against the force of the wind, she traced an arc and inscribed an eldritch geometric pattern within it. The air encircled by the arc glowed green for a moment, then poured out like a phosphorescent liquid flowing down a long-necked bottle towards Pindlebryth. It expanded about the entire group, until a veined green globe encompassed them all.

The turbulence subsided. She called to the others, "We should be able to travel without great hindrance, but the spell can only offer a limited effect. The spell is centered on M'Lord – stay close to him. We should make haste. The spell will weaken the longer I am away from Lenland." Pindlebryth exchanged a glance with Decardan, who nodded in understanding. Pindlebryth signaled, and the party descended slowly into the storm. They flew for hours, often meeting a gust strong enough to penetrate the spell of calming, challenging the skills of the flyers. Just as the steeds began to flutter and stumble in the tyranny of the roiling clouds buffeting the green sphere, they crossed into large column of clear space, centered on Vulcanis Major.

"It's like the eye of a typhoon," observed Pendenar. They descended further in the stillness, and circled the island within the border of the eye. The group leveled out, and Darothien dispelled the emerald sphere around them with a wave of her wand and a single word.

Decardan took out his spyglass, and flew ahead scanning the coastline. Spoils of ragged stone were scattered among long lines of centuries-old pillow lava. On the northeast beach he caught his first glance of buildings. As they continued to approach, he could make out a gigantic pier and the ark described by Vadarog. He signaled the party to descend further and arced towards the jetty.   Though wave upon wave of storm-surge washed against the island, the scale of the port and ark were so great, they seemed unaffected by the tides.   He approached the ark, and circled it twice.

The ark was a ghost ship, emptied of all life.   The ship flew no colors, had no identifying sails on the masts, had no nameplate; the only identifying mark was a plaque twice the size of a Lemming.   It lined the prow of the ark, where a figurehead would normally be.   It was made of a dark black-blue glass with razor sharp edges, and inscribed with strange geometric glyphs.   Several wide gangplanks had at one time connected the ark to the pier, but they had since been pulled up away from the ship.   Three giant hawsers moored the great vessel to the pier.   Scouring the land around the jetty, Decardan saw a wide road lead from the pier to the volcano miles away.   The road split into three and led to cavernous rectangular openings carved into the north, east and south of the mountain.   Scree and crags of old lava flows spilt amongst the road and the entrances.   There was the sound of a mild breeze, but it was discomforting as it made odd whistles, moans and hollows amongst the chaos of tortured stone.

A lone pillar of carved stone, next to the eastern entrance caught his eye.   He could not make out details, but the obelisk was bedecked with pictographs, and was crowned by a half moon of stone with a single word carved into it.

Then he saw the Lemmings.   At first a few, armed with shovels and other tools, arose from behind some wreckage of stone boulders and old lava splinters.   They laconically set to clearing and leveling the ground around the obelisk.   Over time, more and more joined them in their task.   Decardan reined Swifter back to match Voyager and Keen, then reported the scene to Pindlebryth and Darothien.

"Why erect a landmark in such a desolate place?" asked Pindlebryth rhetorically.   "Reconnoiter on ground and signal if it's safe. Don't take any unnecessary risks."

Darothien nodded in agreement.

"Yes, M'Lord," Decardan acknowledged.   He peeled off from the group, and dove to the gathering sleepwalkers.   Swifter nimbly landed amidst the rubble.   Pulling a sword and small shield from his saddle, he walked around the toiling Lemmings.   None seemed to take notice of him.   They merely continued to labor around the stone, making the grounds as smooth as possible, and clearing a way to the nearest minor road.

Decardan called to the Lemmings about him, but his hails seemed to fall on deaf ears. He gingerly stepped into the throng, bracing for the worst; but the sleepwalkers worked around him, as is he were a windblown leaf that would soon be out of their way. It took Decardan a few minutes to circle the column, moving in and out of the workforce. Nothing changed.

He glanced now and then at the obelisk, his head bending to read some of the oddly placed runes, but slightly shook his head, giving up his attempt to understand the writings. He trotted back to his steed and signaled the all-clear. The party descended, and landed nearby Swifter. Decardan remarked pointing back to the laborers, "All seems safe, but the dead look in their eyes makes my tail want to fall off!" He took out his spyglass again, and made one last pivot where he stood to view the landscape. Satisfied, he told Pendenar to stay with the mounts in case a quick getaway was needed.

The three stepped quietly through the enslaved masses, and approached the stone marker. Decardan kept his back to the obelisk and warily watched the somnambulistic crowd employ rake and hand to move the smaller bits of volcanic stone and ash. Pindlebryth and Darothien circled the towering stone, studying the markings. Pindlebryth nearly twisted his ankle on an uneven piece of pumice, but righted himself before he fell. Finally he observed, "I cannot make this out, but I feel this is familiar somehow. But I cannot put my finger on the language."

"I recognize it. It's the language of Fox. See these glyphs here?" she pointed at a small circle of runes, seemingly chasing one another. "They stand for remembrance, or sleep."

"Vulpine? What do the Arctic Fox have to do with this?" sputtered a nonplussed Pindlebryth. A moment later, he turned to regard Darothien. "And how in the world do you know the Fox tongue?" There was no accusation in his voice, but only earnest curiosity. "Graymalden certainly did not teach you that!"

"I am by no means fluent in it. However, I have seen it in contracts where the Fox were concerned."

Pindlebryth pondered how unusual it was that any Lemming would make a contract with a Fox, but he shook his head and tried again to focus on deciphering the obelisk. After a few more minutes, Darothien had a quizzical look when she peered at the top of the stone. "If I recall, the half moon to the Fox is a sign of renewal. Half light and half dark, it represents the struggle of good against evil, the..." She halted with a gasp as she looked at the ground in disgust.

"This is a memorial. A... A headstone for a Fox's grave!" she hissed as she quickly sidestepped off the ground it marked.

In her haste, she stumbled on some loose scree, and fell to her knees. Suddenly, a dozen hands were laid on her. So absorbed in solving the riddle of the stone, they had allowed the sleepwalkers to enclose them. Pindlebryth tried to assist, only to discover that he, too, was being inexorably restrained. He shouted to Pendenar. His heart sank when he saw both Decardan and Pendenar being dragged to the ground with several pairs of hands over their mouths. Their bodies went limp as the sleepwalkers clubbed them with tools and rocks. The prince and the wizard continued to struggle, until blunt pain and blackness also overcame them.

❧⌇⌇❧

As he fought unconsciousness and throbbing pain along the back of his head, Pindlebryth began to perceive a sense of blue light and green darkness around him. An evil odor permeated his nostrils. Opening his eyes, he saw he was inside a large half-domed hall. The floor and curved walls were all carved from an ominous dark green obsidian, shaped and polished to an almost reflective luster. At various points along the walls, sconces held aloft floating orbs of blue light. The two halves of the dome were separated by a wide and deep oblong rectangular channel that ran the entire width of the dome. Out of it drifted curling blue vapours. In the center of the far half of the circle was a large chair on a dais. Not unlike a throne, it also was constructed of obsidian and filigreed ornately with strange symbols in gold. Behind it on either hand were openings leading into barely lit tunnels. A handful of sleepwalkers stood motionless around the dais, some of them holding objects he could not identify.

Pindlebryth tried to survey his half of the dome, but as he attempted to rise from the floor, he found himself bound hand and foot in metal hasps and chains. The slowly diminishing pain in his head pulsed thunderously to a blinding blackness as he struggled to his feet. His feet were chained together with sufficient slack to allow only the smallest of steps, making it quite a challenge to stand. Once erect, he refocused his vision. Around him stood four motionless Lemmings, each holding a staff of wood, with both ends shod in iron. Around his sides, all his companions were similarly bound and guarded. Two portals in the wall behind them led down two more dimly lit tunnels.

Once standing, his vantage allowed him to see wisps of steam rise from a pool of vile blue liquid deep below the edges of the channel separating the two halves of the dome. The syrupy liquid swirled with rivulets of opalescence, and seemed to rise slightly where sleepwalkers were closest to the oblong trench. It exuded a stench of impossible blends of both bleach and ammonia, both acid and lye, burnt flesh and something else that could not identify, nor would he expect to find in nature.

Pindlebryth's companions also started to arise from unconsciousness, and slowly, painfully clambered up to stand. "Where are we?" inquired Pendenar.

"Inside the heart of Vulcanis, I suspect." replied Pindlebryth.

"They've taken all our arms," muttered Decardan with disgust and some shame. Peering over the edge of the dividing pool, he shook his head and snorted out through his snout. "What is that putrid slime?"

"I dare say none of us have seen it before," declared Darothien. "Perhaps it is another of our host's defenses or weapons?"

"And who *is* our host?" pondered Pindlebryth aloud.

As if in response to him, there arose a large chime of glass upon glass. It reverberated throughout the dome and hallways, seemingly originating from nowhere yet everywhere. The sonorous dirge continued until a hooded figure and two attendants entered through the hallway to the right of the throne. The figure's hooded cloak was a heavy cerulean velvet, with a dark cobalt fur border. A delicate right hand held a wand topped with a blue stone that seemed to stare back at the viewer. Pindlebryth realized it was the wand Decardan described from BlueEye's abduction. The figure sat down in the throne, and the two attendants pulled back its hood on either side. The face of Selephylin, aged not even a day since the time of Enorel III, slyly grinned back at the foursome.

"We greet thee, young Prince!" she quipped followed by a small giggle. Pindlebryth and Darothien stared confounded at Selephylin, but Decardan and Pendenar silently bristled with hatred.

Her visage slightly softened with sadness. She sighed, "You were taken at the memorial of my son Selephyrex? We grieve for him deeply. His sacrifice has taken him from Us." After staring at the moat in a moment of inward reflection, she regained her original imperious composure. "But I thank Our dear Hatheron for sending Us his remaining two bastard sons in his place."

"She's quite mad, M'Lord," whispered Decardan. He fumed darkly for a moment, immediately after he realized how easily his voice traveled everywhere throughout the dome. He quickly fell silent again, and his eyes pointed with fire at the witch queen.

On Selephylin's left, a vested sleepwalker emerged from the hallway with a small bundle. They approached the throne until they touched the sleeve of Selephylin's raiment. She looked over and down, and with a graceful flourish of her left hand, she pulled away the top layers of the tiny shrouded figure. "And We bid thee tidings of welcome also, youngest of the cuckold Hatheron." There arose a soft cooing from the bundle in response to the false queen's melodious speech. "We would also indeed like to grant thee a boon, little one. But such would be out-of-place, before those of your own had the opportunity to do so. Come forward, O Prince!" She waved with her left paw once, and two of Pindlebryth's captors shouldered him forward a few paces towards the blue pool. She signaled them to hold, and they did so perilously close to its edge. The steaming foetor began to sting Pindlebryth's eyes.

"We permit thee, young Prince, to make a proper offering." He continued to glare at her, mixed with consternation at her confusing diatribe. She switched her attention to the Lemming next to him, and her charming mask suddenly flashed away.

"We remember you!" Selephylin said with acid in her voice.

She waved her left hand again, then clenched it into a fist. Decardan was suddenly clasped by all four of his guards; by the neck, by the arms, and by the waist. The group marched towards the pool, forcing Decardan along with them. He began to yell curses only Lemmings know, as they edged to the pool.

Pindlebryth's eyes darted back and forth from Decardan's precarious position, to Selephylin's rictus of anticipation, to Darothien's shivers of horror.

Decardan could only finally declare in a loud baritone, "My Prince...!" as the group of five pitched over the edge of the trench. A watery splash was not heard, but rather a sickening impact into thick syrup. Almost immediately, a single scream resonated to the top of the hall. The remaining party struggled against their restraints and captors to peer over the pool's edge.

Pindlebryth roared, "No, Decardan, No! Quickening Spirit, No!"

Cloth, then fur, then skin all sloughed off the bodies where the Living Moat touched. Muscle, sinew and vital tissue dissolved next, but more slowly. The emotionless sleepwalkers offered no struggle. They merely floated lower and lower, as their extremities dissolved. All the skin from his face removed, Decardan's eyes softened. He violently shook his head, in vain hope that somehow the liquid could be thrown off, but his eyes' muscles distended, and their humours spat away in all directions. The melting face of Decardan could scream no more, as he had yowled all the air from his lungs. When he tried to inhale, around him blue tendrils of miasma leapt up a few inches, and probed past his steaming jaw, and dove down his throat. Decardan made one last asthmatic gurgling sound, as the blue liquid forced past his rotting teeth, and coursed down into his gut to continue its work from the inside out. In a few seconds, the foul blue vapour reached a riotous boiling point, and totally occluded the Lemmings' view.

"Lords Below take you, Selephylin you *murderer*! You kill your own kind!" cursed Pindlebryth against her and her atrocity.

Selephylin burst out with an insane laugh, as if she found his pronouncements absurd. Pendenar wordlessly kept himself from retching by clenching his jaw. His jowls distended his open frown into a grimace of disgust. Darothien whined shortly and clenched her fists, her hands aching against her restraints to find and hold her wand and cast something, *anything*. Eventually, the acrid steam began to thin and the group could only discern a few scraps of bone and tendon spin in the eddies of putrescence and finally sink from view.

Quiet was restored, disturbed only by Selephylin's soft tittering. She stood, strode a few steps toward the Living Moat, then uttered a short incantation over her abomination. The steam stopped rising, and started to coalesce. The wand's stone appeared as an eye peering into the bluish-white steam, and began to glow. The steam formed together in small rivulets, then organized into thicker strands as it approached the wand. The tendrils joined together in one translucent stalk drawn into the stone. As more steam was collected, the brighter the stone became, until it shone as a blue diadem. She raised her left arm, and the third attendant placed the swaddled child in her hold.

Selephylin raised her wand and the beaming stone, and declared, "You are no longer BlueEye." Her voice began to increase as she raised the wand to the highest she could reach. "We now bequeath to you name of the newest Selephyrex! We confirm this bequest with his Seal." With that, she turned her wrist, pointing the wand downwards, and plunged the stone into the babe's eye socket.

The three Lenlanders strained again against their captors, as they yelled in disbelief. The child screamed interminably in a piercingly high pitch, until it finally decrescendoed to a gurgle. The newborn finally recalled the reflex to breathe, and began to wail again. Waves of power raced down the wand into the child's head. As each wave expended itself and was swallowed by the eye-stone, a concussion of light flashed around the child, throwing garish blue-green shadows against the obsidian.

But Pindlebryth was not concentrating on the child, but rather the witch queen. With every impulse of the cynosure, the mask of Selephylin was momentarily penetrated, and a new visage could be spied – not just a new Lemming face, but an entirely different structure. The ears were larger and pointed; the irises were black circles set in white almond-shaped eyelids; the eyes were set close and forward facing like a carnivorous predator; the fur was white with black tips; the snout was elongated with enlarged canines.

"An Arctic Fox?" he spurted. His companions all gaped in mute bewilderment.

The pulses of power ceased, Selephylin extracted the wand from the child's skull, but the stone was no longer in the wand. Behind his fluttering eyelid, the blue stone's deep sapphire light leaked through. With each breath and cry, the light diminished in intensity, and miraculously so did the child's mewling. In a scant minute the eerie light was extinguished; and the child, his

tiny energies exhausted, fell into a deep sleep.

"We shall love you as Our very own son, and you shall serve Us as you would your Mother." Her beatific smile and mellifluous tones belied the cruelties that she had just wrought. She released the bundle back to the attendant, ordering her, "See that he has the best of care when he awakens." She dismissed the underling sleepwalker with wave of the back of her hand. She reclined again in the throne, and addressed the party. "Is he not the most beautiful creature? He will surely excel and make proud the many Selephyrex before!"

Her face slowly drained of its rapture, and her voice

flattened to a threatening monotone. "Now I am required to give you a gift in turn, for your sacrifice." The party steeled themselves, waiting for their turn in Selephylin's insanity.

"I offer you all the gift of freedom!" She paused, and looked about, as if she expected thanks for such beneficence. "However," she pronounced, "I first set before you this challenge. You must learn the meaning of Our name Selephylin, and the name of my sons, Selephyrex." She leaned forward with stern intent. "For if you fail to do so by the morrow, you shall meet the same fate as the guard who dared assault My Royal Person in Lenland." One could swear a chuckle escaped her lips, but it was quickly followed by her order to the sleepwalker guards. "Take them to their cell." She waved them away with her left hand then gestured with an open palm to their right corridor. As they were led away, she stood up, flourished her cloak about her, and retreated down the hallway after the child.

The sleepwalkers led the party down their corridor. Halfway down its length, it was no longer obsidian, but constructed of gray-blue basalt with speckles of green. They all continued past a handful of cell doors on either side, to a single door at the very end of the corridor. There they paused as the first two pairs of sleepwalkers, armed with their staves, lined along both sides of the hall. The door was unhasped, then unbarred. The remaining sleepwalkers stood behind the group and stood shoulder to shoulder, an impassable living wall. Slowly a sleepwalker relaxed the ankle chains to allow them, one by one, to move with a less restrictive stride, and shoved them into the room. The door clanged behind the party. Several of the sleepwalkers marched away, but two pairs were left behind to guard the cell door with unblinking, lifeless eyes.

Looking about themselves, the trio saw there was a single sink and two earthen pots of water, a hole in the floor, and four stone slabs jutting out of the walls. Irregularly shaped furs lay flat over each slab. Near the ceiling, an opening set with coarsely wrought iron bars whistled and moaned softly as the storm-whipped winds sped by high above in the night sky. Exhausted, Pindlebryth and Darothien moved to sit on their own slab. Pindlebryth first used his manacles to push the thin, moldy furs off both of their beds of hard stone – only a carnivore like the Fox would think of sleeping on a skin. Pendenar shuffled over to inspect the jars. The water they contained had no odor and seemed clean enough with which to wash. He grimaced as he weighed in his mind the question whether it was potable or not.

Pindlebryth took a couple of deep breaths and coughed to clear the sickening taste and smell of the Living Moat from his muzzle. "All this time, Selephylin was a Fox."

Darothien began to speak, but caught herself and was also forced to cough. "A shapeshifter!" Darothien gasped. "I've heard some Fox have that innate ability."

"Some do. You were right on the mark at the headstone, when you suspected a Fox was involved." He closed his eyes momentarily, and inhaled with a shiver. "You saw it, didn't you? When Selephylin drove the stone into the infant, there were flashes where her Lemming disguise fell away, revealing the Arctic Fox beneath the surface." Pindlebryth rubbed his forehead as he shook his head in disgust. "It fits – when Selephylin murdered Garaden so many years ago, her shapeshifting allowed her to take Garaden's place."

"A Fox... What abomination did she create in her spawn? And she *dared* cast aspersions on the King, you and BlueEye!?" she spat incredulously. "Selephylin named him Selephyrex," Darothien mused, "the same name she gave her own misbegotten child a generation ago. What does it mean? Are they Fox names?"

"I would assume so. But as I said, the Fox tongue is not one I am familiar with, let alone fluent in. I did not study it formally, nor read any of the written form. I only overheard bits and pieces from Fox undergraduates at University. I am however, very interested how you know enough of the Fox tongue, to have foreseen at graveside what we now face."

Darothien fidgeted uncomfortably. "I have discussed this with precious few, M'Lord. Even my closest friend, my tutor and master in the arts, Graymalden, only guessed at my past."

Pindlebryth leaned forward slightly, lowered his voice and tried to show her a willingness to accept, or even forgive if necessary. "Did you commit some wrongdoing?"

"No, M'Lord!" she responded with mild indignation. "There was no wrongdoing on my part. It is just that the answer involves my Name, and parts of my youth that I truly never wanted to remember again."

Beginning to see what might fuel Darothien's reticence, Pindlebryth looked down to hide his embarrassment, but raised his eyes again to meet hers with earnestness. "Please believe that Pendenar and I will have the utmost discretion, if we survive." Pendenar offered as much privacy as he could, and moved over to the door to fix a fearsome gaze through the bars towards the sleepwalkers.

Darothien sighed once, then twice. She turned her head, looking down at the cold gray scrabbled floor. She started softly, "I was born to a poor iron miner and a shepherdess. My father was strong in stature, but had weak lungs from working long hours in the bowels of the earth. My mother also toiled daily in the fields. Despite their labors, they still lived in abject poverty because they could only buy goods from our land-baron's storehouses. Their state was no worse or better than hundreds of families centered around the iron mines. The only families that fared well were those associated with the land-baron, who owned not only the lands of the entire canton, but also the mines they contained. He was the master of all he surveyed, and everyone was his slave. Even his own family, though they were financially secure, were treated no better than the lowest of the low. The only exception was his firstborn son, whom he doted on.

"In time, the land-baron became so influential from the metal wrested from his mines, that he was granted a baronet and ruled the canton."

"The Iron Baron! BrokenTail? That cursed turncoat?" exclaimed Pindlebryth.

"The same. As you know, he began to forge his iron into weapons, and covertly sell arms to other nations. At first, those who found out and questioned the Baron's treachery quietly disappeared. Then as the Baron and his guard grew bolder, dissenters were killed outright.

"My parents managed to hide me, despite my Name of Power dreamed by all of Lenland. But as I grew, I showed strange tendencies. I could becalm the wildest of animals. I could see where things were hidden. I could divine where to dig wells or where to plant crops. Rumors began to grow about me in the canton. Eventually, the Baron's men caught wind of it, and began to search for me. A friend of my father's, who begrudgingly served as lackey to the guards, hinted that the Baron might keep me for himself." Her eyes misted over.

"When he told us that, there was a look in my Father's eyes I had never seen before. All I knew was that he feared for me. It wasn't until many months later I fully realized what it was he feared." She swallowed hard, as the thought of that day choked her.

"Soon after, his friend produced a document stolen from the Baron that panicked my parents. It revealed that the Baron planned to capture and sell me to a count from Vulpinden, who was willing to pay a very dear price. The contract was written in both nations' languages, and I still recall a few symbols of the Fox written language from that parchment."

"Ah!" Pindlebryth surmised, as he scratched his jowl in thought. "That is how you can recognize some parts of the Vulpine language."

"Yes, M'Lord. The next day, while my father labored in the mine under the watch of the growing suspicions of the guard, my mother took me into the fields with the baron's flocks. She attempted to escape into the nearby woods that bordered the next canton. She wanted to pass me and the contract on to her sister who lived beyond the wood, so that I might live out of the baron's reach. But they gave chase and slew my mother..." Darothien closed her eyes, and whimpered as she relived that terrible day. "They mortally wounded her," she began again in a voice choked with emotion, "in a barrage of arrows. She hid me in an abandoned bird's nest in a rock field, before she limped away to distract the soldiers. My aunt somehow managed to find me, wounded and grieving. She spirited me away after the guards found my mother.

"My aunt's family was quite large, and I had many adopted siblings. It was like hiding a tree in a forest, and they became my second beloved family. No one in the baron's employ guessed that my aunt was not my true mother. Years later, we heard news of the baron's arrest and trial before the Royal Court. I and the contract were sent to the CityState to offer evidence. It was there during his trial that I heard testimony how the baron tried to find me. He tortured my father to death." Darothien wept a single tear. "And it was then that Graymalden took me under his protection and tutelage."

"Yes," growled Pindlebryth. "The Iron Baron was found guilty and exiled to one of the smallest islands in the MidSea Archipelago."

Pindlebryth was still a pup when the trial's verdict was handed down. But he could still recall clearly the ethical dilemma that his father, King Hatheron, wrestled with.

Emotions of the day throughout the entire kingdom were so heated, that there were those that called for the Baron's death. But the will of the Quickening Spirit specifically forbade the intentional taking of a kindred life.   The King could not determine a just and equitable sentence to hand down, until Prime Minister Tanderra found a loophole in the first PanGaean Accords – although no nation could lay claim to any part of the Archipelago without release from all other signatories, one exception was made for burial for those who died within its bounds.   The King and the Prime Minister agreed that if the Iron Baron's sentence was declared to be exile for life, the island would eventually be his burial mound, and therefore exempt.

"Every quarter, a supply boat was sent to check on him. Within a year, the supply boat's crew discovered the island was wiped from existence, probably by some giant tidal wave," he concluded.

"A fitting justice handed down by the Quickening Spirit," Darothien nodded in approval. "That is my story, my Prince; and how I know a little of the Fox nation. Now, it is your turn."

"What do you mean?"

"I mean BlueEye! You treat him as if he means nothing to you. You avoid using his name. You come to this island to help save your people, but you do not seem to include BlueEye in your deliberations.   You are greatly distressed by Decardan's malicious demise. Yet when BlueEye is sadistically injured by Selephylin and her evil magick, you concentrate on the witch queen rather than your brother's pain."

Pindlebryth clenched his fists on his knees. "He is *not* my brother! The Quickening Spirit has declared it so!"

"He is not your brother, because he was not given a Name of Power? Consider this – if BlueEye had no Name, would he not be a sleepwalker as other Lemmings? Clearly he is not."

"No one in the nation dreamt his name," protested Pindlebryth.   "And many called my Mother's fidelity into question before the sleepwalker curse was cast, and I returned."

"All right, let us consider the Queen's fidelity. You are upset when Selephylin calls the King a cuckold, which means the Queen has been unfaithful with another in her bed; yet You leave..."

"How *dare* you!" he shouted as he stood in righteous indignation.

"...yet M'Lord leaves no place in his heart for his defenseless younger sibling? Forgive me M'Lord, but how dare *You!* I may have come from a poor family, but it seems the poor treat their own better than those who *claim* to be their betters!" Darothien also stood casting an angry but confused look – she was aghast at her own temerity in castigating her Prince, but she continued. "Either BlueEye is a bastard, as Selephylin accuses, or he is your brother. BlueEye cannot be illegitimate, and the Queen faithful at the same time! Which *is* it M'Lord?

"I have had two families, and I have held every single member precious. Yet you have one true family, which you refuse to recognize. The Iron Baron treated his entire family as detestable slaves, much as you treat BlueEye. Are you and the Baron that much alike!?"

"I don't give a damn about that witch or the Baron! Selephylin deceived and cuckolded my grandfather to make her own bastard, who was never heralded with a Spirit-given Name. She then appears to spirit away another Nameless spawn. It is not I who says I have no brother, it is the Quickening Spirit Himself!"

Darothien and Pindlebryth had long since discarded their composure, and argued further and more passionately, when a pair of manacled hands swept down between them. "I take no sides on this 'discussion', but it seems to me that we have more important issues pressing us." Pendenar tilted his head and nodded upwards, bringing their attention to the barred window. Through the stationary eye of the storm, it could be seen that dawn would soon be upon them.

"Thank you Pendenar, for your alertness," said Pindlebryth, swallowing his anger and returning to civility. He sat back down, as calmly as he could manage. "...and good sense. We have both let our lesser selves run riot. We do indeed have more urgent tasks at hand." Darothien blushed and nodded in silent agreement, and also sat on her slab. A full minute passed before Pindlebryth spoke.

"It seems obvious that their names' shared root of 'Selephy-' indicates a relationship, or a shared experience, or perhaps something else."

"True. There is also something familiar about it I cannot place. It has nothing to do with any arcane arts that Graymalden taught me, but it dimly sounds like something in the contract. Not necessarily a personal relationship, but something about that word makes me think it is some sort of contractual term. Like related functions or relative positions – buyer and seller, or owner and lessee. I wish I could remember more of that document, but it was so very long ago, I was so young, and it was something that I preferred forgotten."

Pendenar, rejoining the group, added a question. "If I may, why is Selephylin offering us an escape at all? She could have doomed us all with a wave of her hand, just as she did Decardan." His jaw clenched shut again, barely controlling his hatred for Selephylin and his loathing of the Living Moat.

"As spells grow in complexity, they eventually exact a price," began Darothien. "They usually require an expensive ingredient, or may sometimes incur some portion of the caster's life-force as payment. If the spell grows even further in its reach or power, something even dearer must be paid, or be risked. I surmise that in order to make the witch queen's spell affect an entire nation, it required her life to be risked. She chose to place a riddle before us as the cost of the gambit. But if that is so..." She blinked suddenly with a revelation. "It suddenly strikes me that the previous Selephyrex's life may have been the cost for some earlier spell." She shook her head, unable to comprehend Selephylin's evil. "Lords Below! Her treachery against the Royal Family and her own makes the deeds of the Iron Baron against the Royal Family and his own pale by comparison."

"The Iron Baron was going to sell you to Vulpinden, you say? Between you and the previous Selephyrex, the Arctic Fox seem to have an obsession with our Names of Power." Pindlebryth shook his head immediately. "No, that's not it. In neither case was the name of Selephyrex given by the Quickening Spirit."

"It may be that with the great magicks Selephylin now wields, she may have hidden or interfered with her own son's and BlueEye's true Names. That's why no one dreamed them. This may be an attempt to access the Names of Power."

"...And why she imbued him with a Name of Fox origin. What hubris, to think she can supersede the will of the Quickening Spirit!"

"Wait," growled Pendenar. "They're returning." The sound of shuffling feet in soft boots preceded the clang of the door's bars and hasps being lifted. The cell door opened and two sleepwalkers with hooked pikes entered, followed by a third.

Each in turn, Pendenar, Darothien and finally Pindlebryth, were faced with two of the three sleepwalkers. The first hooked their hands' manacles with his pike, while the other shortened the ankle chains to their previous length. They were led out one by one, each to four guards with staves. They were marched down the corridor, but they could detect the offensive odor of the Living Moat long before they entered the central dome. They were led within a scant few paces of the Living Moat in the obsidian hall. The familiar toll of the gigantic glass on glass bell sounded, and a hooded attendant entered with Selephyrex cradled in her arms. The babe cooed softly, blissfully ignorant of the terrible events that had passed here. A second thrum resounded, and a cache of hooded sleepwalkers entered, with their mysterious implements still being held firmly in their hands. On the final bell, Selephylin and two attendants entered. The right attendant carried a rich purple velvet pillow on which Selephylin's wand rested.

Selephylin's hood was drawn down, revealing she still retained her Lemming form. Pindlebryth frowned wondering why. Perhaps it was for the infant's benefit.

Pindlebryth could feel the moment of truth quickly approaching. He could see the Living Moat sensed the attendants, trying to rise up along the sides of the pool and attack. Only the mirrored polish of the obsidian prevented the blue ichor from climbing the surface. Their dooms approaching, Pindlebryth silently raced over the clues he and Darothien discussed. A peculiar itch in his mind urged him to believe there was something important in the seemingly paltry conclusions they deduced.

Selephylin lowered herself in the obsidian throne, and addressed the party, saying, "Good morning, favored guests! I hope your accommodations have met with your approval, and you are well rested to face the challenge of the new day!" Pindlebryth barely payed attention to Selephylin's insane drivel. He felt he was close to understanding something important. "Young Prince, your answer is required at this time. What is the meaning of Our Names: Selephylin and Selephyrex?"

"May you perish a thousand times, for every Lemming you have slain!" barked Darothien. Pendenar bared his incisors, and growled loudly.

"Enough of your impertinence!" Selephylin jerked erect out of the throne, and swept her hand from right to left. With a look of angry impatience she strode halfway towards the pool. "I still await an answer from you, bastard Pindlebryth. What is the meaning of our Names?"

In the Prince's mind suddenly burned the singular clue from the obelisk that he and Darothien had not fully understood. It crystallized and led him to the conclusion that made sense, that *felt* correct. The flash of enlightenment emboldened him to pronounce in a voice that almost made the hall ring, "They have the same meaning that they have had several times before. Not once or twice, but for each of the long line of Selephyrex – you are the Master, he is the Slave."

Selephylin, overcome with unbridled venomous hatred, spat a curse in Vulpine as she pointed at Pindlebryth. Following her signal, the sleepwalkers holding Pindlebryth began to drag him towards the Living Moat. However, Selephylin's wand began to vibrate on the pillow. Without warning, it flew from its resting place, and pierced Selephylin from behind. Selephylin looked down at the bloody point of the wand with astonishment, as it drove through her chest and robe.

She stumbled forward a step, and trembled as she tried to regain her balance. She rasped terribly and coughed blood, as she uttered something again in the Fox tongue. Pindlebryth concentrated on her words, even though he could not understand them. Finished, she smiled wanly, and pitched forward onto her hands and knees. Her features swirled and then coalesced to her true form. Before the party was Selephylin, the Arctic Fox. The white fur of her torso showed an ever widening swath of red that spattered on the floor. The wand still skewered her, but she managed to raise her head. Her feral red eyes burned at the prince, but soon began to roll upwards. Her hands became slick with blood, and slid over the pool's edge. Without anything to hold onto, she tumbled into the noisome blue fluid. The Living Moat formed thick pseudopods and tentacles and clamped them down, crisscrossing her body. Dragging her quickly under the surface, a single shriek of agony that seemed to make the whole dome tremble finally trailed off into a boil of rancid steam.

The sleepwalkers stopped. Life slowly returned to their eyes. Some of them began to cough and retch from the blue-white steam as they awoke. Many of the guards dropped their staves, still in a dreamy state. Others used the staves to maintain their balance. The attendants rolled back their hoods.

Those holding the arcane machines dropped them as their bodies rocked slightly back and forth, as if they walked into an invisible wall. The delicate clockworks bent, broke or shattered when they impacted the floor. BlueEye's attendant swayed, then snapped to alertness as she realized she was holding an infant wrapped in rich purple velvet.

Pendenar ordered the Lemming in front of him, "Give me that key!" The Lemming turned to face him but was still confused. Pendenar ripped the key from the Lemming's belt, and set to unlocking the manacles on his feet. As soon as he could, he dashed to the Prince and freed him, then to Darothien, only then undoing his own paws.

"People of Lenland!" said Pindlebryth, "I am Prince Pindlebryth! Move away from the pool, and leave by the doorways behind you!" Some of them still milled about bewildered, marveling at the obsidian hall about them.

Pendenar barked loudly, "Your Prince told you to *move!*"

As the robed Lemmings moved to the carved hallways on their side, so did the Prince and his entourage. Pindlebryth went down the left side corridor, and all the others followed, with Pendenar directing stragglers away from the right corridor that led to the cells. They emerged from the north gate of the volcanic cone, and followed the road that joined the east and south paths. Scores of Lemmings began to emerge, and more continued to wander out from the depths of each of the great corridors. Pindlebryth and Pendenar started to direct the people towards the main road and the coastline.

But Darothien sped along the exterior of the dome towards the east entrance, where she joined up with the attendant still cradling BlueEye in her limbs. She pulled back the velvet coverlet, and examined the babe. He was awake and smiling. But her gaze was drawn to his eyes. The one natural blue eye was still there, but it was paired with the blue stone on the other side. The stone had settled in quite naturally with the flesh and bone surrounding it. She expected to see a bloody wound, only to find his face as clean and supple as the day he was born. As the infant turned his gaze and focused his vision on Darothien, she noticed that both eyes functioned naturally.

"Quickening Spirit! This is magick no Lemming has ever seen before." She broke her reverie and noticed the attendant, who was the wet-nurse while under the witch's spell. Collecting her wits, she ordered the attendant, "Take the child to Prince

Pindlebryth," she pointed, "and stay with Him.   Protect that child with your life. Now go!"

The wet-nurse hustled down the path, her head bobbing between watching her step on the roughly cobbled path, and checking the child in her care. Darothien worked her way back into the obsidian dome, commandeering a Lemming in a tattered uniform along the way. The traffic lessened until they reached the empty domed hall. The soldier held his muzzle against the stench of the Living Moat.

Darothien carefully moved towards where the attendants closest to the pool had stood, and bent over to pick up the remains of one of the intricate machines. It was constructed of finely layered gold, bronze and calcite. But her hand stayed inches away from the artifact. It itched as if a hundred ants crawled over her skin, and her fur was on fire. She instead wrapped her hand in a loose cowl lying nearby. She gingerly picked the broken pieces up without feeling any effect, and handed the bundle to the soldier. "Use one of the robes to fashion a sack, and collect all the pieces. Be sure not to touch them without the robe! And do not approach closer than a body's length from the pool." The soldier acknowledged her request, as she turned down the other corridor. She was intensely alert, not knowing what to expect as she entered the domain of another wizard.   Even so, she still stopped breathlessly in awe as she entered Selephylin's quarters. After a moment, she collected her wits and began to search. She quickly located all their gear out in the open, but she headed straight to hers. She verified her wand was still there, and carried her saddlebag, and as much of Pindlebryth's gear as she could manage.

She paused in the room's doorway, and looked back at the room and a few of the strange objects: a crib scribed with dark arcane glyphs; a set of a dozen strangely angled mirrors interconnected by gold measures, scales, and protractors; a grouping of five gemstones that slowly bounced a tiny ephemeral globe of blue light betwixt them; and many more, all made with the same layering of materials. Part of her was mesmerized with wonder at the magicks, but the wiser part of her experience told her to let them be. She suddenly felt worried with a feeling of foreboding. As she dashed to the great hall, she breathlessly asked the nearest soldier, "Are you all right?"

"Yes, Mistress," he replied. "Is something wrong?"

She was not sure how to answer, when the bell tolled again. But something was awry; the chime developed a dissonance, as if the bell developed a crack or some other defect. As the sound of the ring died away, a chorus of rock crunching against rock could be heard. Fine cracks developed in the uppermost part of the dome.

"You have all the machinery? Then let's get out of here!" With that, they both tucked their tails, took the bags and left the hall.

As they emerged the landscape was covered with hundreds of Lemmings, all heading towards the pier and the ark. Soldiers in ragged garb directed the crowds, and lowered the gangplanks. Above, Pendenar and Keen circled those straying from the masses, herding them toward their escape from Vulcanis. Occasionally, he would hover over the appointed soldiers to get their updated reports and issue new orders. "Grab that cart, and join the others at the east entrance. Look for any storehouses, and collect all the food and potable water you can find. If you value your life, *stay out* of the central hall." He spotted Darothien, and waved at her. He pointed to a jutting promontory near the ark. "Join the Prince there!"

"All right. But tell your men to be careful in the mountain. The structure has weakened and may not at all be safe. And touch no machines of mineral and metal!" They all signaled their acknowledgment, and Pendenar veered away to the next group of uniformed people.

With her soldier in tow, she climbed up the rocks while Pindlebryth was instructing a group of Lemmings. One had made a crude map, and was responding to Pindlebryth.

"Yes, my Prince. I navigated large cargo ships across MidSea."

"Very well, LongBack," the Prince proclaimed. "I give you a field promotion to captain." The whole group was then deputized by the Prince to be the ark's crew and sail all the people back to Lenland. "Captain LongBack, the hardest part of the journey will be steering through the Archipelago. Afterwards, head southeast to the bay near Lenland's CityState."

LongBack was about to ask some questions, when Pindlebryth held up his hand, and broke from them for a moment to address Darothien. "Ah, there you are. The nurse has already taken BlueEye to our steeds. Take him with you on Keen. Pendenar will fly with you, while you see to BlueEye's safety during the journey. Swifter will not accept a new pilot, but will follow us home. We will all take off when I join you with Voyager."

Darothien turned and addressed the soldier that accompanied her from the hall. "Take the sack and secure it to Swifter. And change his saddle blanket to a black cloth of mourning. I will join you momentarily to see to BlueEye's safety during the journey." He took the makeshift robe bag, and stepped back. Darothien did not immediately set off, but faced Pindlebryth again.

"What is it, Darothien?" queried the Prince.

A small grin grew on her face, as she softly said. "You called BlueEye by name." She turned and proceeded to the winged steeds with the soldier in tow.

Pindlebryth also allowed himself a small smile after he shook his head at first in annoyance, then in amusement. Then he returned to the tasks of instructing the new crew, and overseeing the exodus.

Hours passed by as the ark was packed with people, food and water. Virgin sails were located in the upper deck chests, and lashed to the masts. A large battery of newly carved oars, oar locks and portholes were found in the lower decks. Finally the entire mass of Lemmings had finished preparations. The able-bodied sailors amongst the rescued raised and set the sails, threw off the gangplanks and giant lines from the pier, and set the rudder to steer away from it.

The ark refused to move.

Captain LongBack issued orders to break out the oars, and begin rowing. More and more portholes were opened on the side opposite the pier, and oars were threaded through them and began rowing to back the ship away from land. Still the mammoth vessel did not budge.

Pendenar and Pindlebryth sat astride their mounts side by side, overseeing the harbor from the top of a gargantuan mound of eroded pillow lava. Darothien sat behind Pendenar, with BlueEye in a makeshift papoose lashed to Keen's saddle gear between them. Darothien strained her eyes at the ark from their promontory when she told Pendenar, "Something is holding the ark in place. I think I know what it is. Fly me around the ark."

Pendenar faced Keen into the wind and took off. Voyager stamped his feet, anxious to also take to the air. Pindlebryth held both Voyager's reins and Swifter's towline, when he called ahead, "Be careful, both of you!"

Keen gained a modicum of altitude, but then glided down to a height slightly above the ark's railings. As he circled the craft, Darothien kept one hand on BlueEye, uttered a phrase, and made a small glowing green curve in the air about her face with the index finger of her free paw. She cupped the hand over one eye, and scanned the ark through the glyph. When they reached the prow, she pointed at the plaque. "They must break the stone! It brought the ark to the island, and that is what holds it here!"

Pendenar relayed the instruction as he circled the prow once more. Three sailors tied themselves off to belaying pins, and lowered themselves to the plaque. Striking it with hammer, chisel and sword, razor sharp daggers of volcanic glass shivered off. Some cut the limbs of the Lemmings; some sliced and frayed the ropes. The sailors concentrated on the central glyph, and just before the ropes unraveled completely, the plaque split. The plaque cracked clean through, with the sound of a thunderclap. An explosion of blue light burst around the prow, and the ark shuddered away prom the pier. A cry of relief echoed from the hordes on the deck.

Keen stopped circling, and headed back to the promontory. Pindlebryth urged Voyager to take off and join them. Swifter arose and followed in their wake, as the trio paralleled the ark.

Darothien took a long look around the horizon, and tapped Pendenar's back, exclaiming, "The ark was not the only thing that the plaque controlled!" The eye of the storm began to collapse. The dark spiral of whipping clouds became more and more disorganized. Thunderheads peeled off from the giant cyclone, but shrank and became less violent as they ventured into the calm of the eye. More and more clouds sheared away, but evaporated more slowly. The air in the eye began to pick up velocity, and form a weak but building vortex. The ark launched from the pier and plied into wind-whipped waves that began to make even the impressive bulk of the ark yaw and roll. Those who could not secure themselves were ordered below decks.

The wind and seas continued to build in turbulence, when a tinge of red in the sky made its presence known. The setting sun created a silhouette of Vulcanis Majoris, and with it a calming westerly. Within an hour the storm dissipated, and the seas became manageable. The ship sailed easily with the firm breeze, and the hearts of the people were raised in thanks and song to the Quickening Spirit. As the ark wended its way through the maze of the Archipelago, the flying steeds landed on nearby islands, until the ark sailed by. The Prince, Pendenar and Darothien, and Swifter repeated this exercise a handful of times until the ark was free of the Archipelago.

As the ark made to open sea, Pindlebryth perched Voyager on the railing near the bridge and hailed the captain. "Captain LongBack, there is no room to keep our steeds on the ark, and holding them back to pace the ark would exhaust them before the journey is done. I think you can complete the journey easily from here. We will fly on to Lenland, and send back fresh flyers to check on your progress."

"Aye, there's naught much else for M'Lord here. May the Quickening Spirit bless you forever for saving our people." They hailed each other, and Pindlebryth and Voyager rejoined the other steeds, flying at last towards home.

Two giant eyes in the darkness peered at Darothien, without malice, without any emotion at all. Whispers of myriad voices were on the edge of her perception. The eyes glanced left and right, and blinked. She didn't know how it escaped her attention before, but one eye was blue and the other was brown. The indistinct chatter increased, and the brown eye began to waver. Like a reflection in a pond disturbed by waves, the eye's image distorted to the point where it was unrecognizable. The blue eye remained undisturbed, as the brown eye refashioned itself and solidified. Now it was made of blue crystal, and the choir of voices unified into a single word: "Selephygur". The Voice that was many voices repeated the Name until it faded into nothingness. Suddenly the blue crystal eye flashed blood red, as the morning sunlight tumbled through her window.

She rubbed the sleepsand from her eyes, and quickly got dressed. It was the last day of the Week of Remembrance, declared by King Hatheron. When Pindlebryth's group and the ark returned to Lenland, the King called for a day of celebration; followed by five days of mourning, burial and memorial, with a special service honoring the sacrifice of Decardan; ending with a final day of celebration. Surely it was a sign from the Quickening Spirit that He blessed this joyous day with a Name for the infant prince.

She threw on a morning coat against the chill that permeated every wall of the castle. She made her way up the southeast stairs to the royal apartments. A guard accompanied her to Pindlebryth's room as she entered the level. They were about to knock on its door, when it was apparent it was already open. She called for the prince, then entered when there was no answer. They called again as they saw every bookshelf of the prince's personal library was disgorged onto tables and the floor. Every piece of furniture was covered in a chaos of opened books. A second guard came and stood in the apartment doorway. The first inquired, "Where is Prince Pindlebryth?"

"M'Lord left not long ago. He went downstairs."

Darothien thanked the guards, saying, "Ah! I think I know where he is."

She descended and practically ran down both stories of the southwest staircase to the ground floor and the Royal Study. She barely missed tackling Tabarem as she rounded the hall corner leading into the room. Dressed in his usual multi-colored rumpled rags, he leaned on the jamb of the wide doorway watching the Prince, shaking his head with disapproval, but tempered with an amused smirk. "And they say *I'm* mad?" the jester burbled as Darothien passed. "I suppose M'Lord'll leave everything as is when he's finished, for me to clean up after the festivities. Feh!" He turned and stomped down the corridor towards the stairs, his shoes making rude noises with each step.

The Prince was sitting on the lower rungs of the sliding ladder that ran the length of the bookshelves. Like his private study, the floor about the shelves was littered with open works, and stacks of references. He sat with a satisfied smile as he pored through the monograph in front of him.

Darothien gingerly stepped through the minefield of leather-bound tomes about the study, until she seated herself in a plush chair facing Pindlebryth. "What did you find?"

Pindlebryth looked up at her and closed the book, using his

finger as a bookmark. "It is truly unprecedented, that BlueEye was given a Name of Power rooted in a known tongue. That it is also from the language of the Fox, is even more astounding."

"But do you know what it means?"

"As you may guess, the meaning is related to the name that the witch queen originally gave him. But his new Name proves she has no more power over him.

"Recall in the riddle, that their old names meant 'Master' and 'Slave'? This new Name of Power means 'No One's Slave'."

They both quietly chuckled. Pindlebryth's eyes clouded over as he looked directly at Darothien. "Now I truly have a brother."

II – The Prince's Vision

All in all, it was the perfect early summer day – a gentle breeze saying its final farewells to spring, a warm sun brightening the verdant fields and groves with promises of plenty come autumn. Pindlebryth and Voyager flew low over the rolling foothills, taking the time to welcome Lenland, reveling in its sights, sounds, and smells. Much as Pindlebryth enjoyed the environs of academia, Lenland was still, after all, his beloved home. Voyager, always seeming to know the desires of his owner, took even more pleasure in his banks and rolls, climbs and dives.

Pindlebryth had lost the last half of the previous spring semester and the first half of the fall semester, forsaking his studies until his duties in Lenland were satisfied. Only after using the better portion of a year helping in the repair of Lenland and ensuring the security of his family, the people and the land, could he in good conscience return to University at PanGaea.

Upon his arrival at University, he threw himself back with full fervor into his studies. While resuming the work interrupted from the previous lost semesters, he also delved into the new direction of mastering the Vulpine language – a choice that quite perplexed his doctoral advisor, GrayMask. Pindlebryth did not explain his reasoning to him, but he felt sure that his advisor would eventually piece together his reasons why.

By the end of the academic year following the reconstruction of Lenland, he not only resumed and achieved exemplary marks in all his exams and dissertations on the Otter and Ferret languages, but he similarly excelled in the written and spoken Vulpine tongue. Despite initial misgivings over his student's choices, and his concern with Pindlebryth's additional workload of a third language in a single year, GrayMask could not have been more pleased – save for one detail. He did voice a mild reproach to Pindlebryth about the lack of progress on his doctoral thesis.

GrayMask could not be too cross with Pindlebryth however. Pindlebryth, having received his certifications in his fifth through seventh languages in record time, only needed to complete one more course of study to fulfill one of the requirements of eight certificates for his degree. Only after exacting a promise from Pindlebryth to retrain his focus on the completion of his thesis during the coming fall semester, did GrayMask finally wish his prodigy a fond farewell.

But now the spring semester was done, and Pindlebryth was anxious to return home once again, especially to see his younger brother.

Pendenar and Swifter escorted Pindlebryth and Voyager from PanGaea to Lenland. Though their steeds were well suited to ply the long distances over the open MidSea from PanGaea, Pendenar was fatigued from flying those many hundreds of leagues with the additional burden of constant vigilance over his royal charge on the return trip. Nevertheless, once they made landfall, the CityState was not much further.

Upon arriving over the city, they circled the castle once – the North Wing, with its accommodations for guests, living quarters for most of the castle staff, and kitchens; the East Wing that housed the offices and living quarters of the higher government officials, including an infirmary and the archives; and the largest of all, the South Wing. Two great halls and one minor hall occupied most of the ground floor along with a library, study, and an office and dressing rooms adjacent to the Hall of Thrones; the second floor housed the Royal Guard's quarters, common rooms and duty rooms; the topmost floor exterior facing south held several guard stations spaced at equal intervals along its southern wall, cantilevered to afford the best visibility, while the interior facing the inner courtyard held the Royal apartments.

The east and south sides of the castle grounds were mostly open. The eastern grounds were lined with great and ornate metal fences, whereas the southern grounds boasted an impressive hedge labyrinth and several sets of decorative and functional gardens, all encircled by poplar, white birch and quaking aspen trees. To the north of the castle was a line of spruce and fir that separated the castle grounds from the southern portion of the CityState, and offered an excellent break against the winter winds. The West Gate on the perimeter of the castle courtyard was protected on either side with a small guard house. Beyond it were a livery and stables that served the needs of the castle, overshadowed by a large building that housed a battalion of military assigned to the castle and a city guard complement.

Pindlebryth and Pendenar landed their mounts outside the gate. Pindlebryth removed a satchel and his crossbow holster. He then hugged Voyager around the neck, and fed him a salted fish treat. Voyager murmured softly with affection, and wedged his head under Pindlebryth's arm. The two Lemmings then handed their steeds over to the care of the guards on duty. It was then Pindlebryth noticed some castle guards' uniforms had unfamiliar insignia; they were emblazoned with unusual patches, badges and occasionally a sash. Yet, all the other regularly attired guards acted as if all was normal. He was about to inquire of Pendenar about this curiosity, when just inside the gate, they were met with another of the Royal Guard. He saluted both of the travelers, saying, "Pendenar, I relieve you. M'Lord, you are requested at the Prime Minister's staff meeting after dinner this evening."

"I stand relieved, Grefdel." Pendenar replied with the customary salute. Addressing Pindlebryth he acknowledged, "Always pleasant to serve under you, M'Lord," and walked over the grounds to the South Wing.

Turning to Grefdel, Pindlebryth asked, "Where are the King and Queen?"

"They are receiving the Ambassadors from the Snow Goose WetLands. While you were at PanGaea this past year, there have been several official visits to the King from the Ambassadors of all of our neighboring countries. And even a few other nations with which we have treaties."

"Things certainly have been busy in my absence." Pindlebryth held Grefdel with an inquisitive look. "I suppose the Prime Minister shall update me with all manners of news in our meeting this evening?" Grefdel had a look of concern, as if he were swallowing bitter medicine. "Don't worry Grefdel," chortled Pindlebryth. "If you knew the nature of the Prime Minister's business, and could have told me, you already would have. I know better than to ask one of the Royal Guard about any court information they may be privy to, or asked to hold in confidence." Grefdel sighed with relief.

Pindlebryth started towards the East Wing, saying "I would like to greet my younger brother."

"Pardon, M'Lord. But Prince Selephygur is not with his tutors at this time of day."

"Oh?" He stopped mid-stride. "Where then, might I find

him?"

"He'd be at the practice ranges at this time of day."

"Things change quickly indeed! Not just a bookworm now!" smirked Pindlebryth. "Fetch some rides, and we'll go see what draws my brother away from his studies." Grefdel soon returned with a pair of reindeer, and a CityState guard with a symbol of an eagle Pindlebryth did not recognize on his vest pocket leading a third steed.

Grefdel mounted his steed with ease, but the unfamiliar mount gave Pindlebryth pause. He recognized the dwarf caribou breed from PanGaea, where they were commonly used to draw carriages and other vehicles. Originally rescued from extinction due to rogue packs of wolves and ravenous ursine troops in the Polar Bears' Free Hunting regions, they were found to be easily domesticated, and quickly proliferated to widespread use among several countries.

In PanGaea's CityState, where he resided during University, it was common practice to harvest their antlers to prevent accidents and injuries. During their introduction over the past year here in Lenland, however, the reindeer were apparently allowed to retain their formidable looking antlers.

"Grab that," Grefdel said, pointing at the antler nearest Pindlebryth. The reindeer had swiveled its neck to turn one side of its rack towards him. "He'll help you up." Pindlebryth complied, and the beast deftly deposited him on the saddle.

They proceeded out of the castle grounds, to the practice ranges north outside of the city. Within a furlong, Pindlebryth found the reindeer as easy to ride as Voyager.

Soon enough, Pindlebryth found his mind rambling about his beloved countryside. While reminiscing of the days when he trained at these same grounds, they crested the hill into the training valley. Rounding the last rill, he saw a company of troops engaged in several activities.

In two of the farther valleys bordered by forestland, were two lone hills with flags on their peaks. They were surrounded by competing squads each trying to capture the other's flag. In one of the wider plains, several drill sergeants were leading fresh conscripts in field exercises and weaponless combat training. Along a nearby row of hillocks, several squads were performing target practice exercises using all sorts of throwing and shooting weapons.

Overseeing it all was a Lemming Pindlebryth immediately

recognized. They approached him, and all whom the prince passed saluted accordingly. As he rode, Pindlebryth acknowledged their hails, noting that amongst the majority of regular uniforms, there were several with more insignia he did not recognize, and even the occasional doe in a strange uniform. They rode up next to General Vadarog standing on the hillside, and dismounted.

"Greetings general," said Pindlebryth. "It's unusual for a person of your rank to oversee a standard exercise of the troops."

"Greetings, M'Lord!" Vadarog replied as he snapped a salute. "You're quite correct. But there are some new troops I'd like to observe and evaluate personally." He raised a folding set of field glasses to better view the events.

"Ah yes. I've noticed several new faces and uniforms in the ranks. Who are they?" inquired Pindlebryth.

Vadarog surveyed all the troops during their exercises, then folded the binoculars in his vest pocket. He replied with his usual stance and hands clasped behind his back, "There were several companies from across Lenland that we have rotated into our local armed forces during the years since the Sleepwalker Curse decimated the CityState's battalion. The Eagle Company from the canton bordering the Lodges of the WeatherWorn are rounding up their tour of duty, and heading back to their home in two weeks. The Lioness Company from our Eastern quarter will assume their duties." He pointed one arm towards one squad of Lioness does participating in archery drills, then a similar group drilling in weaponless combat. "Those are the two squads that have cycled in early. They will then assist in orientation for their remaining squads arriving later."

"Ah, the exclusive female company," nodded Pindlebryth.

"Correct. While they have little to defend against from our allies the Snow Geese, they do from time to time do battle with rogue bands of Martens and Badger that stray into our lands. They have even brought down a feral wolf scout or two. The Lioness training is quite unique and strenuous. I daresay some of them would put our local troops to shame. Not to mention, they fill out a uniform quite nicely. Ah, if I were ten or twenty years younger..."

"You would be in front of a disciplinary board on charges of fraternizing with a subordinate officer!" quipped Pindlebryth, as they shared a chuckle or two.

They continued to observe the exercises, when Pindlebryth spotted a handful of people not in uniform flanking the firing line of one of the crossbow practice ranges. He shielded his eyes from the noonday sun, but still could not make out any of the individuals. "General, who's that on the range on the left hillside?"

"Oh, he wanted it to be a small surprise for you. Why, that's your brother, Prince Selephygur."

"Lords Above, he's sprouted like a weed while I spent two semesters in PanGaea! What in the world is he doing there?"

"When he is not studying under his tutors, he often joins us for weapons training. Over the past months, he's excelled at several weapons." Vadarog also placed his paw over his brow like a visor, to block out the blinding sun. "I even hear tell he might give M'Lord a serious challenge in the crossbow. I cannot help but to be reminded of history's description of Enorel the Great when I see him wield weapons so well."

Pindlebryth squinted attempting to identify the rest of the party. "And the three beside him?"

"That would be the range instructor, and our field surgeon. Who the other person is, I'm not sure – it may be Sacalitre."

Pindlebryth unslung his crossbow from his reindeer's saddle, and began to descend the hillside to join the crossbow group. The other person was indeed the royal physician, Sacalitre. Pindlebryth wondered why his presence was necessary in addition to the field surgeon. As he approached, something else caught his attention. Selephygur was aiming at the most distant target of the range, usually reserved for the expert archers. Pindlebryth stopped behind the group at several paces, wishing to observe and not disturb Selephygur.

Selephygur stood stock still, held his breath, and released the bolt. The group about him erupted in cheers and applause when the missile struck squarely in the center of the target. Pindlebryth then approached them, saying as he applauded, "A remarkable shot! I daresay, I wouldn't have believed it had I not seen it myself." He nodded his head with a proud smile, and clasped Selephygur on his left shoulder. "Remarkable, indeed!"

Selephygur turned around and exclaimed, "Pindlebryth! You're home! Oh, but now you've spoiled my surprise," he groused with an exaggerated pout. "For that, I challenge you to a contest!" He smiled an impish smile, and saluted his older brother.

"I suspect I am being baited into an embarrassing display. But very well, let us see what we shall see." The two stood side by side aiming at the expert range target. The two princes took their turns at the target, each alternating with the first shot. The contest started to attract the attention of the surrounding troops. One round, two rounds, and a third round passed with both of them hitting the center of the target. It began to be noticeable that Selephygur was almost always closer to the exact center, but both scores were still tied. With each shot, the applause and roar of the onlooking troops grew louder and louder. Finally, in the fifth round, Pindlebryth had the first shot – and missed. He barely was out of the center circle, but there was no doubt it was not a bull's-eye. After a chorus of disappointed cries, the raucous crowd hushed in anticipation.

Selephygur beamed with youthful bravado. "All I have to do now, is hit the center, and I've won!" He loaded and shouldered the weapon, held his breath and began to squeeze the trigger. But suddenly the young prince dropped the crossbow, staggered a step and doubled over, screaming and holding his head in his hands.

"The Prince is down!", "M'Lord is wounded!" cried several soldiers in the assembled crowd. But they were quashed by the range instructor.

"All weapons *down*!" he bellowed. "Unload all weapons *now*!" All those with crossbows and bows unslung them, and all swords were immediately sheathed.

Several Lemmings dashed to the prince to render assistance. Among the first to lend assistance was the field doctor, but the castle physician was already by Selephygur's side. The sawbones instinctively inspected the prince for any obvious wounds, while Sacalitre deftly drew out from his rucksack a large black towel. He calmly folded it lengthwise, and quickly and firmly pressed it between Selephygur's muzzle and forehead. Sacalitre ordered the field doctor to assist by holding the young prince down, then began to fashion the towel into a makeshift blindfold. Selephygur writhed in agony at first, but as the light was blocked from his eyes, he began to calm down, and was soon lying in a fetal position. He was still moaning in pain, but he was stable. Pindlebryth's initial shock at the unfolding events gradually gave way to the deduction that

Sacalitre must have done this several times before.

"Fetch a litter!" ordered the field doctor. A pair of soldiers and a medic rushed in with an impromptu field cot constructed of two poles and burlap wrapped and folded between them. The two doctors and the instructor gingerly lifted Selephygur a half foot, as the litter was slid underneath him. The instructor saw there was no blood; instead, the crossbow discharged into the soil when the Prince dropped it.

Pindlebryth forced his way into the midst of things, and bent down to his brother. "Selephygur!" he pleaded. "Are you all right?" But the young prince just moaned, pressing his temples with both his hands. He rocked back and forth, curled up like an injured infant. "Do you hear me? Selephygur!"

"M'Lord, we need to move him to my infirmary now," said Sacalitre without emotion. The group then proceeded to transfer him to a nearby wagon. But Pindlebryth shadowed the procession closely.

As they gently lowered Selephygur into the wagon, the field doctor inquired, "You seemed prepared for this, Sacalitre. Is there something about this condition I should know?" Before the physician could answer, Pindlebryth wheeled him around and throttled him with both hands around the collar.

"You *knew* about this?" he exploded. "What do you think you're doing? I should have you flogged!"

"M'Lord, calm yourself. Prince Selephygur in is no danger. Until then, please be patient. We need to get him to my infirmary as soon as possible. If you will accompany me, I will explain all after I tend to your brother." Both physicians, as well as Pindlebryth and Grefdel clambered onto the wagon around Selephygur. The wagon began its trek back to the castle, and the physician's surgery in the East Wing. Despite the relative smoothness of the road, every bump and jostle made Selephygur sob anew. Sacalitre took a vial of amber fluid, and dabbed a few drops on Selephygur's lips. The moans of pain partially subsided, and his breathing became somewhat more relaxed. But it was obvious the pain was still throbbing unabated.

"Is there nothing else you can do?" demanded Pindlebryth, grasping at any hope.

"Not here. However, you might help by just talking to him. Take his mind off the situation. Speak to him of happy times."

In a stilted manner, Pindlebryth started to tell Selephygur

of his past year at PanGaea. He kept his voice only loud enough to be heard over the creaks and groans of the personnel wagon, and the clip-clops of the two reindeer that drew it. He spoke of his times with Hakayaa, both in study and in revelry. He described the pranks played by the student body: switching the offices and all their contents of two neighboring professors; rearranging the books in a particularly disliked professor's personal library, and wrapping their book covers with the university student newspaper; and his favorite, infusing the fuel in the Dean's desk lamps with herring oil.

Selephygur's breathing almost became regular, but his paws were still clamped at his temples. Pindlebryth placed his hand on top of Selephygur's head. Careful not to disturb the makeshift blindfold, he stroked his brother's black mane as he described the day trips he and Hakayaa took to nearby cities and counties of PanGaea; hiking up the foothills to the central mountains; exploring the curious monoliths and ruins along its southern coast; and visiting the traveling fairs. Pindlebryth was enthusiastically describing how they gave chase to a cutpurse at the fair, when Sacalitre interrupted, indicating it perhaps was too much stimulation for Selephygur.

They arrived and entered the castle's central court without hindrance. Sacalitre ordered one of the gate guards, "Fetch Darothien, and have her meet us at the Physician's surgery."

The guard selected a private from his command and had him run to do so. The entire crew from the field carried the litter to Sacalitre's offices, where they were met by the infirmary nurse. Four of the party gently lowered Selephygur onto the first sickbed there, as the physician opened one of several glass cabinets, and retrieved a container of brown fluid. He handed the flask to the nurse, and she administered half an eyedropper of the thick syrup past Selephygur's lips, and with a cotton swab, dosed the smallest of drops directly into each of his snout's nostrils. "This is a more concentrated form of the elixir that I gave him on the field," commented the doctor. Selephygur immediately relaxed the death grip on his temples, and began to sleep deeply. "All we can do now is allow him to rest," said Sacalitre. He then asked the field party to escort themselves out, as he placed a ceramic half dome over Selephygur's chest and bent over to listen. But Pindlebryth did not move, nor did Grefdel.

"Doctor, a moment in your front office, if you please."

Anger was barely hidden behind the elder prince's patient whisper and polite demeanor. The trio moved out of the recovery room leaving Selephygur in the nurse's care, and Grefdel softly closed the door. He then crossed the main office to close the outer door, and stood guard in the hallway outside. "Now doctor, explain yourself. You knew this might happen. Why did you allow the young Prince in harm's way?"

"Again, M'Lord, I tell you your brother was in no danger," Sacalitre explained calmly, stuffing his paws in the pockets of his white coat. "Or rather, his symptoms as of themselves pose no danger."

"He's suffered this before, then?"

"Yes. Several times over the past year, but it had always passed with no visible physical harm. The problem of course, stems from that false Eye from Selephylin." Sacalitre gestured towards the chair in front of his desk for the Prince to sit, but Pindlebryth remained standing as he folded his arms.

"It began soon after you left for PanGaea this year. If you recall your own studies at Selephygur's current age, this is the time where one's education branches out. Almost every subject of study is touched on, to evaluate one's aptitudes and weaknesses. History, law and sociology, the arts and the sciences are all introduced to the student. It was during this time in your own education, that your proclivity for languages was discovered. In any case, reading, writing and other close up visual work is stressed. Approximately one month after his immersion studies, he experienced his first migraine. It was attributed to simple eye strain. At first, common pain relievers and a short rest cleared things right up."

A polite knock came at the door. Grefdel opened it slightly to see who the visitor was. He quickly stepped aside as Darothien entered. She produced from her sleeves a triangular prism, a convex lens and a notebook. Nodding to Pindlebryth and Sacalitre, she proceeded into the recovery room. As she sat beside Selephygur, the nurse quietly closed the door again.

"In the meantime, Selephygur's education expanded to include the sciences, and several remarkable things began to occur. In astronomy, he began to plainly see features in the full moon and rough detail in the Red and Yellow planets, which made our telescopes pale by comparison. In the natural sciences, he saw new structures in tissue that we have never before discerned with our comparatively weak microscopes. He saw that all plant and animal tissues were composed of cells. He observed myriads of microscopic creatures that live in a single drop of water. Selephygur described to us how even the blood in our veins is filled with similar cells and organisms. He opened doors of scientific understanding in half a year, which would be the pride of any scientist's lifetime of achievement. It was obvious, that this ability was due to the bejeweled Eye. We all knew he adapted well to it in his youth, including how the gem seemed to grow with the Prince as he grew into adolescence. And as he used it more and more beyond the mundane, he became more adept at using its strange potential. The entire tutoring staff was excited at the prospect of the wondrous secrets his Eye might yet uncover.

"But ultimately, there was a cost. The more he used the unique powers of observation in his magicked Eye, the more the migraines increased in frequency and severity. As you saw today, a severe episode requires total cessation of visual stimuli, and powerful sedatives.

"In the months after the migraines first appeared, we tried several regimens with the Prince. To make a long story short, we found that by restricting the duration and stress of his supernatural vision, the migraines could be avoided. That is, he could do simple reading and writing for almost a full school day; the use of his Eye for weapons training was kept to no more than two hours per day, since the distances involved were only moderately stressful; and any rigorous use of his powers of sight were restricted to an hour per day.

"Curiously, our initial medical examinations during and after the seizures indicated the magicked Eye was *not* the direct cause of the migraines. Rather, it seemed his natural eye was the source of the migraines! At first, Selephygur experienced simple eyestrain and irritation that inflamed the blood vessels and turned his normal eye red. But as he began to gain mastery over the magicked Eye, the normal eye was subject to more and more stress trying to match or complement the gem. Of course, the natural eye is simply not capable of such extraordinary powers. Yet it would still try to balance his vision, until all the muscles around his normal eye seized and cramped, followed by a migraine.

"In time, however, the seizures grew in strength and duration. More alarming was that their character also changed. Selephygur complained the pain seemed to grow into his brain each subsequent episode, and that the pain had moved from his normal eye to the bejeweled Eye. After the most recent attack last month, he said it felt like his entire skull was on fire. Obviously, the diagnosis of eyestrain was not correct. Medicine could not help the young prince anymore, so I asked Darothien for her help.

"Darothien examined the Eye as best she could after each subsequent attack, then again after the migraine ceased. She has made some interesting observations, but I fear neither magick nor medicine have fully uncovered the secrets of how the Eye works, or what it is doing to him.

"Since we could not do much more than blindfolds and sedatives to alleviate the migraine symptoms, we have concentrated on preventing them. We found that beyond restricting the time he uses the Eye, using a simple eyepatch helps deter the adverse magickal effects.

"We thought we had made progress, until today," the physician fretted while scratching the back of his head. "I accompany the Prince whenever he uses his magicked Eye, as he often does during his archery training. But getting a migraine this quickly in the field confounds all previous prognoses."

"Is it not obvious, then, that you must make him stop using the Eye altogether?" Pindlebryth demanded imperiously.

"And monitor him all day long, that he never takes off his eyepatch? How does one control what another wants to see? M'Lord, you forget that unless I can prove his magicked Eye poses an immediate life-threatening situation, there is little I can do short of amputation. And since the use of his Eye is his choice, this is little that you, M'Lord, can do either."

"Very well," Pindlebryth sighed in reluctant agreement. "But why was I not told of my brother's condition while I was away?"

"It is not my place to second guess the decisions of your Father the King, or the Prime Minister. You will need to talk to them."

Pindlebryth clicked his tongue loudly in exasperation. He opened the door to the hallway, and held it open. "Grefdel, I will be sitting with Prince Selephygur for a while. Please notify me when it is time for the Minister's meeting." Grefdel nodded simply, as Pindlebryth shut the door behind him. Pindlebryth paused with his hand on the doorknob to the recovery room, and the hackles of his neck standing up. Looking at the floor, he said, "I am still vexed, doctor – but not at you. I lay this at the feet of Selephylin, the one ultimately responsible. You will please leave us alone. I will call if Selephygur needs you." He quietly opened the door, and the nurse offered her chair next to the young Prince's bed. Selephygur was still quietly resting due to the medicine, and Sacalitre silently motioned to the nurse for her to leave the patient with his visitors.

On the other side of the bed, Darothien had lifted the blindfold over the bejeweled Eye, careful not to shed excessive light on it. She wrote cryptic notes in her book as she examined the Eye. First she used the clear convex glass, then the dark green tsavorite prism, then through both in tandem to peer at the Eye. Within a scant few minutes she lowered the blindfold, and traced a small glowing green circle and a glyph in the air. Lifting the blindfold again with one hand, she manipulated the circle with the other. She had peered directly into the bejeweled Eye for barely a moment, when the Prince rolled his head. Darothien attempted to train the glyph on the Eye again, only to have Selephygur writhe despite his state of unconsciousness away from the symbol. Darothien tried a third time, but was thrice thwarted when the Prince began to twitch in significant pain. Darothien relinquished, erasing the sigil, and exhaling a sigh of frustration. Lastly, she wrote a handful of final notations in her book, then excused herself.

Pindlebryth was left staring at Selephygur with an air of confusion and consternation. His stomach was tight with fearful possibilities. Pindlebryth continued to regard his brother, but soon drew into himself, reviewing what he could recall about the gem of sight.

He first considered the question of how the previous Selephyrex might have passed away. He did not have a true Name of Power, so he would only live a normal lifespan, and would have had no protection against the Eye or its possible hidden side effects. Did the Eye, or the "Seal of Selephyrex" as the witch queen called it, have anything to do with his death? Did Selephyrex use the Eye in service to Selephylin? If so, how, and did he experience the same painful episodes that so afflicted Selephygur now? Did the sorceress create the bejeweled Eye herself? Or perhaps it was some ancient device she had discovered? Did she act alone, or were there others that shared in her intrigue? What plan did the witch queen have for Selephygur in Selephyrex's place, and for the entire Lemming nation for that fact? Pindlebryth left the path that line of thinking might lead him down – for who can know the scheming of the mad? Especially one so obsessed, that her machinations had spanned many generations?

The elder prince had barely scratched the surface, when there was a respectful knock at the door. Pindlebryth bid him enter. Grefdel opened the door and reminded the prince, "It is time, M'Lord, for the Prime Minister's meeting. It is being held in the antechamber to his office. Will you accompany me, please?"

"Good Lords, I was so distracted that I missed dinner. I will have to eat something afterwards, and then apologize to my Father."

"Considering today's events, M'Lord, I'm sure he understands. Nevertheless, we need to go."

"Yes, I will have a few questions for the Minister in private, as well." The pair made their way to the second floor, and entered the antechamber. A large table with ornate woodwork was surrounded with several matched chairs, all occupied save one. As the Prince entered, all rose from their seats and bowed echoing "M'Lord" in unison. Pindlebryth noticed, albeit with some confusion, that the King was not present. He took his reserved seat, next to the Prime Minister, after which everyone took their seats again.

Beside himself and Tanderra the Prime Minister, there were Royal Guard Colonel Farthun, General Vadarog, Admiral Carvolo, Major Domo Melajen, and the Wizard Darothien, all seated around the imposing conference table. Darothien was apart from any side discussions. Instead, she concentrated solely upon her notebook. She studied the new entries there, and flipped pages back and forth to compare them against previous notes. LongBack, accepted into the Royal Guard since his field promotion, wore a Guard's uniform with the smell of new material, and creases that could cut butter. He stood behind Farthun at attention, as did Grefdel behind Pindlebryth. A trio of butlers set out after-dinner tea and cakes for all those seated, then left closing the doors behind themselves.

"Thank you for coming," began Tanderra. "This meeting is to discuss several new developments, so old business will be set aside for now. Before we begin discussions, I must inform you that this information may not be discussed with anyone outside this group, or anyone not privy to the highest security until further notice.

"King Hatheron, Queen Wenteberei and I have recently concluded talks with the leaders and ambassadors of all our neighboring countries of Warrening, the WetLands of the Snow Geese, and the Lodges of the WeatherWorn. The King and Queen have asked me to brief all of you, now that they are complete.

"We have received news from the Arctic Hare and Snow Geese that the Arctic Fox nation is in turmoil.

"The leadership of Vulpinden had been formed many years ago by the marriage of several members of its two largest Pack Clans. These clans were at war with each other at the worst of times, or at an uneasy truce at best, until several marriages of King and Queens, Dukes and Duchesses, Counts and Countesses, and a plethora of Baronies were struck between the rival Packs. The Fox nation was once again stable for many years.

"But a development occurred several years ago, that only now is sending that nation spinning once again into political discord. Our sources inside Vulpinden tell us that its dearest national treasure has vanished.

"It is rumored that this item was imbued with great magick. Vulpine legend says it was an ancient Seal given to the Fox nation from the Quickening Spirit when He bestowed upon them their lands and the power of shapeshifting. But now, each Pack accuses the other of theft of the item, reviving old animosities, leaving that country on the brink of civil war."

The Admiral and General immediately began presenting scenarios; Farthun issued quickly two orders; both were silenced by the Minister's commanding voice, and raising both hands to pause all discussions.

"King Hatheron has treated with the Warrens of the Arctic Hare, whose country insulates us from the northernmost country of the Arctic Fox, in an agreement of mutual defense. If one nation is attacked by the Arctic Fox, the other nation shall come to its aid. Similar treaties have been reached with all our borders' neighbors. General Vadarog and Admiral Carvolo have both taken part in reviewing the details of these agreements. Whereas the opening negotiations were done in secret, we are now notifying the Fox and other nations through our ambassadors of all the completed treaties.

"But now we come to the point that has not been shared with any of our neighboring allies. It is our belief that the device that Selephylin inflicted upon our Prince Selephygur is the very national treasure that has sent Vulpinden into disorder." The room filled with a visceral sense of apprehension.

"Our intelligence sources informed us that Selephylin was a minor countess in the Arctic Fox hierarchy, dismissing her as having only a minor talent for magick." Tanderra's voice took on a slightly sarcastic tone, saying, "Plainly, that intelligence grossly underrated her ability." He cleared his throat, and straightened his sleeves habitually. Several in the room uncomfortably shifted in their seats at Tanderra's comment.

"The leaders of the Arctic Fox strongly suspect she was involved with the disappearance of their treasure, but they cannot locate her – for obvious reasons.

"From what our neighbors have learned, the Arctic Fox still do not know that Selephylin is dead – and we prefer it stays that way as long as possible. For they would undoubtedly blame us for her death, even though it was ultimately by her own magicks. This is also why Selephygur was always made unavailable whenever any ambassadors were in the castle – either by keeping him longer in tutor sessions, or sending him on weapons training. Even our allies had to be maneuvered or distracted from catching a glimpse of Selephygur. We could not risk news of the lost treasure reaching the Arctic Fox. For the same reason, any reports of Selephygur's reactions to the eye-gem had not been allowed to leave the castle."

Tanderra looked intently at Pindlebryth. After a moment's thought, Pindlebryth understood the Prime Minister's assessment of the risks. He nodded his approval at Tanderra, agreeing with the reasons he had not been informed while in PanGaea. But now, something else bothered him deep inside.

The Prime Minister continued, "Selephygur's unfortunate episode today for all to see means this information may not be secret much longer. Therefore, we will also make the following arrangements: there will be an additional regiment from our outlying cantons during this crisis here at CityState, and their tour of duty here will be staggered with the existing regiment already here; also we require that the Royal Guard increase their numbers by four, one for each of the Royal Family, and they will have shift reductions from eight hours to six, to keep the Guards fresh and alert at all times. Accordingly, General Vadarog, you are to select the four most trustworthy of your ranks, and transfer them under Colonel Farthun's command. Also, Major Domo Melajen, you are hereby instructed to make the necessary changes in the Guard's and soldiers quarters, in addition to those already made."

Melajen opened a book in front of him, and flipped a couple of pages to an oversized folding map of the castle and outbuildings. He made some small notations next to the barracks between the main gate and the North Wing, and still more under the South Wing, where the Royal Guard was housed. He laid down his stylus, but left the book open to those pages.

"Are there any questions?" asked Tanderra.

"Several," replied Pindlebryth as he gathered his thoughts. "First of all, when did Vulpinden determine that Selephylin disappeared – when she murdered Garaden and kidnapped King Hatheron's half-brother Selephyrex, or was it when she attacked the entire nation of Lenland?"

"Soon after the time of the Sleepwalker Curse. During the many years between the two events, she was often observed at various political and dress functions. When they noted her disappearance, they also discovered their national treasure was missing."

"How had she lived so long, to be able to attack two generations, and yet age not a single day?"

"Similar to our Names of Power, those Fox with the power of shapeshifting are few, and that Gift also imbues them with long life. We can only guess that she possessed some additional magick to prolong life even further," said Darothien.

"Were our sources able to determine what happened that earned us Selephylin's undying enmity?"

"We've pieced together an educated guess," continued Tanderra. "Selephylin's clan lost a good deal of influence and prestige when the Packs formed the Arctic Fox nation of Vulpinden. Before he was crowned the first King of Lenland, Enorel the Great may have been instrumental in forging the peace between the Packs. We can hazard this hypothesis both from our sources in Vulpinden, and some scant historical notes found by our Archivist's search. Since Selephylin's clan's power and reputation suffered greatly during this time, it would only be natural that she would share in her family's antipathy towards Enorel the Great, even to the point where she considered the offspring of Enorel to be her enemy."

Pindlebryth ruminated while sipping his tea, then asked, "We surely must face the fact that the Fox nation will eventually discover that Selephygur possesses their Eye. What is our recourse when that happens?"

Tanderra nodded towards General Vadarog, who began, "Because of these new mutual defense treaties, we have forestalled any direct action Vulpinden may take. Their military would be spread far too thin to assault us and defend against our allies. Admiral Carvolo and I are close to finalizing our strategies."

Tanderra added, "We are also working with wizard Darothien and archivist WagTail to determine a clearer picture of what the Eye is." He gestured towards the enchantress, continuing, "She believes there may be other hidden powers behind the Eye. If we can uncover them, we may better deal with Vulpinden."

Darothien finished with, "If M'Lord can visit my laboratory, I can inform him what we have discovered so far. Pendenar and I have discussed what passed that fateful day on the island of Vulcanis Major. I also have made several notes on my observations of the Eye. Perhaps after I show you our current understanding, M'Lord may add some details only he noticed from that day, and we might solve its riddle."

"Very well. I will visit later tonight," he replied.

Pindlebryth signaled to Grefdel. He quietly instructed him, "After the meeting, have a small dinner sent to my room. Before I sup, I shall sit with Selephygur again for a short span." He then addressed the group.

"One thing I do not understand. If the Eye is so valuable to the Fox, how is it they only recently determined its loss? Why would they not know it was stolen by Selephylin?"

"Our sources tell us that the Eye was stored in a special vault," said Tanderra. Only three Fox officially knew its existence and location, and those three had the only keys to open the vault. The Eye is brought out of secrecy on the rarest of occasions, and its uses are known only to that cabalist trio. It is therefore feasible that even though it is long after Selephylin absconded with it, only now is its presence missed."

"Selephylin had official access to this vault?"

"No. How she was able to steal the most valuable object to

Vulpinden is a mystery. We only know that the Fox now believe she is the responsible party."

The Prime Minister glanced at all those at the table. "If that is all, then I thank you all for attending," said Prime Minister Tanderra. "Especially you, M'Lord. Our thoughts go with you and Prince Selephygur, and we wish him a hasty recovery. The rest of us shall meet again this time tomorrow to discuss any further responses our nation must take."

Pindlebryth stood and left with Grefdel. As the heavy mahogany doors opened, Darothien collected her notebook and rose, Melajen spun his stylus in his hand as he pored over his castle plans, and Vadarog and Carvolo were reviewing battle scenarios. Grefdel hurriedly relayed his prince's request for victuals to a maid waiting beside the door guards, then resumed being Pindlebryth's shadow. The handmaid curtsied, and turned down the hallway in the opposite direction towards the kitchens. Suddenly out of nowhere, Tabarem appeared down the length of the hall. As he sauntered by the Prime Minister's antechamber with handkerchiefs spilling out of every pocket of his many-hued patchwork clothing, he sang-song to himself. Seemingly without a care in the world, he twiddled the tassel of his hat, repeating "Feh! So many secrets, so many hidden plans," until he turned the corner around the other end of the hallway.

Pindlebryth headed one way to the southeast staircase and the infirmary, while Darothien left the other way towards the northeast staircase leading to her laboratory, still quite deep in thought. When he arrived at the medical section, all was quiet. The physician and nurse were whispering outside the recovery room doorway. The doctor faced him with an emotionless mask. Pindlebryth imagined the doctor would make an excellent international politico, or perhaps as masterful a cardsharp as Hakayaa or Tabarem. Excusing the nurse, the physician began, "The Prince was still in pain as he gained consciousness. We felt it best that we give him another, but smaller dose. We hope he will sleep through the night."

"How long have these attacks lasted before?"

"Each one has lasted longer than the previous one. It's impossible to tell, M'Lord, how long this one will continue."

Pindlebryth rubbed the fur on the back of his neck, hoping to relieve the strain of the long day's events.

"As you saw," Sacalitre continued, "Darothien has also been

observing the Prince after each attack. She believes that medicine in this case is a placebo that will eventually lose its effectiveness." The physician sighed in defeat, looking at the floor and shaking his head. "I am afraid I am now forced to agree with her. Since the Eye is magick in its nature, the best hope lies in whatever magick she can devise to counter it. She has worked tirelessly towards that goal."

"Very well. She already requested to talk to me. Perhaps an answer is finally in the offing." Rummaging through his thoughts, Pindlebryth looked down and to one side, then up and the other side, as if he could peer through the walls at Darothien's laboratory and Selephygur's room. "I shall visit one last time before I retire tonight."

"Very good, M'Lord." The physician bowed slightly as Pindlebryth and Grefdel headed to the northeast stairs.

The underground door leading to Darothien's workspace seemed as damp on the outside as the stairway walls, yet both were bone dry. The door opened into a room crowded with several objects. A glass display case with wooden frame and shelving occupied one wall, a table and chairs dominated the center of the room, display tables stood in each corner, and a door was closed on the far side; all made from the same wood. On what little open wall space was left hung a few tapestries – favorites of Graymalden – and statuettes of various subjects and materials stood on the low display tables. A large ring of wood floated one foot below the center of the ceiling, and inside its diameter was a disc of air glowing with a warm light.

As he entered the room, a statuette of a wolf on the display stand next to the opposite door came to life. It lifted its head and began to howl. Darothien emerged from the far door, and with a "Shh!" and a pat on its head she silenced the statue. It panted twice and wagged its tail, then resumed its original shape.

Fascinated by the golem, Pindlebryth asked, "Did you make that?"

Darothien glanced over her shoulder, and chuckled. "No, that was a gift from Graymalden." She looked at it with a moment of sadness, as she recalled her mentor. "He was endlessly amused by my ability as a child to becalm wild animals. But please, M'Lord, take a seat." Darothien gestured towards the table, as Grefdel stood guard in the hallway. "The door, if you please, Grefdel." Pindlebryth looked over his shoulder and nodded.

Once they were alone, Darothien opened the shelves' glass doors, and took out two pairs of gloves. She donned one pair and placed the second on the table directly in front of Pindlebryth. She then gently took most of the golden, bronze and blue calcite articles from the case and gingerly placed them all within his arms' length.

"I'm sure you remember these items. I would like you to examine these objects and their markings. But have a care – do not handle the objects without these gloves. There is an aura of magick about them I have yet to divine. I dare not touch them directly, nor should you." She arrayed them in four groups. "Also, when you are finished with a piece, please return the object to its original group."

As he donned the gloves, Pindlebryth indeed recognized the objects. They were the bent and broken pieces of the clockwork devices dropped by Selephylin's sleepwalker attendants in the Domed Hall on Vulcanis Major. He picked up one delicately worked piece then another, carefully scrutinizing each one. Placing each fragment back in its place, he noticed Darothien had intentionally arranged them – though no piece touched another, one could imagine their original forms. Each had been a closed loop of one shape or another; the first a simple ring, the others an ellipse, triangle and square. As he proceeded through the dozen or so fragments, Darothien took a seat next to him, and produced her notebook and stylus from within the folds of her cloak.

As Pindlebryth inspected the pieces, he saw they were inscribed with various languages. Each group had writing in two languages; one language he could translate or at least recognize its roots, but the second tongue was a set of petroglyphs that were totally foreign to him. One group's pieces were predominantly inscribed with the Vulpine language, the second group in Snow Goose, the third was likewise Crow, and the last contained sentence fragments of Raccoon, a language he recognized but was not able to translate.

Darothien studied Pindlebryth closely while he continued to examine the broken devices. She remained silent, but it was obvious she anxiously awaited anything he might say. At one time, she inhaled through her teeth sharply as Pindlebryth placed a metal and crystal piece of the broken square back in its place, sat back and paused in thought. Momentarily distracted, he regarded with vague curiosity Darothien, who seemed as if she could barely contain herself. She held her stylus above her notebook, like a serpent rearing to strike.

For several taut minutes, Pindlebryth examined parts of one group, then the second, then the first again. He similarly scrutinized each remaining group of gold, bronze and azure calcite. He compared the fragments of writing between the four groups of broken artifacts. He could do so handily in the language of their neighbors the Snow Goose, and the Vulpine language he was most recently certified in; he could also muddle through the Crow language, that he mostly learned through his friend Hakayaa; but he could only guess at writing that resembled Raccoon language.

"As far as I can tell, they all have the same sentence fragment bound on either side by these pictographs."

"What do they say?" asked Darothien with barely hidden anticipation.

"They say, '...and all its modes, are a Gift to the...' Fox, Wavey, Crow, and what I assume to be the Raccoon."

"Wavey?"

"An old Snow Goose name for themselves." He turned his attention to the unknown writing. "But as for these angular glyphs, I have never seen their like before. I can only postulate about their meaning. The first group of pictoglyphs, before the translatable part, seems to be the name of the gift, and is different for each artifact. But here," Pindlebryth stated as he picked up a pair of broken pieces, "as in each group, after the recipient race is indicated, is the word 'from' followed by the second set of glyphs. This second group is the same set of glyphs on all the ringed artifacts. It is reasonable to assume that word is the name of the benefactor."

Darothien yelped in vindication, as she literally jumped out of her chair. She collected the last handful of pieces from the glass case, and arranged them into a fifth shape – a pentangle. The portion of the ring written in Lemming matched precisely what Pindlebryth translated from the other devices – "...and all its modes, are a Gift to the Lemmings from...".

"Now here is the first of several mysteries," Darothien rasped. She hastily opened her notebook, and frenetically paged to one of the last leaves. It contained several drawings of Selephygur's Eye, and two circles of words written on opposite pages. She tilted the book, so Pindlebryth could see. "These are

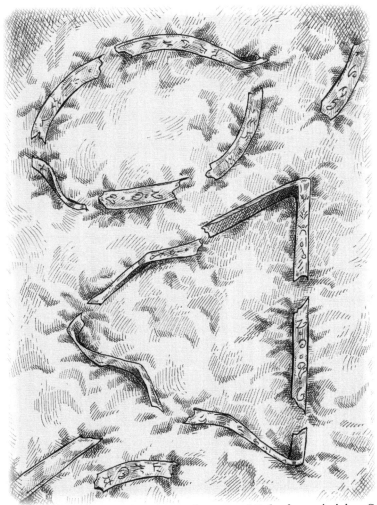

the writings around the circumference of Selephygur's iris. So far I've seen two sets. One when he is conscious, the other when he is asleep during his recovery."

"They seem familiar."

"They should. Look at the very first artifact, the one with the middle phrase in Vulpine. If you piece together the fragments of that first device, its first set of pictoglyphs – the name of the Gift – matches what I see on the Eye's iris when Selephygur is at rest. That proves the Eye is the Gift from the unknown Benefactor. It also proves it is indeed the item Selephylin stole from Vulpinden.

"Do you realize what this implies?" she asked after a pause. Her pitch lowered slightly, "There are five Gifts – one for each of these ringed devices! We can infer that each Gift is different, because each has a different petroglyphic name indicated by its ring. Since the Eye was held by the Fox, and the ring inscribed in Vulpine names the Eye, what is the next logical assumption? Each Gift is held by the nation of the corresponding language. The Crow, Snow Goose and Raccoon each have a unique Gift..."

Pindlebryth blurted with the elation of discovery, "But then the Lemmings have a Gift of their own! But where is it? Who has it?"

Darothien shrugged her shoulders, and only continued, "The entire library of Graymalden contains not even the slightest hint of any of this. And WagTail is unaware of any mention of such a Gift to the Lemmings in our archives – not that I could provide him much information to go on."

She stood, and limned the circle of light floating above the table with her index finger. When her arc was complete, the white light resolved to a translucent milky jade.

"Now for the next mystery. Look at the inner portion of the Fox device again."

Engraved glyphs, now limned with the same jade color, appeared on the previously smooth metal that comprised the inner sides of the ring. Pindlebryth tilted his head to view all the glowing symbols, and tried to assemble the device in his imagination. He glanced several times back and forth between it and Darothien's notebook. It was reflected in his eyes when he realized the solution to the puzzle. "A portion of the inside matches the second set of glyphs in Selephygur's Eye – but only one portion."

"Correct," agreed Darothien. "But you can see there is more. Notice the glyphs on the inside are grouped with spaces between them. I therefore think they are the 'modes' referred to on the outside of the device. There are obviously more modes to the Eye than we've seen to date. But we need to understand this glyph-based language. Do you see any additional clues to identify what language this is?"

Pindlebryth studied the inside for a full minute. Darothien was about to speak again, but he halted her by holding up his paw. He reached for her notebook, and methodically scrutinized through the last few pages, poring over drawings of other contrivances that were unknown to him. One was of a device with delicately balanced gears and levers, and marked rules that slid against one other, to measure items and quantities he could only guess at. The second was a ring topped with five gems – dotted lines were drawn between various stones seeming to indicate beams of light flashing betwixt one another. Three of the gems were labeled as different colors, but two of the gems were notated as being green. He realized there were no glyphs on these pages, and thereby were not part of the problem at hand. But his itching curiosity would not be satisfied without asking. "What are these?"

Darothien settled uncomfortably in her seat. "When I went back to Selephylin's lair to reclaim our travel items and my own magicks, I stumbled into what seemed to be her personal quarters. There I found what we needed, but also saw several self-operating magickal devices – I dared not touch them, but I tried to commit to memory as many as I could. There were more, to be sure, but I had to leave when I heard the roof begin to weaken."

"So, no one was seen operating these devices, and we have no indication what their functions might be." Pindlebryth filed this information away mentally. Perchance it would be meaningful sometime later, when the next layer of the puzzle was ready to be peeled away. He returned to the last pages with the sketches of the Eye exterior and its iris writings. His concentration grew in intensity as he rapidly compared between the pages and each of the various devices again.

After a time, he placed both paws on the table, saying, "It's strange. A solution seems tantalizingly close. But just as I think I see a pattern, or a similarity to our known languages, another portion contradicts a resolution." He exhaled a long sigh, "Maybe it is a Mother Tongue."

"Mother Tongue?"

"Yes. A language from whose roots other languages – or rules of language – had sprouted." Another sigh, and Pindlebryth asked, "Do you remember anything from the time when we first saw these five devices?"

"Only that they were held by the witch queen's attendants, who were stock still. I compared notes with Pendenar, and he agrees – the sleepwalkers holding the devices made no attempts to manipulate them. Nor do either of us remember them changing during the magicks that Selephylin wielded. If the devices are to open a window on the use of the Eye, or a clue as to the nature of the other four Gifts, it was not seen at Vulcanis."

Pindlebryth's shoulders sagged with disappointment, then even more from such a long day's weariness. "Very well. Perhaps an answer will occur to me after a solid meal, and a good night's sleep.

"Nevertheless, thank you for your efforts. You've convinced me that the Eye is indeed from the Fox nation of Vulpinden; that there are four more Gifts held by various nations, and that we now know what these nations are; that these Gifts are from one mysterious benefactor; and that one of the Gifts lies tantalizingly hidden somewhere in Lenland. You've uncovered a plethora of possibilities. I'm not sure I *could* sleep tonight."

He rose from the table. Darothien stood as well, and waved the light to its previous color and luminescence. She curtsied with a heartfelt "Be well, M'Lord," as he took off his gloves and laid them on the table. "But before You leave, let me give one more mystery to add to your dreams." She lowered her voice to barely above a whisper. "...or turn them into nightmares. What if this Mother Tongue you perceived is in fact the language of the Quickening Spirit?"

That gave Pindlebryth pause. He could feel the pinpricks of sweat beginning to break out on the pads of his feet and hands. That was patently ridiculous – Darothien couldn't be sane to consider such a thing, could she? Yet, to consider the possibility that within arms reach were items that would rewrite the belief systems of so many other nations unnerved him greatly. His legs trembled noticeably.

"Perhaps it is best I digest this for a moment." He took his place again in his seat, but Darothien remained standing. He clasped his hands on his lap under the table, in a conscious effort to refrain from touching the pieces of metal and azure crystal. Pindlebryth stared at those device fragments that were in Lemming, and again reviewed the pictoglyphs coupled with them. Try as he might, he could not think of anything to immediately disprove Darothien's conjecture. "Do you think Selephylin arrived at a similar conjecture?"

"That is a secret the witch took to the grave of her own making," Darothien shrugged. She too was visibly shaken by such a revelation. Her mouth betrayed only the smallest of frowns, but her eyes had the look of one facing the Abyss.

Pindlebryth had to take a moment to stop the roots of

astonishment setting in his own mind. When he reached a calm he could sustain, he rose again from the table. "At the very least, this pokes holes in some nations' belief that the Quickening Spirit is a quaint fable, and other nations that pride themselves on being the Quickening Spirit's one and only 'chosen race'. Believe me, I shall think long and hard on what you've shown me tonight. I bid you a good night."

Pindlebryth opened the door, and Grefdel joined him outside. They climbed the stairs, and traversed the East Wing to the highest floor in the South Wing. By the time they reached the topmost stairs, Pindlebryth found he could consider the many discussions this evening in a more tranquil manner. He *had* to – for his brother's wellbeing depended on it.

Striding briskly past Royal Guards all along the floor, Pindlebryth opened the door to Selephygur's apartments. He was sure his new knowledge concerning the Eye combined with something in these rooms would offer an answer. Evening began to fall as he meandered around the study, washroom, bedroom, personal dining room, and the front study again. He drifted to the main window facing the central courtyard, which was wide open with curtains drawn aside. The view was similar to the one from his own apartment's windows, with a glorious view of the sunset over the West Gate and barracks beyond. After a moment's thought, he tilted his head and raised his hand over his brow to better see the buildings beyond the gate. He spied the setting sun shooting rays of red light into and through the plain unadorned windows of the barracks.

He walked along the wall to the double doors that opened to the balcony. Selephygur apparently had a lawn chair and small table placed outside next to them. Warmly lit by the setting sun, they looked quite inviting. It was then Pindlebryth tilted his head with mild curiosity, as he noted the chair faced directly towards the barracks. In addition, the table had more than a dozen water rings left from bottles and glasses over a large portion of its surface. Pindlebryth wondered why Selephygur would spend so much time here. The table was obviously too small to be of any use for writing or to study his lessons.

With Grefdel in his wake, Pindlebryth left his brother's rooms, went one door down the hallway, and entered his own rooms. A maid was waiting, who then finished setting a place for Pindlebryth in his dining area when he entered. Throughout his light and quick meal of a fine stew of lentils and nuts, he turned and considered the view from his own study window and balcony. Even though he was not quite finished, he folded his napkin and stood up. He took one last look out his own window. The sun had fully set, and the lamps of various barracks rooms were lit. Though the West Gate walls hid the first floor of the barracks, he could see blurred outlines of soldiers on the second floor, the Lionesses and workmen in the uppermost floor still working on the changes in the regiment's new quarters dictated by the Major Domo. With a start, he opened his window. He leaned out to get a closer look, without the obstruction of the lead and pewter borders and the thick wavering rivulets in the hand-cut ornate glass. Nodding his head, he watched the silhouetted figures milling about in the barracks. Chuckling once with a note of finality, he shut the window again.

Pindlebryth finally left his quarters, as he and Grefdel calmly walked back to the ground floor of the East Wing to the surgery and recovery rooms. As Grefdel resumed his previous stance outside the physician's offices, Pindlebryth entered the recovery room to find Queen Wenteberei already watching over Selephygur. As he fitfully slept, she sat at the head of Selephygur's bed and softly read aloud from one of his favorite books – a tale of battle and glory, of heroic adventurers and inscrutable villains, of the victory of honor and virtue over loathsome evil. She continued to read, but her eyes showed she was grateful to see him.

Pindlebryth sat down next to her, and smiled faintly as he, too, listened to this favored tale from his youth. He remained with her, until the wee hours of the morning. Occasionally, throughout the story, Selephygur would smile and murmur happily from deep within his dreaming imagination. When the queen finished, Pindlebryth took her hand and said, "Worry no more, Mother. I believe I know how to cure our dear Selephygur." She looked at him pleadingly, but quickly thought better of asking and feeding false hope.

As they both left for their rooms, Pindlebryth took Grefdel aside and instructed him, "I will need to meet Major Domo Melajen, and his chief carpenter tomorrow morning."

Vadarog, Pindlebryth and the Royal Physician applauded as Prince Selephygur once again hit his distant target expertly and directly in the center. Three trios from each of Vadarog's local battalion, the Lioness, and the departing Eagle companies were in a fierce competition of sword, bow and crossbow. Prince Selephygur had almost cemented the win in the crossbow for CityState, whereas LeanShanks of the Lioness had won the sword, and SharpWatch of the Eagle was victorious in the longbow. After the competitions, the groups planned an evening of celebration of all nine participants, to bid farewell and safe return of the Eagle company to their home canton.

One of each group shot their final bolt. LongWhisker of the Eagle hit the target circle but clearly missed the bull's-eye, and RazorMane of the Lioness hit the border of her bull's-eye. The crowd held their collective breath as Selephygur loosed his bolt. All cheered ecstatically as he hit the target dead in the center.

Vadarog spoke aside with Pindlebryth, "Our Prince is performing famously, and once the scores have been tallied, I believe He will carry the day. How did you know He would no longer be afflicted with his migraines?"

"Do you recall the shutters I had Melajen and his carpenters install in the windows of the Lioness company's quarters a few weeks ago?"

"Yes I do," said Vadarog. "I'm still perplexed about the need for that."

The Royal Physician, with a hint of amusement on his face, silently shook his head in mock disbelief. "Surely, General," Sacalitre chided, "you haven't forgotten the halcyon days of your own youth? Or have you forgotten what it was like to be an adolescent, what you spent endless hours dreaming of, and what it was that so easily drew your own eye?"

"And still draws it, apparently?" Pindlebryth laughingly reminded Vadarog.

III – The Lens of Truth

Dear Pindlebryth,

I was so glad to hear of your return to PanGaea late last year. The place was so much grayer and duller without your wit and wisdom. While there was much to learn and much revelry to be had, the times at University just did not have the same panache. I am also very glad to hear that all is well with you and your family. While it is now known among all the nations about the evil that befell Lenland, I can only imagine what challenges you must have faced for almost a full year. You must tell me all about it when next we meet.

I apologize for not being able to greet you on your return to PanGaea, for the BlueHood family business required my presence away from my own studies for a time. Be assured that my troubles are utterly minor compared to your trials in the past, but the family had deemed that I was the only one capable of patching over a spot of bother down in the Southern Lands.

If you can break away from the castle routine, I'd like to make good on a promise made when we last said farewell. Please meet me at the crossing checkpoint closest to CityState, between Lenland and the Lodges of the WeatherWorn. If all goes well with my task, I shall wait for you there on the day two weeks before the start of the Fall semester.

I can stay as long as you can stand me, or at most until we both must leave for University.

Yours sincerely,
Haka

Pindlebryth folded the letter written in Crow, and returned it to his vest pocket. It was worn at its edges and folds from repeated handling. It had been a few weeks since it arrived by courier to the castle, but he found he could barely contain his excited anticipation of seeing his old friend Hakayaa again.

Next to him, Pendenar stood surveying the area with a watchful eye, scanning the groves of weeping willows and birches, under which their reindeer mounts foraged, and the river they drank from that flowed under a nearby wooden bridge. Pindlebryth instead concentrated on the beauty of nature's bounty, and how he would miss it again when returning to University. After the reindeer had refreshed themselves on a portion of food and drink – but not enough to slow them down – they all resumed their journey, over the road's bridge towards the Lenland border.

Pendenar had a look about his face that conveyed either puzzlement or worry. Every jounce of the reindeer's gait made his overly-tight headgear push his eyebrows together, only to accentuate his expression almost to a comical extreme.

"All right, Pendenar," wheedled Pindlebryth, next to him astride his own reindeer. "Out with it. What is on your mind?"

"I am concerned, M'Lord."

Allowing himself a smirk at his refreshingly guileless riding companion, Pindlebryth surmised, "You would be remiss in your duties, Pendenar, if you were not."

"Please M'Lord!" Pendenar admonished, his propriety somewhat bruised. "Why are we meeting your friend at a distant border crossing point, rather than in CityState? And why do we meet this Crow friend of yours along the Lodges border? Could he not just fly as he wills?"

"First of all, we both know we are going to an official Lenland-Lodges checkpoint, so there will be plenty of guards from the Eagle Squadron there to assist if anything runs afoul. Secondly, it is the closest border checkpoint from CityState, so troops are everywhere to be found." Then Pindlebryth rubbed his chin in speculation. "Lastly, he is meeting us as part of a favor that had I asked of him, while he helped me leave PanGaea to rescue Selephygur. I suspect he asked to meet us at the checkpoint, to satisfy his own flair for the dramatic. Please understand, Pendenar; I trust this creature as I might an older brother."

"Very well, M'Lord. But you must appreciate that Lenland is still not fully recovered from its loss, and both General Vadarog and Colonel Farthun require any of the Royal Family be properly attended away from the castle. If they were aware you had left with but a single guard, they would have put a stop to this little jaunt."

Pindlebryth did not respond, but instead spurred his reindeer to a trot. Taken aback by his prince's seemingly irresponsible action, Pendenar urged his mount back to

Pindlebryth's side. But he remained resolutely silent for the short remaining time to the checkpoint, still remaining vigilant even while chewing on his annoyance.

Straddling a river that flowed westward to MidSea, a large bridge joined two facing bluffs on either side. Made ages ago entirely of stonework without mortar, it was testament to the genius of the master architect and mason Henejer. As it artfully bounded between the two countries with lanes wide enough for foot and wheeled traffic, one could not help but to be drawn into a sense of nostalgia. It had stood for several hundred years, and looked like it would weather well even until the end of Time. What artwork went into this edifice, that is so seldom seen in more modern buildings!

The bridge was being well traveled this day. The early days of harvest were upon the lands, and trade across the bridge was vibrant. Such activity surely kept the inspectors of the Eagle Squad hopping, as they monitored all who crossed the bridge and inspected their lading. Despite the beehive of activity, Pendenar and Pindlebryth were spotted as they approached, and were hailed by one of the troops. He rode up to meet them on his own steed with hand raised, calling, "Well met, M'Lord! Major SharpWatch of the Eagle!"

Pendenar trotted forward to intercept the approaching Lemming, and returned the greeting. "Hail, Major. Pendenar of the Royal Guard. How is it you come to know M'Lord?"

SharpWatch sidled up to the pair, "We last met at the castle games. Good to see you again my Prince. "

"Ah yes, quite!" said Pindlebryth. "You won the longbow round, did you not?"

"I am honored you recall! I only wish LongWhisker shared victory in the crossbow as well."

"Tell him he may feel better about that. A few days after the competition, Prince Selephygur felt his advantage unfair, and ceded his prize to the more deserving Lioness squad."

"That's fine news, but I doubt it may assuage LongWhisker's bruised ego. He is certainly quite vocal in his longsuffering!" They shared a snicker or two, but Pendenar remained stolid and watchful.

"But to the business of the day – what brings M'Lord to this crossing?"

"Nothing of great import. I merely came to greet an old friend traveling from the Crow Rookeries."

"Crow?" SharpWatch looked a little perplexed. "I have seen no Crow today. However, there came an elder from the southernmost Beaver Lodges, claiming to have a message from a Crow named BlueHood. Shall I call for him?"

Pindlebryth turned to Pendenar looking as if he now feared a disappointment. Pendenar smirked, clearly convinced this was a fool's errand. "Send him through," Pindlebryth said with a note of discouragement. "I would hear this message."

SharpWatch turned his mount to face back to his post, and gave a piercing whistle with a gyrating hand signal. Presently, a Beaver astride a reindeer trotted forward from the bridge, and met SharpWatch. The Beaver was rather nondescript, except that he looked very old yet smartly dressed. Although the fur of his trunk looked quite pedestrian with an odd tint of bluish-gray, the fur of his head, arms and tail were as black as coal. As the pair approached Pindlebryth, the Beaver took a letter of passing from an inner pocket of his riding clothes, and handed it to SharpWatch.

Pendenar, careful as always, held up a paw to halt, and declared, "Please state your business, Grandfather Beaver." The creature painfully dismounted, creaking and groaning as he reached the ground, and momentarily disappeared behind the large reindeer. But it was not a Beaver that emerged from behind the beast of burden but a Crow – gray feathered over most of his body, with three exceptions of wingtips, tail and a head full of bolt black feathers that glinted a steel blue in the sunlight filtering through the rustling leaves above.

"Hakayaa BlueHood, at your service, M'Lord!"

Pindlebryth fairly bounded out of his saddle, and embraced his friend. All that the nonplussed Pendenar could do was accept the letters of passage being passed to him by SharpWatch. Pendenar had to fairly yank the papers from the sentinel's grip, as SharpWatch was totally absorbed in the novel change that occurred before him.

"Hakayaa, you old farce! You molted to a full shapeshifter! Congratulations!" Pindlebryth exclaimed.

With a sly smile he preened a few feathers and retorted, "Merely fulfilling the request you made of me when you left PanGaea." Motioning towards the papers held by Pendenar, he added, "Hearing that your troubles of almost two years ago were brought down on you by a shapeshifter, my family thought it wise that I have formal papers making an open matter of it.

They have also notified the Crow Embassy in Lenland's CityState to expect me to register these papers with them upon my arrival, so that every official tee is crossed, every jot is tittled, and so on, and so forth..." He rolled his wingtip to exaggerate his complaining, then exhaled in mock exhaustion. Pindlebryth smiled, innately understanding it to be the only protest left allowed to Hakayaa.

Pindlebryth turned to the bemused SharpWatch, "Thank you for bringing your charge to me. This Crow is an old friend of mine from PanGaea, and we shall be on our way to CityState now. Fare you well, SharpWatch."

"Thank you M'Lord." As he turned to resume his post, he added, "Perchance I can give LongWhisker hope to compete with you at the next games?"

"Perchance!"

Hakayaa and Pindlebryth mounted their steeds again, and the three began the return trip to CityState.

"So tell me old friend, what business was so dire it drew you from your favorite pastime of revelry, to your least favorite activity – namely, honest work?"

Hakayaa cawed a small laugh at the gibe made at his expense. "Therein lies a story that is far from simple.

"In a country far south of the Rookeries there is a beautiful lake in the savannas fed by a great mountain river. The lakebed goes all but bone dry once a year during the country's Season of Winds, revealing a richness of diamonds of every size, eroded and deposited from the treacherous mountains above. The lake sustains a great many races during most of the year, so the land is laid claim to by several clans of bush bovidae: impala, gnu, oryx, wildebeest and a few more.

A distant step-uncle badly mismanaged the relations with these clans, placing the family's collection rights over much of the lakebed in peril. I was sent because of my understanding of their histories, and..."

"...and your silver tongue?" chortled Pindlebryth.

"My gift of negotiation, if you please, M'Lord Pindie!"

Pendenar sniffed at such unseemly familiarity, Hakayaa continued without missing a beat.

"...but mainly because of my newly manifested shapeshifting ability. I inherited it from Mother's side of the family. Over many years, we have found the citizens of some nations feel more at ease when we can assume their shape during negotiations. I suppose it makes them feel we share a common bond, and thereby circumvents countless barriers to a mutual understanding. One has to be careful of the flip-side of that coin, however. There are some nations, like Lenland most recently – no thanks to Selephylin – that regard shapeshifters with suspicion.

"As such, Father used Mother's rare talents in the past to smooth the inroads to many countries' families of power, and to expand the BlueHood family business. Between the two of them, we have mining and collection rights to almost all the known gem-producing lands, and nary a single set of crown jewels in the Northern Lands is without some of our work.

"As for the business down south, it was a knotty problem indeed. The whole rhubarb took me most of a whole year to get all the clans once again to treat and trade as one with us."

"And what of your step-uncle?"

"He returned home with me, and has been replaced by a more trusted family member. I can only guess whose toilets my step-uncle is cleaning now."

The two colleagues laughed and recalled favorite stories and remembrances as though they had never been separated. Over an hour passed thus, but Hakayaa ceased soon after they reached the halfway point back to CityState, as he noticed the looks on faces of the travelers and traders heading south towards the Lodges. Most of the passing travelers paid them little heed, only a few recognizing the Prince and bowing appropriately. But occasionally a Lemming or two glared suspiciously at Hakayaa. At first the trio shook it off, but as they drew closer to the home of CityState, more often than not those travelers who were dressed indicating a higher station in society seemed to hold a palpable disdain for Hakayaa. None of which escaped the watchful eye of Pendenar.

As they approached a grove of hickory trees, Hakayaa suggested, "It seems I am not very popular with an increasing number of your citizens. With your permission, M'Lord, I'd like to draw less attention to myself. And to you."

Pendenar also nodded, agreeing it sounded like a good idea.

"All right," conceded Pindlebryth.

They all moved off the road to the side near the grove and halted, except Hakayaa who proceeded into the heart of the copse. As Pindlebryth watched closely with interest, Hakayaa faded between the strobes of light and shadow as he moved through the ranks of trees.

Soon a Lemming with black paws and a head of jet black fur emerged on reindeer-back from the trees. As he approached again, Hakayaa said, "There we are. That should keep undue attention from us. Shall we be on our way?"

"I must apologize for my people," Pindlebryth said as they resumed their journey. "You already know about the scourge of the Vixen witch queen. However, her deceit began long before that. Long ago, she assumed the shape of a Lemming to wed my grandfather. Her malice was so great, and her deeds so evil, that unfortunately many Lenlanders now view any race known to have shapeshifters with suspicion, Vixen or otherwise." He shook his head in chagrin. "I wish it were not so."

With a nod and a look of earnest regret and empathy, Hakayaa silently accepted the apology.

The group resumed their travels in silence, with most passersby not giving them a second look. They soaked in autumn's burning fury in hilltop after hilltop of maple, oak and poplar as the sun began to fall. Even Pendenar began to feel he could relax his vigilance a tad.

"Yours is a most inspiring landscape," finally sighed Hakayaa, breaking the long silence. "Compared to the greater part of my country, comprised of little more than stark cliff faces surrounding endless scrub, the pastoral landscape is quite refreshing.

"But M'Lord Pindlebryth, if you would be so kind, now it is your turn. Could you tell me what has passed with you since we last left each other's company? Remember, I haven't seen you since that day of the sleep-walking Lemmings when you left PanGaea under such dire circumstances.

"At the end of that semester, I was called away to the southern continent. Having been removed from the North for so long, I know only in the most general terms what had happened. I was eminently relieved to hear the crisis had resolved favorably for Lenland – but I have since then heard almost nothing of what your part in it all had been."

"Very well," Pindlebryth began with a sigh. He proceeded to tell Hakayaa the story of Selephylin, beginning with the evils she perpetrated on past and present generations of the Royal Family and the entire Lemming nation. Several hills and valleys passed under the reindeer's hooves as he related to

Hakayaa the horrors, riddle, rescue and escape from Vulcanis Majoris. The only things he did not reveal, were the secret of Selephygur's Eye, and the items that Darothien discovered and collected just before they left the accursed isle. The tale lasted throughout most of the remaining ride to Lenland's CityState and the return to the castle.

"Well, that explains many things – especially why shapeshifters are eyed so suspiciously in Lenland these days."

"I am afraid we have arrived late for dinner," apologized Pindlebryth, as they approached the West Gate to the castle grounds. "That is indeed a shame, for I would like to at last introduce you to my family. They would no doubt thank you for helping me leave PanGaea." The trio dismounted outside the West Gate and handed over their mounts to awaiting guards. Pindlebryth noticed that some guards were members of the latest troop exchange – a squad from the White Ghost platoon. From the lands bordering the Warrening, their uniforms were embellished with an emblem of a polar bear rampant. Passing through the gate, they started towards the South Wing. The reindeer were led back to the stables behind the barracks.

"I suppose we can make do with a small evening meal in the Royal Study. We can start a log in the fireplace, and catch up on the rest of our little misadventures. And maybe even begin to plan some new ones!"

"M'Lord!" Pendenar interjected. "Is that wise? It is quite unusual for anyone outside the castle to have access to the Royal Study and its neighboring rooms."

"I understand, Pendenar," replied Pindlebryth with a hint of annoyance. He was about to remonstrate Pendenar about making him repeat himself concerning his confidence in Hakayaa, when Pindlebryth decided it would be better to merely add, "But it is not entirely unheard of. I will take responsibility."

As they entered the building, Pendenar waved down a servant crossing the courtyard and relayed the Prince's wishes. The three, including Hakayaa still in Lemming form, entered the Great Audience Hall and headed towards the southeast staircase. As they crossed through Henejer Hall, Hakayaa was amazed by the striking architecture of the great room – while the walls were essentially perfectly plumb, almost every brick and block was recessed or protruded out from the overall surface by small amounts. The effect of the construction was mesmerizing and beautiful, if not a mite unnerving.

Pindlebryth pointed out various paintings, busts, and other artworks that graced the gallery. He described the historical significance of several of the pieces to Hakayaa, who found it quite interesting. He even queried Pindlebryth about Henejer himself.

"He was a master architect in the employ of our first king, Enorel the Great. Henejer was our country's best, if not one of the *world's* most prodigious architects. He not only designed and built this very castle, but several other beautiful and cunningly crafted edifices and monuments around all of Lenland.   For example, the bridge by which you entered Lenland was built by Henejer entirely by himself, without pointing or mortar. Similarly, he crafted this entire Hall by himself in secret. It is quite a mystery how he performed both these feats. This hallway was understandably named in his honor."

Pindlebryth and Hakayaa eventually entered the study and sat in the great chairs facing a roaring fire in the hearth. Waiting staff hurriedly set a small repast for the two friends. Pindlebryth and Hakayaa surreptitiously shared knowing smiles as one of the maids made doe eyes at the Prince's guest. First taking a few bites of sandwiches and draughts of mulled cider warmed near the fireplace, Hakayaa then commented almost absent-mindedly as he studied the ceiling. "Yes indeed, you survived victorious to tell quite a ripping yarn, Pindlebryth. It leaves me only wondering what part of the whole truth you chose to omit."

Pendenar nearly choked on the effrontery of this Crow visitor in the form of a Lemming.   But Hakayaa faced Pindlebryth, and they shared a knowing smile – as two opponents might do across a friendly gameboard.

"Come now, Pindlebryth. We've hoaxed far too many fraternities, pulled too many pranks on university stuffed shirts, and had too many games at the PanGaea casinos for me not to know some of your 'tells'. I'm sure you have your reasons, and I am grateful for the limits of the story you did enlighten me with, but in all fairness I would feel dishonest, or at least lax, if I did not let you know I detect something missing." He set aside his dish and mug to a side table, and stood saying, "Perhaps our new guest can shed some more light on the subject." Hakayaa turned and with a bounce in his voice said, "Greetings, m'lady!

You must be the fair Darothien, that your Prince was just telling me about!   Hakayaa BlueHood, pleased to make your acquaintance!"

As she entered in her lime green dress limned with a dark forest green felt border and cloak, she curtsied minimally to him, then to Pindlebryth as he stood. A glimmer of confusion flashed for a moment across her face, as she considered what an unusual name for a Lemming to have. "M'Lord, we had heard you had brought a guest from PanGaea. We bid you both welcome."

"We? Who else?" said Pindlebryth. He craned his head around Darothien to see who the second visitor might be.

"I was escorting Selephygur from a tutoring session, when we passed Tabarem in the East Wing. He was in his usual distracted state, mumbling something about 'barbarians at the gates of his citadel'. Pindlebryth spun to examine the room. To be sure, there was one of Tabarem's wildly colored raggedy hats on a rung of the study's galley ladders that often served as his reading perch.

Selephygur emerged from behind Darothien, carrying a clutch of textbooks in one hand. He was wearing an eyepatch, but from the fresh folds of fur under the laces rather than over them, it could be surmised that it had been hastily donned. Pindlebryth strained to see which patch it was – after a moment he could see it was not the opaque eyepatch which Selephygur wore most often outside the castle, but instead was the eyepatch he used for work. Comprised of thick black lacy material, it was only partially opaque, sufficiently shading the Eye to keep it mostly hidden, yet allowing Selephygur to peer out a small but functional extent for his studies while still preventing his migraines. All Pindlebryth could do was be still, and hope Hakayaa did not notice.

"Hello, Brother!" beamed Selephygur as he happily strode forward. "I'm pleased to meet a friend of yours from University. You did not tell me, however, that he was a Crow of the Rookeries."

Pendenar and Darothien wheeled a surprised glance at Selephygur. Darothien's expression of confusion returned, only doubly so, as she turned back to stare at Hakayaa.

Selephygur stopped and cringed slightly with the sudden realization that something of his doing was amiss. Pindlebryth signaled Pendenar to close the study doors. Darothien in startled wonderment, leaned in to Selephygur and scrutinized his face, and what little she could see of his Eye. "What is it you see?" she asked.

Selephygur's focus glanced back and forth, seeking any guidance from familiar faces, which were frozen in anticipation. All he could do was slowly admit the truth in carefully measured syllables. "Our visitor is a Crow, gray of body with bluish-black wingtips, tail and head."

Darothien permitted herself an uncharacteristic gasp as she turned to Hakayaa, and saw him bow his head, fold his arms together and curl up his torso. Hakayaa suddenly stood erect again as he changed into the form exactly as Selephygur described. His wing feathers made a sound like a towel being snapped as he partially opened his wings. He then quietly folded them back along his sides, after he readjusted his clothing.

"A shapeshifter!" she exclaimed in Pindlebryth's direction.

"Yes." Pindlebryth clattered his mug of cider on its saucer with some exasperation.

"Oh," Darothien flatly muttered. The full realization of what had been revealed, and to whom, became apparent to her. "Oh, dear."

"Yes, 'Oh dear', indeed! Pendenar, do you still have Hakayaa's papers of transit?"

"Yes M'Lord."

"Very well, please see to the door." Pendenar closed the double doors with a resounding thud, then stood facing the group with his paws on his belt.

Pindlebryth turned to Hakayaa, who observed somewhat amusedly, "What trouble am I in now, old friend?"

"Some of your own making," Pindlebryth said dictatorially. He quickly softened his demeanor before continuing. "But neither am I without fault. I should have reminded you to resume your natural shape, when we approached the castle gate." He glanced sternly at Selephygur. "Also, some of our members aren't quite old enough yet to master the necessary art of playing important items close to the vest."

"Oh, don't be too difficult on your younger brother," the Crow quipped, dismissing his friend's criticism with a wave of his wing. "After all, he is only all of, what, two years old? There is so much to learn in such a short period of time, doubly so for a member of the Royal Family. I am sure there is at least one or more events in your own experience at that age, that did not please your father His Majesty." Hakayaa moved closer to Selephygur, examining the patch. "And this must be the wound you received from the Vixen sorceress – except that it is not quite what it seems." Still scrutinizing Selephygur's face Hakayaa asked askance, "Perchance, Pindlebryth, this is the detail you chose to omit from the tale of your adventure?" Glancing at both brothers, he asked, "May I see what has been done to Prince Selephygur?"

Pindlebryth nodded with resignation to Selephygur, who raised the patch away from the socket, revealing the bejeweled Eye.

Hakayaa squinted to examine the item better, but then suddenly snatched a breath and stepped quickly back. "The Lens of Truth? *Great Kyaa!* You have the Lens of Truth!"

"You... you know what this is?" Pindlebryth demanded pointedly.

"And you do *not*? How did this come to be? Is this what the Vixen sorceress did?"

"Hakayaa," Pindlebryth commanded sternly. "We need to know what this 'Lens' is."

He stood erect, but was visibly shaken. "If I may sit. I must sit," he mumbled as he searched for his mug and his chair. He fairly collapsed in the seat, rubbed his brow, took the mug and guzzled it in one swallow. He coughed as his crop enlarged, then passed the liquid down his gullet. As he composed himself, Pindlebryth resumed his seat also, as Darothien and Selephygur inched closer to hear what Hakayaa had to say.

"The Lens of Truth is an Artifact of inestimable age. No one knows for sure its origin. Before today, I would have disregarded it as a myth, a long forgotten lore of legend. As a matter of fact, the only reason I am aware of the Artifacts of Old is because they are a pet crusade of my history advisor at University, Professor DeepDigger. His research into this hobby is regarded by his peers as a crackpot endeavor, and the University always denies his perennial requests for funds to research the Artifacts. Great Kyaa, if he could see this, he would be shouting in vindication from the highest rooftop."

Darothien interjected, "Wait. There's more than one? There are more of these Artifacts of Old?"

"Yes, but each one is different. This plainly is the Lens of Truth, and we've just witnessed one of its mystical powers. It could see through my shapeshifting. I think I recall it having a few more attributes, but I cannot remember them. I'm sure DeepDigger would be familiar with them all. He would also know how many of them there are, and the powers of the other Artifacts of Old."

He stared at the Lens even more intently, then faced Pindlebryth as a swath of realization swept over his face. "This is what the Vixen did? She implanted the Artifact into the young prince's head?"

"Yes, although 'skewered' would be a more accurate description than 'implanted.' At first it was a grisly affair – the witch queen attacking a newborn thus, driving the Eye as we have called it, into his own. But the Lens swiftly cleaved and grafted itself. It has since become almost a natural part of him."

"Indeed. It has grown along with the prince as he has matured," chimed in Darothien.

An ember that began as self-conscious embarrassment in Selephygur slowly grew into an uncomfortable anger. "I'm not an experiment! Stop talking about me as if I weren't here!" he barked.

Darothien turned and placed her hand gently on his shoulder. "We're not ignoring you, my Prince. It is merely that all this passed when you were but a small child. But there is something you can help us with now." She leaned in closer as she asked him, "Is there some other mode, some other strangeness that you have observed with, or through, the Lens?" The young prince was about to answer, when Pindlebryth interrupted.

"Silence," he calmly commanded, making a cutting motion with his right paw. "Too much has already been divulged about this here. Selephygur, if there is more you wish to add, it is best we first discuss it with our father and his Prime Minister."

"Then allow *me* to add some conjectures, in hopes of making amends for this cascade of indiscretion," Hakayaa piped in. He leaned forward in his chair, as the gears turned in his head. "You said the Lens came from the Vixen Selephylin. But where did *she* get it? Our family, while not in seats of power, is however in positions to hear things. One tidbit we've heard is that Vulpinden has lost a national treasure." Pindlebryth remained stone faced, but Darothien failed to suppress the sudden urge to swallow nervously. "It is a reasonable deduction that the Lens of Truth is this treasure. The seats of power in the

Fox nation are in chaos, and they are desperate to reclaim the treasure, so that they may remain in control."

Hakayaa glanced a piercing gaze at the brothers, yet one might sense there was a flicker of worry hidden there. "You've obviously been silent to all outsiders about the Lens, and you have been wise to do so. You have hidden its current location quite well so far. I don't believe Vulpinden knows the Lens is here... yet. But as this crucible of a library has demonstrated, sooner or later the truth will out. And the Fox are on the hunt.

"I dare say, when Vulpinden discovers that you are in possession of their most precious item, they will respond. And respond they will, very quickly. Given their nature, we both know that reaction will not be diplomatic, but more likely violent. You should prepare, and prepare now." Having spoken his piece, he reclined again in his seat, and rested his chin on his wing, deep in thought. His eyes flicked to and fro as a hunted beast; and he frowned deeply, as he considered what might happen next to himself and his friends.

Pindlebryth felt unaccustomed to all eyes looking to him for advice, instruction or succor. But he could do nothing other than what was best for all, and what his duty required.

"Pendenar, take Hakayaa to the North Wing. Give him good accommodations, and see to it that his needs are met. But place a guard on his door and window. Take his papers and register them at his people's embassy, and inform them that Hakayaa will be my guest here at the castle for a few nights. Then return the papers to me. Also, have aides gather the Prime Minister, General Vadarog and Admiral Carvolo, and relay to them they are to join me in the Great Audience Hall on a matter of urgency." Then he turned to Darothien and Selephygur. "Accompany me, both of you, to the Great Audience Hall. Wait there while I gain an audience with my Father. We will have much to discuss."

Pendenar waved Hakayaa to accompany him as he opened the study door. Hakayaa rose again from his seat. As he passed in front of him, Pindlebryth merely said, "Trust me, my friend; as I trust you." Hakayaa shot back a resigned glance, yet managed to work up a troubled smile.

Pindlebryth and the rest followed Pendenar and Hakayaa, only to pass by Tabarem leaning against the wall a couple of paces from the study's doorway.

"You won't find His Highness in the Great Audience Hall,"

he announced loudly.   "He is instead in Tanderra's antechamber, sharing a pipe and some blackberry wine with the Prima Donna Minister.   But do they think to offer Tabarem any?   Oh, no!   They have *important* things to discuss."   He unfolded his arms and strode into the study, merely saying, "Now, excuse me while I look for my hat."

Hakayaa cocked his head at Tabarem, and looked vacantly at everyone else around him.   He was rather baffled that such an odd character didn't warrant a reaction from anyone around him.

The two groups proceeded up the southwest stairs to the second floor.   On their way towards the East Wing, they made their way through the Royal Guard common rooms.   As they passed, several of the guard stood – some with alarm, others with confusion, concern or anger, as they saw in their very own barracks a Crow in the company of the princes.   A stern look from Pendenar was sufficient to let the guards know to keep their comments to themselves.

At the southeast stairs they took their separate ways into the East Wing.   Pendenar and Hakayaa followed the stairway down to the ground floor and the North Wing, while the others turned to the central hallway to the Prime Minister's office.   As they strode forward with speed and purpose, the two Royal Guards stationed outside the antechamber reached over and opened the outermost doors.   Febrile wisps of smoke curled up into the hall from the doorway, as Pindlebryth led the group along an aisle by the long ornate table.   The guards closed the great silent doors, leaving the group in the room.

The King was drawing laconically on a large carved briar pipe, while the Prime Minister was sipping the last dregs from his fluted crystal.   They both looked up from a pair of folders, each of which held several disorganized papers.   "What is all this about?" demanded Tanderra, as he rose dressed in his evening smoking jacket.

"I apologize for interrupting your meeting, but I bear important news.   I beg your patience, until Vadarog and Carvolo can join us.   I have requested that they meet us here," said Pindlebryth, nodding respectfully to his father.

"Very well," snarled Tanderra with some exasperation, his breath scented more with blackberry wine than tobacco. Momentarily, Carvolo and Vadarog hustled into the room, then confidently yet silently took their seats.   The others with

Pindlebryth followed suit and sat in smaller chairs against the walls, but Pindlebryth remained standing.

Once again addressing Hatheron, Pindlebryth began, "My apologies, Father, for imposing on you with such short notice. But Darothien, Selephygur and I have made a discovery that requires your immediate attention." He walked slowly as he talked, until he stationed himself in the corner of the antechamber, so that he could address the entire group.

"As you all know, we strongly suspected that Selephygur's Eye was a valuable item stolen from the Fox nation. We now have information that not only confirms that hypothesis, but also that the Eye is something much more — that it is an Artifact of Old named the Lens of Truth."

King Hatheron remained composed, Vadarog had a glimmer of curiosity across his face, but Tanderra immediately pounced. "Are you saying this Eye is an object whispered of in old wives' tales?"

"Forgive me, but I am not aware of what tales your wives tell you. I am merely reporting what we observed in the past hour." Carvolo, in his chair, smiled at the small jest, but Tanderra was obviously slighted. Not to be deflected, Pindlebryth continued. "We have all witnessed in the past that the Eye, or rather the Lens, has had an ability of superior clarity and focus. But tonight, we observed something entirely unexpected — it allowed Selephygur to see a shapeshifter's true form."

"Explain." charged Tanderra incredulously. "Are you in fact saying, especially in these times, that a shapeshifter has been allowed in these castle walls?"

But Hatheron in an authoritative voice rose, "Calm yourself, Prime Minister. My son informed me weeks ago that his guest was a Crow with a family history of shapeshifting, but that it wouldn't be until his final molt that his aptitude might manifest itself." He then directed to Pindlebryth, "It is, however, distressing to me that this Crow discovers under our very noses the thing we have been trying desperately to keep hidden from Vulpinden."

"Yes. Hakayaa BlueHood was here at my invitation from the Crow nation. May I remind everyone that Master BlueHood has been a comrade of mine since I first attended PanGaea University. Furthermore, he was of great help to me when Decardan and I returned from PanGaea in Lenland's hour of need," Pindlebryth bristled sternly. More calmly, he continued, "He came today to accompany me when I return to PanGaea University. It wasn't until we met at the Lodges checkpoint, that he demonstrated his new abilities to us. During our ride from the borderlands, his presence in my company was drawing undue attention. We all agreed that to keep the passage uneventful, he should assume our shape. However, I failed to remind him to assume his original form when we arrived here in the castle. If there is fault to be found, it is mine. I therefore will personally vouch for him.

"I would also point out that it was his intent to be officially registered at the Crow nation's embassy during his stay here. He is not in CityState under any false pretenses. But as events would have it, he has not been received at the Crow embassy yet – and they are expecting him. Accordingly, I charged Pendenar to inform them that Master BlueHood will be our guest, and we will hold his transit papers during his visit."

Tanderra shook his head, and chafed his paws on the edge of the table. "Oh, magnificent. The Crow ambassador has taken every opportunity to make a nuisance of himself. He has been trying for weeks to cajole his way into my office, on countless trifling matters. Now he will have an excuse that I cannot ignore."

Hatheron leaned to one side in his chair, and rubbed his cheekbone with his fingertips. "Understood. Now Pindlebryth, continue by describing the events in the castle. How did Master BlueHood stumble upon this?" urged Hatheron.

Pindlebryth recounted the incident in the Royal Study to the last detail. "It was then I stopped Selephygur before any more information was revealed in Hakayaa's presence." He turned to Selephygur, softened his tone, and gently asked, "Remember what Darothien asked you last time – were there any other unique or strange happenings that you have noticed with your Eye – that is, the Lens?"

Selephygur sat still and preoccupied for a moment, paging through his memory, his eyes flitting upwards from left to right. "I recall a few instances, when I could observe groups of people talking. For example, when some ladies of the court were chatting over pleasant nothings, or when a few members of castle staff were joking about their personal conquests and other trifles, I found the situation very confusing. For what they said did not match how their mouths moved. It was as if I heard them say one thing, but saw them saying another."

"Thank you, you've done well," quietly assured Pindlebryth, as he firmly squeezed Selephygur once on his shoulder. Pindlebryth then began to pace in thought, rubbing his chin as he did so. "So this Lens has clarity of sight beyond any ken; it can see past the defenses of a shapeshifter; and from what Selephygur tells us, I suspect it can detect when a lie is told. One can only wonder what other powers this Artifact can bestow, and what plans the witch Selephylin had had for it. Is it any wonder the Fox nation considers this item to be so valuable?"

Tanderra's animosity seemed to wane. "All right. Where are you going with this?" he asked Pindlebryth with honest interest.

Pindlebryth paused, standing in place and looking directly at Tanderra. "I want to revisit questions that were raised before in this room months ago. Namely, when will Vulpinden discover we hold their Artifact – if they haven't already? Also, to what end will the Arctic Fox nation go to retrieve their national treasure?

"I think we have the answers to these questions already. Just as we have had ways of hearing news about the Fox's loss of the Lens of Truth, it is reasonable to assume they, as shapeshifters, have even more covert ways to find out we have the Lens in our possession. As for the latter question, we have drawn up new treaties and strengthened existing agreements over the past two years with our neighboring nations for our mutual protection in anticipation of aggression by the Arctic Fox."

"Yes, I recall the discussion. We have them stalemated if they choose to attack," declared Vadarog.

"Ah, but only a military stalemate!" observed Pindlebryth. "Consider all we know. We have something the Fox nation desperately wants returned. They cannot act militarily because they could not handle either offense or defense on so many fronts. They already demonstrated long ago there are those in the Fox nation willing to use shapeshifting to achieve their aims. Are we all that sure they will not use covert means – nay, that they may already have some covert action in play – to discover the location of the Lens, and then to take it?"

There was an uncomfortable agreement between all at the table. Carvolo studied his maps on the table, while Vadarog closed his eyes and drummed his fingers on his crossed forearms. "Then we are agreed," said Pindlebryth with an overshadowing of disgust. "We are speaking of the possibility there is already a Fox shapeshifter spy in our midst."

"Why haven't I seen one before? If a spy is here, why haven't I seen him? Why haven't I seen lies before?" asked Selephygur, with a tremble in his voice, and a paw holding his forehead.

"Because you haven't *looked* for them before," replied Darothien with a faraway gaze. "Your sight with miraculous detail was almost immediately apparent, because your tutors pushed you in that direction from the very beginning. You *wanted* to see as much detail as possible in the small and in the far distant. But you haven't seen lies before, because you did not *expect* people to lie to you. Nor would anyone in the castle have need to lie to you.

"You only saw the discrepancies in others' speech because you tried to understand what you could not hear clearly. And most importantly, you saw Hakayaa in his true form because you earnestly wanted to meet your brother's friend of whom you've heard so much about." Darothien blinked slowly, and focused on the council before her.

"So I echo M'Lord's concern. We must address the possibility of a Fox spy among us."

While most of those seated looked awkwardly to each other to somehow effortlessly solve the problem before them, Carvolo asked, "Given this situation, why do we still allow the Fox embassy to operate within the CityState? Would not its staff have a shapeshifter, and have more easily infiltrated our personnel?"

"Possibly, but if we eject them now without cause, that would clearly show our hand. The action itself would raise Vulpinden's suspicions that we hide something from them." Tanderra made a single brushing motion with his paw. "No, it's better to allow the embassy to stay for the time being. In addition, if they someday find out, I would rather the possibility of a diplomatic solution be as close at hand as feasible."

King Hatheron chose another direction, "Very well, Pindlebryth," he said, tamping out the ashes from his pipe into a heavy lead crystal dish on the table. "We all seem agreed that what you put forward is correct. How do we protect ourselves from this shapeshifter spy, and any number of plots at which we can only guess?" Hatheron poured another dab of tobacco from a pouch he produced from a side pocket into the carved pipe.

As Hatheron struck a match, Pindlebryth posited, "Maybe we have a small advantage here. Only this very day, we discovered some of the true powers of the Lens. The Fox nation might think us ignorant of these powers. Who knows, they may be oblivious to the abilities of the Lens themselves. Might we not put our newfound knowledge to use before they learn of this?"

"I get the feeling you already have an idea how to accomplish this," said Vadarog as he slowly opened his eyes focusing on Pindlebryth.

"Not quite. Only that we must first find who the shapeshifter is. We can later rather concern ourselves with what he or she might do."

"Then the first area we should concentrate on are those on whom we depend on for protection." Hatheron mused between puffs. "General Vadarog, when does the White Ghost squad return to the borderlands?"

"Their tour of duty here at CityState is complete next month."

"Then I propose the following," Hatheron began. "We announce that the White Ghost squad is called back to their original duty along the Warrening border as soon as possible. We also state that a squad or a platoon from the CityState will join them as reinforcements."

Vadarog, genuinely surprised at this order, jerked his head and stared at his King. Pindlebryth cocked an eyebrow, anticipating his father's train of thought. He chimed in, "We stage a review of the troops to select which squad should accompany the White Ghost on their return to their original tour of duty. We also have all the Royal Guard present. As all three groups pass for review, Selephygur looks for a shapeshifter."

"Yes," agreed Hatheron.

Tanderra struggled to make a point. "But what if no shapeshifter is found? Do we still send the two squads, and leave CityState that much less defended?"

"We can let the White Ghost contingent return as planned," Vadarog replied, having returned to his usual inscrutable demeanor. "The bolstering of CityState forces was instituted while our population and our troops were decimated by the sleepwalker spell. That time is long past, and we have since replenished our numbers. I think we will still be safe even with a total cessation of reassigning troops from our other cantons. If there is no shapeshifter found, all the more reason to end the assignment of extra guards in CityState.

"As for our own troops, we can take at least up to a week to decide what to do. If a shapeshifter is found, they simply remain. On the other hand, if we find no shapeshifter, we can safely amend our previous statements by saying the situation is still under review, with the end result also being no relocation of our local troops."

"So be it," said Hatheron with finality.

He turned to Selephygur, and set his pipe in its tray. He steepled his paws in front of his muzzle. "My son, do you feel you can do what we ask of you, to search for a shapeshifter?"

Selephygur swallowed nervously, but answered firmly, "Yes, Father."

"Then We are agreed. We will make the announcement tomorrow." He looked at each of his staff as he addressed them less formally. "Vadarog, have the White Ghost and all the CityState troops ready for review in two days. I leave it to you to manage the logistics so that all troops are reviewed, while the CityState is at no time unguarded. Tanderra, notify Colonel Farthun that the same will be required of his Royal Guard."

Hatheron stood. "The reasons that necessitate this plan are not to be spoken of to anyone outside this room." He approached the doors, and knocked once. The doors swung open as silently as before, each handled by its respective guard.

Pendenar, standing outside, bowed and stepped aside allowing Hatheron to pass. Vadarog and Carvolo stood from the table, and bowed to Hatheron as he passed by. The general then also acknowledged Pindlebryth and Selephygur, saying, "If you will excuse us M'Lords, we need to start as soon as possible on His Majesty's orders."

After they left, Pendenar stood in the antechamber's threshold. Holding a silver tray with papers, a sealed envelope and a silver letter opener, he stated, "M'Lord Pindlebryth, I have returned with Hakayaa's papers, and a request from the Crow embassy."

"And there it is," growled Tanderra, interlocking his fingers tensely.

Pindlebryth took the lot from the tray, and opened the

letter, breaking its embossed seal of the Rookery embassy. He gestured towards the doors, and Pendenar closed them, standing guard inside the antechamber.   As he read, Pindlebryth became agitated. Presently, he looked at Tanderra, and paraphrased the contents of the letter.   "The Crow Ambassador demands to see Hakayaa, to determine his health and that he is treated well. He also demands that we deliver Hakayaa to the embassy for this interview." He threw the paper down on the table in front of Tanderra in disgust. "What cheek! First, he all but accuses me of kidnapping, then he has the gall to make demands! "

"Ambassador Kayawa was always one for theatrics," empathized Tanderra. He picked up the letter and scanned its contents. "He's been assigned to Lenland for less than half a year. I also hear that he was given this appointment just a few weeks after joining the Court of the Kyaa. Which makes me sometimes think the Court made him ambassador, just to be rid of him as quickly as possible."

Pindlebryth considered the Prime Minister. Gone were the abrasive manner and antagonistic debating. Instead, he now saw a person who merely performed his function of assisting the Royal Family. Pindlebryth sighed heavily to regain his composure. "What are our options?" he said as he sat down in a seat across from Tanderra.

"This is an official communiqué, and therefore must be answered officially. There is, happily, no binding requirement on us how soon we must reply. As for his demands, he is within his rights to see Hakayaa. He does not however, have any say where we allow them to meet. Nor is he in any legal position to demand under what conditions they meet. I take it Hakayaa is under guard as we speak?"

"Yes," Pindlebryth chewed on the words, "my friend is being held in quarters in the North Wing, and there are watches on the door and window." Pendenar silently nodded, affirming that Pindlebryth's instructions had been carried out.

"That seems as good a place as any," mused Tanderra. "I would prefer to be present for his interview with the ambassador. However, Kayawa would probably imbue the meeting with more importance if I were. It is probably for the best that you alone – with guards of course – attend the interview. I have other ways to monitor Kayawa, you know." Tanderra seemed somewhat abashed saying, "I believe I can trust you to handle the situation. Just keep in mind – despite Hakayaa being a colleague of yours, your highest responsibility is to Lenland."

"Thank you for your confidence in me."

Tanderra leaned forward. "What's done is done. We cannot change what Hakayaa witnessed. But if you have any sway over your friend, impress upon him the seriousness of the situation, and that Selephygur's secret must remain so. At least for the foreseeable future." To Pindlebryth's surprise, the Prime Minister seemed quite earnest in his desire to help him. Gone were the roles they usually played out when verbally fencing.

"Hakayaa is fortunate indeed to have an advocate in your position." But then Pindlebryth intuitively understood that Tanderra hinted at something else. Almost immediately, Tanderra confirmed his conclusion. "However, there are also others who would not hesitate in restricting him as long as necessary, even others who might pursue his prosecution as a spy." He leaned back in his seat, poured himself a half glass of wine, and with a frown downed it to wash the distaste from his mouth.

"Since you will not be present, what advice can you offer me about the Crow Ambassador?"

"Offer no opinions, personal, overheard or otherwise. Keep to the facts. If you find you must answer him, keep your answers to the barest minimum. He fancies himself a peerless opponent in a debate, but that's only because so many people fold under the bluster of that bastard's tantrums. Again – offer no opinions, even if they might be how much of an ass he is." The Prime Minister planted the empty goblet firmly on the table to emphasize his opinion of the ambassador.

"I will arrange for the meeting to be held in the North Wing's dining hall – for, shall we say tomorrow mid-morning? Although I will be there in spirit, please inform me afterward of anything you deem noteworthy during the conversation with Ambassador Kayawa."

Pindlebryth, deep in worry and doubt, silently rose from his seat, cursorily nodded and exited the antechamber, with Pendenar at his side. He trudged to the North Wing like a condemned prisoner to the gallows. When he arrived at Hakayaa's quarters on the second floor, he asked Pendenar and the guards on duty to wait outside. He knocked, entered and without acknowledging Hakayaa, he similarly asked the guard at the window to wait on the balcony outside.

Hakayaa sat stiffly in a cushioned chair in the main room, watching Pindlebryth until he also took a seat opposite him.

"Hakayaa, what am I to do with you?" Pindlebryth asked as his forefinger traced random circles on the table next to him.

"I know it's a longshot – Let me go?" he smirked.

At another time, Pindlebryth might have been amused, but all he could show now was impatient disdain. "Come now, you and I both know you are in a serious pickle. You yourself surmised that we have the Fox treasure, the Lens. You think that laughable?" Hakayaa quickly felt admonished for his misplaced levity.

"Months ago, we Lemmings came to the same conclusion that we had something greatly valued by Vulpinden, but had no concrete proof. Now that you've confirmed our fear, there is no dispute there will be dire consequences when Vulpinden gets wind of it. Furthermore, despite the fact that it came into our possession solely because of one their own's overarching pursuit of revenge, their huntlust and anger will probably not be assuaged. The result is that your discovery of the Lens makes it far too risky for my brother and Lenland to let you just walk about."

"Yes, and I've had time to think about that. Do you realize I have much at risk also? If the Fox nation learns that I have knowledge of the location of the Lens, my life would be worth little indeed. They would think nothing about capturing, torturing or killing me for what I know. So you see, it is in my own best interests to keep your secret."

Pindlebryth rubbed his muzzle, trying to coolly assess his friend. "Could you even keep it from your own family? Or even those in authority in the Kyaa?"

Hakayaa seemed slightly confused. "What do you mean? What else has happened?"

Pindlebryth knew he was duty bound not to answer – he could not let Hakayaa know that the castle's inner circle was concerned about Vulpine spies. Instead, Pindlebryth pushed himself up from the chair and walked slowly to the window, halting just before it to peer out over the treeline bordering the north side of the castle, and the city beyond. Past the manicured lawns and gardens of the castle, there emanated at first an orderly crosshatch of streets and intersecting avenues. As one got further and further away from the castle, the streets followed the ridges and valleys of the land itself. Soon the complexity of the roadways was not unlike the veins of a leaf. "Isn't that the way of life," Pindlebryth muttered aloud, "Things often start out easy to understand and predictable, but as time moves on the complexity becomes quite daunting." He turned back to his guest, who was regarding him with curiosity and looking for another 'tell.'

"Tell me about your shapeshifting ability. You've hinted at it back in PanGaea, and have demonstrated it plainly. But now I think I need to have a more detailed understanding. What shapes can you assume? What limits are there? Are there other abilities that accompany shapeshifting?"

Hakayaa reclined and described it with a more relaxed look. "As I said before, not all of our people have the Gift. It is mostly inherited along familial lines, although once in a great while a shifter will unexpectedly be born, starting a new line. Some believe the Gift was bestowed directly by the Quickening Spirit, but they are in an ever shrinking minority."

"But what does it allow you to do? Can you assume the shape of anyone or anything?"

"No. We can only shift to a creature we have actually seen. Creatures of our imagination are impossible, and pictures of a desired form will not suffice. Moreover, we can only shift to a creature that is of comparable size and weight – so I could not transform into a full-sized leviathan nor a butterfly, for example. Nor can we shift to assume a specific person's identity. We tend to shift into a single form of that creature unique to each shifter. So, if I were to assume the shape of Lemming again, it could only be the same shape you saw me take on earlier today. It's as if we change into what we might be like, had we been born into that race instead of Crow. It's merely a coincidence that my Hooded Crow markings make me appear as an older Beaver.

"That's as much as there is to know about Crow shapeshifting. I understand that other shapeshifters probably operate similarly, but it is rumored that Fox and Raccoon with the Gift have fewer restrictions."

"There's one I can think of," Pindlebryth snorted. "The Fox shapeshifter can take a specific person's form."

"Really? How do you know that?"

"Selephylin took the place of the doe that might have become my grandmother."

"Oh. I *am* sorry, Pindie," Hakayaa offered genuinely. "As for 'other abilities', those Crow with the Gift have similar boons as those Lemmings with a Name of Power. We age more slowly after achieving maturity, and have a resistance to most diseases and some magicks."

Pindlebryth nodded as Hakayaa spoke, absorbing the details. He then resumed his seat across from Hakayaa. He leaned forward intently. "I may have need for you to assume the shape of a Lemming again in a few days' time."

"Why? What will happen?"

"Nothing I can tell you exactly, until the day itself comes."

"Pindie, I have been fair enough telling you what I know." A look of impatience began to grow on Hakayaa. "I think I deserve to know what decisions have been made concerning me, and what will be required of me."

"Soon enough, my friend. I promise. But please, we have more immediate problems ahead. Ambassador Kayawa has demanded to see you, to determine your well being. We have told him you are my guest for an extended period."

Hakayaa chuckled as his face puckered in distaste, "I'll bet he's raised a stink already."

"Only a small tempest in a teacup so far, but I have been forewarned by others."

"Then I should let you know that I have no great love for this person. My family and he have had a few annoying clashes, and at least one very nasty dealing. He is a consummate bureaucrat – he will insert himself to control things to his liking, regardless of the cost to others. I cannot guarantee I will keep my temper when meeting with the ambassador – but for both our sakes, I will make a go of it."

"That's all I can ask. Just tell as much of the truth as you can – only omit any hints or references to the Lens. I will be there with you, so if he asks any improper questions, or if you are at a lack for words, I can answer for you." Pindlebryth rose, and straightened his attire, saying with a smirk, "...although I seriously doubt that the latter could ever happen to you, you silver-tongued scoundrel!"

Coughing lightly to bring himself back into a more serious tone, he said, "Ring for breakfast tomorrow morning when you are ready. We have arranged your meeting with the ambassador before noon." He strode over to the door, and opened it to the awaiting Pendenar, before looking back to say,

"Sleep well, my friend. We both have busy and trying days ahead of us."

Hakayaa looked at the ceiling, shaking his head with an enigmatic look in his eyes.

Hakayaa was finishing his breakfast of breads, butters and berries, when a perfunctory rap came at his parlor door. He was seated at the small dining table, peering in thought outside the window. From this angle of the North Wing, the morning sun framed the window and balcony in wispy shadow, but beamed to expose a calm pastoral scene beyond the city. The view would have been a perfect study for a painting, had it not been for the guard posted on the balcony.

He methodically wiped his beak, and rose to greet the visitor. He opened to the door to a Lemming he did not recognize, with Pindlebryth and Pendenar behind him.

"Greetings, Mr. BlueHood. I am Tanderra, the Prime Minister of Lenland. Pleased to make your acquaintance. May we?" he said as he gestured back into Hakayaa's room and proceeded in. It was clear he was not waiting for permission. Pendenar closed the door behind them, as he and Pindlebryth also entered. "Forgive me if I do not stand on formalities, but Ambassador Kayawa already awaits us in the dining hall below. I would like to have you speak with him as quickly as possible, so that he is less inclined to believe we are hiding anything from him."

"Which, of course, we are," quipped Hakayaa.

With a momentarily annoyed glance, Tanderra continued, "I take it that M'Lord Pindlebryth has briefed you, that you should be as forthright as possible, with the exception of any information concerning the Lens."

"Yes, yes. Is it still so that Pindlebryth will accompany me?"

"Correct. M'Lord will help to... clarify any responses. I would prefer that I would front for you in that event, but Kayawa would read my presence there as evidence of a political motive afoot, and believe that your original intent at CityState was more than just a visit between friends. Are you ready?"

"As best as I shall ever be. But Pindlebryth has surely

warned you that Kayawa and my family have a history, and I may have trouble keeping a civil tongue in my head?"

"So I've been told. High marks in my book, Mr. BlueHood. But try to keep it in check for all our sakes."

They proceeded along the hallway, with the balcony guard bringing up the rear. Halfway down the hall, they were surprised as a Lemming appeared from behind one of the columns along the inner wall. He was dressed in evening wear of the gentile class, but his clothes looked like they were fitted by an insane or blind tailor. "You who are about to face bombastic bureaucrats, we salute you!" he announced as he bowed low. His crumpled silk hat fell off his head, and rolled down his extended arm, and was snatched up nimbly in his paw. The other Lemmings moved on without much notice, but Hakayaa was baffled.

"What... Who *is* that?"

Pindlebryth replied with a sprinkle of humor, "That is Tabarem. He wears many hats. He fancies himself as an archivist, jester, historian, gadfly, pundit, and a host of other functions, depending on the day, and depending on the hat. He is entitled to live in the castle, witnessed by his Name given him by the Quickening Spirit. And King Hatheron is often amused and sometimes bemused by him."

At the staircase, Tanderra stayed behind as the remaining four descended the stairs to the dining hall. The hallway at the bottom of the staircase led to a large oblong room, with a cupola that was composed of dozens of concentric elliptical ridges. The stonework was cunning and beautifully set with several bas-reliefs depicting the days and deeds of Enorel the Great. Hakayaa began to fully appreciate the craft of the room's stonework, as he realized that the cupola amplified any sound made in the room. The curtains were drawn open allowing in the light from the brightly sunlit courtyard. The furniture was carved from dark cherry wood, including six chairs surrounding a circular table where Kayawa waited standing, with an assistant and a castle guard. As Pindlebryth entered, a butler waiting at the side of the door joined his entourage.

"Greetings M'Lord, and to you Mr. BlueHood," said Kayawa as he bowed minimally. "I take it you are both feeling well, this fine day."

Pindlebryth tried to disregard the saccharine tone of the ambassador. "Quite so, Ambassador. I hope you also are feeling well today." He motioned to the chairs, as Pendenar pulled out the Prince's seat. "Please, be seated," he said as amicably as he could muster. The circular table had six chairs, but only three of them had a separate setting for biscuits and tea with a carafe in the center. He sat down and the butler poured him a cup from the pot. The butler followed suit serving Kayawa and Hakayaa as they took their chairs, then stood in wait at Pindlebryth's side.

Pindlebryth took a calming sip, placed the cup gently back in its saucer, and said perfunctorily, "We all know why we're all here. Shall we begin? What questions do you have, ambassador?"

"A good beginning," thought Tanderra, who sat quietly in a confined and spartan space. It had a single arrow slit window for illumination, a sliding door, and a heavily padded chair placed next to a parabolic depression hollowed out of the wall at ear level.

The Crow ambassador signaled to his assistant who took out a pad of paper and stylus, and began to take dictation. "Why, Prince! What seems to be the rush?" Kayawa said with a generous flourish. "On such a wonderful day, we should take pleasure in such pleasant settings, with such pleasant people." Kayawa breathed on the cup to cool it.

"Indeed. It is such a *pleasant* day, that Hakayaa and I are anxious to attend to our activities."

"No, my Prince! Give him nothing he doesn't ask for!" said Tanderra to himself.

"And what might that be? A walk on the boulevards of CityState? A ride in the countryside?"

Pindlebryth chided himself as he realized how quickly Kayawa wanted to trip him up, to catch him in a fabrication. "We are still catching up on tales of our escapades since last we met. There is indeed much to do before we return to PanGaea University, but we have not decided on what to do first today."

"Besides, I thought you were here to visit *me*," Hakayaa added humorlessly.

"Very well." Kayawa turned in his seat towards Hakayaa. "You have been treated well, I take it."

"But of course. Were you expecting otherwise?"

"Is your freedom to move about hampered in any fashion?"

"I wouldn't put it that way. I am accompanied by a castle guard wherever I go."

"So you *are* restricted!" Kayawa seemed to champ at something inconsequential.

"No less than I might be, than when I visit the Court of the Kyaa. Speaking of which, how long has it been since you have seen your fellows at court? I am sure your presence is sorely missed," said Hakayaa slipping in a sly barb with a touch of sarcasm.

Kayawa's aggravation grew, by the set of his beak, and the focus of his eyes. "Not that it is any of your business, but I often receive letters from my comrades, about how much the Kyaa feels the absence of my wise counsel."

"What is Hakayaa trying to do?" thought Pindlebryth. "Perhaps he's trying to goad him, or to keep him unbalanced, on the defensive rather than offensive?"

But Kayawa was unswerved, and pressed on with growing spite in his voice. "I hear that during your trip through Lenland, you adopted the visage of a Lemming. Did you feel in any peril, traveling through this foreign land? Were you asked to change because the Lemmings find the Crow so distasteful?"

"No!" blurted Hakayaa, becoming more upset. "I did so, to avoid drawing attention to myself or the Prince during our travels."

"As I explained to Hakayaa," added Pindlebryth, "our country suffered greatly due to a Vixen witch, whose evil deeds began and ended with shapeshifting. It is understandable, then, that our people still hold a suspicion about shapeshifters in general.

"I, however, do not. In fact, I congratulated Hakayaa on becoming a full-fledged shapeshifter."

Hakayaa silently nodded in agreement. "It was, in fact, *my* idea to shift into the guise of a Lemming."

"I see." said Kayawa as he slipped back into an overly ingratiating tone. "Have you been asked to shapeshift again at some future time?"

Hakayaa became subdued, and quietly admitted, "Yes."

Tanderra held his breath.

Kayawa immediately leaned forward to press the issue. "And what have you been asked to do?"

Pindlebryth interrupted, "There were no explicit requirements or instructions, per se – merely that he might assume the form of a Lemming again. Just as he changed during our travels to CityState, he may want to do so again if and when we go out and about."

Tanderra nodded to himself again. It was the truth, yet wrapped in sufficient misdirection. Kayawa looked askance at Pindlebryth, assessing how far he wanted to pursue this point. Pindlebryth kept up his show of earnestness, despite the pounding in his chest. He felt like he was playing a bad hand at the PanGaea casinos.

Thankfully, Kayawa and Hakayaa turned their attention back to each other. "I have heard on good authority, Mr. BlueHood, that you have had little activity at all during your visit here. That you, in fact, have been confined to your room since you arrived." Kayawa turned with a glint in his black eyes and a sudden sharpness in tone to Pindlebryth. "My Prince, is this any way to treat a good friend?"

"Listen here, you *toad!*" Hakayaa exploded. "I have been treated well, and have no complaints about my stay here at CityState. If you have any valid questions, by all means, air them out and pose them now. Otherwise, Ambassador *Tadpole*, keep your machinations to yourself, and away from me, my family and my friends! I find your attempts to find intrigue in innocent events contemptible, even for a *polliwog!*"

"What is going on?" thought Tanderra, as he fought to remain silent in his berth. Pindlebryth was also visibly taken aback by the sudden tirade. He had never seen his friend lose his composure so quickly, and so vehemently.

"As you wish, sir," Kayawa replied oily, with a satisfied smirk on his face as if he had just eaten one of the frogs that Hakayaa was ranting about. "I do not want to upset a member of the House of BlueHood so. Please understand that I am merely concerned about the safety and comfort of one of the Kyaa's most preeminent citizens."

Murder was in Hakayaa's eyes. He angled his head at Kayawa to draw a bead as if he intended to fly across the table and attack. He shook his head slightly, and then glowered also at his host. But after a moment, a look of surprise and embarrassment was in his visage. He drew in a breath and calmed himself, and the raw emotion washed away.

"Then we are finished?" flatly asked Hakayaa, returning his attention to the ambassador.

Kayawa stood, saying, "Quite. Enjoy your time here at CityState. If you need the services of our embassy, do not hesitate to engage us. I wish you success at University and all your endeavors. My best regards to your family's health!" He bowed, and took a few steps back. He ruffled his right wing, and his assistant closed his notebook. "Good day, to you also, M'Lord." He rigidly turned about, and exited the dining hall by the glass doors leading into the central courtyard, followed by his assistant and the castle guards assigned to them.

When the doors closed behind them, Pindlebryth turned to Hakayaa and observed, "I think I just saw a rather spectacular example of one of your 'tells'."

Hakayaa chortled at his misstep. Pindlebryth could not tell through the feathers whether he was blushing or not. "I did try to warn you, after all. Kayawa and our family have a history that does not endear him to me."

"Not to fret, my friend."

"As for 'tells', I wonder what you were not telling Kayawa, when you answered for me about shapeshifting. Not that I fault you for it, Pindie, but I could tell something else is behind the curtain."

"Now that this small task is over, we can discuss that in my rooms," Pindlebryth concluded just before he finished the last of his tea.

"Fair enough. But I'll need to get a few things from my room first."

The two got up from the table to return to Hakayaa's room, when their attention was drawn to the inner courtyard. A strange gust of wind yowled along the walls, and rattled the windows of the room. It whistled through the risers and bleachers being erected in the yard by workers for the upcoming martial review, then blew past the Ambassador and his assistant.

He was nearly bowled over by the rush of air, and his notebook flew out of his wing. The book landed open, and the stiff wind shuffled the pages, like it was paging back and forth through the whole volume. After the wind died down, the two Crow tried to regain their composure and collected their things. It was then Pindlebryth caught a glint of green emanating from Selephygur's window.

Pindlebryth chuckled and Hakayaa laughed outright at the events as they unfolded in the courtyard. Kayawa dove on the notebook as if his very life depended on it, while the assistant hopped and ran after the herd of scattered papers.

"Perhaps there *is* a Quickening Spirit, after all! And He has a sense of humor to boot!" jested Hakayaa. The two clapped each other sharing their humor and relief, and proceeded towards and up the stairs. Hakayaa seemed a mite surprised when Tanderra rejoined them at the top of the staircase. As Hakayaa went into his room, Tanderra paused outside with Pindlebryth. "What was *that* all about, M'Lord?"

"I don't know exactly. But I suspect I'm going to have a long talk with my brother. And possibly one of his tutors."

"I beg your pardon?" Tanderra shot back in confusion.

Pindlebryth only then realized that Tanderra could not have seen the mischief in the courtyard from the secret listening room. "Oh, I was thinking of something else." Pindlebryth cleared his throat softly. "Yes. I've never seen Hakayaa so flummoxed – what makes it so unusual is that he's been quite unflappable in many tight situations. I'll see what I can find out." Pindlebryth started to get an itch in back of his mind.

"So what do you have in mind with regards to Hakayaa's shapeshifting?"

"I'll tell you by this evening, if he agrees to it."

"As you deem best, M'Lord. You know where to find me." Tanderra soliloquized softly, "Who knew the Crow hated frogs so?" and left as Hakayaa emerged from his rooms, with his jacket folded over one wing, and a book in the other.

"Shall we?" Hakayaa said, as he started off with a jaunty pace. The pair, with their guards, made their way through the East and South Wings, wending their way to Pindlebryth's chambers.

"I couldn't help but notice the intricate and curious stonework of the public room where we met with Kayawa," said Hakayaa as they walked. "No matter where I stood or sat, every voice and footstep sounded as if it were right next to me. Quite a feat! The quality of the masonry reminded me of the ornate bridge where me met yesterday, and the art gallery. Obviously more of Henejer's handiwork."

"Quite an astute observation, Hakayaa. If you spent a few days in our archives, your head would spin with the range and elegant wizardry of Henejer's accomplishments. Sadly, many of the secrets of his masonic craft are lost – he took them to his grave. Many have since tried to duplicate his techniques, but all have failed."

As they entered his rooms in the South Wing, Pindlebryth rang the velvet bell strap just inside the door. The two then cleared aside several works in foreign languages that cluttered the dining table, and settled in around it. Hakayaa hefted one pile from the table and placed it on the floor next to the voluminous bookshelves. Taking a small handful of books from the top of the pile, he tried to file them as best as he could. He tilted his head to read a few of the spines on the shelves.

"What? No literary works from our country?" rebuked Hakayaa, as he stood facing the library. He turned to face Pindlebryth, and set his wings akimbo in mock effrontery. "I'm horribly disappointed!"

"Sorry, but I only know the colloquial Crow speech that you have often used. I fully plan to formally learn your language, possibly next semester." With a scrap of sarcasm, he added, "Then perchance you can enlighten me about these great works written in High Crow. I might even make it a project to translate them into Lemming."

"An excellent idea! You might even succeed at selling half a dozen copies!" Hakayaa chuckled, and joined Pindlebryth again at the table.

"During lunch, let me tell you what I'm planning for tomorrow," said Pindlebryth. "Once we are finished with lunch, we can go for a ride. After dealing with that blowhard of an ambassador, we both can do with some fresh air to soothe our spirits."

The waitstaff entered and served lunch, and the two friends relaxed. But the itch in Pindlebryth's mind did not abate.

Selephygur looked like an animated clothes tree as his butler finished adjusting his formal dress uniform. He was still fussing over the last details of his task as Pindlebryth, Tanderra, Darothien, Hakayaa and Pendenar filed into Selephygur's rooms. Pendenar moved to stand by his fellow guard LongBack, who kept a constant vigilant eye on the young prince. Selephygur swatted away the butler, as Pindlebryth commanded, "Please leave us." The poor Lemming was about to protest about the cuffs still being the wrong length, but he held his tongue, bowed and excused himself from the room.

Once they were alone, Pindlebryth went to Selephygur and

greeted him by clasping both his shoulders. "Brother, the hour is nigh. Are you ready do what we have asked?"

"Yes, brother," solemnly replied Selephygur.

"How long will you be able to function, inspecting the troops through your eyepatch?

"Two hours easily. Three hours with minimal pain."

"Good, we should need less than two hours to do what we need to do today. If you are ready we shall begin immediately."

Selephygur nodded, and removed his eyepatch.

Darothien stood in front of Selephygur, and gently guided his head towards her with her paws. "Now my Prince, relax and concentrate on me."

"Hakayaa, if you please," said Pindlebryth.

He bent over, curling his wings over and around his head and body. His appearance reminded one of a large feathered egg. He slowly straightened as the feathers shrank in size and faded into transparency. He finally stood erect, and before the group was the Lemming that Pindlebryth and Pendenar had seen before – gray fur over most of his body, except for his black paws, neck and head. Darothien stepped aside, out of Selephygur's field of vision.

"Selephygur, what do you see?" asked Pindlebryth in a low soothing voice.

"A Lemming. The same as you do."

Darothien spoke up, with command in her voice. "Now *look* at him. *See* him. Look at him, *wanting* to see him as he really is."

His brow furrowed in concentration. "Yes. I see him as a Crow."

"Excellent," said Pindlebryth. Now scan the room, examining each of us, wanting to see everyone as they really are. Tell me what you see."

Selephygur slowly pivoted and named each person, one by one.

"The guards as well."

He looked at them, then again one last time at Hakayaa to double check. "Every one except Hakayaa is a Lemming."

"Put your working eyepatch back on. Any changes?"

"No. It is a bit more difficult with the patch in the way, but I can manage it."

"Good. Now you and LongBack accompany Tanderra and Hakayaa. You will first review the guards waiting for us on the floor below us.

"As you examine them, Hakayaa will remain in Lemming form, and be your control, your proof. While you still see him in Crow form, you can be assured that you are examining the guards correctly. It is imperative that you see both Hakayaa and your target at the same time. If you spot any irregularities, do not overreact, but calmly bring it to Tanderra's and LongBack's attention. Do you understand?"

"Yes," Selephygur replied as he adjusted his patch, and combed his fur over its strap. He grinned broadly with innocent excitement.

"Some of these first guards will be with us during the review in the courtyard below," explained Tanderra. "The others will relieve the guards currently on duty throughout the castle. Those guards on duty now will then be in the review on the grounds outside. They and all of our troops will file past the reviewing stand."

"So we will be assured that none of the guards are shapeshifters," followed Selephygur.

"Correct," continued Pindlebryth. Hakayaa will be seated one row ahead of you, so that you may continue to prove all the remaining troops. Again, if you see a shapeshifter amongst the troops, alert Tanderra immediately but quietly. We do not want an outsider to know of the Lens, or your ability with it. Do you understand?"

"Yes." Selephygur tried not to sound impatient, though he felt his brother was hovering and being overly didactic.

"All right, off you go. Once you approve the guards downstairs, follow Tanderra who will lead you past all the castle staff, who are waiting for review in Henejer Hall, and finally take you to the review stand. I will join you there presently."

Pindlebryth inched slightly closer to his brother, and spoke more softly. "Selephygur, our security very much depends on you now. Not just you and I, but Mother and Father also, and everyone in the castle. I am very proud of you this day. Do well, and keep safe." Selephygur returned Pindlebryth's embrace in earnest, then stepped back and bowed his head in acknowledgment. Pindlebryth saw the four to the door, but held the door open. "A moment, if you please, Pendenar."

He glanced quizzically between the two, but Pendenar left Pindlebryth and Darothien alone. Pindlebryth moved to the window facing out over the courtyard and the new and finely embellished review stand. But Pindlebryth was focused solely on the North Wing's dining hall doors across the grounds.

"What was that hijinks with the ambassador yesterday?"

Darothien moved to within a pace behind Pindlebryth. "Oh, you saw that." she replied with a small mischievous lilt in her voice. "I was seeing Selephygur to his room after lessons were complete for the day, when we heard a commotion clear across the commons, loud enough even to pass through the windows of the dining hall in the North Wing. We could easily see Hakayaa was greatly distressed, and that you were not having a pleasant time either. When the ambassador and his assistant exited onto the grounds... Forgive me! I couldn't help myself from tormenting those Crow, returning some discomfort in good measure to them."

Pindlebryth chuckled, "And this was not Selephygur's idea?" He waved his hand, shuffling away any polite denial on Darothien's part. "Never mind. That's quite alright. The two of us enjoyed your sport."

"The contents of the Crow's book intrigued Selephygur," continued Darothien. "So I obliged him, and fanned it with a zephyr. He didn't say how much of the book he was able to focus on, or what part of its contents he could read. I am sure if it was important, he would have brought it to your attention by now."

"I see." Pindlebryth heard a horn outside sounding a command, followed by the gathering troops snapping to attention. They quickly tightened their ranks in formation at the far end of the commons near the West Gate. "We had best be going. The review is about to begin."

The pair, followed by Pendenar, hurried down the spiraling stone staircase at the eastern end of the top floor hall, down to the ground floor. Making their way through Henejer Hall of the South Wing, the castle staff was about their business and leaving the room in all directions. "Since there is no undue commotion, apparently they had all passed Selephygur's gauntlet," thought Pindlebryth. The trio exited the castle through ornate folding doors of stone and glass, onto the central courtyard behind the review stand. Constructed of temporary wooden and metal structures, most of the stand was festooned with banners, bunting and multi-colored flourishes bearing the Lenland heraldry.

The two circled around to the front and climbed the stand

into their seats. Pindlebryth sat next on Selephygur's right, while Darothien took her assigned place one row lower. Tanderra was already seated by Selephygur's left, and Hakayaa sat on the next lower row betwixt them. Pendenar, along with the other guards already reviewed and approved by Selephygur, stood in a row wrapped along the entire length and sides of the review stand. Two Royal Guards holding polearms, and with crossbows slung on their belts, served as the entry guards on either side of the center steps leading into the review box.

Pindlebryth surveyed the tableau, and seeing nothing that required his immediate attention, closed his eyes and deeply inhaled to calm himself. A breeze bearing the aroma of late summer blossoms made Pindlebryth's muzzle quiver.   An abundance of autumn anise, garden phlox and sequim lavender wafted throughout the entire atmosphere.

In the distance he could hear the flying steeds in their stables outside the West Gate beginning to complain. They probably were not used to being left mostly alone, and probably some were late for their feeding. As the climbing sun drove out the last of the moisture from the air, he could single out the call through the air of his own dear petrel, Voyager, keening from behind the walls. Soon, the flying steeds quieted down.

Refreshed, he reopened his eyes just as the bugle and wood drums announced the review.   As rehearsed, Hatheron ascended to the front podium and began his prepared speech – due to two years of peace and plenty enjoyed by the CityState and all of Lenland, the additional platoons pressed to duty around CityState were no longer necessary. The White Ghost platoon could return to their home along the borders with the Warrening.   In a further act of good will, He and General Vadarog would now review the troops to determine which platoon would be first to have the honor of reciprocating, of serving a period in the cantons that assisted CityState in her time of need.

Selephygur understandably began to fidget – he was not used to the long-winded orations called for by such occasions, and wanted to use the Lens as quickly as possible.   King Hatheron finished in the time allotted him, and General Vadarog assumed the podium to order the review to begin.

Again, the bugle and drums announced a different tune for the exercise, but the wooden and gourd drums continued the moderate beat for the march. As each platoon approached the stand, its block of troops peeled off their lines behind their platoon standard bearer. Each line performed a right face, and formed a single file, turning along a line eight paces from the stand. As each Lemming passed through the line of sight formed by Selephygur's and Hakayaa's seats, the young prince scrutinized them. After each squadron passed, they formed sixteen paces away from the stand, and slowly began to fill the courtyard block by block from the West Gate inwards.

First passed the Red platoon, the pride of the CityState soldiers, followed by the Blue and Green platoons. Bringing up the rear was the White Ghost platoon from the north, and finally the rows of Royal Guards relieved by the guards proved by Selephygur.

Without warning, as the standard bearer of the White Ghost stepped forward to become the pivot point for the first line of his platoon, Selephygur whispered to Tanderra, "Something's not right." Pindlebryth turned towards his brother to hear more clearly. Feigning to shield his eye from the sun, Selephygur furtively adjusted the patch to get as precise a view as possible. "I see a Fox!" he hissed. This time Pindlebryth heard the warning, as it was loud enough for both to hear.

As the bearer approached the stand, Tanderra signaled Pendenar at the corner of the review stand. Suddenly, Vadarog declared, "What's that on the standard?"

He intended for only the Royal Family to hear, but a few more heard his exclamation. The standard had a grapefruit-sized brass globe atop the center, couched in a life-size bronze polar bear paw. Almost in unison several heads snapped to look directly at the standard bearer. Pendenar signaled four guards at attention to accompany him as he marched along the front of the stand behind the bearer.

The standard bearer quickly glanced about and saw what was taking place, and immediately recognized the situation was becoming dire for him. He took a step back and wielded the standard like an atlatl.

Pendenar yelled the order to "Halt!"

The drum beat stopped, and the remainder of the White Ghost platoon stopped unaware that the order was not directed at them. Those on the first line were stunned at the sudden turn of events, at the threatening action of their fellow soldier. Others were quicker, and rightly assessed the situation after a moment's hesitation. Still, even though they sprinted at breakneck pace like Pendenar and his fellow Royal Guard, they were not speedy enough to stop the attack.

The bearer launched the brass globe towards Prince Selephygur. It arced high through the air, but not high enough to be out all the guards' reach. One of the review stand guards jumped and struck the globe with a glancing blow from his polearm. The globe careened off its mark past the young prince and to the far side of Tanderra. Hakayaa leapt back between Tanderra and Selephygur to shield the prince. The globe clanged against the railing to the side of Tanderra's seat and exploded.

A shock wave, far stronger than one might expect for such a small globe, pulsed across the stand. The wooden railing splintered violently, knocking several guards on the ground to their feet, and tearing the nearest guard in half. Shrapnel caught Tanderra full in the face and body. Hakayaa and Selephygur fared much better, due to the shield of Tanderra's crumpling form. Intense heat and thick black smoke issued from the explosion, causing blinding confusion and panic in the stand as the acrid screen enveloped them all. Pindlebryth could barely see the darkened forms of Hakayaa pulling Selephygur away, and the fallen Tanderra was but a dim nebulous shadow silhouetted by half a dozen burning embers.

The cacophony of screams, orders barked and countermanded, the melee of fists and weapons from the courtyard, the patter of falling fragments of wood and metal, the overturning of chairs, the pounding of footsteps up down and across the vibrating wooden beams underfoot – all fell to the wayside of Pindlebryth's consciousness, as he thrust his way to get to Tanderra. One side was unwounded, but his left face and chest were in bloody tatters. He moaned softly in and out of lucidity. Pindlebryth hovered over him, tearing off his own sleeve to fashion a bandage, when he was alerted to a new unexpected sound.

Selephygur cried with a gurgling, guttural yelp. Pindlebryth could only see two black forms surrounded by swirling gray and black clouds. One was larger, and hovering over the other. Pindlebryth could only look in shock and disgust as the large shape quickly lunged at the head of the supine form. Selephygur screamed in agony, as the other leapt up into the air.

"Hakayaa! *No!*" screamed Pindlebryth.

Darothien produced a flash of green from her wand, and whistled up a wind. Through a hole in the smoke above the fracas, Pindlebryth could see Hakayaa completing his shapeshifting into that of a peregrine falcon. The Lens of Truth, with bits of tendon and skin still attached to it, dangled from the falcon's beak. The great bird swallowed the bejeweled Lens into its crop, and let out a keening cry, before bolting up and away at astonishing speed. Its cry at first held a shout of success, but as it died in the falcon's throat, Pindlebryth heard in the fading call overtones of loathing, shame and regret.

Pendenar appeared through the dispersing smoke, trailed

by one of the entrance guards wielding his polearm. He leaned over Tanderra and tore cloth from the hanging shards of bunting. He deftly folded Pindlebryth's torn sleeve into a compress, and tied it with bunting over the gashes deep in the Prime Minister's flesh that continued to lose the most of his lifeblood. Fashioning a tourniquet from the cords of his epaulets, he glanced at the guard and shouted above the din, "Get the Royal Physician and a medic *now!* The Prince and the Prime Minister are wounded!"

Pindlebryth desperately shouldered over to one of the review stand guards, and clutched at his belt. He tore off his crossbow gun, and fumbled for the bolts. Through sheer instinct he loaded and aimed, but it was too late. He fired anyway. The bolt arced true, but fell to the ground, far short of its mark. He slammed the gun to the ground in utter frustration.

Pindlebryth then pivoted over to his brother. Selephygur was trying to silence his yelling through clenched and grinding teeth, as blood coursed between his paws and the torn eyepatch from his empty eye socket. The elder prince followed Pendenar's example, and tore bunting and wrapped it around Selephygur's wound anchoring it around his head, forming a temporary field bandage. Forcing down panic made Pindlebryth's breath quick and shallow, and he incoherently sobbed with every exhale.

As the smoke continued to clear under the new stiff breezes, Pindlebryth looked over the courtyard. A circle of troops stood around near where he last saw the treacherous standard bearer. All had lowered their weapons. Farthun and Vadarog paced inside the radius of the circle, yelling and gesturing wildly. Guards collected a handful of medics and shouldered their way through the crowd, and up the review stand. The medics ordered the Red, Blue and Green standard bearers to combine wooden planks with their flags and poles to make field cots. The clearing smoke revealed the physician Sacalitre was off to one corner finishing a makeshift splint to Queen Wenteberei's leg. When it became apparent to him that more urgent needs required his ministrations, he left her with King Hatheron holding her hand, and lurched up to join the medics on the other side of the stand. He quickly triaged Selephygur, and judged that his injuries were not mortal. Selephygur was loaded onto one of the quickly constructed pallets, as the physician began to treat Tanderra's wounds. Sacalitre kept applying temporary bandages as Tanderra was transferred to his own pallet. Tanderra fell into shock, and the field doctor covered him with a field blanket to keep him warm during transport.

"To my surgeries immediately with them both!" he directed. He looked around to find any other life-threatening cases, but Pindlebryth urged him on.

"Go! See to them now! If the shapeshifter is still alive, I'll see he is brought!" he sputtered. Sacalitre acknowledged the command, and ran alongside his patients' litters.

As the last of the injured were whisked away, Pindlebryth and Hatheron stood and descended into the crowd. Pendenar cleared the way, parting the troops as they pressed on. The three of them looked down on the wrecked body of the shapeshifter. In death, he reverted to his original Vixen form. His neck was broken and a deep and vicious blade wound scored across his spine, apparently as he attempted to run and disappear in the crowd of confusion.

A faint keening suddenly caught Pendenar's attention. He and Pindlebryth looked skyward to see the rapidly shrinking form of the peregrine Hakayaa, as he receded westward beyond the city. "Fetch my petrel! Prepare Voyager immediately!" desperately ordered Pindlebryth.

"It's no use, M'Lord," replied a troop coming from the stables. "The aerial cavalry has been sickened – some sort of drugged feed. I saw the White Ghost standard bearer by the stables soon before formation – he must have done it then." He also raised his head, and followed Pindlebryth's line of sight. "Besides, even Voyager could not catch a beast of that speed."

Pindlebryth looked inside of himself – frustration, pain, hatred, disappointment, fear and sorrow answered. But the itch in the back of his mind was gone.

He looked at his father the King, the visage of implacability. He searched for recrimination or anger, but saw none. He found there was already enough inside himself.

"This is all my fault. My plan. My deed. My error. How could I not see this? How could I allow this to happen?" came Pindlebryth's thoughts amongst the maelstrom of events and possibilities around him. How did he allow himself to be ensnared in all this? He planned for most of his life to be a linguist, a translator, a diplomat – to assist his country by being expertly fluent in the languages of every nation important to Lenland. Instead, he found himself in the center of disastrous events, fashioned by his own hand. He was surrounded by developments filled with struggle and strife, which could easily lead to another catastrophic crisis for his homeland. Quickening Spirit, how did this come to pass?

He turned to look back at the review stand, and latched onto the slowly approaching Darothien. She paced toward him as though she were merely a spectator watching her own personal nightmare. Their eyes locked and shared an unspoken bewilderment. She shook her head in disbelief and dismay at the disaster surrounding them all.

Pindlebryth arose out of his musings as droplets of blood fell off his brow. He gradually became aware of the unmistakable stench of burnt fur, and realized some of it was his own. He lightly dabbed his temple with a paw, and it came back moist. A small wound from the blast scarred his temple, but only now did he pay it any attention. More of his blood dribbled onto the red-stained grass as he picked up the broken remains of the standard. He examined it, and found a hidden release switch along the length of the pole. It retracted the nails in the bear claw holding the bomb in place. He guessed the mechanism also somehow armed the globe. He threw it onto the body of the Fox spy.

"Take all that to the morgue," instructed Vadarog. "I'll have the field surgeon look at the body when he has completed more pressing matters." He looked up at Farthun, then the King.

"I will be at the surgery with the Queen, the Prince and the Prime Minister," growled Hatheron. "I will discuss options with you, Colonel, along with General Vadarog and Admiral Carvolo this evening." His voice quivered with threatening, "I want answers. And how we shall reply."

There it was – the recrimination. Pindlebryth not only felt it, he *knew* it. His presence at council was not required.

A medic started to tend to Pindlebryth, wrapping a bandage across his brow. With his canteen, he washed the carbon from the fur on Pindlebryth's face, arm and chest, looking for unexposed wounds. But Pindlebryth paid him no mind – it was his shoulders that hurt. They slumped as if weight of the world were planted directly on the back of his neck.

But then he felt the gentle touch of Darothien's hand there. "Go. They all need you."

He tilted his head and eyes toward her in appreciation, and nodded slightly in commiseration and thanks. He began to plod as if he were in a trance to the East Wing and the first floor surgery. Order slowly continued to return to the field. Vadarog ordered the medics to tend to the last of the wounded. He assigned a detail to cover and take away the remains of the guard obliterated in the blast, assigned other groups to break down the review stand, and still others to obtain reindeer-drawn carts to haul away the debris. The sense of confusion in the field finally ebbed away, as it was replaced by tasks on which the troops could concentrate. But Pindlebryth could not fully quench his personal panic yet.

He entered the outer waiting room of the surgery. He crossed the empty room to peer through the window of the side door into the operating room. Sacalitre was ministering to Selephygur, and the field surgeon was tending to Tanderra. Both had a bottle of the physician's amber tranquilizer opened next to each patient, and nurses periodically applied it to hemispherical cloth masks over their muzzles.

Selephygur seemed to be out of mortal peril, and was breathing slowly and steadily. In contrast, the Royal Physician bent over him, working frantically. Pindlebryth could see, past the doctor's shoulders, streaks of red emanating outwards like a bloody starburst on the cloths surrounding Selephygur's head. Tanderra was far worse off, and was still wracked with spasms of coughing. He was lying on his right side while the field doctor worked on the burned left side. With each cough, fresh gouts of blood sprang from his muzzle. He lay in tatters of bloodied and blackened cloth cut away to expose the wounds. He could barely make out what the field surgeon was saying through his mask. "His cranial injuries are very severe, and several of his organs are badly bruised or torn. I will have to perform further exploratory surgery. At the very least, I'm afraid he'll lose part of one of his lungs."

Sacalitre was busy stretching and grafting skin across exposed muscle and bone around Selephygur's eye socket. "I will assist as soon as I am finished here," he said reservedly without looking up.

"Don't be long," shot back the field surgeon.

Pindlebryth stepped away from the surgery door as a nurse emerged to procure more vials, bandages, metal implements, and other needs from the outer room cabinets. After the nurse returned to surgery and deposited her armfuls into a steaming cabinet, Pindlebryth opened the doorway to the patient recovery room. His mother wore a freshly fashioned cast about her ankle, and his father sat beside her. His attention seemed to be directed at her cast, but he was lost in thought. A moment later, Hatheron looked up, and Pindlebryth reacted by bowing and stepping backwards out the door.

"Son. Please, don't go," implored the Queen. She raised her hand and reached for him from her bed, but he continued to back out of the room. He felt he could not face his father. The door creaked shut, but he could still hear their two voices as he backed past the surgery entrance.

Held by indecision, he wanted to plead with them, to tell them how sorry he was, to repent of placing his brother and so many others in harm's way; another part of him wanted to crawl away into the darkest, farthest recesses of the castle; yet another part mindlessly raged, wanting to kill something – anything. Most of all, he couldn't understand why he had been betrayed by a friend as close as any brother. Nor could he tolerate all the questions that came unbidden.

Why did Hakayaa tell him about the Lens, only to steal it in such a violent and despicable manner? Was he in league with the Fox nation? If so, why? What detail did he miss, that might have helped him foresee and prevent this calamity? Pindlebryth grabbed with his fist at his vest over his heart. He wanted to rend his clothes, when the door to the recovery room opened.

The backlit form of Hatheron stood in the doorway momentarily, as he regarded Pindlebryth. His face was calm and sedate, but his eyes flitted like those of a caged animal's. Without a word, he walked over to the surgery door and peered in. He bowed his head, and almost painfully exhaled and inhaled.

"What are we to do, Pindlebryth?"

Pindlebryth could only offer a stunned silence. He did not know how to reply – he had never seen his father like this.

Hatheron turned to face him. "Today my youngest was attacked. I almost lost both my sons. And I might still lose a trusted friend." He shook his head, looking at the floor. "By the Quickening Spirit, there will be a reckoning," he growled. He returned his gaze to Pindlebryth, but his eyes were different. "I wanted someone to blame. Anyone. Forgive me, I wanted to blame you."

The fear and panic grew again by leaps in Pindlebryth, but Hatheron continued, stepping closer to him.

"But the truth in all this is – before I could blame you or anyone, I also must blame myself. We both had a hand in creating the plan to unearth the spy. You may have filled in the details, but we both saw the same need. Never forget that both Tanderra and I approved of the plan." Hatheron cast a long worried look back at the surgery.

Pindlebryth's emotions began to ebb, and he presently found the courage to speak. "I just do not understand Hakayaa, Father. I've known him for several years – long before we were ever attacked by Selephylin. He's helped me through thick and thin. How could be turn on me now? On us? How could he do this unthinkable cruelty to Selephygur?"

"We may never find his reasons. Only now, he has made himself an enemy of Us, of Lenland. Join us tonight when we meet to discuss our response to the Fox and Crow."

Hatheron returned to the surgery entrance, and looked again through the door. Nurses now tended to cleaning up and bandaging Selephygur. Both Sacalitre and the field surgeon were hovering over Tanderra. They and two guards who volunteered to assist were working furiously over his chest.

Pindlebryth simply sobbed, even though there were a confusing myriad of emotions vying to speak. There was a small twinge of relief, hearing his father no longer blamed him, but it was quickly swallowed up by the maelstrom of sadness, hatred and remorse that still remained.

He wandered aimlessly throughout the castle. He lost track of time. He could not remember the path he took to his rooms, or how long he took to get there. He was sitting at his study table with two books in front of him, when he was brought out of his fugue. Roused by the sound of Pendenar knocking at his apartment door, he found himself still staring at the opened book written in Crow on top.

He hesitantly entered, after Pindlebryth barely whispered admittance. "M'Lord. News about your brother. He is out of mortal danger and recuperating. The doctor has finished as much as he can do to reconstruct his face. But it will take several days for healing to complete."

Pindlebryth reacted not at all, continuing only to stare at the book. "What about Tanderra," inquired Pindlebryth in a listless, apathetic voice.

"He died in surgery, M'Lord."

"How?"

Pendenar shuffled his feet. "The doctors tried to save the lung, but the damage was too extensive. There was shrapnel everywhere, and part of his abdomen was also scrambled by the shock-wave of the blast."

Pindlebryth looked up at the ceiling. His jowls ached from holding back any show of emotion whatsoever. "Thank you, Pendenar," he whispered. "Please leave me be for a while."

"But your presence is required at... Yes, M'Lord." Pendenar suddenly felt it best to leave his Prince a moment or two to himself. He bowed and left the room, and quietly closed the door behind him.

Pindlebryth looked down at the topmost book again. It was Hakayaa's journal. Open to the last entry, a lone inscription said simply:

Forgive me.

IV - Trials and Transformations

Pindlebryth snapped out of a dreamless sleep, woken by his brother's panicked outcry. As Selephygur lay in his bed in the recuperation room, his arms first thrashed about, then both paws clutched at the bandages around his head.

He jumped to his feet to his bedridden brother's side, and along with an orderly pulled Selephygur's arms away from his bandaged face, holding them firmly until he returned to full consciousness and clarity. Selephygur rolled his head, a wide swath of cotton wrapped around it, holding a thick gauze pad over the wound and an opaque disc of cardboard over the remaining eye. The young prince relaxed, save for his labored breathing from the sudden exertion.

"It really happened, didn't it?" he asked of no one in particular between gulps of air. His arms lost their tension, and Pindlebryth and the orderly released them.

"Yes, brother. I am afraid it did."

Sacalitre hastily entered the room.

"Pindlebryth?" Selephygur called, turning his face towards the sound of his brother's voice. "How long have you been here?"

Pindlebryth held his paw firmly. "Yes, it's me. I've been here since the council broke late last night. We met in the Prime Minister's antechamber, and had to..."

"Quiet, please!" ordered the Royal Physician, as he placed his ceramic half-dome over Selephygur's heart and bent down to place his ear on the flattened upturned side. Satisfied, he stood erect again and examined the bandages, straightening out any displacement that his patient caused. "I'm glad you've calmed down much more quickly this time. These night terrors will pass soon."

"I still don't understand why I am forced to remain in this bed, bandaged like a mummy," Selephygur pouted.

"Two reasons, my Prince. Until you can awake without a panicked episode, you must remain here with my staff. We can't afford you tearing off your bandages every few hours. Secondly, I want your eye totally immobilized. If you use your remaining eye, the remaining muscles and tendons in your other orbit will naturally be stimulated to track along with it, even though it is empty. Then all their sutures and the rest of my delicate work on the surrounding skin will be torn apart."

"That I understand well enough. It is bad enough to remain motionless like a lump of clay, but to be also imprisoned in hospital away from my own room now is... is..."

"Frustrating?   Intolerable?   Damned   inconvenient?" Pindlebryth smirked. Selephygur pouted with an exaggerated frown, and crossed his arms petulantly.

"...adding insult to injury! Next thing you know, I'll be spoon fed again. Will I also need help to hold myself when I use the toilet?"

"Only if you stand up," interjected the physician.

The two brothers snickered at the ridiculous turn of the conversation, and Selephygur relaxed his arms and his air of annoyance. LongBack also sniggered quietly standing at the recovery room door, until Pendenar silenced him with a stern look. Pindlebryth cleared his throat, indicating the need to be serious again. He nodded to the physician, who collected the orderly and guards, leaving the brothers alone in the room.

"Sacalitre tells me that the facial and superficial sutures can be removed three days from now, but the work inside the orbit will take at least an additional week to heal. Be thankful you have a Name, or healing would take even longer." He clasped his brother's paw firmly one last time. "I will ask the doctor again how soon you can be allowed to recuperate in your own room, and maybe even be taken for a constitutional occasionally."

Pindlebryth turned to leave, but Selephygur would not release his paw. In fact, he gripped it even more firmly. "Why? Why did he do this to me?"

Pindlebryth sagged, then sat, nearly falling back into his chair. His eyes focused on long-past memories. "I wish I knew."

"But he was your *friend,* damn him!"

"I *know*!" Pindlebryth threw down his brother's paw. "I've known him for years. I want to believe something or someone forced him to injure you. To take the Lens by force. To throw away my loyalties. But I am simply at a loss." If his younger brother were not in the room, he might have cried. "I cannot begin to say how sorry I am for letting this happen."

"This was not your fault, brother."

Pindlebryth saw Selephygur's face take on aspect that burned though his bandages – like it hid a deeply buried anger.

"You and I were both deceived. You more so, because he took advantage of your trust. Do not feel your confidence is too easily earned. I have heard many times of your exploits, and they plainly show that this was not the simple con of a bucky-come-lately. He may have hatched these plans for a very long time – perhaps even since the time of your victory against Selephylin. Or he truly did not know we had the Lens until we met, and he decided there and then to throw away your trust.

"But that does not matter. Whatever his reasons for committing this treachery against myself – against both of us – I sometimes find myself hoping that I am the one to mete out the fate what he so richly deserves. Not just an eye for an eye, but tenfold that." Spite, malice and the pain of his torn face spilt out. "A hundred times!"

Selephygur's words somewhat unsettled Pindlebryth – his brother was so fixated on his hatred, that it threatened to warp his view of the world, and poison his every subsequent word, thought, or deed.

"Calm yourself, brother. I can only imagine what you are feeling. But you are in no shape now to go gallivanting about like an avenging angel. The best thing for you to concentrate on is healing. Both body and mind."

Pindlebryth clasped his brother's shoulder one last time as a farewell. He was about to turn to leave, when Selephygur reached up, his paw in return feeling its way along Pindlebryth's arm to his shoulder.

"How is Mother?"

"She will be bedridden for a while. What we thought was a simple sprained ankle, has turned out to be a torn ligament. I will let her know how you are improving." He released his brother, and opened the door to leave.

"As for Father and myself, it will be a very interesting day. And that's putting it mildly. We expect there will be quite a bit of feathers and fur flying in the Great Audience Hall today. But first, we must meet with our own ambassadors." Before he disappeared through the door, he looked over his shoulder and bade one last time, "Be well, Selephygur."

As he left, LongBack sidestepped back into his prince's room, and closed the door. Selephygur faced the warmth of the morning sun streaming through the window.

"Oh, you're not leaving me behind that easily," he muttered. He turned as best as he could approximate towards LongBack. "My Father the King habitually starts events at the top of the hour. Please fetch me a walking staff at the bottom of the hour, LongBack. I think that you can take me for my 'constitutional' at that time, while my brother and Father are occupied with our diplomatic corps. Tell the good doctor that I promise to only sit quietly and listen to the world around me."

LongBack nodded out of habit, then followed it with a verbal acknowledgment as soon as he realized its pointlessness. He immediately found Sacalitre and the orderly waiting just outside of the recuperation room.

Leaving the infirmary, Pindlebryth climbed the spiral staircase to the second floor and proceeded to the South Wing, with Pendenar in tow. As he entered the barracks, several Royal Guards interrupted whatever they were doing at the moment, and snapped to attention facing the prince with their smartest salutes. Pindlebryth waved them all down, signaling to merely continue their routine. He paused as he crossed the common room's large window facing the central courtyard. He observed silently, as the various countries' ambassadors and each of their small flotillas of assistants and attachés made their way to the Great Audience Hall below him. Each group was bounded on four corners by members of the Royal Guard and the army. A colony of Beaver from the Lodges came in first, followed by a down of Arctic Hare from the Warrening, then a gaggle of Snow Geese, and a skulk of Arctic Fox. He could easily see that their leader, assumed to be the ambassador, strode quickly under a full head of steam, and looked like he was on the verge of foaming at the mouth. Straggling behind them all was a murder of Crow. Their entourage looked smaller than the other diplomatic parties. After a moment of reflection, Pindlebryth understood why – the group was not led by Ambassador Kayawa, but by his assistant. The assistant seemed quite unsettled and almost timid. Pindlebryth narrowed his eyes as he wondered where the ambassador was. He fully expected Kayawa to be just as furious as the Fox ambassador, given that both were pressed to mandatory attendance here this morning by Royal demand. But then it struck him – did Kayawa have the temerity to refuse the demand, or was it something else? In any event, his assistant was going to be dragged over the coals.

Pindlebryth reflected how he had planned to be a multilingual diplomat *par excellance,* but now was chagrined that he had seldom taken part in actual negotiations with the neighbors of Lenland before going to University. He regretted not paying closer attention to the few he had attended. Instead, he now had to rely on others' experience with dealing with these diplomats, these sharks in fine couture and obscuring masks. Normally, such an onerous duty was handled by Tanderra, but he was now resting with the Quickening Spirit. Now the task would be shared by his Father and himself.

Pindlebryth did not relish in the least what lay ahead. He shook his head in distaste with a slight frown, and turned heading towards the southwest staircase, nearly bumping into Farthun's batman.

"Nay I be of assistance, N'Lord?" the Royal Guard inquired in his curious fashion. Pindlebryth always had to suppress a smile at the accent of his particular canton to the north, which made him sound as if he suffered from a continuous cold.

"No thank you, Gangon. Merely on my way from the physician's rooms to meet Father, while avoiding the arriving ambassadors. I take it the colonel is already there."

"Very good, N'Lord. Yes, Colonel Farthun is with His Najesty, awaiting their guests downstairs in the Vestment Room."

Past Gangon's shoulder, Pindlebryth spied two Lemmings escorted by a guard through the barracks. The two were well dressed, but their bleary eyes betrayed them, indicating they also had had a long sleepless night. Gangon noticed Pindlebryth's focus had shifted past him, and turned to see what drew his attention. "Ehh, our own emissaries assigned to foreign lands have also arrived. I had best not delay you further, then." He stepped aside, letting Pindlebryth and Pendenar join the two diplomats assigned to the Fox and Crow nations. The group walked unhurriedly to the door that opened to the southwest stairs that led up to the Royal Family's living level, and down to the royal offices.

"I trust your journey went well," offered Pindlebryth.

"Yes, quite, M'Lord," said the diplomat assigned to the Crow nation. "Although I am more used to travel by reindeer or by ship, I found my overnight flight by air rather exhilarating."

"I wish I could say the same, M'Lord," the other Lemming

from the Fox lands said between muffled belches. "Flight has always disagreed with me, but one does not ignore His Majesty's command. Fortunately, one of my staff packed a flagon of ginger tea for me to quiet my stomach."

They made their way to the ground level, down the staircase to the Vestment Room and other secured rooms behind the Hall of Thrones. One of the diplomats said, "My escort on the flight told me of the tragic events that occurred yesterday. First of all, let me offer condolences on behalf of both of us to you on Tanderra's passing. Also, I sincerely hope your brother the Prince is faring as well as can be expected?"

They halted on the midway landing that had a locked door to the Guard's Gallery above and behind the Hall of Thrones. Pindlebryth responded with his eyes fixed on the ground, on the walls, at the door; all so he did not have to look the ambassadors in the eye. "Thanks greatly. I am afraid that I only recently truly got to know Tanderra, but what little time I had with him made me realize what a fierce friend my Father and Lenland had. As for my brother, he is resting quietly and the doctor has great hopes for full use of his remaining eye, and minimal disfigurement."

The visitors were about to ask another question of Pindlebryth, when the chime of the clock in the CityState main square, softened through the stone exterior walls, could be heard. A trio of guard descended the stairs, and nodded to the Prince and the diplomats, as they unlocked and entered the gallery door.

"We had best not keep my Father waiting," Pindlebryth recommended. They reached the ground floor and turned into a short hallway past the pair of doors opening into the Royal Study, and finally to the spacious Vestment Room. The office was sparse, but was offset by the elegant workmanship of the various pieces in the room. A desk and a ceiling-height armoire were the largest pieces of furniture about the room, dwarfing a set of chairs and end-tables. In facing corners were a globe of rich wood, pearl and gold, and a thin cabinet filled with books of law. In a third corner was a fireplace with a cheery little fire, and a swing-arm holding a kettle just beginning to steam. Paintings were centered on each of the walls, each depicting a landscape of each of the four corners of Lenland. On the wall opposite where the group entered was an ornate metal door fitted with a lock handle that could only be operated with the royal signet. A metal plaque was placed between the door and the armoire. Small circular openings spaced evenly along the ceiling dispersed reflected sunlight to illuminate the room. A member of the waitstaff was preening the official vestments still on their stands in the open armoire.

One emissary remarked to the other, "Sunlight shining into an entirely enclosed room? Another example of Henejer's genius, no doubt."

The King was behind his desk, signing and sealing with his signet a small handful of documents. He finished by dusting it with fine sand from a small cylinder, then blowing the document's inked granules onto the floor. Farthun was pacing back and forth along the length of the room.

"Good morning, your Majesty," greeted both the emissaries. Pendenar and the other guards took their positions at the open hallway door, and the opposite closed door that opened onto dais of the Hall of Thrones. "As we just said to M'Lord, may we offer You our heartfelt best wishes for the recovery of young Prince Selephygur, and condolences on the passing of your friend, Tanderra."

Hatheron surveyed the pair with a drained look in his otherwise august visage. It reflected not just the exhaustion of the body, but also a weariness of the spirit. "Thank you, but we first have much business to tend to before the hour is up. Some of it may not be to your liking. Be seated." Pindlebryth stood in front of a chair to the right of Hatheron's desk, while the two visitors sank into plush chairs across from him. They had alert looks about them, like schoolchildren awaiting punishment from their headmaster. Hatheron arranged the four papers on his desk into a neat pile, and inspected the topmost sheet one last time.

King Hatheron addressed the diplomats. "You've no doubt been told what transpired yesterday in the courtyard. What you have not been privy to is the long and heated discussions that took place last night between Myself, Pindlebryth, and my three military leaders." Farthun stopped pacing, and stood a few paces behind the visitor's chairs as Hatheron continued. "I'm sure you agree what the Fox and Crow committed are tantamount to acts of war. But cooler heads have prevailed, and it was decided that we need you here. You've brought with you back to Lenland those documents you've deemed most important and relevant to the situation?"

Both affirmed their actions.

"Then know this. You have been officially recalled, and the embassies to these countries have been closed." Their looks of shock and dismay were apparent.

Pindlebryth continued as Hatheron handed him the papers. "During your flight, precautions were taken to assure the safe return of all our citizens from their assignments. They are instructed to leave our mission's grounds by midnight tonight, and are bringing with them what material they can save. Any remaining documentation is to be destroyed."

Clearing his throat, Hatheron pointed with his pen. "These are your new assignments." Pindlebryth handed out the top two documents, the first one to the diplomat returned from the Crow.

"Amadan, your experience with the Crow, and previous experience with the Fox makes you the best choice to fill this position," said Hatheron as he returned his pen to its holder and stood. "Congratulations, Prime Minister Amadan."

The astounded Amadan sputtered, then shakily stood to give his most reverent bow and accepted the document. He looked in surprise all about him, including the now-rising Talenday next to him, who extended to him a salutary paw. Pindlebryth handed the second document to Talenday, while Hatheron continued.

"Talenday, your experience with the Fox, and familiarity with many other embassy missions makes you the best choice for an ambassador-at-large. Since we are closing our embassies in the Fox and Crow CityStates, any diplomatic contacts you lead will occur here, or at our embassies in neutral countries. In the happenstance that these two nations wish to sue for opening relations again, you will be Our voice."

Amadan and Talenday found their voices, and both expressed their thanks to Hatheron. Talenday remained ebullient and swept away by the heady turn of fortune, but Amadan was the first one to set aside his emotion and come to a realization. "Highness, if You've decided to recall our embassies abroad, what of their embassies here in Lenland?"

"They, too, will be closed."

"But how?" he blurted while leaning forward. "And without expressly intruding upon their grounds?"

"The agreements enacted by my forefathers will be honored. We shall not invade by force. But have no doubt, there are other tools available to Us." Hatheron glanced knowingly at Farthun, who nodded solemnly. Hatheron's voice contained a shadow not unlike the sound of crushing gravel. "Mark my words. They *will* leave by midnight, the same time we leave our embassies."

Amadan and Talenday shifted nervously in their seats. They feared the precedent set by this radical action, but dared not question their liege. They could only hope that his action would not be overly perilous.

Pindlebryth read the two remaining signed papers, and a look of weathered patience came over his face. He placed them wearily back on Hatheron's desk. The orders contained therein were a necessity, but he also feared their consequences – both for Lenland, and himself personally.

"And now gentlemen, please return with your escort to the guards quarters above. You will be brought to your seats in the Hall of Thrones at the next hour, after all the other emissaries are seated." Looking at them unblinkingly, Hatheron added, "I trust you will have your wits about you. Today will continue to be a challenging day."

As the two rose from their seats again, Pindlebryth asked in a lower tone, "Before you go, there is something that perplexes me. Have the Fox and Crow ever worked together? Do you think they could have conspired to attack in concert yesterday?"

The visitors looked at each other momentarily with a look of startled puzzlement. Amadan responded, still with a look of confusion. "That would be highly unlikely. There is an undercurrent of animosity between those two nations. They are civil enough to one another, but both races think themselves superior to all others because of the Gift of Shapeshifting among their elite families.

Talenday chimed in, "I would agree. They would rather compete to attain a specific goal, to keep it under their sole control, rather than share it with any other races. Especially if that race were also shapeshifters."

"I see. Thank you, gentlemen. And now, if you would return upstairs with your guide." Pindlebryth motioned to the rear door.

They turned to Hatheron, thanking him again for their new opportunities to serve Him and Lenland. They exited and their escort closed the door behind them, but not before Talenday muttered, "I think I could use more ginger tea!"

Farthun began slowly pacing in thought again, observing, "I don't think they fully expect what is to come, but they know it will be not just unprecedented, but may be as perilous as dancing on a knife's edge. They will not be alone. Several in our and others' governments will be surprised."

"I don't give a tinker's damn what the other nations may think!" Hatheron stated firmly, pounding on the desk making his pens, inkwell and dusting cylinder clatter in their silver holders. "They should instead all breathe a sigh of relief, that We do not go blindly into a war of retaliation and revenge!"

Pindlebryth interjected, pointing to the papers on the desk, "I agree we need to take these steps." He closed his eyes momentarily, until he was sure he could retain his composure. "Those involved will answer for the crimes committed yesterday. But we must be prepared. All the nations represented here today, both friend and foe, will not just be surprised but also extremely nervous. While we will not be formally declaring war, they all will feel threatened. And countries under these circumstances will do equally or even more surprising things – almost surely more surprising than we can anticipate."

Above them they heard the muffled tamping of footfalls emanating from the ceiling, near the wall separating the Vestment Room from the Hall of Thrones. Farthun observed, "The guards are in place in the gallery above. You had best prepare, Your Majesty, M'Lord." Taking his cue, the butler took out the vestments one by one from the armoire for Hatheron and Pindlebryth.

As he was draped with the embellished and embroidered symbols of his reign, Hatheron stared absently at the crown and sword he would wear. The Sword of Enorel was slung reverently in its scabbard, scribed with images of a totem. Legend told that these were the visages of five Angels, both benevolent and terrible, that were sent by the Quickening Spirit to inspire, counsel and guard the first liege of Lenland.

The crown, resting on a velvet dome, was fashioned with an entirely different motif. Made for Hatheron for the day of his coronation, it was an affair of several precious metals and gems. The circlet was festooned with holly leaves of gold with silver veins and stems, and a small red ruby at the base of each leaf. Small leaves of maple were similarly interwoven, with sapphires at the base of each of them. The center of the crown featured a pair of large curled oak leaves of platinum, holding a great emerald between them. Hatheron contemplated the crown, and silently asked the Quickening Spirit to see him through this day.

Upstairs, the diplomats were returning through the guards' common room when they spotted the young Prince sitting in a chair next to the large window, with a walking staff across his lap. Amadan led Talenday, who had an increasingly pale look about himself. They greeted Selephygur, but cut themselves short when Selephygur turned in their direction, and they saw the full extent of his bandages.

"I'm sorry, sirs," LongBack interceded. "I am under doctor's orders to keep the young Prince as quiet as possible."

"That's all right, LongBack. Let them see part of the results of what happened yesterday," Selephygur said through a frown.

"Begging the Prince's forgiveness," Talenday hastily said as he bowed and continued down the guard's living quarters. He frantically reached for a small handkerchief up his left sleeve, and quickly shielded his muzzle, as he mewled, "My, oh my!"

Amadan remained momentarily, only to add, "I am sorry to disturb you my Prince. I only stopped to wish you a speedy recovery."

"What was taken cannot be recovered," Selephygur snapped.

Amadan wanted to explain that he merely meant well, but looking at the Prince, he could only guess at the physical damage and deep emotional wounds hidden by the bandages. He knew no words of consolation – under these circumstances they could only worsen their first impressions of each other. He nodded quietly and withdrew, and forthwith caught up with and accompanied the distressed Talenday.

When they had left the common room, LongBack whispered, "They're gone, my Prince. It's now or never." Selephygur stood and steadied himself with the staff in his right paw. LongBack took the other paw, and placed it on his shoulder. They walked calmly from the commons room into the hall that led to the southwest stairs. Checking that they drew no undue attention to themselves, LongBack shuffled the Prince onto the landing and closed the door behind him. Breathing a short sigh of relief, LongBack turned around backwards, and led the Prince down, stair by stair, to the next landing and the galley door. He rapped twice, then twice again. A panel indistinguishable from the rest of the parqueted door recessed then swung back. A voice commanded from the dark square.

"LongBack? You're not authorized to be here."

"But surely *I* am allowed," sternly stated Selephygur. "He is my assistant this day. Open this door."

The panel closed, followed by the sound of the door being unlocked from behind. It opened into a dimly lit and cramped corridor that turned almost immediately to the left. The two entered, and the door was bolted behind them. LongBack waited a moment until his eyes adjusted to the meager light coming from a handful of vertical slits in one wall. The shoulder height slits opened high above the floor of the Hall of Thrones, and offered a full vantage of everything beyond the four thrones and the three-stepped dais separating them from the audience floor. Inside every other slit was a crossbow mounted on a gimbal ring. The bow of the unusual weapon was vertical, and could turn to aim at any point visible through the slit. There was a guard stationed at each of the three crossbows, and they were all looking at the newcomers. "A seat for the Prince?" asked LongBack.

"There are only these," said the squad leader, pointing at seats attached to the wall at each crossbow, and one similar small bench in the corner next to the door.

"I'm sure that will do." Guided by LongBack, he found the bench, and sat quietly, still holding onto his walking staff.

"If I may be so bold, to what honor do we owe this visit?" the guard asked while nervously looking between LongBack and Selephygur.

"Oh, just following the physician's orders to sit quietly and rest."

The squad leader and LongBack exchanged glances and raised eyebrows, as if wordlessly saying to each to the other, "I hope you know what you're doing." He sidled past LongBack to resume his station along the galley.

Below, Pindlebryth raised an eyebrow and looked upward to the ceiling when there was the muffled sound of the gallery door closing a second time. But his attention was quickly brought back to the task at hand, as the butler draped his sash and epaulets on his shoulders. That being the last of the dress apparel, the butler set to brushing off fur, dust and other imperfections, real or imagined.

Farthun walked to the plaque next to the Hall of Thrones door, raised it, and leaned forward to peer through the silvered glass. "All the audience orderlies are in place, Your Highness." The noon bell tolled. The butler put away his brush, and collected the dome holding the crown. Pindlebryth removed the crown from the dome, and placed it on his father's head.

"The emissaries are entering now," reported Farthun. Group by group, each mission was guided from the Great Audience Hall to their table. They were followed by Amadan and Talenday, who sat at their own table nearest the dais, where General Vadarog and Admiral Carvolo stood awaiting them. Next to them was an empty chair, bedecked with a black wreath. Lastly, Darothien approached the dais and stood opposite the Tipstaff, who held a full height ebony stave shod with steel on the bottom and crested with an ornate gold symbol of Lenland.

The butler handed the sling to Pindlebryth, who then, holding the scabbard, offered the Sword of Enorel to his father. Hatheron took it and slung it about him, and lashed the other end to his belt, angled to be drawn at a moment's notice. Hatheron then moved to the door, steeling himself for the duties that befell him this hour. His face became more inscrutable with each step. Pindlebryth lined up behind him. When the attendees were all seated at their tables, Farthun said, "They are ready now, Your Majesty."

Hatheron drew a deep breath and opened the door, one hand clenched to hold the signet against the lock, and other to open the handle. Once unlocked, Farthun took the door as father and son strode through. Farthun closed the door from within the Vestment Room, holding the handle to keep it unlocked. He looked over his shoulder, and ordered, "Pendenar, take the other door, and ensure no one enters until the King returns."

King Hatheron and Prince Pindlebryth entered the Hall of Thrones at the rear of the dais. The floor was covered in deep purple velvet, textured with a repeating geometric pattern. The wall was a network of copper and gold stripes in front of a dark background. The vertical copper stripes were a couple inches wide and were separated by the same width. Inlaid over the copper were gold rays of similar width that converged to a sunburst behind the center throne's headrest. The whole array effectively hid the arrow slits of the Guard's Gallery above.

The Tipstaff sounded his verge on the floor three times, and called, "Hail to King Hatheron, Scion of the Line of Enorel the

Great, King of Lenland, Protector of the People, Defender of the Land!" All the attendees stood, and bowed as Hatheron took his throne, followed by Pindlebryth taking his place on the lesser throne to his right.

"There is much to be done today, and little time left to do it, so I shall be as quick as possible. Yesterday was a dark day for Lenland. We mourn the loss of a member of this court, but moreover an important and dear friend." Hatheron gestured towards the empty chair and wreath, then cleared his throat. "If that were not enough evil to befall Lenland, members of the Royal Family were also foully injured, and cannot attend these proceedings. Queen Wenteberei is rendered lame for a time, and Prince Selephygur has been partially blinded." Murmurs began to rise from the assembly, as many of the attendees glanced at the two unoccupied thrones to Hatheron's left.

"It has been observed by many witnesses, and cannot be refuted, that the fiends that perpetrated these treacheries are from the Fox and Crow nations." The room broke out in calls of condemnation, and tables being pounded. The Crow delegation kept their heads lowered between their shoulders, but the Fox party members remained stock still. Only their eyes betrayed any movement, as they calmly surveyed the room with a continued air of superiority.

The noise rose even further in volume until the Tipstaff intervened. He pounded his verge on the floor again several times, commanding in an authoritative voice, "Silence in the Hall! There will be *silence*!"

Order was quickly restored, and the King continued. "Last night, I ordered the immediate return of our ambassadors to the two countries of Vulpinden and the Rookeries of the Kyaa. In addition, I have ordered that as of midnight tonight, all members of our embassies to these countries are to be recalled, and return to Lenland forthwith." A handful of gasps echoed about the hall.

"Much as Prime Minister Tanderra richly deserves a day – nay, a week! – of mourning," Hatheron boomed, "Lenland cannot stand still in these tumultuous times. I have therefore appointed that Amadan, previously the Ambassador to the Crow nation, be set as the new Prime Minister of Lenland. Also, I have decreed that Talenday, formerly the Ambassador to the Fox nation, be appointed to the new station of Ambassador-at-Large. His main function will be that of liaison to those nations with which we have no current relations. His function will be carried out only here in Lenland, or in friendly third-party nations, where we have embassies." Hatheron allowed a moment for the information to sink in, perhaps even to see which of the audience could anticipate what that information foretold.

"And now to the business that is even more distasteful. We declare all members of the embassies of those two nations, Fox and Crow, are under sanction. At midnight tonight, We will rescind all their diplomatic immunities. Therefore, all members of the Fox and Crow nations must leave Lenland by midnight tonight. Their embassies are to be closed."

The crowd reacted with calls of "No!" and "Fie!" and the like. The Fox ambassador rose, his tail curled in anger.

"The perpetrator was not operating under orders of any kind from our government!" he howled. "Furthermore, Your Majesty cannot take the lands of any embassy. They have been granted to us in perpetuity since the time of Enorel!"

The Tipstaff smashed his verge on the floor once, and bellowed, "Order! You are out-of-order, sir!"

"Your protestations are moot," replied Hatheron. "Your precious lands will be left abandoned." He leaned forward, and menace filled his voice. "It matters nothing that the Vulpine fiend that blasted Us with an infernal device was or was not sanctioned by your government. His example, and the example of Selephylin years ago, clearly prove that the Fox nation has little control over its citizens abroad, elite or otherwise. Therefore, all citizens of Vulpinden must leave by midnight tonight. The members of your mission will be escorted without harm to the harbor town of Cape Ark, where you may arrange whatever departures you choose. Similarly, because of the criminal who blinded the Prince, the Crow mission must also leave our borders by midnight tonight.

"As for the embassies' grounds, We will honor their sanctity, and will not enter them. However, starting at midnight tonight, they will be policed by Lenland's forces, and no traffic will be allowed in or out. So you see, you both may leave your missions in peace, or remain there and starve."

A stunned silence spread across the room.

"The choice is yours," Hatheron intoned with doom.

The Fox ambassador retook his seat. He looked as if he were ready to bite through iron nails. The Crow still remained silent, but their attempts to feign an air of dispassion were in vain.

"Furthermore, any citizens of Vulpinden or the Rookeries of the Kyaa found in Lenland after midnight tonight will be arrested and held for interrogation.   In addition, any shapeshifter found while attempting to conceal their identity will be tried, punishable by death!"

Pindlebryth surveyed the crowd. Many were still dazed by the events passing in their presence. He noted even Darothien was alert with a look not unlike prey freezing in front of a predator. Pindlebryth had an eye on his father, who finally noticed the empty chair at the Crow's table.

"Where is the Crow Ambassador?   Why is he not in attendance at Our specific request?"

The ambassador's assistant rose, filled with apprehension. "Begging Your Majesty's pardon. I am his assistant, Eekaya. Ambassador Kayawa was recalled last night back to the Court of the Kyaa."

The newly appointed Prime Minister's neck snapped to attention, and looked between the Crow, and Hatheron. Standing, he interrupted the Crow. "Your Majesty, if I may?" Turning back to the assistant, he reiterated, "Kayawa, you say? Of the Rookery House of Kakaan?"

"Yes, Minister?" the underling replied with a note of indecision.

"That is not possible!" Amadan burst out. Speaking towards the audience, he continued. "Just this previous week, I paid Kayawa a convalescence visit in his home. He had been selected to be the Kyaa's ambassador to Lenland, but he has lain in his sickbed for the past six months!" The Crow assistant was flabbergasted. Focusing on him, Amadan pressed on. "How long have you been assigned to the Crow mission?"

Eekaya fumbled for an answer, his mind in obvious turmoil. "I have been serving this station for a year and a half. Each of our staff has been here for at least a full year as well. "

"Have you ever met Kayawa back home in the Rookeries, before he arrived in Lenland?"

"As for myself, no."   The Crow turned to survey the remainder of his seated group, and they all to a single craven bird were shaking their heads, or had no response.

"Your Highness!" Amadan declared with alarm, facing the King. "We all have been duped by an imposter! The Court of the Kyaa debates to this day over whom to appoint as ambassador to Lenland."

"I am surrounded and vexed by Shapeshifters and imposters! Quickening Spirit curse them all!"

Pindlebryth sat in silence, recalling his meeting with Hakayaa and the false Kayawa two days previous. He couldn't allow himself to think that the two worked in concert. His outward stoic mask of calm belied neither the fear nor hope of what might happen next. It was out of his hands, as long as his father was angered thus.

"I am loath to add, Your Majesty, that Kayawa – the true Kayawa – suspects he had been poisoned," Amadan declared.

"A Ravenne assassin was in my CityState all this time, and within these very walls the day before the attempt on my kin?" Hatheron grew fiercer by the second. Vadarog and Carvolo silently echoed his outrage. Pindlebryth sat motionless in quiet consternation at the thought he had been within arm's length of one of the feared Crow merchants of death.

"And passing his orders to his lackey from the House of BlueHood, no doubt!" Standing, Hatheron wrested the crown from his head, and looked at it with burning hatred. Pindlebryth's heart sank.

"The same House that crafted this for my coronation!" Hatheron raised his hand, and smashed the crown on the velvet floor. It bent severely, shivering several of the smaller gems from their mounts, sending them flying in all directions. It bounced off the dais, and clanged onto the hard floor, where the large central emerald simply fell out of the deformed oak leaf setting.

"I retain the Crown of Lenland, but I will wear none made by that house of vipers!" he said, pointing accusingly at the destroyed headpiece. Breathing with exertion, he then pointed outwards with his left paw, while his right shifted to grip the hilt of the Sword of Enorel.

"I now give you a gift, you nation of bitch-cubs! You have long been searching for your lost emblem of pride, the Lens of Truth?" The Fox ambassador was thunderstruck. Amadan and Talenday looked at each other in utter perplexity. A feeling of incredulity grew in the rest of the audience. "That confounded trinket was stolen by Selephylin, who mercilessly grafted it by her foul magick to the young Prince Selephygur. It was that very Artifact that was cruelly ripped from his head by Hakayaa

BlueHood. You will be gladdened to know it is now in the possession of the Rookeries of the Kyaa!"

The Fox ambassador jerked to attention, as though he were stung on the nose by a wasp. He began to shout accusations at the table of Crow. In return, they remonstrated in total confusion, pleading ignorance of these affairs. The other embassies called and pounded their tables again. Several calls to order by the Tipstaff were fruitless, and did not quieten the ensuing pandemonium one whit. Darothien watched the Tipstaff and considered if she might be required to glamor the audience to calmness.

Finally, the Fox ambassador shouted above the din, "We retire from these proceedings, Your Majesty!" He stormed away from his table, with the rest of the mission jumping out their chairs to follow in his wake. As he passed their group, he blasted at the Crow around their table, "You flight of cackling cormorants! This will not be forgotten, nor forgiven!" All eyes watched as they left.

The Vulpine ambassador barely noticed, as he passed through the exit, a shrouded figure standing in the rear of the room. The shape stood quietly, accusingly staring at him from behind the deep shadow of the hood. The ambassador almost stumbled when he glanced again, seeing two irises of red encircling glistening pupils peering from the inky blackness. The Crow assistant was likewise unnerved, as he led his party from the room, besieged by the jeering crowd.

Pindlebryth knew the revelation spoken by his father meant a death sentence for Hakayaa – there would now be two nations with a price on his former friend's head. And if the Kyaa were truly not complicit in yesterday's attack, a third nation would join them in seeking to capture him – any one of which would inflict anything on him to gain the Artifact. He looked at Hatheron as he collapsed back into his throne. He could not tell if his father's mouth was shaped into a snarl or a grin.

With the last of the Fox and Crow out of the Hall, the shrouded figure bent his head forward and dropped two halves of a bright crimson agate geode into one paw. Polished to bring out the color of the agate ring and silica center, they were trinkets common from the lands of the old Iron Baron. With his free hand, Tabarem pulled back the shroud from his face and inhaled deeply. "That should put the fear of the Quickening Spirit in them!"

Darothien tilted her staff towards her face, so that her sleeve would hide her amusement at Tabarem's uncanny ability to be where things of import occurred, and in his own twisted way slip in the last barb.

Hatheron once again stood, his previous calmer demeanor concentrated about himself as he addressed the remaining contingents. "My friends, let me again state that we keep the door open to negotiate with the Fox and Crow nations, but not on our contiguous soil. We hope that we may count on your hospitality to meet with them on neutral ground within your lands. However, let me be plain. We will not look favorably on any nation that harbors the Fox or Crow within their missions here in CityState. Good day to you, and may the Quickening Spirit protect us all."

Hatheron wheeled and returned to the Vestment Room. Inside, Farthun opened the door in anticipation of His Majesty's exit, then closed and locked it after Hatheron and Pindlebryth had exited the Hall of Thrones.

Darothien watched silently as the diplomats milled about and gossiped, and remained until the guards ushered the last of them out of the Hall. She, too, was about to leave when she felt something pull at her. She stopped and looked around with her head tilted and ears twitching. The Tipstaff inquired of her, but she assured him all was well. Exhaling, Darothien closed her eyes and cleared her mind.

She held out her hand, and walked about in a curving pattern. She stepped tentatively at first, then more decisively towards the pull. She almost felt giddy – this feeling reminded her of her youth, and the game her old family and neighbors made of finding lost items or dowsing for a well site. The Tipstaff stood in silent wonder – he had heard of the trances of wizards, but had never seen one before. She took a few more steps, slighter in gait as she approached the source. She opened her eyes, and spied where the emerald centerpiece of the crown had fallen. It began to vibrate, to rustle about on the floor, then suddenly leapt into her waiting hand above. She examined it more closely. It had no magick she could sense, but she had the unmistakable feeling she was supposed to have this – perhaps to somehow use the gem. She remarked absently to the Tipstaff to clean up the rest of the crown, then made her way to her workplace, absorbed as the emerald's glittering facets revealed their secrets to her.

Pindlebryth and Hatheron handed their garments of office to the awaiting butler. Colonel Farthun looked at his liege with dismay and shame. To think an assassin was within these walls – and he above all never suspected.

"Well, you certainly struck the hornet's nest!" Pindlebryth exclaimed in exasperation.

Hatheron leaned on the desk with his fists. "I lost my head," he said shaking it slowly in self-condemnation. But then he paused, saying, "But in hindsight, it may have been fortuitous, after all. Think of it. We no longer have to worry about keeping secrets from the Fox or the Crow, and wait with trepidation for the moment they decide to move against us."

"But at what price?" Pindlebryth exclaimed.

"Do you not think that weighs on me?" Hatheron locked eyes with him. "Yes! They killed my friend. Yes! They injured both my wife and my son, who were innocent in all this. And may the Quickening Spirit curse them for their criminal deeds. But think! Their sword has struck, they took their attack. It is now the Court of the Kyaa who will spend many sleepless nights wondering when the Fox will strike."

He regarded Pindlebryth in utmost seriousness. "Much as I would relish strangling the life out of them with my bare hands for what they have done to me and mine, I must think more for the whole of Lenland." Hatheron sat behind his desk, exhausted by the audience following a sleepless night. Pindlebryth sat opposite him. The butler turned from the fireplace with a prepared silver set, and served tea to his King and Prince.

"Perfect timing! Bless your heart, WildEye!" Pindlebryth said emphatically. Father and son took a moment to calm themselves over the fresh hibiscus tea. Hatheron took another long thoughtful draught, then broke the pause.

"By revealing what we knew about the Lens, we made the best of a bad situation. We are no longer anyone's target. If the Fox and Crow are both vying for the Lens, as Amadan suggests, then they will be at each other's throats. On the other hand, if they are somehow in this together, Lenland could not stand against both of them anyway. And by revealing the Lens, I also reveal their motives. Since this all took place in such a public fashion, the Fox and Crow will have a much larger theater of countries watching their next move, all of whom are our allies." He put down his cup, and sighed, "Not to mention – if I didn't force them to leave quickly, we would still be in there dealing with endless posturing and diplomatic discourse."

There was a knock at the door. Farthun held up his paw to wave the butler away, and he opened the door. The leader of the gallery guards saluted in the hallway, then leaned in to whisper something to Farthun. Farthun dismissed him and closed the door.

"It seems there was one more person in the audience. Prince Selephygur listened in from the gallery."

Pindlebryth was nonplussed. "I left him in the infirmary! What was he – How?" He snapped his cup down, and scowled slightly. "I will deal with this. It seems I need to have a talk with my brother." He stood and found that the tea was having a marked effect on him. He resisted the urge to stretch and yawn, saying simply, "But first, I will sleep for a day."

"Go on ahead. I will wait for Vadarog and Carvolo, who will undoubtedly want to confer with me sooner rather than later." Farthun opened the door for Pindlebryth, who wearily trudged up the multiple flights of stairs to the top level. Pendenar, who looked not too much better, trailed behind him. As he passed by his parents' quarters, a nurse was quietly closing the door as she left, telling Pindlebryth that the queen was finally asleep and healing well. Acknowledging the hall guard, he entered his own quarters.

He allowed his shoulders to slump, then began to stretch. He froze abruptly when he realized he was not alone. Selephygur sat at the front room table, with LongBack standing behind him. In the hall, Pendenar sensed something was amiss, and moved quickly into the doorway. Although momentarily startled, he relaxed but threw the hall guard a peeved glance.

"What fun, eh, Pindie? I could practically hear the ambassadors sweat!" Selephygur cracked a smile, as he juggled his staff from hand to hand as it pivoted on the floor.

"What did you think you were doing?" Pindlebryth placed his arms akimbo, a useless gesture considering his audience. "If you were heard and had given the gallery's existence away, Father and Farthun would have your pelt! That gallery is not public knowledge."

"But I *didn't* fumble, and our precious security measure remains safe. Besides, I couldn't stay away."

"You mean you didn't trust us to tell you everything that transpired."

"What! How could you think that?" Selephygur stopped playing with the walking staff after nearly dropping it. "You misunderstand – I had to hear for myself how the Fox and Crow reacted. I *had* to." Selephygur's emotion and conviction grew more solid.

"You don't know how good it felt to hear those foreigners assail each other for a change. I am tired of being the one who suffers. The one who suffered from Selephylin, the one who needed help to overcome the Lens, the one who daily battled its blinding pain, the one kept in hiding, the one who needed protection from the outside world. The dirty little state secret." He stamped the staff on the floor. "You once told me my name means 'neither master nor slave'. I think it's time for me to be treated that way! Time to act like it! I think it's time for me to stop being a slave; targeted by, or hidden from every country on this continent!"

Pindlebryth stood over his brother and put his hand on the young Lemming's shoulder. "And what about *this* country? What about us?" Selephygur's youthful exuberance and anger stumbled, as he tried unsuccessfully to mouth an answer. "Enough, *Master* Selephygur. We will discuss this later. But for now, you need your rest, and so do I." He looked around the room. "Pendenar, please take the young prince to his bed in the infirmary. If he does not stay in bed, Sacalitre has my permission to strap him in. If he cannot sleep, please have the archivist fetch one of the treatises on the evolution of Lenland civil law, and one of his tutors to read it to him."

"Oh, that's quite alright, Pindie," Selephygur hemmed hesitantly. "LongBack can take me back to the..."

"No, I have another task for him. Off you go, Pendenar. And please send in the hall guard as you leave. Thank you kindly." Pendenar had a smirk on his face, as he assisted Selephygur from his chair and into the hallway. LongBack stood at attention as he pointlessly looked pleadingly like a lost pet at Selephygur. Pindlebryth was draping his vest on a chair, when the hall guard reported.

"Ah, there you are. Please go now and inform Colonel Farthun that LongBack here will be pulling hall guard duty for the next twenty-four hours. LongBack, wake me one hour before midnight. I will need a quick snack then as well. I wish to observe the Fox and Crow exodus.

"Carry on!" He waved them both out of the room, and

closed the door. He walked over to his bed in the next room, swept his suspenders off his shoulders, and collapsed on top of the covers.

Darothien walked as a somnambulist, with the emerald in one hand, and her staff in the other. It rhythmically tapped on the floor as she wended her way to the East Wing and down the stone steps to her laboratory. As she entered the front room, the granite wolf statue whined a greeting, then fell silent as she continued to the workrooms beyond.

She placed her staff next to the inner door, which she then latched shut. Moving to a table crowded with apparatus of all sorts, held the gem above a small curved dish made of bronze, gold and lead supported by an intertwined nest of tripod legs. With her free hand, she pulled a tube from a rack and emptied its mercurial syrup into the dish. Uttering a few words, she released the stone, and it began to slowly rotate above the liquid.

"All right, what are trying to tell me?"

From a velvet lined case, she produced her prism and convex lens. She examined and peered into the gem with several combinations of her tools – first each separately, then one for each eye, finally using the pair in tandem, lens through prism, and prism through lens. She settled on using the prism alone, and produced her wand. Focusing both wand and prism on her subject, she inquired half to herself, "You have no magick of your own. But you want to be something. Do you want to be a tool of body, spirit, or of mind?" After a few minutes more of manipulation, she quietly exclaimed her satisfaction. "Or just of sound?" She placed the glassware back in its case, pronounced a short series of words that sounded more like a waterfall than speech.

The gem rose a few more inches, whereupon Darothien inscribed a wispy green circle around the gem. The gem ceased its slow rotation, and the circle locked in place around it. The wraithlike ring began to spin in the air around its axis, with the gem at its center. It increased in speed and coalesced into a translucent solid band, until it fairly began to whine. A thread-

thin line of lime green appeared along the surface of the gem, tenuous at first but growing in brightness. Nodding with satisfaction, Darothien put away her wand, and set to other tasks. She moved from table to sink, from workbench to books on podiums.

She felt the first pangs of hunger, and realized she had worked away the entire afternoon, when she heard a knocking at the outer door. She left her book, quickly checked the progress of the encircled gem, and went to answer the outer door. The wolf statue whined again, and even wagged its tail until Darothien commanded it to stillness.

She opened the door to a Royal Guard, who straightforwardly reported, "Please come with me to the infirmary. The Royal Physician needs to consult with you about Prince Selephygur."

"What seems to be the matter? Is the young Prince in pain?"

"No. Beyond that, I can offer nothing. I have been simply asked to escort you to the infirmary as soon as possible."

"Wait outside." Darothien went back to the inner room, and collected her velvet glassware box, and tucked her wand into her sleeve. She accompanied the guard up to the ground level to find Sacalitre examining the Prince and his bandages.

"Good evening, my Prince." Darothien gently put her hand on the top of her student's head, where his black crown of fur was encircled by bandages. Regarding the doctor as he listened to Selephygur's heart with his ceramic dome, she watched quietly as he then examined his patient's mouth and ears. "What seems to be the problem, Sacalitre?"

He sat straight in his chair next to the bed, and folded his arms. "Nothing that I can tell. Prince Selephygur has been having nightmares again."

"No!" interrupted his patient. "They are not nightmares. At least not like the ones I have had that relive the day of the attack. These are different!" He was not angry, but strong in his conviction.

"What can you tell me, then?" asked Darothien with earnest interest.

He tilted his head as he strived to recall. "I see things as if through a fog. Sometimes I see the face of my attacker, Hakayaa. Sometimes I see a field of sand and boulders bordered by a dark ocean. Other times I see smoke rising through large holes in the roof of a structure, into a clear star-filled night sky.

"But unlike my nightmares, I hear nothing, I smell nothing. I can't speak, nor can I even move. I can only see things."

Darothien opened the velvet box, and used the prism. She scanned the Prince's head and shoulders, then strained to look at his face hidden by the gauze. She shook her head in disapproval, and remarked, "I see nothing I haven't seen before. Sacalitre, can you temporarily remove his bandages?"

"Mmmyes, but let us take some precautions." He called for a nurse, who dimmed the room by closing the curtains, then assisted the physician in carefully removing the bandages. Darothien spun the prism in her hand as each layer of gauze was unwrapped.

"I think I can see something," she said calmly. "Can you remove the paper disc over the wound?"

Sacalitre was reluctant to accede to the request. "The inner wounds are packed, and removing them may open them back up. Are you sure that's necessary?"

"Just remove the disc, then, please." Sacalitre nodded, and the nurse coaxed the disc from the underlying cotton and cloth. The back of the disc and the packing were dark with fresh blood, and parts were black with dried blood. It crackled softly as it was coaxed and peeled off the underlying clotted cotton. Darothien rotated the prism once more, and saw more clearly a blue glow in the socket, dimly radiating from behind the gauze. She stared at it in rapture and repulsion, until Sacalitre coughed to bring back her attention.

"Are you satisfied?" asked the physician tentatively.

"Not entirely, but I think I've seen enough for now. How long until the bandages may be entirely removed?"

"As early as six days. But they will need to be regularly changed. If you wish, you can examine the Prince at that time."

"Yes, please." Darothien looked around, and asked the nurse, "If you would, can you give us some privacy?" Sacalitre nodded the nurse out of the prince's room.

"What do you see, Darothien?" Selephygur asked with some trepidation. Sacalitre involuntarily peered into the socket and its bolus of gauze and clotted blood. He shook his head as he convinced himself nothing was out of the ordinary.

"There seems so be some residual magick behind the bandage. And it bears the color of Selephylin's work." A doubt then struck her. "Or maybe the Lens."

"There was no part of the Lens remaining when I started treating the wound," professed Sacalitre. He almost sounded indignant.

"I don't know..." ruminated Darothien as she tapped the end of the prism against her mouth absentmindedly. "My Prince, I will visit each day. Try to remember and describe to me any more visions you see, and I'll examine you when they change your bandages and dressings." She rose and took a step back. "With your kind permission, of course, Doctor.

"Do not grieve yourself, my Prince. Together, we will figure out this puzzle." Darothien returned the prism to its case. Then she and Sacalitre left, while the nurse returned to reapply a fresh disc and pressure bandage.

Waking from a disturbing dream about Vulcanis Major, Pindlebryth was roused from his slumber by a knock at the door. Despite sleeping soundly for the entire afternoon and evening, he had barely moved a muscle since his head hit his pillow. He opened the door, and blinked a few times at the light in the hallway, and the silhouette of LongBack. The guard was only beginning to show the first signs of fatigue, but then his long day was only half done. Rather, he kept as brave a face as possible to prove to his Prince his vigilance and stamina. "It is one hour before midnight. You requested to be woken?" A maid stood behind him with a small tray with a granola and some fruit juice.

"Yes, LongBack." He accepted the food and glass, saying as he pushed the door closed with his back, "Have my guard ready to accompany me in ten minutes." He wolfed down the granola and juice, then freshened up quickly. He changed his shirt and put on fresh vest. He was donning a jacket against the night air, when he heard a knock again, and bade Pendenar to enter.

"I wish to observe the Crow eviction. Is everything on time?"

Pendenar nodded, but then shrugged his shoulders slightly. "There are many dissidents amongst the Crow – some who are protesting that this is a ploy to murder them, or to steal their state secrets, or even wilder conspiracies. As a result, there are a few tenants who threaten to stay behind."

"I suppose that is their choice to starve. Who is overseeing the task? Are any of our diplomatic corps there to assist?"

"All but the main gate of the embassy is cordoned off, and the roofs are being watched. General Vadarog is there to assure that all the Crow are handled with kid gloves, until the midnight deadline. Amadan will be joining us, as he feels his expertise with Crow language and culture can coax the stragglers to comply."

"Excellent! The very person I wanted to talk to." Walking

with a quick pace past Pendenar, Pindlebryth exclaimed, "We had better bustle if we are to catch him as he leaves!"

Dashing down to the central court, they were in time to join Amadan in a carriage leaving from the West Gate to the Crow embassy located amidst the central neighborhoods of CityState.

Amadan was lost in thought in the cabin, but snapped to alertness, shuffled over to one side and greeted them as the two hoisted themselves inside. Pendenar closed the door, and the driver called to the reindeer, who initially lurched then steadily pulled the carriage off at a trot.

"I'm afraid this could be a rather messy business, M'Lord. Are you sure you wish to be at the Crow embassy during the King's decreed action?"

"I will only observe at a discreet distance, which I'm sure will greatly relieve Pendenar." Pendenar pierced his charge then Amadan with an unblinking stare dripping with long-suffering. Pindlebryth had several competing impulses how to answer the Prime Minister. With difficulty, he resisted the desire to directly inquire about the Ravenne imposter, or the Fox spy, or about BlueHood. "Actually, I am here to talk to you, Amadan.

"I have trouble understanding how the Court of the Kyaa and the Crow embassy here did not realize that the real Kayawa's place had been filled – nay, usurped – for several months by an imposter."

Amadan peered out the window facing into the CityState, then returned his attention to Pindlebryth. "That has been troubling me as well. It would be easy enough for the imposter to send communiqués home to the Court and forge the signature of his assistant. That way, the Court of the Kyaa would not be any the wiser of the usurper. But any communication from the Court over the past several months would be addressed to the assistant as the 'acting ambassador'. That may have gone unnoticed for a few weeks, attributed to a slow inefficient bureaucracy, but it would raise suspicions if it continued for the entire time the imposter was here. I am forced to a disturbing conclusion."

"Someone in the Court of Kyaa knew that the imposter was here! And was covering for him!" Pindlebryth immediately deduced.

Amadan jumped excitedly in his seat. "Exactly! But that's not all. It means this same courtier was complicit in the real

Kayawa's poisoning. The Kyaa had better watch his back."
Pindlebryth sat back and looked heavenward, as the gravity of
the conclusion sank in. Amadan rested his chin on his hand, as
he chewed on his thoughts. "But why? Why would someone in
the Court send a Ravenne?"

"I do not know. This conspirator obviously covets the Lens
of Truth. But I could never conceive that even the Crow would
go to such lengths as poison, sending an assassin against
another Royal Family, and..." Pindlebryth found he couldn't
continue, and give voice to Hakayaa's betrayal.

"King Hatheron castigated the Fox ambassador today about
that 'Lens of Truth.' What is it?"

"A magickal item, capable of powers that we were only
beginning to understand. It originally belonged to the Fox
nation, but we came in possession of it, not knowing its history
or pedigree. Once we discovered its true nature, we started to
take security precautions – we did not want Vulpinden to learn
we had it."

"Only to have the Crow snatch it away. BlueHood might
have sensed the Fox's presence."

The carriage took a sharp turn that nearly unseated the
three riders. Pendenar, leaned out the window to glimpse a
crowd forming at the end of the street.

"What do you mean, 'sensed'?" Pindlebryth demanded.

"Hatheron said it was a BlueHood that took the Lens. That
family is well known for its dominant trait of shapeshifting. He
probably felt the other shapeshifter was near, and decided at
that moment to act."

"I had not been told of that ability. How is it you know?"

"Almost every influential family in Kyaa has a shapeshifter
in the family, or in their employ. Some families of lower lineage
will blackmail or otherwise press them into service. I've noticed
several of their abilities merely by being observant. In this case,
they cannot tell another shapeshifter merely by looking at them,
but can sense them if they concentrate when another's ability is
used close by."

Something deep inside Pindlebryth reeled. Lords Below
take him! Hakayaa knew! He *knew* both the Ravenne and the
Fox shapeshifter were there. And he had kept it from him!
Pindlebryth struggled with himself as he was inexorably forced
to the realization how deeply he had been betrayed. He tried to
understand why a friend of so many years turned on him, but

his attention was grabbed when Pendenar ordered the driver to stop the carriage.

"You there!" he bellowed to a constable on the corner. "What is going on down the street?"

There were a few Lemmings walking in the same direction as the carriage. They were dressed in all sorts of attire, ranging from evening wear to coats hastily drawn over bedclothes. The constable advised them several times to stay back as he made his way to the carriage. "A crowd is forming around the Crow embassy. So far, they are just onlookers, curious to see what is causing all the activity so late this night."

"Fetch a castle guard as quick as you can," said Pendenar pointing at a squad of guards marching in double-time towards the embassy.

The riders all poked their heads out the windows to look down the street. Gas streetlights were aided by several torches in iron baskets held aloft by soldiers and city guards around the embassy gate. Two lines of guards had their hands full keeping the crowd away from the line of Crow as they exited carrying bundles and boxes. The diplomatic staff was being perfunctorily ushered into a line of waiting carriages. As each was filled, it rolled down the boulevard, only to be replaced by the next conveyance in line. Pindlebryth and Amadan caught a glimpse of the Crow assistant ambassador vehemently railing at the unflappable Farthun. Behind them, every room in the embassy was lit, and the flickering light from around the building revealed every embassy chimney belching columns of thick smoke and glowing cinders.

"No doubt the staff are destroying all documents and material they cannot carry with them in diplomatic pouches," observed Amadan. "And it looks like Farthun could use some help."

The constable corralled a guard from the squad leader, and brought him to Pendenar.

"The Prime Minister needs to assist Colonel Farthun. Stick with him, and bring him back if the situation turns ugly." He looked sideways at Amadan sternly as he added, "You may use force, but only whatsoever you must."

Amadan opened the door, and he and his guard hastened towards the embassy and soon disappeared amongst the confusion of the crowd. Pindlebryth started to step out of the carriage, but was restrained by Pendenar's arm. "Your Father would have my head, if I let you venture any closer. I am afraid this will have to do, M'Lord."

Pindlebryth continued to strain to look into the growing crush of people. He stood on the step by the carriage door to get a better view, and finally saw Amadan join Farthun and the assistant ambassador. The Crow gesticulated his wings wildly. It struck Pindlebryth odd that the timid assistant he saw in the Hall of Thrones was acting so extravagantly now. Amadan quickly engaged the assistant ambassador, trying to placate him. But the more he tried, the more bellicose the Crow became. The volley became more and more heated until a loud crash of glass and wood resounded from the second floor. One of the rooms flashed once then flooded with orange light. Almost instantly, its windows shattered as great tongues of fire leapt out and licked up the side of the embassy. The fire quickly spread across the upper floors, and a huge wall of smoke and embers flew up into the sky. Soldiers on the roofs of neighboring buildings scurried to stamp out any burning debris that landed there.

Constables blew their whistles, which soon were soon joined by a chorus of similar trills that communicated down the streets. In response, one bell of a fire company, then another and another, began to ring.

Farthun barked at the guard, and gestured back down the street. The guard wrestled Amadan away from the sudden panic. Some onlookers ran away from the scene, while others of the crowd pressed in to watch the conflagration. Still others started to throw objects at the Crow's carriages, as the crowd was overtaken by a mob mentality. The guard and Amadan returned, whereupon Pendenar summarily loaded the Prime Minister into the carriage, then himself jumped inside and ordered the driver back to the castle.

Amadan tried to protest but was silenced by Pendenar. "You've done all you could, Minister. Farthun has his duty now, as do I." The carriage completed its turn with difficulty in the active street. As it was about to get on its way, a great rumbling erupted from behind them at the embassy. Stones began to crumble, and a half dozen windows cracked then imploded on the ground floor. Fire did not gush out of the newly broken windows, but the upper stories blazed with renewed vigor with the onrush of fresh air from below, and the chimneys fumed even more furiously.

Groups of Crow appeared on the roof, and scrambled to fly away. The surrounding rooftops' soldiers, some with bows drawn, directed the Crow to join the carriages at the gate below.

One reindeer-drawn steam engine trundled past the Lemmings' carriage and down the flagstone road towards the fire, then another one. As they increased in number, the chorus of engine bells were abruptly drowned out by the chime of the CityState clock tolling midnight.

"What did Eekaya have to say?" asked Pindlebryth as he peered through the carriage's small rear portal. The ground and middle stories of the embassy began to disgorge rolling plumes of steam, as the engines set about their work. But the entire top floor was ablaze, as the timber crackled and roared with unfettered abandon.

"He was frightened."

"Frightened? It looked as if things were ready to come to blows."

"That's the way Crow behave – their braggadocio rises up when they are fearful. He was begging for political asylum, which of course is impossible at this point. It seems he came to the same conclusion we did – that he was the dupe for a Ravenne, and that someone in the Court of the Kyaa conspired with him and BlueHood. He is deathly afraid of returning to his homeland. He believes that he will be poisoned or meet some similar fate. Since he unwittingly worked so closely with one of the assassin class, he believes he is a loose end that they will want to tidy up."

Amadan chuckled quietly to himself, but then felt slightly ashamed. "I shouldn't laugh. Eekaya is in quite a predicament. It's just that he was so agitated, that he tried to insult Farthun and myself, calling us 'mottled eggs'. As if such a thing would mean anything to a Lemming..." Amadan leaned closer to the rear portal to watch the blaze, until their carriage turned a corner.

"Mottled eggs? What in the world does that mean?"

"Oh, Crow insult one another by referring to one's shell before they are hatched. For example, a weakling would 'have no egg tooth'. A dullard would have come from a 'soft shell'. And someone of disreputable birth would come from a 'mottled egg'."

Pindlebryth slammed back in his seat to face Amadan. "Quickening Spirit! *That's* how BlueHood communicated with the Ravenne."

"I beg your pardon, M'Lord?"

"I presided over a meeting between Hakayaa and the false ambassador. BlueHood threw several epithets at him, all related to frogs. I assumed they were insults meaningful to Crow. He even focused on the young ones, using words like 'tadpole' and 'polliwog'." Pindlebryth snapped his fingers in recollection. "Even Tanderra remarked it was unusual that Crow hated frogs so."

"Frogs? That makes no sense to a Crow. Frogs are food to them, not an insult."

"Precisely! The references to young frogs indicated the Lens was in the possession of a young one – that Prince Selephygur was the target!" Pindlebryth closed his eyes as he recalled the whole of the meeting. "It makes sense now!"

The two rode in silence for a time, while Pendenar watched the streets for any sudden impediments to their return to the castle. Amadan finally quietly suggested, "Perhaps you had better tell me more about this Lens of Truth. Though everyone knows of your and Darothien's rescue of the people from Selephylin at Vulcanis, I feel I have not heard the full story where the Lens is concerned."

After a long pause and a deep sigh, Pindlebryth began to tell the story again, including everything that was kept secret from the public and especially the peoples of other nations. He had scarcely relayed the last of the island adventure when the carriage arrived at the castle gates.

"Accompany me to my rooms, for there's more to tell." The group quickly made their way to Pindlebryth's apartment, whereupon Pendenar closed the door and took up his usual place by it inside the room. Pindlebryth bid Amadan sit, while he fetched a decanter and two glasses from underneath a countertop in a side room.

"Usually I have chamomile at night, but I daresay we both could use something stronger." Pindlebryth poured himself a half snifter of brandy, and placed the open decanter and the other empty glass in front of Amadan. Pindlebryth collapsed in one of the plush chairs in front of his book cases, then Amadan sat slowly in the other, then poured himself some brandy.

Pindlebryth rubbed his eyes, then sniffed his clothes. The stench of smoke could faintly be detected. He sipped a portion of the brandy, then began again, telling Amadan of the powers that the Lens bestowed to Selephygur and lastly recounted the night when Hakayaa told the legend of the Lens and the Artifacts of Old.

Amadan listened intently, and concluded by taking a draught from his snifter. He swirled the liquid in the glass, as he pondered. Then looking at Pindlebryth he asked, "Tell me of Hakayaa."

Pindlebryth did not reply for a good time, as a torrent of happy memories, sadness, pain and hatred all vied for attention. "We met at PanGaea University, and quickly got on together. We were thick as thieves through many an adventure. But we also often had stimulating discussions that lasted long into the night, as we deliberated over any and every topic – from the ridiculous, the epicurean (where to find the best food), to questions as heady as the meaning of existence, or the current state of the world. In that category, I would look at it from the vantage point of countries' languages, whereas he as a student of history, would…"

Pindlebryth stopped cold, as something in his bookshelves caught his eye. There in the center of a four volume work on the history of Lenland, was a book he did not recognize. He rose and approached the shelf, tilting his head to read the title on the spine. Pulling the book out, he returned to his chair and put down his glass. He read the title out loud – "Eekah and Kaiya."

"Hmm," Amadan mused as he inhaled the vapors from his glass. "One of the lesser known classics of Crow literature. I didn't know your expertise in languages extended to that nation's higher culture."

"It doesn't. I can get by with conversational Crow, but there is much I do not know. It is a language I have not yet formally studied. What is this work?" He scanned through pages of writing that looked like disorganized scratches to the untrained eye. "A sonnet? A novel?" Pindlebryth handed it to Amadan, who skimmed through the pages.

"A libretto. Believe me, Crow opera is an acquired taste, and is a tooth-jarring experience for those who are not familiar with their music. 'Eekah and Kaiya' is a dreary three-act tragedy, based on an equally tiresome Crow novel about two ill-fated friends, both in love with the same hen from a warring family. One of the protagonists' closest kin is kidnapped by an interloper from the hen's family. He is ultimately forced to betray his friend. The two acts of treachery draw the families into a blood feud. Just when you think things couldn't get any worse..." Amadan looked up from the book. He was going to continue, but thought better of it.   Pindlebryth was thunderstruck, staring off into nothingness.

"Please leave me. I... I need to think," Pindlebryth whispered without moving a muscle.

Amadan swallowed the remainder of his drink, and placed the glass and book on the table between them. "Yes, M'Lord. Thank you," he said as he bowed, and Pendenar escorted him out of the room.

After a few breaths, Pindlebryth stood up and took the libretto. He regarded it as he rolled it over in his hand. Just when he made up his mind to face Hakayaa's deeds and judge his motives, it was all thrown into disarray again. How like that blasted mocking magpie to keep him off balance! With a fiery outburst and an inarticulate shout, he flung the book at the shelves, then smashed the snifter against the wall.

Frustrated by the physician Sacalitre's requirement that he remain under observation in the patient recovery room, Selephygur felt sure that he, like LongBack, was being punished for their ill-advised foray to the Hall of Thrones' gallery.

The guard in charge of Selephygur was changed twice over the previous day. Starving for any news, be it of import or petty gossip, he pestered each new guard. Each time, he also made sure to ask of LongBack's situation. It was reported during the first shift that LongBack was still on his punitive duty in the royals' apartments' hall, and by the third shift he was sleeping the sleep of the dead. Neither guard could tell Selephygur when LongBack was to have some free time, only that he was slated to go back immediately to duty elsewhere.

What little respite from monotony Selephygur was allowed usually came an hour or so after mealtime. The guard and the medical orderly on duty led him on a short walk around the castle commons. Otherwise, Sacalitre strictly kept Selephygur within the confines of the recovery room. When he asked when he might be released to his own apartment, Sacalitre answered time and again, "We'll have to see about that."

It became increasingly difficult for Selephygur to simply remain still in his bed, but the medical staff kept vigil to ensure he remain as quiet as possible. As a result, the sheer boredom that only youth seem to be able to fully experience often led him to think fancifully of what doom he would inflict on Hakayaa. They ranged from the ridiculous to the most deliciously poetic. But the one common theme Selephygur seemed to always return to in so many of the various fantasies involved blinding Hakayaa. So vivid were his machinations, that he could easily visualize the pitiful state in which he would leave his attacker.

So immersed in this singleness of thought, Selephygur well-nigh jumped out of his bed when the visage of Hakayaa became as clear before him as a cold crisp breeze.

Behind the Crow was a domed wall, lit by crude flickering fires. The wall was a dark and glossy stone, though heavily cracked. In places, the cracks widened to gaping holes, through which a drenching rain fell. Selephygur's gaze centered again on Hakayaa, when suddenly the visage of Hakayaa returned his gaze with a look of astonishment. Selephygur gasped, before all went spinning into darkness.

He had been so absorbed in the vision, that he flinched again when Sacalitre asked, "Are you all right, my Prince?"

"What? Oh, Sacalitre." Selephygur breathed deeply. "It's you."

"I am here also, my Prince," chimed Darothien. "It looks like we gave you quite a start there."

"Did you have another nightmare?"

Selephygur sternly replied, "It was *not* a... It was not pleasant." He sighed again, hoping to hide the disturbing experience of his vision. He was not ready to divulge what he saw, let alone discuss his growing suspicion.

"All right, then. It's time to change your bandages, and both Darothien and I thought she should look again at your wound. Now relax, this won't hurt a bit," the physician cajoled. After the orderly drew the curtains closed, Sacalitre clipped the outermost bandage holding the gauze and paper discs over Selephygur's orbits. As he wound down to the last part of the wrapping, he slipped in his fingers to hold the gauze pad in place. Selephygur felt the pressure over his face, and could see the slow leaking of dim light grow in his good eye. "If you would, please hold the pad in place, while we look at your wounds." The doctor gently took Selephygur's hand, and guided it to the gauze pad. "Don't let too much light in. Your eye is now accustomed to the dark, and too much light might shock you. All right?"

"Yes, Doctor."

Sacalitre removed the disc, and began to peel away the first layers of cotton, pressed and clotted with brown blood and seepage. Using a dental mirror, he illuminated the rim of the socket by the meager light filtered from the window. Using a pair of cotton pads, he wetted the bare skin, washed it a gingerly as possible, then dried it off. "Excellent. The resected skin layers around the socket are healing nicely, and should easily accept and hold a glass eye. What do you see, Madame Wizard?"

Darothien had her prism and convex lens at the ready, and leaned in face to face with the prince. "There is definitely something behind the remaining gauze. If you would, please proceed doctor."

The physician and Darothien switched places. "Now, Prince Selephygur, please hold still. This may sting quite a bit." Sacalitre used a pair of forceps to remove the woven gauze and pressed cotton buried in the socket itself. Both were entirely dyed with colors ranging from hardened black blood to relatively fresh red. But as he extracted the last of the bolus, Selephygur had no reaction.

"Was that it? Are you done? There was no pain. Not one jot," reported Selephygur.

Sacalitre's brow furrowed with puzzlement. He took the mirror again, to examine the interior of the empty socket. "Lords Above. It is entirely healed! This is unheard of – even those with a Name cannot heal a wound that great in the space of a single day." He spun the mirror around to scan the entire inside of the orbit. "This is quite amazing," he said, almost with the excitement of a child with a new toy. Suddenly, he stopped his inspection. "Hello. What's this? Darothien, have you ever seen the like?"

She leaned in again. Speaking a single word, she tapped the end of her prism, which began to glow with a ghostly green light. She held the prism to illuminate a portion of the socket. Indeed, the physician was correct – the wound was entirely healed, and all the tendons and tissues had neatly sealed themselves back into the surrounding fibrous tissue. But something caught her attention, making her stop and shift the prism to closer examine the area. Strange filaments of blue stone had intermingled with the tissue, and formed a fine latticework inside the empty orbit. The finest lines began near the edges of the socket, which then combined like veins with other strands until they all converged at the rear of the cavity.

"No, I have not," she whispered in awe.

"Tell me! What do you see?" commanded Selephygur.

Darothien described the structure in his orbit, down to the finely structured spiderweb of stone. After a moment she mused barely aloud to herself, "The Fox kept the Lens hidden in a vault. Never to be used..."

Sacalitre ventured an idea he barely believed could be true. "My Prince, I am going to remove the disc, and gradually remove the bandage on your good eye. Let us know when you can sense movement. While the physician partially removed the bandages, he moved his remaining hand back and forth. Almost immediately Selephygur said, "You're moving something up and down."

Sacalitre placed his hand directly in front of Selephygur's eye. "Now, without moving your head, try to follow my hand." He moved his paw again, slightly at first from right to left, then up and down. He repeated the exercise with increasingly wider ranges. Looking into the socket, he could see its remaining muscles flex slightly, as they tried to track Selephygur's vision. "Do you feel any pain?"

"No. None," flatly came Selephygur's reply.

Sacalitre looked at the orderly, then at Darothien. Shrugging his shoulders, he said, "If you're ready, I can remove the entire bandage."

"Absolutely!" Selephygur replied, barely containing his anticipation. Sacalitre slowly removed the last layers of the bandage. After each layer, he asked Selephygur if he felt any discomfort, but there was none. Finally, the last layer came off, and Selephygur squinted as he adjusted to the subdued light.

He smiled broadly, saying simply, "Finally! I can see!" He swung his legs out, and stood facing the window. Ignoring the sputtered warnings from the physician, he took a few unsteady steps and tried to draw the curtains open. The first time, his paw grasped empty air, but he quickly focused and correctly judged the distance and gripped the drawstring. Instinctively shielding his eyes against the sudden onrush of light, he pushed open the window. He took a deep breath of freedom, only to make his snout wrinkle. "Smoke?" he asked. He scanned the sky directly above the castle, and saw a slowly rising wispy column of grey rising beyond the north roof. "What happened last night?"

"Apparently there was an accident at the Crow embassy. In their haste, the staff touched off a blaze that leveled most of the building," Darothien answered.

Selephygur began to chuckle, then let out a single laugh. "Oh, that's rich!"

He continued to titter as Darothien added, "A few Crow suffered burns to their feathers, but there were thankfully no fatalities."

"Of course, of course," Selephygur clucked before regaining his composure. He did not want to let either of them know his real desire to break out into unbridled righteous laughter. Quickly changing the subject, he stated, "I take it that I can be discharged forthwith." He looked around for his clothing.

Sacalitre fumbled inside his white coat's pockets, and produced Selephygur's old eyepatch. He rubbed his chin before responding and handing over the eyepatch. "A moment, my Prince. I'd like to repack the socket, just in case any wounds open – although that now seems unlikely. Report back tomorrow, and we can begin fitting a glass eye for you. I'm assuming you don't want to wear the patch anymore than you have to. We'll also go over the additional steps to your daily toilet, to care for the eye." Sacalitre sat the Prince down, and gently placed fresh cotton and gauze inside the cavity. He then handed the eyepatch to Selephygur, who slung it on with the ease and familiarity of putting on old gloves. "I will ask you to stay in the castle, preferably on your apartment's floor. The less undue stimulus the first day out, the better. "

"It is probably best that you aren't seen outside the castle anyway, given the events of yesterday and last night," recommended Darothien.

"Very well." Selephygur donned the dressing robe in the corner next to his guard. "If there is a problem, I shall have my guard send for you or an orderly." He carefully and methodically walked as he left the infirmary and rounded the corner following the hallway to the southeast stairs. He then asked his guard, "Where is LongBack?"

"He is on duty at the West Gate. His shift lasts until dinner time."

"When you are relieved by the next shift, please go and notify LongBack I wish to see him in my apartment at his first opportunity." Selephygur climbed the first few steps easily, but his monocular vision led him to stumble once or twice as he tried to navigate the stairway past the second floor. As they entered the third floor of the South Wing, Selephygur took a moment to stretch, muttering, "I've been sedentary for far too long!"

Once in his rooms, Selephygur immediately pulled the bell strap next to the door. He then walked around his rooms, and stretched his arms and back.

"Lords Above, it is good to finally be out of that sterile room," he groused at the guard. He looked out the window for a while in thought, periodically looking again at the billowing tapers of smoke and steam from the embassy. He began to slowly pace back and forth in front of the window, reveling in the poetic justice of the blaze. Occasionally he paused and looked longingly at the barracks level beyond the West Gate where the Lioness squad once resided.

When a maid came in response to his call, Selephygur simply asked for some scones and ginseng and ginkgo tea. When she returned holding a tray with the biscuits and a steaming pot, he sat down and dismissed both her and the guard. He quietly but intently quaffed two cups. He poured a third, then closed his eye and steepled his paws in thought.

Selephygur found himself thinking that he was beginning to be comfortable with the darkness. But comfort was not his reason for waiting alone. He set his mind to reach out, to try to experience what he saw before. He searched for the unique feeling when he had his visions. Several minutes passed by, and he exhaled in disappointment. He opened his eye, stretched then relaxed, and quaffed some more of the tea tonic. He resumed his position of concentration and searched again. He tried to recall the feel, the touch, the flavor of the vision. This time, rather than actively trying to search for it, he let it come to him.

His vision slowly grew in brightness with yellows, oranges and reds. He did not force it to focus, but rather willed the vision to know he was open to it. The colors slowly grew into focus for him to see it was rapidly changing, ever in motion. In moments, he realized he was looking at fire. It swirled about, and beyond it was dim flickering diffuseness. Only then did he realize he was not looking at fire, he was seeing from within the fire. Thankfully, there was no sense of burning or of heat. He tried looking to his left and right, only to lose the vision abruptly.

Opening his eye, Selephygur looked about his room. Satisfied nothing had changed, and the sun had not moved appreciably, he finished his cup of tea and settled in to try once more. This time the sensation of his nerves aligning came readily. After a time spent opening his mind and focusing on the peculiar perception, he once again saw the fire. This time, however, from inside the fire he saw elongated shadows undulate against walls. They were like glass, but riddled with great breaches to the outside, and crazed with countless tiny cracks. The ragged openings showed dawn was slowly approaching, with wisps of heavy fog sifting through them. Selephygur again tried to look to one side or another, and found that he could turn this time. A large log lay charred and broken in halves on either side of him. At various places along the circular wall were archways leading off into darkened hallways. Beyond the glowing coals at the base of the fire, he thought he could see a depression in the floor, long and leading straight from side to side. As Selephygur tried to perceive more, he suddenly spied Hakayaa.

As the Crow approached, he looked more harried and wild-eyed than before. He moved stiltedly, and Selephygur could see that his clothes hung about him in tatters. Hakayaa proceeded to bend down, and picked up a large glossy stone. The accursed Crow knelt closer, then began to strike at him with the rock repeatedly. Each impact shook and rocked Selephygur's view, but there was no crack of injury, no sting of pain.

Selephygur, however, was wrenched out of the vision by a loud knock at his apartment door. He shook his head to restore his wits about him, and checked that his eyepatch was still in place.

"Come in," he said.

Hatheron and Pindlebryth entered, all smiles. Selephygur rose, but had to suddenly steady himself on the table as he fully stood. His visitors immediately protested not to exert himself, but he held up one paw and blithely assured them, "It's quite all right – I guess the tea is a bit heady. Please sit!"

Hatheron approached, and clasped his youngest son by the shoulder. "It does me good to see you up and about. You are well? You must have been sound asleep – we knocked several times."

"Yes, but I'm fine and well rested," Selephygur played along with his father's assumption. "Sacalitre had no more reason to keep me, although I must visit him tomorrow to satisfy his worrisome nature."

"I understand he was taken by surprise at how quickly you healed, and Darothien detected some lingering glamor in your healed wound."

"Yes," Selephygur replied thoughtfully. "I accept it as a residual benefit from the Lens."

Hatheron and Pindlebryth exchanged glances. "Again, I'm glad to see you bushy-tailed. I wish I could speak with you longer, but several of the diplomats from the remaining nations wish to be assured from Tander... Amadan and myself, that Lenland had nothing to do with the leveling of the Crow embassy."

"It couldn't have happened to nicer people!" gibed Selephygur.

Hatheron leaned in and lowered his voice. "Between the three of us and the walls, part of me agrees with you." Leaning back again, he continued, "But decorum requires that Lenland be more sympathetic. I think I will leave the sympathy to Amadan. I merely will keep an impassive front. Keep yourself well, my son."

Hatheron left with his escort, leaving Pindlebryth alone with his brother.

"And what say you, dear brother?" Selephygur said teasingly.

"Your concern for Mother is touching." Pindlebryth looked somewhat dour, and held his paws clasped behind his back.

"Oh! I *am* sorry. I just find myself preoccupied. I'm sure you understand. How is Mother?"

Pindlebryth ambled around the room, and Selephygur turned to follow him as he did. "Doing well. Sacalitre thinks she may walk small distances by tomorrow. She asks constantly about you."

"I suppose I should visit her before day is done, then. However, I now find myself suddenly wanting to get some fresh air and stretch. Care to accompany me for a walk around the grounds?"

"You didn't seem strong enough to stand a few minutes ago, let alone take a stroll."

"Precisely my point. All that lying around and sitting does me no good." He walked purposefully to the door. "Shall we?"

Pindlebryth regarded his brother cynically for a moment, but then simply shrugged, and walked down the hall with him. Selephygur's guard accompanied the two as they made their way slowly and carefully down the stairs and outside into the central courtyard. At Selephygur's insistence, Pindlebryth regaled him with his recollections from the embassy blaze the previous night. They had circled the yard and made their way to the West Gate as Pindlebryth finished. The gate guards saluted as Selephygur walked through, but his own guard began to protest.

"My Prince, remember the Royal Physician asked you to stay within the castle today."

"Oh, please. I am merely going to the barracks. Surely Sacalitre could not begrudge me this. The barracks may be a separate building, but it is considered part of the castle, is it not? Besides, surely I am safe surrounded by regiments of Vadarog's soldiers?" he said with mock petulance. Pindlebryth shrugged at the guard, and accompanied his brother. The group made their way to the north of the gate into the barracks ground floor and the gymnasium, where various pairs of soldiers were sparring with wooden swords, and some with fencing foils.

Selephygur made his way to a wall, and collected a sword. He found a practice post wrapped in straw and thick rope, and attained a stance. His guard and Pindlebryth shared a concerned look. Selephygur swung, and roundly missed the post. A snigger or two could be heard in the room. Those soldiers were quickly jabbed by their partners, a reminder it was not their place for any comment whatsoever.

Selephygur approached the post with a few small steps and felt out the location of the post with his sword. Once he was in range, he took his stance again and made several practice swings. The first few strikes hit solidly, but as he sidestepped and thrust, riposted and sliced, his blows grew farther from his mark until he glanced off the post, and he nearly lost his grip. He renewed his position and stance, and had at it again. But desperation, quick exhaustion, and frustration all combined to make him even more quickly lose his balance.

He was shakily positioning himself a third time, when Pindlebryth sidled up to him and suggested, "I think you've had enough exertion for your first day out."

"No!" Selephygur argued vehemently. He took the smallest of moments to adjust his eyepatch. "I have to do this."

"And so you shall, but not now," Pindlebryth urged in quiet but stern tones. "You've made your point. You also have made a small spectacle of yourself. No need to go further, and make an ass out of yourself." He firmly grabbed Selephygur by the arm. At first he resisted, but Selephygur started to breathe heavily. He relaxed his stance, and fumbled with the sword as he tried to return it to its peg. "Let me take you back to your room."

Unnoticed by them as they left the barracks, a fencer was quietly sitting in a corner and removing his fencing uniform. As Vadarog removed his fencing helmet, he regarded Selephygur, then nodded to himself as he came to a decision.

Pindlebryth led him back into the South Wing, then addressed the guard. "Please see my brother makes it back to his room, and lies down for a while. I unfortunately must take my leave here – I am asked to see Darothien's latest discovery."

He stood as the guard carefully guided Selephygur down the hall to the stairs to the upper levels. Concern washed over him as he observed his brother critically – he did not seem lethargic, just unsteady due to the loss of depth perception. When Selephygur was out of view, Pindlebryth turned about, and headed towards the underground level of the East Wing. Preoccupied with worries about his brother, and a nagging flicker of indecision about Hakayaa, he opened the deceptively damp-looking outer door to the laboratory, and strode into the anteroom. Immediately the stone wolf jumped up on all fours, and stood howling on its pedestal. The sound made Pindlebryth blink and rouse himself back to the present moment. He stood quietly and politely until Darothien opened the inner door.

She silenced the wolf, and commanded it in the arcane language of wizards at which Pindlebryth could only guess. The wolf sat, and regarded Pindlebryth with a piercing stare. "Come in, M'Lord. But first, allow him to sniff your palm." Pindlebryth with a hint of a bemused smile, approached and did as Darothien bade. The wolf leaned forward, sniffed rapidly several times, growling once then snuffling as if to clear its nostrils. It then wagged its tail and returned to its original position of watchfulness. "There! From now on, he will allow you to come into the inner room whenever you like, whether I'm here or not." She paused for a moment, putting a finger to her chin, and looking upwards mischievously at the ceiling. "Enh, unless this door is latched from the inside."

"Thank you," Pindlebryth replied with a note of true appreciation in his voice. "You left me a message that you had something to show me?"

"Actually, something to give to you," she said as she walked towards a table in the middle of the laboratory. "I can't explain it in any way that would be meaningful to you. I can only say that this gift *wants* to be given to you." She led Pindlebryth to an apparatus, above which two emeralds hovered above a liquid filled basin. Each were separated from the other by a spinning green wheel of arcane energy. It was only after closer inspection, that Pindlebryth realized the gems were two halves of what had been the main stone from the broken royal crown. It was split perfectly in half, with the cleaved faces mirroring each other. Inside the green wheel were two glowing wheels of argent energy spinning in the opposite direction, which pulled the metallic liquid from the ornate dish of bronze, gold and lead. They spun the liquid into fine filigrees of silver onto the edges and faces of both halves of the gem. After a few mesmerizing seconds, the wheels flashed out of existence, leaving the two silver and emerald devices hovering over the emptied dish.

Darothien gingerly touched and gently pulled one stone from the air and inspected it. Satisfied, she nodded and indicated Pindlebryth should take the other. He was unsure at first, but he plucked the slowly gyrating stone from above the dish. He looked quizzically at Darothien.

"See the flat mirrored surface? It has been cleaved perfectly from its partner. So perfectly in fact, that if the two halves ever touched without their silver casing, the gem would seal itself back together.

"Place the flat surface to your ear, like this, M'Lord." He mimicked Darothien, who then moved her half in front of her mouth. "Your gem allows you to hear whoever speaks into the flat of this gem." Pindlebryth eyes widened as Darothien's voice resounded like a tiny vibrating glass in his ear. He smiled a tickled smile, like a child who finally sorts out how a new toy works.

"Similarly, I can hear whatever the holder of the other gem speaks into it." She returned her gem to her ear.

"Like this?" he said with playful hesitation as he held the gem in front of his mouth.

"Precisely!" Darothien smiled with satisfaction. She pulled open a drawer underneath the table, and produced two small velvet boxes. She placed her half of the gemstone in one box, and closed it. She then offered the second empty box to Pindlebryth. "That one is yours, this one is for Selephygur. I'll give it to him when I next see him."

"Oh. I thought... never mind," said a crestfallen Pindlebryth. Checking himself that he did not pout, he looked up and around the entire lab. "Why do you suddenly trust me to allow unfettered access to your work rooms? I myself am afraid to touch anything, lest I set off any number of tricks, traps or whatnot. Or even worse, inadvertently destroy some project you are toiling over."

She had a hint of pain in her otherwise simple smile. "Perhaps it is merely another thing I cannot explain. I can only say that this room told me there may come a time when you need to be here, and I might not be."

⌒⌒⌒ ⌒⌒ ꙮ ⌒ ⌒⌒ ⌒

When Selephygur was escorted back to his apartment, he dismissed the guard in a huff. He found his newfound impairment intolerable, and swore by the Lords Above he would overcome it. He rapidly swept about the room, and went to a small closet near the hallway door. He rummaged about for a moment or two, and emerged with a decorative walking cane. He then paced around the room, the cane in one hand, and the other outstretched. He went from wall to wall, object to object, practicing how to judge space and depth with just one eye. He often jarred his wrist when he misjudged the proximity of an item as the cane solidly impacted it. He was starting to improve his ability when there came a knock at the door.

In exasperation, he snapped, "Come in!" at the distraction. LongBack cautiously opened the door. Selephygur immediately changed from annoyed chagrin to gladness, and bade him enter and close the door behind him. LongBack was exhausted, and looked like Colonel Farthun had run him through the wringer. Selephygur lowered the cane and walked toward him, welcoming him in.

"Welcome, old friend. Please sit. I would offer you something, but I'm afraid all I have is some cold tea." LongBack accepted the chair, but politely declined the drink. Selephygur joined him and sat across the table, hanging the cane on the back of his chair. He earnestly asked him what discipline his brother and Farthun had subjected him to, listening intently as LongBack described his tasks for the past two days.

"But enough of my troubles. What of you, my Prince? I'm glad to see that you are out of the leech's room. I've heard you've healed far more quickly than anyone expected – that's excellent news! You certainly look none the worse for wear. How have you spent these past two days?"

"I'll tell you soon enough."

"Then why did you request that I come to your apartment?"

"I need to ask you some questions," Selephygur said as he settled in the chair. He leaned his elbows on the table, and rested his chin on his paws rolled into a ball. "Tell me of Vulcanis."

LongBack seemed a mite incredulous. "The sorceress' island? Again? Surely, you've heard the tale of that day from Prince Pindlebryth, Darothien and even Pendenar at least a dozen times."

"Yes, but I want to hear your story. What was it like to fall asleep? And to wake up on the island? Where did you wake up? Can you describe the island and its fortress?"

LongBack looked at the ceiling, as if there was a long-forgotten script written in the air above him. "My Prince, I will tell if you need me to. But it is something I do not wish to dwell on."

"Please, LongBack. I think it is important."

LongBack closed his eyes, and sighed in resignation. Looking again at the ceiling, he began. "I was working along the harbor, helping my crew load freight, when we all heard a strange siren's voice sounding over the horizon. It was strangely compelling, and the last thing I remember is dropping several crates on the deck, diving into the water, and swimming to the west. I felt like I couldn't help myself. I couldn't stop, and I didn't care. For the longest time I was lost in dream. I've tried several times to remember what happened afterward, and how I got on the island. But like a dream, it became dimmer and foggier the harder I tried to remember it. I have no idea how long I was a sleepwalker. I can only guess it was three or four days, relying on the stories that have been told. Then I awoke to the sound of a woman's scream." LongBack's spine shivered, making him sit ramrod straight in his chair.

"Even now, the thought of that shriek makes my blood freeze." He swallowed with difficulty. "When I came to, I was a scullery slave stirring a large pot of lichen, mosses and kelp in a stew that was to be our mess. I was amongst several other Lemmings, none of whom I recognized. We were confused, and started milling about and exploring this strange place we found ourselves in. We found huge store rooms, others found rows of sleeping quarters, torture chambers, and still others found the central dome."

"Can you tell me of that place?"

"I was not there myself, but I spoke with others on the ark on the return trip home. The first thing that every one talked about was the horrific smell from some vile blue filth in a long rectangular pool. They also spoke of the throne in the one half of the room, and also the sheer size of the dome." He clicked the fingers of one paw. "There was a soldier that accompanied Darothien back to the dome, after the witch's spell was broken. He said the dome was made of some shiny volcanic material. I think he called it 'obsidian'. There were four hallways that led out of the dome. Darothien followed one hall to the witch's rooms, and another hall led to holding cells." He sat for a moment in the chair, chewing his lip and trying to remember more. "After that, the whole place shuddered and rumbled, and your brother the Prince led us out of the maze of rooms inside the volcano. Outside was just as bleak – dark and foreboding skies, grey and black sand, endless fields of dark rocks, the pier and the ark."

"I see." Selephygur leaned back and collected his cane, and stood to walk over to the door. He pulled the bell strap, and resumed his seat at the table. Presently, the maid knocked and opened the door. Selephygur asked for fresh ginger and gingko tea, and some more fruit and nut scones.

"On the island, my brother put you in charge of the ark's return. One thing I don't think I was ever told. Why did you not return to your life of the sea? Why did you elect to apply and become a Royal Guard?"

LongBack considered his answer for a while. He began when the maid returned with their refreshments. "My Prince, I... Forgive me, but I do not wish to answer that just now." He looked desolate and grieved.

"Oh," Selephygur realized, speaking softly. "You lost your family in the spell." He sipped his tea, suddenly losing his appetite.

"Yes," LongBack choked. "My wife drowned in the harbor. And my son..." He sat sullenly, and made no move to look up or consider the food.

"Forgive *me*, my friend. I didn't realize. I didn't know. If it still means anything after all this time, you have my condolences."

"Thank you, my Prince," LongBack gurgled, then cleared his throat. "If I may be excused, I only have a short break between gate duty, and whatever next task Colonel Farthun has for me. I think I may be reporting late already." He stood, barely glancing at Selephygur, bowed and left the room. He was gone long before Selephygur realized he was still holding his cup. At a total loss for words, he left his room to moodily pace the hallways. A strange balance – almost akin to an equation Darothien might teach him – involving LongBack, Hakayaa, and his brother Pindlebryth revolved within his mind.

It was close to dinnertime when Selephygur emerged from his introspection, when he recollected the strong suggestion his brother had given him. He stopped, and tried to brush all his thinking and planning to the side. He proceeded down the hallway, knocked on the doors before entering his parents' chambers, and spent an hour with his mother. She was out of her sickbed, but sat in an opulent lounge chair with her splinted leg resting on a similarly plush ottoman and an extra pillow.

"Ah, welcome my dear! So good to see you. Sacalitre told me that you had healed far earlier than he expected. I'm so glad you are doing so well. As for myself, they tell me I can take short walks tomorrow." Her beaming face was contagious, and Selephygur soon couldn't remember why he expected this to be a bothersome and boring exercise. Queen Wenteberei called for dinner for themselves, and they reminisced and relaxed for over an hour.

More than once, however, the conversation turned to the

past two days. Selephygur quickly changed the topic each time. However, when their discussions turned to it one last time, Wenteberei plainly asked, "What is troubling you, my dear?"

Selephygur dabbed his mouth with his napkin, and dropped it on the plate. Looking down at the table, he let out a long sigh.

"I am conflicted about what to do, or even what to feel." He balled up his right paw into a fist. "I want Hakayaa punished for what he did to me, to Tanderra, and to you. I want him blinded or *dead*. No one knows how much Hakayaa has taken from me – not just my vision, but all the abilities the Lens gave me! The sights I've seen, the discoveries I've made, the new worlds of science I've opened – who knows what else I could have done with the Lens?

"But what confuses me is that I cannot tell where Pindlebryth stands on this."

"True enough," admitted the Queen. "One minute, he seems filled with malevolence toward his one-time friend, yet a little while later he still has hope that all his misdeeds can somehow be explained away."

"Even now! After all that has passed?" Selephygur asked with incredulity.

"Selephygur, you have so many who hold you dear. Especially Pindlebryth – he was ecstatic the day your Name was revealed to all of Lenland. But consider that you have something he never did – an elder brother. Someone who helps, guides and commiserates with you. You know you can talk to me or your father about anything, but parents also know that there are some things that will only be shared by brothers and friends.

"Pindlebryth had no elder brother of his own. And being a possible future leader of Lenland, means that the oh-so-many who want to claim him as a friend end up being nothing of the sort. Many sought his friendship only as a path to consolidate their own finances or power. Others tried to insinuate themselves romantically, not because of love, but only so that they could live in the lap of luxury. So, try to understand your brother and Hakayaa have spent so much time, trust, sad troubles and happy times together, that they have a bond not unlike how you regard Pindlebryth." She paused to sip some dandelion tea.

"How would you feel if it was Pindlebryth who attacked you instead of Hakayaa? You couldn't forget your years of experience together and simply decide you would hate him forever and ever, could you? Would you not at least try to understand your brother?"

Selephygur was speechless, and suddenly more troubled than when he was pacing about the halls hours ago.

"Well, I think we've both reached the end of our energy today," yawned the queen. As if on cue, a knock on the door sounded, and a nurse and maid entered to prepare Wenteberei for bed. "Good night, my son. Sleep well. And think on what I've said."

Closing the door behind him, Selephygur realized he was indeed tired from all the day's activity. He returned to his rooms, prepared for bed, and quickly fell into a sound sleep.

But only a few hours of rest found him. In the middle of the night, he was set upon by another vision.

Hakayaa lay sleeping on a smooth black floor, riddled with rubble and scree. Domed walls vaulted upward on all sides, and were cracked and broken in several places, allowing starlight to twinkle through. Hakayaa looked progressively worse than before – his clothes were almost non-existent, and patches of feathers were missing across his body. Peering over a circle of rocks and small piles of ash, he saw the long and straight depression in the floor he had envisioned before. His heart leapt into his throat when he saw alongside the depression, a raised platform and a toppled throne on it.

Some motion in the periphery caught his attention. He turned to see Hakayaa wide awake and staring directly at him. With wide-eyed panic, the Crow scrambled backward on all fours. As he scuttled away, his beak moved soundlessly, but Selephygur could easily see that he was screaming.

He sat up in bed, his feet and forepaws drenched in sweat. "I know where he is!" he blurted out loud in the dark.

By the gibbous moonlight coursing through the apartment windows, Selephygur clambered out of bed and carefully lit an oil lamp on an end table. He then quietly made his way to his closets, leaving the lamp just outside the door. He methodically rifled through the racks until he found some riding clothes. After he put the last parts of his leggings and calf chaps on, he picked up the lantern, and crossed his bedroom to a small cabinet. Pulling open a lower drawer, he pulled out a locked box. After undoing the lock, Selephygur took out two matching daggers. He slipped them into the straps on his leather forearm guards, and tied them tightly. Dousing the lamp, Selephygur tiptoed to his front door. Nearly walking into several items along the way, he realized he could not do what he needed to do alone. He disliked the thought of imposing on his friend a second time, but there way no other way for it – necessity required it.

Steeling himself with a deep breath, Selephygur opened the door and headed out with determined resolve. The hall guard greeted him with a quick bow of the head, but Selephygur strode brashly on, without acknowledging his presence. He made it to the staircase, and suffered a mild attack of vertigo. He was not dizzied by the stairs, but he had to carefully and deliberately guide his steps down while holding the handrail.

Once on the second level of the South Wing, he padded down the dorm hall. He squinted to read the nameplates on doors by the dim light of a single lit sconce in the hall. Stopping at the desired door, he furtively looked both ways, and held his breath to listen. Hearing only the muffled snoring emanating from several rooms, he carefully opened the door in front of him. He entered quietly, leaving the door behind him ajar less than an inch. He crept to a point between a pair of bunks in the dorm room, one on each of his left and right. Confounded by the choice in the dark, he shuffled to the window, and slowly opened the curtain, allowing in some reflected moonlight. Looking back at the beds, he still could only barely make out the profiles of the guards, as the moon shone away from the window. He chose one, and hoped for the best.

"LongBack!" he whispered. He leaned even closer and shook the sleeper's shoulder. "LongBack! Wake up!"

The sleeper snuffled once, and rolled over, pulling a blanket over his head. But Selephygur was nothing if not persistent.

"LongBack! *Now*!" Selephygur murmured hoarsely.

The sleeper began to snore, at a volume Selephygur didn't quite believe was possible. Selephygur's heart leapt into his throat when a muffled voice behind him gurgled, "Batten down the hatches!"

Selephygur straightened up with a start, and wheeled around when he recognized the familiar voice. LongBack rolled over, groaned a totally unrecognizable question, then propped himself up on one arm as he looked blearily at his visitor. He was about to hurl a few choice words that would have made his old shipmates blush, but he snapped fully awake when he realized who it was.

"My Prince?" he whispered in kind. "What are you doing here?"

"LongBack, I'm sorry to rouse you. Even more so, that I have to ask you a favor. It will quite probably get you in even more hot water than before, but I need your help. I need to do something, but I can't do it alone. I can count only on you."

LongBack glanced at his snoring roommate, and sat up, rubbing the sleep from one eye. "You don't need to ask twice. What's afoot?"

"Get your riding gear, and bring your weapons. We're flying westward."

"Over MidSea?" he grunted as he pushed his blanket, and pivoted his legs out of bed.

"Precisely. I'll wait for you at the stairway."

A few minutes felt like an eternity, as Selephygur stood just inside the stairwell. Finally, LongBack emerged from his room, ready for action. LongBack wordlessly and instinctively took the lead as they climbed down the steps, and headed to the central courtyard doors of the East Wing. LongBack checked the yard and the moon declining in the northwest, then instructed Selephygur, "Follow me and stay in the shadow along the North Wing."

They almost reached the end of the wing, and would lose their cover as they approached the West Gate. Selephygur asked, "How do we get past the gate guards without notice?"

"Maybe we don't. They aren't scheduled to change until morning. Take the lead, my Prince. And don't rush. We'll just have to brass it out for the rest of the way to the stables."

Selephygur adjusted his eyepatch, and walked ahead with LongBack one step behind and to the left. When they stepped from the manicured lawn onto the crushed gravel path near the gate, the guard delivered a snappy salute. Selephygur wordlessly waved past him, and the two continued without missing a step. LongBack glanced back to see another guard join the first, standing just outside the doorway of the gate station box. The newcomer looked at them, then began talking to the guard on duty.

"We're in for it now," rasped LongBack. "WhipTail just came out and spotted us. He's a stickler for protocol, and he'll wonder why he wasn't notified about you leaving the castle tonight. He'll have someone on our tails if we don't move quickly." They made their way along the northern path past the barracks to the stables. Selephygur waved aside the stable watchman, and he started to look for a mount for two, as LongBack collected saddles, tack and some supplies. Selephygur was about to bring out the albatross Keen. LongBack caught up with him, and unabashedly corrected him. "You don't want Keen. He's not the spring chicken that he was two years ago. Besides, albatross need thermals to climb and fly fast. He'd have trouble attaining altitude at night. We need this one – Mariner's a good night flyer, and can carry two in a pinch," he suggested as he opened the gate of a roseate tern's stall.

As they started to put the saddles on the bird, the watchman came up. "My Prince, what are you planning?"

"That does not concern you. It is sufficient that I need this mount now."

"Yes, my Prince. LongBack, I need you to sign for taking Mariner."

"No, he doesn't. LongBack, continue preparations." Selephygur tried to shoulder past the watchman, but he was faced with the log book.

"I'm sorry my Prince, but it is the rules. The troops requisitioning must sign."

"Oh, very well. *I'll* sign."

"My Prince, only troops or guards may sign..."

"I will remind you that I am attached to Blue Regiment, an archer directly under the command of General Vadarog." He tore the pen out of the watchman's hand, and wrote hurriedly. Looking over his shoulder, he ordered LongBack simply, "Come along."

They led Mariner outside, and LongBack mounted the front saddle and took the reins. "Belt yourself in – don't want you falling off!" Selephygur pulled himself up into the rear saddle, but almost lost balance. Righting himself, he secured himself in with the leather hip strap. LongBack pointed Mariner into the prevailing breeze, and snapped the reins to take off.

They had circled a couple of times to climb, and started westward when Selephygur began to nervously giggle. "Whoo! I don't believe what I just did!"

"That indeed was an interesting act to watch. But you should have let me sign the log."

"No. This is all my idea, and I should take the

responsibility. Besides, I told the truth – I made no false claims. And you are merely executing your duty to protect me as best you can."

"Ah, the truth. I believe you are only an *honorary* member of Blue Regiment. Not that I don't appreciate the effort, my Prince. But I'm afraid Colonel Farthun may not agree with your thinking. He still may have no choice but to drum me out of the guard."

Selephygur suddenly became stern. "I will *not* let that happen."

They were silent for a while as Mariner continued westward. "Where exactly are we heading?" LongBack inquired.

"Vulcanis Majoris. Head northwest."

They quickly reached the coast, and wheeled past the harbor of Cape Ark. They could still see by the setting moon the remainder of the ark as it rested half a league west of the port. Although used temporarily to house many of the rescued, it was abandoned after a few weeks because no one would stay on that accursed ship longer than necessary. It was set afire and adrift, but an ocean swell forced it against the rocks in the wide westerly cove just north of the harbor city. The lumbering hulk lay there ever since, half-burned and half-scuttled against the jagged rocks.

They remained on their northwestern tack for several hours. Both LongBack and Selephygur often checked to see if they were followed, but the night sky made it difficult. In the act of doing so, Selephygur was once stricken by dizziness, when several low cumulus clouds swept between them and the dark but calm ocean below.

Selephygur's curiosity had been eating at him ever since their misadventure began. He needed to ask LongBack something, but could not figure out how to broach the topic. Finally, at the risk of being ogreish, he decided there was no other way than to be direct.

"Why are you helping me, LongBack? You already have said you know the consequences of aiding me, especially after what happened at the gallery." Selephygur paused to think, wondering if he dare ask something that pointed to a darkness in LongBack. "As a matter of fact, why did you join the guard at all?"

"My Prince, the MidSea Archipelago is coming over the

horizon."

"Don't change the subject!" Selephygur scolded. Almost immediately he regretted his ill-mannered response. He gripped the side of his saddle with one paw, and clasped LongBack's shoulder with the other. "I cannot thank you enough for helping me, but this goes beyond any reason I can fathom. Why are you doing this?"

"Prince Selephygur," said LongBack as if he already knew the answer to the question, "what exactly is it you plan to do once we get to Vulcanis? The answer to both our questions may be the same."

Selephygur was stunned. Could LongBack have known all along? And still without complaint join him on this dark task? He took a deep breath, sighed, and relinquished to answer first. "Hakayaa is at Vulcanis. I mean to... I don't know. I haven't decided if I want to kill him or just blind him. In either case, I cannot do it alone. Half-blind myself, I would surely fail. I need your help. You're the only one I feel I can trust, even for this vengeance." A silence fell, filled only by the rush of the wind, and the regular flapping of Mariner's wings. LongBack's shoulders tensed, even though he only loosely held the reins.

"While we returned to Lenland on the ark, Darothien showed you to all the crew and many of the people rescued. You were so... you were a beautiful child. You looked just like my own son BlackBrow, and I longed to see my family again.

"But neither my son nor my wife were on the ark. When we made port in the town that grew to become Cape Ark, I and countless others searched the crowds for our families. I left my old shipmates to hunt for my wife high and low in the city, and then in the surrounding countryside. But she was nowhere to be found. Becoming mad with worry, I ran to our home miles from the town. When I arrived, the door was open and the house was overrun with vermin. Like everyone under the witch's spell, my wife mindlessly left our home. And just like hundreds of other lost souls, she must have drowned heading west into the ocean. My shipmates followed me to my house to find me," he sobbed, "grieving over the starved and partially eaten corpse of my son.

"That night, all of Lenland dreamt your Name of Power. I saw your eyes again, and once again I was reminded how much you looked like my own son. It was then I swore I would do everything in my power to protect you. There was nothing else

I could think to do. So, I enlisted and requested to become a member of the Royal Guard – your brother wrote a letter of recommendation to Colonel Farthun, and I was accepted." He lowered his head, and recalling the pain and grief, he shuddered it away.

"My Prince, I failed you."

"What?" said Selephygur, sitting erect in surprise.

"I should have been there to protect you. Something in me went mad, when that Crow attacked you. I should have been there! Not on some pointless detail, standing at attention on the courtyard field!"

"You were not at fault, LongBack. You were following orders."

"After the attack I lost my head. I felt I had lost my son again. In blind rage, I was the one who killed the Fox shapeshifter – I sliced him in the back."

LongBack raised his head, wiped his face, and checked behind their trail. He cursed, snapped the reins and applied the spur to Mariner. "We're being followed. That damned WhipTail must have alerted his superiors." Selephygur turned around and tried to see. Out of force of habit he tried to focus the Lens on the three far off specks, but shook his head with chagrin when he realized that was not possible anymore.

LongBack guided Mariner to dive, and circled around the nearest cumulus. Staying relatively on course for Vulcanis, he then flew from cloud to cloud, trying to use them as cover. They flew past the first few outlying isles and atolls, then dove lower to use the cones of the smaller volcanoes as cover.

Selephygur looked back down their trail again. This time he more easily spotted their pursuers against the first gleams of dawn. "They're slowly gaining on us. They know where we're going, we might as well just make a beeline for Majoris as fast as possible."

LongBack called back, "I wonder who it is, and how they knew where we were headed."

"It doesn't matter. The dice are rolled. Just get us to Vulcanis as fast as you can!"

They swooped even lower to gain speed, and LongBack repeatedly slapped the reins on Mariners' neck and goaded her with his voice. The massive cone of Vulcanis Majoris crept over the horizon, and LongBack renewed his urgency.

When they flew over the dark sands of Majoris, Selephygur

advised, "Do you know where the central throne room inside the dome is? Fly around the cone. There should be a large gap in the cone wall near the ground that opens up into the throne room." They circumnavigated two thirds of the way around the cone, until Selephygur pointed, "That's it! Set down near there!"

LongBack landed Mariner close to where the wall of the cone jutted out of a field of loose rock. He immediately dismounted with the reins still in one hand. Rummaging through a small pouch behind the hollow in the saddle leg rest, he produced a dried fish. He tied off the reins on one of the larger rocks, and tossed the fish to Mariner who speared it with his bill, and set to it with relish. Selephygur clambered down with little difficulty, and went ahead, lumbering thru the slabs and slag. Pulling a sword and its scabbard from the saddle, LongBack turned to see Selephygur already scrambling away. The Prince stepped surefootedly, but kept one hand out occasionally grasping a nearby stone to ensure he kept his balance and perspective. By the time he reached the opening, LongBack easily caught up with him. Together, they carefully and quietly crawled up to the edge of the broken wall to peer inside.

Great cracks and breaches peppered the entire dome, even to the top of the cupola. Piles of rubble and debris were scattered under each fissure and hollow. Stray winds from the ocean made the dome reverberate with whistles and moans. A foetid stench wafted out of the structure, and wrinkled their snouts. It rose from the rectangular depression scored through the center of the dome. An eerie blue glow reflected near the center of its long side walls. Of the four hallways that had opened into the dome, the two halls beyond the rectangular pool had collapsed, leaving only the two doorways behind the toppled throne.

A dark figure shrouded in a torn cloak sat facing away from Selephygur and LongBack, shivering next to the throne dais. It twitched sporadically, and mumbled in front of a circle of gathered stones, inside which were the ashes of a campfire long since dead. LongBack and Selephygur cautiously crept through the jagged opening in the wall. They approached within two arms' length of the creature, when Selephygur scuffed against a torn belt and its buckle.

The head of the figure slowly turned around. It looked sidelong at them, at which time the eye nictated once, then twice. The head jerked towards them, and its beak and feathers could clearly be seen. It jumped up, and the cloak fell aside. What few clothes the figure still had were rent, and most of the feathers below the neck were plucked. What few feathers remained lost their color – their steel blue tinge had begun to fade with a blanched grey. The sickly emaciated creature stood facing them with a large rock in the tip of its stubbled and curled right wing. It nictated its eyes again in disbelief at Selephygur, and lurched forward, screaming.

"You're dead! I *killed* you! You haunt me! All these days and nights you haunt me! You *see* me! Away spirit!" With a guttural yell, he charged at Selephygur. LongBack leapt and tackled the bird. He forced the rock from its grip, and pinned the beast's wings behind him. He stood up, dragging the bird up with him. The Crow sobbed uncontrollably and drooled as he stared in abject fear at Selephygur.

"Let me die! Let me die!" he weakly pulled at LongBack, trying to run towards the rectangular pool.

LongBack said firmly, "Now, my Prince. Now!"

Selephygur drew a dagger from his forearm guard, and clutched it firmly in his fist. He stepped towards his prey with murder in his heart. But after a few steps, he hesitated, then stopped, his mouth agape. He was horrified at the sight of this pitiful creature driven utterly mad. Selephygur recalled how each time he saw Hakayaa, the Crow seemed to sink lower and lower into a pit of fear and despair. But he simply was not prepared to see his nemesis so consumed by insanity.

"Kill me! Revenge yourself! Let us both be at peace!" Hakayaa wept and gibbered as he writhed in LongBack's hold. His eyes pleaded with Selephygur for an end to it all.

Selephygur shambled in shock towards the Crow, still not fully comprehending the wreckage in front of him that once was Hakayaa. He stopped a pace from the Crow, and shakily raised the dagger to strike. It suddenly occurred to him that it might be a kindness to end Hakayaa's cruel nightmare.

He had never taken a life before. Just as quickly as he considered the mercy or malice of what he had so long fantasized, he was beset by the repugnance of the act. Other thoughts crowded in – nothing would be the same. How could he face his parents, his brother, himself?

There was a flutter of wings. LongBack cried out to warn Selephygur. He wheeled about, dagger held threateningly in a defensive stance. Two Crow alighted through the largest holes in the dome walls. One directly in front of Selephygur, standing where they had entered the dome. He wore a black leathern sleeveless jerkin slung with two small pouches. A second similarly clad Crow had landed on the other side of the pool, and had already strung and armed his shortbow. Selephygur squinted at the first Crow, as a third one landed on the far side of the dais, and withdrew a sword.

"I know you," Selephygur grunted. "I saw you in the central courtyard. You were the ambassador – the Ravenne."

The Crow cackled and said with amusement, "Oh, this is hilarious indeed!" He laughed heartily, and stepped down from the obsidian rubble. "I expected Pindlebryth to come to the rescue, but here instead is the Pup Prince ready to do in his adversary!" He took a step further, and cocked his head. "No..." He stood fully upright again. "Oh, no! He's still debating whether or not he's got the stones to do it!"

"Selephygur... *lives*?" stuttered Hakayaa.

"Stand aside, pup. Hakayaa and I have unfinished business. And tell your lackey no surprises, if you please. Otherwise my friend may lose his grip of the arrow aimed straight at your heart." He stepped to the opposite side to better see Hakayaa. "Hakayaa, my friend. How poorly you look."

"Keeyakawa!" mewled Hakayaa.

"You had us puzzled for quite a while. You were not at the appointed place, you naughty cockerel. We had many of my brethren searching high and low along the borders and coasts of Lenland.

"My sister! Hayake! Where is she?!" Hakayaa sniveled as he struggled against LongBack's clench.

"But of course. You may have your precious sister back – you have but to give me the Lens.

"You have inconvenienced me, oh so much, Hakayaa. I had a hunch that Pindlebryth would search you out – for revenge or to forgive you, it mattered not. But to have the pup fly past us in the ark was indeed fortuitous." The Ravenne Keeyakawa circled around Selephygur until he was a few paces from Hakayaa. "But come, Hakayaa. All will be forgiven, and your delicate sister shall be free. You have but to give me the Lens."

"Hayake..." sobbed Hakayaa again.

Selephygur pivoted to follow the Ravenne, but he looked inwardly, trying to remember something – something he saw in the courtyard.

"I hope it was not in your clothes," continued Keeyakawa in a tone reminiscent of a slithering viper, looking at the shreds of cloth scattered across the entire dome. "That would truly be the proverbial needle in a haystack. And I sincerely hope you didn't throw it away." He stretched his neck to see better into the pool, and the thing it contained. "Oh, certainly not there, I trust. Otherwise, we might need to send someone in to fish it out," he said leering at Selephygur.

"Fire," capitulated Hakayaa, as he slumped in surrender and exhaustion. LongBack released him, and he collapsed to crouch on all fours.

Keeyakawa glanced at all three of his captives, then signaled to the third Crow. Keeping his sword pointed at LongBack, he approached the campfire and stooped to stir the ashes with his foot. He soon stopped, and extricated the Lens buried underneath a broken charcoaled log. He blew off the crumbling gray and black dust, and tossed it to his superior. Keeyakawa snatched it effortlessly, inspected it, and quickly sealed it in one of the pouches slung over his shoulder.

He was about to speak again, when a spark of recollection and discovery washed over Selephygur's face. "I saw you," he said half-questioningly. But after a moment's thought, he was sure. "As you left the palace, I saw you. And I saw your book. It was only a fleeting glimpse as the pages blew past, but it was enough for me to see. It may have been written in that scratch you call a language, but it had several drawings, and even a map or two. One of the drawings was the Lens, next to a map of Vulpinden."

Keeyakawa closed his beak, and focused on Selephygur. His eyes momentarily revealed grave apprehension. But Selephygur continued.

"You knew the Fox had the Lens, and that Selephylin lost it to me two years ago. The book had drawings of four other objects, and crude maps of the countries next to them. One of them was Lenland... You think we have another of the Artifacts! In fact, you know which country has each one." He took a breath as the realization rushed in on him. "You mean to steal *all* the Artifacts!"

"No! You can't! You *mustn't*!" whimpered Hakayaa, looking astonished at Keeyakawa.

"My, my! The lad has spunk and some brains, after all! It is a pity that your discovery will cost you your life." He raised his left wing to point at his archer.

A blur and whistle shot across the room, but it was the archer who fell back with a crossbow bolt squarely through his heart. Pendenar charged from the fractured opening behind Keeyakawa, as Pindlebryth emerged from the shadow in the hallway right of the dais. Dropping his crossbow, he unsheathed his shortsword and ran to attack the sword-wielding Crow closest to his brother. The Crow wheeled around to meet Pindlebryth's blade. As Pendenar dashed towards his target, Keeyakawa cocked his right wing, and three small metal rails extended along each of his wing's largest feathers. He raised his wing to his eyes, and snapped it forwards at Selephygur, flinging the darts at his torso. He then leapt, spreading his wings to fly out a large opening near the top of the dome. Pendenar swung at his target from behind, but it was fruitless as Keeyakawa flew above his reach.

The rail-darts sped toward the Prince. With an explosion of frantic energy, both LongBack and Hakayaa jumped to Selephygur. Hakayaa sprang from his crouch, and arriving first, shoved him out of harm's way. One dart pierced his abdomen, and another his shoulder. The third rail-dart struck LongBack in his upper arm.

Pindlebryth parried and feinted against the attacks of the last Crow. He thrust and hacked as opportunity allowed, but the Crow's style of swordplay was foreign and unpredictable. He struggled and was forced back, blocking the Crow's assaults. A flurry of slices and jabs maneuvered Pindlebryth near the edge of the rectangular pool, and forced open a hole in Pindlebryth's defense. The Crow was about to thrust into that weakness, when Pendenar charged in and skewered him from the side. The Crow grimaced and grabbed at Pendenar's sword, then collapsed with the momentum of the blow over the moat's edge.

Pindlebryth tensed, immediately expecting the screams and boiling stench reminiscent of the fate met by Decardan and Selephylin. The Crow instead fell onto a swath of blue crystal salts that filled most of the trench, his body crunching the dehydrated remains of the Living Moat.

But the abomination was not wholly desiccated. A shrunken ponding of the noisome mass sensed the blood filtering along the nearby cracks and crevices of the translucent white-blue salts, and it rapidly flowed upwards to ensnare its prey. Tentacles of blue gelatinous fluid extended from the monster, and grasped the wings and legs of the Crow. Hissing azure steam and acid pain roused the Crow back to consciousness as he was being eaten alive. He screamed in terror and anguish until he was dragged bodily, thrashing into the rancid blue slime. Its volume grew and extended a few inches beyond its previous size, reclaiming salts around its enlarged border. Tantalized by fresh life, it tried to surge up the walls of its prison, but the pool's mirrored vertical surfaces offered it no traction for it to climb.

Selephygur clambered back to his feet, and looked back to see both LongBack and Hakayaa in a jumble prostrate on the floor. Both began to quiver as he stumbled towards them. Kneeling next to him, Selephygur cried out LongBack's name. Pindlebryth similarly dashed to Hakayaa's side.

Selephygur turned his friend over, to see with shock LongBack's eyes rolled up, and red froth beginning to flow and spray from his muzzle. Shivering even more violently, he crumpled into a fetal position. He was about to pull out the rail still sticking out from LongBack's arm, when Pendenar intervened.

"Don't touch it! It's poisoned!" He knelt down, and wrapped his paw with the torn belt Hakayaa had cast aside. He pulled the rail out, and a black syrup hung between it and the wound. He threw his wrapping and the rail into the pit, but more black ichor wept from the wound. Pindlebryth tore out the two rails from Hakayaa's wounds using a glove. Following Pendenar's example, he also cast his glove and the darts into the blue pool. "We've got to get that poison out quickly!"

LongBack's body wracked with one last great spasm. He coughed, and crimson sputum and foam sprayed from his mouth and nostrils. His eyes tried vainly to focus, but all he could do was peer at the ceiling and utter, "RedTress... BlackBrow! I... found you." He smiled wanly, then lay still.

Selephygur sat back on his heels, and simply whimpered, "No. Please, LongBack, no."

Pendenar placed his paw above LongBack's heart for a short period, then clasped Selephygur on the shoulder. "I'm sorry, my Prince. He's gone."

Pindlebryth looked at his brother with sympathy, and wanted to console him, but time was of the essence. "Pendenar!

Go to our petrels, and get both medic kits." Pendenar nodded, and launched himself at a sprint. He scrambled up the hillock of rubble and obsidian out the opening where he entered the dome.

Pindlebryth removed his riding vest, and rolled it up into a makeshift pillow. Placing it under Hakayaa's head, he rolled him on his side to make sure he didn't choke if he started to foam and bleed from his beak. Pendenar returned quickly with two small boxes of lacquered wood, reinforced and hasped with metal edges and corners. Handing one to Pindlebryth, he opened the other.

"What are we looking for?" asked Pendenar.

Pindlebryth opened his box, and began to rummage through it. "Anything in a glass bottle – Ah, here! Antiseptic! Perfect!" He unstoppered the small vial, and poured its contents over and around the wound in the abdomen. He then took a nearby small rock and smashed the flat bottom of the vial. Shaking loose any remnants of broken glass from the remainder of the vial, he raised it and jammed it over the wound. A beaded circle of blood formed around the oozing wound. Pindlebryth then leant down and began to suck on the mouth of the vial. Black syrup and pus swelled out of the wound. Pindlebryth continued until the black poison gave way to blood. He removed the vial and wiped off the poison with his remaining glove. Pouring half of his water canteen to wash off remaining poison, he then layered patches of gauze over the red circle. Pendenar followed suit with his kit on Hakayaa's shoulder wound.

"Selephygur, help us move Hakayaa outside," requested Pindlebryth.

"No," he replied, still looking down at LongBack's motionless form.

"Selephygur, help us – he saved your life!"

"I will not leave LongBack," he sobbed through gritted teeth.

Pindlebryth sighed in exasperation and resignation. "Then there's nothing for it. Where's the rest of the squad, Pendenar?"

"They only had terns and albatross to ride over the ocean. They couldn't keep up with Voyager and Swifter. My guess is they should arrive in about a quarter of an hour."

"We're sure there are no other Crow?"

"We both only saw the three flyers ahead of us."

"Alright." Pindlebryth stood up, and collected his sword. He walked over to the arched doorway, keeping the sword out in case Keeyakawa had doubled back. "Wait here with Selephygur. I'll be right back."

Pindlebryth entered the shadowy corridor, and went a short distance until he came to the apartment. He entered the living quarters, and walked past the broken gap in the wall to the outside, where he first entered the cone. The daylight was stronger now, and lit the rooms sufficiently to explore. The rooms were dilapidated and musty, and quite muddy where rain had poured through the cracks and holes in the walls and ceiling. He pushed on through a dressing room, and found himself in what he realized was witch queen's laboratory that Darothien once described.

He padded carefully around the tables and tools of the craft. There were stands and crucibles, tubes and bowls. Pindlebryth remarked to himself, "I suppose some tools of magick are common to all wizards." He started and angled his sword threateningly when a small stream of pebbles coursed down from the ceiling. Satisfied that he was alone, he sheathed his shortsword.

Moving as carefully as he would in Darothien's laboratory, he spied a glint of gold. He sidled over to a table where intricate devices set. One contraption was composed of sliding bars, graduated rules and weights. But it was bent from falling rubble, and looked quite unusable. But his eyes widened when he saw the ring. It was appointed with five jewels equally spaced along its upper rim. It was reminiscent of the ring described in Darothien's notebook, except that all the gems were dark and no bolts of lights flitted between them. He reasoned it had run out of whatever energy Selephylin had imbued it with, but recalling Darothien's cautions against touching it, he picked up a rock and poked at it. Even though it did not react, he was determined to remain cautious. He returned to the apartment room adjacent to the laboratory, and collected a dusty pillowcase. He then carefully enveloped the ring in the cloth and tied it off in a knot.

When Pindlebryth returned to the central dome, Pendenar was hearing the squad's report. They had seen a single Crow leagues away, flying southerly. Then, having made one final assessment of the situation, Pendenar occupied himself with instructing the squad detail.

"Take this Crow to the shore, and wash out his wounds with sea water. Then do the same with LongBack's body. Be sure to use your riding gloves, then throw them away to prevent poisoning. Dress and bandage the Crow's wound. Place LongBack on one of the albatross to return home to Lenland. We'll join you shortly."

"Have a care! Be respectful with him!" ordered Selephygur in a quivering voice. "I want him to have a hero's burial." Pendenar nodded at the squad in agreement.

"The Crow is not to be harmed." added Pindlebryth as he picked up his crossbow then joined Pendenar and Selephygur.

The squad brought in two bedrolls, and ported their charges over the rubble, filing through the opening to the outside of sand and rock.

Selephygur stood next to Pindlebryth. Watching as they left, he shuffled from one foot to another, then adjusted his eyepatch. "Pindlebryth, I now understand why he did what he did. He had to ransom back family from that Ravenne."

"I know. I heard Hakayaa and the Ravenne when I first approached," said Pindlebryth with a frown.

Selephygur struggled to find the words to explain what was inside him. "I found when push came to shove, I did not have it in my heart to kill him." He sighed one last time, as he came to a resolution. "And now that I know his reasons, he need fear no reprisal from me. However, I don't think I can wholly forgive him. Just keep him out of my way."

"Easily done," retorted Pindlebryth. "If Hakayaa were to return to Lenland, father would have his head – no matter how much you or I pleaded. He'd be forced to follow through on His edict, if only to make an example of him."

Pendenar folded his arms, and walked to within a couple of paces of the rectangular pool. "M'Lord, look at this."

Pindlebryth joined him, followed by Selephygur. The three discarded rails lay close to the Living Moat, but the creature kept its distance from them as it ebbed and flowed.

"It's as if the creature knows it's poison. Perhaps it can be killed?"

"Look at the crystals. The monster is far smaller than before, but grew when it ate. It must have starved since we last came here," Pindlebryth added. He rubbed his chin contemplating the undulating mass. "It's too dangerous to fiddle with, and we don't have time or the resources to figure out how to kill it. I'd rather just let time do its work."

"If the poison is strong enough to affect this slimy thing, why did the Crow not die? He took two darts, and both were direct hits, not just flesh wounds," Selephygur said angrily.

Pindlebryth looked at the Living Moat, his brow furrowed in thought. "The Ravenne, what was his name – Keeyakawa? He expected that it would be I that would lead him to Hakayaa. He then tried to kill you, brother. Perhaps the poison is most lethal to Lemmings. It may have killed Hakayaa eventually if we didn't remove it. He may still succumb to it, given his haggard condition. Again, only time will tell."

He faced Selephygur. "Go, accompany LongBack's body to Lenland. Pendenar and I will consider what to do with Hakayaa."

"One last thing, brother," requested Selephygur. "How did you find me? How did you know where to look?"

Pindlebryth's eyes blinked in embarrassment. "Lords Below, I totally forgot! Darothien must be going insane with worry!" He collected his vest where Hakayaa had lain, and opened up a side pocket. He produced the emerald and silver device she gave him. He turned the flat side to his mouth, saying, "Darothien, can you hear me? Darothien?" He shifted the device to his ear, then winced as the gem emitted a shrill noise.

"Alright, alright. Darothien, listen carefully. Selephygur, Pendenar and I are fine. LongBack is dead. Hakayaa was poisoned and may still succumb to it. Yes... *Yes.* Selephygur will return by the end of the day. Pendenar and I will follow afterwards. We will talk later... *Later!*" He clasped both of his paws over the device.

Pendenar looked sidelong at Selephygur, with a thin-lipped wide-eyed expression that he often used to suppress a smile. Pindlebryth ignored him, and answered his brother. "Darothien created a device from Father's discarded crown, which allows people to talk over any distance. When we formed the squad to follow you, Darothien took your old bloody bandages from Sacalitre from the previous day, and used them back in her laboratory to divine where you were. She guided us westward, then over MidSea. When we arrived at the Archipelago, it was obvious to us where you were headed.

"Now it's your turn. Tit for tat, brother. How did *you* know where to find Hakayaa?"

Selephygur looked around the crumbling remains of the obsidian hall. "What everyone thought were nightmares were visions. Sacalitre and Darothien found the Lens left a trace of itself in my wound. One last gift from the Lens, I suppose.

"I found that if I concentrated, I could see what the Lens saw. At first, I did not understand what it was that I saw. But after I recalled the descriptions of this place over the past year from you, Darothien, Pendenar and LongBack, I finally realized that Hakayaa was hiding here in Selephylin's dome."

"Alright, off you go. We'll be along presently." He lifted the knotted pillowcase to Selephygur. "Take this to Darothien. She will want to see this as soon as possible. It may help us understand more about the Artifacts." He pulled it back slightly as Selephygur reached to take it. "Do not open it. Darothien herself was afraid to touch it two years ago. It seems to be quiescent now, but there's no need to tempt fate. Just deliver it to her, and assure her that no one else has touched it either. Promise me you will only allow Darothien to open this."

"Very well, brother. I promise."

Pindlebryth allowed Selephygur to take the makeshift satchel, saying, "By the way, Darothien also has a gift waiting for you."

Selephygur turned to follow the squad outside, with Pindlebryth at his side. At the base of the pile of loose rock, he paused and picked up a fist-sized piece of jet black obsidian. He examined it, and placed the volcanic glass in his vest pouch and left. Pindlebryth assisted him over the rubble, until a guard helped him outside through the wall.

As Selephygur was about to cross the breach, Pindlebryth said, "I'm glad you are safe. I'll see you again soon at home." The younger prince and the guard headed carefully down the other side, and towards the waiting flying steeds.

"You don't think he would...?" worried Pendenar.

"No. Selephygur's word is good. He won't harm Hakayaa. And he'll not open the bag. But he's obviously got a use for that rock.

"Now here's what we need to do. I will leave immediately with Voyager. Select a guard and another petrel to escort me to PanGaea's CityState – they can return to Lenland as soon as I'm situated. In the meantime, send the rest of the squad back to Lenland as soon as possible. Ensure your most trusted guard of the squad is paired with Selephygur on Mariner. You will stay here on Vulcanis with Hakayaa, until near sundown."

Pindlebryth handed him the silvered emerald. A soft but tinny voice was still periodically calling out from the device. Pendenar looked confused at the device, then decided to also simply close his paw over the gem.

"Talk with Darothien and have her work with Sacalitre, to find anything to help Hakayaa overcome the poison. Then secure him for the ride on a tern, and bring him and this... talking gem... to me at my apartments at PanGaea. If Hakayaa survives the flight, we have work to do."

V - The Pieces Fall

Pindlebryth sat at his desk, rolling a fountain pen between two flat paws. His study in PanGaea had been recently cleaned and all the furniture freshly polished. Everything on his desk was still cared for and in near-pristine condition, except for the ink stain that had spilled and dried on the blotter a few years before.

He stared at the large deep indigo patch in meditation. How long ago it seemed, and how such a small thing heralded so many adventures – and who knows what misadventures to come?

Pindlebryth had heard how one's life flashes before their eyes in times of danger or death, but in the relative safety of his study it seemed the course of the past two years thundered in his head every time he focused on the mottled blotch. The sleepwalking of his people, the deaths by drowning of BlackEars, TwitchNose and so many others, the kidnapping of Selephygur, his rescue at the cost of Decardan's life, the destruction by his hand of Selephylin by turning her magick against her, the Lens of Truth, the wonderment of the manifold discoveries it gave Selephygur, though only at the cost of his suffering torment, the betrayal by Hakayaa, the emotional chaos it threw Pindlebryth into, the theater of distrust the nations fell into at Hatheron's revelations and edict, the danger of twice facing members of the Ravenne and nearly being done in by them, the death of LongBack, the redemption of Hakayaa for Selephygur's sake, all swirled and swarmed about his mind.

And now Hakayaa's life was in the balance. Even if he survived the trip from Vulcanis, his fate still rested ultimately in these hands rolling a stylus.

Or, to be more precise, in the hands of BroadShanks.

Pindlebryth had not made close ties with her and HighStance, the staff that had taken the positions formerly held by BlackEars and TwitchNose. They had been recommended by the Lenland embassy in PanGaea, and had been exemplary in the performance of their duties. But he found himself reluctant to become too familiar with them. In fact, Pindlebryth had previously made only two specific requests of BroadShanks – never to make TwitchNose's quickbread, and never to replace the blotter on his desk. He reflected on the contradiction of those two orders. He preferred not to suffer the pleasant memories that the former brought, but he held onto the painful memories the latter represented.

This day, however, after hours absorbed in feverish planning during his solo flight, he found the number of people he could count on for help over the next few days in PanGaea to be embarrassingly few. After so many months of avoidance, he had found himself in the unnerving position to issue a flurry of instructions to his two staff on his return.

"HighStance, go to an apothecary you trust, and get medicines and antidotes for poisoning."

HighStance, standing rail thin and a full head above Pindlebryth, looked almost comical standing at attention, only to slouch a bit as he blanched and blinked in surprise. "M'Lord! Are you all right?"

"Yes, yes," Pindlebryth said impatiently, dismissing his concern with a wave. "Pendenar will be bringing the patient soon."

"Who is this patient, if I may ask? Why doesn't Pendenar take him to hospital?"

"This is an issue of some delicacy."

"Very well." HighStance seemed a trifle unsettled at suggesting, "But you will find that BroadShanks is more adept where medicine is concerned."

"Oh, I see. Well, fetch *her* then. I will explain the situation to her. Meanwhile, make up the spare rooms – one as a sickroom, and the trophy room for Pendenar. Then keep an eye out for them. Pendenar will be landing on the roof late this evening with our guest. Help him bring the patient to the sickroom as soon as they arrive. Please see to it now." HighStance bowed and left to make his preparations.

Presently, BroadShanks knocked on the doorjamb as she entered. Her pudgy frame bunched and stretched her uniform taut as she curtsied. "M'Lord? HighStance said you wanted to see me about a patient we will have under our care?"

"Yes. Pendenar will be bringing him this evening. I need you to tend to his wounds. He has been poisoned."

"Oh my dear! What with?"

"We know not, other than it was some black liquid on a

weapon. We were able to remove most of the poison from his wounds and wash them, but who knows what the toxin has done to him already. The poison was instant death for one Lemming in our group."

"Heavens!" she interjected, placing her paw on her cheek.

"...but it apparently does not affect Crow as quickly."

"A Crow? Who is our patient?" She seemed almost afraid to ask. "Do we know him?"

Pindlebryth batted the question aside. "In a moment. Is there an apothecary you can trust?"

BroadShanks blinked rapidly as she returned to the question at hand. "We already have some of what I'll need. I can get a few of the other things I'll need from the chemist, and I can bring a healer who has the most wonderful array of herbs and mixtures."

"*No!* Listen carefully. You must not bring anyone, must not tell anyone – *Anyone!* – what business you're about. You must not even hint that we have a visitor. Just get what you need and hurry back.

"Your patient is Hakayaa."

"Oh no! The poor dear!" BroadShanks interrupted, raising both her paws to her mouth.

"HighStance is preparing a sickroom for him. Now hurry along. Evening will soon be upon us, and he will need your full attention."

"Gracious!" she blurted as she kneaded her paws together with worry. "We haven't seen him for over a year. He's always been a bit of a rapscallion, but he's never gotten into serious trouble. Whatever happened to him?"

"Are you not listening to me?" Pindlebryth bristled, his fur on his head and hackles beginning to rise. "I have told you all you need to know for now, and time is against you. Make the utmost haste to get what you need, and tell no one why. *No one!*"

He stamped his foot, and BroadShanks scurried away quickly with an expression of both reproach and alarm, making small exclamations to herself as she hustled down the hallway and down the stairs.

Pindlebryth collapsed behind his desk, rubbing his brow, as he heard his apartments bustling with noise. HighStance was busily preparing the sickroom for Hakayaa and rearranging the trophy room across the hallway for Pendenar, while

BroadShanks scampered about the floor below collecting a coat and basket, and dashing out the front door.

He was engrossed with rolling his pen back and forth again, planning what to do with Hakayaa when he heard the beat of wings approaching in the dim twilight. A rasping of claws on the roof sounded through the ceiling above the stairwell. HighStance bounded up the stairs to the third floor, and unfolded the ceiling's ladder to the roof. Pindlebryth quickly forgot his meditation on the stylus and blotter, and hurried out of his study to look up the stairs.

HighStance collected a cot from storage, climbed up the ladder to open the hatchway to the roof, then stepped out of view to assist Pendenar. Pindlebryth climbed the stairs, and could soon hear the two of them exchanging instructions. They soon reappeared in the hatchway with an unconscious Hakayaa limply draped between them. HighStance guided Hakayaa's feet down the ladder, while Pendenar precariously hefted Hakayaa down by the shoulders. Hakayaa was covered with a blanket with an extra layer wrapped around Pendenar's paws to ward against accidentally touching the poisoned shoulder wound.

Hakayaa's damp blanket offered little protection against the cold air, and the Crow shivered terribly. Pendenar's jerkin and clothes were dry by comparison, yet had telltale water stains, and his fur was matted and windblown. Pindlebryth assisted by laying down the cot, and the others placed Hakayaa on it.

Pindlebryth allowed himself a great sigh of relief at seeing Hakayaa still alive. Pendenar descended the staircase first to bear the brunt of the weight, and held his end of the cot level with his head, while HighStance bent over with his end. Keeping Hakayaa as level as possible down the stairs and the hallway, Pindlebryth lent a hand turning the corner into the sickroom. As they transferred Hakayaa's clammy body onto the bed, HighStance removed the dank blanket. He covered him with fresh sheets and a warm blanket, but Hakayaa continued to shiver.

"Where is that blasted BroadShanks?" complained Pindlebryth. Pendenar moved one corner of the bedsheets back, and slowly removed the field bandage from one of Hakayaa's wounds. Around the wound, the flesh was darkened almost to lifeless gray, and some skin sloughed off with the bandage. A guttural moan arose from Hakayaa in his unconsciousness. There was a small circle of moist black blood dotted around the wound, where the teeth of the broken glass vial had pierced the skin. Beyond the circlet, his flesh had more color.

The front door opened and slammed shut, and thunderous footfalls could be heard bounding up the stairs. BroadShanks leaned in the doorway – in one paw she held her basket, in the other she clasped the blouse over her chest as she panted heavily. Between gasps, she wheezed orders to HighStance. "Get towels from the washroom and fill a basin with water." She lurched over to the bed and looked at the wound, and the remaining bandage on the second wound. "And bring the mortar and pestle from the kitchen." HighStance disappeared down the stairs.

"Oh dear, we've got to keep him warm! This shivering helps to spread the poison." BroadShanks pulled a heavy comforter from a cedar chest below the window. "What's this ring?" she demanded, pointing at the wound.

"We sucked out the poison with broken bottles. We had to cut into the skin to get a good seal," replied Pendenar.

"Good. The cuts around the wound allowed more of the poison to escape."

"Do not touch the black liquid. Burn the bandages, and anything that comes in contact with it," said Pindlebryth.

HighStance arrived with the towels and basin. He soon returned with a jug of fresh water and the mortar and pestle, as BroadShanks started to pull various vials filled with liquids and powders, and bunches of leaves and blossoms tied together with twine from the basket, setting them on the bed and floor. She bumped into both Pendenar and Pindlebryth as she grabbed the mortar, and started to mix the various items about her. "HighStance, wash the wounds. Every one else out! *Out!* Everyone out! You busybodies let me do my work!"

HighStance took off his outer jacket, and rolled up his sleeves. Wrapping his hands in towels, so as not to touch the blood and remaining traces of the black ooze, he set to work assisting BroadShanks, as the other two filed out.

"Pendenar, what happened on your way here? Were you followed?" asked Pindlebryth just outside the room, as he kept his gaze fixed on BroadShanks.

"No, M'Lord. But the trip was a bit dicey. I steered my tern to avoid a building storm out at sea, but we were besieged by a torrent of sudden downdrafts. I had a terrible time controlling my tern with Hakayaa strapped behind me, what with the unpredictable winds. He's no Mariner, to be sure!

"In one instance, we were caught in a strong squall spun off from the main storm. A handful of times, Hakayaa stirred from his delirium, and yelled things in Crow-speak that I couldn't guess at. That made the already skittish tern even more frightened and difficult to control."

Pindlebryth turned his attention directly to Pendenar. "Hand me the Talking Gem." Pendenar fumbled for it, and pulled it out a pouch from a side pocket. Pindlebryth took the pouch, keeping the gem inside of it. "Did you use this? Did you contact anyone?" he demanded.

"No, M'Lord. I already had my hands full en route. No time to chat with Darothien or Sacalitre."

Pindlebryth's eyes closely examined Pendenar. "Then you did speak with Sacalitre."

"Only before we left Vulcanis. I told him and Darothien to expect Prince Selephygur and his party, and that you and I would follow at some later time. The physician gave me pointers on preparing the poisoned wounds for travel. But I spoke with no one during the flight."

Pindlebryth relaxed a little. "Alright then." He turned to again peer through the doorway at Hakayaa. HighStance was washing the wounds, and BroadShanks was stirring a yellow-green poultice in the mortar. A few moments later, she turned around and threw a packet at Pendenar. "Make yourself useful, and brew a tea with this." Pindlebryth dismissed him with a nod. "And mind you! Don't you drink *any* of it! It's only for Hakayaa here."

BroadShanks reached into her basket and opened a jar of turbid liquid with something squirming on the bottom. Pindlebryth could not help but to grimace as she pulled leeches out of the jar with small wooden tongs, and placed them around the wound. Each of them quickly latched onto the flesh and began to feed. Once both of the gray skinless sores were encircled with the glistening creatures, she worked the poultice into the open wounds, which though cleaned were beginning to weep afresh. Hakayaa's eyes snapped open as he screamed in pain. He tried to flail about and out of bed, but HighStance threw himself over Hakayaa's legs and uninjured shoulder and held him fast. He thrashed his head back and forth, and spied

Pindlebryth. He cried out in Crow at Pindlebryth.

Astonished, Pindlebryth took a step back further into the hallway. He gulped, and said softly to himself, "I've been thinking the same thing, my friend." He pivoted on one foot and dreamily strode down the hallway back into his study. He sat behind his desk again, trying to shut out the sounds of groaning and whimpering from across the hall. Pindlebryth lost track of how many minutes passed, until Pendenar politely knocked on the study's doorjamb.

"BroadShanks and HighStance seem to be handling our patient well. After I fetch Hakayaa's tea, they won't require anything more of me. Is there anything you need, M'Lord?"

Pindlebryth looked up at Pendenar with tired eyes. "Only a good night's sleep. But I don't think that will come easily for me." He sighed and rubbed his eyes. "You look as if you could use sleep as well."

Leaning forward, Pindlebryth finished, "But first take your mount to the stables down the length of this street, near the fire station. It's called the "Double Eagle", and they take excellent care of their charges. I have already secured Voyager there for the next few nights. As I instructed HighStance and BroadShanks, tell no one of our visitor. At least, not yet. Tell those two I'll have some announcements tomorrow morning."

Pindlebryth reclined back in his desk chair, as Pendenar bowed and left. He stared aimlessly at the ceiling, but still heard Hakayaa's request echoing in his head. Pindlebryth didn't know which disturbed him more – that Hakayaa would think of such of a thing, or that he had entertained the same idea as his raving lunatic friend.

He could not tell how long he sat in his study. What seemed like hours plodded by, punctuated by moans and cries from the sickroom. In one instance, Pindlebryth had tired of merely sitting and thinking about what he needed to do tomorrow, and he opened the sickroom door to satisfy his curiosity and concern. Hakayaa was no longer shivering, but was panting heavily. He was now covered by two heavy quilts, save for where the wounds were cleanly bandaged, and up to his neck where his feathers were still intact. HighStance stood at the foot of the bed, and BroadShanks sat huddled next to Hakayaa's chest.

"How is he faring? Is he overheated?" Pindlebryth ventured. BroadShanks turned around with a flash of anger, but she promptly quelled her emotion.

"The leeches have done their work, and my medicines are flushing out the remaining poison.   Every hour I have HighStance towel his legs dry. Filthy stuff!" Hakayaa began to moan softly with each rapid breath. Pindlebryth noticed a small pile of cloths stained yellow at the corner of the bed, and a mound of dead, shriveled leeches. "His flesh seems to have gotten some of its color back. What in the world happened to all his feathers?"

Pindlebryth did not answer, but approached close to Hakayaa, and awkwardly whispered something in Crow. BroadShanks and HighStance exchanged glances and shrugged their shoulders as Pindlebryth repeated his question. Hakayaa's eyes fluttered, and focused cross-eyed on Pindlebryth.

"Pindlebryth? Is that you?" Hakayaa coughed trying to speak in a mishmash of Crow and common tongue.

"Yes, I'm here, old friend," Pindlebryth replied in common.

"Selephygur!" he yelped as he tried to sit up, but quickly collapsed back onto his pillow.

"Oh, no you don't!" quibbled BroadShanks, as she leapt up and began to tuck the sheets and covers firmly under the mattress to hold her patient down.

"Selephygur – is he... alive?"

"Yes, thanks to you. He's flying back to Lenland. And with a large entourage to ensure his safety."

"Go-oo-ood," Hakayaa exhaled with a rattling wheeze.

"Hakayaa, I have to ask you again." Switching to the best Crow speech he could manage, he asked, "Did you mean what you said about your death?"

"Yes!" he exclaimed in common tongue. "Only way... all... be safe..." His eyes rolled up and went wall-eyed, whereupon he passed out, panting even more heavily.

"What was that all about? Are we in danger?" BroadShanks inquired, with more than a little nervousness.

Pindlebryth continued to ignore her barrage of questions. He placed his paw gently on Hakayaa's faded gray forehead, silently prayed to the Quickening Spirit, then turned and crossed the hallway to his study, leaving an annoyed BroadShanks to wonder what just happened.

He paused just outside the doorway, to see Pendenar climb the stairs, his face and arms freshly washed, with a small pot of tea. He wordlessly placed the pot on the end table next to BroadShanks, and then made for his own room. Pindlebryth surmised he must have taken a cold bath from the sink in the mudroom downstairs. He was suddenly aware he had not slept for just over a full day, and the weight on his eyelids quickly became ever so enticing and nigh overpowering. Over his shoulder he requested of HighStance, "When BroadShanks can spare you, draw me up a bath before bed."

Back in his study, he paced slowly back and forth in an attempt to remain awake. He tried to focus on all the factors that pulled and pushed him in so many directions, but there were too many to find a solution, let alone an elegant one without risk and loose ends. He struggled to balance whatever means and resources were available to him, against all the problems that he faced in simultaneous contention: the safety of himself and his family, and all of Lenland for that matter; the manifold threats posed by an unknown member of the Kyaa court willing to use the Ravenne to collect the Lens and possibly all the Artifacts of Old; and last but not least the safety of Hakayaa and his family.

The ancillary questions that were swept along with these only added to the cacophony in Pindlebryth's head. What purpose did all the Artifacts serve when held together, and why did Hakayaa fear it so much? Who was it that coveted them, and why were they willing to set nation against nation to achieve that goal? What part did the witch Selephylin have in this scheme? What was the Artifact the Ravenne believed to be hidden in Lenland? The mountain of unanswered questions exhausted Pindlebryth's already tired mind. He was certainly thankful when HighStance finally informed him his bath was ready.

When he woke up the next morning, he could only dimly remember the bath, the bed and the blissful comfort of his pillow. His nose twitched to the wonderful smell of cooking, frying, baking and brewing. The morning sun had already climbed half way up the sky – he must have slept soundly for an inordinate amount of time. His body and spirit obviously needed it, for he felt quite refreshed. And more importantly, he found he woke up with what seemed like an answer for his immediate problems. "Is this the best solution?" he asked himself. "Maybe, maybe not," was the only reply his mind echoed. But it was the only solution he had with so little time left.

Still in his nightgown, he crossed the hallway to see Hakayaa. Pendenar, still wearing his riding jerkin, sat at the foot of Hakayaa's bed. He stood to greet his prince.

"I thought you were going to sleep," Pindlebryth voiced with concern.

"I did sleep for a while, but the others needed a rest from their all-night vigil."

Hakayaa was sound asleep and breathing much more easily since his arrival. BroadShanks' ministrations obviously did their work quite well overnight. He had regained much of his color, and his bandages were fresh, obviously replaced during the last hour. The room however was filled with an odd rank smell. A moment's observation showed Pindlebryth it came from the towels and old bandages, charred to ash in the sickroom's fireplace. Pindlebryth coughed against the odor, and resisted the urge to sneeze. He instead put his hand over his snout, and asked Pendenar to remove the offensive cinders at the earliest opportunity. Nodding to himself that everything else was right for now, Pindlebryth let Hakayaa sleep. He would need, however, to try to talk to him before he set to his tasks this day.

Returning to his room, he dressed and went downstairs to the kitchen. Passing through the dining room, he saw his usual place set with plates, glasses and silver. In the previous year, he usually would simply take his seat and be served his meal. But something moved him to not set himself apart this day.

He found BroadShanks mincing about the kitchen, bouncing like pectin as she juggled several items on the counters, stovetop and oven. HighStance was dressed with his jacket hung on one post on the back of his chair and a work-apron on the other. He was savoring his breakfast on a small table filled with breads, jams and butter, pancakes and syrup, juice and tea, before setting about his daily tasks.

Pindlebryth closed his eyes, and inhaled deeply the ambrosia wafting through the room. His stomach growled loudly enough to make both his staff stop and take notice. They gawked momentarily with a small amount of surprise, and watched agape as Pindlebryth rifled through a cupboard. He tried to remember as best as he could where the plates and cups were kept, but he found rows of glassware instead. Only then did he realize that he had not familiarized himself with the workings of BroadShanks' kitchen since he returned after Lenland's reconstruction.

He looked about, feeling a mite foolish, but BroadShanks guessed what he was looking for and handed him a plate and cup from a cabinet closer to the staff table. He took them and sat in the empty third chair across from HighStance, who still watched him with bemused bewilderment over a bent newspaper.

"Please," he said as he gestured to BroadShanks to join them. She regarded him with her hands on her hips, then raised them in surrender and shook her head. She took a pot off one of the stovetop plates, and sat down at the place awaiting her at the table. HighStance folded his paper away, and joined in as the three of them began to fill their plates.

"I wanted to thank you both for all you've done. It is certain that Hakayaa would not have survived otherwise. When we're finished with breakfast here, please join me and Pendenar upstairs."

BroadShanks set aside her annoyances, slights, and frustrations from the night before, and heartfeltly replied, "You're quite welcome, M'Lord." She took a long draft of some peach nectar, then resumed. "I must say though, that last night fairly reeked of cloak and dagger. What in the world had happened to Hakayaa – and you?"

"And in what misadventure have you involved us?" interjected HighStance.

"Shush, you ridiculous rodent!" scolded BroadShanks.

"No, no. HighStance has a perfect right to ask that. Despite the fact it all occurred within just under one week, the answer to both those questions is a long story." He sighed wistfully. "Long indeed. But you nonetheless deserve to know what has transpired in Lenland."

Amidst a sumptuous feast of shortcakes, jams and bread, juices and tea, Pindlebryth related all that had happened since Hakayaa arrived in Lenland such a short time ago. BroadShanks periodically arose from the table, and brought more tidbits to the table.

Between platefuls Pindlebryth told HighStance and BroadShanks of the curious powers of Selephygur's eye, the arrival of Hakayaa, his revelation of the Lens of Truth, the meeting with the false Crow ambassador, the attack in the courtyard and the death of Tanderra, Hakayaa's assault on

Selephygur, the exile of all Fox and Crow from Lenland, the embassy fire, and finally the trap set by the Ravenne on Vulcanis, the rescue of Selephygur, the death of LongBack, and the redemption of Hakayaa.

The story was peppered throughout with BroadShanks' exclamations of "Oh, Dear!", "Gracious!", and the like. More than once she interrupted with comments and tangents that had only the most tenuous connections with Pindlebryth's account, usually to be countered by HighStance's reproach to "Mind your place, doe! Be quiet and let M'Lord finish!" Pindlebryth was unaware how hungry he had been until he realized BroadShanks had brought him a third helping of oatmeal with hazelnuts.

After he finished his story, he folded his napkin, and concluded somberly, "Thank you, BroadShanks, for the wonderful repast." He took one last sip of tea, then stood and said, "HighStance was right. I may have brought you no end of trouble. There is much to do, and I need your assistance again." Before he crossed the doorway into the dining room, he added, "Join me and Pendenar in Hakayaa's room when you're finished cleaning up."

When the two came upstairs to Hakayaa's room, Pindlebryth had taken the seat held by Pendenar, who had since moved to one side of the doorway. The air was noticeably better, after Pendenar had removed the foetid char in the fireplace, and opened the room's windows. They were wedged ajar by a paw's width, so that a modicum of fresh air could enter without disturbing the curtains.

"He's looking worlds better, BroadShanks. Thanks again to you for bringing him back from the edge. What was in that mixture?"

"Oh a little of this, a little of that," giggled BroadShanks. She fanned herself with one hand, reveling in the praise. "Some castor and ginger, but mostly yellow-bird's-nest to counteract the poison, and of course I used leeches to draw much of it out. And the tea had ground beets, parsley and milk thistle to help flush out the rest.

"Oh my, what a mess *that* was! It would have been so much easier if birds could sweat!"

"I daresay, Sacalitre could not have done as well in one day," Pindlebryth remarked.

"That quack!?" blurted out BroadShanks. "He's gotten lazy

now that he's accustomed to treating only Lemmings with Names, who mostly heal themselves anyway!"

Pendenar blinked with surprise, then lowered his chin struggling to hide a smirk. HighStance patted her on the shoulder. "Now dear, don't work yourself into a tizzy. He wouldn't be the Royal Physician if the Quickening Spirit had not ordained it. Besides, I think M'Lord has something more important to discuss."

"Yes, quite correct," Pindlebryth said flatly.

Pindlebryth turned to Hakayaa, who began to murmur. His eyelids slowly opened, and his brow lowered against the meager light afforded through the curtains. He moved his head to look away from the light, and Pindlebryth.

"Shouldn't we let him rest?" suggested BroadShanks.

"He can rest later, but for now he should not be left alone, and I need to brief all of you. So it is best if everyone is here. If Hakayaa is aware of us, all the better. It is best if he hears this as well."

With his paws steepled in front of him, he said, "Hakayaa is dead."

Gesturing at their patient, he said, "Allow me to introduce to you Kaiya."

He looked at each of his dumbfounded audience, and continued, "Hakayaa, who gave his life to save my brother Selephygur, passed away during Pendenar's flight here from Vulcanis. Already weakened by the poison, he could not withstand the flight from Vulcanis, and succumbed quietly. Unfortunately, Pendenar's path crossed last night's storm, and was almost downed by a squall's sudden downdraft. Hakayaa's body was lost over MidSea." He took a deep breath, allowing the announcement to sink in on the group.

"That is all anyone outside of this room need know. You are to tell no one otherwise, unless commanded by me, King Hatheron or Queen Wenteberei. Hakayaa is *dead*. Is that understood?"

HighStance and BroadShanks stood and nervously nodded in astonishment and trepidation, while Pendenar nodded only once.

"My wishes alone should be sufficient for you, but I feel you have some right to know why I find this necessary. The Ravenne pressured Hakayaa to help them steal the Lens of Truth by threatening his family. If the Ravenne, or their masters, know Hakayaa remains alive, they or someone else might try again to use him to get at the Royal Family. Or they may try to use him to obtain the second Artifact hidden in Lenland. At the very least, his family remains in peril if Hakayaa lives. At worst, any Fox still unaware that the Crow now have their precious Lens would torture Hakayaa."

Pindlebryth looked at his Crow friend, to see his glance returned. He blinked once, and acceded with a small nod. He turned again and regarded his fellow Lemmings. "I and Pendenar need to leave for Lenland within two days. I expect to return to PanGaea in time for the start of the next semester. However, before I leave I will need to talk to Hakayaa's advisor at University. He told me Professor DeepDigger is an expert in the lore of the Artifacts. I am sure I will need to divulge Hakayaa's 'death' to him, in order to gain his assistance in solving the mystery of Lenland's lost Artifact."

"Word will get to the authorities sooner or later. What do you plan to do about that?" asked Pendenar.

"Why, we're going to tell them. Our first audience will be our embassy here in PanGaea's CityState," replied Pindlebryth looking soberly at Pendenar.

"How do we inform the Crow embassy?" reminded Pendenar.

"Oh spot and bother! They are forbidden now to enter our embassy, aren't they? It will take too long to try to coordinate a meeting on neutral ground in two days. We'll have to leave it to our ambassadress, Quentain, to relay the information to them. Regardless, I daresay I wouldn't receive a warm welcome from the Crow.

"And of course the local authorities will eventually hear of it." Pindlebryth took a moment to calm his racing mind. He still couldn't shake the nagging itch he was missing something else. "If anyone comes here asking questions, we cannot let them find here someone who is presumed dead. Is there some other place we can move our patient?"

After a moment, HighStance spoke up. "I have a friend with a cabin in the woods far west from here, where we've taken holiday once before."

"I don't know if he can withstand another flight," retorted BroadShanks.

"No need," a croaking voice whispered. The group faced the bed to see a Lemming with severe red mange looking back at them. Pindlebryth cocked his head at the sight, recalling the Lemming that Hakayaa had shifted to days before in the woods of Lenland. It was difficult for Pindlebryth to be certain, but the Lemming before them seemed to be nothing like the shapeshifted Hakayaa he saw before. This Lemming was thinner and wan, and what little hair was present was piebald. Given that Hakayaa told him that Crow could not shapeshift to specific or different identities, Pindlebryth was only more confused by the apparent contradiction.

After a few seconds, the nearly featherless Crow reappeared in the bed.

"Can he hold that for a longer time, say at least one minute?" wondered Pendenar.

Hakayaa nodded ever so slightly. Pindlebryth searched Hakayaa's eyes, and surmised, "I think so. That may all he need do. Anyone who sees what seems to be mange will not want to examine him too closely, nor for any period of time." He looked again at BroadShanks to add, "Just make sure that whoever comes to visit is told it *is* mange, and give our patient 'Kaiya' ample warning to prepare. Shuffle any visitors out as quickly as possible, so our patient may rest quietly."

"What was his name again?" inquired HighStance.

"Kaiya." He turned with a small grin to Hakayaa. "It's a small joke between him and myself. It's apparently a pivotal character in a bad Crow opera."

"But how do we explain a sickly Lemming here, in the home of a Prince of all places?" protested BroadShanks.

Pindlebryth stood up from the chair. "I think we should leave Kaiya to his much needed rest, while we discuss details in my study." Regarding Kaiya's prone form, he asked, "Will you be all right for a few minutes? Kaiya?"

The Crow nodded ever so slightly. Leading the way, Pindlebryth took his three compatriots across the hallway. He sat behind his desk, and steepled his paws again, while he abstractly regarded the ink blot.

"To answer your question, BroadShanks, perhaps you should explain Kaiya as a friend or relative from the countryside. That should be difficult enough for anyone to verify."

HighStance interjected, "I have a second cousin that works on the farms on the west coast of PanGaea. I haven't seen him or his family for years. Will that do?"

"Excellent! The story shall then be that he has fallen on hard times, and was returning to Lenland. You housed him here while he traveled home, but expected him to be gone before I returned for the next semester. For anyone who asks me, I will seem appropriately put out and upset that I found him here when I prematurely returned, and will insist that he be gone when the semester begins.

"That much actually is true – for his own good, he should be gone as soon as possible. Is it likely, BroadShanks, that Kaiya will be free of the poison by the time I return in two weeks?"

"Difficult to say. I have not dealt with poison before, and by your orders I cannot talk with my herbalist friend for guidance." Her nose twitched as she switched between indignation and worry.

"We can only hope then, that you can help him heal quickly on your own experience. The longer he remains, the greater the chance someone can poke holes in our story, before Kaiya has a chance to start his new life."

He looked introspectively at the bookshelves, when another thought struck him. "After we finish with the embassy, decorum requires I bear the bad tidings to the BlueHood family directly. To my knowledge, they have no summer home here in PanGaea. The next best thing is to visit Hakayaa's old house. Perchance a family member is visiting there now. If not, the only alternative that is left me during the next two days is to inform the staff at Hakayaa's house. A Mr. and Mrs. ..."

"SootBeak!" groused BroadShanks, as she folded her arms. "If you want something to be spread about, she's undoubtedly the one to talk to. She never stops gossiping!" HighStance stood silently and rolled his eyes with the utmost forbearance. "If you tell her about Hakayaa, she'll find a way to notify the BlueHood family faster than any embassy. With her wagging tongue, I wouldn't be surprised if the very Court of the Kyaa hears of it by the time you return to Lenland!"

"I agree," Pindlebryth snickered. "She certainly missed her calling as a town crier," he said while shooting a knowing smile at HighStance. "At any rate, they have known me for many years, and I believe they will trust me where Hakayaa is concerned." He soon resumed a look of abstraction, as if he were thinking of two things simultaneously.

"I've taken enough of all your time, now. BroadShanks, sit with Kaiya for a while more. We've left him alone too long already for my liking. I will join you presently. HighStance, set out my best day clothes in black. Then arrange for a carriage in one hour. Pendenar, sit with me for a while. We have some matters to discuss." The two left, and Pendenar closed the door of the study behind them. He then stood in front of the desk, with his paws clasped behind him.

"Please sit, Pendenar," Pindlebryth said with some rigidity.

"I may not, M'Lord."

"If you do not, then you force me to stand. Now sit."

Pendenar wavered, then pulled a chair to him, and sat with resignation.

"Do you know what you'll tell the authorities?" Pindlebryth asked with a softer voice.

"Yes, I believe so."

"Good. Use this hour before we leave to solidify your story. But don't just rehearse the words over and over. Picture what happened. Add one or two personal observances or details. See and hear the tale of your misadventure over MidSea, until you half-believe it yourself. That way, when you describe it, it will seem all the more real to the listener. More importantly, you won't sound rehearsed if you are asked to repeat it. If you are pressed further for more details, simply say you were focused on staying airborne, or you simply don't recall."

"I understand, M'Lord." Pendenar nodded respectfully, but he looked as if Pindlebryth's advice left a stale taste in his mouth.

"I hope you do. You may have to testify to that effect. Remember, no one else is to know the truth about Hakayaa-Kaiya, unless I, the King or Queen command you."

Pindlebryth leaned in closer over the desk. "After we finish our deposition with the embassy, we must repeat our story to the SootBeaks. But before I begin with them, I'll find some way to keep Mrs. SootBeak busy. Follow my lead, and distract Mr. SootBeak. Tell him you're concerned about my security, safety, and such – and that you wish to inspect and secure the front and back doors. I will need sufficient time to search for something in Hakayaa's study. In the off chance – actually, with Mrs. SootBeak, it is a near certainty – that they ask about details about the trip from Vulcanis, you'll have to do the talking. So I ask one last time – are you up to this?"

Pendenar stood to leave, saying, "Yes. Is that all M'Lord?"

"No, there is one more thing. Don't clean your uniform and

riding gear. Left as they are now, it will lend credence to your story, as if you came directly from travel, and haven't had a chance to prepare."

Pendenar saw the wisdom in this, nodded his acknowledgment, and after a moment's thought tousled the fur on his head. He opened the door and headed to his own room, while Pindlebryth rose and crossed back across the hallway to the sickroom.

Standing next to the bed, opposite BroadShanks, he saw Kaiya had fallen back to sleep. Pindlebryth regarded him obliquely, as he mulled over the many tasks and challenges set before him over the next few days. After a few minutes, HighStance tiptoed into the room. One arm cradled a small stash of fresh towels, linen, gauze and bandages, the other held the familiar basket filled with fresh jars of powders and unguents, and a bottle of freshly brewed tea. Setting them on the end table, BroadShanks quietly set about mixing a fresh poultice. HighStance left, then almost immediately returned with a basin and fresh water jug. He whispered across the bed, "Your clothes are ready in your room, M'Lord."

BroadShanks pulled her chair next to the bed, and delicately but deliberately removed the bandages, while HighStance poured water into the basin behind her. Tossing the blood-stained and pus-encrusted bandages on the floor, she set about washing her patient. First she washed the day old leech marks, which were healing nicely. After dabbing the wounds clean, she applied some more of the ointments she concocted to fresh bandages, and wrapped the wounds closed. Kaiya winced from the sting of the salve as BroadShanks secured each bandage, and eventually clawed back to consciousness.

"I'm sorry dearie, but it can't be helped." said BroadShanks as she rolled up her sleeves. She handed HighStance a sheet, and unfolded the towel. "HighStance, if you would, please?" HighStance crossed by the foot of the bed to stand next to Pindlebryth. He rolled back the covers, and grasped Kaiya by the shoulder and the hip. BroadShanks took a deep breath and held it, while HighStance rolled Kaiya onto his side. Pindlebryth could not help but to be moved by his friend's abject and pathetically gaunt form. Small goose-bumps, and small fibrous spindles could be seen barely poking through areas of his naked featherless skin. Underneath his body was the old towel, soiled with the morning's discharge. The pungent effluvium made Pindlebryth's eyes tear, as he stepped back from the bed and fought down the urge to retch. As HighStance gently rolled him, Kaiya stirred and muttered, "Oh bother, not again."

"Believe me dearie, no one will be happier than me when you can take your first steps out of your bed," needled BroadShanks. She deftly replaced the old towel with a fresh one, and HighStance rolled him again onto his back.

She exhaled explosively, then collected the soiled cloths. HighStance covered Kaiya with a clean sheet, and primped the bed. Each of the two then poured water onto the other's paws over the basin while they washed.

Clearing his throat and a bad taste from his mouth, Pindlebryth added, "I need to set about my meetings today. But I will need to talk to Kaiya before Pendenar and I leave for the embassy."

Pindlebryth returned to his room. After opening the window for some fresh air, he made past the wardrobe HighStance had prepared on his clothes tree, and opened the closet. From the vest worn yesterday, he pulled out the small pouch. He regarded its light heft, and set his jaw as he unfolded the small sack and pulled out the Talking Gem. He first put it to his ear and listened, but could hear no voice. Alternating positions between talking and listening, he called.

"Hello? Darothien?" Several times he repeated the cycle of calling and listening, but he still heard no response. "Piss and vinegar!" he spouted. Pindlebryth shook his head, sat on the side of his bed, and toyed with the gem between one paw and the other. He resisted the temptation to shake it vigorously, as if that might fix something that was broken. After a few minutes he tried several times again to call for Darothien, but there still was no reply. He was about to return the Talking Gem to the pouch, when he felt it vibrate and give the most delicate squeak in his hand.

"Darothien?"

"Pindlebryth, is that you? It's Selephygur. This is wonderful! It actually works! Darothien gave me this gem when I returned from Vulcanis. We've been trying to contact you ever since. Where are you? Are you all right?"

Pindlebryth allowed himself a weak smile at the excitement he heard in his younger brother's voice, fondly remembering the exuberance and wonder of Selephygur's earlier years, and his own youth. But it was soon shouldered aside by the memory of his dour and severe brother he left on Vulcanis, after he weathered so many trials and misfortunes. Pindlebryth wondered if he was about to add to them.

"I am here in PanGaea, with Pendenar."

"What about... Hakayaa?" said Selephygur, the tone of his voice changing suddenly from delight to guarded displeasure.

"He... did not survive the trip." Pindlebryth swallowed the sudden taste of gall. He had never lied before to his brother, but he didn't expect it to have such a physical effect on himself. "He succumbed to the poison in the Ravenne's dart."

A pause spread across the distant emptiness. "I know he was your friend, and in the balance of things I guess I owe him some thanks. For your sake, I am sorry to hear that." Pindlebryth could hear a sigh, but could not tell the emotion behind it. "Where is... he?"

"Pendenar lost him at sea, when he was struck by a sudden storm. His mount could not carry both him and Hakayaa's deadweight in the cloudburst. We are going to the authorities within the hour to report the incident."

"Will you be able to return for the memorial? It is to honor Tanderra as well as LongBack, and is being held two days from now."

"I have already made plans to, yes." Pindlebryth felt glad he was already sitting down. He felt sick to his heart, having lied to his brother. "Selephygur, I must go now. Look for me in two days."

"Take care, brother. I look forward to seeing you again. Oh – and I will have a small surprise for you by then!"

"Goodbye," said Pindlebryth curtly, as he firmly stuffed the Talking Gem back in its pouch. He found he could not maintain his composure, and he certainly was not in the mood for small talk. His stomach was tied in a knot, and he felt even more nauseated than in Kaiya's sickroom. In a way, he drew a small comfort in that he did not face Selephygur directly. He also felt a glimmer of gratitude knowing he would fail miserably as a diplomat, who seemed as practiced in the art of lying to others as easily as drawing breath. But the glimmer soon faded with the realization that he had chosen a path that was not all that dissimilar.

Pindlebryth rose and went again to his bedroom window, drawing a deep breath. He looked out over the city, and could see the buildings of the university near the center of the CityState. The distaste of the falsehood of Hakayaa's fate still fresh in his mind and throat made the impending task of repeating it at least twice more it even more unpalatable. Closing the window, he put the gem in an armoire drawer. He changed into the black attire set out for him, save his jacket, then left his bedroom and returned to the sickroom.

Pindlebryth found HighStance sitting next to Kaiya, reading his ever-present newspaper, *The Facade*. He never quite understood how that yellow rag still managed to flourish in the otherwise respectable journalistic circles of PanGaea's CityState. Pindlebryth pulled up the opposite chair, but not before checking the floor where BroadShanks left the waste cloths. Thankfully, it was washed and mildly redolent of borax. A soft breeze fluttered under the bottoms of the closed curtains.

"HighStance, would you wait outside for moment?"

"Yes, M'Lord." He folded his paper and stuffed it into a large pocket in his apron, and politely closed the door behind him as he stepped into the hallway.

Pindlebryth leaned over the bed, and called "Kaiya? Kaiya." When he didn't respond, he patted him on the cheek lightly at first, then more firmly and called his new name with a mote more force, "Kaiya!"

Kaiya stirred, and in a few moments turned his face and focused his eyes on Pindlebryth. He was obviously still weak, but Pindlebryth could see the glimmer of calm alertness.

"Oh, yes. That's to be my new name." He smiled wanly at Pindlebryth.

"Not just a new name. You'll need a new persona, a whole new identity and history. I will leave that up to your own wiles and ingenuity.

"But I need to ask you a third and final time. Is this what you *really* want to do? Have no illusions about this, my friend – it will make both our lives more difficult." Pindlebryth clasped Kaiya's good shoulder. The skin was no longer slick and clammy, but rough and stubbled as the stalks of new pinfeathers began to grow.

"Absolutely. Otherwise, I could again be used against you and your family. And anyone else who tries to befriend you may similarly be turned." Kaiya inhaled deeply with a husky wheeze. "I'm sorry, Pindie – but your life just became much lonelier."

"That's no great loss. You haven't seen or spoken to the daughters foisted on me by their fathers, the Dukes, Barons and magnates who hope to wheedle their way closer to the throne. They are all quite fetching, but most have a mind as barren as a desert, and the others have the moral compass of an eel." They shared a small laugh, but it was cut short as Kaiya convulsed with a hoarse cough.

"I'm sorry, I shouldn't tax you so. We'll talk later, Kaiya. But there is one thing I must know now. Pendenar and I are going to your house to inform the SootBeaks of... Hakayaa's demise. I know you have emergency funds somewhere in your study. You accessed them once to pay off a sizable debt you incurred during a particularly bad run of luck at the casinos three years ago. You'll need them again now to start your new life, since you can no longer seek support from your family. Where I can find them?"

His wheezing marginally worse, Kaiya struggled to reply. "The bookshelves – the second case from the right, the fourth shelf down, the eighth book from the left. Touch nothing else." He coughed again violently. "There are other stashes, but they are trapped."

Pindlebryth could only guess at what snares Hakayaa had put in place – it could be something as humorous as squid ink in the eye, or poison sumac dust, or something more diabolical. In any case, he was not going to satisfy his curiosity and test their existence.

"Very well. Now rest." Pindlebryth opened the door, and was about to ask HighStance back in when BroadShanks shouldered past him with two baskets. She placed the basket with medicine next to Kaiya's bed and then took her seat producing a set of crocheting needles and yarn out of the basket on her lap. "Kaiya, I still have many questions, but they can wait. Or perchance Professor DeepDigger can answer them."

"Good." Kaiya coughed one last time, closed his eyes and began to breathe more easily.

Pindlebryth left the sickroom to collect his black jacket. He then called for Pendenar as he descended the staircase to the ground floor. Waiting at the door, still in his apron, HighStance dashed out the door to the street gate and proceeded to call a carriage.

Pendenar joined Pindlebryth at the ajar doorway, with his uniform still rumpled from the journey, as Pindlebryth suggested.

"Are you ready?" Pindlebryth ventured.

"I was about to ask you the same, M'Lord."

The carriage pulled up and the two climbed in. HighStance instructed the driver, who promptly drove his fares away, heading to the embassy.

Pindlebryth sighed with assignation. "I don't know how much background I will have to explain to Quentain – if starting from Vulcanis is sufficient, or everything from the past week is necessary. I hope she has received word of all that has happened in Lenland. It will make things easier it we are not the ones to break the news about King Hatheron's order deporting the Crow and Fox." He put his paw to his chin, as the carriage turned and continued to rumble down another cobblestone street.

"If the order was sent by our fastest couriers, it's conceivable she has received it by now. But even if she has received the order, M'Lord, I'm sure she will be anxious to know how such an order came about."

"Such a discussion could consume our whole day, and we have much to do and little time to spare. We can only hope the order will be self-explanatory, and let the ambassadress sort out the details of how to officially inform the Crow about Hakayaa."

The carriage took another turn onto a more well-traveled paved boulevard, towards the financial and government districts. Through the window, Pindlebryth could catch sight of the spires of PanGaea University. "And then there's the matter of talking to Professor DeepDigger. Hopefully he can finally shed some light on the Artifacts that have been the cause of all of Lenland's woes." Even though it was nearing the lunch hour, Pindlebryth still found he was quite full from this morning's sumptuous breakfast. "I'll visit his office this evening after supper."

"Alone?" Pendenar said incredulously. "I don't think it is wise for me to leave your side for long periods."

"I think I can be safe in PanGaea University," Pindlebryth fussed. "After I repeat for DeepDigger the story of Hakayaa, hopefully for the last time, I think he and I will spend a long time together. Poring over books and papers, discussing esoterica, and so on. It's going to be pretty dry stuff."

"Your pardon, M'Lord, you know that I cannot let you go alone."

"Do you propose to hover around me forever? Will you be my ever-present guardian during the entire upcoming semester?"

Pendenar chewed on his response for a moment. "Of course not. But it is too soon after the attempts on the lives of you and the entire Royal Family. And surely no one can predict what the Ravenne are planning next. Even if you are correct and there is indeed no threat here in PanGaea, after the rough and tumble events of the past few days, I would find a night of tedium somewhat refreshing."

Pindlebryth cocked his head in slight surprise and skepticism at Pendenar's forthrightness and rarely seen sense of humor. He soon found himself chuckling at his guard's assessment. He leaned on an elbow, and continued to dreamily watch out the carriage window at the mundane affairs passing by on the street.

"Traffic is light today," Pindlebryth finally remarked. "Lords Above, I cannot remember what day of the week it is."

"Perhaps it is merely due to the fact the university is between semesters."

"Oh. Quite right. When I return in a few weeks, it will be much more crowded. That reminds me, I'll have to inform my advisor of my continuing language studies. I think it obvious that my next language to master is Crow."

Pendenar closed his eyes, trying to recall something from the day at Vulcanis. He opened them and asked, "Prince Selephygur said something about 'all the Artifacts'." His muzzle made a clicking sound. "Now that I think about it, the day we met Hakayaa, he said there were five Artifacts. If Lenland has one hidden, and the Crow now have the one from the Fox, and possibly more, who have the others?"

"That is an excellent question. Whoever they are, I suspect I will need to master their tongues as well, if I haven't already. If DeepDigger cannot help us answer that, then we will have to rely on Selephygur's memory of what he saw in the Ravenne's book. There are several other things I need to discuss with... Oh. Here we are. Your wits about you now, Pendenar."

The carriage stopped at an iron gate on the side of the street, and a uniformed Lemming approached. He was about to ask their business, when he spied Pindlebryth and Pendenar's uniform. "Good day, M'Lord."

"Greetings. Is the ambassadress available now?"

"Yes, but just.   She and her staff have a luncheon appointment with the Warrening ambassador.   But I'm sure she'll make time to see you, M'Lord."   Stepping back from the carriage, he called to his fellow guard and the driver, "Proceed!"

The carriage wended its way up a short curving lane to the embassy main entrance, where a portico was supported by four fluted columns.   The flag of Lenland draped from the roof, and ruffled lazily in the gentle ocean breeze.   One of the pair of guards stationed at the great ornate doors opened the carriage door and assisted the two out.   Pendenar instructed the driver to wait, after which the embassy guard pointed to where he and his carriage could park.   The second guard opened the door and escorted them to a desk in the vestibule.

"M'Lord!   It's good to see you again!" chimed the floor concierge sitting behind his desk.

"Good morning, QuickEyes," Pindlebryth responded.

"I must say, I'm a little surprised to see you here this early. The University doesn't start its next semester for two more weeks."

"Yes, I'm afraid I'm here on official business.   I need to the see Ambassadress Quentain immediately."

"She and her assistants are preparing for a luncheon meeting at the Warrening embassy."   His face lost its smile, as he tried to relay empathy and disappointment.

"Yes, I've heard.   Perchance is she meeting with a Crow delegation?"

He was genuinely surprised at Pindlebryth's seeming leap of intuition.   "Why, yes she is!"

"Then you *have* received a communiqué from Lenland today," Pindlebryth remarked, looking to Pendenar.   Focusing on the concierge, he said, "It is urgent that I see her beforehand. What I have to tell her bears directly on Lenland's situation with the Rookeries."

"I will see if she's ready to receive you."   QuickEyes got up and proceeded a few paces down the main corridor, when Pindlebryth followed him and interrupted.

"Take us to her now.   I must insist she receives us forthwith."

Though visibly shaken, QuickEyes nonetheless continued through an impressive set of double doors leading to the ambassadress's office.

Pindlebryth, without breaking step, quietly whispered aside

to Pendenar, "What good is being a Prince, if you don't throw your weight around once in a while?" Pendenar's eyes widened with a ghost of a snort.

Behind the doors, several voices could be heard in animated discussion. The concierge politely knocked on the doors, but the voices continued. Pendenar marched up to the doors, and pounded thrice. As he opened the doors uninvited, all the voices save one stopped.

"What in the world?" boomed a loud contralto. "QuickEyes! I told you I was not to be disturbed until... Oh!" Ambassadress Quentain quickly lost her indignant head of steam, and stood up in a shot. The two assistants, sitting across the desk from the ambassadress over a pile of erratically strewn documents, turned and nearly jumped out of their skins.

"M'Lord! Forgive me! I would not have..." Quentain began.

Pindlebryth brushed the onslaught of excuses and formalities aside, and strode in. QuickEyes quietly closed the doors as he left, while both assistants moved aside and proffered their seats. Pindlebryth sat in one of the chairs, as Pendenar stood behind him, paws clasped behind his back. Pindlebryth cut directly to the heart of the matter.

"I am told you are to meet with the Crow at the Warrening embassy. I presume you have heard the latest from His Majesty?"

Without a word, one of the panicked assistants delved into the pile and produced a letter bearing the seal of the new Prime Minister, Amadan. Next to it was another letter with the royal insignia relaying the news of Amadan's appointment. Hardly glancing at the papers, Quentain replied, "Yes, concerning the expulsion of all Fox and Crow from Lenland. It is not, however, forthcoming on details."

"And a Crow entourage are waiting with their Arctic Hare counterparts at the Warrening embassy to discuss these developments with us," chimed in one of the assistants.

"Yes, and we have little time left to prepare. My contacts warn me that the Crow are fit to be tied. Any information you can provide will help strengthen our negotiations."

"Let them stew in their indignation. What I and Pendenar were witness to make the Crow as innocent as baby timber rattlers." Pendenar sighed heavily. The moment Pindlebryth dreaded was finally upon him. "I shall try to be as succinct as possible. It started with an attempt on the lives of the Royal Family in the very castle of CityState…"

Pindlebryth spoke quickly, and yet somehow managed to summarize all that had transpired in the courtyard and afterwards, and why King Hatheron imposed the exile. He continued by recounting Hakayaa's part in all the intrigue, through to the final confrontation with the Ravenne at Vulcanis.

Quentain sat back in her high-backed chair and exhaled in disbelief.

But Pindlebryth was not finished. "As if you haven't already enough on your plate, there is also the reason I came to see you today. Hakayaa BlueHood did not survive his wounds. Though I am no authority on international law, it seemed proper – under the circumstances of the Crow exile – that you should be the first authority to be informed."

"Quite correct, M'Lord. Did he pass away on Vulcanis?" inquired Quentain.

"No, we lost him en route to PanGaea." Pindlebryth looked over his shoulder at Pendenar, and nodded to him to add his part. As Pendenar stiltedly told his portion of the fabrication, Pindlebryth looked down at the pile of papers on Quentain's desk. Pendenar hemmed and hawed several times, and barely sounded convincing. Pindlebryth locked his focus on one particular paper, hoping he could hide his consternation at Pendenar's difficulty behind a mask of solemn bereavement.

Mercifully, Pendenar finished with the details of the agreed upon fiction still intact. Pindlebryth took a handkerchief from his vest and pressed his sweaty palms on the cloth as he unfolded it and wiped his eyes.

Quentain looked at both of them twice, and finally offered, "My condolences, M'Lord, at the loss of your friend." She gathered a few of the wildly strewn papers on her desk, and assembled and tamped them into a small sheaf in her hands. "The Crow, and maybe other authorities, may want more than just my word. Considering these events, I agree it would be problematic for you to join us at the Warrening embassy. And at such short notice, it would be impossible to guarantee your security and safety. If the need arises that the Crow will not be satisfied, would you both be willing to sign affidavits?"

"My word should be sufficient, Ambassadress. And I shall vouch for my guard," Pindlebryth replied emotionlessly.

"You put me in an awkward position, M'Lord," Quentain

quipped tersely. After a tense breath, she relented. "But I suppose it will have to do." Her assistants flickered glances around the room, daring not to attract attention to themselves, or insert themselves into the discussion again. "You do realize, M'Lord Pindlebryth, that today's events must be reported to the new Prime Minister?"

"You have your duties. I would not have it any other way," said Pindlebryth as he rose abruptly. Pendenar snapped to attention, while Quentain and her assistants scrambled to their feet. "Now if you will excuse me, I have my own unenviable task to attend to – notifying the BlueHood family. If memory serves, they usually winter here at the end of the fall semester. You wouldn't happen to know if any members of Hakayaa's family are here early?"

"No, I don't believe I've heard anything," replied Quentain.

"Then I shall pay a visit to his staff in the meantime, until I can offer my condolences to the BlueHood family directly. Good day and good luck, Ambassadress Quentain."

"And to you, M'Lord."

One of the assistants had already moved to the door, and opened it as Pindlebryth and Pendenar turned to leave. As they crossed the threshold, Pindlebryth stopped, and as an afterthought added, "Oh, and one last thing. Will you also have one your staff notify PanGaea University of Hakayaa's passing?" With that, he strode out into the hallway, filled with stern purpose. They ignored QuickEyes and the other staff as they left, and stood impatiently, while the guard outside summoned the waiting carriage. Pindlebryth perfunctorily gave the address of Hakayaa's house to the driver as he and Pendenar clambered into their seats. Once the carriage was on its way, Pindlebryth relaxed and breathed a sigh of relief.

"I don't think Quentain found you very convincing, Pendenar."

Pendenar looked like he had eaten a sour persimmon. "Forgive me, M'Lord, but I am not used to ly... I find... deception to be..."

"Enough. I understand what you are trying to say," said Pindlebryth, perhaps a mite too sternly. He mollified his response by adding, "Besides, it proves to me that you are more trustworthy than I could ever hope for.

"When we arrive at Hakayaa's old house, let me do the talking. Mrs. SootBeak will see right through you and would eat you alive. Just keep Mr. SootBeak preoccupied for a while." The two Lemmings fell into silence as the carriage trundled on. The estates, mansions, and smoothly paved roads gave way again to cleanly cobbled streets as they left the central districts, into the residential areas. As they rolled in front of the walkway to their destination, Pindlebryth's unease grew into apprehension. Whereas he had not had many dealings before with Quentain, the SootBeaks were more familiar with his mannerisms and comportment. Convincing them about Hakayaa's demise would be a bird of another feather.

As they exited the carriage and made their way to the front door, Pendenar rushed ahead to knock. Before the door opened, the increasing volume of a chattering hen could be heard.

"Honestly, I don't understand why you spend so much time over there. Believe you me, there's plenty to do around here, you..." She turned towards the door, and the surprise in her face and voice were clearly evident.

"Prince Pindlebryth! My word, it's so good to see you! It's been so long since we saw you last! When you missed that year at University, we all wondered if you were going to come back at all. Even Master Hakayaa was worried, although of course he would never admit it to anyone. But then again, we haven't seen him since before last semester, either. He got pulled away to fix some problem in one of the mines, I am told. Goodness, listen to me go on! Please, come in, come in!"

Pindlebryth attempted to divert the conversation, but instead, all he and Pendenar could do was to follow the chattering Mrs. SootBeak into the foyer and main hallway. Once they entered, Pindlebryth shivered a bit and his nose wrinkled at the odor of what was cooking in the kitchen. Pendenar, not accustomed nor prepared for the strange and overpowering smells, coughed heavily. Pindlebryth turned his head towards Pendenar, with his paw over one side of his mouth held a handkerchief over his nose. "I forgot to warn you, Pendenar, that the Crow diet is quite different from ours. They often eat foods we would never think of touching."

Mrs. SootBeak must have heard them, or simply recalled the preferences of their guest, as she quickly apologized. "Oh! I'm so sorry Pindlebryth! If I had known you were coming, I would have held off lunch for Mr. S. and myself. I'll have him toss it out this minute!"

Pindlebryth immediately saw his opportunity. "No, no, Mrs. SootBeak. That's not necessary. I wouldn't want your meal to go to waste." Pindlebryth tried to swallow, but he suddenly felt as if he had eaten a rancid bit of cheese. "Hmp!" he gurgled. "If you could just cover it up, and perhaps if we could go upstairs to the study, away from the kitchen, I'm sure that will be sufficient." Looking at Pendenar, he saw he was not faring much better. He thought it strange that a battle seasoned fighter like Pendenar who had experienced bloodshed that would make a lesser Lemming swoon, would be nauseated so.

"Oh thank you! I was making one of our favorites – it's the most delectable stew of... Oh, no! Perhaps I shouldn't say!" She was making her way to the stairway, but as she took the first step up the flight of stairs, she leaned over the banister and raised her voice to a level that Pindlebryth was sure could be heard two houses away.

"SootBeak, you inconsiderate lout! Take the pots off the stove and cover them up! Close the kitchen door and open the windows!"

Mrs. SootBeak fairly hopped up the staircase to the first door, but Pindlebryth took slow steps, trying not to breathe too deeply. Mrs. SootBeak hurried into the study, threw apart the curtains, and swung the windows wide open. A waft of fresh cool air poured into the room from the bottom of the curtains, as the warmer air in the room pushed out through their tops. The Lemmings entered the room, and both exhaled in relief, then gulped in the fresh air. Mrs. SootBeak leaned on the window jamb, short of breath and panting with her hand over her chest. After a moment, she caught her breath and opened another window in the adjacent wall.

Between the two windows stood a circular table covered in red felt. Mrs. SootBeak removed a turntable filled with columns of multicolored chips, and pulled out Pindlebryth's preferred chair at the gaming table. Pindlebryth gratefully sat in his chair and exhaled deeply again. There came the sound of feet climbing the stairs, and Mr. SootBeak sheepishly poked his head in. In broken common tongue, he awkwardly asked if everyone was all right.

"Yes, you foolish fowl! You just *had* to have your stew today, didn't you? Now throw it out, before you make our guests sick!" Mrs. SootBeak scolded.

"No, please don't," Pindlebryth persuaded her a second

time. "But now that you're both here, there is something important I need to talk to you about. Are there any of the BlueHood Rookery here in CityState?"

"No, not now," said Mrs. SootBeak. "However, we have heard that Hakayaa's uncle HeaKea may visit this month. Or that his sister Hayake is traveling all about the continents, and may visit sometime this year. I sometimes wish his parents would come and visit. It's been over a year since they have come to PanGaea, and..."

"Very well, then." Pindlebryth broke in. "I am afraid I have sobering news for the BlueHood family, and in lieu of any family members here, I'll have to inform you instead. I have informed my embassy, who will pass it on to your embassy. But I felt it proper to inform those closest to Hakayaa myself."

Overcome by a sudden wave of apprehension, Mrs. SootBeak's left wing sought out to hold her husband's for support. "My dear Prince, what are you trying to tell us?"

"In a moment, dear Mrs. SootBeak. But first, there are a few details to attend to.

"Pendenar, please take Mr. SootBeak. Check and secure the rooms of the house." Looking at Mrs. SootBeak, he added, "And I would be most thankful if you brought some of your wonderful cranberry tea. Bring cups for all of us, if you please." Pindlebryth turned to peer out the window while the three of them left the room. He mused nostalgically about the nights he, Hakayaa and others spent around this very table. Saddened by those spirited times long gone, he quickly sobered as he heard Pendenar's and Mr. SootBeak's voices downstairs. He quietly got up and scanned the rows of books in the shelves starting next to the windows.

He tried to concentrate and recall Kaiya's instructions, when he was distracted by a commotion downstairs. Cocking his ears at the noise booming up the stairwell, he raised his eyebrows and grimaced as he discerned several sounds – of Pendenar becoming ill, the fuss raised by Mrs. SootBeak, and Mr. SootBeak clattering about with a bucket.

As the din slowly subsided, Pindlebryth closed his eyes for a few seconds, recalling his bedside talk with Kaiya. Opening them again, he began to scan the books. From the second right case, he went down four shelves and touched the top of the eighth book from the left. He was about to pull the book out, when he paused, and realized something didn't feel right. He tilted his head to read the title along the spine – "Geologies of the Nations". If this was one of Hakayaa's hiding places, it was much too obvious – furthermore, it just didn't fit the Crow's twisted sense of humor.

He pondered his instructions, and whether Kaiya, through the haze of poison, magick and malnutrition, had recalled his instructions correctly. With newfound determination he started again, but this time from the second shelf from the left, and eighth book from the right. This time, the title printed on the spine made Pindlebryth smile, albeit with a certain disturbed embarrassment. He could barely guess what the original contents in the Crow language of a book called "Forbidden Pleasures" might be.

Checking that he was still alone, and all the voices were still downstairs, Pindlebryth held his breath, closed his eyes, and pulled the book from the shelf. Just as gingerly, he opened the book, then breathed a sigh of satisfaction. Carved into the inside of the book, was a rectangular cavity. Stuffed into the hollowed out pages was a small velvet pouch with a leather drawstring. Prizing the tightly packed sack from the book, he deftly slid the book back into its place in the shelves. He unwound the leather lacing, and glanced inside the pouch. Pindlebryth nodded his head as he saw the contents that jam-packed the velvet purse – diamonds in the rough. Untraceable in their current form, when cut and polished they truly would be worth a king's ransom. If sold one by one, a person could easily move from city to city, from country to country without leaving a trail.

Pindlebryth tied the pouch back up, and stuffed it into a pocket inside his vest next to his heart. Taking his seat at the gaming table, he resumed his position staring out the window with barely a minute to spare as Pendenar and SootBeak passed by the study door to secure the rest of the second floor. Pendenar walked with a slightly unsteady gait from his ordeal downstairs, but was nonetheless strong enough to continue his distraction with Mr. SootBeak.

Eventually, Mrs. SootBeak and her finest tea set rattled up the stairs. She entered the room, placed the set on a side table and spread a finely embroidered linen cloth over the red felt table. As she poured two cups, she visibly shook the teapot with trembling dismay, wondering what news Pindlebryth had for her. She was so distracted, she filled the cup to overflowing.

Apologizing profusely, she replaced the cup and saucer with a fresh set, and poured anew.

Mr. SootBeak and Pendenar entered the study. Despite Mrs. SootBeak's requests for Pendenar to also take a seat and have his tea, he politely refused. He instead stood between Pindlebryth and the window, keeping a watchful eye on the street below, and the rooftops beyond.

Pindlebryth gestured an invitation to the SootBeaks. "Please join me for tea."

"Lord Pindlebryth, we mayn't! It just is not *done*."

"Please humor me." He gripped the handle of the teapot with one paw, and was about to take a third cup. Mrs. SootBeak placed her wing above the top of the pot.

"Oh, very well. But I will *not* have you pouring my tea. People will think I'm putting on airs." She sat down in a huff, and took the overfilled cup for herself and poured another for Mr. SootBeak. Unlike his better half, he had no compunction about sitting at the table. He was about to sip from his cup, when Mrs. SootBeak slapped his wingtip.

"Mind your manners, you oaf! Guests first! And if you spill any on the linen or felt, I'll pluck your back!"

Pindlebryth obliged them by gently sipping the smallest of tastes from his cup. He savored the curiously delicious brew, only to faintly sense an acrid aftertaste at the back of his throat reminiscent of the vapors of the Crow's inedible stew. The Crow each imbibed the tea — Mrs. SootBeak took a dainty sip, while Mr. SootBeak downed half his cup with gusto. Mrs. SootBeak flashed him a disdainful glance, then rolled her eyes at her husband's ever-flowing lack of etiquette.

"Now, my dear Prince Pindlebryth. What is troubling you so, that you have our other guest and Mr. SootBeak checking all the doors and windows? It smacks of so much huggermuggery, if you ask me," she said as she theatrically fanned herself with her napkin. "And all this falderol makes me wonder even more what has recently happened to you and Master Hakayaa." Mrs. SootBeak didn't know if she should feel compassion for her guest, or be wary of things she found unpleasant intruding into her world.

Pindlebryth coughed away the aftertaste, put down his cup, and dabbed his mouth with his napkin. "This... is not easy for me to say. In the past few days, there have been attempts on the life of my brother, myself, and the rest of the Royal Family."

Mrs. SootBeak's mixed look of empathy and abhorrence melted away to one of enraptured attention.

"And there was a time when I suspected the worst of Hakayaa, but he finally comported himself with dignity and courage until the..." Pindlebryth sighed as he found himself filling with latent anger at all the events that passed, and what he was about to describe.

Mrs. SootBeak looked at him pensively, fearing the worst of his tale. She reached over the table, searching to again hold her husband's wing for support.

Pindlebryth wove his tale of truths, half-truths and deceit to protect his friend, their employer. He was mildly surprised that the story became easier with practice. Despite this, he could not relax one whit as he sympathetically talked to the SootBeaks. The comfort that initially began to seep into his psyche, was washed away by a sudden thought – is this lie the pebble that starts an avalanche, even one that would smash and eventually corrupt his ideals? He steeled himself as he began to describe the fight against the Ravenne at Vulcanis.

Mr. SootBeak was unreadable, but Mrs. S. became rather agitated at the mention of the Ravenne. She shivered with apprehension, and could not control her gasps of troubled dismay. She became quite frantic when Pindlebryth told them that Hayake BlueHood had been a hostage of the Ravenne, then she ultimately burst into tears when Pindlebryth told of the fateful poisoned darts meant for Selephygur, that killed his faithful guard LongBack, and Pindlebryth's dearest friend Hakayaa.

He paused while Mr. SootBeak rose to comfort his wife. He marveled at how the Crow, the target of years of endless bullying and insults, could still harbor affection for his mate. Pindlebryth sipped some more tea to savor the bittersweet moment, only to be distastefully reminded of the tea's slight notes of carrion absorbed from the SootBeaks' lunch.

She closed her eyes and wept, and pulled a white kerchief from inside her maid's uniform. Holding the cloth awkwardly over the spiracles at the crest of her beak, she simpered quietly, "Where?" She coughed and sprayed loudly into her handkerchief, and sniffled until she could talk more clearly. "Where does the body of Master Hakayaa lay now?"

Pindlebryth put down his tea, and mustered what empathy he could, slowly meting out his response. "Mr. and Mrs.

SootBeak, it is my sad and terrible duty to inform you that Hakayaa was lost at sea. He succumbed to his wounds and the poison as we tried to transport him to the nearest help, here in PanGaea. To make matters all the worse, his body was lost in a storm over the MidSea between Vulcanis and PanGaea."

Mrs. SootBeak screeched a shrill "No!" and shook violently, succumbing to even more wretched weeping.

"Pendenar and I have made a report to our embassy this morning. They will disseminate our official statement to the Crow embassy and PanGaean authorities today." He breathed finally, "Please accept my heartfelt condolences at your loss. He was an invaluable and stalwart friend, and I shall miss him sorely as well."

Mr. SootBeak pulled his chair next to his wife's, and sat with one wing enfolding his inconsolable wife. Then with an unsteadiness in his voice that Pindlebryth had never heard before, he said, "Thank you, Lord Pindlebryth, for all help. Bringing us saddest news. I think is nothing more we can ask of you. I... Could you...?" His voice, his composure, and command of common tongue all failed him.

Pindlebryth took his cue to stand and offer, "We will see ourselves out. Again, I am so sorry to be the bearer of these sad tidings. Please let me know if there is anything else I can do." Pindlebryth let himself out of the room, as Pendenar gave a curt bow to their hosts, and shadowed Pindlebryth down the stairs. As Pindlebryth waited, Pendenar marched quickly out the door, and took a cavernously deep breath of the fresh outside air, then proceeded to the waiting carriage. Pindlebryth slowly walked to the carriage door opened by Pendenar, but paused. He produced a PanGaean coin and flipped it to the driver.

"Thank you for you troubles. I think I'd rather walk the rest of the way home." Slightly alarmed, Pendenar quickly closed the door and double-timed to catch up with Pindlebryth.

"Is this advisable, M'Lord?", his eyes moving back and forth incessantly wary of potential threats.

With his head down in thought or disgust, Pindlebryth replied, "After dealing with the SootBeaks so harshly, and with the cloying aroma of their food still in my nostrils, I don't think I would fare well in a moving carriage. I would feel better if I simply walk it off."

"What about meeting with DeepDigger at University?"

"He will have to wait until tomorrow morning. I don't think

I could face a display like that twice in one day." They silently trod the several blocks and turns to his own apartments. HighStance met him at the door, and took his outer garment. The sound of BroadShanks in the kitchen barely registered on Pindlebryth as he aimlessly wandered into the front parlor, where he promptly collapsed on a richly appointed divan. After taking several deep breaths, he leaned forward and began massaging his brow. As he worked the tension between his temples away, HighStance returned with a tray holding a crystal decanter and glass. He unstoppered the glinting bottle and poured a draught of a sweet smelling amber liquid.

"Some hazelnut liqueur M'Lord? You look as if you could use it."

Pindlebryth accepted it, sipped a small portion, and reclined again on the divan. "Thank you, HighStance. It indeed helps." After taking another deep breath, and savoring the drink's aroma, he asked, "And what of our visitor?"

"He's recovering quite quickly."

"That's not wholly unexpected. As a shapeshifter, he has strong recuperative powers."

"Ah. I don't think I will tell BroadShanks that. She attributes his remarkable improvement to her knowledge and adeptness in the healing arts."

Pindlebryth chuckled softly. "Well then. If he's doing so well, then I think I should talk to him now." He stood up with glass in hand, and grabbed the decanter by its neck in the other paw. "Bring another glass, if you please." He arched his back to stretch, and went into the hallway. Pendenar was about to follow him upstairs, but Pindlebryth waved him to stay. Upon reaching the sickroom door, he placed the decanter next to a bouquet of peonies and hydrangeas on a side-table in the hall. Knocking on the door, he simply announced "It's me." After a pause, he opened the door and scooped up the decanter again.

Kaiya was sitting up in bed, and looking quite alert. His skin, previously covered in prickly stubble, was now thickening with small quills and featherlets.

"HighStance was right," said Pindlebryth as he placed the decanter and glass on the end table and took one of the bedside chairs. "You are recuperating quite nicely." He could not, however, help but to notice that Kaiya was still rail-thin – much less than he would have believed a full coat of feathers would normally hide.

"Yes. I've even taken a few steps out of my bed now and then. Your maid cum nurse is unsure whether she should be angry with me," Kaiya mused with a wry tone. "On one hand, she is displeased that I am out of bed without her permission; on the other hand she is rather relieved she needn't be constantly changing my sheets."

"Has she been feeding you well? You're thinner than I would have imagined."

"As best as she can with a Lemming's diet. She's been feeding me bushels of nuts and berries, but I could murder a bowl of one of Mrs. SootBeak's stews."

Pindlebryth shook his head as the memory of the aroma of stewed meat assaulted his snout again. He could barely stifle the sneeze that came with it.

"And now you realize why I couldn't ask BroadShanks to even entertain the notion of a Crow's diet in her kitchen." He sighed wistfully. "Under the circumstances, I suppose nuts and seeds are the best foods to quickly regrow my plumage."

Kaiya drew a wheezy breath to speak again, but was cut short by a series of rattling coughs. He grasped for a cloth under the pillows, and expectorated into it. Catching a few gasps, then steadily deeper breaths, Kaiya then looked at Pindlebryth with a concerned, pleading gaze. "Was there any news of my sister, Hayake?"

"I'm afraid not. Mrs. SootBeak was of the opinion that she was traveling. She was not even aware of her having been kidnapped, until I told her of the events at Vulcanis."

Kaiya sighed in disappointment and frustration.

"I will try to find out what I can," Pindlebryth tried to assure his friend, "although it may take some time. Father's decree prevents me from visiting the Crow embassy directly, but I can have our embassy request this information through indirect channels. The only other venue I can foresee is that the SootBeaks find out for us."

HighStance knocked at the ajar door, and brought in a second crystal glass. As he placed it next to the decanter, Pindlebryth added, "Thank you, HighStance. Please close the door behind you."

Pindlebryth looked out the window at the sun casting ever-lengthening shadows until HighStance closed the door. Assured that they would not be disturbed further, he reached into his vest pocket and produced the pouch from the library and handed it to Kaiya.

"'Forbidden Pleasures'?" Pindlebryth added with a weak grin. "That's rather an unusual title to find amidst so many otherwise nondescript books. I might think a thief might take a book with such a title just as an amusement or an evening's diversion." He twisted in his chair to pour a small dram of liquor into the empty glass. "And so much more interesting than a work on 'Geologies of Nations'."

Kaiya snapped his head up from the pouch to look wide-eyed at Pindlebryth. "You didn't pull *that* book, did you?"

Pindlebryth chortled and handed the glass to Kaiya. "No. Something told me that you might have recalled your directions incorrectly."

"Sorry about that! But I am glad to see I'm finally beginning to rub off on you, Pindie." Kaiya tilted his head to sniff the potable, then took a sip. He immediately sputtered at its unexpected strength, but swallowed the rest, closing his eyes as he welcomed the familiar warmth in his throat. He tried to place the goblet back on the table, but it was out of reach. Pindlebryth took the glass and set it aside.

"I'd offer you more, but I think one sip is enough for now. Aren't you going to inspect the contents of your prize?" Kaiya undid the knot in the leather cord that cinched the pouch, and beheld the dozens of rough diamonds within. Pindlebryth gasped in surprise as Kaiya popped two of the smaller stones into his beak and swallowed them down into his crop. "It helps with digestion," he commented sheepishly, "and one can never tell when I can use them again in a pinch."

"You'd best keep the rest hidden for now," Pindlebryth suggested.

Kaiya resealed the pouch and considered sliding it between the two pillows propping him up for a moment. "Could you put these with my clothes, please? They're in the cedar chest under the window. BroadShanks would happen upon it too easily here in bed."

"Clothes? You had none when we brought you here!" Pindlebryth sniggered as he almost spilled his own glass.

"HighStance packed some for me, for that day when I'm well enough to go. He thought it best if I leave as a Lemming when I do," Kaiya said as he lifted the cache of gems to Pindlebryth. "His clothes are a bit tall for me, but they'll fit my frame now."

Pindlebryth obliged him, and secreted the pouch between a jacket and waistcoat he found in the chest. When he resumed his seat, he took one final swig of the sweet and burning hazelnut, but then noticed a quizzical look from Kaiya.

"Speaking of finding things, how in the world did you find me on Vulcanis?" Kaiya asked hesitantly.

"I'm more interested in why you went there."

"I barely remember going there. Maybe I went trying to find a place to hide the Lens. Or maybe I went looking for the reason why Selephylin needed the Lens, or perhaps a way to destroy it, or even..." He took a deep and solemn breath. "Or even a way to destroy myself. I was so confused and torn apart inside, I don't think I even remember making the decision to go there."

Kaiya looked at his friend with a sadness in his eyes, that Pindlebryth believed he never saw before. "I don't expect Selephygur to ever forgive me, but in the heat of the moment, I took the Lens to *protect* him."

"Protect?"

"Yes. The Fox certainly demonstrated no compunction against using deadly force to regain their precious Lens. And if the Ravenne themselves ever got ahold of Selephygur, he was as good as dead anyway. Or worse. Taking the Lens as I did was the only way I could think of to keep him *alive*."

He shook his head violently to whisk away the cobwebs and the madness that overtook him in those dark days. "That day drove me to insanity. Between the need to save my sister, and the remorse over attacking your brother, I panicked and ran blindly away. But, if *I* didn't know I was going to Vulcanis, how did you? One of your intuitions?"

"No, it wasn't I who followed you there. It was Selephygur."

"But how?" said Kaiya, as he sat up straighter, his eyes bright with curiosity.

"He saw you. He had dreams, and sometimes daytime visions of you and your surroundings. It was as if he could still see with the Lens in those visions."

"Lords of the Air!" Kaiya exploded. "He saw me? He *saw* me! And here I thought it was part of my madness! I *did* see the Lens move and look directly at me!" He leaned forward as a wave of nausea swept over him. He hastily grabbed a towel rolled up next to his pillow, and retched into it. "I guess I can't hold my crop just right now..." He soon recovered with a sheepish grin, wiped off the gorge of stones with the remainder of the towel, and placed them on the outer coverlet next to his friend. Pindlebryth regarded with stones with a raised eyebrow and aversion accompanied with the aftertaste of bad cranberry tea.

But Kaiya did not settle back in a comfortable posture. He held Pindlebryth with a look of trepidation mixed with earnest concern. "Do you realize what Prince Selephygur has? Do you understand the advantage this gives us?"

After a moment of thought, Pindlebryth caught on to Kaiya's meaning. "Yes! Selephygur can *see*! Even removed by leagues or more of distance, he can still see what the Lens sees."

"And he might be able to see who has it now. He can find out the Crow who is behind all this! The one who kidnapped my sister, the one who orchestrated the attack on your family, the one who recruited the Ravenne – the one who is trying to amass all the Artifacts!" He coughed with the sudden excitement. Catching his breath he continued, "This is something no one could expect. It's not recorded in any archives that I or DeepDigger have found."

Pindlebryth struggled to recall something the old Prime Minister Tanderra had said. "Ah! That might explain why the Fox nation kept the Lens of Truth hidden away when not in use. It was too risky to allow it, and perchance a previous owner, see what he was not meant to see!" He stood up and began to pace. "I've got to tell Selephygur as soon as possible. I'm sure he doesn't realize the advantage we have."

"Nor the possible danger it puts him in, if anyone outside your trusted circle finds out. You're heading back to Lenland soon, aren't you?"

"Yes. Right after I meet DeepDigger tomorrow."

"That may not be soon enough. Your brother needs to be tight-lipped about this. The Ravenne have their own spies, in addition to what information gathering resources the Court of the Kyaa may bring to bear."

"Fear not," Pindlebryth countered with a knowing grin. "I have a way to get word to him immediately."

Kaiya looked at him unabashedly. "Oh? What trick do you have up your sleeve?"

Pindlebryth stood over Kaiya and clasped him on the shoulder. He then produced a monogrammed handkerchief from a pocket, and collected the two stones. Placing the handkerchief with the pouch of stones in the cedar chest, he responded, "Maybe later. For now, you have your secrets, and I have mine." Pindlebryth was sick to his core with secrets and the lies they forced him to tell. But something led him to believe this secret of omission over the Talking Gem was necessary and should be kept strictly in his family and the most trusted castle staff.

"But there are a few more things I must ask you." He sat again leaning forward, steepled his paws, and looked Kaiya squarely in the eyes. "All the years that I have known you, you never mentioned a peep about the Artifacts until your visit to Lenland. But in the past weeks, they have dominated almost your every waking moment. Have you been keeping this secret from me all this time?"

"No, not at all," Kaiya said feigning a mock hurt expression. He quickly resumed a serious demeanor as he continued. "The year that you were away from PanGaea was indeed a lonely one. Our usual haunts in the casinos and grand balls no longer held quite the same atmosphere of merrymaking. If that was what my future in PanGaea and the Rookeries held, then I wanted to improve my situation. And much as it might be difficult for you to believe, I returned to my studies. At first, I latched onto DeepDigger's affectation for the archives as a way to get into his good graces, and make my stay at University an easier one."

"Ah! That sounds more like the old Hakayaa I knew," Pindlebryth observed sarcastically as he sat back and folded his arms in an imitation of disbelief.

"But as the year passed, I found his studies and discussions about the Artifacts to be quite compelling. I was a mite surprised as you might expect, that what started out as a dodge, became an earnest and diligent subject of study. In time, it was in fact DeepDigger who advised me to not spend so much time on the study of Artifacts, and concentrate more on those studies which would actually help my degree. He was concerned that the time I spent with his research material would reflect badly on me with the rest of the history department, and become problematic come time for graduation."

"Fair enough. But now to the nub of the problem. On Vulcanis you became most agitated when you realized Keeyakawa or his master was intent on collecting all five Artifacts. What would happen if he were successful? What exactly was it that you feared so awfully?"

Kaiya sank back into the pillows, and stared at the ceiling. "I almost hesitate to answer – you might think me still stricken with the madness that overtook me on that island." He sighed, the trembling in his exhalation revealing a deep and disturbing fear. "The writings aren't clear about how it comes to be so, with the little that I have read. They are frustratingly obtuse about the final outcome. They speak of a cataclysmic bane, or an extraordinary boon. But about one thing the archives are painfully exact. It would be the sharp and sudden end of one era, and the beginning of another, spanning the entire world." Kaiya bowed his head, and closed his eyes as he drew in a breath with a final shiver.

"But why then would someone endeavour to do this? Why would anyone want to bring together all the five Artifacts?"

"Because they would have the power to control the outcome – to recreate the world in whatever image they desire."

Pindlebryth looked again out the window, as the gloaming dusk began to herald a dark and starless evening. His mind wandered as he tried to assimilate the magnitude of Kaiya's fear for quite a few moments, until he realized his mouth was slightly agape, and his vision was unfocused, as if he were trying to perceive an unknowable but dreadful future.

"If you feared this, why did you keep the Lens if you could not destroy it? Why not just drop it into the depths of MidSea?"

"Oh, poor Pindlebryth. Cooped up in Lenland and PanGaea all of his life," needled Kaiya. "In my travels to our many business interests around the world, I have seen things that would challenge the conception of the world held by many in the Northern Lands. Not only are there many peoples in other lands that have never heard of PanGaea, but our family have also had dealings with other races of the air. Do you think the Snow Goose and Crow the only races with flight and language? Do you think the peoples of the Northern Lands are the only ones capable of the spark of intelligence and civilization?

"There are creatures in this world you have yet to even dream of. Most are unintelligent beasts, but a choice few are not. There are leviathans of the ocean, as large as anything built by the shipwrights in the Lodges of the WeatherWorn. And I have seen that spark of intelligence in their eyes! Even if I were to consign the Lens to the deepest part of the Cetacean Ocean, who knows what undersea race would find it? Who knows what unforeseeable ruination from the deep it might bring upon the world?"

Pindlebryth regained his composure when he heard a small bell rapidly ringing from the floor below. He stood, realizing he had not eaten since the morning, and his appetite came roaring to the front of his attention. Pindlebryth tried his best to keep it at bay.

"Is there anything else you can tell me about the Artifacts?"

"Not that can be summarized easily. It's best if you talk to Professor DeepDigger directly, and see his books for yourself. You'll have to visit him at his home on Arbor Drive for that. The university does not look favorably on his predilection for Artifact research, and considers it a foolish hobby and a waste of time and resources. They have therefore forbidden his archives on the campus grounds."

"But why? We have seen the proof that at least one Artifact exists."

"It's not the Artifacts themselves that the Board of Regents refutes, but rather they frown upon the more metaphysical and occult attributes that DeepDigger ascribes to them. They have made it plain to the professor that his avocation is an 'exercise in ungrounded hysterics', and that if it in any way affects his duties at University, they will find some technicality to revoke his tenure."

Animated voices could be heard in the hallway. While the door muffled the discussion, it was clear that BroadShanks was energetically yet essentially amicably arguing with someone.

"Considering what we've just been through, they could not continue to hold that position."

"Ah, my friend. You underestimate the difficulty in making people see what they refuse to see."

"Very well. Although an attitude such as theirs rankles me, the Regents are not my bailiwick. I'll arrange to meet DeepDigger at his home tomorrow." Pindlebryth opened the door and left him, saying sardonically, "And now I leave you in the care of your mild-mannered nurse." Pindlebryth was barely through the doorway as BroadShanks shouldered her way past Pendenar, carrying a steaming bowl of porridge piled high with nuts and berries, and a large cup of tea that smelled with a subtle tincture of medicine.

BroadShanks fussed over her charge and prattled tirelessly, while ignoring Kaiya's dismayed complaint that he "will never be able to taste Mrs. SootBeak's cooking again."

Pindlebryth made his way to his room, where he found that HighStance had laid out his dinner attire on the bed, and set out a clothes tree for his black formal suit. He took a small bit of comfort that he did not need to be tended and dressed as he changed his own wardrobe. That was a custom he put up with when at the castle, but he preferred not to waste his staff's time and energy when away from Lenland's CityState. Besides, he needed the privacy to talk to Selephygur. He thought it strange that he could not bring himself to use the Talking Gem until he was fully dressed again.

"Selephygur?" he ventured. "Brother! Are you there?"

However, after several attempts, his frustration with the gem quickly grew as the device remained stubbornly silent. After a moment's thought, he realized it was late at night back home in Lenland, and Selephygur was probably away from his room or sleeping. Pindlebryth secreted the gem away in its place again, and resolved he would try again first thing the coming morning.

Downstairs, Pindlebryth fairly devoured the awaiting dinner that BroadShanks had prepared. He found he missed having a dinner companion to discuss events and plans for the future in confidence. While he would welcome Pendenar's company at the table, his guard's sense of duty would make him feel it above his station or outright improper. Even BroadShanks might be tolerable for a short while. And HighStance, who was waiting at the table's end, would be preferable, but he was about to be otherwise engaged.

"HighStance, please arrange a meeting with Professor DeepDigger at his residence on Arbor Drive tomorrow morning. Inform him it is of the utmost importance that I talk to him after morning meal. Make sure he understands I wish to see him at his home alone, not at University."

"Is there a letter or card you wish me to deliver?"

"Just one of my cards. I think Pendenar would want no undue publicity. Just let DeepDigger know he may expect me and Pendenar."

HighStance bowed quickly, and left to collect his outerwear. He took a deep breath of the fresh evening air, and left as Pendenar descended the stairway. "Who was at the door, M'Lord?"

"HighStance is running an errand for me, to arrange a meeting with Professor DeepDigger. We'll go talk to him tomorrow immediately after breakfast." He finished the last draught of wine with his meal, and added, "I think I'll turn in early. I will need to have my wits about me tomorrow."

The day did not start well for Pindlebryth. He slept fitfully, filled with dreams of foreboding, often degrading into delirium where his family, Kaiya and Darothien all met unkind and sometimes grisly fates. When dawn mercifully coaxed his eyes open, he rose from his bed and immediately tried several times to contact Selephygur. To his mounting annoyance, the Talking Gem was obdurately mute each time. Frustrated again and again, he practically threw the gem and its pouch back into its drawer. He dressed awkwardly and mechanically, as though he did not feel comfortable in his own pelt. And to top it all off, although breakfast was filling, it was strangely unfulfilling. HighStance and Pendenar both saw that their prince was in a moody state, and thought it best to be silent and leave him be. Only BroadShanks broke the silence, with almost continuous observations about the wonderful morning, the courses in the morning's fare, how well Hakayaa – Oops! – Kaiya was recovering, and all the busywork that she would be tending to today. But none of it penetrated Pindlebryth's senses.

He remained in his fog of worry and doubt long after breakfast, until Pendenar roused him out of his funk as the carriage rounded the corner onto Arbor Drive. The lane was short and the carriage quickly rolled up to the front of a house in need of paint and several days' work of mending.

An odd shutter leaned away from the wall on one good hinge, another window was crazed in one corner pane. The hedges and trees around the property were badly in need of pruning, and patches of sawgrass and weeds ran rampant across the ill-kept lawn. As Pindlebryth and Pendenar approached the front door, they noticed brass and stone work that had remained neither cleaned nor polished for several years. Pendenar knocked on the door, which rattled in its frame. After a second and third summons, the door finally creaked open. Pendenar clapped his paws together to shake off the patina of rust that came off from the doorknocker.

They were met by a Ferret charwoman, who eyed them suspiciously, and with nary a greeting she unconsciously smacked her lips as if she were tasting a tidy morsel. With a begrudging frown, she nodded and let them in. She closed the door behind them, and unceremoniously called up the stairs, "Perfesser! Yer visiters are here!"

A resounding tenor emanated from a side room near the bottom of the stairs, making the Ferret squeak and jump. "You needn't bellow so, Miss Roan. I can hear you from here. Please show our guests in."

The pair followed the charwoman into the room where they found Professor DeepDigger. He was an ermine with an immaculately groomed moustache, whiter than the rest of his fur. Its ends flowed along his jawline giving him an appearance not unlike that of an ancient dragon. He was pacing around a set of chairs and a couch, along with two end tables encircling a long low-slung table. A small pile of books and dozens of loose papers perched precariously on one of the heavily worn and distressed end tables. As he paced with a handful of papers, a myriad of dust motes swirled about him in the sunlight beaming in from the east window. He was well dressed, but his rumpled suit, waistcoat and all, looked as if he had slept in it for several weeks.

He stopped in aimless trudging, vainly attempted to straighten his clothes, and barked, "Miss Roan! Where are your manners? Take our guests' coats!" He then greeted them in a tired voice, "I am so pleased to finally make your formal acquaintance, Prince Pindlebryth. We had met before in passing at the Dean's Dinner when you first joined the University. Your doctoral advisor Professor GrayMask also has often spoken highly of you." A perceptible waver entered into his voice. "Hakayaa BlueHood also had regaled me with tales of your exploits together." In a slightly louder voice, he added, "Miss Roan, please bring us some brandy. From the glass cabinet, if you please – not the cupboard." Turning toward Pindlebryth he haltingly commented, "You'll have to excuse her. She's somewhat deaf." DeepDigger cleared his throat, acting as if it was irritated from the dust. "I know why you have come, Your Highness."

Pindlebryth felt vaguely uncomfortable. He was about to speak when Pendenar interjected, "Professor, the proper address is 'M'Lord'."

"My apologies. I stand corrected." DeepDigger's moustache twitched at the interruption. "But returning to the purpose of your visit – I have already heard of Hakayaa BlueHood's untimely passing. I have tried to occupy myself, burying myself in work, but I am afraid I cannot concentrate." He tossed his handful of papers on the already precarious stack of books and papers, and a few stragglers fluttered down onto the musty carpet.

Pendenar stepped forward. "If I may be so bold, if you have heard the whole story, then will you permit me to ensure the house is secure?"

The ermine was taken slightly by surprise, but acceded to Pendenar's request with several small nods. "Yes, of course." Pendenar bowed and left the room, following Miss Roan. Regaining his composure, DeepDigger turned to Pindlebryth. "I beg your pardon if I have offended you or your friend – I confess I am a mite confused."

"Do not be overly concerned. My guard Pendenar tends to be very protective, and sometimes a stickler for protocol. To be fair, your mistake is a common one."

"Ah, yes." DeepDigger put his right paw to his muzzle, and tapped it rapidly. "The underlying reason is coming back to me. I understand it translates into common tongue as the 'Quickening Spirit'?"

Pindlebryth felt even more uneasy, and somewhat defensive. He slowly and warily replied, "Yes."

"Ah! Put yourself at ease. I am not one who offhandedly belittles the notion of the Quickening Spirit. In my line of research, it is a recurring, if not an overarching, concept that is referred to quite often." In a lower tone, and almost commenting to himself, "Almost to the point where I sometimes wonder if I am becoming a believer myself."

"If that be the case, Professor, then no offense is taken. But, did Pendenar assume correctly – have you heard the whole story?"

"Well, I am not sure how anyone could answer such a question. I can only suppose, that by asking me, there is something concerning the sad event you wish to discuss."

"Yes. But first, how did you come by the news?"

"By two separate venues, actually. I was informed late last night by my department Regent. He relayed only the basics – that Master Hakayaa passed away overseas, and the body was lost. Later, I heard a much more detailed and lengthy report from Miss Roan, who in turn had spoken to Mrs. SootBeak in the morning marketplace." Looking past Pindlebryth's shoulder, he announced, "Ah! Speaking of whom, here she is with our brandy." With Pendenar a few steps behind her, she brushed various papers and knickknacks on the crowded table aside, and placed her tray in the new open space.

Pindlebryth was immediately reminded of the prediction from BroadShanks about Mrs. SootBeak's dissemination of news. He could only guess, however, about the accuracy of DeepDigger's information after it had been told and retold.

DeepDigger took the decanter and poured a portion of the brandy into two of the glasses. He was about to fill the third glass, when Pendenar declined the potable as he was on duty.

"Normally I do not partake this early in the day, but if you would be so kind as to join me in a toast." He waited for Pindlebryth to raise his glass, then cleared his throat. "To Hakayaa BlueHood. A fine student, and a dear friend. His wicked wit belied a kind heart. The world will be that much smaller without him."

Pindlebryth returned the toast, then braced himself, expecting an inferior liquor, but was pleasantly surprised by the excellent bouquet and flavor of the drink. He found himself thankful that DeepDigger steered Miss Roan specifically to the glass cabinet. DeepDigger took out a handkerchief and swatted the pillows on the couch across from the seat where he had been working, and motioned for Pindlebryth to take a seat. He did so, but found his nose involuntarily twitching from the cloud of dust raised.

"Thank you, Miss Roan. That will be all. So, M'Lord Pindlebryth, what additional news brings you here this morning?"

"Have you heard how Hakayaa met his end?"

"Yes, that he was poisoned by assassins." DeepDigger shook his head, still in disbelief and on the verge of tears. "*Poison*! How could he meet such an evil end?"

"He died shielding the intended target, my brother Prince Selephygur, from a Ravenne. But what you haven't heard yet is this – the accursed Ravenne assassin is still at large, and he made away with an item that Hakayaa recognized as an Artifact."

DeepDigger's head twitched as if someone yanked his

moustache. "An Artifact, you say?"

"Yes. A few days before the incident, we had only thought of the Artifacts as the stuff of legends. But Hakayaa identified an item Prince Selephygur possessed as the 'Lens of Truth.' He went on to describe to us many of its powers and abilities – some of which we actually observed in practice. He also said that you were an authority on the Artifacts, and would have a more detailed knowledge of such things."

"You... you actually *had* it?" The questions began to spill out of DeepDigger in a torrent. "And you say it actually exhibited powers? It's not just an intricate and ancient sculpture? You have proof! Finally a living witness! How did you come by this device? What things did it do?" The professor had a look of wild excitement in his eyes, as one might in anticipation of finding a box filled with gold. "But, I thought the Lens was in the possession of Vulpinden."

"It was. But that is an entirely different story. Suffice to say the Lens had been stolen by a Vixen witch, who attempted to use it to destroy the Royal Family of Lenland and enslave all of Lemming-kind. She failed, of course, otherwise we would not be having this conversation."

"Ah! That's what happened two years ago – the Lemmings' march to the sea. I recall that dark day." But DeepDigger's brow furrowed with incomprehension and awe, as he began anew to pace behind the chairs. "The Lens did all that?"

"I can only presume so, combined with some of the Vixen's own magick. I am not knowledgeable in these things.

"What brought events to a head, was that someone in the Rookeries of Kyaa learned Prince Selephygur was in possession of the Lens. Whether it was the Ravenne themselves, or they acted as some other party's agent, we do not know.

"But before the Ravenne assassin escaped with the Lens, he revealed something that alarmed Hakayaa utterly."

"And what, pray tell, was that?" said DeepDigger, stopping in his tracks.

"Someone is planning to amass all five Artifacts."

"Flood the Burrows!" DeepDigger almost jumped out of his pelt. "Do you know what that means? What exactly did Hakayaa say?" He began pacing still more rapidly, stroking his moustache in thought and watching Pindlebryth fiercely as he explained.

"You have to understand – when we found Hakayaa on

Vulcanis, he was lucid one moment, and raving the next. Given his familiarity with the Artifacts, I had to give credence to his fears." Pindlebryth began to feel once again the nervous ache in the pit of his stomach, as he faced revealing what Kaiya told him after Vulcanis from the comfort of his sickbed, but representing it as something Hakayaa told him on Vulcanis. He wasn't sure if it was due to the fact he was lying again about Hakayaa's death, or he was being infected by DeepDigger's nervous energy, or a lurking fear that DeepDigger would paint a picture even gloomier than the one Kaiya described. "He alluded to the end of the world."

Pindlebryth recognized the look that overcame DeepDigger – Hakayaa showed the same incredulous dread at the revelation back on Vulcanis. He stopped in front of his chair and collapsed into it. The sudden movement of air fluttered several papers off their unstable piles, but DeepDigger paid them no mind.

Pindlebryth allowed DeepDigger a few moments to compose himself, before continuing. "I'm sorry to impose on you at such a time, but I need your help. I, the Royal Family, and possibly all of Lenland have been thrust into this affair, and we have little with which to defend ourselves."

DeepDigger looked at Pindlebryth with pleading eyes, as if he were about to be plunged into nightmare. "Oh yes, you had best believe it can affect Lenland! Hakayaa was correct. It may endanger the entire world." He sat erect, and took a moment to preen his face and moustache, then cleared his throat. "You must excuse me – it is quite overwhelming!

"The entire body of academia doesn't deny the existence of the Artifacts, but rather they simply regard the Artifacts as exquisitely created totems of government authority, or racial superiority. I've worked so long to research and collect clues, trying for years to prove to my peers that the widely held version of their history has erased something wondrous and important," he said breathing shallowly and rapidly. Almost panting, he added, "Then to find in one fell swoop that solid evidence exists of the power of Artifacts – only to learn that the same proof for which you searched tirelessly and railed against disbelievers and sneering skeptics, now augurs the End of All Things?"

Pindlebryth mused aloud to himself, "Perhaps history has intentionally erased evidence regarding the mystique and power of the Artifacts for that very reason." He shook his head to clear it, and focus on the task at hand. "But what is done, is done. I need your help. The Ravenne have drawings of all the Artifacts, and maps that roughly indicate where they are. What most concerns me, is that they believe Lenland still has one – its own Artifact."

DeepDigger regarded him quizzically. "But, you *do*."

Pindlebryth was abashed. "But where? Until a few days ago, we did not even conceive we *had* an Artifact, let alone that any existed! That is why I am asking your help – we need to find that Artifact before the Ravenne do. We need to protect it, or perhaps even move it from where their maps indicate it is.

"Hakayaa said he had read something he called your 'archives'. Where do you have these references?"

The professor stood, and marched towards the hallway, and bellowed in his piercing tenor, "Miss Roan!" There was a scurry of footfalls out of sight, until she rounded the corner.

"Miss Roan, your services are not needed today. Please gather your things, and I will see you at the usual time tomorrow morning." He stood and impatiently watched as she disappeared back the way she came. She reemerged with a shawl and a light coat, cap and her bag, and hurried out the front door.

"G'day to you all, sirs," she jabbered curtly as she sped past, obviously conflicted at being unceremoniously ordered out of the house, but on the other hand having gotten the rest of the day off. Pendenar followed her to the front door, and locked it behind her.

"Follow me," DeepDigger intoned with little emotion as he began to climb the staircase. Pindlebryth and Pendenar followed him as he rounded the upstairs hallway and climbed the second set of stairs. At the top of the staircase was a padlocked door to what was ostensibly an attic. There were no windows at the platform, and the only light came from the second floor below. On either side of the door were hung a pair of intricately constructed lamps. The base of each hung from the wall, to which was attached a pivoting fulcrum. In turn the arm held a hurricane lamp, which was weighted to hang aright. DeepDigger removed one of the lamps from the wall, and pressed a raised square button just below the bottom of the glass enclosure. A tiny amount of wick rose from its central slot, and a spark inside the glass lit it. For its size, the lamp quickly spread a remarkably bright and steady light.

"Please take the other lamp." DeepDigger reached in his waistcoat, and pulled out a watch. Fumbling at the other end of its chain, he produced a watch fob and two keys. "Please be very careful inside my sanctum. Many of the items you will find there are irreplaceable." He selected the larger of the keys, and unlocked the door. With some effort he pushed it open with a long rusty creak, and entered in. Pindlebryth took and lit the second lamp with cautious unfamiliarity, and followed.

Inside was a windowless room, barely large enough to contain two people. Peering inside, Pendenar stayed outside of the room, and stood to the side of the landing to look past the two flights of stairs and monitor both the room and the lower floors' hallways.

The walls of the remodeled attic were festooned with shelves and bookracks, containing binders of loose papers, scores of books in various states of disrepair and decrepitude, several small statuary and models, and a handful of dioramas. Pindlebryth momentarily regarded the statuary, but felt strangely disturbed at the peculiar stances of the subjects. Nor could he shake the feeling that their visages were oddly familiar.

On the bottommost portion of the center bookrack was an oblong metal panel with four hefty metal disks with recessed handles, one in each corner. A small desk was wedged into a tiny workspace, with two books resting on its blotter: one a crusty antique tome that fairly radiated an aura of extreme age, and next to it a notebook filled with miniscule and frantic scribbling.

Pindlebryth scanned the spines of the books and the labels of binders and scrolls that could be read without disturbing them. He found only a handful were in a language he was familiar with, all the rest were in what he vaguely recognized as Raccoon. His heart sank into disappointment as he surmised that most of this unique find of a library was currently unknowable to him.

It was then that he noticed the state of the room – although crowded and pungent with the scent of old vellum, it was immaculate. Not a single mote of dust could be found on any surface of wood, stone or glass. And even though it at first seemed claustrophobic and chaotic, he soon appreciated that there was a place for everything, and everything in its place.

DeepDigger went behind the desk and opened the topmost

drawer, from which he produced two pairs of white cotton gloves. He placed one pair across the desk, and proceeded to put on the other.

"Please use these gloves to handle anything in this room," he directed as he might someone in a classroom. Pindlebryth donned the gloves, only to find they were ill fitting for a Lemming, and the fingertips were stained beige from touching countless pieces of parchment and binding.

DeepDigger looked misty-eyed around the room, and reflected, "There have only been three people besides myself in this room. Yourself, Hakayaa, and my mentor. He was a wise old Raccoon who knew so much more than I about the Artifacts. It was a sad day indeed when he passed on so many years ago. He knew his end was soon in coming, so he gave the entire portion of his library on the subject of Artifacts to me. I have since added my own meager contribution to the collection – much to the dereliction of the rest of my estate. I sometimes wonder if that old rascal in turn was bequeathed his mentor's library."

"Raccoon?" Pindlebryth mused. "That is the language in which most of these books are written? I barely recognized it."

"Yes, that is so – although the present-day Raccoon language is quite different from ages past. In their history, they wrote many treatises about the Artifacts. Sadly, only a small amount survives to this day. Most of which are within these walls. Several of these books refer to other works that had been destroyed by ignorant mobs and politicians, had dry-rotted and crumbled to dust in nameless vaults, or are otherwise impossible to find.

"I had a meager working knowledge of the Raccoon language from living near our country's border with Esepanauk in my youth. I later learned a little more from my mentor, and from studying his library. Hakayaa told me that you are fluent in many languages, and adept in some others. Do you know the Raccoon tongue?"

"Frustratingly, no," Pindlebryth replied with a grimace. "Lenland unfortunately never initiated relations with Esepanauk."

"Oh," DeepDigger replied with disappointment. "I had hoped you might. There is much written there that I simply am not able to translate on my own. And I have been most anxious to find anything they may have written concerning their own

Artifact. However, I am afraid I might lose my tenure if I approached any of the language professors at University for assistance, and the Regents got wind of it. So I muddle on as best as I can."

DeepDigger gingerly stepped over to the bookshelf. "Now where to begin?" he muttered, as he ran a finger along the wood starting from the top shelf. With a small exclamation of satisfaction, he stopped in the middle of the second shelf, and carefully pulled out a tome with a threadbare binding. He set the book on the remaining open space on his desk, and slowly and carefully paged through it.

"Prince Pindlebryth, you had touched on the subject of the Quickening Spirit earlier." As he continued his concentration on the pages of the book, he continued, "Could you elaborate, specifically how that affects the succession of your country's monarchy?"

A glimmer of impatience grew in Pindlebryth. "How does this help us, exactly?"

"Humor me, M'Lord," DeepDigger patiently replied as he turned each precious page one by one.

With a sigh of exasperation, Pindlebryth began. "The Quickening Spirit enters the dreams of the entire nation of Lenland the night after the monarch's passing. It is in that dream that the heir is named, for all to know."

"I suppose it makes the rite of succession much less contentious."

"Quite so. Although historically, the heir to the throne thus far has been an offspring of the current monarch, there is no guarantee that it will always be so."

"Ah, that explains the whys and wherefores of Pendenar's remonstration."

"Yes. There is no contention or rivalry, let alone any double-dealing to usurp the throne. In addition, it is nearly impossible to ransom or threaten the new monarch-to-be, as the successor has a Name of Power and therefore already resides in the CityState or castle directly. Any false pretender with machinations on the monarchy is simply ignored, and in at least one case, banished outright."

"Oh, that would be the Iron Baron of Lenland?"

"Correct. Curious that you know of him."

"I am a professor of history, after all!" said DeepDigger as he looked up at Pindlebryth with a smirk. "Besides, his exile was notorious in several countries. Especially when it was learned he was banished to the MidSea Archipelago – many countries argued it contravened the PanGaean Accords."

DeepDigger stopped paging, and leaned closer to the page to which the book was now open. He seemed to be searching for something as he spoke further. "If I am correct, the Quickening Spirit is also responsible for allotting various members of your people these Names of Power."

"Yes, that is so."

"That is the Quickening Spirit's gift to your people, just as he gave gifts to the other First Speakers."

"The what?"

"According to this record set down many centuries ago by the Raccoon, the Quickening Spirit chose five races to be the 'First Speakers'. To these people he gave the gift of their own language, and a unique talent to assist themselves, and a Seal to prove their covenant. To each of these peoples, he also gave an Artifact. Five First Speakers, five Artifacts, five Seals, five abilities, five languages. Of course, there are many more languages than that today. Over the ages, many other peoples learned how to speak, and evolved their own dialects and sub-tongues. Even the Polar Bear have their own spoken language – although they have no written language. Perhaps because there are no reeds or trees to make paper in their northern wastelands."

Pindlebryth was momentarily distracted by the sound of Pendenar snickering outside the tiny study.

"The point is, each of the First Speakers was given several Gifts. Not only language, and the Artifacts, but also special faculties. The Crow, Fox and Raccoon, each have the ability to shapeshift – although each race has unique restrictions on how they may use it. The Snow Geese have the ability of unerring location – they never get lost, and they instinctively know where to find anything in the world, with the exceptions of Artifacts. And the Lemmings have the gift of, as best I can translate from this Raccoon passage, 'communal knowledge'. Your people can share thoughts or decisions to affect the common good." DeepDigger was about to twirl his moustache in thought, but caught himself before he might contaminate his cotton gloves. "Furthermore, yours is the only people where the Gift, from one extent to the other, is born into the entire populace – every other Gift manifests only in a small portion of individuals and family lines of that race. It must have been this ability that the Vixen witch somehow perverted to enslave your people.

"But such an aberration could not be done solely by mortal magick, although possibly so in tandem with an Artifact. She must have employed some power of the Lens of Truth to wreak her mischief."

DeepDigger pointed to a paragraph in the book after he spoke, and he moved aside for Pindlebryth to read. Pindlebryth squinted at the book as he unsuccessfully tried to make sense of the curious but impenetrable writing of the ancient Raccoon.

"Wait, Professor." Pindlebryth shook his head. "You said we Lemmings have an Artifact. The Crow also believe we have an Artifact. And I've seen the remnants of age-old ringed devices that also indicate we have an Artifact." He held out his paws beseechingly. "But we know of no such thing. We don't know where it is, and we certainly don't even know what Artifact we are supposed to have!"

"Ringed devices? You've seen these? What did they look like?"

"We possess the broken pieces of five of them. They were broken when the Vixen died by her own magick. Our wizard brought them back with us from the Vixen's lair."

"What else did they tell you?"

"Very little. Each had engravings in the various First Speaker languages, but much of the rings' writings were glyphs, the like of which I have never seen before."

DeepDigger inhaled sharply, and his face belied he couldn't believe his ears. "For so many years, I've looked in vain for items other than books and writings. And here, you had not only an Artifact in your possession, but also the five Seals!" His legs momentarily gave out underneath him, but he was able to right himself by leaning against his desk.

With renewed energy, DeepDigger scanned the room about him, and focused on a grey book with an unwinding spine on the topmost shelf. But first, one by one, he delicately collected each of the books already on his diminutive desk, and deliberately slid it into its place on the shelves. Over his shoulder he asked, "Can you read Vulpine?"

"Yes, I am fluent in the Fox tongue."

"Excellent." DeepDigger deftly slid the grey book from its place, and carried it with both hands to his workspace. He methodically opened the book, wincing involuntarily as the spine creaked.

"This is a work translated into Fox from the original Raccoon text I previously showed you. My own ability in Vulpine is quite rudimentary, but good enough for me to see some major differences. I can tell it is inferior in two aspects: firstly, like any such work, there are phrases, idiomatic expressions, inferences, and myriad other phrases that are lost in translation; secondly, a large amount of information concerning the Fox's Artifact, the Lens of Truth, is omitted. Like many First Speaker races, they jealously guard such information. But since you already have had experience with the Lens, that omission is moot. Perhaps later you can help me make a full comparison between the two texts.

"However, this text has one thing the original Raccoon tome does not."

DeepDigger pulled back the first sheet to reveal the title page. Surrounding the title were diagrams of the Seals.

"That's them! The ring with five sides is the one that was for the Lemmings. Can this book help me decipher the glyphs?"

"Sadly, no. That is a language lost to antiquity. Some zealots call it the 'Holy Language of the Quickening Spirit'." Pindlebryth blinked, as he suddenly recalled Darothien had reached the same conclusion. "Of course, proof of such a claim is not forthcoming."   Seeing Pindlebryth's disappointment, DeepDigger added, "But for now let us at least answer one of your previous questions."

He paged slowly until he came to a page with the first word stylishly illuminated with gold leaf and exotic inks. "The Lens of Truth is listed first, out of sheer Vulpine pride." DeepDigger turned a scant few pages to the next illuminated section, and stepped aside and invited Pindlebryth to read as he spoke further. "The Crow received the Prism of Persuasion, which imbues a power of personality. The bearer not only can be a charismatic force, able to win any argument, debate, test of wills, but also can dominate and lead large groups with unquestioning loyalty." He methodically paged to yet another section, the beginning of which was similarly embellished. "The Snow Geese were given the Vessel of Sorrows, a receptacle for memories of the living, and possibly even those of the dead. The text goes on to say the user has the ability to manipulate the emotions of others."   With the next section, he said, "The Raccoon were allotted the Ring of Fortitude, the primary purpose of which is to sustain the life of the bearer against disease, poison or weapon. It also has the ability to make the mind of the bearer an unassailable fortress – as if it is meant to be a defense against the effects of the other Artifacts. And finally," he announced with a flourish turning to the last section, "the Lemmings were given the Orb of Oblivion. At first blush, according to this somewhat biased record, it seems to be the least powerful of the Artifacts. It can be used to make the bearer or another individual forget."

Pindlebryth paused following DeepDigger in the book. "On reflection, this is probably why the Artifact has been lost."

"An interesting theory. But the manuscript goes on to refer to another ability. However, it fails to describe what that power is. From the Fox translation, one might be led to believe the Orb made the writer forget what that power was. But the original Raccoon implies the omission was purposefully made."

"Most peculiar indeed. So is there nothing else in this library that can help me learn more and possibly locate this Orb?"

DeepDigger scrutinized Pindlebryth for a few seconds. He gathered the loosely bound book, and placed it back in its proper position. "If I may beg your indulgence?" he asked as he went to the door. He began to close it, but was stopped as Pendenar rushed over and blocked the door.

Pindlebryth likewise took his scope of DeepDigger, assessed his intent and responded, "It's all right Pendenar. Please wait for us." Pendenar stepped back, with obvious concern and a measure of distrust in his eyes, as the professor closed the door.

DeepDigger squatted down in front of the large metal box built into the bookcase. One by one, he turned the dial in each of the four corners to seemingly random positions. As he did so, Pindlebryth noticed each dial was marked with an arrow on the recessed handle, and gradations like a clock face along its circular edge. When DeepDigger finished with the last tumbler, he selected two of the handles and pulled. The entire metal face rolled out barely a paw's width then stopped with a firm click. DeepDigger then took the smaller key at the end of his watch's chain, and unlocked a latch hidden inside the drawer. He pulled open the drawer to its full extent exposing a large solitary tome inside a compartment lined with white sandstone.

"This is my prize possession, and I must ask that you not handle it." He lifted the untitled book with reverence, and laid

it on his desk. As DeepDigger began to leaf through it a page at a time, the pages made a sound unlike paper or parchment or even vellum, but almost like a sail being unfurled. Pindlebryth stepped closer to view its contents. He was immediately struck by two differences – there were diagrams with notations not unlike those of a blueprint, but more surprising, the book was written in Lemming.

"You didn't say you had any books in our language!" he exclaimed.

"Is *that* what you see?"   He regarded Pindlebryth's expression for a moment, then added, "To me it is written in the language of my people, and Hakayaa observed it was written in his native Crow."

"So... it is perceived by each reader in their own language? Astounding! I think our court sorceress would give almost anything to see this! I, too must confess I find it quite maddening to have such a treasure in front of me, and to be forbidden to touch it."

"Well, then by all means, M'Lord. Help yourself," DeepDigger said with a knowing smile as he stepped aside. Pindlebryth eyed him suspiciously, but regardless stepped closer and attempted to turn the next page. An orange spark danced between his fingers, as he recoiled in pain. The sensation was like that of touching metal after walking over a woolen rug, and he could detect a whiff of ozone in the air.

"My apologies, but it is not my doing. The book seems to know who its owner is. Now, if you will permit me."

"How did you come by this item?"

"Perhaps one day I will tell you that particular misadventure, but only when my already precarious tenure would not be at risk."

DeepDigger resumed revealing the contents page by page. Pindlebryth breathlessly scanned each paragraph, but frustration mounted with each turn of the page. Although he could make out the magicked words in their excessively baroque cursive script, he found their disjointed context confusing. With time, he might be able to make sense of the entire work, but he soon realized he could not glean much meaning from it in the day left to him.

The main thrust of the first part of the book seemed to be a severely condensed history of the creation of the Artifacts in long ages past. Following it were verbose sections of annoyingly cryptic descriptions of the Artifacts and their abilities.

Pindlebryth soon found himself simply overwhelmed by the enigmatic writings, and began to focus more on the diagrams accompanying the text. He tried to commit to memory the diagrams of the various Artifacts, but he found he was distracted by other drawings that were paired with each Artifact.

They were not of a device or mechanical in nature, but were renderings of some sort of living creature. They stood erect with strange extremities that resembled arms and legs, but what was more curious about their stature were those additional appendages that appeared to be wings. Most disturbing of all was each creature's visage. It was simultaneously beautiful yet terrifying.

That familiar yet vexatious itch in his mind made him look around the study. He fixed his gaze on one of the statuettes on the shelves. As he recognized it was a rendering of the same creature, a sudden realization fell in on him like a thundering waterfall. He had seen this face before.

"Professor, what are these creatures?" he blurted out impatiently.

"These are the five Angels of the Artifacts. They were messengers sent by the Quickening Spirit, each to deliver the Artifacts to chosen representatives of their respective First Speakers. They are purported to have names, but they cannot be uttered by any mortal tongue."

"I have seen them all before. Their faces are inscribed on the scabbard holding the Sword of Enorel."

"Indeed? Most interesting."

"So another of our legends is true?" Pindlebryth spoke unsteadily, barely able to dare believe it himself. "These Angels were not only bringers of gifts, but also of wisdom – they were advisers to our first King." He steadied himself against the desk, careful not to touch the book, and took a deep breath. "Show me the Orb of Oblivion."

DeepDigger's shoulders sagged. "I'm afraid you will be disappointed." He turned the next page that displayed a drawing of a small portion of a sphere with no distinguishing marks. Most of the Orb was depicted as covered with a cloth. The covering was embroidered with glyphs and sigils that resembled Darothien's arcane magick symbols.

Pindlebryth rubbed his forehead, and felt as if his mind were about to break into splinters. The fate of his friend Hakayaa, the threat of an apocalypse, the revelations of the Artifacts, and the frustration of the impenetrable mystery surrounding the Orb all pounded at his temples. "What is that draped over the Orb?"

"A shield of some sort, to protect the holder from the Orb." DeepDigger gently parceled several pages at once to turn to the last chapter. "Read this section here." Pindlebryth attempted to do so, but it was as enigmatic and disjointed as the rest of the codex. After standing by and observing Pindlebryth's consternation, DeepDigger summarized what he understood.

"Some Artifacts, though none besides the Orb are named outright, have an effect on their users. This reaction is brought on by each use of the Artifact, and in some cases their effects might even be brought on by touch. Some Artifacts affect the mind, others the physical body, some both. Moreover, the consequences are cumulative in many cases."

Pindlebryth felt his legs tremble, his mind filled with a myriad of possibilities and dire apprehensions. How many times had Selephygur unknowingly and innocently used the power of the Lens? What changes were imposed on him by being constantly in the most intimate physical contact with the Lens for the first several years of his life?

"Furthermore, the book goes on to describe a certain strange and unique *strength* in each Artifact. The best way I can describe it, is that each Artifact has wants and desires. If you will, a *will* of its own.

"The Orb of Oblivion has the strongest will of all the Artifacts – it wants to be alone, to be secreted away. Anyone who touches it directly may be overcome by that overarching desire. How the Orb manages to do this is a mystery, but the book states that this cloth protects the bearer from that coercion."

"So, you are telling me that the Orb may be impossible to find."

"I'm afraid so. I can't help you with finding where the Orb might be. However, I do recall having some record of who was originally entrusted with each of the Artifacts. Perhaps that can give you a clue where to start looking."

"Would that not be King Enorel the Great?" puzzled Pindlebryth.

"Not necessarily. But before we answer that question, there is one last thing this codex has to offer." DeepDigger ruffled to the last page of the tome. Pindlebryth looked about the room with some trepidation. Though the lamps' flames were undisturbed and their light undiminished, the tiny room seemed noticeably darker. Returning his attention to the book, the professor was pointing to the middle paragraph on the page. Pindlebryth tried to piece together the impenetrably obtuse prose. Though it made little sense as a whole, he did see several phrases that he recognized, sending a thrill up his spine – an admonishment against bringing all the Artifacts together, a warning of great bane or great blessing, and a repeated reference to the End of All Things.

"Now you see why our friend Hakayaa was so upset. Why he tried to keep the Lens from the Ravenne."

DeepDigger closed the ponderous book with reverence, and placed it back in its stone and metal drawer. Pindlebryth still stared at the empty desk. Lost in indecision, his mind balked at accepting the proof that had lain in front of him. He slapped the sides of his muzzle with his paws, snapping himself out of his malaise.

"Wait. One item I have not seen in this book, is a depiction of a circlet with five gems," said Pindlebryth before the book was fully locked away. "Found in the Vixen's private quarters, it was a perfect circle with five prongs rising at equal intervals, and a solitary glowing gem set on each. The five gems were originally of different colors, although when I most recently observed it, the gems were colorless and dark."

"Oh? Where is it now?"

"I have sent it on ahead for our wizard to examine it."

DeepDigger rubbed his knuckles on his moustache for a moment, then commented as he looked at his library, "I don't think I have come across such an item. It must be something that your Vixen witch had constructed. If your wizard does divine something about its nature, I am most interested to learn about it, too."

Returning his attention to the metal drawer, he closed it and locked it with his key. After spinning each of the dials, he returned to the library's outer door and opened it.

"You see? Safe and sound," he reassured Pendenar. "Now to the task at hand." He sidled back and forth along the bookshelf, shuffling through one manuscript, then another, then a loosely bound sheaf of papers, all the while mumbling to himself, "No," then "That isn't it," and "Where are you? Ah! Here we are!"

DeepDigger placed a book hand-labeled in cursive "Compendium of Recipients" on his desk and began to leaf through its chapters. Pindlebryth observed each chapter was written in a different language. He could recognize the chapters in Fox and Crow, Snow Goose, and what he assumed was Raccoon, until the final chapter was reached. It was written in Lemming.

"You will have to read for yourself here, my ability to read Lemming is practically nonexistent."

Pindlebryth leaned in and drew a surprised breath. "It's written by Gazelikus! He was the Wizard of Lenland's first Royal Court." He was about to jump to the conclusion that the great wizard of old was the trustee of the Orb, but something made him read on. Holding his finger just above the pages so as to not damage the paper or inks, he scanned the text, flitting back and forth along groups of lines, until he came to the answer he needed. He stepped back, looking incredulously at what he just read.

"Henejer? The Orb was entrusted to King Enorel's Royal Architect? That makes no sense at all! Why was not Enorel the Great its recipient? Or Gazelikus himself? Either would have been a much clearer choice, I would think."

"Who knows what the Quickening Spirit or his Messengers intended? Unless you pretend to know their minds, M'Lord," DeepDigger chided.

Pindlebryth shot DeepDigger a cross momentary glare, which quickly softened as he took the chastisement in the spirit it was meant. "It's all just so much to take in."

Pindlebryth continued to digest Gazelikus' writings. He had hoped it would contain insights about Enorel or Henejer, or hints about where the Orb of Oblivion might be hidden, but he was to be disappointed once more. The only paragraph that caught his attention was a description in maddeningly general terms about how he, Gazelikus, created a cloth to protect Henejer from the Orb. At the end of the chapter, Pindlebryth closed the book, closed his eyes and tried to breathe a sigh of finality. But he was not assuaged – his mind still reeled with concern for his brother. There was so much about which he had to warn Selephygur, his family and Darothien.

What changes were already manifest in Selephygur? In fact, was any of the original Selephygur still intact? What affect did the Lens continue to have on him, when he saw through the Lens remotely? How would he and his family react when they were informed not only of his ability, but also its potential harmful reaction? Would they try to capitalize on its capacity to spy, regardless of that cost? Pindlebryth could feel the cotton gloves begin to wick away the perspiration on his paws.

He wanted to ply DeepDigger for more information, but he feared a detailed conversation would lead him to fully divulge Hakayaa's initial treachery, thereby sullying DeepDigger's memory of him – all the while fearing he might let slip

Selephygur's current ability and peril, and clues that Hakayaa was still alive in the persona of Kaiya.

Pindlebryth looked around the contents of the confining room one last time. "I must leave for home within the day. You've given me much to think about during my trip. But rest assured I will return before the next semester begins. I will undoubtedly have several more questions that we may need to research here further." Pindlebryth removed his gloves and handed them back to DeepDigger.

"My door is always open." DeepDigger placed the last book back in its place, and left both pairs of gloves on top of his desk. He collected the two lamps, and one by one, hung them on the outside wall. As he set them in their places, the wicks retracted and the light was snuffed. The trio descended both sets of stairs, with Pendenar separating his charge and DeepDigger. As Pindlebryth donned his coat hanging next to the front door, Pendenar swatted Miss Roan's dusty paw prints off the collar and shoulders.

As his guests left, DeepDigger cursorily said, "Until we meet again," and returned to his parlor, beginning to pace once again. As Pindlebryth and Pendenar stepped into the waiting carriage, they could see DeepDigger occasionally pass his grime-fogged windows, twirling his moustache in thought.

By the time the carriage arrived at his apartments, Pindlebryth said nary a word, under the concerned and watchful eye of Pendenar. His mind was spinning with an overflow of new information, new concerns and fears, and new doubts. On top of it all was that familiar and nagging itch of intuition that told him he was overlooking an important connection.

As he trudged from the carriage to his front door, he tried to calm himself by taking several deep breaths of the cool afternoon air tinged with salt from the ocean breeze. He scanned the skies to the west to see if the weather for traveling tomorrow morn would be favorable. He took some small comfort that the deep blue sky was streaked only occasionally with the highest clouds. Pendenar shepherded him to the front door, as HighStance opened it to greet him and collect his outerwear.

Still lost in thought, Pindlebryth climbed the stairs to his room, and found the Talking Gem where he left it. He began to absentmindedly pace about the room, as he attempted to call

Selephygur. After hearing nothing for the first few attempts, he caught himself in mid-stride, and forced himself to set along the edge of the bed facing the southern window. On the third effort, he breathed a happy sigh of relief as Selephygur answered.

"Pindlebryth! I finally got you!" Selephygur exploded. "This device of Darothien's is wonderful, but it is bloody frustrating! I've been trying to reach you all day."

Pindlebryth resisted the urge to laugh, but did manage a sympathetic smile. "You don't know the half of it, brother. Likewise, I've been trying to reach you since I arrived here in PanGaea. Listen – are you alone?"

"I've got so much to tell you. The arrangements for..."

"Selephygur, be still! Are you alone?"

There was a moment of silence from the gem, then a cautious, "Yes?"

"Have you told anyone about how you found Hakayaa on Vulcanis? Have you told anyone that you can still have a connection with the Lens?"

"Only poor LongBack."

"Good. Tell no one else for now. We will inform Mother and Father and Darothien when I arrive tomorrow. But not until then."

"All right," Selephygur said slowly and cautiously.

"And one other thing. Do not attempt to see with the Lens again. There may be a danger associated with it."

It was obvious from his tone that Selephygur fought urgent curiosity as he responded simply, "I understand." After a short silence he ventured, "Are you all right, brother?"

"Yes, I am fine. But over the past two days I have had to notify the authorities and many of Hakayaa's friends of his passing. It has been quite draining, and I look forward to being home again."

"We all look forward to seeing you. The memorial will be the morning after you arrive. May your travel be speedy and uneventful."

"Thank you, Selephygur." Pindlebryth sighed with resignation, "I am afraid I must go. I have a few loose ends to tie up here, and then of course I must prepare for the trip if I am to be home in time. I look forward to hearing all your news when I land. Keep well."

"You as well, dear brother."

He wrapped the gem, and laid it on the bed. He then went to his closet and pulled out his riding gear, and a few sundry garments he might need for the trip.

He pulled the velvet strap to call for HighStance, who arrived as Pindlebryth was placing the last of his travel wardrobe on the bed. "Be good enough to have Pendenar go the Double Eagle stables and prepare Voyager and his own mount for departure before sunset. Make sure we have overnight rolls packed."

"Very well, I'll inform Pendenar. He's already spot cleaning his uniform and riding gear."

"How is Kaiya doing?"

"He's resting soundly after having a meal and chamomile tea laced with BroadShanks' latest concoction. I don't think Old Bellows in the Eastern Bay lighthouse could wake him, even if it blew directly above his bed."

"Alright. If you would, please also have BroadShanks prepare meals for our journey."

"Very good, M'Lord. Do you know when you will be returning to PanGaea?"

"I couldn't say, exactly. I hope to return as soon as possible after the memorial, so as to study more of Professor DeepDigger's library before the next semester starts in two weeks. However, I have much work that may detain me in Lenland until the first day of classes."

HighStance bowed, and set about his errands. Pindlebryth made quick work of packing, as he had made the trip from PanGaea to Lenland and back several times, and had been on bivouac dozens more. He took special care in placing the pouch with the Talking Gem securely in an inner pocket of his rucksack. In the hallway, standing in front of Kaiya's door, he could look partway into Pendenar's room, and see that he too was fully prepared for travel – even to having freshly cleaned his riding gear.

Pindlebryth quietly opened the door to check on Kaiya. Though sound asleep, he had still managed to ruffle his covers and sheets all askew. Pindlebryth stole to his bedside and tried to arrange the bedding. His body from the neck down still only had the barest of gray pinfeathers, featherlets and quills. Kaiya had attempted to shield his eyes under his topmost limb, but it did not afford the shade that a fully fledged wing would have. Despite the ministrations of BroadShanks, Kaiya still looked lean to the point of being emaciated. He tried to imagine the body of the old Hakayaa, and how his past blue, gray and coal-black plumage filled out his form, but he could not envision how Kaiya would even approach the old Hakayaa's bearing and posture. What wasted Kaiya's body so – was it the proximity of the Lens, as DeepDigger forewarned? Pindlebryth quickly dismissed that. For if it were so, surely Selephygur would have suffered infinitely more. Either the Ravenne's poison or something else ravaged Kaiya's body. Perhaps Selephygur had something Kaiya did not – perhaps the spell by the Vixen witch queen somehow guarded Selephygur against the Lens. He sorely wished he could ask DeepDigger's advice on this point, but the risk that such a line of questioning would reveal that Hakayaa was alive was too great.

Pindlebryth clasped him on the shoulder one last time, and quietly whispered, "Goodbye, Kaiya. Take care of yourself until I return." Closing the door behind him, he went downstairs and made his way to the kitchen. He savored the aroma that greeted him even from the far end of the dining room, and was smiling as he breathed in deeply the steaming bouquet of savory and spice.

BroadShanks barely looked up from her counter where she was mixing and pressing out granola and hardtack, saying cynically, "It's mid-afternoon, M'Lord. And I'll wager you haven't had a midday meal. It's a wonder we both don't waste away with worry! I have something for you and Pendenar at the breakfast nook." She pointed over her shoulder with her rolling pin. "Your meal for travel will be ready within the half-hour." She placed a tin holding the nut and grain goods into the oven, and let the door close with a slam. "Now where is that layabout HighStance? He promised he would help me wash up!"

Pindlebryth leisurely ate the meal of salad, seeds and breads. He was just about to finish, when Pendenar and HighStance came downstairs from the roof.

"Voyager and my tern are hitched and ready to go. I was also able to get their feed provisions from the stables."

"Have a seat here, Pendenar." Pindlebryth motioned to the chair across from him. "When you're finished, we can load up and be on our way." He leaned back in his chair, occasionally sipping from his mug of mango juice, alternately watching Pendenar wolf down his meal, and BroadShanks and HighStance cleaning the counters, stove, mixing bowls and utensils. Quicker than he expected, Pendenar finished and declared, "We can leave at your convenience, M'Lord."

"Oh no, you don't!" scolded BroadShanks, her voice suddenly reaching a commanding soprano. "You'll have to wait for your meal to settle, or you'll be sick before you're out over the sea! Besides, your travel meal still is baking. I don't know where these bucks get the urge to rush, rush, rush!" She continued with a litany of complaints, instructions, neighborhood news, and commands as she tended to her beloved kitchen. Both Pendenar and Pindlebryth looked to HighStance for help, who could only give them a wise glance that spoke volumes – as if to say "pay attention, or suffer the consequences." Within a few minutes, a timer rang a single chime. BroadShanks pulled out the tin baking sheets, and a wave of delicious warmth bathed the entire room. As she deftly wrapped the baked goods into parcels with cloth, she said "Alright, you can get your things collected and outfit your rides. These goodies will be ready by the time you're ready to leave."

The trio quickly evacuated the kitchen to each of their preparations – Pendenar and Pindlebryth both donned their riding gear and outerwear, while HighStance collected the sacks and rolls and took them to the roof. He returned with BroadShanks' freshly prepared meals, as the others packed and strapped their luggage to their mounts.

After Voyager pestered Pindlebryth to be petted, the two Lemmings double-checked their tack and climbed astride the steeds. The mounts stretched their wings and tails, and arched their necks from side to side. Just before they departed, Pindlebryth said, "I cannot say if I may be back in a few days, or just before classes begin. Make sure Kaiya gets the best of care. Remember he is to have a minimum of visitors, and only if he can maintain the guise of one of us Lemmings."

Voyager and Pendenar's tern held their wings aloft and apart, and crouched low. They then one after the other darted to the edge of the roof, and sprung upwards as they leapt off the edge of the building. Though the sun was dropping towards the horizon, the ocean breeze still afforded the mounts a goodly lift. Off they soared, circling a handful of times on the rising thermals from the city, before they both headed eastward over the sea.

VI - Farewells and Introductions

As soon as Pindlebryth arrived back home, he was surrounded by a whirlwind of activity and distractions. Soaked to the skin by the pelting rain, he was weary to his bones. The all too brief rest he afforded himself on one of the myriad of nameless isles in the MidSea Archipelago barely mitigated the exhaustion that wore on him mightily. Both Pindlebryth and Pendenar fared worse than either of their steeds, as one had kept watch as the other and their rides slept. As it was, they arrived at Lenland's CityState with little more than an hour to spare before the memorial began.

No sooner had Pindlebryth been hastily ushered into his rooms, then he was set upon by his butler and an assistant who quickly relieved him of his riding clothes, waterlogged from the rain and sea spray. After washing his fur and toweling him off rapidly, they dressed him in his mourning attire. Pindlebryth's shoulders sagged as he resigned himself to what he considered a necessary indignity. Pendenar himself was about to take his leave to change into his dress blacks, when Gangon entered the rooms with another of the Royal Guard. They both were dressed in immaculate black uniforms that carried a strong scent of cedar and naphtha. The silver buttons and insignia of country and rank were polished to a high luster.

"Grefdel, you are to accompany N'Lord to the nemorial, and remain with him during his stay. Pendenar, report to Colonel Farthun at his quarters immediately after the proceedings. He eagerly awaits your report about the events at Vulcanis. Dismissed."

As Pindlebryth's head popped out from his undershirt as it was pulled over him, and he added, "Be sure to preserve the honor and memory of my friend."

"Absolutely, M'Lord," Pendenar acknowledged. With a salute to Gangon, he quickly wheeled around to leave. Gangon rapidly glanced betwixt the two, wondering if he missed something of import, or an inside joke. After a moment of perplexed thought, he simply shrugged his shoulders and began to review the plans for the memorial with his Prince.

Pindlebryth interrupted as Gangon described the chronology of each of the royals' detailed movements planned for the ceremony. "We are having the memorial in the city hall square?" he blurted incredulously. "Need I remind you what happened the last time the Royal Family was all gathered in our own central courtyard? At least that area had a modicum of security!"

"No one has forgotten, N'Lord. But King Hatheron felt it was a necessary show of stability that we do so. He and Prince Selephygur were both adamant that we clearly demonstrate to the people that we are not cowed by the previous attempts on their lives."

"Even so, it makes me feel uneasy."

"I understand, N'Lord. Nay I...?"

"Yes, yes. Continue." Pindlebryth snaked his head back and forth to keep concentration on Gangon, while the two attendants buttoned his shirt and trousers. He found it easier to understand him through his accent, if he could keep him in a clear line of sight.

"The visiting ambassadors will in be the first section cordoned off nearest your platform. Of course, the Crow and Fox ambassadors are absent. However, the new Snow Goose ambassador and his family will be in attendance."

"New ambassador?"

"Oh, dear – that's right! GanderLord Ambassador Onkyon was installed just two days ago. The previous ambassador was recalled, and Onkyon was formally introduced to King Hatheron during a small state dinner yesterday. And before you ask, Darothien has examined him to the best of her ability. She is reasonably sure neither he nor any of his family are shapeshifters."

"Why was Ambassador Ankuu recalled?"

"There was no official reason given. But there are rumors that the departing ambassador was requested to assist in the defense of a family nember against a charge of treason. If that weren't excitement enough, the ambassador's idiot son went nissing during the dinner. Tabarem found him later, standing quietly in Henejer Hall, and brought him to the attention of his governess and Darothien."

Pindlebryth's butler stopped in his preparations, and holding Pindlebryth's long black greatcoat with gold insignia and piping, held Gangon with a look of reproach. "Lieutenant!

I'm sure M'Lord does not need to hear this backroom gossip. He has more pressing needs."

"Harrumph," Gangon coughed, politely covering his muzzle. He fumbled with "Quite correct," before proceeding with the rest of the memorial's itinerary. Pindlebryth occasionally had to ask for a review and clarification of the proceedings' details. Midway through the seemingly endless list of arrangements, the butler left the final details of fitting with the dressing attendant, and returned with a cup of concentrated Pu'erh tea. Pindlebryth greedily gulped down the brew, and almost immediately felt it wash away the fatigue of the many sleepless hours behind him.

"There! You are ready for the proceedings, M'Lord!" proudly announced the dressing attendant. Despite his pronouncement, he continued picking at nibs, pills, dust and other imperfections.

"We must bustle, N'Lord," added Gangon. "The Royal Family is already assembling in the audience hall." He proceeded to lead Pindlebryth and Grefdel down the southeast stairway, through Henejer Hall toward the Great Audience Hall.

It was in Henejer Hall that they discovered Darothien. Dressed in a coal black dress and long shawl that seemed to soak up the light around her like a sponge, she stood in the center of the hall. She slowly precessed as she examined the stones of the four walls, peering intently through her green prism. Occasionally she would pause, and approach a portion of a wall, and if need be, temporarily move aside the portrait or bust that blocked her view.

The walls and floor of Henejer Hall were composed of blocks of stone of various sizes, all larger than the breadth of both a Lemmings' paws. The mosaic of stonework was even more impressive, in that no mortar was used. Each block was inscribed with a bas-relief of a different object – a tree, a teardrop, a bee, a hammer, and countless other such mundane items. Each was inset with minerals of various colors, shades and striations. Along the walls, the stones jutted in or out from the overall plane of the wall in a random pattern. At one point, she ceased rotating and took a step back, and turned her prism on the floor.

So absorbed was Darothien by her examination of the crenelations in the walls and the patterns in the floor, she wasn't aware of Pindlebryth's and the others' passage until they walked almost directly behind her. When she became aware of the pad-falls behind her, she turned around and her expression of fastidious concentration exploded into relief. She dashed towards Pindlebryth and clamped him in a hard embrace.

"My Prince! We were all so worried about you! Prince Selephygur told us what happened on Vulcanis. He told me he had spoken to you, but he has refused to divulge any further details. I couldn't help but to assume to worst." She released him, and forced a calm over herself. She looked at the floor with embarrassment, when she realized that Gangon and Grefdel regarded her with looks that confirmed that such displays were simply not done.

Pindlebryth smiled kindly at her, saying "Thank you for your concern. But I assure you I am just fine. A bit weary from my travels perhaps, but otherwise quite well."

"I am so relieved," Darothien's voice quivered, as she slid the prism into the folds of her sleeve. "May I also offer my condolences on the passing of your friend, Hakayaa. I can hardly guess as to what his motivations were, but all of Lenland is glad that in the end he made possible the safe return of Selephygur."

Behind him, Grefdel cleared his throat.

"Thank you," Pindlebryth said as he warmly clasped her paws in his. "I appreciate your kindness." Her hands were trembling slightly, and Pindlebryth got the sudden and distinct impression, that if he were not a royal, she would have slapped him directly in the face before embracing him. He looked solemnly and pensively in her eyes, and with a little of his own embarrassment, slowly let her go of her hands.

Pindlebryth moved to the side, and squinted slightly at the wall, as if he could see what Darothien was looking at.

"What do you find so interesting here?"

Darothien turned around, and gestured open-handed at one of the walls, arrayed with several large portraits. "This is where we found Unkaar yesterday."

"Unkaar?"

"GanderLord Onkyon's son. When his governess and I came upon him, he was standing here, quietly staring off into open space. He also stood with his wings outstretched and moving slowly up and down, forward and backward. It was almost as if he were trying to catch a wind. It was most strange and captivating to watch. I came back to see if I could understand what interested him so much."

"It may have been nothing of import. I have heard that he is an idiot."

"An unfortunate title, and I would take a care who you repeat that to. His governess informed me he was born deaf and dumb, but I sense he is not lacking in intelligence."

"I stand corrected. I wish we could speak more now, but matters are pressing. But please join me and my family after the memorial. There is much I have to tell all of you."

Two guards opened the ceiling-high doors, and the troupe entered the audience hall. Outside, it could be seen through the courtyard doors' windows that the remnants of the storm – the very same one that caught Pendenar flying to PanGaea, and that he and Pindlebryth braved on their return to Lenland – were quickly scattering before the westerly wind. Diagonal columns of sunlight occasionally poked through the clouds and the southern windows of the hall. Unpredictable bursts of wind made the windows in the hall creak and shudder.

Amidst the ever-changing light and dimness were Hatheron, Wenteberei and Selephygur in a semicircle. Along with Prime Minister Amadan, they were receiving their final instructions from Colonel Farthun. Pindlebryth and all of his family were dressed in black with gold piping and details, but Hatheron wore a royal purple sash across his chest, with the Sword of Enorel strapped to his side. Pindlebryth noted that not only Hatheron wore a simple gold band as a crown, but also Wenteberei. Pindlebryth wondered what happened to her crown, the sister to the one fashioned by the BlueHood family that his father had dashed to the floor. It was then he noticed his mother stood with a cane, and still favored her injured leg. Her healing was coming along quite nicely, much faster than that of a Lemming without a Name.

Selephygur had his back to him, but Pindlebryth did not see the familiar eyepatch loop around his head. Pindlebryth took the only open place, and stood to the right of his brother. His curiosity was piqued as to what Selephygur had done to replace his eyepatch. Farthun was reviewing details that Gangon had told him earlier, so he allowed himself the luxury of craning his neck forward to see what Selephygur wore over his missing left eye. He was instead distracted by Tabarem, dressed in a dark grey woolen outfit, overcoat and overly-large three-cornered hat. He was slowly walking around Farthun and the Royal

Family, and staring alternately at the floor and the vaulted ceiling. Somehow the crafty gadfly had edged himself into the hall when Gangon and the others entered.

When he finished his review, Colonel Farthun joined General Vadarog, who stood close to the doors leading into the central courtyard. Vadarog seemed to be giving instructions or trying to persuade Farthun on some point. They both occasionally turned to look out the windows in the direction of the gate to the courtyard. Eventually, Farthun nodded in agreement.

Vadarog opened the courtyard doors, and a gust of wind poured into the hall. He stepped outside, and signaled the West Gate. An entourage of reindeer and riders leading a large open carriage pulled outside of the courtyard doors. Behind them was a smaller less ornate carriage, followed by another rank of riding guards.

As King Hatheron approached the doors, Vadarog turned towards him. "I must again protest, Highness, about the wisdom of addressing your subjects in the open CityState central square. Colonel Farthun and I cannot guarantee your safety."

"It seems these days, Our safety is never guaranteed." Hatheron regarded Vadarog with a fatalistic sadness in his eyes. "Besides, if an attack is made, the ensuing panic in the populace would cause more loss of life, injuries and damage than if they were cooped up in the central courtyard."

A pair of guards preceded Hatheron and Wenteberei into the central courtyard. Followed by their sons, then Farthun and Vadarog and finally Darothien and Amadan, the entire formation slowly made their way to their conveyances, allowing for Wenteberei's hobbled gait.

As Pindlebryth climbed into the first carriage, he hesitated a moment as he looked straight into Selephygur's face. He had a glass eye – not one made for an aesthetic cosmetic appearance, but rather one made from the piece of jet black obsidian he collected at Vulcanis.

Selephygur staunchly regarded his brother for a moment as he held his grief inside. It struck Pindlebryth then that his brother was truly no longer a child. More than that, he seemed to have a new and hardened edge to him. He concluded with some apprehension that this was not the effect of the obsidian eye, but rather it reinforced the appearance of what was already there.

Guards closed the doors, and a pair of riders left the rear formation to move alongside the royals' carriage. When the others had taken their places in the second carriage, the procession circled around and left the courtyard through the iron West Gate.

"Father, Mother – Selephygur and I need to talk to you as soon as possible after the memorial. While in PanGaea, I have discovered more about the reasons for the attacks on Selephygur. I've asked him not to divulge any of this until we can all discuss this in private. I also require Darothien to be present to counsel us, but no one else."

A flare of anger sputtered across Hatheron's face, but he quickly calmed himself. Pindlebryth knew that look – Hatheron wasn't angry with anyone in particular. Rather, he was bracing himself for something he expected to raise new problems. "The Vestment Room, then – immediately after we return to the castle."

Pindlebryth looked behind at the carriage that followed them. He was momentarily puzzled when he realized Tabarem was not among its occupants. He stretched to one side, and shook his head in mild disbelief. Tabarem brought up the end of the procession riding a reindeer colt. The gait of the young and inexperienced steed made Tabarem's overly large hat flop about like a pancake.

Promptly at the chime of eleven, the entourage arrived in the CityState central square. A large crowd of the citizens of CityState and surrounding cantons stood, filling the main square. Open rows and columns between sections of the throng were patrolled by the Royal Guard and the army's Blue, Green and Red Squads. At the front of the center of the crowd was a small section cordoned off with brass pillars and chain, where several ambassadors and other dignitaries from the Beaver, Arctic Hare, and Snow Goose nations stood in front of their chairs. Ambassador-at-Large Talenday was seated between the emissaries of the Geese and Hare, talking to one, and constantly sniffling due to the other's dander.

Pindlebryth scanned the Geese for new faces, and spied who must have been Ambassador Onkyon, wearing the seal of his office on the outside of his black coat. He furrowed his brows when he realized neither wife nor son sat with him. The carriage stopped at the raised platform festooned with black bunting and heavy drapes, erected on the steps leading to the city hall.

At the end of the clock tower's chiming, a brass choir began to play a funereal lament. The royals and their entourage left their carriages, and stepped in time with the dirge to the raised platform. Looking at the chairs and the speaking podium, Pindlebryth felt a slight shiver as it reminded him of the stand where Tanderra and a guard lost their lives on that fateful day of violence.

A wind whistled over the roofs and vanes of the buildings surrounding the square, as the remaining storm clouds high above raced inland to the east. Pindlebryth glanced at the sky, and wished that the clouds would last a bit longer, as they seemed more befitting a day of mourning. It was then he noticed there were soldiers stationed on the roofs of almost every corner of the buildings lining the square. He felt marginally better, seeing that Farthun and Vadarog tried to make their situation as secure as possible. He climbed the few stairs and assumed his place before his seat. He was about to bow his head in reflection, when a stream of sunlight, roving between the rolling clouds, ran across Darothien. Her black gown seemed to draw the light into itself, while diminishing the ambient light all about her. As the shaft of light moved on, shards of green shimmered within the fabric of her shawl, growing quickly in intensity, then quickly winking out. Pindlebryth wondered what magick she wove to cause such an effect. When the entourage took their places on the platform facing the crowd, the Royal Family sat, followed by their company.

At the end of the dirge, Hatheron rose and approached the podium. A hush gathered over the crowd as he began to speak. His eulogy for Tanderra was artful and heartfelt, but for some strange reason it did not interest Pindlebryth. He began to feel both agitated and tired at the same time. He felt most uncomfortable sitting for all to see on the platform. His Father's wishes be damned, he imagined the eyes of a hundred sharpshooters and bomb-throwers focusing in on him. Hatheron spoke on, careful to describe the hateful event of that day, but thankfully did not yield to the rage he had shown afterwards in the Hall of Thrones. He reiterated his proclamation of exile of all members of the Fox and Crow nations, but did not use the speech to foster a desire for retaliation or further violence by his people.

And yet Pindlebryth became increasingly unable to maintain his concentration, as the effects of his Father's droning wore on and the Pu'erh wore off. He was reasonably sure he didn't nod off when the polite but muted and sparse applause from the multitude punctuated the end of his Father's speech. After the crowd's response subsided, Hatheron formally declared the next three days as a period of national mourning.

Next Selephygur stood, then took his place at the podium. At first, a handful of people in the crowd craned their necks to see the young Prince, then uttered words of wide-eyed surprise as he regarded his audience. Pindlebryth assumed that, like him, they had never before seen Selephygur with his striking obsidian eye. But the exclamations quickly died down as the Prince began to speak.

To Pindlebryth's ear, Selephygur's remembrances of LongBack seemed rough and overly rehearsed. But it quickly became apparent that what Selephygur lacked in experience at public speaking, was more than overcome by his conviction and emotion. He spoke of the calamity that befell LongBack's family in the dark days brought on by Selephylin, and how he essentially adopted Selephygur, and protected him in his lost son's stead. When Selephygur finished, a mixed but full-spirited reaction of wailing and firm applause resounded from the multitude. Pindlebryth found that even he was affected, as his torpor weakened and his attention was held fast by his brother's speech.

Selephygur then bowed to the throng, and returned to his seat. The drums and brass started the refrains of another traditional funereal march, as they formed ranks in front of the carriages. Two color guards in front of the platform raised flagstaffs as tall as themselves. A soldier carried the insignia of Lenland, and a Royal Guard carried a flag bearing their insignia. Their pennants at half-mast, they hitched the staffs to their belts. Holding their pennants with elbows angled outwards and paws facing away, they began to march to the beat of the chorus of drumbeats. They fell in line behind the brass choir already marching in formation. Behind them were led two riderless reindeer with the largest antlers outfitted with black saddle and tack.

As the Royal Family filed into their carriage, Pindlebryth

took Darothien aside and instructed her to meet them in the Vestment Room upon their return to the castle. The entourage, having reassembled, followed the band and the reindeer through the city to the southern annex of the CityState. The ambassadors and other dignitaries followed in their own carriages, which in turn were trailed by a sizable portion of the crowd from the square. The straight road began to turn this way and that. The procession eventually took a southwest road, past forks to the east and south, wending its way into an open field spotted with copses of trees. The parade road led them to a row of four mausoleums. The first building was the final resting place of the kings and queens of Lenland. The drum and brass band halted between the third and second buildings. The lead carriage stopped in front on the second mausoleum, reserved for the heroes and honored dead of Lenland. The steps to the mausoleum doors were lined on either side with Royal Guard at attention.

The Royal Family and the occupants of the second carriage climbed the stairs to the crypt chambers inside, where they paid their silent respects to the two laid in state. Pindlebryth looked about the mausoleum, and nodded in approval when he noted two bays draped with black sash waiting next to the sealed – albeit empty – bay set aside for Decardan.   Hatheron and Selephygur accepted wreaths from guards just inside the gallery, and placed them on top of the glass covered caskets of Tanderra and LongBack. The long line of delegates and other visitors snaked outside, slowly trudging past the caskets after the Royal Family and company paid their final respects. The formal ceremony completed, the castle entourage boarded their two carriages and commenced back to the castle.

When they returned to the central courtyard, Amadan, Talenday and Vadarog headed for the East Wing, while Hatheron and the others made for the Vestment Room. As the door from the Vestment Room to the Hall of Thrones could only be opened from inside the office, their path was indirect – through the Royal Guard quarters on the second floor, then down the southwest stairways.   When they arrived, with Farthun and Darothien following behind, a servant was already waiting in the Vestment Room to relieve Hatheron and Wenteberei of their crowns and vestments of office.

"Off with you, then. We require privacy," said Hatheron sternly. "We can take care of our things." The butler placed his brush in the armoire and left, while Hatheron gently hung his sash and the Sword of Enorel in their places. He collected Wenteberei's crown and placed both it and his own on their domed receptacles. Pindlebryth addressed Farthun as he and his brother draped their sashes and epaulets away.

"You also, Colonel, I'm afraid. Please close the door after yourself, and standby."

Farthun was disconcerted by the request, but after he glanced at Darothien, who stood her ground, he nodded to Pindlebryth in obeisance. "Yes, M'Lord. I would only remind you and Your Majesties that there is a dinner with the visiting dignitaries in an hour."

"Hopefully we won't be that long," Pindlebryth said tersely.

Farthun looked through the doorway one last time at Hatheron, who sat behind his desk. He nodded once to dismiss him. Darothien moved a chair next to the desk by Hatheron's side, asking Wenteberei if she felt like sitting. She gracefully accepted, it being quite apparent she tired of the strain placed on her healing leg.

When they were finally alone, Pindlebryth turned to Selephygur. With a stern look, and casting his paw towards his brother's eye he sputtered, "*This* was the surprise to which you alluded when I was in PanGaea? I tried to warn you not to draw attention to yourself, and instead you make a public display of yourself that is sure to be the talk of all Lenland!"

Pindlebryth expected the old Selephygur to respond with an innocent sheepish grin, but instead he remained phlegmatic. "Father himself has made it plain with today's open ceremony that we will not be intimidated by those in the world that would do us harm. I happen to agree with his wisdom."

Pindlebryth regarded Hatheron and Wenteberei, and did not hide his annoyance at the situation. "Then it is definitely for the best that I tell you all of my news now, before any more missteps are made." He walked over to the inlaid and lacquered globe, and spun it to display the MidSea. "Selephygur had followed Hakayaa to Vulcanis. And how did you know he was there, brother?" he grated in an exasperated didactic tone.

"I had seen visions and dreams of him there," Selephygur responded flatly.

"But you no longer had the Lens. Who have you told of these visions?"

"Only LongBack, then you and Pendenar at the island.

Sacalitre and Darothien knew about my visions, but Sacalitre believed they were merely nightmares induced by the trauma of Hakayaa's attack."

"No one else?" Pindlebryth demanded impatiently. "Be sure of your answer."

"No, no one else. Not until now." Selephygur began to look and sound defensive. Hatheron and Wenteberei sat quietly, calmly listening. But Darothien leaned forward, observing intently with her head slightly tilted.

"There's at least that, then." Pindlebryth's shoulders relaxed a little before he pressed the issue. "Have you had any more of these visions since you returned to Lenland?"

"Nothing definitive. Some indistinguishable blurs of color and darkness. But then, I haven't been trying."

"The let me repeat the admonishment I gave you while in PanGaea. You are not to discuss any more visions with anyone outside of this room. Your life may depend on it."

"Selephygur's life? How so?" interjected Wenteberei alarmedly.

"Selephygur still has a connection with the Lens." Pindlebryth paused to allow his declaration to sink in. "That is why he was able to find Hakayaa so easily. He had visions of Hakayaa at Vulcanis. He can still see with the Lens. My research at PanGaea confirmed this – some Artifacts may make physical changes in their host the more they are used. Selephygur was in constant use of the Lens for over two years. So it is confirmed to my satisfaction that Selephygur continues to somehow have access to the Lens of Truth." He paused to see if anyone else in the room had the epiphany of the next logical conclusion.

"Then he can see who is in possession of the Lens now!" blurted Darothien.

"Yes! He can spy on those who harmed him," Hatheron mused.

"Exactly. And we may for the time being have an advantage over the Ravenne, the Crow, or whoever is behind all this. This is why it is imperative that no one else know of Selephygur's ability. If the Ravenne ever found out that they in turn were spied upon, they wouldn't hesitate in tracking down Selephygur." He turned again to his brother. "And now you know why that little trinket in your head is such an unwise exhibition."

"I must disappoint you, Pindlebryth," Selephygur argued. "While I agree that my visions should be closely guarded from now on, I do not share your concern over my eye. It is a cosmetic accessory, nothing more. The one has no relation to the other."

Pindlebryth studied Selephygur for a moment, then shook his head and exhaled in capitulation. "Then at least promise us this. Whenever you have another vision, tell one of us as soon as possible. Even if it has images you may not understand at the time. And especially if it reveals to you someone you recognize. Time may be of the essence if we are to protect you."

"I can take care of myself."

"Your performance at Vulcanis indicated otherwise."

Anger flared momentarily in Selephygur's eye and brow. But he quickly restrained himself, as he could see he was being baited into proving Pindlebryth's point. Instead, he answered in sardonic satisfaction, "I believe the same could be said about you."

"Enough!" sputtered Hatheron as he stood with his fists on his desk. "We remain under threat from agents unknown, and it is not productive, let alone seemly, that you two bicker so."

"Quite right," Pindlebryth acceded. "For there are other dangers I have uncovered. Not only to us or Lenland, but much larger in scope." Facing Selephygur again he asked, "Do you remember what you said to the Ravenne assassin at Vulcanis?"

"That he planned to locate and collect all five Artifacts? Or that he knew of an Artifact in Lenland?"

Pindlebryth pressed him further. "The former. Now do you recall what Hakayaa said when you reached that conclusion?"

"Yes – he became even more agitated in his madness, and said that the Ravenne mustn't do so."

"He may have been driven mad, but what if his insanity was caused by a truth he found impossible to bear?"

"It has been a long day, Pindlebryth, and there is much We have yet to endure before it is done," Hatheron complained. "I tire of this riddle."

Hatheron's dissatisfaction made Pindlebryth cautious and reflective. With all that had happened recently – the fight at Vulcanis, the hiding of Kaiya, and the iconoclastic research with DeepDigger – life was at a frenetic urgency. Even when reviewing all his discoveries during his flight back to Lenland, the exigent crisis seemed so real and utterly palpable. Now, when faced with explaining it to a potentially skeptical audience, the menace seemed more like a dream, a tissue of phantasms. Doubts and contradictions grew louder and louder inside him, until a glint caught his eye.

He walked over to the armoire and took the Sword of Enorel in its scabbard. He ran his paw over the faces of the five Angels carved in the metal inlay, and took a deep breath while he organized his thoughts.

Addressing Hatheron he began, "Do you recognize these archetypes?"

"Of course," he responded with a small amount of incredulity. "If I and Archivist WagTail taught you anything of legends and history, it was that those are the faces of the Five Angels that led Enorel the Great to become the First King of Lenland."

"Would you be surprised to know that others from several races throughout history have also seen these beings?" Pindlebryth again paused, seeing that his audience was dealing with varying levels of shock and confusion. "I have seen carvings and statuettes of these creatures – not just of their faces, but of them in their entirety. Several books from different lands also speak of the Angels.

"Have you ever wondered why there were five Angels? Now add to that the knowledge learned by Selephygur that there are five Artifacts. Furthermore consider that there are five races, we Lemmings included, which possess faculties and powers, endowed by the Quickening Spirit.

"There are too many multiples of five for it all to be coincidence. I had only a short glimpse into the ancient documents and the knowledge secreted away within them, but what I had seen quickly brought me to the inescapable conclusion that each Angel gave one of five original races its Power, its language, and its Artifact. I cannot say if Enorel indeed met with all five Angels, as our legends say and this scabbard suggest – such a story may yet lie in the details of other books I have not seen. But I was able to determine this – a single Angel gave the Lemmings their own Artifact. But he gave it to Henejer. Not Enorel, not Gazelikus. By wisdom I cannot hope to know, the Angel bestowed an Artifact upon Henejer."

"Pindlebryth, you befuddle me," Wenteberei said with obvious confusion in her eyes. "You say at the same time, that our legends are false and true."

"Only parts of them. Like many legends, they are embellished over time and telling. But within them still lies the germ of truth. The problem is to discern which is true, and which is distorted from the truth that they once held."

"Poppycock!" exploded Selephygur. "You have spent so much time reading your books and other fairy tales, that you now believe them to be true."

"Do you doubt your own experience, brother? Do you question the abilities beyond your ken that the Lens had given you? Or what you saw in the Ravenne's book? Do you also question the sacrifices made by Hakayaa and LongBack, to protect the knowledge you may possess?"

Selephygur bristled at the mention of Hakayaa in the same breath as his beloved LongBack. The hackles along his head and neck rose at attention.

"Do you now deny that they died protecting you from Keeyakawa, after you yourself declared out loud that he and his fellow Ravenne were trying to amass all five Artifacts?" Pindlebryth scolded. He did not wait to see Selephygur's reaction. Regarding Hatheron again, he held both ends of the scabbard in each paw, and placed it on the center of his desk. "I have confirmed that about which Hakayaa had warned us – that a great calamity will befall all of us if any one person gains all five Artifacts. It makes me believe each of these five Angels gave each race their unique Artifact – and to help keep them separated, they also granted the five races of Lemming, Goose, Raccoon, Fox and Crow the gifts of their different abilities and their different languages."

"Other than the books that only you have read, what proof do you have that Hakayaa's warning was more than just the raving of a lunatic?" charged Selephygur, his arms folded over each other in a display of dismissiveness.

"Perhaps I can shed some light on that," piped Darothien as she glided from behind Wenteberei to the side of Hatheron's desk. "Pindlebryth, do you recall the bejeweled ring of magick you sent me from Vulcanis?"

"Of course."

"When I first saw it after we rescued Selephygur as a pup, beams of light exchanged between the five gems. I recorded in my journals that two of the gems were green."

Pindlebryth looked upwards in recollection. "Yes, I recall

seeing that in your journal. But when I found retrieved it from Vulcanis, all the gems were uniformly dark."

"It was a delicate operation, but I have since succeeded in filling the device with new energy, and it began operating as before – but with one important difference. Only one of the green gems remains green, but the other green gem is now red. 'Selephylin's Crown', as I call it, now has two red gems."

Pindlebryth began to rub his brow in thought. "But what does it mean?" asked Hatheron.

"My guide to the books, Professor DeepDigger, had seen no record of such a device as Selephylin's Crown. The witch queen must have created it for her own purpose."

"Which is?" Hatheron pressed impatiently.

"I believe the crown's purpose is to track what race currently has each Artifact," Darothien ventured. "The crown is inscribed with the same arcane glyphs that identified each Artifact on the odd-shaped rings carried by her attendant slaves. The color of each gem represents the race in possession of the respective Artifact. Selephylin placed the Lens in Selephygur, and after we rescued him, the Lens was for all intents and purposes now in our possession. Now, consider that green is the color favored by the magick of Lemming wizards. This has been so for myself and Graymalden before me, and all the way back to the Lemmings' first wizard, Gazelikus. According to Graymalden's journals, yellow is the color of Geese wizardry, blue is the color of Fox magick – which we have seen with our own eyes – and red is the color of Crow magick.

"The crown is in agreement with what we already know. The Crow hold the Lens, in addition to their own Artifact."

"That would be something called the 'Prism of Persuasion'." Pindlebryth commented editorially.

"But that still is not proof," sulked Selephygur.

"I was not finished, my Prince," Darothien gently corrected. "Similar to the manner that I used to divine a second use for the center jewel in Hatheron's broken crown, I have discovered an underlying function of Selephylin's device. She intended to wear it, somehow to control the five magicks, perhaps even the Artifacts themselves. That's why I had dubbed it 'Selephylin's Crown'."

Pindlebryth felt a shiver of dread run down his back. He finished Darothien's train of thought. "That corroborates the last finding in the ancient books, and confirms Hakayaa's worst fear. There was a curious book that appeared to be written in whatever tongue the reader spoke, and it spoke of the end of the world. If all five Artifacts were held by the same person, the world would suffer a cataclysm. If that wasn't spirit-withering enough, it went on to tell that there was a way that the holder of all five Artifacts might influence the change according to his or her own will.

"Like the Ravenne, it seems this was Selephylin's original intent as well." Pindlebryth could sense his brother was going to object yet again, but continued, refusing to let his brother break Hatheron's attention on himself. "It doesn't matter anymore if we believe this is sufficient proof of wild conjectures. The inescapable fact is that Selephylin believed it, and the Ravenne's master believes it. They will stop at nothing to gain all the Artifacts, including the one supposedly in the Lemmings' possession – named the 'Orb of Oblivion' according to that magickal book. We must find it before they do.

"As if that weren't enough we had to fear from the Ravenne, we must now ensure they never find out about Selephylin's Crown, for they would surely go to any length to procure that as well."

Pindlebryth found he was breathing heavily, but no one intruded on his silence. Even Selephygur relaxed his arms, perhaps indicating he might be less obstinate. "The most immediate problem we now face is that we have too few clues to guide us to our own Artifact." He faced Selephygur, with earnest sincerity. "We need you to try to remember any details from the Ravenne's map that would help us locate the Orb." Turning back to the rest, he added, "And the life of Henejer himself needs to be examined for any evidence that may indicate the Orb's location."

Hatheron stood and nodded in agreement. "I will instruct WagTail to research his archives and report to you." He scooped up the Sword of Enorel, and reverently hung it again in the armoire.

Darothien chimed in, "I will also check the writings of Gazelikus, to see if they offer any help, Your Majesty."

Looking at them all, Hatheron concluded, "As for the issue of Selephygur's visions and Selephylin's Crown, I concur that we shall not speak of them outside of this circle." Turning to his family, he added, "But now the hour draws nigh, and we have dinner with our ambassadors and emissaries."

Darothien opened the door, and seeing it was clear, bowed as the Royal Family exited. Down the short corridor, between the Royal Study and the southwest stairwell that served the Royal Guards' floor and the royal apartments, waited Farthun and the servant. Farthun trailed the family up the stairs, while the servant hurried back to the Vestment Room to ensure that everything was in its proper place.

While ascending to the guards' level, Wenteberei called for Darothien. She hurried past Pindlebryth and Selephygur to her side. "I understand you and Ambassador Onkyon's governess collected his gosling Unkaar in Henejer Hall. Have you discerned how he got away from his governess, and why he was so interested in Henejer Hall?"

Selephygur grumbled and roasted in his own thoughts, but Pindlebryth strove to listen to Darothien. He thought suddenly of the last time he had the itch in the back of his mind at DeepDigger's, and found himself also wanting to understand the reason why he found Darothien earlier this morning in Henejer Hall.

"Yes, my Queen. He somehow discovered the secret passageway in the dining hall in the North Wing, when her back was turned. Tabarem found him, and soon brought it to my attention. Tabarem tried to put on his usual act of the old curmudgeon, but I could tell when he returned with the governess, he was very interested, even concerned about Unkaar. When I found him, Unkaar seemed fascinated by the pattern of carvings in Henejer Hall. Even with the governess' help, the three of us found it quite a task to tear the gosling's attention from the walls. I spent a good portion of this morning examining that area and more, but I could find nothing untoward about it. I even made notes of the bas-reliefs on the stones he was most interested, but apparently he could see something I haven't yet."

"His mother had the Gift of Location. Perhaps he has it too."

"Had? What happened to the ambassador's wife?"

"She died soon after childbirth – if that's what one can call egg-laying. I spent a bit yesterday speaking with the governess, but she was understandably circumspect about revealing much information about the Ambassador and his family. But I was able to fill in the blanks after talking with Talenday, who has had some dealings with the Snow Goose nation.

"Six generations ago, there was a plague that decimated the population of the Snow Geese. They called it 'The Scarlet Influence', and though it exacted a heavy toll on the general populace, it all but wiped out those who had the Gift. Those fortunate few that survived began to marry within other families with the Gift in order to preserve it. They obviously were successful, but at a cost. Decade upon decade of intermarriage resulted in physical difficulties in every offspring who also had the Gift, which became more pronounced with each new generation. Unkaar's mother suffered from salpingitis, a disease of childbearing, and Unkaar was left deaf and dumb."

"Unkaar must have the Gift," reasoned Darothien, "as it certainly would explain how he so quickly discovered the secret passageway. But I am afraid I can offer no guidance on what he was looking at in Henejer Hall."

The group made their way through the guards' barracks on the second level, and Gangon called the floor to attention as soon as he spotted them. Hatheron waved them at ease, but addressed Gangon. "Is everything ready for dinner?"

"Yes, Sire. The guests are assembled in the dining hall in the North Wing. You will be announced as soon as you arrive." Gangon selected two guards to accompany the group as they proceeded on through. As they passed through the East Wing, Darothien took her leave, and descended to her laboratory.

They paused as they approached the door, and a group of attendants descended upon them to brush, groom and ensure their bearing was fit to receive their audience. The doors opened, and a swell of chamber music poured out of the hall. The music stopped, and the Royal Family was formally announced by the Tipstaff. The eight musicians, grouped in a far corner of the hall began to play a fanfare for their liege. As Hatheron and Wenteberei greeted the various emissaries, they thanked them for coming and slowly made his way to their chairs at the head of the table. Pindlebryth and Selephygur stood by seats on either side of the long table next to their parents. As decorum required, the roomful of attendees took their places at the table, and all sat only after Hatheron and Wenteberei did so.

Waitstaff entered with trays and tureens of various dishes, tailored to each race's preferences. Pindlebryth wrinkled his nose at the recollection of the acrid stench of things coming from Mrs. SootBeak's kitchen that were barely fresh enough not to considered carrion, and was grateful that there were no Crow dishes served this meal. Happily instead, dinner was served with carafes of Lenland's finest wines, including one from the northern highland that Pindlebryth decidedly relished as his favorite. That, along with a selection of neutral music neither sad nor joyful, seemed to prevent the mood at the table from becoming too sullen. Pindlebryth, however, found himself quickly tiring of the small talk that pervaded the mid-afternoon meal. When the waitstaff brought in the desserts, they had to scramble to also fill the goblets of everyone at the table as Hatheron called for a toast. He stood and raised his glass, as did all the attendees.

Hatheron's voice was audibly shaky as he pronounced, "Ladies and Gentry, I give you Tanderra and LongBack, Lenland's favored sons. Their talents, service and courage will be sorely missed by myself, my family and all of Lenland."

"Tanderra and LongBack." echoed the audience. When all were seated again, the waitstaff served the desserts of spiced granola cakes, topped with flaming brandied blackberries. But soon after the dessert plates were set out, the rear doors opened, and Darothien strode through. She made straight for Hatheron, and had a worried look on her face. She whispered something to him, looked at Pindlebryth with a nod, then stood waiting in the corner across from the musicians.

Hatheron thought for a moment, then looked at Onkyon and regarded him for a space while the ambassador was otherwise occupied in conversation with his counterpart from the Lodges. It was then that Hatheron seemed to have a flash of insight. He signaled Farthun, who came quickly to his side. This time, Pindlebryth could hear, "We will be leaving dinner presently. When our guests in turn leave for their embassies, take GanderLord Ambassador Onkyon aside discreetly, and inform him that We wish to speak with him before he leaves. Then bring him to Us at the Hall of Thrones."

"Alone, Sire?"

"He may bring an assistant if he wishes, but as this is a rather delicate issue, it may be best if he does not."

Farthun nodded and joined Darothien in her corner. When the Royal Family was finished with their pastries, Farthun crossed to the other corner and spoke with the conductor, who signaled his musicians to close with a coda at the end of the musical phrase. Hatheron then rose, followed in kind by his audience. He dutifully and formally thanked them all for attending this solemn occasion. As they bowed, Hatheron motioned for his family to accompany him. Following suit, Darothien trailed them out the doors by which they entered. The two guards who ushered them to the hall remained past the doors, and Hatheron curtly addressed them. "Accompany us to the Great Audience Hall."

They all made their way silently until they reached their destination, when Hatheron issued a second instruction. "Remain outside until Farthun arrives with the Snow Goose ambassador." They closed the doors leading from the audience hall to the Hall of Thrones after their charges entered. Hatheron and Wenteberei took their places on their dais thrones, while the three others stood in front of them.

"Pindlebryth, you mentioned the names of three of the Artifacts. What are the names of the remaining two?"

Pindlebryth glanced at Darothien before replying. She was pacing slowly near the base of the dais, but she kept both Hatheron and Pindlebryth in her vision. "The Raccoon possess the Ring of Fortitude, while the Snow Geese have the Vessel of Sorrows."

Selephygur raised one foot onto the dais, and leaned on the raised knee. As he intently listened to the conversation, he locked his false eye on Pindlebryth. Pindlebryth immediately saw through the ploy that his brother attempted, trying to upset him by keeping the unblinking obsidian eye towards him. Hatheron looked at the floor and nodded his head a few times, trying to familiarize them all in his mind. After a respectful pause, Pindlebryth ventured, "May I ask why you wish this information, Father?" He wanted to also ask about Darothien's news, but he hoped that it would be forthcoming regardless.

"I am not totally sure yet. I have my suspicions, but I will need to confirm them from Ambassador Onkyon. If he gives the answer I think he shall, you shall have your answer as well." He ran his paw under his muzzle, and squinted slightly as he asked Pindlebryth, "Did you know the previous ambassador from the Snow Goose nation?"

"Only by name."

"A pity. GanderLord Ankuu was a good spirit. We had built a rapport during the many years he served as the WetLands

ambassador. I believe even Tanderra took a liking to him.
Onkyon seems to be cut from the same cloth, but it is far too
early to be certain of such a new acquaintance."

Pindlebryth thought momentarily about the recalled
ambassador, and he began to sorely realize that he had
squandered many opportunities and resources over the years.
He had otherwise kept his mind entirely focused on the study of
languages, and largely ignored those few people who spoke
them. As a result, he now paid the price of having no one
outside of the castle he could rely on – neither as a confidant, as
an information source, as a sounding board, nor simply as a
friendly ear he could bend. He currently could count only one,
but now that single person had to be treated as dead to the
world.

He regarded Darothien and wondered if one day they might
share the same level of trust. But part of him felt slighted that
she did not yet trust him enough, evidenced by the news she
had shared with only his father.

A knock at the ceiling high door was followed by Farthun
opening one door, and slipping deftly between the small gap.
"Ambassador Onkyon to see you, Your Majesty. Will you
receive him?"

Hatheron nodded, and Pindlebryth, Selephygur and
Darothien took their places at the base of the dais. The door
opened, and Onkyon entered. One could see beyond the doors
that his assistant waited outside. He had a perplexed look on
his face, as Farthun closed the vaulted doors and waited inside
with paws clasped in front of him, leaving the ambassador's
assistant with the attendant guards behind. Onkyon stopped
three steps before the dais, and bowed. "You sent for me, King
Hatheron?"

"Yes, GanderLord Ambassador Onkyon. Thank you for
coming so quickly despite the inconvenience. We also greatly
appreciate your attendance at today's memorial service."

"You and your family, especially Selephygur, have my
deepest condolences. It is never easy to lose a friend or a loved
one."

"Quite so." Hatheron inhaled quickly and coughed loudly,
to separate the pleasantries from the rest of the meeting. "But
time is pressing, and I have news concerning the Snow Geese
nation. In a show of good faith, I wanted to inform you of it as
soon as possible – rather than letting you wait for a

communiqué from your own government that may or may not arrive."

Onkyon, lowered his bill and stared directly at Hatheron warily. "Yes, King Hatheron?"

"We have just received word that your national treasure, the Vessel of Sorrows, has been stolen." Hatheron and Darothien intently studied the face of the ambassador. The rest of the Royal Family stared wide eyed at the King. Even Pindlebryth could not keep his surprise entirely concealed.

"Indeed," intoned Onkyon, who remained utterly stoic. "That would be most unfortunate to lose such a symbol of our national heritage. I do hope the guilty parties are found and brought to justice swiftly."

"We fear that is highly unlikely, sir. We also happen to believe that the Vessel is already in the clutches of the same people who tore the Fox nation treasure, the Lens of Truth, from my son bodily, and killed LongBack. The very one we honored today! The blackhearts We speak of, of course, are none other than the Crow."

Onkyon was not swayed from his impassive demeanor, and seemed to measure out his words. "I recognize these are trying times for Lenland, Your Majesty, and you and yours have suffered many dark deeds. I have the utmost sympathy for your losses, but the strictures of my office require at this time that I remain circumspect. I shall of course, report your findings and advice to my superiors, and await their reply. Until that time, what other would you have me do?"

Hatheron pulled back to rest against his throne. He pulled down on the whiskers on his left side, as he tried to assess the new ambassador and adjust his tack. "How well did you know your predecessor, GanderLord Ankuu?"

Onkyon relaxed his stance a mite, and folded his wings at his side. "We both served in the GanderLord House of Parliament. Depending on the issue we often debated on the same side, and sometimes against one another. I find him quite forthright, and eminently adept in statecraft."

"I'm glad to hear so. I also have found him to have a high moral character, and I respect him greatly. I had just remarked to my son, Pindlebryth, that even Prime Minister Tanderra, who did not easily take a shine to people, considered GanderLord Ankuu a friend." Hatheron paused as Onkyon nodded in appreciation. "I do hope his reputation will not be sullied by events back in the Snow Goose nation."

"What do you mean?" asked Onkyon, with an eyebrow raised.

"We understand that Ankuu, who also had a stellar record as an outstanding solicitor before being called to public office, has returned home specifically to defend his brother-in-law in court. Moreover, We hear the charge against the poor soul is treason.

"We have the utmost regard for GanderLord Ankuu, and are confident that there can be no reflection of these charges on him. Unfortunately, I am sure there will be smaller minds amongst your citizens that will quickly assume guilt by association."

That seemed to unnerve Onkyon. Hatheron saw an opportunity, and came to the point of insight he had earlier. "Could it be that GanderLord Ankuu's client is accused of stealing the Vessel of Sorrows?"

Pindlebryth wasn't sure who was the more surprised in the room, himself or Onkyon. But Hatheron leaned forward to sit erect, and followed where his instinct led him. He said in a calmer, more supplicant tone, "I understand this is a great deal to have thrust upon you so soon after accepting your new position. But we have a common friend, overshadowed by a common threat. Return to your embassy, and issue what communiqués you need to confirm what I have said, and help GanderLord Ankuu. But return to Us, so that we may strive together to help return your national treasure to you, and you may help Us in turn. I fear the Crow are not yet finished with Lenland."

Hatheron signaled Farthun, still waiting dutifully by the door. He advanced to respectfully escort Onkyon back to the entrance where his assistant and guards waited beyond. As Farthun closed the door, the receding pair of Snow Geese could be heard talking in rapid peeps and bill snaps.

Pindlebryth turned to his father with a look of wonderment. "How did you know?"

"Hmm?"

"About it being Ankuu's brother-in-law having stolen the Artifact?"

"It was an educated guess. It was soon after Ankuu's departure that we heard from Ambassador-at-Large Talenday that the brother-in-law was brought up on charges of treason. I also know something of Ankuu's family. Ankuu's mate and her brother were very close until her unfortunate demise. I could easily believe that Ankuu could not bear the thought of his in-law's distress, and that Ankuu would be obliged to help him to the best of his abilities.

"As far as the actual deed, the brother-in-law may have done it, or he may have been somehow forced to assist – we may never know. In any event, I believe the timing of Darothien's discovery indicates that the Vessel of Sorrows was only recently physically handed over by the actual thieves from the Snow Goose nation to the Ravenne.

"If Onkyon is indeed anything like GanderLord Ankuu, then he will persuade assistance from the Snow Geese on our behalf. What remains to be seen, is what form of cooperation we may expect, and how soon it may come."

Selephygur looked with mild exasperation at the doors and declared, "Well, I for one cannot stand by, idly hoping and waiting for help that may not come. Good day, Father... Mother." He strode with purpose to the doors and let himself out, but leaving the door wide ajar. Farthun watched Selephygur as he left, then turned back to Hatheron. "By your leave, my King, I have several tasks that require my personal attention." Hatheron nodded, and Farthun followed Selephygur, closing the door behind him.

Pindlebryth could feel himself growing more and more upset at his brother's behavior. Each argument, each contradiction, each slight in of itself was a trifle, but together they became quite irritating. Pindlebryth exhaled in exasperation, regarding his parents in frustration.

"Why is he so contrary? Did something happen to him since his return that I am not aware of? When I spoke to him from PanGaea, he sounded most anxious to see me. Now, he is nothing but antagonistic."

"He is still upset. His duties today wore on him since his return. I will speak with him when he has calmed down," offered Wenteberei.

"That probably would be for the best. I can't seem to talk to Selephygur anymore. Either I end up upsetting him, or he upsets me. He reminds me of..."

"He reminds *me* of another son that was quite contrary when he decided he was no longer a pup. He needs time to find himself again."

Pindlebryth looked at his mother with a shake of his head. At last, his shoulders sagged in surrender to her wisdom, as he exhaled. "Amongst other things, the long journey, the duties of the ceremony, compounded by food and drink have just about worn me entirely out. I need to retire to my apartment, before I collapse outright in a stupor. Good evening, Mother and Father." He could not muster even the weakest of smiles of appreciation, but at least he no longer frowned.

Hatheron simply looked at the door after Pindlebryth closed it, and asked, "Wenteberei, do you think I pushed Onkyon too far too quickly? Will he help us?"

"You are asking a lot of him on faith and little else. But I think he will seek out advice from GanderLord Ankuu, who will vouch for your character. In the end, I believe Onkyon will be an asset. But only time will tell how much sway he has with his parliament."

Hatheron sat staring off into the distance, frozen in place except for his stroking of his whiskers.

Pindlebryth slept soundly the rest of the day and the entire night. When he woke, he could remember the events of the entire previous day with crystal clarity, up to and including the gathering in the Hall of Thrones. But his memory of last nights' events dimmed increasingly after he left the hall, walked through the other halls of the South Wing, the corridors and the stairwells he had frequented so often before. As he looked out his window at the last of the sparkling dew that had collected on the rooftops of the North Wing and the central yard, he could not recall exactly how he made it to his bed. He had been so weary of mind and body, he could not even recall if he changed into his bedclothes and made it into his bed with or without assistance.

He was, however, still pleased overall at the luxury of having had slept late. Finding a fresh toilette pitcher and bowl set out along with a change of casual wardrobe for the day, he prepared and dressed himself. Looking one last time out his window and balcony at the damp but drying courtyard lawn, Pindlebryth pondered worriedly if his brother was in a fairer mood this morning. He opened the door to find Grefdel standing across the central hallway dutifully waiting for him. At first, Pindlebryth wondered if he had waited there all night and morning, but he discounted that thought when he realized Grefdel was far too bushy-tailed to have done so.

"What is your pleasure this morning, M'Lord?" asked Grefdel politely in his resounding baritone.

"I guess I have risen too late to have breakfast with my family."

"I'm afraid so, M'Lord. They all have already gone about their business for the day. But I'm sure that the staff has kept things warm for you in the dining room."

Pindlebryth shrugged his shoulders, and crossed the hallway diagonally and entered the dining room separating his parent's rooms from his and Selephygur's. Standing next to the south window was a chef, with his arms folded and back to him, looking outside over the landscape. While he had seen this chef before, he was of the opinion that he was an assistant of the head chef's. As he entered, the chef came to life. Pindlebryth expected this assistant to be nervous and fumbling the first time he served, but he was instead pleasantly surprised as he brought his cooking station to life. He deftly took a small spade of charcoals from the hearth and placed his pan over it, and began to make a string of crepes. He opened several small covered dishes filled with sweet pastes of pecan, sunflower seeds and hazelnut, with several syrups and preserves. Pindlebryth was familiar with most of them, but there was a fruit compote he did not recognize.

"Those are delicacies from the south we rarely see: banana and pineapple, in a light caramel sauce. Save that for last, your stomach will thank you! And your usual tea, M'Lord," he added as he set before him a cupful of Pu'erh.

Pindlebryth found himself amused by the chef's exuberance, but he quickly felt fairly drunk on the long line of sweet delicacies. "This calls for something different. Could you whip up some coffee for me?"

The chef seemed to anticipate his wishes, and wholeheartedly complied, rendering a cup out of a press in scarcely a minute.

Pindlebryth invited Grefdel to try one of the crepes, who refused on principle. Pindlebryth looked to the chef, saying, "Make him one anyway. I often have to eat alone at PanGaea, but I prefer not to while back here at home." The chef presented Grefdel with a crepe with pecan paste, topped with the compote. With a forlorn sigh, Grefdel accepted. But the speed at which he bolted it down filled the chef with disappointment.

With an amused grin, Pindlebryth asked, "I take it, that you will be accompanying me when I return to PanGaea?"

"Yes. I also have orders from Colonel Farthun to remain with you there."

"That may raise some eyebrows. The PanGaean authorities take immense pride in looking after their dignitaries and notable visitors. Having my own protection will raise objections."

"They need not know. Before I enlisted in the guard, I was raised on the farmlands to the south. When in PanGaea, I will function as your gardener, as far as any outsiders need know."

Pindlebryth chuckled, "Oh, indeed? Then you will find a fast friend with my housekeeper, BroadShanks. Just be careful she doesn't run you ragged endlessly tending the backyard." After a gulp of coffee, Pindlebryth changed the topic. "Where is my family now?"

Grefdel placed his empty plate on the corner of the chef's station. "King Hatheron is with Prime Minister Amadan and Ambassador Talenday; Queen Wenteberei returned to her bed, as her leg still bothers her quite a bit after all of yesterday's exercise; General Vadarog and Colonel Farthun collected Prince Selephygur, and are currently with him in the barracks gymnasium."

"That's unusual," Pindlebryth muttered as he put down his empty cup. "What do they want with Selephygur?"

"I'm sure I don't know, M'Lord."

"Very well. I'll first go to see Darothien, then check on what doings Selephygur is up to. But first..." Pindlebryth relished his last crepe of sunflower paste and compote. As he rose and left the dining room, he said to the chef, "You were absolutely right. The compote was the perfect finish to a wonderful breakfast!" The chef beamed back at him.

With Grefdel in tow, Pindlebryth took the most direct route to Darothien's laboratory in the lowest part of East Wing. At the top of the stairs to the entrance, Pindlebryth told Grefdel to wait. He pattered down the stairs, and opened the strange door that looked wet with condensation, but still was dry to the touch.

The front room was as it ever was, and the wolf statuette next to the laboratory door yipped once, then stood at attention, panting and wagging its tail. Pindlebryth had dealt with wolves and the occasional coyote in the wild, but he did not know how to interpret the statue's stance. He only recalled that Darothien instructed the magickal totem to allow him entrance. From that he reasoned that the statuette's stance was not threatening. But still, a small part of him couldn't help but to wonder what the wolf would do if an unrecognized intruder attempted to gain entrance to the laboratory. He looked at the display case to the left, and saw the strange and broken ringlets and the fine cotton gloves to handle them, but Selephylin's Crown was not to be found. Pindlebryth then advanced, and warily opened the door to the laboratory.

His sense of smell was assaulted with the odors of burning alchemy, the permeating sting of the smell after a thunderstorm, and still other scents he did not recognize. In the center of the main table was the crown, brilliantly lit and flashing with activity. Around it flew three globes of green energy, and to the side was Darothien observing the device through her prisms and lenses. She was mumbling softly, and a stylus with a glowing green nib danced, writing line upon line of fresh ink in her open notebook. The rest of the room was dark, and the spinning shadows thrown from the crown and the globes made him dizzy. As he approached Selephylin's Crown, Pindlebryth immediately confirmed what Darothien had reported to Hatheron the day before – three of the five gems were flaming crimson, while only one gem was glowing green and the last was a deep indigo that seemed difficult to focus on. And the ringlet indeed seemed the right size and shape to snugly fit the head of a Fox.

He was about to address Darothien, but held himself silent as he thought better of it. Instead, he moved to stand directly across the table from her. She was oblivious to his presence, as she concentrated on the activity in and around the crown. She presently lowered her prism, and the stylus came to rest flat between pages. Only then did she realize she had company.

"Oh! I beg your pardon, M'Lord. How long have you been there?"

"Not long at all. I just came to see the crown for myself." Gesturing with his paw, he commented, "This whole assembly is quite hypnotic when it is in operation."

"Yes, isn't it? Unfortunately, this spell is the only way I have found to make the crown operate safely. If it weren't for my prism and lenses, I couldn't examine it for long without getting a terrible migraine." She raised her palm, and with a word, the globes slowed to an undulating hover. She sat back, and turned away from the equipment. "By the by, Graymalden's notes mention nothing about Raccoon magick. Am I far off the mark by assuming the indigo gem represents their race?"

"Not at all. That is what I would surmise."

"Then they at least are still in possession of their own Artifact."

"Thank the Quickening Spirit for that."

Darothien scratched her muzzle in thought. She darted a glance at Pindlebryth, looking as if she were almost embarrassed to say something. Pindlebryth tilted his head at her with an expression that promised he would not be offended.

"I am afraid I am ignorant of much of the political goings on in Lenland. Why is there no Raccoon embassy here in the CityState?"

Pindlebryth leaned back slightly with a crooked smile to assure her he thought no less of her because of her question. "We have no embassies of *any* of the lands from the west of MidSea. After the land of PanGaea was set aside, it quickly became the arena of neutrality where nations – even nations at war – could practice diplomacy. In addition to the embassies that the Northern Lands maintain in PanGaea, the eastern nations have additional missions here in Lenland for simple expediency."

After considering the explanation, she picked up her prism again, and looked sidelong at the crown. "I have been trying to wheedle more secrets from Selephylin's Crown, but I have been only able to get random scraps that seem to be the unconnected parts of a larger puzzle. Between my lack of further progress with the crown, and inability to uncover what drew Unkaar to Henejer Hall, I feel the answers are maddeningly close but still just beyond me."

"I know what you mean," Pindlebryth sighed with new frustration. "I have had that same feeling since I left DeepDigger's archives. I feel I am missing something. I *know* it! And now that you mention him, I can't help but to think the missing piece also has to do with Unkaar."

"Ah yes. These archives you spoke of." Darothien got up from her stool, stood and stretched, balling her paws to press against the small of her back as she arched slightly backwards. After a moment, she straightened back up, and groaned with satisfied relief. "Please tell me about them. Perchance they might point me in the right direction."

At first, Pindlebryth was mesmerized by the flashing gems and whirling globes, but he suddenly caught himself dumbly staring across the table at Darothien's form as she stretched. "Ah yes," he stumbled back to his wits, lowering his muzzle in embarrassment. Darothien smiled to herself, but did not draw further attention to the awkward moment.

He cleared his throat, and focused on the matter at hand. "I've already explained at last night's meeting all the relevant discoveries I've made. All that remains are my impressions, feelings, and a sense of something I haven't had since I was pup."

"Which is?"

A look of unguarded truth came over Pindlebryth's face. "A sense of wonderment. And yet, the discoveries in the archives – and so many of them in such a short time! – so challenged my conception of the world, that it shook me to the core. I felt as if I were drowning." Darothien looked at Pindlebryth expectantly, eagerly waiting for him to continue. "All about me were carvings and statuettes of the Angels that ministered to Enorel the Great, and there were drawings of them in one of DeepDigger's books. Not just works wrought by Lemmings, but almost every culture. And their faces all looked like those five Angels depicted in the emblems on the scabbard holding the Sword of Enorel.

"I read stories from every language about how each Angel gave an Artifact to each nation. I suppose a researcher trained to be more of a skeptic might regard them as a universal legend adapted over generations by all peoples as their own. My guess is that how the Regents of PanGaea University view them.

"But both you and I have seen an Artifact, and know its power is real, not mere legend. And we both have lived through what extremes the desire to obtain that power will drive some to."

Pindlebryth went on to describe everything he saw and read. Darothien leaned forward, enraptured by his description of the magickal codex perceived by the reader as written in their native tongue. He continued for quite a while before ending with his revelation that Henejer, not Gazelikus, was the recipient of the Orb of Oblivion.

Darothien's eyes flashed wide with recollection at the mention. "So that's what he meant!" She jumped up and quickly crossed to a pedestal holding an ages-old book already open. She fingered a satin bookmark and turned to the place it marked. After scanning the page for a moment, she exclaimed, "Here! – one of Gazelikus' personal notes scattered throughout his alchemy and sorcery reference works. He wrote about being envious of Henejer, that he coveted a Gift that was given the architect, but he felt should have been given to him instead. He rails on about it for quite a while, filling an entire page's margin. He goes on to say that he was foolish to honor Henejer by giving him a tool to use with the Gift, and later thoroughly regretted it. The curious thing is, at the end of his rant, he admits he can't seem to recall what the Gift and the tool were."

"That's the power of the Orb. It wants to be alone. It makes people forget about its existence. How it managed to be recorded at all in the archives is something of a miracle." Then it hit him. "Wait! Gazelikus doesn't remember what he gave Henejer?"

"No." Darothien peered closely at the book to read verbatim. "Here it is. 'Henejer took both the Gift and the tool I had made for him, and he has not been seen since. Curse his greedy hide! The longer he is gone, the more difficult it is to recall. What spell did he cast on me? Or is there an Angel who hinders me? Every power at my command, every spirit, magick and alchemy has failed me.'" Darothien leaned back and looked quizzically at Pindlebryth. "Curious, isn't it?"

"Somewhat – but probably not for the same reasons as you might have. I read in a book entitled 'Compendium of Recipients', a passage from Gazelikus himself. There he stated essentially the same thing you found, except he described to a small degree the Gift which of course was the Artifact – the Orb of Oblivion. The only information about it that survives today is that it does not want to be found, and will cause people to forget of its existence. He went on to mention the tool he created, an enchanted cloth that was to be draped over the Orb to protect the user from its effects.

"What I find interesting, however, is how your passage

differs from the Compendium. There he seemed to be in full possession of his faculties, but here his memory fails him. I cannot help but to conclude it was the Orb itself that somehow affected him, despite how he vehemently attributes his failing memory to Henejer's machinations."

"Powerful magick indeed," commented Darothien. "But that is what one would expect from an Artifact." After a moment, her head snapped up, and she excitedly added, "Do you think Unkaar has found the Orb?"

"Sadly, no. DeepDigger told me the Snow Geese who have the ability of unerring location are not able to find Artifacts. If such a thing were possible, the Ravenne would have employed a Snow Goose to find and take the Lens from Selephygur, long before resorting to threatening Hakayaa's family. They might have also used a Snow Goose to find the Orb hidden in Lenland."

Darothien's shoulders slumped with disappointment, as her expression lost its hopeful intensity. "So what was it that drew Unkaar to Henejer Hall?"

Without warning, Pindlebryth smacked his paw against his forehead. "Imbecile! I am an imbecile! It was in front of me all this time! Since the time I was in DeepDigger's archives, I *knew* I was missing something!" Pindlebryth moved to the table end, so he could see Darothien without the Crown and the mystical globes intervening. "Snow Geese with their gift cannot locate an Artifact, correct? But the protective cloth fashioned by Gazelikus is *not* an Artifact. So..."

Darothien's look of excited discovery reignited immediately. "...Unkaar was drawn by the magick of Gazelikus' Cloth!"

"Yes exactly!" Pindlebryth agreed excitedly. But he suddenly looked in thought to his side and shook his head, while waving his hand downwards as if to hold the idea down. "It is enticing to think it is here in the castle. But what real proof do we have that it is? You had been scanning the hall for some clue about Unkaar's obsession, but had found none." He held Darothien fast with a piercing gaze. "If you cannot find it, what recourse do we have?"

Darothien slipped her prism into its customary place inside one of her sleeves, then steepled her paws in thought. "Why not just see if Unkaar could find it with his own talents?"

"Not until we know we can trust Ambassador Onkyon."

"Well, then," said Darothien as she folded her arms into

their opposite sleeves. "Now that I know of the cloth, and that it was in the possession of Gazelikus and Henejer, I suppose I could search Henejer Hall again. But knowing Gazelikus, it is quite possible that the cloth is somehow shielded, even from magick. He was quite clever when he wanted to keep something hidden. That could be why he could not find it later, after he forgot what it was. The only other tack I could take is to search my own library, and engage WagTail to help me research the archives for some clue."

Pindlebryth felt a mite distressed, as he had somewhat naïvely hoped that Darothien would produce a solution from somewhere hidden within the folds of her draping sleeves.

"Can we disassemble that wall?" Pindlebryth pondered aloud.

"First of all, I doubt that anyone would be willing to take apart something Henejer built, for fear they might not be able to restore it. Secondly, the walls there are made without mortar. One mistake, or removing a keystone, might bring the entire wall down."

All he could do was to sullenly add, "Between my father's request to delve the archives for Henejer, and you looking for Gazelikus, WagTail will find himself quite busy." Mimicking Darothien, Pindlebryth also folded his arms. "I may be able to help in that effort for a few days, but I will have to return to PanGaea soon. There are so many more books in DeepDigger's archive that I haven't even opened. And there may be something concealed there that would help us find Gazelikus' Cloth. Given its propensity to remove itself from memory and recorded history, I don't hold much hope of finding much more about the Orb along that particular line of inquiry. But the cloth..."

Pindlebryth tapped the side of his muzzle in thought and affirmed, "The cloth may be another story." He nodded to himself, observing, "DeepDigger's expertise is in history, and he has already admitted his command of languages is somewhat weak. Even if he could help a little, he would not necessarily know the meaning of idiomatic expressions; or when a phrase is meant literally or rather is indicative of a localized dialect; or a dozen other eccentricities inherent in languages. So if things weren't challenging already, I now additionally have two more languages to master during the coming semester while trying to use them to find what we need."

They both stared at Selephylin's Crown and the hovering globes of arcane energy, as if peering into its core might offer a miraculous alternative.   After a few moments, Pindlebryth shook his head to fend off its hypnotic effect.

"First, I think I shall see if Selephygur has recalled anything from the Ravenne's book of maps. That is of course, assuming he will even talk to me." He regarded Darothien with cheerless concern.

"It's not just you, M'Lord. Normally it would not be my place to say, but you mustn't believe Prince Selephygur is angry with you alone. He has turned dour in the past few days, and has been terse with many people in the castle. He has even begun to let me know he tires of me as his tutor."

He placed his hands gingerly on the table, and leaned in to ask, "What brought about this change in him?"

"I don't know. Perhaps the loss of LongBack had time to finally sink in. He was quite fond of him, you know."

"Yes, I could see how it affected him on Vulcanis. But there was more. So much has happened to him. Since his very birth, so many calamities had befallen him: Selephylin taking his eye, the years of pain he endured from the Lens, the attack by the Fox shapeshifter and then Hakayaa, the Ravenne slaying LongBack in his stead, and finally his frustration when he decided for my sake not to avenge himself on poor deranged Hakayaa. Is it any wonder that he thinks the entire world has become his adversary?"

"He really believes that?"

"Yes, he said as much in his sickbed after Tanderra was killed. And I could feel that resolve strengthen on Vulcanis. It just surprised me how he changed towards me in the short span of two days. When I spoke with him by the Talking Gem from PanGaea, he seemed so anxious to see me, but then he was almost belligerent when I returned." Pindlebryth's paws clenched into fists on the table, but then relaxed again. "Queen Wenteberei had said she would talk to him, but I think I need to talk to Selephygur for myself. And this time, do so without regarding him only as my little brother."

He was about to turn to leave, when instead he reminded himself of a thought he had in the Hall of Thrones. He was terribly alone – isolated from his closest friend and sole confidant, no other friends that he didn't keep some secrets from, and now isolated from his brother. He resolved that this was a situation that needed to be repaired. He took a few steps toward Darothien, and took her hand. "I also wanted to thank you."

"For what?"

"For helping Selephygur, for helping my father, and for helping me. You…" He gulped and took a resolved breath. "You have been always there when I needed help and counsel." Pindlebryth took a step back, and bowed to her. Dumbfounded by his gesture, Darothien stood agape at him as he left. Only after the door closed behind him and the guardian statue whined pensively, she muttered, "You are welcome, M'Lord."

As Pindlebryth climbed the curious stairs that looked wet and slick, but were firm and surefooted, he looked towards the ceiling in embarrassed frustration. At first he couldn't understand how he could feel so awkward. But in a moment, part of himself realized why he felt like this. It was only that the exigency of all the other events couldn't allow him to admit to himself the reason. Things were complicated enough.

When he reached the top of the staircase, he asked Grefdel, "Where did you say I might find Prince Selephygur?"

"Before you woke, he left with Colonel Farthun and General Vadarog for the barracks."

"Right – the gymnasium. Let us be off." He started towards the courtyard with Grefdel trailing a few steps behind. When they strode towards the West Gate, Pindlebryth squinted against the brightness the late summer sun high in the sky. There was no hint of the storm that he raced against over the MidSea, and which cast a somber note over yesterday's memorial.

When they reached the barracks, Pindlebryth was puzzled that so few soldiers were there. He inquired a passing sergeant where he might find General Vadarog, who responded he was still in the gymnasium. He found Pendenar and Gangon standing outside its doors. Gangon blocked the doorway and shooed away a few privates who seemed curious as to the activity inside.

"Good norning, N'Lord! Please go right in – General Vadarog was hoping you night find your way here."

Raising his eyebrows, he wondered what Vadarog and Farthun had planned. Pindlebryth hesitated a moment when he heard the familiar ring of steel blades clashing and sliding edge against edge. He entered and saw Selephygur and another

Lemming he did not recognize engaged in a sparring match of fencing. Pindlebryth became somewhat alarmed that neither were wearing fencing gear. Vadarog and Farthun stood by leaning against a wall, watching intently and occasionally commenting quietly between themselves.

Selephygur, still sporting his obsidian eye, parried and riposted quite clumsily against a clearly superior opponent. The young prince's fencing partner strode calmly around him, and smartly guarded and feinted, and handily swatted away the thrusts and slashes that came at him. Finally, he did not miss his opening when the opportunity presented itself, and he unceremoniously swatted the prince's behind with his blade. Farthun and Vadarog beamed and trembled slightly as they forced themselves not to laugh at the prince's painful lesson. The newcomer scolded Selephygur, saying, "No! You must learn not to depend on your good eye like that! It tricks your depth and can unbalance you. Use sound! The movement of your opponent's feet, the whir of the blade as it cuts through the air! Let your peripheral vision increase your advantage! The Quickening Spirit put our eyes and ears towards the sides of our heads for a reason!"

While attempting to concentrate on his opponent, Pindlebryth could easily see that Selephygur was enraptured with gleeful abandon, despite the thrashing he was receiving.

Vadarog caught sight of Pindlebryth and Grefdel entering, immediately stood aright and clapped twice to halt the bout. At first, the stranger had a murderous look as he swung about towards Vadarog. Obviously put out by Vadarog's temerity at interrupting, he would have lambasted him if Vadarog hadn't already started walking towards Pindlebryth. Instead, he turned again to Selephygur and saluted with his rapier indicating the lesson was over for the time being. Vadarog spread his arms wide, one to beckon Pindlebryth to come in, the other to introduce the stranger. "Good morning, M'Lord. May I introduce Duke Trevemar, come all this way from the NearWarrens canton. He is one of Lenland's greatest swords in the fealty of King Hatheron."

Facing Pindlebryth, Trevemar saluted again and snapped the sword to his side as he bowed. When he arose, he corrected Vadarog, "*The* greatest sword in Lenland!"

Vadarog immediately responded with a sarcastic taunt. "Who suffered an even greater loss!" From his tone,

Pindlebryth could easily tell Vadarog's barb was one borne of a long-worn friendship.   But then, as Pindlebryth regarded Trevemar, he quickly realized what Vadarog meant.

Trevemar wore an eyepatch over his left side.

"I'm sure, dear general, you recall I was facing three opponents on that day when the Iron Baron finally fell. Two of them were his firstborn, and his personal guard – both of whom were far superior to the usual milksops in his employ. No one has touched me since I dispatched them."

To prevent himself from staring, Pindlebryth looked instead at Selephygur.   He was breathing much more heavily than Trevemar.   Unlike Trevemar's bare blade, his rapier had a protective button inserted on the end.   When Selephygur realized he had an audience, his previous demeanor of distaste, wariness and disdain from yesterday returned.   Pindlebryth inwardly pouted as he realized he would not make much progress attempting to talk with his brother at this time.

"I am honored to make your acquaintance, Duke. Your reputation precedes you.   But I see you are engaged with Selephygur and I have come at an inopportune time. I have work of my own to attend to as well. Perhaps we can talk at some later time.

"Selephygur, I will be leaving for PanGaea again in a few days. I would hope we can both find a goodly amount of time to continue yesterday's discussion." Selephygur's frown increased in intensity.

As he turned to leave with Grefdel, Farthun shoved himself away from the wall, and piped up, "Let me see you out, M'Lord." They left, and paused outside as Gangon and Pendenar closed the doors to the gymnasium behind them.

"Pendenar gave me a full report of what happened at Vulcanis on his return. My condolences to you, M'Lord, on Master BlueHood's passing. I know he would not be mourned by many in Lenland, but I feel sorry for him nonetheless. We do, after all, owe him a measure of gratitude for having sacrificed himself to save our Prince Selephygur."

Grefdel looked at Farthun with a strange look of confusion.

"Thank you, Colonel." Pindlebryth at first felt the familiar pang of conscience over the continued deception on Hakayaa's behalf, but kept an emotionless mask lest he give away his thoughts. He could only hope that Pendenar was convincing as well. Pindlebryth forced himself not to glance at Pendenar to reassure himself. He reckoned his conflict of emotions had lessened, but couldn't help but to wonder if that was a good thing or not.

Farthun shuffled his feet awkwardly, then changed the topic. "Vadarog was also present when I received Pendenar's report. It seemed that it reinforced an idea that Vadarog had since Selephygur lost the Lens. "

"To introduce him to fencing lessons?" Pindlebryth ventured, recalling the last time he accompanied Selephygur to the barracks.

"Yes, but more than that. Selephygur always had a strong interest in the military, and had a natural talent in weaponry. Therefore, in light of his loss of vision, Vadarog felt it apropos to make sure that the young prince be adept in self-defense in general."

"Considering all that Selephygur has gone through, I would concur. If I had the time, I might avail myself of it as well. I'm sure Pendenar would have told you that my own close quarters skill was lacking."

The thought of criticism distressed Farthun, and he shifted his weight nervously. He glanced momentarily at the door as the sound of swordplay and Trevemar's commentary resumed. "Since Trevemar was here to attend the memorial, Vadarog took advantage of the opportunity to ask his long-time friend to tutor Prince Selephygur in the military arts."

"He certainly has the perfect perspective to be an excellent teacher for Selephygur."

"Yes, that was precisely Vadarog's thinking."

Pindlebryth immediately thought, "Then he also might be the one person Selephygur would open up to." Facing Farthun, he said, "Very well. I think Vadarog has taken the correct steps to best protect my brother. And Selephygur seems to have taken a liking to Duke Trevemar. I hope he takes advantage of advice Trevemar may also offer on many topics beyond just swordplay."

Since it was not his place to criticize Selephygur, Farthun instead could only shake his head as a comment on the young prince's behavior towards Pindlebryth.

"Carry on then, Colonel Farthun. As for myself, I will be spending much of my remaining time performing research in our archives before I must return to PanGaea."

"Very good, M'Lord," acknowledged Farthun. "At that time,

Grefdel will be assigned to accompany you back to PanGaea."

Pindlebryth and Grefdel had already started for the outer doors, when Pindlebryth called over his shoulder, "Yes, my new gardener has already informed me!"

While crossing the central court, a thought occurred to Pindlebryth. As he continued walking, he asked Grefdel, "You were assigned to Selephygur between the time of his return from Vulcanis, until my return from PanGaea. Correct?"

"Yes, M'Lord."

"During that time, did you happen to notice any sudden changes in my brother's mood during that period?"

"None that come to mind. He was quite upset and grieving during that entire time." They had made it most of the way to the East Wing, when Grefdel recalled, "Although he was rather irritable the second night after his return. When I asked him if everything was all right, he said he had had a bad night's sleep."

"And he's been that way ever since?"

"Yes, I'm afraid so, M'Lord."

"Did this start before or after he sported his new eye?"

"Before."

Befuddled, Pindlebryth grimaced slightly. He had hoped the cause of Selephygur's antagonistic behavior would have a simple cause – perhaps some residual magick on the obsidian from the witch queen's fortress. At least such a cause would be one that could be easily remedied. Despite that, he decided that it would still be prudent to have Darothien examine – discreetly, of course – the obsidian eye for any leftover dweomer.

The castle archive was a crowded affair, placed in a large rectangular cupola above the second floor's northeast corner. The only windows it had faced north, so that the rooms were functionally lit, but direct sunlight almost never shone in. On those few days of summer when it did, WagTail would perennially move books and scrolls away from the windows, so that their precious contents would not yellow from exposure.

The archives consisted of a large storage room, and a much smaller reading room. The storage room was stocked with countless high shelves separated by walkways barely wide enough for a Lemming to maneuver. Most of the shelves were already crammed with tomes, scrolls and binders full of loose papers. It was WagTail's favorite pastime to fret over what to do on that fateful day when the last shelf was full. The smaller reading room was fitted with a pair of rectangular tables, their accompanying stools and chairs, and a small writing desk and grandfather clock in opposite corners. Both rooms had the curious quality in that their temperature was moderate and humidity was low throughout the whole year – during the coldest winter, or the hottest humid summer, or the drenching thaws of spring.

Lanterns and other contained flames were allowed in the reading room, but were strictly forbidden in the archive proper. As a result, the storage room was closed from dusk to dawn for many generations, until Graymalden presented the archivist of his day with an enchanted lamp. Made in the same fashion as his laboratory's outer room's ceiling lamp, a ring mounted within the lamp generated a disc of glowing air until the lamp was upended.

WagTail emerged from the archival storage room pushing a small cart with several books, and the lamp on top of the stacks. Immersed in a biography of Henejer, Pindlebryth barely noticed the archivist as he emerged like a greenish-white wraith from the darkening repository behind him. Pindlebryth sat with his head propped up with both paws, his elbows sharply angled on the table. Bookended by two lamps, he looked up as WagTail stood beside him and deposited the new volumes on the table's closest open space.

Pindlebryth sat straight again, and stretched his back. Despite their utilitarian appearance, he appreciated how comfortable these wooden chairs could still be.

"Is that the last of them? Additional information on the life of Henejer?"

WagTail nodded his head with a patient smile.

"What about any drawings or plans of the castle?"

WagTail moved over to the table corner, and patted a sheaf of tubes bearing the crest of Lenland. He then swept his gaze around the reading room and momentarily looked concerned. Grunting softly, he pointed around either side of Pindlebryth.

"Oh, Grefdel? I asked him to stand outside. I'm afraid PanGaea has spoiled me. I find it difficult to concentrate on my reading when I know there is someone watching my every move."

WagTail looked down self-consciously.

"Oh, I'm sorry. I was not referring to you! And I'm certainly not going to throw you out of your own archive. In fact, you're quite welcome to..."

There came a polite knock at the door, and a butler brought in a tea service. Looking perplexed, he glanced about the room, but could not find a place to set his tray. WagTail quickly set about to clear off a smaller circular table, stacking the displaced books onto an empty chair.

"As I was about to say, you're quite welcome to some tea – ginseng and lemon. I find it helps keep me alert, but won't leave me with a sleepless night."

After they were served, the butler let them be. As they sat quietly sipping their beverages, Pindlebryth regarded WagTail. His eyes were closed, and his head was tilted to listen to the steady heartbeat of the clock. His jowls curved up once again into that small but unmistakably placid smile that spoke of a guileless spirit. Pindlebryth wondered how one who had witnessed so much evil, and suffered so much during his lifetime could still be so peaceful.

WagTail had been the Iron Baron's secretary of affairs, but on one fateful day he had somehow displeased his lord. His subsequent reward, for whatever the infraction, was to have his tongue burned out, and to be left to rot in the Baron's disease-ridden dungeons. When the Baron was captured at the end of that dark time of the easternmost canton, his dungeons were flung open, and WagTail was discovered and rescued. Such a pitiful picture was he, that King Hatheron ordered Sacalitre to personally oversee his recovery. When he was restored to health, and his previous situation was eventually made known, Hatheron further granted him the position of the Royal Archivist at the castle, despite him not having a Name of Power. Time had proven his was a good decision, as the Quickening Spirit had yet seen fit to destine a Name of Power to someone who desired the office.

Pindlebryth finished his tea, and reapplied himself to the task at hand. He had already gone through more than a half dozen biographies and architectural treatises, but not a single one had a reference to the Orb, or to a cloth or any other gift made to Henejer from Gazelikus.

He had high hopes when he found a biography that was comparatively unvarnished. Although it begrudgingly acknowledged Henejer's mastery of stonework and architecture, it was exceedingly uncomplimentary when describing his personality. It alleged that Henejer had stolen from the Royal Trust, had plagiarized ideas from colleagues, and had betrayed several friends to achieve his position. Pindlebryth thought that if any work would bury a hint on the cloth's whereabouts, it would be in the sections where it discussed the falling out between Henejer and Gazelikus. Unfortunately, he could unearth no such clue.

Under the curious and watchful eye of WagTail, Pindlebryth took a break from reading by clearing off a portion of the second table, and unrolling the castle plans and architectural drawings from their sealed tube. WagTail silently assisted Pindlebryth in this task, as the large scrolls were brittle with age in places, and needed to be gently coaxed to lie open. The drawings were of a general sort, giving an overall view of the castle layout floor by floor, without much detail.

Pindlebryth scrutinized the area of the ground floor around Henejer Hall, and shook his head as he concluded that there was little useful information here. He looked up, and asked of WagTail, "Are there more detailed drawings of the rooms, specifically Henejer Hall?"

WagTail put a finger to his temple and scratched in thought for a moment, then rummaged through the tubes from the small pile he had brought from the archives. He turned each, looking for a label, and when he happened upon the specific one he was searching for, he opened the cylinder and produced several sheets of parchment paper. As he unfurled each of the nested scrolls, it was plain the drawings had much more detail than the overall plans.

First was of the Great Audience Hall, and the second was of the dining hall in the North Wing – Pindlebryth could see that the detail included the secret listening room that Tanderra had used weeks ago, and the secret passage that Unkaar had uncovered. Another depicted the various Royal apartments and still another detailed the archive itself.

Inside the walls of the archive was a system of ducts carrying water and air, surrounded by a mixture of sand and other minerals. The water, air, and insulation all served to maintain the temperature of the room. The water came from the spring under the castle, which also served the kitchens. Furthermore, the insulation collected condensation to drains under the floor, keeping the archive as dry as a desert. Pindlebryth noticed WagTail patiently waited with more drawings, and reprimanded himself to not be further distracted from his goal.

They continued until WagTail unrolled the last of that tube's contents. He then searched the pile, looking for another label similar to that on the first tube. He and Pindlebryth eventually depleted the entire stock of tubes and drawings, only to find that specific plans for Henejer Hall were not to be found amongst them.

Pindlebryth collapsed in a chair and thumped the table with a fist. "Lords Below take Henejer! Stymied by him again! Why was he trying to hide this?" He rubbed his brow and then his eyes with both paws in complete consternation. He leaned against the back of the chair and sulked. Staring off into nothingness, he desperately tried to think of where to look next.

WagTail waited a few moments, then made to collect the drawings back into their tubes, but Pindlebryth waved him off. "No, leave them be. I may yet find a clue later buried amongst this chaff."

WagTail bowed and stepped back, waiting to hear what Pindlebryth next required. But his prince merely sighed, and turned to WagTail, saying, "Is it alright for me to leave these here for the time being? Will anyone be using the archives tomorrow?"

WagTail shook his head, held up three fingers then pointed to the clock in the corner, and scribed circles in the air.

"Ah, you're not expecting anyone during the three days of mourning?"

WagTail nodded, and touched his nose with his right index finger.

"Then I'll let you retire for the night. I will remain for a little more, to see if any brainstorms come to me. Otherwise, I will head off to bed in a little while as well. I'll extinguish the lanterns when I leave."

WagTail bowed again, upended his lamp, then hung it next to the entrance of the archive storage room. As he opened the door to the hallway, he stepped back just at the moment Darothien was about to knock. She nodded to Grefdel, then entered the room but looked away from WagTail, as if she were almost afraid to look him in the eye. WagTail bowed one last time to both of them, and softly closed the door as he left.

"M'Lord," she said perfunctorily as she pulled her wand from her sleeve.

Pindlebryth glanced back and forth between Darothien and the door WagTail had shut, and tilted his head at her as he leaned back against the chair. "What is the matter, Darothien?"

Darothien looked at the floor and muttered softly and slowly with difficulty, "WagTail grieves my spirit."

Pindlebryth immediately took her meaning, or at least he believed so. "WagTail has been in the service of King Hatheron for many years, and is one of the meekest Lemmings I have ever met."

Darothien shuffled nervously, and looked about at the explosion of books, papers and maps strewn about the reading room. "I know, I know." She stepped carefully around the table, focusing on the books. "But even after all the years that I've resided here, I just cannot bring myself to face him directly."

"Granted, he was in the employ of the Iron Baron. But surely, you cannot believe he was in league with that wretched creature, let alone was a willing participant in his many crimes against Lenland and its people."

"No, no! It's not that at all."

Pindlebryth fixed his gaze even more intently at the sorceress.

"There is something submerged inside WagTail that I cannot bring myself to look at. Whenever I am near him, I feel an open wound buried deep inside his spirit. Like a scab that is still fresh, and will bleed anew if I get too close."

"The Iron Baron left similar scars on several people." Darothien still did not look up from the table, and failed to see the gist of Pindlebryth's observation. But Pindlebryth was not going to belabor the point. Instead he asked simply, "What are you looking for here? WagTail has probably already brought it out from the archive for me."

Darothien didn't answer, but instead muttered a few words to her wand. After a moment a small cone of green fluorescence emanated from its tip. She put the base of the wand next to her ear, tilted her head towards the table, and began to listen intently to the books. Pindlebryth watched silently, engrossed by this new magick. She methodically and deliberately went from stack to stack, and moved the wand from top to bottom of each pile. She had finished with the column that Pindlebryth had most recently pored through, and was about to move to the next. Darothien paused as if she heard the wand say something, then returned to the column. She scanned the array again even more carefully until she stopped at a book in the middle of the pile and closed her eyes in concentration. She then stood erect, and extinguished her wand by passing her paw from its base to its tip.

She pulled the book, entitled "An Architectural Digest of the Works of Henejer", and laid it open to the first page on the table. Darothien pulled a chair and sat, then used her wand again. Speaking a series of words that sounded to Pindlebryth's ear like rushing wind, she pointed her wand at her free paw. A dim green bulb grew at the end of the wand, then when she completed the spell, it fluttered from the tip of the wand to her palm like a firefly. It landed and spread a diffuse green glow across from the base of her wrist to the tips of her fingers. Darothien placed her paw edge down on the table, with the palm facing the book. Darothien slid the wand back into her sleeve, and in the same motion pulled out her prism.

Staring at the book through the prism, the glow in her palm intensified ever so slightly. The topmost page on the book began to tremble, and then turned. Darothien remained stock still as page after page began to flip over in an ever increasing rate. Then without warning she extinguished the glow by clenching her paw into a fist, and exclaimed, "There!"

Pindlebryth stood up from the chair, and moved to stand next to Darothien. He hoped to see what she had discovered, but the body of text and diagrams looked nondescript, like the rest of the material he had examined. Darothien pointed and underscored a passage with a finger.

"There! What do you see?"

Again, Pindlebryth saw nothing especially noteworthy. "Just a quote from Henejer about the technical difficulties of designing and building the hall that now bears his name."

"Yes, that's what it says *now*." Still looking with the prism, Darothien drummed the line with satisfaction. "But there is an illusion cast on it, hiding the original text, overwriting it."

"A palimpsest! What does the hidden passage say?" Pindlebryth asked with growing excitement.

"The author asks Henejer if there was an overarching theme

to his work throughout Lenland. Henejer responds with, 'I always held dear to me two guiding principles: to set the world aright, you must turn my world upside down; secondly, I merely asked the stone to forget.' "

Darothien lowered her prism to look at Pindlebryth. "The author then dismisses the comments as the prerogative of an erratic genius."

Pindlebryth plopped down in the chair next to Darothien, and let out a harrumph. The two of them were silent for quite a while, looking at the book then each other, both their minds racing to discern the meaning of Henejer's statement.

"What could he have meant? Ask the stone to forget?" Darothien wondered out loud.

Two dissimilar ideas came together and formed an itch in Pindlebryth. "Even if Henejer referred to the Orb of Oblivion, how do you make an inanimate object forget?"

Looking again at the writing that obscured the original, unsure of what to think, Pindlebryth asked, "Was it Gazelikus who did this?"

Darothien passed her paw between the prism and the page. "It feels like his doing. But why would he hide this? "

Pindlebryth scratched his jawline, which began to ache from clenching his teeth over the past two days. "Any number of reasons, I fear. He resented that the Orb was given to Henejer, instead of himself. Maybe he was covetous of the Artifact. Maybe he saw a change come over Henejer, and he feared what he what would do with the Orb. Or he could have reconciled with Henejer at some later time, and assisted him in hiding the Orb and any reference to it. I could postulate any number of scenarios."

Pindlebryth sighed with resolution. "I need to return to DeepDigger's library, to learn as much as I can about the Orb, Henejer and Gazelikus." He pointed at Darothien's sleeve, where she secreted the wand. "I certainly could use your ability to find what I need the books to tell me."

Darothien smiled for a moment, but then had an inquisitive look over her face. "You've said on several occasions the need to return to PanGaea. What is it that keeps you here?"

It was immediately obvious that Pindlebryth was plagued by worry. "Selephygur. I tried before sequestering myself here for the day to talk to him, but he was otherwise engaged. It was plain to me that even if I could pry him away, he would be in no mood to talk to me. So I wonder if I should wait to try again tomorrow."

Darothien lowered her head to hide her initial disposition of disappointment at his response. Having seen a glimmer in Pindlebryth's attitude towards her, she began to ask herself how long she needed to wait for Pindlebryth to accede to it, or if she could help him to see.

Ultimately, she forced herself to accept certain realities: that it was not her place to be so forward, as Gangon had reminded her yesterday; and that all the troubles that weighed on Pindlebryth's mind outweighed her hopes for herself. All she could do was swallow and sublimate her frustration. Almost immediately, another thought took its place. Filled with trepidation, she faced Pindlebryth directly and braced herself for what could only distress Pindlebryth even more.

"I'm afraid that would do little good." She reached within a fold in the front of her flowing gown and produced Selephygur's Talking Gem.

Pindlebryth looked at it with marked dismay.

"I'm so sorry to show you this. Prince Selephygur returned his Gem to me earlier today while you were here in the castle archives. He made it plain to me that he did not wish to talk to you – not even through this medium." She proffered the Gem to Pindlebryth, who at first moved to accept it from her, but then halted and returned his arm to his side.

"No. It's probably best that you keep it for now. When I return to PanGaea, we will need to keep in close contact with each other if we are to have any hope to solve this mystery quickly." He rubbed his palms together, and then looked at her plaintively. "Besides, while I am far away from Lenland, it would comfort me to have a friend with whom I could talk from time to time."

Darothien smiled a delicate smile, though she was much more eminently gladdened that the glimmer she had sensed before in Pindlebryth had returned. She wanted to pursue the point, wanted him to say more; but she knew that beginnings were fragile things.

"I would be happy to," she replied simply. Pindlebryth watched with interest as she returned the Gem to its place in her gown.

After an awkward silence, Pindlebryth rested his forearms on the table, and looked over the hordes of books and papers layered across the tables. "I only wish I understood why Selephygur is so resentful. I at first wondered if something I said or did upset him so, but you and Grefdel have told me his mood had abruptly changed before I returned from PanGaea. We already know the Lens has changed Selephygur physically, as he can still see through the Lens with focused concentration. I fear the Lens may also be responsible for this change in his temperament."

"It's almost as if he is going through a withdrawal of sorts," Darothien mused. "If a person is used to a condition or persistent stimulus, he can exhibit irritable or even irrational behavior when it is removed."

Pindlebryth stood, and regarded Darothien with sad resignation. "If such is the case, then there is little any of us can do. We will just have to wait and be patient with my brother until this phase passes. If the change is more permanent however, I will rely on you to keep me abreast of his condition while I am away."

Darothien stood and was about to curtsey as Pindlebryth left, but he paused before opening the door. Turning sideways, he turned to look back at Darothien. "I was going to stay in the archive for another day, but I now think I will leave for PanGaea tomorrow. Would you care to join me after breakfast for a ride through the forest trails southeast of the castle? I would like to be able to take away with me at least one pleasant memory from my visit this week."

"Very much so, M'Lord," Darothien beamed. Pindlebryth smiled wanly, opened the door and walked down the hallway, with Grefdel in his shadow.

Pindlebryth retired to his rooms, and for the first time in a very long time, he was able to put out of his mind the burdens that swarmed around him, and slept peacefully.

"Greetings, Father," saluted Pindlebryth as he entered the family's dining room, as Grefdel waited outside. He then walked over to Wenteberei, who accepted his kiss. "Good morning, Mother." As Pindlebryth sat down, the waitstaff served the plates of the morning meal. He noted that in addition to the usual breakfast fare, there was included one his mother's favorites – a simple bread made from alfalfa sprouts topped with honeycomb.

"Someone seems rather chipper this morning," quipped Wenteberei.

"Yes, I suppose I am. Darothien and I are riding in the southeast forest this morning."

Hatheron and Wenteberei exchanged a knowing glance and tried to hide a smile. Pindlebryth looked at the empty place setting and inquired, "Where is Selephygur this morning? He's not still sleeping, is he?"

"No," Hatheron replied. "He took a light meal in his own room, then went to join Trevemar for tutoring in the sword again. I hope his absence at the table does not become a habit."

Pindlebryth regarded Wenteberei, who for some reason sat still, and had not eaten any of the food in front of her, not even the alfalfa bread. "What is the matter, Mother? Did you have occasion to talk with Selephygur yesterday?"

Her chest heaved with a great plaintive sigh. "Only for a bit. He was in no disposition to respond beyond single word answers. Perhaps he will open up to us in the next few days."

A pained look came across Pindlebryth's face. "I'm afraid I will not be able to help in this matter, at least not immediately. I plan to fly back to PanGaea later today. The matter of the Orb and the Crow will not wait. I must return to my research there.

"Darothien will continue to delve through our archives in her attempt to find further clues about the Orb that Henejer or Gazelikus may have left. If only her wizard's power did not wane away from Lenland – she would be a great help to me with my own research."

"Is that all?" Hatheron inquired after sipping some juice. Wenteberei kicked her husband lightly under the table with her good leg, while maintaining an innocent smile.

"In addition, I find that I must ask a favor of you. If Selephygur becomes civil again and deigns to talk with you, help him recall where he may have seen the location of the Orb in the Ravenne's book."

"What do you mean, 'if'? Do you believe he will continue to withdraw into himself?" Wenteberei fretted.

"Possibly. Remember, Artifacts have the power to change the user. It is decidedly plain to me that the Lens has already affected his attitude, and I fear may have affected his mind as well. If he continues to remain detached, you might make progress by asking Trevemar to engage him."

Pindlebryth and Hatheron took a few more bites of their breakfast, but Wenteberei remained still. "Very well, then. You must go where you feel your duty to Lenland calls you." The three of them finished their meal in silence. Even Wenteberei finally partook in the meal, relishing her bread and honeycomb. Through the windows, the peal of the clock in the city square could be dimly heard. Pindlebryth excused himself, to change into his riding clothes. As he and Grefdel receded down the hallway, Hatheron looked at Wenteberei, remarking quietly aside, "I was beginning to wonder when our son, whom the Quickening Spirit decided to bestow such remarkable intelligence, would finally take notice of the obvious." Wenteberei chortled softly in agreement.

When he and Grefdel arrived back at his rooms, Pindlebryth yet again endured what he perceived as the indignity of being assisted into his riding clothes. At least, he thought, he wouldn't have to undergo this ritual a second time today, as his riding gear was also fit for flying. When his butler was finished, he ordered that his bags from PanGaea be ready and packed on Voyager upon his return from his morning's ride.

Darothien was already in the stable, assisting the reindeer wrangler in adjusting the steed's tack and saddle. She wore a pair of dark brown pants made of hemp, a pair of sturdy boots, and a long green jacket. Stable workers brought out reindeer already fitted for Pindlebryth and Grefdel.

"Good Morning, M'Lord," chimed Darothien.

"And to you, fair Darothien," echoed Pindlebryth in a tone that almost might have been described as playful. "Shall we be off?"

As they all mounted their rides, Pindlebryth noted with some curiosity that Darothien did not ride sidesaddle. After a moment, he recalled hearing that such was not the practice in the eastern cantons, then shrugged his shoulders and put it out of his mind. The group trotted from the stables along the western wall of the castle and followed the path of crushed gravel that bordered the South Wing. While Pindlebryth and Darothien soaked in the sunlight pouring from the east, they simply enjoyed the tableau of greenery speckled with dots of brown signaling the oncoming fall, and each other's company. Though they were quite oblivious to anything else, Grefdel however looked up to the windows of the topmost floor. From the dining room, King Hatheron looked down upon the riders, and he and Grefdel exchanged nods of acknowledgment. The trio followed the path as it wended past a hedge maze, through a gated hedgerow, and finally joined the southern road from the city square. They continued on the road for a little over a mile, and took an easterly fork, away from the mausoleums where Tanderra and LongBack lay. Then as copses of trees gave way to a lush continuous verge on either side of the road, they veered off the main road towards a bridle path to the southeast. As they entered, Pindlebryth and Darothien slowed their mounts to a walk, and Grefdel quickly pressed past his charges to take the lead.

The path followed a smooth line curving towards the south, until it paralleled a brook, where it widened. Pindlebryth sidled next to Darothien's mount, and took a deep breath. The air was invigorating, filled with fragrances of the ripe fruit of summer's end, the sweet scent of fresh water, and the tang of imminent fall. Glints and spots of sunlight appeared and disappeared all through the verdant grass, as a gentle breeze swayed the trees' canopy to and fro. The calls of wild birds could be heard from far away, nearby, and despite their passing close by, even in the trees next to the path.

"I haven't been along this way for quite a while. It's also been far too long since I merely took the time to..." Pindlebryth paused. "To just *be*." Darothien looked sidewise at his profile. She was gratified to see he was looking all around with an unabashedly innocent grin.

"I have never been down this path. It *is* quite beautiful," she agreed.

Pindlebryth moved his reindeer to the side of the path, and pulled two pears from a low hanging limb. His reindeer sauntered back to her side, and he offered one of the fruit to her. She accepted with a smile, "Thank you, M'Lord."

"Gangon's not here. You needn't be so formal," he teased. He paused, to watch her bite into the fruit. He continued to smile, perhaps not as innocently as before, as he found he was quite stricken by Darothien's green eyes as they scintillated in the sunlight.

They rode on more slowly, letting Grefdel get quite far ahead, but still never entirely lost from view. Pindlebryth figured that was more Grefdel's doing, allowing him to keep an

eye on their safety, but still allowing them a modicum of privacy. As they finished their pears, they approached a thicket where a number of white birch trees grew. Pindlebryth reached for his water-skin behind his saddle, but Darothien interjected.

"Wait! There's something better." She pressed with her knees to steer her mount towards the birches, where she dismounted. Pindlebryth watched with interest as she walked slowly around the closest of the trees with her right paw held out, level with the ground. She slowed and began to hum to herself softly, soon stopping near where a network of roots had percolated along the surface. For a moment she closed her eyes, and turned in place, as if her paw were leading her. She opened her eyes, and spoke a word.

It seemed a tinge of green left the leaves of the birch, and coursed down the branches and trunks of the birches. A faint limning of green encircled a small area on the ground. Water began to burble out of the rough circle and quickly fill a depression bordered by criss-crossing roots raised on the ground. She bent down, cupped her paws, and drank. "Ah! The sweetest water there is."

Pindlebryth hopped off his steed, and joined her. Down on his haunches, he cupped his paws and sniffed. There was a scent unknown to him, but it nonetheless smelled inviting. He took a sip, and tasting the tinge of sweet birch, he glanced at Darothien and smiled and drank it fully. He and Darothien took a few more handfuls, when Darothien placed her hands in the pool, and splashed Pindlebryth's face.

Sputtering with mock outrage, he reached down into the pool to do likewise, but Darothien had already jumped up, and skirted past the nearest tree. Her head poked out from behind, and with an impish grin slid back behind the trunk. Pindlebryth abandoned himself to the child's game of hide-and-go-seek, and leapt up to pursue. He reached the tree that Darothien hid behind, and quickly circled around it, but she was not there. Looking around and back again in confusion, he spotted that Darothien had somehow moved two trees further away from the path. He scrambled to the second tree, only again to be left searching emptiness. Scanning around again, Darothien had managed to be behind yet another trunk two trees over. As she slipped away from view once more, Pindlebryth took a deep breath, and ran. But he did not stop at the particular tree where Darothien last appeared. Instead, he ran to the fourth tree away.

Rounding from the opposite side, he caught her. He let loose an exclamation of satisfaction as Darothien squealed with surprise. He held her fast by the wrist, and pulled her closer. They both smiled, and their eyes met as if they both said 'yes'. Together they closed their eyes, bowed their heads and pressed the sides of their muzzles against one another.

Pindlebryth was about to whisper something to Darothien, when the rough pounding of hooves came rushing towards them. Grefdel rode up with reins in one paw, and a spyglass in the other.

"Forgive the intrusion, M'Lord. But we have a visitor."

Pindlebryth took Darothien by the paw and hurried to their mounts. "Where?"

Grefdel gestured towards the sky with the spyglass. "A solitary flyer, circling around. It looks like a Snow Goose."

"Solitary?" he echoed. Pindlebryth looked inquisitively at Darothien, who could only shrug her shoulders. He strained to catch a glimpse of the bird through the canopy, but could not.

"There's a glen ahead, where we can get a better view. We should ride as if everything were normal, unawares of prying eyes." Grefdel waited for the pair to get astride their reindeer, then led them at a moderate pace further along the path. A few minutes passed until they approached an open swale of grass. They stopped just before they left the shade of the trees.

Pindlebryth lowered his head to scan more directly upwards through the opening. They didn't wait long until a silhouette floated past the opening and began to circle, leading away from the brook. Grefdel's reindeer began to stamp its hooves as if it were impatient. He firmly stroked the side of its neck to calm it down and silence it. Within a minute the bird circled again over the opening, flapping its wings continuously. It quickly banked away from the brook before disappearing a second time.

"That is no Snow Goose," whispered Pindlebryth.

"How do you know?" asked Darothien quietly.

"Snow Geese never fly alone," Grefdel replied.

"They usually circle only to land, and then only near bodies of water," chimed in Pindlebryth cautiously.

"Also... it doesn't seem to be flying right," noted Grefdel. "It doesn't look wounded, but I've never seen a Snow Goose fly like that before."

"It's a Crow," Pindlebryth hissed.

By force of habit, he looked behind his saddle for his crossbow. There was none, and Pindlebryth remembered with some aggravation at himself for letting his guard down. Pindlebryth glanced at Darothien, who likewise was nonplussed without her wand.

"Here!" Grefdel pulled two crossbows, one from either side behind his saddle. He tossed one of the crossbows to Pindlebryth, followed by a capped quiver of bolts. They cocked their weapons, loaded a quarl each, and waited.

Pindlebryth raised his crossbow in anticipation of a third appearance of the interloper. He was closely watching the skies when it appeared yet again. Its path had shifted and its circular path was larger, which made it obvious the bird was searching for them. The Snow Goose seemed low enough to just be inside the range of a crossbow. Grefdel and Pindlebryth raised their weapons, and waited for their best shot.

Pindlebryth was about to fire, when a doubt crept into his mind. What if this was Hakayaa? He tried to convince himself that although Hakayaa might be well enough by now to no longer be bedridden, he was in no way well enough to fly all the way from PanGaea. He was still wrestling with the dilemma, when Grefdel's shot whistled skyward.

It was a clean miss, but at least it did confirm that the target was within range. "We're committed now," Pindlebryth thought to himself.   He held his breath to aim, as he prayed, "Quickening Spirit, please let that not be Hakayaa."

He shot true, but did not hit the target squarely. The quarl ripped through one wing. A flurry of feathers fell from the bird, and within moments it underwent a change. The long graceful neck foreshortened, the cygnet wings thickened and moved forward on the body, and the white and gray shape molted to black. It stopped circling, and lost altitude. It tried to limp along, but suddenly veered directly towards them. An object dropped from a claw headed directly for them.

Grefdel yelled, "Cover!"   He kneed his mount and interposed himself between the object and Pindlebryth. It hit the ground and exploded in a soft concussion. A great cloud of grey and orange smoke spread thickly and rapidly.   The reindeer bucked and nearly threw Grefdel off before trying to bolt. Grefdel dropped his crossbow. Then with one hand on the reins, the other pulling the reindeer's antlers to the side, he managed to bring it under control. As he rejoined his charges, the reindeer's side quaked and shivered. Pindlebryth glanced skyward, and could barely see through the rising smoke that the Crow limped directly to the south until it disappeared from view for good.

Darothien saw the broadside of the reindeer and exclaimed, "Grefdel, are you all right?"

Pindlebryth turned to look at the guard, and saw several shards of glass sticking out of his riding chaps. Grefdel swiped them off with his glove. The reindeer took the brunt of the grenade, as several slivers of glass were embedded in its coat. Fortunately, only a few of the glass fragments drew blood.

"I'm fine. Stay here, M'Lord." Grefdel dismounted his reindeer, and handed the reins to Pindlebryth. He ran directly into the center of the glen, where he circled around for a few moments, searching the ground.

Darothien also dismounted, excused herself, and disappeared into the thicket.

Grefdel stooped down to pick something up from the tall grass, then jogged back to Pindlebryth. He handed over a glove-full of black Crow feathers. "Blood. He's not badly wounded, but he will find it difficult to fly any distance."

"Lords Below!" spat Pindlebryth. "What did he think he was doing here?"

Darothien soon returned with a fistful of witch-hazel. She separated the roots, and rubbed the leaves and bark together furiously in her gloves. Meanwhile, Grefdel retrieved his dropped crossbow. He then loaded it, and handed Pindlebryth the remaining bolts from his quiver. He refilled the empty container with shards of soot-covered glass he gingerly pulled from his beast. The reindeer whinnied and complained when the few that sunk into skin were removed, but it stood fast.

"He's moving slowly. Shouldn't we pursue?" Pindlebryth champed with more than a little anger.

Capping the quiver shut, Grefdel said, "No, M'Lord. We had best get back to the castle. There's no telling if our friend may return with others."

Darothien cupped the bark in her paws, and uttered words that sounded like boiling water. When she opened her gloved paws, the bark was dried with a tinge of green. She gently took pinches of the material and gently pasted it over the wounds. Within seconds the bleeding stopped. The reindeer whickered with relief.

Grefdel elected to walk aside his reindeer, rather than ride it. After Darothien climbed back onto her mount, he led Pindlebryth and Darothien back down the path towards the main road and ultimately the castle. As they neared the road, Grefdel's reindeer's breathing became labored. Grefdel faced a conundrum – he wanted to slow his pace to make it easier for the reindeer, but did not want to unduly delay getting everyone back to the safety of the castle. Maintaining his walking pace, they made it to the road and turned north. By the time they reached the fork, and rejoined the light traffic on the main road, the reindeer was beginning to stumble. Darothien moved forward to suggest, "I think there is more I can do to help the poor creature."

But it was too late. The reindeer whinnied and its legs began to tremble then buckle. Violently bringing up the contents of its stomach, the poor creature also lost control of its bowels. Its eyes rolled up, and it collapsed in the middle of the road. Within seconds, its gulping breaths stopped.

"Ravenne!" Pindlebryth cursed between grinding teeth.

"They dare enter Lenland again!" exclaimed Grefdel. He spun around, and looked around at the sparse populace on the road.

Darothien began pulling off her gloves, turning them inside out as she did so. "Grefdel! Take off your gloves and chaps. There may be poison leeched onto them." He speedily unlaced his leggings, while Pindlebryth opened his saddlebag and emptied it.

"And burn everything poisoned when we return," added Pindlebryth, holding its flap open. Grefdel and Darothien complied and dumped the capped quiver, leggings and both their gloves into his saddlebag.

Spotting a wagon drawn by two reindeer, Grefdel ran towards them hailing the driver with his arm. "Stop! Your Prince needs your assistance!" Amidst the yelp of surprise and protests, Grefdel began unhitching the closest of two drafts-deer. The Lemming, driving a wagon-load of grain, continued his complaints until Pindlebryth and Darothien joined them.

"Is there a problem?" Pindlebryth demanded. The merchant was struck dumb when he realized the gravity of the situation. "Wait here with the fallen reindeer. Make sure you or no one else touches it until help arrives from the castle. Do you understand?" The rider looked vacantly at Pindlebryth, and said nothing.

"*Do you understand?*" Pindlebryth shouted. The merchant nodded in silent and shocked agreement. "A detail of guards will return presently to collect the carcass. Your reindeer will be returned to you at that time, and then you may be on your way."

"Yes, my Prince!" stuttered the driver, finally finding his voice.

When the reindeer was unhitched, Grefdel pulled the full length of its reins from the driver's paws, and cut them to a short length with a knife. He leapt astride the beast without a saddle, and called to Pindlebryth and Darothien.

"M'Lord! Let us be off!" He looked skyward, and seeing it was clear, he motioned Pindlebryth and Darothien to precede him. While constantly scanning the sky, the road ahead and behind, Grefdel followed close behind as the trio galloped back to the castle.

Racing to the southern hedgerow, Pindlebryth yelled to the watch at the gate as they approached. Two guards scrambled to open the gate and close it behind them again. Grefdel shouted an order over his shoulder to lock down the entrance and admit no one until further notice. They sped along the south of the castle, until they returned to the stables. A few soldiers from the barracks followed them, giving chase after they saw the trio race past.

Grefdel, Pindlebryth and Darothien dismounted and simultaneously barked orders to the stable hands and the soldiers around the stables.

"There is a fallen reindeer along the southern road, just before the first fork," Grefdel shouted. "You'll find a farmer merchant waiting there. Take a wagon to collect the poisoned carcass, then burn it."

Pindlebryth unslung his saddlebag and threw it on the ground.

"Burn these with it. Take Grefdel's mount and return it to the merchant, and help him to hitch it to his wagon again," concluded Pindlebryth.

"Enough, my Prince!" said Grefdel as forcefully as he dared. "I think it best you get inside. I shall report the attack to Colonel Farthun."

Immediately Grefdel was besieged with questions by his fellow soldiers. He bellowed over the cacophony of voices, "We were attacked by a Ravenne! Lock down the West Gate and all other entrances. No one except castle personnel is allowed to enter. Where is Colonel Farthun?"

Pindlebryth and Darothien bustled through the West Gate, and headed towards the East Wing. Grefdel soon followed hot on their heels. Once inside, Grefdel ran to the stairs leading to the South Wing's guards' quarters. Pindlebryth and Darothien stood aside to let him pass. He turned to her and said, "I need to see my father. You go inform the Prime Minister." He had the look of murder in his eyes as he turned to follow Grefdel, but Darothien did not let go of his paw. He stopped and faced her again with angry defiance. She held him fast, hugging him with her whole being, holding her head against his chest. Before he had a chance to react further, she released him and dashed away down the corridor.

For a split second he stood dumbfounded. More properly, he was confused, fighting a dilemma between what he wanted to do, how he could have responded, and the necessities that needed his immediate attention.

He watched as Darothien rounded the corner, then turned to go his own way. He bounded up the stairs to the top floor of the South Wing, and dashed to his parents' rooms. A butler was leaving with an empty service tray, leaving one of the double doors ajar. Pindlebryth pushed his way past and pounded on the door, but did not wait for a reply. He pulled the door fully open to see Wenteberei and Selephygur sitting on either side of one corner of the table, and Hatheron at the other end with two sheets of paper.

Wenteberei stopped talking to Selephygur, who glared at him with no small indignity, while Hatheron looked up with inquiring alarm.

"What's wrong, my son?" he ventured.

"We have been attacked by a Ravenne spy."

Hatheron bolted upright out of his seat, crumpling the papers in his fist. "Are you all right? How did this happen?"

"We were followed by what seemed to be a Snow Goose, but Grefdel and I spotted it for it was. When we attempted to bring it down, it threw a grenade and retreated. It was only slightly wounded, but the grenade had traces of poison which killed Grefdel's mount."

"We must see Prime Minister Amadan." Hatheron stormed out the room, with Pindlebryth following. Selephygur also stood to leave, but Wenteberei placed her paw over his, persuading him to remain with her.

"Darothien has already gone to inform Amadan, and Grefdel is reporting to Colonel Farthun."

Hatheron was angrily silent as they walked. They left the top floor, one of the hallway guards trailing close behind them until they reached the Prime Minister's anteroom. They burst in upon Darothien and Amadan, who were already engaged in an animated conversation. Hatheron marched up to the long central table, and pounded it with the fist still holding the crushed papers.

"Amadan, get Vadarog to post watches, night and day, around the entire Snow Goose embassy. They are to report if any members of the embassy are wounded, and if possible apprehend them."

"But they have immunity," Amadan protested.

Hatheron shoved a nearby chair away and stalked right up to Amadan's face. "Don't you think I know that! If you spot them, hold them for questioning," said Hatheron, growing in intensity. "Do what you have to do, use any legal tactics you can to delay them, but do not allow them back onto their grounds!"

"Yes, your Majesty."

"I'm not finished! Have your staff, your spies, or anyone you need to find out if anyone in their embassy is missing or wounded. I want to know if there is a Ravenne amongst his staff.

"And you, Darothien, be on call to examine anyone Vadarog brings you from that embassy staff you haven't already checked." Darothien shrank under the weight of Hatheron's booming voice.

"If that doesn't convince Onkyon to make a damned decision, then he's totally useless, and I want him out of the country!"

Hatheron turned, looking as if he could spit acid, and tromped out of the room. As he receded down the hall, he could be heard bellowing for Colonel Farthun. Amadan glanced at Darothien and Pindlebryth with indignation battling contriteness, then turned around and walked into the waiting room between his and his undersecretary's offices.

"Tell Vadarog I want to see him here within the half-hour, and get a carriage for us," said Amadan as he leaned through the doorway into his undersecretary's office. "Then get back here yourself, along with Talenday. We have an official letter of protest and possibly some warrants to draft."

Scuffling could be heard beyond the door. Moments later, Amadan's secretary scurried through the anteroom on his errands with only the slightest bow as he passed by.

"If you will excuse me, M'Lord and madam," Amadan concluded as he shut his office door behind him leaving Pindlebryth and Darothien alone.

Darothien regarded Pindlebryth for a while, her head turning to one side and another, while he stared at the table rubbing his jowls deep in thought. Finally, he looked at her and hazarded a speculation. "I don't think the Ravenne's original intention was to attack us. He could have done so earlier, if he so desired. I think he was initially just trying to observe us. He attacked only when we attacked him and he needed to escape."

"Why would he follow us? We were doing nothing out of the ord... well, nothing he would be concerned about."

"Perhaps he needed to know what we were doing, such as looking for the Orb."

"But they have their map, which is more than we have. Why would they need to follow us?"

"True." Pindlebryth folded his arms in thought, staring at the table again. "But Selephylin's Crown still indicates they do not have the Orb, correct? Perhaps their map is not as accurate as they thought. Which means we may have a little more time on our side to find Gazelikus' Cloth and the Orb."

Pindlebryth rounded the table to be next to Darothien. "I hate to leave, but we are in a race. I have to go back to DeepDigger's archive. Perchance I will pay the Raccoon embassy in PanGaea a visit as well.

"I'm counting on you to continue to search our archives. Remember to help Selephygur recall the details of the map. Even if their map isn't accurate, it at least will tell us where the Crow will be searching."

They hugged each other firmly, and nuzzled again. Pindlebryth inhaled deeply and withdrew, but kept his paws on her waist. He found he wanted desperately to be able to remember every aspect of this goodbye – her look, her smell, her touch.

Darothien released him adding, "Keep the Talking Gem next to you – next to your heart, so I will always know you are well."

"And you. It will constantly remind me of you." Pindlebryth hesitated, then at last turned and walked out of the room, where Grefdel patiently awaited at a respectful distance from the anteroom's doors.

"How long have *you* been there?"

"Not long, M'Lord. Colonel Farthun is inspecting the castle grounds' lock-down. Are you still planning to return to PanGaea?"

"Yes. As soon as possible, if not sooner. Get Voyager, your mount and a fresh set of riding gear ready now, before that blasted Crow has a chance to report to his superiors."

"I don't think Colonel Farthun or General Vadarog would agree that is wise."

"It is not their decision, and I'm in no mood to explain it to them," said Pindlebryth as they rounded up the stairwell to the top floor of the South Wing.

"Yes, M'Lord." Grefdel stopped, then turned to go back down the stairs when he was assured there was a full contingent of guards along the main hallway.

Pindlebryth threw open the door to his rooms, to find a maid and butler finishing the packing of the belongings he had brought from PanGaea. He undid one of the largest bag's side pockets, and fished around. Presently, he pulled out a pouch, and removed the Talking Gem from it. As Darothien asked, he buttoned it in his left breast pocket of his riding jerkin.

"Get me my riding coat," he ordered the butler, who retrieved it from the closet, and held it up and out for Pindlebryth to don. Pindlebryth quickly swept it on, his usual distaste for such menial assistance not even coming close to crossing his mind. "Take these bags to the stables immediately, and have them loaded onto Voyager."

He looked out his window, first down at the inner courtyard, then up at the skies. It was well in the afternoon, and the skies looked calm. "Thank the Lords Above," he muttered to himself. The skies were mostly clear, with only a smattering of high cirrus clouds. It would afford them little to no cover during their travel, but on the other hand, it would be equally difficult for them to be followed unnoticed. The clouds crawled slowly eastward indicating a headwind from the west, which made it almost a certainty that they would have to pause overnight somewhere in the MidSea Archipelago.

He turned to leave but halted abruptly when he saw Selephygur leaning against the door jamb.

"Where are you going in such a hurry?" he asked with a sardonic grin.

"To PanGaea, of course."

"Not running away, are we?"

"What?!"

"To some it would seem that at the first hint of danger, you tuck tail and fly off, leaving everyone to deal with it."

Pindlebryth's temper began to rise at Selephygur's smarmy tone, but he still managed to rein it in. "You have no idea what you're talking about."

Selephygur pushed off from the doorway, and stepped closer to his brother. "Then why are you going to PanGaea at this moment?"

"This is no secret to you. I go to research where the Henejer hid the Orb, and to find Gazelikus' Cloth, and any further clues to stop the Ravenne from taking the Orb."

"Oh, your precious books. Come brother, why are you really going?   Afraid of something – or *someone*?" Selephygur prodded.

Pindlebryth began sounding as if he was chewing mill grist. "To protect Lenland. If your remaining eye were any good, you would see that is exactly what everyone around you is doing, too." His voice grew in clarity and volume with each sentence. "Why do you think Vadarog brought Trevemar here? Because he likes you? Or might there possibly be another reason? Why do you think Pendenar and Grefdel risked their lives for me? Why do you think LongBack risked his life for you?"

Selephygur became visibly incensed, his paws clenched in fists, but he stood his ground.

"To help protect Lenland's future, that's why!" Pindlebryth fumed.

Pindlebryth stormed past his brother but halted as he entered the hallway. In a more level tone, he added, "You told me once that you were tired of the way the world treats you. You've had more knocks than most, I give you that. But the world is not going to start treating you well because of your protests. The only ones you can count on not to take advantage of you are your parents and myself, your family."

He sighed, and looked straight and true at his brother. "It's time to stop being a pup. Make LongBack proud – and his sacrifice *mean* something."

He left, heading for his parents' rooms. Selephygur growled and pounded the doorjamb with his fist. But after a moment, he leaned his head against it and closed his eyes.

Pindlebryth explained his intent and said his goodbyes to Wenteberei, and left. Hatheron had not yet returned, so he asked her to inform him when she next saw him. The afternoon was waning, and they both agreed that it was best if he leave as soon as possible.

As he passed through the West Gate, he saw the guard was doubled, and a lot of activity could be heard from the barracks. When he arrived at the stables, Voyager keened happily and shoved his head between his chest and his arm. Pindlebryth in turn lovingly stroked the neck of his petrel. Voyager pulled his head out, and began to take Pindlebryth's arm in his beak and playfully, gently gnaw. Looking around, he was somewhat surprised to see two other birds saddled and prepared for flight. He was about to inquire, when Grefdel and another guard emerged from behind a wall with provisions.

"Colonel Farthun insisted we have at least two guards accompany you for the flight. A prudent precaution, given today's events," said Grefdel, anticipating Pindlebryth's question.

"But PanGaea authorities will not stand for that. They do not allow soldiers from other countries. You have your cover story as my gardener. But what about his?"

"Jarjin here will accompany us to the Archipelago. When we are assured we are not followed, he will return to Lenland while we proceed to PanGaea."

"Well enough then. Let us be off before we lose anymore light. What moon shall we have tonight?"

"The last quarter."

"Alright. At least we'll have some light to see if anyone is tracking us."

They stocked their provisions and their travel bags, then mounted their steeds. Pindlebryth pressed a paw over his breast pocket to ensure the Gem was still safe and secure. With his nod, the troupe set off without ceremony.

The headwind grew in force as they approached the shoreline, but then abated appreciably once they were over the open MidSea. Every dozen leagues or so, Jarjin and Grefdel would move their terns to exchange places around Pindlebryth and Voyager. When Grefdel took the lead, he would scan the air ahead, and Jarjin would periodically check the rear. As the sun sank hazily into the west, they no longer stayed in single file. Sometimes they would maneuver to Pindlebryth's sides, and other times beneath and above him. Pindlebryth himself would occasionally scan the horizon and air about them, but most of the time his mind was wrapped up in the riddle of the Orb, or drifting off into daydream about Darothien.

They made good time, and landed on a particularly hospitable island of the southern part of the Archipelago. The eastern beach was dotted with knots of palm trees, and a small grove of bushes was several yards past the line of high tide.

They landed next to a rocky outcropping, where Grefdel and Jarjin quickly set up camp. The birds were tied to the trees, and their gear removed. Circling rocks for a fire, they collected driftwood and built two small lean-tos. They were placed on the east and south sides, to hide the fire from prying eyes. Once the fire was going, Jarjin collected two flat rocks and a few coconuts, placing one rock in the middle of the fire and the coconuts on top of that. Grefdel took a large bag of dried fish to the terns. Removing Voyager's reins and hitch from the tree, Pindlebryth took one of the fish, and held it up for him. Voyager trilled with anticipation. With a childlike grin, he threw the fish towards the ocean. It never hit the water, as Voyager launched himself and caught the tidbit in midair. Pindlebryth left Voyager to have his fun and sat next to the palms, watching with innocent pleasure. Voyager dove into the water, and with a great splash flew back out with a fish in his crop, and dove again. When he had his fill, he returned to Pindlebryth, and moved his bill up and down his side as if he was preening his master. Pindlebryth tied him again to the palms, and took out a thinly toothed comb from Voyager's tack and saddle next to the trees. After giving Voyager a quick preening and a mild rubdown, he rejoined his fellows.

Pindlebryth sensed Grefdel's unease. He kept scanning all the horizon that he could see from the north to the south.

"What's wrong, Grefdel?"

With a tense inhalation, he replied, "It is nothing M'Lord. Just some unpleasant memories. This island is very similar to the one on which the Iron Baron was marooned. I just can't seem to shake the foolish notion that a rogue wave might eradicate this island as well."

After some thought, Pindlebryth countered, "I wouldn't be too concerned. If some such event were to occur, our mounts would sense it long before we would see it. That's something we have the Baron didn't."

The coconuts cracked with a resounding pop, and Jarjin nimbly removed them from the rock. He took his knife, and wedged it into each crack, and gingerly forced them open. He kept the halves horizontal so as not to let the milk spill, and placed them on rocks away from the fire to cool. The delicacy made a wonderful end to an otherwise rough meal.

Grefdel and Jarjin took turns keeping guard while the others slept. The morning arrived without incident, and they were awakened by the terns' shrill calls greeting the predawn sky. Grefdel scanned the horizon with his spyglass, while Jarjin broke camp and saddled the birds.

"The skies are still clear. We should leave before the sun rises," advised Grefdel. Before they took off, Grefdel changed his flying jerkin with guard insignia to a plainclothes riding suit. They all took off, circled the island twice to gain altitude, then went their separate ways – Jarjin to the southeast and home, and the others towards the northwest to PanGaea.

They resumed their flight as before, except Grefdel would occasionally loop around Pindlebryth to scan the entire horizon. By the midpoint of this second leg of the trip, Pindlebryth found he could think no more about the Orb. Besides, he felt it was irresponsible to allow himself the luxury of daydreaming. He thereby occupied himself with looping and scanning the skies in turns with Grefdel. As they approached PanGaea, the cirrus clouds gradually gave way to towering cumulus with their bottoms sheared away. Nearer the shoreline, they dropped down to a few dozen yards above the water, taking advantage of the boost from a building tailwind.

They arrived in PanGaea without incident, and landed at the Double Eagle, the stables that Pindlebryth often employed. Collecting their bags, they hired a carriage to his apartments. Pindlebryth assisted in transferring their baggage from the steeds to the carriage, all to Grefdel's confused chagrin.

"Grefdel, you will find that there are some things done for me back home, that I will do for myself here."

Pindlebryth tried to relax during the ride, often rubbing his neck made sore from the constant craning left, right and behind during the flight. He determined the first thing he would do back at his abode, would be to have BroadShanks prepare several hot towels for his stiffening neck.

He looked at Grefdel, who was still as alert as ever, his eyes seemingly trying to observe everything outside. "I think you can relax now, Grefdel."

"Yes, M'Lord. But I am only taking in the sights. I have not been to PanGaea before."

"Well, try not to look like a tourist when we're out and about. Accompany BroadShanks and HighStance when they make their rounds for their errands. They'd be happy to acquaint you with the CityState of PanGaea."

Pindlebryth sat back and arched his shoulders, hoping to

stretch out the kink that was building in his neck. He started to think about what else would be waiting for him. He was sure he would have to spend a good portion of the day telling Hakayaa what had passed back home. He wondered if Hakayaa was indeed no longer bedridden, and how his health had progressed. Then suddenly, with a start, Pindlebryth sat bolt upright.

Hakayaa!

He looked at Grefdel, who still was looking alternately out through the left and right windows. How could he be so forgetful, spending so much time being distracted by daydreams? He leaned forward, and wondered how Grefdel would receive the news.

"Grefdel? What I am about to tell you, is known only by a few people. I have sworn them to secrecy, as I must now require of you." Pindlebryth paused and sighed languidly, as Grefdel focused on him with inquiring eyes.

"Hakayaa is alive."

"The Crow?" He gulped incredulously. "The one who ripped out Prince Selephygur's eye?" If they were not in a moving carriage, he might have leapt to his feet in furious indignation. Pindlebryth was somewhat taken aback that Grefdel would be so upset – he had been Selephygur's guard only since his return from Vulcanis. "The Crow responsible for LongBack's death?"

Pindlebryth interrupted, his face a study in stoic resolve.

"Who told you *that*? No need – it was my brother, wasn't it?"

Grefdel nodded, containing his anger.

"Hakayaa and LongBack *both* shielded Selephygur from the Ravenne. The poison they used was deadly to Lemmings, but still quite injurious to Crow. Hakayaa's wounds laid him out on a sick bed for several days. Selephygur owes his life to Hakayaa just as much as LongBack."

Grefdel's jaw moved up and down, as if he was chewing his tongue, or wanted to say something in protest but dared not open his mouth. He composed himself then muttered, "We were told he died over MidSea and was lost."

"No, Pendenar brought him to PanGaea under my care." The carriage started to rumble with the sound of the cobblestones of his neighborhood, so Pindlebryth quickly summarized the aftermath of Vulcanis. "When you return to

PanGaea, you can verify Hakayaa's self-sacrifice with Pendenar. But until that time, I must swear you to silence about this. If the Ravenne find out Hakayaa is alive, they may kill him or put his family in peril again in another attempt to manipulate him. For his protection, we have created the persona of Kaiya for him."

Grefdel still was obviously perturbed, but he acceded, "I understand, M'Lord."

The sudden knot in Pindlebryth's stomach abated and eventually disappeared, as he summarized Kaiya's story and situation to Grefdel. He assuaged the anger at his nearly disastrous forgetfulness, by rationalizing that he was simply not practiced in the fine art of deception.

The carriage rounded the final corner, and stopped in front of his building. Paying the driver, Pindlebryth took a few of the bags that they unloaded, and Grefdel the rest.

The pair walked up to the door. Pindlebryth was about to knock, when a visibly upset BroadShanks flung open the door. She bunched the corners of her apron in her paws, kneading them nervously. Her voice trembled and cracked with emotion as she tried to speak.

"Oh, M'Lord! He's gone! He's left us! During the night! I don't know what to do!" Pindlebryth let slip his bags, and with frowned determination ran through the foyer and up the steps two at a time. BroadShanks minced behind him to the bottom stairs, still chattering hysterically. Pindlebryth paid her no mind. Turning the corner, he burst into Hakayaa's sick room.

The chest holding his clothes was emptied, and the window open. Confounded, he looked this way and that around the room, until his eyes fell upon the end table next to Hakayaa's sickbed. On it lay a paper, folded once with a single rough diamond as a paperweight. Pindlebryth moved aside the stone, and unfolded to paper to read.

BroadShanks and HighStance,
A small token of my thanks for your kindness and care. Apologies for leaving so unceremoniously, but this way R will not find me easily. Please tell P not to look for me – it's best that way.
Remember me as,
K

Pindlebryth folded the paper and collected the diamond. He climbed down the stairs slowly, in somewhat of a daze. It was strangely quiet downstairs, until he passed the hallway entrance to the parlor. HighStance and Grefdel stood over BroadShanks, who had collapsed on the divan. She was breathing heavily, but periodically took sips of water from a glass held by HighStance.

"She'll be all right now," pronounced HighStance as BroadShanks' breathing got under control. Pindlebryth handed the note and the diamond to HighStance. He sat next to her, read the note aloud to her then handed her the paper and diamond.

She got slightly more agitated again, babbling, "That silly Crow! I *knew* I should have kept a closer eye on him. Just because he can walk around and climb stairs without assistance, he thinks he can go out to face who-knows-what? Oh, I'm sorry M'Lord! I know how you wanted to see him again. Forgive me!"

Pindlebryth patted her on the paw, then the shoulder. "It's all right, BroadShanks. I have a feeling that when he wants to see me, or if I really need him, he'll show up again." He wondered if what he said was really true. BroadShanks blew her nose on her apron, and cried.

A knock came at the door. "Now what?" said HighStance. He put down the glass, and left the room to answer the door. He returned presently with a card of introduction, and handed it to Pindlebryth.

He read it, looked at BroadShanks, and pointed at the note and diamond. "Hide those," he instructed HighStance. He turned, and strode briskly to the door.

In the foyer stood two figures, the first was an immaculately dressed Crow, the smaller one stood behind with a long cape, its hood drawn over the figure's head. The Crow bowed, saying, "Heakea BlueHood at your service, Prince Pindlebryth. I was Hakayaa's uncle. We are here on BlueHood family business. Allow me to introduce..."

The smaller one stepped forward, and lowered her hood. "I am Hayake BlueHood, Hakayaa's sister. I'm afraid we have a favor to ask of you."

Heakea added, "Actually, more of a business proposition..."

VII - Flight

Pindlebryth burst out of the language department's auxiliary hall and dashed down the pavement leading to the much larger DarkMane Languages Center, nearly bowling over two other students as he turned and skidded around a corner bordered by an opaque wall of arborvitae. His reference books, strapped together and slung over his back, held down only a portion of his student's robes as they fluttered and whipped back and forth while he ran. Blurting out a halfhearted apology to the underclassmen, he continued unabated. His feet crunched on the dry leaves left on the walkway from a recent windstorm. He sprinted for only a few more paces until he spied one of the University's Regents across the Students' Union quadrangle.

There strode DarkMane himself, a self-aggrandizing fop of a Badger who strode confidently in his robes of office. His gown was bordered with red and was overlaid with a floor-length purple velvet sash, and he bore them as if he indeed were royalty. Next to him were two professors, and all three of them seemed to be engaged in an energetic discussion as they walked. Pindlebryth did not fully recognize the two accompanying DarkMane, only that they were members of the history department. From their mannerisms, it was quite obvious that one, an Arctic Hare, was subservient if not positively sycophantic to DarkMane; while the other, a Ferret, was demonstrably at odds with the Regent. The Hare clutched a valise, holding it tightly against his chest with both arms. His drooping long ears pivoted from side to side as the other two fellows argued. As the Ferret engaged DarkMane vociferously, he waved about an envelope crushed in his paw.

Pindlebryth slowed precipitously, and followed quietly from a distance as they headed down the lane on the other side of the quad, towards the hall that bore the Regent's name. He tried to eavesdrop on what they were saying, but they were too far away.

While it was not altogether unusual to see a Regent out and about the University grounds, it was however decidedly uncommon to see one publicly involved in a heated argument.

The sycophant hounded the other professor, chiding him mercilessly, then vigorously nodding his head in agreement whenever DarkMane spoke. The three continued quarreling until they stopped just outside the hall's main entrance steps, where DarkMane loudly burst out, "Good riddance to him! That ne'er-do-well was a dark blot on this institution, and I..." He realized too late how unseemly such an outburst was. Becoming drastically circumspect, he accordingly lowered his voice and moved to the far side of the broad stone steps. Despite his precautions, Pindlebryth had approached close enough to catch him remark in an acidic tone, "I cannot believe my fellow Regents are allowing the University to bestow such a blaggard an honorary degree! And his mentor is little better – a useless dreamer who continues to squander department resources, and is already poisoning another student with his fantasies! I will be glad to see the back of him!"

The Ferret was about to protest further, but DarkMane immediately cut him off.

"I will not have this discussion again, neither inside nor outside of closed doors!" He lowered his voice to a growl. "The decision has been made by a majority of the Regents. His tenure is to be revoked!"

"No doubt at your behest," complained the Ferret.

"Regardless, let that be an end to it!" DarkMane and his lackey climbed the stairs into the hall, while the Ferret wheeled about and stormed back down the walkway. Pindlebryth waited until DarkMane was out of view, at which point he resumed his dash to the main hall of the linguistics department. Once inside, he scanned the main lobby to ensure he would not run into DarkMane, then proceeded to bound up the stairs to a gallery off of the main auditorium. He halted outside the gallery door to catch his breath and out of habit began to straighten his attire before entering the room. But he caught himself, thought better of it and undid his actions, further ruffling his clothing for good measure. He opened the door and slipped in. Seeing that the class had started without him, he swung the door closed with an audible click.

Several heads turned towards him, many of them with blatant schadenfreude wrapping wry smirks across their faces.

"So glad you could join us, Master Tardy," said Doctor GrayMask in Raccoon authoritatively. He peered disapprovingly over the pince-nez at the end of his sloping snout. "If you would be so kind, please take your seat."

"Your pardon, Professor," Pindlebryth replied likewise in Raccoon, albeit in a sloppy drawl. "Doctor Keewa's lecture series on Classic Crow Literature went a bit long today, and afterwards we were discussing..."

"That will be all," declared GrayMask imperiously. Pindlebryth noted there was also a tinge of tired sadness in his voice. "Wait for me at my office, immediately after this class."

A suppressed snicker emanated from one of the other students as they all resumed facing the professor. Pindlebryth found a seat, and unbound his notebook to join the Conversational Raccoon class in progress. The rest of the class period went without event. Pindlebryth was never called on during the verbal exercises and discussion, and he got the distinct feeling he was being ostracized from activities – not just for today, but quite possibly for the remainder of this class's semester.

At the top of the hour, Old Pan rang from the central administration building of the campus, and GrayMask punctually closed the session in mid-sentence. Several of the students were surprised at such behavior, as it was common for GrayMask's sessions to continue a few minutes past the top of the hour. Regardless, GrayMask solemnly gathered his folders and his ornate mahogany cane from his podium, and unceremoniously left by the gallery's rear entrance as everyone else was still rising from their desk-rows. Another nameless student whistled absently, enjoying the situation that someone other than himself was the focus of GrayMask's ire.

Refusing to give anyone the satisfaction of making eye contact while his fellow students left, Pindlebryth slowly wrote his last entries into a notebook, and methodically collected his papers and books, reslinging them in the book strap. When he was finally alone, he sighed and walked slowly out of the gallery and up the flight of stairs to his advisor's office. He could easily guess what was in store for him. There were several signs over the past weeks that storm clouds were brewing, and the behaviors of DarkMane and GrayMask proved to Pindlebryth that things were about to come to a head. But he had long since chosen this course and set it into action. Having prepared all that he could have up to this point, all he could do was to let things play out.

When he arrived in the waiting room outside GrayMask's

office, Pindlebryth was mildly startled to see the DarkMane's toady standing outside the closed door to the office. The flop-eared Arctic Hare stood with both paws in front of himself, still clasping his valise as if his life depended upon it. Beyond the door he could hear the erratic staccato tapping of GrayMask's cane on the floor, and the muffled voice of DarkMane. After a moment, the rap of the cane stopped, and DarkMane sounded like he was lecturing GrayMask, or perhaps giving him a series of instructions. Pindlebryth could not glean much from the discussion, except for a few spare words here and there – "enormous gift to the University," "obvious bribe," "concerns were swept under the rug," "reputation ignored," and the like. Disdain practically dripped from his voice, as he droned on for several more minutes. Unlike Pindlebryth had observed outside, DarkMane never raised his voice. GrayMask himself hardly uttered a word, except to simply respond with either a barely perceptible "Yes, Regent," or "No, Regent." DarkMane finished with a curt final sentence, after which he opened the door. The Hare deftly stepped aside. If he had groveled in abject servitude as DarkMane emerged from GrayMask's office, Pindlebryth would not have been surprised in the slightest.

"Ah, M'Lord Pindlebryth," DarkMane acknowledged him with barely a nod, as he extended an expectant paw towards the Hare.

"Regent," said Pindlebryth simply.

DarkMane's lackey opened the valise, which was filled with several envelopes. He rifled through them in order, produced one with the PanGaea University Regents' seal, and handed it immediately to his superior, who in turn offered it to Pindlebryth.

"There is a special ceremony this weekend. The Regents request the honor of your attendance. Good day to you." Pindlebryth accepted the invitation, as DarkMane left with a small flourish and his Hare scurrying behind. Pindlebryth watched him leave, noting how the black and beige stripes down DarkMane's face lent an easy air of menace to the Badger's face. He also concluded that DarkMane was one of the few persons he had ever met who mastered the ability to simultaneously be respectfully polite, and yet leave one with the distinct impression of being insulted.

Though the door was left wide open, Pindlebryth respectfully knocked. GrayMask stood behind his desk, his cane laid across the arms of his desk chair. He waved him in with an opened envelope similar to Pindlebryth's, not looking up as he continued reading the contents of his own invitation. Pindlebryth took his seat in front of GrayMask's desk, and noisily dropped his bundle of books on the floor next to his seat.

Like so many professors' offices at University, the desk was covered with a chaos of books, periodicals and papers – theses to be reviewed, grants to be processed, and the ubiquitous paperwork associated with being head of a department. He tossed the invitation on top of the burgeoning pile in the center of his blotter, and took his cane.

With one paw clenching his knee, and the other firmly gripping the elegantly carved head of his cane, the old Raccoon eased himself with a grunt into the chair, quickly settling into the depressions in the seat's upholstery worn over the years. Holding the top of the cane with both paws, one over the other, he looked cynically at Pindlebryth as if to say, "What am I to do with you?"

Indeed, there were dozens of questions and complaints running through his mind. Instead, GrayMask simply inquired in Lemming, "Aren't you going to open your envelope?"

Pindlebryth considered the envelope diffidently before responding. "I can guess what it is. I had heard Regent DarkMane haranguing another professor earlier today. I assume it was about the same topic that he was discussing with you." Pindlebryth broke the seal on his envelope and nodded as he saw the contents were the same as the invitation GrayMask had lobbed onto the mound of papers on his desk.

GrayMask leaned forward in his chair, and rested his chin on his hands wrapped around the cane's handle. His gaze grew into one of annoyance. He found he quickly grew tired of Pindlebryth's air of indifference.

"I understand Hakayaa BlueHood was a close friend of yours. I have even heard he may have saved the life of your brother. Your invitation is to the ceremony where he will be granted an honorary doctoral degree from this University – an honor this institution rarely bestows, even if it is a posthumous one. You have nothing to say on the subject?"

Pindlebryth folded the invitation and stuffed it into an inner pocket of his student's robe. "He was also responsible for the attack on my brother that partially blinded him." He shrugged his shoulders as if the two events were of little matter.

GrayMask leaned back in his chair, as the cushions quietly breathed against his weight.   He shook his head almost imperceptibly, and sighed in disbelief.   His pince-nez were clamped so firmly, that his snout whistled as he exhaled.   "I've wondered for quite some time on how to have this discussion. The Pindlebryth I thought I knew would appreciate it if I were forthright." GrayMask shifted in his seat.   He had given similar talks to many an errant student in the past, but he never before had to remonstrate a person of royal standing.

Pindlebryth easily surmised GrayMask's discomfort.   He remained seated in a relaxed posture, keeping an unemotional mask.   A mannerism he learned early from Hakayaa at the casinos, he knew it would only further infuriate his advisor, but it could not be avoided.   He could not let anyone, especially GrayMask, know his aloof demeanor was a front, albeit a painful one.   He only wished that GrayMask might later understand the need for such impassive, almost disrespectful, behavior.

"You have become an embarrassment.   Your academic future is in jeopardy."   GrayMask paused to see what effect those two statements might have on Pindlebryth, but he saw none.

GrayMask had placed high hopes upon this candidate, for both altruistic and selfish reasons.   Pindlebryth's natural ability for languages was evident the very day they first met and spoke together.   The young prince had petitioned the linguistics department, requesting their most tenured professor as his advisor.   During their initial interviews, Pindlebryth's ability to appreciate the beauty of both the vernacular and high speech of various tongues, the innate ability to see patterns and relationships in the various dialects had shone through. Although GrayMask was aware of this student's family and history, which exposed him to almost an entire continent's language pool, his mostly self-taught ability to read, write and speak fluently in so many tongues was still a wonder to observe. Though GrayMask knew his tenure was secure, association with this brilliant student would have surely increased his prestige in the department, with the Regents and possibly the entire University.   GrayMask made the decision the very day of Pindlebryth's interview, that he would accept him as an advisee.

As Pindlebryth concluded each semester, GrayMask was further assured he had made the right decision.   Ultimately, when Pindlebryth selected and began work on his dissertation, he displayed a capacity to almost intuitively deduce connections across disparate tongues. Pindlebryth was such a unique find in the academic community, that GrayMask never ceased to be impressed, despite his jaded experience. Both their positions in academia seemed assured.

However, Pindlebryth's sudden change this semester was putting both their reputations at risk.

"Both you and I know you only need one last language to complete the doctoral requirement of fluency in eight written and spoken tongues. Although you switched without warning your selection at the very beginning of the semester to Crow, I approved your decision. But you went against my advice, and have taken a plethora of courses clearly not necessary to achieve that aim. Not only have you signed up for additional topics in Crow that, as far as I can see, add little to your functional understanding of the Crow language, but you are also auditing a slew of courses in my own language of Raccoon. Since you are only auditing them, I have little say about them.

"But consider what you are doing. Your professors report to me that you are not completing any work associated with your required courses. Your grades will suffer as a result, and will have a deleterious impact on your degree. You had been on track to matriculate with the highest honors, but a spate of low grades will erase all that.

"Furthermore, from what I can see, you have not made one whit of progress on your dissertation on the common roots of Ferret and Otter. If it is not completed in timely fashion, your degree will be at best only delayed; at worst, the Regents may reject your entire body of work, and deny you any degree at all!"

GrayMask had almost worked himself into a fevered pitch, leaning forward again in his chair and holding his cane's head in a grip so strong, his hand began to cramp. He calmed himself with deep breath, and both he and the chair wheezed as he relaxed and whistled again through his snout.

"I have had this lecture with many students before, who were the children born into families of power, position, status or wealth. All of whom were spoiled layabouts that expected everything to be handed to them." Pindlebryth looked GrayMask in the eye as if he were insulted being compared to such people. GrayMask felt a tinge of satisfaction, finally hitting a nerve, finally seeing a crack in his facade.

"Oh, like any student, you've had your moments of extracurricular rowdiness and mischief. Several clever pranks and escapades have been attributed to you and your partner-in-crime Hakayaa, but never proven. But they were all harmless when all was said and done. Simply put, before this semester, you were an exemplary student and doctoral candidate.

"But now I have serious doubts concerning you; not only as far as your career is concerned, but about you yourself.

"Where you had been outgoing and gregarious, you now are withdrawn. Except for your attendance in classes, no one ever sees you about the University grounds.

"Where you had been scrupulously honest and industrious, you are now elusive and furtive. No amount of coaxing from professors seems to get you to produce work, and I certainly have not been able to get you to move one iota on your thesis – yet you still seem to lavish desperate attention on every subject, every class, every exercise. And as soon as your last class of the day is over, you disappear to who-knows-where.

"You have made no attempts to garner new friends inside or outside of the student body, and you have let most other relationships lapse – save for two. You spend much of your time with that little coquette you've got squirreled away at your apartments. A commoner without a Name, no less!

"Oh ho!" chortled GrayMask at Pindlebryth's raised eyebrow and wrinkled smirk that spoke volumes.

"Your private life is not as private as you may think!" the old Raccoon scolded. "Whereas some may not care about your dalliances, and you yourself may not give a fig about anyone who *does* gossip about it, I cannot help but to wonder if she is at the heart of your problems. Or is she just another symptomatic response to the loss of your friend?

"Therein lies the puzzle you task me with." GrayMask leaned forward again, and placed his cane directly in front of him on his desktop. "What is it that drives your reclusive behavior: the loss of Hakayaa, this tufthunter that has you wound about her finger, or is it something entirely different?"

Pindlebryth looked sad for a moment, but said nothing. GrayMask rose out of his chair with a grunt, and meandered about his office assisted by his cane.

"Blast it, Pindlebryth! I am genuinely concerned about you. During the time of the mass suicides of Lenland, my first thoughts were about your welfare. I tried contacting you as soon as news of the tragedy reached me, but you had long since left to answer the need of your country. When you subsequently took a nearly year-long sabbatical during Lenland's reconstruction, I wished you nothing but success – but I also hoped for a speedy return. Needless to say, I was positively relieved when you *did* return to University. I would be dishonest if I didn't admit my hopes were tempered with apprehension – there was always the concern about performance after a student's prolonged interruption. However, I found it remarkable that such a dire misfortune only seemed to redouble your efforts towards your education, as you completed your work on all your previous languages handily, and easily mastered the Vixen tongue during that year's semesters to boot. All was further proof of the strength of your talent, even more so your character and determination.

"But ever since the passing of Hakayaa BlueHood, you have become this..." he said as he broadly gestured, "...this walking contradiction." He paused, and he was slightly surprised that he was again breathing rapidly. GrayMask found the whole situation maddening, and he could feel his dander rising. He sat on the edge of his desk next to Pindlebryth.

"What I'm trying to say is, I wanted to help you at times when I could not. Now, I can see you are wrestling with some problem. Even one as blind as a bat could see you are in trouble. This time, I *can* help. But only if you would let me. Only if you follow my advice."

Pindlebryth shifted in his chair, and craned his neck to look out the window behind GrayMask as if he were distracted by something outside more interesting than this meeting.

"You don't seem to appreciate what a precarious position you are in." GrayMask picked up his invitation from the top of the mound of loose papers on his desk, and tossed it back on the pile. "You might have escaped the Regents' notice for a bit longer, but now that this matter of his posthumous degree has been forced upon them, your past association with Hakayaa is weighing against you.

Pindlebryth chuckled out loud and cheekily observed, "Forced upon them? So, the Regents *aren't* all-powerful, after all!"

"Money talks, as if I needed to remind you. Somehow the BlueHood family has wielded sway over several heads of state from both sides of MidSea, all of whom are requesting – nay, demanding – that PanGaea University confer this degree. It is even rumoured these nations all threaten to withhold their annual benevolences to the University. All except Lenland."

"It is well known that there is little love lost between my family and the Crow nation." Pindlebryth pretended to stifle a yawn. "I am, on the other hand, somewhat surprised that King Hatheron has not threatened to withhold funds if Hakayaa's degree *is* in fact conferred."

"To sweeten the pot, the BlueHoods themselves are coming to PanGaea to present a gift of their most treasured pieces to the University," GrayMask continued. "The University cannot resist the prestige that an event opening a large display featuring the legacy of the BlueHoods would bring." GrayMask rubbed his chin, and tilted his head as he pondered out loud. "What amazes me is the suddenness of this whirlwind event – the arrangements for the ceremony and the reception afterwards are being made most hastily. The University is practically bending over backwards by scheduling the event weeks before the end of the semester."

"Perhaps the Blue*Bloods* wish to spend as little time here as they can stomach."

"M'Lord!   *That* was uncalled for," GrayMask scolded indignantly, but Pindlebryth maintained his attitude of apathy. "Your relationship with the deceased notwithstanding, perhaps it was not a good idea for the family to extend an invitation to you. I trust that you can behave yourself during the ceremony?"

"That depends on the quality of the food and drink at the soiree afterwards."

GrayMask could feel his hackles rise again. "If you raise a fuss at either event in front of the Regents, you would almost surely seal your fate here at University."

Out of the blue, GrayMask pointed an accusing finger at Pindlebryth.   "And don't think I don't know about your association with Professor DeepDigger! He and his peculiar beliefs have been blacklisted for years. The Regents hold that he and his frivolous interests in historical items of questionable repute somehow contributed to Hakayaa's demise. And now, with this embarrassment about Hakayaa's degree, I wouldn't be surprised if the Regents may take it out on DeepDigger one way or another."

"Then DarkMane didn't inform you that DeepDigger's tenure will be revoked?" Pindlebryth observed with a tone that bordered on insolent. GrayMask's eyes widened, and flashed with surprise, then empathy, and finally anger. He stood up from his desk's edge and slowly walked back to his chair.

"If the Regents knew how much time you have been spending with DeepDigger, your standing with them would be far lower than what they are already considering. Your future at PanGaea would assuredly be very bleak indeed. Or short. Or both!"

Pindlebryth sat up in his seat, straightening his robe flaps with his paws over his thighs absentmindedly. He looked straight at his advisor with a plain face and asked mechanically, "Is there anything else, Doctor GrayMask?"

GrayMask collapsed against the back of his chair, exhausted. "We are nearing the end of the semester. There is still time for you to pull yourself out of this rut." He lowered his head, and peered over his glasses. Slowly he shook his head and sighed, saying with somber finality, "You won't let me help, will you?"

Pindlebryth wasn't exactly sure if it was a question or a statement. He rose out his of chair with slow purpose, and replied, "I will take one bit of advice – I will behave myself at this event. I would be obliged if you kept the Regents' collective nose out of my other business. Other than that..." He trailed off the sentence, shrugged his shoulders, collected his books and turned to leave. As the door shut, GrayMask leaned forward in thought, one paw grasping his cane and his chin cupped in the other hand.

Pindlebryth strode down the hall. After he turned a corner, he exhaled and rubbed his eyes. He genuinely was fond of GrayMask, and it was exceedingly difficult to close himself off to his advisor. He started again down the hall and the stairs, trying to assuage the knot of guilt in his gut.

As soon as he was far enough away from DarkMane Hall, Pindlebryth began running again towards the west side of the campus. Cutting across between two greenhouses and through a hole in a hedgerow separating two dormitories and a sporting practice field, he ran along a northerly street until he spotted Grefdel standing next to a carriage. Although he was dressed in street clothes, Pindlebryth could tell Grefdel had his customary dagger strapped under his left sleeve. Tossing his books into the awaiting open door, he instructed the driver to go to Arbor Drive. The carriage sped off the moment Pindlebryth and

Grefdel clambered into the vehicle, and slammed the door shut.

"All things are going as planned. Not even my advisor GrayMask suspects anything. He believes that the entire Royal Family holds the BlueHoods with the utmost enmity. In fact, I fear I may have overplayed my hand with him – ironically, by underplaying it."

"Do you think he may piece things together before it's time?"

"I don't think so. It is all coming together this weekend. There is, however, one additional fly in the ointment – DeepDigger is about to be sacked."

Grefdel's eyebrows knitted in confusion. "How can the University give him the boot? I thought he had tenure."

"He does, but a certain Regent can make it very uncomfortable for anyone he wishes to be removed. If DeepDigger loses his standing, he cannot stay in his house provided by the University. And there is still much that I need to translate in his library. If only..." Pindlebryth looked thoughtfully out of his window, as he considered possibilities.

"You're not about to suggest that he move in with us, are you?" Grefdel blurted out incredulously. "We have little room to spare as it is, and it is too close to the end to have anyone outside our circle find out what we've been planning."

The two slid in their seats as the carriage rounded a corner, and slid back again as the carriage swerved to avoid a large pothole in the road.

"You are absolutely right of course. We are too close to the goal to take such a chance. BroadShanks is about to bust as it is." Pindlebryth leaned towards the opposite window as they turned onto Arbor Drive. Suddenly, he exclaimed, "Lords Below!" He moved to the opposite side of the cabin, and leaned out the window. "Driver! Keep going – do *not* stop! Take us back home." The carriage sped up perceptibly, and took the next fork in the road.

Grefdel looked alarmedly at Pindlebryth, then out the window down the receding Arbor Drive. "What happened?"

"Do you see the carriage already at DeepDigger's house? An Arctic Hare, Regent DarkMane's errand boy, was at his front door. He must not see me with DeepDigger, or he'll report it to his master." He banged his fist on the seat cushion. "Piss and vinegar! I'll have to come back sometime later. I only hope they won't evict him immediately."

Grefdel wanted to probe further as to what happened at the University that upset Pindlebryth so, what changes to their plans it might forebode, along with a host of other questions. Seeing the foul mood Pindlebryth was in, he instead sat quietly, waiting on his brooding prince.

The carriage halted in front of the walkway to his apartments, but Pindlebryth sat motionless, lost in thought. It was not the usual itch in his mind that often warned him of something amiss that distracted him. Rather, he was in a melancholy about what irreparable damage may have been done between him and GrayMask. After a moment, Grefdel gently nudged him out of his trance.

Still preoccupied, Pindlebryth went up the flagstone path to his door, well-trimmed with lines of late-blooming marigolds and twinspur. Grefdel collected the parcel of books, and paid the carriage driver, who quickly pulled away to seek his next fare. Grefdel opened the door for Pindlebryth, and followed him in. Before the door closed, Pindlebryth was embraced by a stunning beauty of a Lemming, dressed in red and deep maroon taffeta, cinched about her waist with a satin and lace belt. If Pindlebryth didn't know better, her outfit would convince him of GrayMask's opinion that she was indeed a strumpet.

"Pindie! So glad you're back!" she said, as she playfully touched Pindlebryth's muzzle with her fingertips. The touch of her crimson satin gloves made his whiskers twitch and shiver curiously. Pindlebryth smiled sheepishly, and could feel the sweat begin to bead on all four of his paws. "You know," she purred cheerily in the curious accent of northern Lenland, "I've had a narvelous time in the narkets today, and…"

"Oh, leave him be, GraceTail! Ah, there you are Grefdel!" chimed in BroadShanks. Her voice rang out with an almost musical lilt as she emerged into the central hall from the kitchen. Fresh from the mudroom, she held a wooden tray holding a dozen small cups of woven reeds, each of which contained a perennial bulb in soil. The delicate flowers threatened to topple over as BroadShanks minced down the hall. "The tulips and hyacinth are ready to be planted. Madam WhiteSocks says we're to have a deep frost in two weeks, and her arthritis is never wrong! And half the garden still needs to be turned over, too."

Grefdel closed the door with an authoritative thud and declared, "This is not the best time."

"Yes," agreed Pindlebryth. "The University has caved in and is scheduling everything for this weekend – the degree ceremony, the opening of the BlueHoods' display, and a reception afterwards. We have much to prepare, and little time left." Pindlebryth moved the young doe aside gently by the waist, and proceeded to go up the stairs. "I'll be back down after I change out of my robes." Grefdel followed him up the stairs with the strapped bundle of books.

"Oh, but BroadShanks, it is such fun to watch M'Lord fidget!" GraceTail remarked, her northern canton accent absent. BroadShanks simply rolled her eyes and disappeared back into the kitchen.

From the kitchen BroadShanks could still be easily heard, "Now give me a hand with these bulbs and the rest of the goods from the market."

"What? In these clothes?" GraceTail rebuffed her.

Upstairs, Grefdel stopped HighStance, who was leaving Pindlebryth's room after laying out his change of clothes. "You had best break up those two downstairs, before they get into it again."

"Yes, the two of them do enjoy getting under each other's skin," he replied as his shoulders drooped in resignation.

As HighStance plodded downstairs, Grefdel deposited Pindlebryth's books in his study. He then went to Pindlebryth's bedroom, and stood attentively just outside the doorway, watching his prince as he hung up his student's robes and put on a house jacket. "Is there a problem, M'Lord? Anything I can help with?" he ventured. Pindlebryth didn't look at Grefdel directly, but stared introspectively at the floor with a plaintive solitary look on his face. Grefdel lingered for a moment, still hoping Pindlebryth might elaborate on what occurred at University, or even open up and share the burden of his thoughts.

Pindlebryth went to his bedroom window and looked out over the view of PanGaea's CityState it afforded him. He was struck with a pang of something – not quite homesickness alone, but that mixed in with something else. After reflection, he found he missed the unconfused and straightforward sense of purpose that his old bedroom's view of the castle courtyard instilled in him.

"I can still recall how ill at ease my first deception made me feel. And now I find myself wrapped in lie upon deception upon pretense. I am tired of all these lies!" he said with a sudden growl in his voice and his paws clenched momentarily into fists. "I will be ever so glad when it all can be put behind us." Pindlebryth sighed heavily, and rubbed both his eyes with the backs of his paws. "I sometimes wonder if the Quickening Spirit is testing me, to decide if I am fit to one day rule Lenland."

Grefdel responded with a kindly set to his eyes. "I am sure He already knows the answer, M'Lord. Rather, I prefer to believe He is trying to reveal to you what that answer is."

Pindlebryth opened his eyes, regarded Grefdel with an inquiring and introspective look, and marveled at his insight. He stood savoring the moment of serenity for a short while before replying with a simple but heartfelt, "Thank you, Grefdel."

Straightening his clothes again, he made for the door. "Go check on Voyager and Clarion. Make sure they're ready for flight tomorrow. On your way back, circle past DeepDigger's house. If the Hare has left, ask DeepDigger what his visitor wanted. Inquire delicately – I fear the Hare may have just given the professor his walking papers." Pindlebryth walked past Grefdel and the staircase, to his study at the other end of the hall. Grefdel followed him with his eyes, sighed sympathetically, went downstairs and then outside as Pindlebryth had requested of him.

Pindlebryth stood in front of his desk, and unbundled his books. He perused through the assigned texts: a compendium of Crow short stories from that race's earliest classic writings to modern literature, a collection of noteworthy speeches recorded throughout Crow history, an introductory primer to the Raccoon tongue, and a collection of landmark pieces of journalism that GrayMask had compiled over the previous decade from his home nation of Esepanauk. He considered applying himself to his studies while his classes were still fresh in his mind. But despite HighStance having finally managed to calm the brewing maelstrom downstairs, he would not be able to concentrate, knowing the clock was ticking.

There came a knock from the front door below. A small ruckus between BroadShanks and GraceTail resurfaced over who would answer the door. But eventually, decorum won out and soon afterwards BroadShanks met Pindlebryth standing at the open door of the study.

"Begging your pardon, M'Lord, but there is a gent from the University who needs to talk to you." She handed the visitor's card to Pindlebryth, and waited for a reply.

"What does *he* want?" Pindlebryth hissed under his breath rhetorically as he read the card. Stamping down the stairs with vitriol in his eyes, he was met in the foyer by DarkMane's Arctic Hare flunkey. "Yes, Mr. WickerWit?" he curtly demanded of the Hare, snapping his card back at him.

"*WhiskerWidth*," the Hare corrected him coolly. The Hare returned the card to his vest pocket then waited a moment until BroadShanks disappeared back into the kitchen. "Regent DarkMane would appreciate a reply to his invitation as soon as convenient," he said in a syrupy voice. Pindlebryth was sure what he actually meant was 'immediately.'

"You may tell your master that I will attend the ceremony, and the opening of the display. I will also bring a guest to the reception afterwards."

"Ooh! Where are we going, N'Lord?" piped up GraceTail giddily from just outside the kitchen, before she was unceremoniously yanked back in by BroadShanks.

"Very good, M'Lord. Thank you for your patience." The Hare looked past Pindlebryth where GraceTail had popped out, and with one eyebrow raised, he snickered quietly. He bowed as Pindlebryth glared at him, turned and let himself out.

Pindlebryth turned around and was met by GraceTail.

She looked very tired, not only in her eyes, but also in how she carried herself. She coughed demurely, and spoke in a much more subdued tone. "I wish I could be there for Hakayaa's ceremony."

"You know you can't. It would raise questions if you became emotional for someone who is supposed to be a stranger to you, and we certainly cannot risk you losing your concentration in such a public forum."

The pang of remorse overcame Pindlebryth again. How one deception, even for the best of causes, affected so much of his life and inflicted pain on others!

"I know," GraceTail whined melodramatically. "It's just that I haven't seen my parents in so long. I cannot wait to see them again."

"So you've said several times," Pindlebryth replied beneficently without reproach.

"If you will excuse me, M'Lord, it has been a very tiring day."

I need to rest a little, and collect myself before dinner."

"Of course." Pindlebryth nodded, and watched her go upstairs. Even as spent as she was, he couldn't help but to think how beguiling she still looked as she ascended the staircase, step by step. He continued to watch her, his mind wandering as a young Lemming's fancy is wont to do, until she reached the top of the staircase. There she loosened her belt, and removed her red gloves. They hid her only physical defect – she had no nails, and the fur on her hands was absent. She clenched her paws, bent over into a tight crouch, and began to twist herself about her whole torso. Starting slowly then increasingly violently, until her body and the very air about her vibrated and blurred, she abruptly sprouted feathers and stood fully erect again. The feathers smeared from a reddish gray to coal-black, with a ring of blue around her neck. As she stretched her wings, it became obvious that they were clipped along their tips.

"Rest well, Hayake. I'll have BroadShanks wake you when dinner is ready. Grefdel should have returned by then, and after dinner all of us can review the day's events, and plan any necessary changes." It occurred to him, as it had often times before, what Hakayaa had told him about the restrictions of Crow shapeshifters. If Hayake was as ravishing in her natural form as she was in the shape of a Lemming, then she must also be a striking beauty indeed to her fellow Crow.

Grefdel and Pindlebryth banked along the coastline south of PanGaea's CityState, where the beaches were smooth, serene and sloped long and slowly into MidSea's depths. They flew high above the shoreside, and caught a sea-breeze thermal that wafted them even higher. Pindlebryth was both invigorated and calmed by the scent of the ocean air, unsullied by the myriad odors of civilization. The mid-morning sun warmed them against the cool of the high altitudes. Grefdel, for the moment, was happy to let Pindlebryth enjoy a fleeting moment or two of serenity. But it was already late in the morning, and there were things yet to be done. They followed the coast for a few minutes more, before he intruded on Pindlebryth's contemplation.

"No one was at DeepDigger's house yesterday. Was he there

this morning, M'Lord?"

"No. His housekeeper Miss Roan told me I had just missed him. She did not know where he went, but said he was expected back around noonday."

"Good. I was afraid he might have done something rash. I sometimes wonder if he has his marbles mixed."

"Now, now, Grefdel. His world has just been turned upside-down. With all that has passed in recent years, I can only hope I am at least that sane when I reach my old age. At any rate, I must meet with him before the ceremony tomorrow. I'll try his house again later this afternoon."

Soon Voyager and Clarion slowed their rhythmic flapping then stopped, stretching their wings out with feathers foiled downwards. They had found the sweet spot where the wind alone would keep them aloft and stationary.

"Good. They can rest a bit," observed Grefdel. "They don't get to fly as often as they should, and they are out of shape."

"Will Clarion be able to complete the trip?"

"The MidSea Archipelago shouldn't be too difficult for her. The prevailing winds should become westerly over the open water, giving us a good tailwind. And the skies in that direction look clear as far as we can see, so we shan't be caught by a storm. But I had best be on my way, before she tires out."

"I'll fly with you down to Elbow Spur." The two careened in unison to the south, and resumed following the coastline. After several minutes they spotted the landmark. The beaches gave way a hundred yards inland to modest cliffs of stone and soil. A large outcropping of granite jutted out from the sandy coast. Behind were a dozen or so smaller granite hillocks, left behind as the granite behemoth was pushed along by some long-since vanished glacier. Its peak rose barely a hundred feet above the cliffs, separating the shoreline heading directly northwards, and the southern beach that angled away at a westerly arc.

"Fly due east from here, and you should be able to spot each other as you approach the first western islands of the Archipelago. I'll let them know you've left PanGaea, as soon as I land."

"I still feel like I am abandoning my post by leaving you now, M'Lord."

"I can appreciate that, but you've been in PanGaea too long. You are known to too many in the CityState and possibly the University, and there would be no explaining why my gardener accompanies me to the reception. Besides, between the BlueHoods' reception and the Beaver's sloop, there are already going to be too many Lemmings about. We cannot unduly risk drawing attention to ourselves. You will have to be satisfied with your part at the end, riding in with the cavalry. Or so to speak."

Grefdel hesitated in his saddle, holding his reins as if he were undecided about something. He turned to Pindlebryth with a look of concern. "Watch Hayake."

"Why?" replied Pindlebryth, looking a more than a little surprised.

"It's nothing I can put my finger on. But anyone who spent that much time with the Ravenne, even as a hostage, has to be scarred somehow."

"First you're concerned about DeepDigger, and now Hayake? Is there anyone you are *not* suspicious of?" Pindlebryth regarded Grefdel with mock exasperation, but relinquished. "Very well, Grefdel. Consider me warned. Now go – have a safe journey."

Grefdel reluctantly said farewell, saluted his prince, and then gently peeled off towards the east. Clarion and Voyager called to each other – a wistful keening as if they too were saying their farewells. Pindlebryth began circling down towards the rounded top of the granite peak. Even after he landed with Voyager at the top of the promontory's pinnacle, he followed Grefdel's and Clarion's progress as they grew smaller and finally fell below the horizon.

Pindlebryth exhaled, closed his eyes for a moment, and searched his mind. Try as he might, he could not feel the familiar itch that often warned him something was amiss. He opened his eyes again, and shook his head, wondering what it was that discomfited Grefdel so. He pulled out his Talking Gem from its secure place in his riding jerkin's inside pocket. He spoke into it a few times, always holding it to his ear afterwards, until he heard a reply.

"Darothien? All is well. Grefdel just left from Elbow Spur. Is everyone able and ready to fly today?"

"Yes. SharpWatch will meet with Quentain. LeanShanks, LongWhisker and I will board the Beaver's sloop after nightfall."

"We were able to get both LeanShanks *and* LongWhisker? Grefdel will be relieved to hear that."

"You will have to ask Pendenar how he managed that."

"I will. I wonder what Colonel Farthun or General Vadarog had to say," Pindlebryth chuckled. "I had best cut this short. I don't want to be away from PanGaea's CityState on my own for any extended period of time. Just meet the boat twelve miles from the East Harbor. The owner takes the sloop for a nightly evening jaunt, and is expecting you. The moon is almost new, but the boat is well lit — you should have no problem finding it. You'll be over the horizon from PanGaea, so you should not have to worry about prying eyes. All of you stay below decks until the sloop leaves harbor again tomorrow night. Is there anything else before I go?"

"Just... be careful." After a pause, Darothien added a simple but heartfelt, "I miss you."

"And I you. Good luck to us all."

Pindlebryth slipped the Gem back into his jerkin pocket over his heart, as he had promised Darothien so long ago, and buttoned it shut. He scanned around the peak, and saw the only others in the vicinity were two lonely Otter beachcombers walking along the shore, holding each others paws, and occasionally stooping to pick up a shell. He snapped his reins, and gave the command to Voyager to ascend. Voyager extended his wings, and dove off the point towards the sea. The sea breeze was strong and building in the late morning sun, and Voyager used it with only a little effort to begin climbing again. As they turned north back to CityState, Pindlebryth scanned the surrounding skies, making sure they were free of any other flyers. Halfway to CityState he could feel through his legs that Voyager was breathing harder than usual.

"Grefdel was right. We should have flown more often."

The return flight was thankfully uneventful. Pindlebryth breathed a small sigh of relief as he fed Voyager a dried fish treat, and handed him off to the stable hand at the Double Eagle where he rented two stalls. When the stable hand inquired about Grefdel, Pindlebryth simply replied he was on a trip, and did not know when he would return.

He hailed a cab, but was still undecided where to go first — the University, or directly to DeepDigger's house. A carriage soon pulled up, with a driver that Pindlebryth had employed several times before. As he climbed into the cabin, he thought it best to go directly to DeepDigger's abode, as he did not want to make the extra trip to his apartment to collect his student's robes just now. If that meant he had to wait for Professor DeepDigger, so be it.

The ride passed quickly, as the wind circled around the cabin through the open windows on either side. The scent of the city reminded him he was already missing the clean ocean air. After asking the driver to wait for him, Pindlebryth walked up the path overgrown with grass and weeds. He felt the house looked even more dilapidated than ever, and wondered if the same would be true for DeepDigger himself. He rapped the door three times with the rusty knocker, and clapped off a small cloud of oxidation from his paws. After a few moments, the door opened with a long grating scritch from its hinges. Miss Roan, looking as dour as ever, poked her head from around the door, which apparently she had to pull open using both hands.

"Me master ain't home yet, M'Lud Pindlebryth," she rasped.

"That's alright. I'll wait a little while, if I may." He entered through the foyer, and walked into the parlor. It was festooned with even more books and papers than before, and a few of the columns of books had fallen over like a cascade of dominoes. Like the rest of the house, the room had a slight chill to it. The fireplace was cold, and the firewood caddy was empty. Finding a recent academic periodical, Pindlebryth swatted the seat and back cushions of a chair, raising a cloud of dust. He sat down, and began to pass the time by perusing assorted books within arm's reach.

Pindlebryth leafed through several books, but found he was fascinated by a comparison of the various belief systems in the world, authored by a self-proclaimed devout agnostic. While reading a humorously inaccurate chapter dealing with Lenland's "preoccupation with a Quick Spirit," he was startled when a raucous clamor arose outside. He rose from his chair, and tried to glimpse through the gray-streaked front window what the commotion was, but it apparently ended by the time he could wend his way back through the maze of piled books. All he could see was his driver shaking his fist in the direction the house. A scratching and fumbling sound came from the front door, followed first by a jostling of the door handle and finally pounding.

Miss Roan must have also heard the furor outside, as she was already lugging at the door as the second round of hammering began. An untidy figure stumbled in as the door creaked open under his weight and Miss Roan's efforts.

"Perfesser! Yer *snookered*!"

DeepDigger pushed off from the door and stood erect, but swayed slightly. "Yes, I suppose I am!" he proclaimed, quite pleased with himself. Pindlebryth watched him lumber past Miss Roan, clomping erratically down the hall past the parlor quite unaware of his visitor. Presently, Pindlebryth could hear the sound of glassware being rattled and bounced inside a glass cabinet, along with Miss Roan's protestations.

"Perfesser! You've got a guest!" she shrilled. "M'Lud Pindlebryth is in the front room!"

A thud and the careless slamming of the cabinet door resounded over Miss Roan's scurrying about and fretting. Preceded by his irregular footsteps in the hall, DeepDigger rounded the corner into the parlor, one paw holding a pair of glasses with a finger in each, and a decanter in the other. The bottle of fine brandy was still as full as it was the last time DeepDigger offered him a snifter when they first met, but Pindlebryth doubted the bottle would survive the day.

"Congratulations are in order, M'Lord! I am no longer in the employ of the 'versity. You care to join me?"

Pindlebryth raised a paw to decline. "Thank you, no, Professor. It's a bit early for me, and I haven't had any lunch yet."

"Oh, I had a wonderful repast! I spent the morning divvying up my classes to my fellows – well, now my *ex*-fellows – in the history department. Afterwards, they treated me to a feast at the Belled Bull. We toasted each other's health, wealth, and... and several other things."

DeepDigger lurched towards the chair Pindlebryth had just vacated, and nearly toppled into it, even though he miraculously managed not to disturb a single pile of books. The contents of the decanter sloshed wildly, and the glasses clinked so loudly that Pindlebryth feared they might break. He set the glasses on top of the closest tower of books, and popped off the cut crystal top of the decanter. He set the stopper on another column, but it rolled off and thumped on the carpet. Pouring himself a large draught of brandy, he raised the glass to Pindlebryth and to several of the pillars of books as if they were also friends in attendance, and toasted himself.

"To a life down the loo!" DeepDigger pronounced flippantly, and downed half the glass.

"Surely Professor, you can't believe that."

"Oh, but I do! The Regents gave me the old heave-ho, and had the custodial staff clear out my office yesterday. The movers plopped down the contents here last night. They've even scraped my name off the office door window. Here's your hat, and what's your hurry? And to add insult to injury, I have to vacate this house by the end of next week." Suddenly, the good-natured grin left DeepDigger's face.

"With the Regents having blackballed me," the professor rumbled, "I will be locked out of work in my field anywhere in PanGaea, and anything I try to publish is certain to be refused by any reputable journal. I probably wouldn't even be able to get a position teaching grade school, in this city or any other!" He leaned back in the chair and tried to focus on the ceiling. "I'll probably have to go back to Dookinger with my tail between my legs."

"Did DarkMane inform you of your dismissal?"

"No, he wouldn't dirty his paws with such a menial task. The head of the history department broke the news to me yesterday. Then WhiskerWidth gave me my eviction notice."

"I've had the displeasure of meeting him."

"Yes, yes. DarkMane's sniveling rabbit." DeepDigger's head shook back and forth, half rolling on the back of the chair. He stopped suddenly, shot Pindlebryth a look of unfiltered anger. "But it was DarkMane who had his pawprints all over this!" He stood, teetering precariously. "That dictatorial cretin has had it in for me for years!" he boomed. He punctuated the statement by gulping down the last of the brandy, and smashing the empty glass in the fireplace. Holding his forehead in his paw, he collapsed back into the chair with a fresh cloud of dust.

Suddenly, Pindlebryth's heart sank, and the pit of his stomach began to cramp. Here again yet was another casualty of his deception. Hayake was in mourning for her brother. And now through no fault of his own, DeepDigger was being held responsible in part for the fiction that was Hakayaa's death, and was paying a terrible price. A pang of guilt overcame Pindlebryth so strongly, that his jaw began to ache and his throat constricted.

Happily, one possible solution to ameliorate DeepDigger's predicament became immediately apparent.

"Might I make a suggestion, Professor. I need more time to examine the books from your library upstairs, and no doubt your assistance would be invaluable. After all, I cannot even read your master cryptograph without you to open it." He stepped closer to DeepDigger.

"Come with me to Lenland. You can stay in the North Wing of the castle in our CityState, and I will see that you have unfettered access to our historical archives." DeepDigger looked up at him slightly cross-eyed, when another thought crossed Pindlebryth's mind. "Lenland has no standing embassy with Dookinger. If you are open to the idea, perhaps I could persuade my father and Ambassador Talenday to petition Dookinger to make you their first ambassador to our country?"

DeepDigger's jaw went a little slack at the proposition. Then his mouth closed and opened twice, as if he were debating what to say. He at last responded in a noncommittal tone, "I will have to think on it."

Too late Pindlebryth realized that what he intended as a reparation was quite outlandish, and instead could only be interpreted as charity – or worse, pity. DeepDigger's pride would accept neither. He hastily added, "I ask this only because I desperately need your help. We both know the danger if the Five Artifacts are brought together."

His plea was met by continued silence.

"Please let me help you, Professor." Pindlebryth and DeepDigger remained frozen for quite a while. Pindlebryth felt miserable that he could not help someone who selflessly risked and lost what little he had. Then a thought struck Pindlebryth – GrayMask had made a similar offer. His advisor begged him to accept his help, and he refused. The parallel made the pathos of DeepDigger's situation sting only more.

"It's best if you leave, and not return," DeepDigger grumbled suddenly.

Pindlebryth felt as if he had been slapped. "*What*?" he spluttered.

"Oh, I did not mean it to sound that way," DeepDigger immediately apologized. "WhiskerWidth made it plain that I am to have nothing more to do with you. When he was here yesterday, he imitate... intimanated... inni... he *threatened* things could go badly for you, unless I stop filling your head with my 'silly ideas and baseless dogma'." DeepDigger fumbled for the decanter and second glass, and squinting at the bottle's remaining contents, proceeded to empty it.

Pindlebryth could only hang his head in resignation and sigh. Apparently GrayMask's fear about the Regents was well-founded, if only realized too late. "Very well. At any rate, I trust you will still allow me to send someone to help pack your belongings – hopefully for a trip to Lenland." He paused to see if DeepDigger was persuaded in the slightest. Seeing no sign, he added, "As you ask, I will take my leave of you for now. But my offer still stands. And believe me when I say that I do not care one whit what the Regents think or do. There is simply too much at stake.

"Good day, and be well, dear Professor." He clasped DeepDigger's shoulder for a moment, but the professor remained unmoved. Pindlebryth then walked into the foyer and said farewell to Miss Roan as she shouldered the door closed behind him.

DeepDigger leaned forward holding his head in both paws, and couldn't decide if he wanted to laugh with reckless abandon, rage at the top of his lungs, or weep piteously.

A whole day had passed, and sleep evaded Pindlebryth for most of the previous night. He had been plagued by thoughts that would not be silenced, and worries that blossomed into half-dreams, all of which ended in catastrophes that jarred him back to wakefulness. And yet, rather than feeling drained and inattentive, he was strangely invigorated after his sleeplessness.

He sat in the richly upholstered cabin of Lenland's embassy carriage alert and restless, like a caged beast. Across from him sat Ambassador Quentain, whom he regarded sternly.

"I still don't understand why you must accompany me to Hakayaa's degree ceremony."

Quentain straightened her elegantly appointed dress of white with lavender sashes and charcoal side panels. She coughed demurely through a matching lavender fan, and held him with a look of skepticism. "I or someone from my office must attend any PanGaean state function involving Lenland. Since you are attending a formal event at PanGaea University, that makes it a state function. The University simply followed protocol, and extended an invitation to my office." She glanced sidelong at Pindlebryth while she turned to watch the CityState streets roll by. "...even though from what I've gathered recently, the University is doing their utmost to keep the ceremony as small and unnoteworthy as possible.

"But you, of course, should know the embassy's duties. Is there a reason M'Lord does not wish me to accompany you?" She allowed herself a small knowing grin. Pindlebryth wondered to himself if it was a pastime of all females to torment playfully. "Or perhaps there is someone else M'Lord would prefer by his side?"

Pindlebryth concluded if he answered naming either GraceTail or Darothien, that it would lead the conversation into two vastly different topics, neither of which he cared to discuss. At first he thought to simply ignore her question, but he decided to turn the tables, and make Quentain take the defensive position.

"I understand that SharpWatch paid you a visit last night. Is there somewhere else *you* would prefer to be?"

Quentain crossed her legs, turned back to him, and knitted her paws together in her lap. "He made a surprise sweep of the embassy last night, verifying everyone's credentials to ensure there are no shapeshifters amongst us. Your father certainly is resolute in his disdain for Fox and Crow."

"He has a right to be. And he is not the only one."

Quentain eyed Pindlebryth up and down his entire length, as if she were trying to assess an inconsistency. Pindlebryth was aware of this, but stolidly maintained his composure. She leaned slightly forward to ask a further question, but was distracted as the carriage turned off the main thoroughfare. "Ah, we have arrived at the University."

Pindlebryth looked out at the passing halls – the auditoriums, libraries, galleries and lecture halls in which he had spent so much time. He wondered how much longer he might be able to frequent them. "Who will be accompanying you to the reception?" Pindlebryth asked. "Come to think of it, do you know where the reception is to be held? That information was not included on the invitation," he continued, feigning ignorance of the answers to both of his questions.

"SharpWatch was most adamant. I can't say I understand his security concerns, but he insisted that he escort me to the reception. Perhaps he also wants to keep a watchful eye on you. By the way, where is Grefdel? I did not see him at your residence, when the redoubtable GraceTail introduced herself." Quentain giggled, recalling GraceTail's ebullience and her northern Lenland accent.

"I sent him back home. The PanGaean authorities were beginning to sniff around, suspecting that he was more than just a gardener. We both know how PanGaea frowns on members of any country's militia or security within their borders for extended periods of time." Pindlebryth looked down in a moment of reflection. How easily half-truths had become for him, he mulled to himself. Though his emotions churned between revulsion and a sense of satisfaction at such an accomplishment, he was ever conscious to maintain his mask – which only fueled the biting irony of his internal debate.

Pindlebryth regarded Quentain as an honest sort, and part of him wanted to confide in her – but he did not want to subject her to the risks. He knew if the PanGaean government suspected she was complicit in what he had planned, her position would be in question and she would be sent packing to Lenland in a heartbeat. He looked back up to see Quentain studying him again.

"As to your second question, I've been informed that the reception will be held at the CityState North Shore Marina. Shall SharpWatch and I collect you this evening for the reception?"

"No, that will not be necessary, thank you. I have made my own arrangements," he responded flatly.

"As you wish, M'Lord," she concluded, ostensibly watching the scenery, but keeping one eye on Pindlebryth.

The carriage pulled up in front of the museum attached to the Hall of Natural Sciences. Pindlebryth's hackles rustled as he spied WhiskerWidth among a few others waiting for them at the entrance. He noticed that his beige fur was beginning to shed, and was being replaced by thick white tufts, a sure sign that winter was approaching. He felt mildly grateful, as WhiskerWidth's copious shedding provided a socially acceptable reason to keep his distance from the despicable toady.

Pindlebryth was not the only one agitated. Quentain snapped open her decorative fan, and whispered guardedly to him, "See that Crow in uniform? He's a Warder!"

"I know."

"You *know*?" she said with a start, barely able to keep her voice down. "What in the world are the Kyaa's marshals doing here?"

"The official story is that the Kyaa wants to absolutely guarantee the BlueHoods' safety. In actuality, he was pressured on many sides, within and without the Rookeries, to grant the BlueHoods this time away from his country, and he wants to make sure they return."

Quentain regarded her prince, somewhat befuddled. Because of his past with Hakayaa, Pindlebryth might be aware of any number of past dealings between the BlueHoods and the Kyaa. Grefdel might have advised Pindlebryth regarding matters of their security before he left, but unless he somehow knew the BlueHoods, his insight would merely be conjecture. Quentain had trouble accepting either of those two possibilities. She closed her fan with a flick of her wrist and a resounding snap.

Valets and pages assisted them off the carriage and escorted them inside the museum to a large gallery near its center. As he and Quentain entered the room, Pindlebryth felt several pairs of surprised eyes fall upon them. He quickly gathered that they were the only Lemmings present amongst those assembled, and that their presence was somewhat unexpected, given the current relations of Lenland with the Rookeries of the Kyaa. He ignored their curious stares, and proceeded to walk nonchalantly about the gallery.

Paintings of PanGaean landscapes graced one wall, while the adjoining walls on either side held artworks depicting wonders of the Northern Lands, both east and west of PanGaea. The only ones he recognized were the Three Sisters Falls from the Lodges south of Lenland, the ring of thirty-two giant sequoias that encircled the Warrening CityState at every major and minor point of the compass, and Lenland's own Valley of Giants, a field of granite megaliths surrounded by a ring of cliffs over a dozen leagues wide. In each of the four corners of the hall were busts of the founders of PanGaea University. Standing around the largest bust was a quartet of musicians, playing a series of simple chorales on their reeds and recorders. A wide and warmly carpeted walkway encircled the outermost portion of the room, allowing the growing number of visitors to view all the artworks. One step lower was an equally wide concentric walkway, separated from the outer one by a banister. In the very center of the room was a bare but richly polished wooden floor, holding a table, a podium, and a host of chairs with seating cards arranged in a pair of semicircles facing the podium. On the table were a small black lacquered easel, a single lit beeswax candle on a spiral scrolled onyx marble candlestick, and a large black cloth embroidered in red craftily folded into the shape of a nesting bird.

This room was familiar to Pindlebryth, as he had attended a few chamber concerts here. Although at those events, the orchestra held the center pit, and the audience was seated in the concentric walkways. The only thing in the room unfamiliar to Pindlebryth was the fourth wall. Apparently for this occasion, it held a handful of paintings – some quite amateurish, and others positively primitive. Ambling past them, he viewed the first few along the wall. The first he did not recognize, but after a moment of consideration, he believed he recognized the scenery of the second landscape – it seemed to depict the dry lake bed gem field where Hakayaa had been sent on family business one and one half years ago. He inspected the brass nameplates along the bottom of the frames, only then confirming that these indeed were scenes from the great southern continents. Pindlebryth scanned the room, slowly filling with diplomats and other observers. He recognized members of all the races of the civilized Northern Nations, but there were no members of the strange and wonderful races of the south that Hakayaa had described to him over a semester ago. He wondered what this new set of artwork might signify.

Pindlebryth focused momentarily on Quentain, who was engaged conversing with a member of Vulpinden's embassy staff. All about her were furtive glances and a cloud of guarded remarks, most of which relayed surprise that Lemmings would attend a ceremony to honor a Crow.

If he were given to paranoia, Pindlebryth might have been suspicious or even irritated with Quentain for speaking so familiarly with any member of that race, but he recalled a statement she had often made in the past. "Politicians make a career out of talking when they have nothing to say. It is the lot of ambassadors to talk when they do not want to."

The crowd reached a peak of about two dozen, consisting of three distinct groups. The majority of the attendees were from the University – all the heads of each major department of the University were spoken for, including GrayMask and the Ferret that Pindlebryth observed arguing with DarkMane the day before. GrayMask kept to himself, however the Ferret looked about warily, occasionally glancing at DarkMane with obvious animus.   Pindlebryth felt disheartened and ashamed momentarily as he realized that DeepDigger was not invited, and would quite probably have been barred from attending had he tried.

The next largest group consisted of official representatives from each nation that supported PanGaea, mostly ambassadors and other notable politicians.   The remainder was a mismatched pair of a Beaver and an Otter – two business partners and longtime friends of the BlueHood family.   They kept to themselves for the large part, but occasionally engaged various ambassadors, ostensibly to keep the machine of international business well oiled.

A page entered and ostentatiously announced the Regents. The first four Regents entered, each of them gladhanding and cheerily greeting their guests.   They were followed by the fifth Regent, DarkMane, who looked as if he were chewing on a bitter fruit.   After a few minutes, one of the Regents chatted up Quentain, and was about to offer his condolences to Pindlebryth, when the page announced the arrival of the guests of honor, the BlueHoods.

They walked in slowly and stately, followed by two Crow wearing the formal uniforms of the Crow military.   The two soldiers took their place on either side of the entrance and stood at what Pindlebryth assumed was parade rest.   The BlueHoods greeted the Regent President, and all in the room bowed to them, even Pindlebryth.

Mr. and Mrs. BlueHood were dressed in fine but plain black clothes of mourning, save for he with a red cravat pinned in the center with a large blazing diamond, and she with a pendant necklace comprised of diamonds holding a central ruby larger than her eyes.   Age wore on them well – he walked with a cane built for show, but that could still bear weight, and she shuffled along at his side with only the hint of a hunched back.   Through her veil of mourning, one could still see that one of her eyes had a milky tinge to it.   Similar to her daughter, the ends of her wings had been clipped, albeit more severely.   Pindlebryth thought he began to understand why Hayake wanted to see her parents so badly.   Despite their impairments, and the obvious weight of what must be a bittersweet time for them, they still bore themselves nobly.

They greeted each and every one of the attendees, although in Pindlebryth's case, they simply but respectfully nodded their acknowledgment to him. The pair eventually took their seats, and at the behest of the Regent President who took the podium, the musicians completed their refrains and filed out of the room as everyone else followed the BlueHoods' example.

The Regent greeted the guests in a formal and solemn tone. After formally – and needlessly – re-introducing the guests of honor, he proceeded to eulogize Hakayaa BlueHood in extravagantly superlative terms. Pindlebryth quickly found the content of the soliloquy was so inaccurate by exaggeration, it proved to anyone close to Hakayaa that the Regent knew absolutely nothing about him. The almost laughable errors were the sole feature of the Regent's speech that Pindlebryth could use to combat the sonorous drone of his voice. His interminable ramblings mercifully concluded by calling Mr. BlueHood up to stand next to him. The Regent undid the pleated cloth to reveal a diploma framed in densely veined myrtlewood. He presented the degree of letters in history to the audience, handing it to the guest of honor, and bowing to him and Mrs. BlueHood. He rested the framed document in the table easel, and the single candle flame flickered silently, giving the vellum a warm glow. Mr. BlueHood took the podium, and spoke briefly. Pindlebryth found he was anxious for the elder BlueHood during his delivery, for though it was short, it was nonetheless obvious that he still wrestled with his grief. After thanking the University for the honor bestowed on his late son, he closed his remarks with an invitation.

"I would be honored if all in attendance would join us immediately afterwards in the central hall of mineralogy at the end of the hallway to view a display in my son's honor. The BlueHood estate hereby donates to PanGaea University a collection of gems, jewels, along with wrought and mounted items, that were to be a portion of Hakayaa BlueHood's inheritance. My wife and I believe that this would be the best disposition of our son's wishes."

Pindlebryth's shock momentarily poked through his adopted mask of indifference. Moved by the difficulty with which the BlueHoods restrained their grief, it took all his discipline and concentration to stamp down the guilt that churned in his stomach. Already tortured by refusing to display the slightest empathy for the pain endured by Hakayaa's parents, he was overwhelmed by this magnanimous gesture. The only reprieve of solace he could afford himself was the hope that he might one day soon be able to tell them that Hakayaa was alive but in hiding for their sakes. But he could not wallow in depression, as he became aware he was being watched.

Quentain leaned forward slightly with an expression of inquisitiveness and concern. Resuming his facade as best he could, he stretched his paws and pretended to stifle a yawn. Before he turned his attention back to Mr. BlueHood, he also became aware of DarkMane glowering with utter disdain at him.

"We also extend to all attending and their guests an invitation to an observance in honor of our son after sundown. The main ballroom of the CityState North Shore Marina is at your disposal until midnight." The guests rose as Mr. BlueHood collected his sobbing wife. Two University ushers moved to the seating area, and row by row indicated the order by which guests should follow, as the BlueHoods and their uniformed escort slowly walked to the display hall. Pindlebryth and Quentain were among the very last to be escorted from the room. Before he left, Pindlebryth examined the framed document, and amused himself with the thought that Hakayaa got his degree before he did. When he finished, two Crow in black raiment bearing the BlueHood family crest extinguished the candle, and collected the framed award.

The hallway was quite long, and they passed several side doorways that opened into various rooms holding exhibits of geology displays, dioramas of various land and sea environments, and finally a rich catalogue of crystals and stones, both precious and semi-precious, still encrusted in raw outcroppings.

Refrains of music could be heard wafting from the great display hall at the end of the hallway, and Pindlebryth could spy the musicians had moved there during the ceremony. Next to the entrance of the great display room, was a table with a pair of servants offering flutes of champagne to each of the guests. Quentain graciously accepted her drink as they entered the display hall, Pindlebryth less so.

As he entered, Pindlebryth was struck by the dichotomy of stately elegance and cold functionality in the room. Although the room was beautifully appointed with ornately scrolled molding and sculptured ceiling, there was a deep metal groove running the full height of the doorway. Glancing around the border of the entrance, he saw the lintel hid all but the lowest portion of a formidable steel portcullis. A heavily reinforced affair, it was riveted at every intersection of its crosshatched bars, and could be lowered to the floor, where a metal plate locked it in place. Pindlebryth doubted that he could get anything larger than his arm through the openings of the woven metal bars. He could only guess where the lever that controlled the gates had been hidden. Of the four doorways in the room, two were fully closed with their portcullises down. He chortled with disdain at the security guards at each corner. Pindlebryth remarked audibly to Quentain, much to her embarrassed dismay, that he wondered whether the guards were a show of force to impress the BlueHoods, or were instead necessary to protect the gems from the upper crust of society.

Strutting like one of the contemptuous delinquents that GrayMask had alluded to, he went from case to case cursorily looking at the enclosed items, only to quickly move on as if he were bored. As Pindlebryth took in the display, he had to restrain a gasp. He had previously seen several examples of the BlueHood artworks, including of course the crowns of Lenland, but the size of the gems, the complexity and beauty of the bejeweled pieces far exceeded anything he had ever seen before. In his wildest dreams, he would never have guessed at the size and caliber of the collection. And this was but a small portion of Hakayaa's inheritance? Small wonder then indeed, Pindlebryth marveled, how easily the BlueHoods coerced so many heads of state to pressure the University for what in return was a pittance of a gift.

Pendants, bracelets, eggs, statuary and headpieces befitting of emperors were covered by thick reinforced glass enclosures fitted over heavy rectangular marble and granite stands bolted into the floor. He quietly sampled all the pieces, as Quentain by his side intercepted and conversed with several of the other guests. Pindlebryth found himself again struggling to maintain his air of complacency – only this time he fought the enormous urge to laugh, imagining the flustered look on Kaiya's face as he learned his birthright was being given away in this manner.

Within a short period, Pindlebryth quickly tired of the crowd of guests, and suggested to Quentain that they take their leave. Pindlebryth downed the last of his drink and was about to make a beeline for the exit, when Quentain interposed herself and quietly corrected him in a lightly scolding and didactic manner. "We mustn't leave without thanking our hosts,

M'Lord."

"Quite right," Pindlebryth acceded. He calmly approached the BlueHoods, bowed slightly and thanked them on both his and Quentain's behalf.

"Thank you for attending, Prince Pindlebryth," said Mr. BlueHood. His wife turned to look at Pindlebryth with her good eye. "I certainly hope to see you at the reception. My wife and I hope you would be able to share any fond memories you have of our son with us." He leaned forward slightly, and in a softer tone added, "Especially those that would make our other guests uncomfortable!" He chortled in the queerest manner, laughing through the spiracles in his beak.

Pindlebryth returned a heartfelt but weak and pained smile with a nod. Next to him, Mrs. BlueHood gently sobbed, "Hakayaa spoke to us often about you. Thank you for being his one true friend." A small respite of appreciation came over him – at last there was one thing said today that was true. He was about to bow and take his leave, when she like her husband also leaned forward. Pindlebryth stooped slightly, and she whispered into his ear in a flat unemotional tone, "Take care. The tall one is a shapeshifter."

Pindlebryth rose slowly, his eyes widened slightly and suddenly piercing. "Thank you Madam BlueHood. You have been most helpful and gracious." As he and Quentain left the room, Pindlebryth surreptitiously glanced around the room, and marked the taller of the escorts.

Once back in the embassy carriage, Quentain resumed her game of chatting up Pindlebryth, and occasionally good-humouredly needling him.

"Such a wonderful array of finery. I knew the BlueHoods had amassed a fortune that rivaled any kingdom, but to actually see such examples that put lesser kingdoms to shame!" The pair swayed in their cabin seats as the carriage rounded the corner onto the main thoroughfare, leaving the University grounds behind them. Pindlebryth was lost in his thoughts and paid little heed to the baits and prods that Quentain used to try to provoke a response out of him.

"...and for their age, the BlueHoods are looking quite well. Pray tell, what was that all about with the Matron BlueHood? A new contract to be worked out between their businesses and Lenland perhaps? It is no secret that she is the real brains behind the BlueHood dynasty juggernaut."

"There has been a change in plans," Pindlebryth declared, looking her straight in the eye. "I want you and SharpWatch to collect GraceTail and I for the reception this evening."

"Certainly, M'Lord," she tittered, with a grain of anticipation. "Might I inquire why the sudden change?"

Pindlebryth's response was as hard and final as iron. "No." Gone was the pretext of bored indifference. Pindlebryth's jowls flexed repeatedly as he clenched his teeth, his eyes darting to and fro in desperate concentration.

"I *knew* something was afoot!" she exclaimed, clapping her fan into her gloved paw. "I've known you since you were a pup, and I could not believe that you could turn into an indolent malcontent in such a short time." But Pindlebryth maintained a humorless stare. Quentain quickly dropped her amused manner, and became as deadly serious as she now observed Pindlebryth to be. "Forgive me, M'Lord," she apologized. "Tell me what you need me to do."

Pindlebryth reached into his vest, and pulled the Talking Gem out of the pouch tied into the inner pocket. Quentain eyed the device with keen interest as he put it to his ear. She thought she recognized the emerald inside the silver frame, and was about to ask Pindlebryth about the trinket when he held up a paw for her to keep silent.

"Darothien? Darothien!" he spoke into it. He again held it to his ear, but shook his head and put the Gem back into its pouch and pocket. "Lords Below! There's too much noise." He reached upwards, rapped on the ceiling of the cabin and bellowed, "Driver! To my house as fast as you can!" The carriage lurched as the driver applied the lash with a crack.

"I will have more instructions for you when all four of us are en route to the BlueHoods' reception. When we arrive, behave as if everything is normal."

"Normal! How can I act normal when *you* are not?" she protested.

"I must play the part of the fool in public for the time being. But I can let you know this – once at the observance, follow SharpWatch's instructions. Do not ask questions, do not debate it, just *do it*! Our lives and the lives of others may be at stake." Pindlebryth fell silent for a while, as he fell back into furious thought.

"That's all?" Quentain blurted impatiently.

Pindlebryth shook his head as he returned to the

circumstances at hand. "No, but I cannot explain everything just now. The BlueHoods gave me information that put some plans in flux. I will have more instructions when we ride to the reception."

"But you've got to give me something more, M'Lord!"

"All in good time, Quentain. In the meantime, don't bog down SharpWatch with questions. But do inform him there is a shapeshifter in the BlueHoods' escort. And make sure you wear those evening gloves!" As the carriage rocked to a stop in front of his house, Pindlebryth bounded out the cabin door. Dashing towards the front door of his house, he did not take notice of Quentain's flabbergasted half-smile at his apparent non sequitur.

GraceTail descended the staircase, a captivating study in red. The sun was setting, its warm ambiance only intensifying the crimson and magenta hues of her costume. Her gown flowed about her, accentuating all the right places. The gown's generous shoulders framed a plunging neckline, and sleeves that ended above the elbow. Tether straps buttoned at the bottoms of the sleeves looped to the ends of long elegant gloves. The dress had both sheer and thicker woven layers, that made her look like a delightful package to be unwrapped, tied with a deep burgundy belt sash. Topping her head was a small matching crimson hat jauntily tilted forward in place with a stenciled metal and wooden comb, which underscored her sassy Lemming public persona.

Pindlebryth was somewhat impatiently waiting for her in the foyer. When she arrived at the landing at the bottom of the stairs, he ceased his pacing and was riveted speechless by the sight. He was not the only one affected, as GraceTail had also successfully stopped HighStance in his tracks. He was transfixed as he held Pindlebryth's outer coat like a statue with his mouth agape.

BroadShanks followed GraceTail, fussing after the gown's small train and the bow of the belt tied behind, and primping the shoulders to remove unwanted folds.

"Pindie, whatever you pay BroadShanks, you should double

it! She is an amazing seamstress!" She sashayed to the left and right in rapid succession at the landing, making the gown sway back and forth. BroadShanks had stopped a few steps above her. Momentarily stunned that GraceTail had actually paid her a compliment, she quickly scooted down the last of the staircase, and scolded her husband.

"M'Lord may look, but *you* are spoken for, you lecher!" HighStance's head quivered like he had been splashed with cold water, and quickly took advantage of the moment to drape the overcoat over Pindlebryth. BroadShanks maneuvered around GraceTail to fetch her outerwear.

"I fear you are going to attract *too* much attention, Hayake."

GraceTail curtsied slightly. "First you are supposed to say, 'How beautiful you look, Miss GraceTail!' Then I reply 'Why thank you, N'Lord!'" she taunted as she stood again. "I am merely playing the part that we have created these past months. And I am firm believer in hiding in plain sight. Trust me, the more outlandish I look, the more the other guests will avoid looking closely at me."

"It's not the guests I am worried about now. Just keep your distance from the Warders assigned to your parents, especially the tall one. Remember your mother informed me he's a shapeshifter."

"That *is* unfortunate," GraceTail complained. "But I doubt if he will be looking for me, or any other shapeshifter. Uncle HeaKea has been conspicuously throwing his weight and money about the CityState and its LakeShores in the Lodges of WeatherWorn this past month. The Court of the Kyaa believes I am hidden there under his protection after the Ravenne released me."

BroadShanks draped GraceTail's coat over her shoulders, adjusted her crimson hat and reseated her comb. She then bustled into the kitchen, and almost immediately reappeared with a small vial of golden liquid, and a lit candle.

A knock came at the door. BroadShanks let out a peep as she jumped at the sound. With a nod from Pindlebryth, HighStance peered through a side window, then opened the door to the awaiting SharpWatch. Handsomely dressed in an immaculate dress uniform, he greeted his prince. "It is good to see you again M'Lord. It's been a long time since the bridge at the Lodges border." His amiable demeanor quickly grew serious. "I take it that it was necessary to bring Ambassador

Quentain into this..." he trailed off as he caught sight of GraceTail.   Catching himself with only some mild embarrassment, he quickly bowed. "Forgive me, m'lady. We have not been introduced."

Pindlebryth immediately jumped in, fearing that SharpWatch might make a bit a fool of himself. "May I introduce SharpWatch of the Eagle Squad. SharpWatch, this is Miss Hayake *BlueHood*," he emphasized. "She is in disguise."

"It is a good thing then, that we will be the only Lenlanders at the reception. She would have the unfettered attention of every Lemming buck within sight!"

"Ny dear SharpWatch, you do turn a doe's head!" GraceTail said playfully as she batted her eyes at him.

BroadShanks proceeded to bustle about the ground floor, lighting a lamp in each room. Pindlebryth held out his arm beckoning his two companions to the door. "We had best hurry, sundown will soon be upon us."

BroadShanks called from the parlor. "Yoo-hoo, M'Lord! Don't forget your tincture of ginger and peppermint!" She trotted into the foyer, and handed the vial to Pindlebryth, who dropped it into a pocket of his overcoat.

Pindlebryth coughed to get SharpWatch's attention. "As you were saying, we will need Quentain's help at the reception. Is everything prepared on your end, SharpWatch?"

SharpWatch immediately became attentive and all business. "Yes, M'Lord. The materials for the raft are all assembled, and ready to sail. Also, Darothien requested a few supplies – a barrel of light fuel oil, and one quarter of a cord of white pine. They have been delivered to the sloop."

"I wonder what Darothien has up her sleeve," Pindlebryth mused.

"I'm sure I don't know, M'Lord. I asked her, half in jest, if she needed a brazier or something for a fire, and she quite sternly replied, 'That's not what it is for!'," said SharpWatch, moving aside from the front door.

"Did you get the parcel for GraceTail?"

"Yes, I met with the Beaver quartermaster in the market this morning. We were not followed, and I inspected the contents. The package is waiting for her in the carriage."

HighStance held open the door, as the trio exited the foyer for the embassy carriage. BroadShanks remarked to HighStance, "He gets so terribly seasick." She sniffled and waved goodbye as he closed the door.

"Don't worry, my dear," HighStance reassured her. "I'm sure he'll come back to us safe." He put his arm around her to reassure her, but it was not helpful. She broke away, and scampered back to her kitchen, crying, "Oh my poor prince! Madam WhiteSocks said he faces a perilous voyage, and she's *never* wrong!"

SharpWatch held the cabin door as Pindlebryth assisted GraceTail into the carriage, then secured it behind him after they all joined Quentain inside. It was quite confined in the carriage with all four of them. Pindlebryth found himself thankful that the style of large hoop skirts that were popular in some countries never caught on in the circles of high fashion in Lenland.

SharpWatch knocked twice on the ceiling of the cabin to get the driver's attention. "To the Royale at the CityState marina," he commanded. The carriage rolled away slowly, but picked up speed after it turned a corner to head bay-side.

"Good evening, M'Lord," Quentain said coolly. Pindlebryth eyed her, and got the distinct feeling that not only was she seething with nervous energy beneath her calm exterior, but that she was reveling in the anticipation of whatever lay in store.

"I'm sorry to have brought you in on this at such a late time. Or to have you brought in at all, ambassador." He turned to SharpWatch. "Madam BlueHood informed me at the ceremony that one of the military guards assigned to her, ostensibly for her protection, is a shapeshifter."

"So the ambassador informed me," replied SharpWatch, though it was plain that he did not understand its importance.

"Crow shapeshifters can detect others of their kind if they are in proximity, and concentrate on looking for them. Also, though she did not specifically say so, we have to be prepared that he might also be a Ravenne. So, we must keep him away from GraceTail."

"GraceTail?" exclaimed Quentain, looking at her as if she were a stranger.

"Hayake BlueHood at your service, ambassador," she said with a grin as she extended her paw. Quentain was too floored to accept the greeting, but simply stared at her for a moment.

"*That*'s why you always wear gloves! And why *you*," nodding at Pindlebryth, "wanted to make sure that I also wore gloves."

"Hiding in plain sight," repeated GraceTail with satisfaction.

"Do your parents know you are here?" Quentain asked excitedly.

"Yes, they do. And that's all we should say on the subject," Pindlebryth interjected with finality.

SharpWatch looked even more perplexed as Quentain closely examined GraceTail's gloves.

"Crow hens with shapeshifting have their wings clipped," Pindlebryth explained to him. "It is a... tradition they have."

"The word you're looking for is *barbaric*," quipped GraceTail. "After every yearly molt, our wings are clipped so that we cannot fly for long distances. All in the name of arranged marriages," she spat. "It also allows us to be easily recognized even when we shift into another form, making it more difficult to escape those loveless pairings."

Quentain nodded vigorously as she chimed in. "At least the tradition is better than what it was in generations past. The current practice replaced the truly distressing custom of pinioning."

"Pinioning?" Pindlebryth asked. He was somewhat familiar with the term from flying with Voyager and his studies in Crow literature, but his understanding did not clarify Quentain's use of the word.

"Yes," GraceTail answered with disgust. "The female offspring of any known shapeshifter had their metacarpals removed at birth." Seeing that Pindlebryth was now as equally confused as SharpWatch, she added, "Imagine half your fingers were hacked off."

"Is that what was done to your mother?" asked Pindlebryth not bothering to hide a grimace. GraceTail simply nodded, to which Pindlebryth added apologetically, "I was only told your mother couldn't fly. I assumed it was because her feathers were clipped like yours. My apologies, I didn't know of your custom."

"It is not *my* custom!" GraceTail seethed. "We are wasting precious time!"

"Quite right," Pindlebryth agreed. "Quentain, we all have our parts to play. Here is yours. Keep an eye on the Warders, especially the tall one. If he gets too close to GraceTail, or begins to nose around, keep him distracted."

"Yes, M'Lord." Quentain began to smile again with

excitement. Pindlebryth began to think that she must be terribly bored with her official position in PanGaea. If they made it out of this, he would have to see what he could do about that.

"There is one other thing, Quentain. During the evening, I've arranged a distraction to preoccupy the Warders, and get as many of them away from the BlueHoods as possible. It's best if you do not know what it is, so you can act surprised with everyone else. Just stay with us regardless what happens, until all of us leave. As soon as that opportunity presents itself, we will escort you and GraceTail back to this carriage. SharpWatch and I shall distract the driver until he, Hayake and I can proceed separately to the *Peerless*. You will remain with the carriage."

"The *Peerless*?"

"A racing sloop owned by LogSplitter, a Beaver business partner of the BlueHoods. You might have met him at the ceremony today? He takes his pride and joy out for a moonlight circuit outside of the bay every night. He has also arranged to lease his berth next to the *SlipStream*, the ship that brought the BlueHoods to PanGaea.

"When SharpWatch and I bring you to the carriage, you will help GraceTail with the contents of her package," he said pointing to the parcel underneath her seat. "You will then return to the embassy, and await word from me. If all goes well, I will be back by tomorrow morning. But rest as best as you can tonight. You will need to be on your toes tomorrow, for the Crow ambassador will in all probability lodge a formal complaint at our embassy against me. If things go especially well tonight, he will want my head."

"Then why return to PanGaea at all?" Quentain protested.

"Three separate bits of unfinished business." Pindlebryth sat back in his seat, sporting an impish grin. "But foremost, I want the satisfaction of seeing the Crow squirm under the screw for a change, when they realize they cannot prove a thing!"

The scent of ocean air tinged with the odors of the harbor marketplace had been building as the carriage drove on, and soon the sounds of harbor business could be heard. Amidst the hubbub of a hundred voices and the occasional shouts of mooring crews could be heard the clanking of loading hooks, the rustling of loosened sails being collected into their shrouds, and the bells of the various ships.

Though the carriage followed a boulevard that paralleled the harbor's edge a few blocks away, the pungent reek of the fish and cargo markets was still quite prominent. Quentain covered her snout with a daintily laced and monogrammed handkerchief, while GraceTail smiled, closed her eyes and inhaled deeply.   She exhaled loudly and pronounced, "Goodness, I missed that! Now I'm getting quite hungry!"

Pindlebryth countered with a needling smirk, "One might even say ravenous?"   Quentain's nervous energy must have been contagious, as both GraceTail and Pindlebryth both laughed at his terrible and almost tasteless pun.

Mercifully for the Lemmings, the stench of the harbor marketplace abated as they approached the northern side of the bay.   The prevailing northwestern breeze washed away the offensive odors with a refreshing aroma of firs and spruce from the mountains beyond. The land breeze was still surprisingly warm, as it rolled down from the deep green foot hills peppered with deciduous trees seasonally ablaze with reds, ambers and golds in the waning twilight. As the carriage passed through the outer gates of the CityState marina, the oily flicker of street lanterns gave way to the steady light of gas lamps. The last of the tall wrought iron fixtures were being lit by groundskeepers as the carriage arrived at the main clubhouse.

The Nautical Royale Clubhouse, simply called the Royale by its members, stood on the center of a large rock outcropping leveled by its builders several feet above the highest tides. Around the impressive cedar and redwood building was a beautifully groomed area of white and coral river stones, surrounded by walkways of cut granite. Under each window was a rugose rose shrub, and the doors were adorned with miniature saffron-colored gingko trees. On two sides of the Royale, several sets of granite stairs connected the walkway with boardwalks that led to the various piers comprising the marina.   The carriage passed by the third quadrant of the marina, which boasted a well manicured lawn with several gazebos and small pavilions, before stopping in front of the Royale itself.

Moored to the piers closest to the building was the schooner *SlipStream*. With three masts and a jib, it towered over all the other boats in the next several slips, and was large enough to take two side-by-side berths normally used by smaller boats. One of the flagships of the Kyaa's Navy, it cut an impressive figure. Though not nearly one of the largest nor most heavily armed ships in the Rookeries' fleet, it still had a respectable gunnery, and was mainly bred for speed. All in all, it was more than a match for most any pirate vessel that dared to cross it.

Pindlebryth quickly understood why this vessel was chosen for the BlueHoods: it simply was the logical choice of transport for the BlueHoods and their valuable gifts from the Rookeries of the Kyaa to PanGaea. Though not a sea-faring type by any stretch of the imagination, Pindlebryth still could appreciate the beauty of the ship. In his opinion, however, the sleekness of line and craftsmanship was marred by the choice of figurehead – a menacing rendering of the Kyaa himself.

The carriage was sandwiched between two others as it joined the progression that had formed in front of the clubhouse. After a valet assisted one of the Regents and his spouse out of the conveyance ahead of them, the embassy carriage took its place in front of the building's entrance.

As the valet approached them, Pindlebryth leaned into GraceTail, whispering, "Be strong. Remember, you cannot show the slightest sign that you knew Hakayaa." GraceTail inhaled sharply, held her breath and closed her eyes as she steeled herself, and nodded rapidly. She exhaled slowly as she adjusted her hat's comb, then ran her paws down her lap to straighten out any bunches of material in her gown.

Pindlebryth and GraceTail, then SharpWatch and Quentain exited the carriage and paired themselves along the carpet leading to the open doors of the main lobby. Pindlebryth adopted an air of cocky indifference and GraceTail imparted a wide-eyed but street-wise excitement as they stepped into the crowd within. Behind them, a dour Regent DarkMane accompanied by an equally glum Badger sow emerged from their carriage. Pindlebryth did not know if DarkMane was married to his severe looking guest, and he quickly decided he did not wish to find out.

They were greeted enthusiastically by the president of the marina club, as butlers collected their coats and outer garments. Pindlebryth and GraceTail shared a glance of mutual satisfaction as the finely dressed and immaculately groomed Otter stumbled and stuttered in greeting the prince's partner and her outlandish evening wear. Pindlebryth repressed a snicker, as he finally realized that GraceTail had been sarcastic in her praise of BroadShanks' acumen as a couturier.

The group was guided by an usher down a hallway to the reception ballroom. Along the hallway was an array of paintings of various ships, under each of which was a display case. Quentain noted one of the paintings' labels identified the *Peerless*, and its matching display case contained several ribbons and two racing trophies. One was from an annual national contest in the Lodges, the other larger one awarded by this very marina. An inkling of what Pindlebryth might be planning began to grow in her mind.

The opulent ballroom was bathed with warm light from arrays of gaslight wall sconces. Several small circular tables and chairs dotted the room, with several in a row along a wall of sliding glass doors. All the tables were trimmed with black bunting, and the glass wall was almost entirely enclosed with dark blue draperies. A few of the transoms above the doors were opened, leaving the whole room scented with the pleasantly refreshing combination of salt air and conifer.

The most striking feature in the reception hall was the central display. A table was set with several articles of Hakayaa's clothing from his youth and later years, selections from his library, and other memorabilia. The framed diploma conferred to Hakayaa had been transferred from the museum to the end of the table, completing the collage that spanned his lifetime. At the table's center stood a portrait of a younger Hakayaa BlueHood. Its frame was festooned with an oblong ring of holly so dark it was almost black. Twined all about the wreath were rows of full autumnal blossoms of azure monkshood and blue leadplant.

Upon entering the room, Pindlebryth and GraceTail paid their respects again to the BlueHoods. Pindlebryth's unease was piqued by the tall Crow Warder behind them, and two others standing watchfully in opposite corners of the room. GraceTail was also immediately aware of this first challenge of the evening, and defended by keeping Mrs. BlueHood between herself and the shapeshifter Warder. Pindlebryth observed GraceTail showed no undue emotion, despite being distracted by Mr. BlueHood reminding him to relate any tales of misadventure with Hakayaa.

As SharpWatch and Quentain in turn paid their respects, Pindlebryth and GraceTail were offered refreshments by the marina waitstaff and invited to partake from the many small tables laid out with various cakes, biscuits and other light fare.

The pair then milled about the room among the other guests, Pindlebryth playing the bored delinquent, GraceTail the flighty fortune hunter. Quentain and SharpWatch were not far behind, making sure they were always in a position to intercept the Crow Warder.

As Pindlebryth walked along the long memorial table, he inspected the various books. He was suddenly struck with a twinge of nervousness. He wondered if anyone had known about and searched the library for Hakayaa's cache of uncut diamonds, or worse, what they might think when none were to be found. He quickly pushed his fear aside, reasoning that the missing cache could be explained away by any number of nights at the casinos when luck eluded them. Pindlebryth finally put it to rest with a grin by imagining that whoever searched the library set off one of the tricks and traps it contained.

A long night of dreary hobnobbing and avoiding GrayMask, DarkMane, and the Warders was occasionally made tolerable by Mr. BlueHood. Finally acquiescing to his requests, Pindlebryth told two tales, taking care to make it sound as if he were an unwitting bystander to Hakayaa's hijinks. The first story revolved around some mischievous prankster who wrapped Old Pan's clapper with pillows, and how the partially deaf tower keeper didn't notice the problem until the school day was more than half done. He saved the second tale involving the substitution of disappearing ink in some Regent's inkwells until DarkMane was in earshot. Pindlebryth found DarkMane's reaction of choking on his drink quite satisfying. GraceTail laughed appropriately at all the proper places during his anecdotes, leaving Pindlebryth relieved and impressed at her control of the conflicting emotions of levity and loss.

He was about to start on a third anecdote, when a commotion arose at the hall entrance. The marina president and a trio of distressed and fidgeting university staff clogged the doorway, trying to hide their frantic motions to attract the attention of the Regent President.

Finally alerted to the disturbance, he walked over and met with the officials. After he sternly admonished the group for their untimely interruption, one of them – a guard from the museum – nervously whispered into the Regent's ear. The president's transformation was immediate, his attitude of annoyance changing to near panic. Glancing nervously about the room, he wanted to gather the remaining Regents as unobtrusively as possible. He quickly realized this was a fruitless task, as all eyes in the room were upon him. The look of dread on his face when he glanced at the BlueHoods spoke volumes.

"May I please have the attention of all the Regents," he commanded, as he rang two empty glasses together. He motioned for his people to follow, then retreated into the hallway without. The Regents placed their assorted teas, spirits and cakes on the nearest tables, and hurried to follow, leaving their spouses to gape, conjecture and gossip. One minute later, the president returned searching for the Warder captain standing with the BlueHoods. He beckoned the tall Crow away from his charges, and spoke to him in hushed tones. The captain blurted out an expletive, and pointed at the two Crow under his command.

"Accompany the Regents to the museum. You report back to me immediately on the situation, and you," he said looking at the other, "assist with the investigation." The two saluted, then accompanied the Regent back outside. This drew Mr. BlueHood's attention, as he thumped down his glass on the nearest table, and strode with alarmed concern to the Warder as fast as his cane allowed.

LogSplitter, sporting a black suit bearing the insignia of the marina, broke away from talking about business affairs with his Otter partner near the entrance and moved towards Pindlebryth by a meandering path.

"I must say, M'Lord, a master stroke! Sheer genius!" he whispered.

"Whatever do you mean?" sputtered Pindlebryth barely under his breath.

"Why the BlueHood gems, of course!" he replied quietly, barely reining in his excitement. "However did you manage..." He stopped mid-sentence as he realized that Pindlebryth's surprise was sincere. Quentain and SharpWatch joined Pindlebryth to hear what was transpiring.

"What happened to them?" Pindlebryth insisted.

"They're gone! Every last one of them!"

"I assure you, sir, I have nothing to do with this!" he protested through gritted teeth, glancing rapidly between Mr. BlueHood and the remaining Crow Warder as a truant child might peek at a teacher. "Now go about your business, before you draw undue attention!" he hissed. The astonished Beaver stepped back, and wandered away glancing worriedly at the BlueHoods.

Quentain began covertly, "But if this distraction was not of your doing, then what...?"

A deep, almost visceral pulse interrupted her, rattling the glass doors, and making the drapes near the open transoms flutter and blow into the room. An orange glow flickered and grew quickly into an intense undulation, throwing a dance of amber light onto the ballroom ceiling. Several guests hurried to the doors and threw aside the drapes, and crowded around to witness the excitement outside. Columns of light and heat from a large bonfire beamed into the ballroom, casting tormented shadows of the attendees against the opposite wall.

A raft bearing several large barrels had struck the prow of the *SlipStream* as it faced the open bay. Some of the pine barrels had burst, and splashed large swaths of their contents onto the front and side of the vessel, and the raft itself. The tar and oil spread slowly across the hull as the flames licked upwards. Someone on the Crow ship rang the vessel's alarm bell, while a bosun piped the call for all hands on deck. Several crewmates began by trying to douse the flames with water, but the pitch was impervious to it, and clung to the hull like a slimy black barnacle. Various members of the crew had to dodge being sprayed by splotches of burning fuel as another barrel burst with a thrumming sound. The splattering oil was peppered with dots of brilliant white incandescence that hurt the eye.

As the conflagration grew in size, the crew of other boats scurried to protect their own vessels, and smother any small fiery pools that splattered onto the pier between them and the *SlipStream*. Fortune was with them, as the prevailing evening land breeze helped to contain the spread of the flames. Those hands that could be spared from tending after their own vessels assisted the plight of their brothers aboard the *SlipStream*.

In the ballroom, the press of the curious grew as more of the guests, including Mr. BlueHood, Pindlebryth and the Warder captain, were enthralled by the tableau unfolding before them. As the Warder pressed closer to watch the fate of his ship, Pindlebryth and Mr. BlueHood quietly fell back. When clear of his keeper's field of vision, Mr. BlueHood signaled his wife and LogSplitter.

She was standing by the portrait of Hakayaa, touching the

end of one wing to her beak, and then caressing the beloved face in the portrait. Her eyes nictated rapidly, which Pindlebryth surmised was the Crow equivalent of crying.

In the doorway, LogSplitter nervously scanned the room and about the hall for any unduly curious eyes looking their way. Seeing none, he impatiently motioned for all of them to hurry. Mr. BlueHood spread a wing around his wife's back and coaxed her away from her farewell.

Together with all four Lemmings, they hastily exited into the hallway.   The BlueHoods surprised everyone but Pindlebryth with their spryness. Had Pindlebryth been in a less dire situation, he might have laughed at the images of Mrs. BlueHood legging it in her mourning clothes, and Mr. BlueHood using his cane to hop and glide. Once free of the ballroom, the troupe dashed outside and split up. LogSplitter pointed the BlueHoods to his sloop and disappeared back into the Royale, as the Lemmings sprinted to their carriage.

The embassy carriage was now last in the line of remaining conveyances not already taken by the Regents, and in proximity of both the clubhouse and *Peerless*. As soon as she emerged from the Royale, GraceTail wasted no time in tearing off the bow about her waist which hindered her movement. In one move she cast the sash aside and rent the side of the gown so she might not slow the group down. Quentain brought up the end, though she did not lag too far behind as she was vigorously dragged along by SharpWatch. Their driver watched in quiet bewilderment as the two does clambered into the carriage in a most unladylike fashion.

SharpWatch gave instructions to the driver, keeping one eye open for any signs of the Warder captain leaving the Royale. Pindlebryth slammed the door and spoke his last instructions to Quentain through the open window.

"SharpWatch, GraceTail and I will take our leave of you now. As soon as any Warder emerges from the clubhouse, attract their attention, then race back to the embassy. Give them a good chase." Quentain nodded in agreement as the two bucks moved to the back of the carriage. When they were assured of a clear path, the two dashed to the nearest stairs to the boardwalk. They halted sufficiently partway down the stairs, so they could watch the Royale and their carriage without themselves being seen.

Quentain's ears twitched as she heard GraceTail tear into

the parcel. When she turned to look, a naked GraceTail faced her, hastily donning a baggy pair of pants, a black sailor's cap with the *Peerless*'s insignia and an oversized navy blue peacoat. Quentain gaped for a few seconds as GraceTail curled up and shapeshifted into the form of a Beaver.

"Grand meeting you, Quentain! Thanks for all your help!" she rattled off in a whisper, as she straightened her hat, and closed her perfectly fitting coat. She was about to open the carriage door, but paused for the shortest of moments, as if she were forgetting something. With a click of her tongue, she retrieved her hat comb from her old costume, tucked it into the pocket of her heavy coat, and quietly exited out the opposite door. Glancing up to make sure the driver did not see her, Hayake plunged her hairless paws into her coat pockets and ducked behind the carriage.

Strolling down the walkway as if she didn't have a care in the world, she meandered towards the stairs. She was just about to reach them, when a scuffle could be heard at the entrance of the Royale. Bursting out of the doors was the Warder captain, with murder in his eyes. He looked rapidly this way and that, looking for any trace of his charges. Hayake continued to saunter to the stairs, hoping not to attract his attention. She didn't even have time to worry if she was far enough away from the Warder for him to sense her shapeshift, when Quentain noisily beat on the roof of her carriage.

"Driver! To the embassy! Don't spare the reindeer!" she hollered. With a crack of the reins and the snap of the whip, the steeds reared and bolted the carriage away. The driver expertly maneuvered the carriage, avoiding the remaining conveyances, but had to roll over the closest walkway to swing fully around. River stones were shoved out from under its wheels as it turned and sped away, digging unsightly ruts into the marina grounds. Spying the discarded red bow and sash between him and the carriage, the Warder yelled a command to halt. Cursing in Crow, he took a few running steps, and took to the air. Within seconds, the carriage and the Warder careened past the outer gate then around the nearest stately house, and finally out of view.

Hayake laughed to herself as she watched the Warder give chase. She eventually made the stairs, but not before she saw out the side of her eye LogSplitter as he emerged from the Royale. He stuck out his chest as proud as a peacock, and took a deep satisfying breath as he stuffed an envelope into his club jacket. He nodded and gave a sloppy nautical salute to Hayake, and began to follow her to the stairs.

Once the four were all out of sight of the Royale, they dashed down the remaining stairs, and tore down the boardwalk to the *Peerless*. Both Hayake and LogSplitter fell behind Pindlebryth and SharpWatch, waddling as fast as their Beaver's gait would allow. Just as they arrived at the *Peerless*'s dock, another barrel burst into a fireball on the far side of the *SlipStream*.

A few hands were trying to push the raft away with catchpoles and long-oars from the vessel's lifeboat, while others smothered the fire by draping water-soaked tarpaulins over the walls of burning pitch. One brave soul crawled out above the flames to undo a thick waterlogged rope someone had lassoed around the figurehead, holding the raft fast against the side of the schooner.

Sailors from the neighboring boats scooped pails of water from the dock and threw them in vain at the growing curtain of fire. They scrambled for cover, and the deck hands ducked below the *SlipStream*'s railing as another barrel blasted its contents over the vessel and raft. A fresh stream of flaming tarballs and white-hot pebbles showered them all, and immediately yelps of pain and alarm were soon accompanied by the stink of burning fur and feathers. Once the unfortunate few stamped out their knots of scorching hair and plumage, they applied themselves anew against quenching the fire.

The tarps, though drenched with seawater, proved less than effective. Once they were removed or holes burned through them, the freshly exposed white-hot embers flashed again to blinding argent life, rekindling the surrounding pitch.

Pindlebryth and the others bounded over the handrail onto the *Peerless*. As LogSplitter assisted Hayake aboard his sloop, Pindlebryth saw the final crew member scale over the opposite rail. A naked Beaver holding a small dagger between its bucked teeth rolled over the rail from the water onto the deck. After he shook the excess water off his fur and tail, he handed the dagger to LogSplitter and winked at Hayake.

The second that all were on board the *Peerless*, the bosun pressed his finger against his nippers and whistled shrilly, piping a call to the deckhands. The small contingent of crew loosed the moorings, and unfurled the front sails. They slapped wooden handled metal levers into winches at the bottom of the masts and smartly hoisted the remaining sails. The first diamond-shaped sail raised on the aft mast fluttered in the light wind, but the triangular sails raised on the fore mast and jib immediately snapped taut. LogSplitter took his place behind the wheel near the very aft of the sloop, and barked out a command to the hand on the aft mast to leave his remaining sail be, and assist the others to trim the mainsail and staysails.

Pindlebryth looked back up towards the Royale in anticipation of a chase. To him, the sloop pulled away at an agonizingly slow clip from its pier. But the sloop finally did clear the last of the pilings, and soon all the front sails were set and billowing out nicely.

The deckhand drawn away from the aft mast returned to his task. As he did so, LogSplitter checked the compass inlaid in the wheel's gearbox and lashed the wheel. He then wobbled over to a chest built into the deck on the wheel's fore. He unlocked its lid, and gathered four steel rods, all with angled ends. Despite his tottering gait, LogSplitter's sea-legs allowed him to nimbly move around the deckhand who was busy raising the last aft sail. LogSplitter then inserted the first of the rods into holes into a set of three interlocking toothed steel rings around the base of the mast. The rings had a rich grey patina, except around the hexagonal holes that accepted the rods, where the fine protective covering was scraped away from use. The deckhand tied off his last knot for the rigging, then took the remaining rods from LogSplitter. He continued inserting them as LogSplitter did, with the short angled ends pointing back at the mast.

LogSplitter fetched a spyglass from the bosun and rejoined Pindlebryth. He scanned the marina and skies above it, and pronounced, "We're still in the clear." Without a thought, he handed the scope to Pindlebryth, adding, "Be a good lad and.... I mean, M'Lord!" he corrected himself with an embarrassed chuckle. "Cry out as soon as anyone follows us. I should see after our guests." He waddled away to the central cabin, giving new commands to a crewman who was catching his breath after raising the front sails. As LogSplitter bent over to open the slanted doors that led to the cabin, he paused at the top of the steps to cover his ears. Old Bellows, in the shield wall lighthouse at the far southeastern corner of the bay, fired up its lantern and sounded its first horn of the night. Before he disappeared below, he motioned to the bosun and reminded him, "Take the wheel. Douse all our running lights as soon as we leave the bay. Let's not make it easy for the Crow to find us."

SharpWatch stood next to Pindlebryth, and held out his paw. "I can take watch, M'Lord. Go down below with the Beaver." As Pindlebryth reluctantly handed over the glass, SharpWatch added, "And watch GraceTail, I mean Hayake. She looks as if she could use a friend."

Pindlebryth turned to follow LogSplitter, but he stopped dead in his tracks. There was that itch again, scratching away at the back of his mind, digging away at something he had missed. He demanded over his shoulder to SharpWatch, "What did you say?"

SharpWatch stammered, "Nothing," unsure of what might have upset his prince. "Merely that Hayake seemed quite a jumble back at the reception. First she was on the verge of being emotional, then she was as smooth as glass, then she would have the strangest look at Mrs. BlueHood. I just thought that with all she's had to go through, an old friend might be comforting for her."

Troubled by SharpWatch's words and how they mirrored Grefdel's admonition, he hurried after LogSplitter. He took the stairs down into the cabin two at a time, as they were built for a Beaver's foreshortened stride. The staircase led to a cabin built only half below the deck. Portholes along the top of the inside walls opened onto the deck level outside. Along either side of the cabin were long benches with fitted cushions tied to rungs in the walls behind them. The benches were latched down over each seat to cover long storage bins, and above them recessed ladders led to beds along the portholes. Forward of the bunks and opposite the stairs were three doors, one to storage, one to the head, and a center doorway leading forward to the mess and galley.

Along the port bench sat the BlueHoods and across from them on the starboard bench was LogSplitter. Hayake had shapeshifted back to Crow, but still had on her loosely fitting peacoat and pants. She was bent over, placing her head on her mother's lap. Hayake's eyes were fully nictated as her mother cooed and stroked the plumage of her head and neck. Sitting on the bench opposite them, LogSplitter had just begun to strike up a conversation with Mr. BlueHood.

"What a day! Hoo! We actually made it safely away, didn't

we?" The vest under LogSplitter's jacket looked like it was about to burst as he stuck out his chest again in proud accomplishment.

"It's not over yet," Pindlebryth interjected. "We have to make our rendezvous."

"Pindlebryth?" came a call from the galley. Darothien emerged with a look of relief and a cautious smile on her face. The two awkwardly walked towards each other under the pitch and roll of the boat, and embraced. Behind her stood LeanShanks and LongWhisker in the center doorway, also glad to see their prince again.

"Indeed a happy reunion," observed LogSplitter as he winked at the BlueHoods. "Lenland's wizard spoke of little else since her arrival!" he chortled.

The sloop pitched again, and yawed slightly against a sudden side current. The portholes went dark as the lights on the deck outside were extinguished one by one.

"Ah! We've made it out of the bay." LogSplitter rose from his bench to dim the lanterns hanging from the ceiling on either side of the mast. LongWhisker returned to the galley and shortly emerged again, holding several water flasks. Another blast from Old Bellows resounded in the cabin, reaching a crescendo before waning as it passed along the starboard side.

"You had best be on deck now," said Pindlebryth to his squad members. "SharpWatch is keeping an eye out for Crow. I'm surprised we got this far without being given chase." He turned to stand aside Darothien and allow LeanShanks and LongWhisker to pass. LongWhisker gave Darothien and Pindlebryth each a flask, as he and LeanShanks shoved theirs under their belts.

Pindlebryth faced the BlueHoods, adding, "Congratulations to you as well. You played your parts brilliantly, and seem to be none the worse for wear."

"Actually, there are a few items that still concern me," Mr. BlueHood retorted, rubbing his aching hip. "We have left so much behind. Not only Hakayaa's belongings and inheritance, but several members of our loyal staff. We have hired private couriers to deliver them their continuance pay, and letters promising them a place with us again when we get settled. But I'm afraid that Hakayaa's inheritance will be confiscated by the Court of the Kyaa as recompense for the damage to the *SlipStream*, and as punishment for our defection."

"The fire should not have damaged their ship too much. It was meant as a distraction – to disable, not destroy," stated Pindlebryth.

"The fire should still leave them seaworthy, but only just. With repairs, they can still limp home. But if they give chase, they will be taking a terrible risk." LogSplitter agreed.

"And I think the University will not release such a magnanimous gift without a fight, regardless what the Kyaa demands," Pindlebryth concluded.

"Eh, about the inheritance," coughed LogSplitter interrupting. "I am afraid I must be the one to bear bad tidings on that matter." He sighed heavily, bolstering his courage. "The disposition of Hakayaa's inheritance may be moot." He coughed again, and adjusted his collar as if he were trying not to choke on his news. "The University has been robbed. Every gem and jewel from the BlueHood display has been pinched!"

"What!" Mr. BlueHood looked at LogSplitter in shock and confusion. "No wonder that Warder was so blasted evasive!"

"I overheard the museum guard spill some of the juicier details before all the Regents left. It happened sometime between one of the guards' rounds. All the glass cases were crushed, and their contents taken. But the thing that really has them stumped was that all the portcullises were still locked down. No sign of a forced break-in whatsoever!"

The ship pitched forward again, and the sound of the jib and the yardarms swinging to catch a new prevailing wind filled the cabin. As the square sail billowed and fluttered trying to find their fullness, LogSplitter declared with confidence, "Ah, it feels like we've caught the Westerlies. The *Peerless* should really move now!" He opened one of the portholes, and called out in a booming voice. "Spin the mast!"

Pindlebryth felt slightly unwell. He patted his jacket pockets and muttered, "Blast! I left my coat back at the Royale!" He swallowed and tried to ignore the turmoil growing in his stomach. It was only slightly better to concentrate on the itch that SharpWatch prompted, than to worry about his sea-legs and fret over losing BroadShanks' tincture.

"Oh! I almost forgot," said LogSplitter patting his own pockets after the fashion of Pindlebryth. He quickly produced an envelope, and handed it to Mr. BlueHood. "A curious old fellow gave me this, and said you dropped it in your hurry to leave."

Mr. BlueHood accepted the unfamiliar envelope. "This is not mine. Who did you say gave it to you?"

"Some lanky gray Crow valet from the Royale. Strange — now that I think of it, I've never seen him at the club before."

Mr. BlueHood looked askance at LogSplitter, and after eyeing suspiciously both sides of the envelope, he carefully opened it. He unfolded the letter within, and held it between himself and his wife as she turned her head to be able to use her good eye. The two had barely read the first few lines, when they exploded in unison.

"Great Kyaa! HAKAYAA!"

The entire cabin was intently focused on the BlueHoods as they read, and they all jumped in surprise to one extent or another at their outburst.

Hayake reacted most emphatically, jumping from her reclined position and standing like a shot with her plumage ruffled in startled consternation. She folded her right wing under her oversized peacoat, over her heart as if she were about to faint. After a few deep breaths she relaxed, and her feathers began to lay flat again.

Pindlebryth began to tremble. For the longest time, he knew this tower of deceit would collapse under its own weight sooner or later. He had hoped against hope that he would have some control over what time to inform the BlueHood family, to soften the blow for them once they were safely settled in their new life away from the Rookeries of the Kyaa. It would have been less than honest, all contradictions aside, to ignore that he preferred to have such a heart-to-heart at a time of his own choosing, to allow him to save face. But to have instead Hakayaa himself bring the tissue of lies crumbling about his ears left him speechless.

"You told us he was *dead*!" screamed Mr. BlueHood, waving the envelope at Pindlebryth as if it were a weapon.

Hayake echoed the sentiment. "How could you do this to us? You're worse than the Kyaa!"

Mrs. BlueHood had snatched the letter away from her husband and continued to read as he and her daughter leapt into their tirades. While still staring at the contents of the message, she firmly called out, "Quiet, you two. You should read this." She did not have to shout to be heard above the rest of her family — a feat that was not lost on Pindlebryth, Darothien nor LogSplitter. The effect was almost immediate.

The two Crow held their tongues for the moment, though it was quite apparent that they were barely able to contain their rage.

In her most matriarchal tone, she began to read the Crow writing aloud as she moved the paper back and forth close to her eye.

Miya & Piya,

Thanks ever so kindly for the family gifts. (A wonderful creature is the rock python from the southern lands – terribly strong, and just our size, too!) I will surely put my new trinkets to better use than the University ever could. The University may have what's left of them back when I am done with them, or this world is done with me – both of which I plan to be a very long time!

Thanks also for the degree. I am sure it will open doors in those countries where K's reach does not extend.

Do not hold any of this skullduggery against P. In fact, you owe him (and all those with him in PanGaea) a great debt of gratitude, as do I. After all, it was they who saved my life, and it was at my request that he keep this secret. If in fact P ever does succeed his father, you could do a lot worse than calling his country your new home. And wouldn't that stick in you-know-who's craw!

Must dash.

I'm sure P will fill you in on all the details...

H

LogSplitter tilted his head to listen, and closed his eyes in concentration as he tried to translate her speech. Darothien drew her wand from her sleeve, and spoke to one of its ends a sound like a dozen whispers. The tip began to emanate a cone of pale green lambency again, as it did once before in Lenland's archives. She then held the base of the wand close to her ear as Mrs. BlueHood read.

The anger that so palpably radiated from the two Crow waned by degrees with each sentence. When the letter was done, both of them had collapsed back in their seats. Mr. BlueHood looked at his wife as if he were beseeching her for understanding, while Hayake sat with her head down and her eyes nictating rapidly. Darothien stood stock still, only extinguishing the wand after she realized she was staring at Pindlebryth in disbelief. Old Bellows sounded with a note of finality in the receding distance.

Mrs. BlueHood lowered the letter, then turned her head to the left and right, alternately regarding Pindlebryth with her good then her translucent eyes. "Regardless of what our son may believe, what are we to think, M'Lord? We have placed our livelihoods and lives in your hands. Have we made a mistake to do so?"

Pindlebryth sat down on the bench across from her. The pit of his stomach was as turbulent as the cabin in the *Peerless* was becoming. Yet despite the movement of the cabin and the swaying lanterns casting dim yet disorienting shadows, the thought of finally ending the fabrication of Hakayaa's death reduced the grip of nausea on him. His eyes did not focus on anything or anyone about him, but rather they had the appearance of one who was looking inside himself. He tried to collect his thoughts, but Mrs. BlueHood would not be that patient.

"What do you say, M'Lord Pindlebryth? Why this elaborate charade?"

Pindlebryth looked her squarely in her eye and began. "When he visited Lenland, Hakayaa attacked my brother and stole an Artifact, the Lens of Truth. On Vulcanis, we learned he did this only because the Ravenne held Hayake hostage. We were ambushed by the Ravenne, and they managed to take the Lens."

"This much we already know," she said glaring at him with her milky eye.

"When it became clear they meant to leave no witnesses, Hakayaa took a poisoned bolt meant for my brother. Though the poison was instant death for Lemmings, it was still strong enough to leave Hakayaa's life hanging by a thread. We treated him as best as we could on Vulcanis, but he needed more care than we could give him there. Travel was dangerous in any regard, but we had little choice. Flying to Lenland would have been less stressful, but my father's edict would doom him if he were found in our country. Therefore, we had to fly back against the prevailing winds to PanGaea. Hakayaa barely made the trip – it was a near thing.

"It was on his sickbed that he concocted the notion of his death. He was convinced that as long as he was alive, and you remained in the Rookeries, the Kyaa or whoever controlled the Ravenne would not hesitate to use Hayake or one of you to extort his obedience again."

Mr. BlueHood leaned forward with his chin resting on his cane, but Mrs. BlueHood remained motionless. "Where is our son now? And who was that Crow who spoke to LogSplitter?"

"One and the same, I'll warrant. I do not know why, but Hakayaa underwent a striking transformation after Vulcanis. I did not see its completion, as I had to travel back to Lenland, and Hakayaa left the care of my staff before I could return. Whether his striking change was the effect of the poison, long-term exposure to any number of latent magicks in Selephylin's dome, being so long in close quarters with the foul life-eating creature there, or the combination of all of them together — I cannot guess. But know this. The last time I did see Hakayaa, he bore little resemblance to the son in the painting you left back at the Royale." Pindlebryth sat back with a wistful look in his eye. "I'm not even sure *I* would recognize him, were he standing in front of me now."

LogSplitter shifted his weight from foot to tail to foot, trying to understand Pindlebryth's story. Hayake however was incredulous.

"Lens of Truth? Life-eating creature? What nonsense is this?" she said in shrill voice. But she quickly fell silent as Mrs. BlueHood touched her wing. She whipped about, looking sternly at her mother, but Hayake instantly recognized that look. When the Matron BlueHood eyed someone as she now observed Pindlebryth, she was making a final decision and she was not to be trifled with or interrupted.

"You have told us how. Now tell me *why*," said Mrs. BlueHood with steel in her voice.

Pindlebryth's ire flared momentarily, not being accustomed to being given direct commands. But it was quenched when he reminded himself that such mistrust was perhaps well deserved. Pindlebryth considered that simplicity was the best response. "Hakayaa and I had each other's backs through thick and thin. What kind of friend would not help when the need was so dire?" He inhaled with a shiver. "He trusted me."

There came a rap at the hatch. It opened just a crack, and SharpWatch spoke quickly though the gap in the doors. "There is a squad of Crow giving pursuit. We need Darothien on deck."

LogSplitter jumped up and extinguished one lantern, and reduced the other to a bare flicker. SharpWatch opened the hatch doors as Darothien scurried across the cabin and up the handful of stairs. Pindlebryth nodded to Mrs. BlueHood and followed Darothien outside.

As he stepped outside, he breathed a sigh of relief. Free of the confines of the cabin, he breathed in deeply the crisp salt air, and his nausea left him. He dared not relax however, as LeanShanks held out to him a sheathed shortsword and his crossbow and quiver. He promptly tied the shortsword to his belt, slung the quiver around his back, and took the crossbow. He cocked the weapon, but did not yet load it with a quarl.

Once Pindlebryth was out of earshot, LogSplitter made one last comment before leaving the cabin himself. "I have spent some time with all the Lemmings on board, and many others at Vulcanis. They could not all show such devotion to him, nor continue to do so, if there was any subterfuge in his heart."

"Piffle," she reproached. "*They* were not in this cabin, and the sorceress is in love."

LogSplitter set his jaw and clicked his nippers together against her cynicism. He climbed out of the cabin in an annoyed huff. He then turned around and called down before closing the hatch, "Lock these doors behind me."

Hayake softly and tenderly took the envelope and letter from her mother, and reread it before folding it and placing it in her coat. Mr. BlueHood dutifully went to the hatch and did as LogSplitter asked.

Activity around the aft mast caught Pindlebryth's attention as he emerged from the cabin. Two Beaver were at opposite levers around the mast's ring assembly. They had flipped the ends of their levers, so the short bent end was inserted, and the long lever arm swung out. As they pushed the levers back up against the mast, the topmost toothed ring rose. They then set to the other two levers, again flipping them to set their long arms point outward. Instead of pointing them up, they heaved against them, and the middle ring and starboard yardarm rotated clockwise. Returning to the first levers, they lowered them back down and turned the top ring counterclockwise. The top ring and the port yardarm spun, setting the diamond sails like a scoop to best catch the wind behind them.

SharpWatch returned to the aft and resumed his watch, as LogSplitter took his place at the wheel beside him, relieving the bosun. SharpWatch scanned just above the horizon between port and stern. "They were flying low, staying in the earth's shadow. Which makes them difficult to see against the night sky." Moments later, he exclaimed with satisfaction as he found the flock of Crow again, their dark cloud making the stars behind them wink in and out.

The bosun opened the wheel chest, and hefted out several large objects. He retrieved two quarter-barrels of oil then several armloads of short wooden planks, all of which he placed at the tail of the sloop. He upended one of the barrels, grabbed one of the metal levers around the aft mast, and hammered around the barrel plug until he was able to pull it out. Using the lever, he set to splitting the lid to leave half of the barrel's top open. When he finished, he tossed the metal lever back to a deckhand who inserted the lever back into position on the ring.

Darothien took her place by the chest and slipped her wand out from her sleeve, standing at the ready. She stood facing forward, but turned her head to listen to SharpWatch.

Tense seconds clicked by in silence. SharpWatch then declared, "They've spotted us, no doubt about it. They've turned and are heading straight for us. They'll catch up to us easily in a few minutes."

"Straighten the mast!" barked LogSplitter. Two deckhands around the aft mast heaved against the levers, setting the aft yardarms pointing straight out to port and starboard. As they did so, the sloop slowed marginally.

Darothien turned towards the diamond-shaped sails of the aft mast, and scribed an arc in the air with her wand. A circle of green poured from the tip of the wand and floated in front of her as she traced. When it was complete, she scribed a symbol of intertwined shapes within it. The limned air quickly grew in size and brightness, filling out from the original circle to a disk then a sphere. If the Crow weren't already heading towards them, the brightening glamor lined with veins of living green energy would have surely drawn their attention.

Pindlebryth nodded in recognition, recalling when Darothien had used this same spell to carry them safely through a raging storm to Vulcanis so long ago.

But he was astonished when Darothien changed the spell.

She uttered a chant that sounded like the rush of a twister, and jabbed her wand at the sphere. It contorted in upon itself, and began to spin – first end to end, then from front to back. Darothien shook with fevered concentration, and the pulsing globe convulsed with increasing frequency to the point where it seemed it would tear itself apart, until it finally changed with a concussion of sound into an oblong torus. Shaped like an apple that had its core removed, it moved into position behind the sails under the bidding of Darothien's wand. As it did, the veins of green energy spun from front to back along the exterior, returning through the core toward the front of the torus again. It continued faster and faster, and the sound of rushing wind increased – though anyone on board would be hard pressed to say if the sound came from Darothien or the ring. Every one aft of the spell soon felt the pull of a strong tailwind, and the sails billowed out to their straining point.

The sloop lurched as the ship picked up a sizable jolt of speed. Spray coursed over the prow of the *Peerless* and showered down over the deck as the ship plowed into wave after wave. LogSplitter let out a whoop of delight as the ship sped on. "She's bucking like a wild animal, but she loves it!" he exclaimed, as he gleefully wrestled with the wheel to stay on course.

Darothien stopped her chanting abruptly, and panting from the exertion of the spell, dropped her arms. She looked up again to ensure the torus blew steadily against the sails, then moved portside and began the process anew.

LogSplitter and half the Beaver crew watched in frozen wonder as she drafted a second sigil and transformed it into another torus. LogSplitter couldn't help but to utter a warning cry as she visibly strained against the second torus. The two rings of coursing power deformed and seemed to be attracted to one another. Darothien exerted her will as the sound of two howling winds reached a deafening level. With a final yowl of effort, she pulled the second torus away from the first's proximity, and they resumed their shapes. She guided the second torus with her wand, giving it a wide berth around the first. Visibly shaken, she pointed her wand beyond the prow of the ship, and with a flick of her wrist suddenly tilted and partially submerged the ring. The tail end of the ring scooped up seawater from in front of the boat, as its front sprayed a steady stream off to the starboard side. Its mist dripped off the jib and fore staysails, but a good portion of the spray still swirled past them and began to soak the deck.

Eddies formed on either side of the ring swirling in opposite directions, their outer edges deflecting the waves that had crashed repeatedly against the bow of the *Peerless*. Darothien with a final wave of her wand, pulled the torus closer to the prow, and fixed it there. The crew staggered again and cheered as the sloop pulsed forward with another gain of speed.

Exhausted, Darothien tottered back to the chest and sat down to catch her breath. She leaned forward and held her head in one paw as her wand dangled from the other. Pindlebryth rushed to her side, and knelt in front of her.

"Are you all right?" he asked, almost afraid of the answer.

"Yes. Fine," she panted. "Just... took a lot out of me. I've been away from Lenland too long."

Pindlebryth took his flask and offered Darothien some water. She took a swig, and returned it with thanks. She reclined against the wheel gearbox, closed her eyes and exhaled through pursed lips. She opened her eyes again and admired her handiwork. Pindlebryth sat next to her, and followed her gaze to the tori. "When did Graymalden teach you that spell?" he wondered aloud, as he leaned his shortbow against the sea chest.

She retorted with a little pride and mock indignation, "He didn't. I took his spell, and crafted a new one."

Pindlebryth raised his eyebrows with a renewed sense of admiration. "Lords Above!" he marveled. "It took Graymalden almost five years before he could craft his first new spell."

Darothien shivered from the fine mist coating the deck and almost everyone on it. Pindlebryth sidled closer to her, and put his arm around her. She pressed against him, appreciating his warmth against the chilling mist.

"The Crow are off the port quarter. Still advancing on us, but not as quickly. They'll be here in a few minutes," SharpWatch pronounced.

"I'll guarantee they're alone! There is no way that the *SlipStream* could keep up with us now!" LogSplitter boasted. He turned the wheel clockwise, and the *Peerless* edged starboard until the Crow were directly behind them. Darothien looked up at her spells but relaxed again when she confirmed they turned in lockstep with the sloop.

"If luck is with us, they'll be exhausted by the time they reach us," said Pindlebryth. He stood and loaded his crossbow. Darothien struggled to get up. "Don't strain yourself," admonished Pindlebryth, but Darothien brushed it aside.

"There's still work to be done, and I have a few more tricks left."

LeanShanks and LongWhisker moved to either side near

the stern, and cranked their crossbows. They stood silently, straining to catch sight of the approaching threat.

Darothien strode purposefully to the port corner of the cabin, where she might see the Crow as they neared, and still have clear views of where she had left her spells and the materiel on the stern. She looked fore and aft for the bosun, and spotting him she commanded, "To your place!" He went to the stern and picked up one of the short wooden planks. Wielding it like a hammer in both hands, he stood at the ready next to the half open barrel.

Barely a minute went by, every Lemming standing still and facing where SharpWatch indicated. LogSplitter occasionally glanced over his shoulder when the compass and wheel did not command his full attention. All the while, the other Beaver were occupied trimming the sails, trying to eke out every last knot of speed.

"I see them!" cried LeanShanks, pointing her paw then hefting her crossbow. The others followed suit and loaded their weapons. SharpWatch returned the spyglass to LogSplitter, who did not take it, but instead called for one of the crew. "My hands are full," he said loudly. "Keep an eye on the horizon, in case another flock comes from another direction." SharpWatch handed the glass off to the sailor, then loaded his crossbow.

"Don't let the tallest one on board!" shouted Pindlebryth above the din of the winds. "He's a shapeshifter, and might be Ravenne!" He stepped to the side, to have a clear shot away from LogSplitter.

"Dead astern, they're in range!" declared SharpWatch, firing first. He barely winged the closest Crow, and was almost finished reloading when the others caught sight of them. LeanShanks and Pindlebryth fired into the approaching squadron. Neither of them hit, and the Crow halved their distance to the *Peerless*.

The sound of rushing wind grew behind Pindlebryth. He turned while he reloaded to see Darothien tugging the torus away from the prow of the ship with her wand. It breached out of the water, whipped around faster and nimbler than a cave swiftlet, and sped with such velocity that it sang until she placed it above the Crow. The light from the emerald torus shone down on a dozen or so Crow, their black feathers glistening with a green corona. Clearly seeing their targets, the archers fired again in succession, with all four hitting their marks. As they cranked and reloaded their crossbows, Darothien whistled the torus directly down into the flock.

It enveloped one of the Crow, like the eye of a needle around a thread, and spat the Crow out of its mouth. The hapless bird spun with a broken wing into the sea, as the torus weaved upwards again. The quartet fired again, this time only Pindlebryth bringing down a Crow, the remaining quarls being a clean miss and two winging hits. The Crow were nearly upon them, and all but Pindlebryth dropped their crossbows and drew their shortswords. Pindlebryth adeptly loaded and fired his crossbow one last time before he was forced to abandon the weapon. The bolt streaked straight at the tall Warder captain, but as he banked and dodged, it solidly struck a Warder behind him.

The torus chased after the captain, but he continued to weave and circle, refusing to be ensnared by it. Darothien whipped her wand down at the stern of the ship, and the torus sped to a few feet above the bosun. The Beaver ducked instinctively, and shook visibly – either by fear of the spell, or from the gale-force wind whipping about him. The Warder captain flew around the torus trying to get to the sloop. But Darothien smiled for just a moment before she shouted at the bosun.

"Now!"

The bosun struck the half open barrel like a drum for all he was worth, and a large gush of oil shot out of the barrel's mouth. The torus rotated abruptly, far faster than the captain could maneuver. It vacuumed up the spray, and then almost immediately the entire remaining contents of the barrel. The mouth of the torus pointed in front of the captain, and disgorged the entire torrent of oil. Too close to evade, he plowed directly into the drape of clinging liquid. The weight of the oil dragged him out of the air, and he slammed into the aft railing of the *Peerless*. He tried to clamber over the rail, but he could not gain purchase. He slid into the roiling water below, thrashing for any hold but finding none. The bosun threw the wooden plank in the sea after the captain, taunting after him, "*I'd* throw you an anchor, but *she* bids otherwise! You winged snake!" He tossed the empty barrel off in the direction of the Crow with the broken wing, and was about to open the second barrel when the remaining Crow dove onto the combatants on the deck.

They harried the Lemmings, hovering directly above them and clawing at their faces. The Lemmings tried to strike and stab at their foes, but the birds' legs were armored with tightly woven slats of lacquered wood which deflected the blows. Darothien reeled in the torus and drove it into the midst of the flock. Some peeled away from the melee, while the other half were driven onto the deck. They pulled their own shortswords from scabbards lashed to their backs and engaged the Lemmings. One Crow each landed in front of Pindlebryth and Darothien.

Pindlebryth parried his opponent, and backed away to the side, interposing himself between Darothien and the other Crow. Darothien continued to direct the torus, chasing those few Crow still in flight, while Pindlebryth sliced and riposted the attacks against him and Darothien. Forced back by the pair of weapons, he feinted to one side. Both Crow concentrated on Pindlebryth and went for the opening, unaware of an attack on their rear.

LogSplitter lashed the wheel and tackled the Crow closest to Darothien, bundling his legs from behind in both arms. The Crow did not fall, but turned to slash at LogSplitter. Too late he realized he was the target of a diversion, as the bosun cracked the Crow's skull with a solid blow from his plank. As the Crow collapsed in a heap, Pindlebryth saw his opportunity on his own opponent's open side, and stabbed with all his might. The sword drove deep into feather and flesh. As the Crow began to double over, Pindlebryth pushed the fowl off with his foot, withdrawing the bloodied sword.

A crewmate near Darothien pulled a belaying pin out of a handrail. He and Pindlebryth interposed themselves between Darothien and the two remaining Crow as they dove, in their attempts to find an opening to attack the sorceress. Darothien paid them no heed, as she maneuvered the ring in a tight circle. As it chased one Crow, it suddenly peeled off and intercepted the other and vomited him into the sea. The force of the dive was such that the Crow simply floated on the water unconscious, its leg broken and one wing almost entirely denuded.

The bosun went to the stern, tossed his plank to the Crow that Darothien had downed. Grabbing a fresh plank, he charged in with it in full bloodlust to assist the trio of Lemmings, only to hold back at the last minute. LeanShanks had already dispatched her opponent with a disemboweling stroke across his belly, and charged in to assist her comrades. SharpWatch matched his Crow's sword blow for blow, parry to parry. LongWhisker was beginning to flag as he was bleeding from an arm and a leg. But the Crow were also fatigued from their flight. Whereas the pair was building an advantage against LongWhisker and SharpWatch, they were forced to fade back against an additional opponent.

LogSplitter regained the wheel, and cried out, "They're outnumbered! Why do they still fight?" Darothien, Pindlebryth and the crewmate all ducked a raking dive from the sole flying Crow. The bird continued in tighter and more desperate circles, trying to keep Darothien and the others off balance. The two Crow at the stern fought like lunatics, even though they were now surrounded two against four, and being forced against the aft rail.

LogSplitter's question was answered in less than a minute as the crewmate holding the spyglass called out, "Ship ho! Portside!" Another schooner, the twin sister to the *SlipStream* in every aspect approached diagonally, under full tacking sail and bearing down on them rapidly. Suddenly flashes of light and smoke jumped from the front of the schooner, and the report of cannon fire could be heard as plumes of water exploded short of, and in front of the *Peerless.*

"They were waiting for us over the horizon, and saw our light!" LogSplitter exclaimed. "What do the BlueHoods have that is so blasted important?" He spun the wheel to turn away from the schooner, but with no one spared to tend to the jib and staysail rigging, the *Peerless* was slow to turn.

A second pair of flashes lit the side of the schooner, and another volley came their way. One shot flew clear over their heads, but the second shattered the beam at the bottom of the staysail. The crewmate with the glass staggered back and fell with a bloodied face and neck, pocked with splinters and shrapnel. He clamped a paw over a large gash between his neck and shoulder, and tried with the other arm to tear his shirt and fashion a field bandage. The sail flapped like an injured bird, held marginally in place by what was left of the rigging.

"They've got our range. They'll pound us for sure next round!" whined LogSplitter, straining against the wheel.

The Crow that harassed Darothien darted away toward the schooner, and in a final act of desperation the two Crow against the aft threw their swords at their attackers as they dove over the railing. They flapped for their lives, barely skimming the water, as they too turned towards their ship.

"Turning your tail on a sorceress?" growled Darothien. "*That* was a mistake!"

She raised her wand again, and sent the torus screaming to the schooner that had now set a course almost parallel to the sloop. It zoomed past the retreating Crow, scattering them and buffeting one into the sea. The ring grew furious in spinning brightness as it positioned itself in front of the schooner's main mast, a few feet above the deck. Most of the Crow on the rigging about the mainsails flew off in fear, cawing and chattering as they landed on nearby yardarms. A few braver deckhands desperately tried to tend the nearest sail before the raging wind from the torus tore it apart, but Darothien spun the torus in place, blowing the remaining Crow off the rigging or into the water. Though the torus was blowing mightily, it was too low to hamper most of the sails or the schooner's speed. Darothien then turned to the second torus and drove it away from the *Peerless*'s aft sails.

"What are you doing?" cried LogSplitter. "We need that to run and maneuver!"

Darothien uttered a sound like the rush of a cloudburst, and sent the second torus keening after the first. In a few heartbeats, it was upon its target. The two deformed as they neared each other, stretching like they contained magnets drawing them together. They then collided, detonating in a flash of blazing green fire. The blast was strong enough to ripple the sails on the *Peerless*, as the bottom of the schooner's mast shivered into a hailstorm of splintered wood and wrecked metal. The Crow on the neighboring masts were knocked off their perches, and they all fell like rag dolls. The top of the mast toppled forward, while its bottom swung backwards. Pivoting on what little rigging remained between the fore and aft masts, it slammed onto the deck of the schooner, smashing into the bridge. The top of the mast continued to collapse forward like a great oak in a forest, tearing the fore sails before finally crashing across the deck.

The schooner lost its speed quickly. It fell back and veered away, as the untended wheel spun counterclockwise.

Most of the schooner's crew lay unconscious or badly wounded about the deck and in the water. Those few that still had their wits about them, moved laboriously and painfully. A wild cheer arose from the sloop from all aboard except for Pindlebryth. He sheathed his sword and rushed to Darothien's side as she collapsed from the exertion. She lay on the deck, her chest heaving like she had run a marathon. Pindlebryth reached for the wand that had slipped from her hand, but paused above it. Even though Darothien granted him unprecedented access to her laboratory in the castle, he still thought it unwise to touch a wizard's most prized device. He took her paw in his, and molded her hand around the wand. He scooped up her figure and carried her to the cabin. Kicking the hatch, he commanded, "Open the doors!"

Mr. BlueHood threw open both doors, and Pindlebryth bore Darothien's limp form down the ungainly stairs. He ignored the questions that peppered him from Mr. BlueHood and Hayake, and gently laid her down on the starboard bench and propped up the cushion into a makeshift pillow under her head.

"Is she all right?" Hayake repeated. She shivered as the night air poured down into the cabin. She stood up and lifted her seat on the bench, and pulled out a red blanket stowed in the bin under her seat. She wrapped herself in the blanket over the peacoat she already wore.

"What happened up there? Are we still pursued?" demanded Mr. BlueHood again.

"Obviously not!" scolded Mrs. BlueHood, as she stood and continued to look out one of the portholes. "The *Vortex* is crippled. They'll be lucky to make to port in PanGaea." She looked over her shoulder at the hatch. "How are *we* faring?"

LogSplitter descended into the cabin, and replied, "We took a hit on the staysail, but the crew is jury-rigging it. One crew member is down but alive." He stood aside as a Beaver assisted his wounded and pale crewmate into the cabin. A large compression bandage was held in place by strips of cloth wound over his shoulder and under the opposite arm. LogSplitter motioned for the BlueHoods to move off the bench, and the two Beaver hefted the wounded crew into the bunk above the bench. He moaned with relief as he finally relaxed on the bed.

"And LongWhisker is being tended to above. His wounds are not as severe." LogSplitter spotted Darothien lying exhausted on the other bench. "How is our wizard? She really taught those bloody Crow a lesson they'll not soon forget! And not a single one of the blackhearts she thrashed were kill-"

Realizing the BlueHoods were listening to every word he said, he coughed loudly in embarrassment. "Not to worry, Lady BlueHood," he recovered, albeit a bit more reserved. "We can still make our rendezvous."

"I'm all right," came a weak whisper. "Just need to rest," Darothien wheezed. "Just for a little..." she trailed off. Though she was prostate with exhaustion, Pindlebryth was relieved to see that she breathed normally and restfully. He pulled a blanket off of the bunk bed above her bench, and draped it gently over her, pulling its ends over her shoulders and then her feet. He addressed LogSplitter while still watching Darothien. "Fetch LeanShanks in here. I want her to watch Darothien."

LogSplitter obeyed and LeanShanks entered the cabin almost immediately. "See that she is cared for." He stood and looked her squarely and soberly in the face. "Do not leave her side," he ordered, then left the cabin without further ado. He needed the open air, as nausea arose in his gut, and the nagging itch declared itself again.

LogSplitter had resumed his place behind the wheel, and set the *Peerless* again on a course due east. The *Vortex* had since passed below the horizon, and the sloop plied steadily onward. LogSplitter pulled a lantern from the chest next to the gearbox, lit and hung it near his wheel. One of the crew followed suit, and lit the lanterns on the four corners of the cabin. Pindlebryth walked up to LogSplitter, surveying the ship and the activity of the crew along the way. Despite the broken boom under the staysail, not to mention the deckhand's and LongWhisker's wounds, he thought they came out of the ordeal quite well.

Now that they were no longer in a fight or flight situation, Pindlebryth looked with curiosity at the aft mast, and the ring assembly at its base. He remarked to LogSplitter, "I'm not much of the seafarer, but I do not believe I've seen such a mechanism on a ship before."

"Nor will you anywhere else. It's a gadget of my own design," LogSplitter beamed with pride. "We Beaver are excellent shipwrights, but not the greatest of climbers. So our ships have various ways of moving the yardarms and trimming high sails, which forgo the need for us to scale to such heights. That little gem is what made the *Peerless* win so many races."

"What metal is that? It's not bronze or brass, but it does seem to be well suited to the sea."

"Ah! That's phosphorous steel. It doesn't rust, but grows a patina that seals the metal against salt. My metallurgists and I came up with that, too."

"Metallurgists?" asked Pindlebryth, wondering what LogSplitter's vocation might be.

"Yes. My business specializes in unique metals. We make most of the settings for the BlueHoods' gems and works of art the world over." He leaned over to Pindlebryth, as if to share a joke. "By the by, we also fashioned the metal liners inside the barrels that focused the pitch towards the *SlipStream* but leaving all the other ships unscathed."

"And the burning rocks?"

"Ah! You've found me out! That's white phosphorous! Not only does it forge with iron to yield excellent steel, but in its pure state it has the particularly nasty tendency to burn when exposed to air. Mixed with magnesium it makes an excellent fuse, don't you think?" LogSplitter laughed, recalling the mayhem he and his crew caused that night.

"Do you think the Royale will let you back, after tonight's escapade?" he probed. But LogSplitter only chortled all the more.

"*Them*? Most of the people in that club have barnacles for brains. As long as we stick to the story that I took the BlueHoods safely away from the attacks at their insistence, they won't be any the wiser."

"Hmm," Pindlebryth mused. "Still, Hakayaa obviously knew you were up to something." LogSplitter suddenly stopped laughing as he regarded Pindlebryth, looking as if the prince had just spoiled the punch-line to his joke.

The both of them were startled and looked up at SharpWatch as he called back from the prow, "Ship ho! Dead ahead!" The others of the crew momentarily halted keeping trim on the sails and sweeping off the debris from around the staysail. LongWhisker hobbled over to SharpWatch as he lowered LogSplitter's spyglass and pointed to faint lights on an approaching ship.

LogSplitter looked up at the night sky, and observed. "Wait a minute. It's too early." He checked the compass in the gearbox, and noted the *Peerless* was still true on its easterly heading. He then craned his neck over the wheel, trying to get a better look at the silhouette of the approaching ship against the starry sky. "We shouldn't be meeting our rendezvous for another hour or so." He called out to the crew and alerted them. LongWhisker and SharpWatch drew out their swords.

The BlueHoods emerged from the cabin. Once Mr. BlueHood assisted her to the floor of the deck, Mrs. BlueHood corralled the nearest crew and bid him to fetch the spyglass. She looked at the approaching ship, and declared, "That's not necessary. That is our contact." Hayake stepped out onto the deck with her blanket even tighter around herself, and peered over the roof of the cabin into the night.

LogSplitter glanced back and forth between his passengers and the ship. "It is?" He squinted at the approaching lights, and tilted his head. He remarked slowly, and not quite sure of himself, "That's not one of my merchant vessels. And it is not flying any colors."

"And where's their escort? Where are Grefdel and the others?" Pindlebryth demanded.

"Be at peace, young prince," chided Mrs. BlueHood. "You have your surprises, and out of necessity, we have our little secrets as well. Stop the ship," she commanded. Pindlebryth frowned with consternation. After a moment of hesitation, LogSplitter ordered his crew to drop the sails, but keep their paws on the sheets in case a quick getaway was called for.

Mr. BlueHood took one of the corner lanterns from the cabin, and swung it to and fro. After two cycles, he hid the lantern behind his back. Pausing for only a moment, he swung the lamp again thrice before holding it behind himself once more. He continued for several sequences, sometimes swinging twice, thrice or even four times. He finally stopped and returned the lantern to its fastenings on the cabin exterior.

The crew watched silently at their stations as a lamp on the approaching schooner blinked on and off several times. LogSplitter hung on his wheel, ready to make a run for it at the word of the BlueHoods or Pindlebryth.

The lamp fell silent, and Mrs. BlueHood declared, "All is well. Prepare for a visitor." After a few minutes, the sound of feathered wings in flight could be heard over the sound of the waves rhythmically slapping against the hull of the sloop. At first only their shadowy outlines were visible, but as they approached the ship, their white plumage became apparent. Three Snow Geese landed behind the cabin next to the BlueHoods. The lead Goose approached and greeted the BlueHoods, while the others remained behind him. He had striking markings on his face – two teardrop shaped patches of black around his eyes. Behind him, one Goose slung a shortsword across his back, while the other carried a satchel on his.

Pindlebryth approached the leader of the group, with a glimmer of recognition. "Ambassador...?"

"Ah, felicitations to you also, Prince Pindlebryth. GanderLord Ankuu at your service. But I am ambassador to Lenland no longer. GanderLord Onkyon now fills that capacity." Ankuu had a plaintive and wounded look on his face.

"My father has spoken of you fondly, and will be glad to hear you are well. You are still seated in the WetLands Parliament I trust?" Pindlebryth inquired.

"Yes," he replied as his countenance brightened marginally. "I still serve in that capacity at least." Ankuu turned to the BlueHoods, adding, "But this day I function in that and another capacity: first, as a member of Parliament, I have successfully petitioned my government, and am here to officially grant the BlueHoods political asylum in the Snow Goose WetLands; secondly, as the BlueHood's solicitor in the Snow Goose CityState, I am here to deliver them a legacy to which they now have final claim in the eyes of the law. My instructions were quite specific – to deliver this immediately after their asylum had been granted, and they were free of any and all influence from the Fox and Kyaa."

Mrs. BlueHood stepped forward, and said flatly, "The item, if you please, M'Lord Ankuu." The Goose nodded, and honked over his shoulder. The Goose behind him shed his backpack, and removed a locked cedar box, inlaid in silver with two insignia: the BlueHood family crest, and a second one of some Vulpine origin. The box passed from Goose to GanderLord to Mr. BlueHood, who produced a key from his vest pocket.

Pindlebryth signaled SharpWatch, and instructed him, "Fetch Darothien up here. She needs to see this." SharpWatch hurried down below as Mr. BlueHood unlocked and opened the box. The contents of the small chest were wrapped in a black silken cloth.

Mr. BlueHood held out the box to Pindlebryth, as Hayake moved around her mother to better see the contents. Mrs. BlueHood said sternly, "As we agreed, M'Lord Pindlebryth, here is your reward for returning our daughter to us, and helping us escape." Hesitantly at first, Pindlebryth gingerly pulled the silk aside.

Atop a five pointed star of gold rested an enormous black gem. The fingers of the star radiated outward from the center, and arched downward like the contours of a dome. At first, Pindlebryth thought it resembled a five-legged golden spider. But his skin shivered and the fur on his back rose as he recognized the glyphs inscribed along the curved rays of the star. They were of the same language as those on Selephylin's broken Five Rings, and her Crown.

"Go ahead, it won't bite!" Mr. BlueHood remarked reassuringly.

Pindlebryth held out his hands to accept the box, when a screech pierced the night.

"No! It belongs to *him*! He commands it!" shrieked Hayake.

Pindlebryth fumbled for the chest, as Mr. BlueHood collapsed suddenly in front of him. Still clasped in her wing, the metal tines of her stenciled comb protruded from his back. She had already shed her blanket and peacoat, and climbed over her father's crumpled form. Totally naked, she charged Pindlebryth with red fury glowing from her eyes. She tore and pecked at his face, trying to blind him. Surprised by the suddenness and ferocity of her rabid attack, Pindlebryth stumbled backwards. He managed to clamp the box shut, and clutch it under one arm as Hayake violently grabbed at it. Taking another step back, he unsheathed his shortsword and fended off the berserk Crow.

Mrs. BlueHood knelt over her husband, who coughed up blood, and gasped violently. SharpWatch scrambled out of the cabin, and assessing the situation fast as lightning, leapt over the two of them.

Hayake flapped aloft and scrabbled at the chest with her claws. Pindlebryth successfully batted away her first attempts, but she grasped the box on her third try. She began to flap furiously, pulling the chest out of his grip. But her apparent victory was short lived, as the Ankuu's companions swooped in on her from above, while SharpWatch tackled her legs. The lot of them piled onto the deck. Even though the bodyguard and envoy pinned her down and SharpWatch held his sword to her neck, she still thrashed like a lunatic. Her eyes burned like two red-hot coals, as she yelled to be let go and screamed aloud again and again that 'he' must have the headpiece. The Goose

bodyguard struck Hayake where the top of her beak joined the skull, and she fell silent. Her eyes nictated shut, and the eerie ruby glow faded from behind them.

Mrs. BlueHood wailed suddenly, and all turned to see her collapse and weep over the still form of Mr. BlueHood. One of the Geese crouching over Hayake pivoted to examine the body of her father. He listened at the keel bone for a heartbeat, and touched his abdomen with one wing, and his spiracles with the other to feel for respiration, but there was no sign of life. He looked at Ankuu and shook his head.

At the door to the cabin, LeanShanks propped up

Darothien. "Take me to her," she said softly, taking out her prism and pointing it at Hayake. The pair slowly walked over, pausing a moment to bow her head at the deceased, and bend over to embrace Mrs. BlueHood. "I'm so sorry..." started Darothien, but Mrs. BlueHood shook off her arm, and stopped her outburst. They both stood, Darothien a little shakily, and Mrs. BlueHood slowly and deliberately.

She cleared her throat, and in her cool matriarchal tone said, "Mr. LogSplitter, if you would be so kind, pull the *Peerless* aside Ankuu's ship. We shall transfer over to their vessel."

LogSplitter sullenly went to the wheel, remained silent and kept his thoughts to himself as he steered. Soon the ships were close enough to lash together and throw out a makeshift gangplank between the two. With Mrs. BlueHood's permission, the Geese envoy and bodyguard bound and gagged Hayake, and were about to cover Hayake's modesty with the peacoat, but not before Darothien stopped them and examined Hayake with her tsavorite prism. She looked back and forth across Hayake's entire length, and stopped as she noted something askew in her eyes. She delicately plied back one of the membranes, and gasped. She held up her paw and LeanShanks helped her stand up as she slipped the prism back in her sleeve. She backed away, to stand next to Pindlebryth as two additional Geese alighted next to Ankuu.

"She has been ensorcelled by something very powerful. I believe it was the Prism of Persuasion." At the mention of the Artifact, Pindlebryth felt the itch in his mind snap.

"Ah! Fool that I am! I should have seen it! She always wore red!"

Darothien nodded in agreement. "And all Crow magick is red, as we witnessed in her eyes."

"Grefdel and SharpWatch both warned me to watch her. Lords Below!" he exclaimed as he punched his leg. "The Kyaa and the Ravenne used poor Hayake as another pawn in their pursuit of the Artifacts."

Mrs. BlueHood laid her wing across the faces of Hayake followed by her husband, then stood next to Ankuu. The four Geese transported Hayake and Mr. BlueHood over to their vessel, leaving Ankuu to say his farewells.

"Before you take your leave, M'Lord, I must ask," insisted Pindlebryth. "Why are you here assisting the BlueHoods? You may be their solicitor, but this is far above and beyond the duties of your profession."

"Restitution for crimes committed?" he shrugged. "Restoration of some semblance of honor to my family name? Vengeance against those who caused my brother-in-law's demise? Any of those will do." His shoulders slumped as he spoke.

Pindlebryth inhaled sharply and nodded, recalling the circumstances under which Ankuu had left his post in Lenland.

"I was not able to adequately defend my beloved wife's brother in court, and he was executed for treason."

"So it is true then. The Kyaa has the Vessel of Sorrows."

Ankuu regarded Pindlebryth with mild surprise. "You know of it?"

"The Kyaa – or someone in his court – is amassing all the world's Artifacts. He will soon come after ours in Lenland. We hope the item in this chest holds the key to prevent that from happening."

"Then use it well indeed, young prince," pronounced Mrs. BlueHood. "This gem was cut and the mounting was crafted and inscribed under the specific directions of Selephylin. She paid us quite handsomely for it, but we only heard of her death after we completed the work. The gem in the center of the device is a carbonado – a black diamond. She brought it to us, wrested from the heart of an even blacker stone that fell from the sky generations ago in Vulpinden."

She lowered her veil of mourning again, and sighed so hard, that she almost broke into tears anew. But her iron will asserted itself once more.

"Before today, I was content to live in exile from the Rookeries for the rest of my days. But this day, I learned the son I believed dead was instead hiding from the Kyaa. This day," she repeated with increasing venom, "the Kyaa has driven my daughter mad with magick. This day, the Kyaa has made me a widow. This day," she uttered with fearsome finality, "the Kyaa has made a sworn enemy.

"I will use my last breath, and every last penny of the BlueHood dynasty to bring down the Kyaa, and any who stand with him."

She marched over the gangplank, leaving both Pindlebryth and Ankuu speechless. Pindlebryth broke the silence, asking, "Where are you taking the BlueHoods?"

Ankuu shrugged again. "I don't know. I'm sure she will tell

us when we embark." A moment later Ankuu exhaled through his spiracles, and opened his mouth to taste the air. He then bowed slightly, and parted saying simply, "May all three of us be successful against our common enemy."

The gangplank and lashings were quickly removed, and the two ships silently went their separate ways. Pindlebryth ambled back to the wheel, and stood next to LogSplitter for several minutes. He tried to think, but his mind was a jumble. He was only cursorily aware that the ship was quite active, once it resumed their original course to the east.

Only twice did his mind focus on the happenings about him. The first time, he slowly became cognizant that LogSplitter was whistling a happy tune.

"What makes you so carefree?" he asked, slurring slightly.

"Oh, I think the future will be very bright," he replied, continuing on to whistle his aimless melody.

"I would have thought otherwise. Did not Mrs. BlueHood just vow to use everything she had to bring down the Kyaa? I would think you would be out of a job."

"On the contrary!" laughed LogSplitter. "The BlueHoods still have enormous stashes of gems hidden around the world. They've quietly moved much of their holdings out of the Rookeries ever since Hakayaa died... appeared to die. And who do you think will be making the fittings and artworks for the BlueHood inventory? Me!" He checked his gearbox compass and adjusted his wheel. "Even if they don't need me – which I seriously doubt – the Kyaa will not go down without a fight. And what do you need to make weapons? Steel!"

"Have a care, LogSplitter," cautioned Pindlebryth. "That's what brought about the Iron Baron's downfall."

"Not quite, M'Lord. That rogue sold weapons. I merely make specialized alloys. What others make of my metals is beyond my control." LogSplitter chortled to himself, eminently satisfied with his legally sound – if ethically questionable – logic, and started to cheerily whistle again. The meandering tune lulled Pindlebryth back into a half-asleep trance.

The second time Pindlebryth roused himself to the moment at hand was when Grefdel, and a few other Lemmings from the Royal Guard and military arrived. Riding a brigade of terns, they escorted the ship that was originally intended to ferry the BlueHoods to the Lodges of the WeatherWorn.

As the parties arrived, LogSplitter explained to the

exasperated captain and the even more angry Beaver ambassador, that the BlueHoods had made separate plans and had already left. A woodworker from the vessel came aboard the *Peerless* to oversee fashioning a makeshift staysail boom from the remaining planks the bosun had collected.

Pindlebryth suddenly felt very tired and very hungry. In a fog, he gulped the remainder of his water canteen, and stumbled down the stairs into the cabin. Too fatigued to be affected with seasickness, he raided the galley finding a few biscuits of millet hardtack, then summarily collapsed on the port bench opposite the exhausted Darothien, who slumbered peacefully on the starboard bench.

When he awoke, Grefdel was sitting across from him, listening to one of the *Peerless'* sailors describe their adventure. LogSplitter snored peacefully in the bunk above them. As he propped himself up, Pindlebryth noted the sun had already risen, and surmised from its position that the *Peerless* was on its way back to PanGaea.

"Good Morning, M'Lord," Grefdel said, interrupting the crew member. The guard sat with legs crossed, and a curious lop-sided smile. "Darothien and the rest have flown back to the Archipelago. After a night's rest, they'll take the chest back to Lenland. What's in there must pretty important to warrant such an escort."

"Thanks, Grefdel. It is," he said, rubbing the sleep from his eyes. Pindlebryth yawned, and drowsily smacked his lips, suddenly aware that he could taste Darothien on them.

VIII - Aftermath

"This is unacceptable!" cried the Crow ambassador. Ever since the meeting began mid-morning, he gestured more and more with his wings, until it seemed at times he was about to take flight. His assistant sitting next to him seemed a bit on edge. He kept one wing and a paperweight on a pile of documents in front of him, to prevent them from scattering when his superior gesticulated.

Quentain and Pindlebryth however, were as placid and polite as could be on their side of the conference table. Sitting between the two groups at the head of the table was the Dookinger ambassador to PanGaea, a Ferret whose white ermine fur and generous beard lent him the distinct air of wisdom and authority. Against a far wall sat another fellow citizen of Dookinger, the Regent President. His elbows rested on the chair arms, and his deep chestnut paws were steepled together as he carefully watched the discussion.

"I must renew my objection to an outsider being privy to this meeting," the Crow ambassador firmly protested, pointing towards the Regent.

The ermine calmly and simply responded, "Ambassador Kayka, my government requires an observer, even in informal talks as these. I am allowed some latitude, however, in whom I chose as my second." The Ferret splayed his hands as he surveyed the room. "Be at peace, Ambassador. There will be no written record of these proceedings."

Pindlebryth successfully hid a yawn as the sun streaked through the windows of the conference room in the Ferret embassy. Though the current political situation required that Lemming and Crow meet on neutral ground, Pindlebryth still wished that they could have met in an embassy of a country openly friendly to Lenland. He yawned again, but this time he did so without restraint. Despite the fact he had slept an entire night and day on the *Peerless* and another full night in his own bed, it seemed his body wanted even more rest. Little wonder, while he digested an overstuffed belly. The positively effervescent BroadShanks had made a breakfast fit for a returning victorious emperor, and in enough quantities to feed a whole platoon.

"Are we boring you, M'Lord?" demanded the Crow. He flapped a wing so close to Pindlebryth's face, that his fur rustled.

"Not at all, Ambassador Kayka. I often yawn when I am fascinated," Pindlebryth replied matter-of-factly. Quentain shot a pleading glance at Pindlebryth.

"Please, everyone. We are here to discuss things like civilized people," the ermine coaxed. Attempting to defuse the situation, he calmly added, "Perhaps we are approaching all this the wrong way. Ambassador, what is it that you are looking to achieve during this meeting?"

"My government demands an official apology from Lenland, and Prince Pindlebryth deported from PanGaea!" he shouted.

"An apology for what, if I may ask?" ventured Quentain.

"Have you not been listening? Can you not read?" cried Kayka.

He was about to launch into another tirade, when the ermine rapped twice politely but firmly on the table. "*I* have, and *I* can," purred the mediator. "But the list of grievances you bring forward is a long one. I for one, would find it helpful to all parties if you would enumerate them one by one rather than all at once, and allow the representatives from Lenland to respond to each one in turn."

Forcing himself to a calmer state, the Crow continued. "My apologies," he replied through a clenched beak. Turning to Quentain, he started slowly. "It is our contention that M'Lord Pindlebryth abducted three of our most prominent citizens, the BlueHoods, from the CityState North Shore Marina."

Before Quentain could reply in an official capacity, Pindlebryth responded out of turn, much to her annoyance. "Abducted? How can I abduct someone who approaches me for assistance? How can I abduct someone, when they depart at their own volition? On a vessel that they themselves arranged?"

"You speak of the *Peerless*," the Crow said as he read a paper his assistant sheepishly handed him, "owned by one LogSplitter?"

"I refer to an unidentified vessel, arranged by the BlueHoods themselves that conveyed them to asylum in another country."

"This ship had no name? Flew no flag? What country

would that be? Lenland perchance?" the Crow bounced back dripping with sarcasm.

Quentain quickly replied, trying to gain control of the dialog. "I assure you, Ambassador – neither the BlueHoods, nor any other Crow, is harbored in Lenland. Not while King Hatheron has ceased all direct formal diplomatic ties between our countries.

"We can however respond thusly: I am sure the country that granted them asylum will announce it to all interested parties, once the BlueHoods have arrived safely at their destination. Given that a third party has already made attempts on the lives of several members of the BlueHood family, and that the family is currently grieving the loss of their patriarch, I'm sure you will understand their precautions."

The Crow gasped and leaned away with a flourish at her veiled inference. Pindlebryth eyed the Crow critically – he found he could not quite tell if he was forthright in his indignation. As the Crow immediately recovered to press another point, he decided this politician did not deserve the benefit of the doubt.

"The entire Crow nation mourns the passing of Mr. BlueHood. As long as we are on the subject of regrettable losses, what say you about the damage to ships and the grievous injuries to members of the Kyaa's Navy, and the deaths of many of the members of the guard detail assigned to protect the BlueHoods?"

Pindlebryth pounded the table. "Mr. BlueHood did not merely 'pass away!' He was murdered – stabbed in the back by his daughter, Hayake. I and several others witnessed the event, and the circumstances which strongly point to the intervention of Crow magick!" Quentain was taken aback by Pindlebryth's reaction, thinking how much he resembled his father when roused. But before she could interject, Kayka quickly stoked the flames of heated argument even higher.

"Several survivors from the *Vortex* witnessed the effects of Lemming magick as it crippled their ship, and incapacitated most of her crew! How do we know that Hayake BlueHood was not under the spell of the Lemming sorceress?"

Pindlebryth's hackles stood straight up on the back of his neck at Kayka's attempt to impugn Darothien. A ferocious contempt overcame him, none of which escaped Kayka's nor

Quentain's notice.

"You *dare*? The color of the spell belies the source. Who else but the Kyaa's Vizier would be behind her murderous deed!"

"So you admit that the Lemming sorceress, by the color of her spell, attacked our guards and sailors! What was she doing on board the *Peerless* to begin with?"

The Ferret once again rapped the table with his palm gavel. "Please control yourselves. I will have order." He stroked his white beard, and gestured towards Quentain. "I believe it is your turn to respond to the accusation of Crow casualties?"

"Thank you, Ambassador," said Quentain. "First of all, let us call things for what they were. The detail assigned to the BlueHoods were not merely guards, they were Warders. They aggressively pursued the *Peerless*, and refused to turn away after several warning shots."

"Warning shots!" the Crow exploded. "They were fired upon directly! There was no 'warning' implied! They..."

"If I may continue," Quentain demanded with a commanding shrill in her voice. "We concede there were three opening shots, but none caused injury. Any reasonable person would call that a warning shot. Only after the interlopers kept advancing, and they were seen to carry weapons, was deadly force used. The fact that they were Warders, yet did not identify themselves as such before or after boarding, is not something that can be held against the *Peerless*."

Pindlebryth maintained a silent and watchful gaze. He thanked the Quickening Spirit that the first volley fired by those on the *Peerless* was indeed a trio of misses, as it helped bolster Quentain's case. What troubled him, however, was Quentain's and LogSplitter's misrepresentation of when they knew they were Warders. Such an interpretation could not be disproved, but it worried him nonetheless.

"I would remind everyone that this incident took place far outside of Eastern Bay, in the open MidSea. Therefore, LogSplitter as captain of the *Peerless*, and all others aboard were entirely in their rights to react as they saw fit against perceived acts of piracy.

"As for the *Vortex*, did her crew also inform you that they fired upon the *Peerless* without provocation? By the maritime statutes endorsed by both our countries and PanGaea, the

Peerless and its members were again entirely within their rights to defend themselves, even to the use of equal deadly force.

"So, Ambassador Kayka, Lenland agrees these deaths are indeed regrettable. But the responsibility for them cannot be laid at *our* feet."

Pindlebryth felt a glimmer of vindication as the Ferret ambassador nodded almost imperceptibly to Quentain's reasoning. However, the Crow was not similarly impressed. He was about to pursue the point with reckless abandon, when the Ferret interjected, "What is your next grievance, Ambassador?"

"In good time. Ambassador Quentain, where is this LogSplitter person? He seems to figure prominently as a witness, but authorities have not been able to locate him."

Quentain pulled out a valise that rested against her chair and placed it with a resounding slap on the table. "LogSplitter is en route to the Lodges of the WeatherWorn to tend to urgent matters of business on behalf of the BlueHoods, while the *Peerless* is in dry-dock for repairs. In the meantime, we have his affidavit about the entire incident. It describes the events of the evening in question, beginning after the fire at the marina, and ending with the *Peerless* leaving the *Vortex* behind."

"My staff is transcribing copies of it, one of which we have for your inspection." She opened the valise, and handed a single sheet to the ermine. "M'Lord Pindlebryth has reviewed the document, and is willing to testify as to it veracity. The original will be surrendered to the PanGaean authorities, if these negotiations fail."

"Well played," thought Pindlebryth to himself as the Ferret began to read the transcript. Quentain made it sound as if Pindlebryth would confirm the written deposition in its entirety. And indeed he could, as long as he was not asked certain questions.

LogSplitter was scrupulously honest in his sworn declaration, but had to be reminded to strictly pertain to only what he witnessed and his own actions during the melee. Thankfully, LogSplitter's loyalty to the BlueHoods guided his pen to leave out any details about his involvement in their conspiracy to defect, and all inconvenient references to Hayake or Ankuu.

"How convenient that this statement has no details concerning Mr. BlueHood's demise, or the country that has spirited our citizens away," Kayka grumbled.

Quentain simply stared back at Kayka, like a parent waiting for a child to finish a tantrum. While the Ferret ambassador continued reading the document, the Crow pressed on. "There were several diversions during the night in question. First, the BlueHoods' legacy gift to the University was stolen in a remarkable and inexplicable fashion. Then the *Vortex*'s sister ship, the *SlipStream*, sustained considerable damage from fire.

"We cannot help but to wonder what hand M'Lord had in all these events. With one misdirection after the other, is it any wonder the BlueHoods' escorts were distracted, allowing them to escape their protection?" The ermine paused in his reading to hear Quentain's response.

Pindlebryth felt a surge of satisfaction, despite the Crow's refusal to acknowledge that the guards were Warders. For Kayka was no longer lobbing inflammatory accusations pell-mell, but instead was reduced to only couching his questions in vague innuendo.

"In the first case, M'Lord was in plain view of several witnesses at the Royale," said Quentain looking at the Regent President. "The Regents themselves can attest that M'Lord was present when we were all alerted to the robbery of the BlueHoods' collection. I am sure we all have read the police report on the incident, and I will testify that I can provide an alibi for M'Lord. To wit, I and two other persons were in a carriage heading to the reception at the Royale at the exact time the burglary occurred.

"In the second case, M'Lord was still at the Royale, although the Regents had left by then. But I'm sure their spouses and other guests will attest to the fact that M'Lord never left the ballroom, before the *SlipStream* was attacked.

"Lastly, M'Lord left with LogSplitter and the BlueHoods as the *SlipStream* was burning. His paramount concern was for the safety of his own guests and the BlueHoods. He had no time to worry about anything else."

"Ah yes, his guests. We have been trying to locate your two compatriots from the Royale. Where are they? How may we contact them?"

Pindlebryth decided it would be best if he answered directly. "SharpWatch is already back home in Lenland. As to my personal guest, GraceTail, I am afraid I have lost track of her and do not know where she is. It seems she had little stomach for such excitement." While that was full of obfuscation, Pindlebryth smiled inward to himself, satisfied that his statement was still essentially true. To Quentain's mild surprise, he threw out one last misdirection. "You don't think she may have had something to do with all this, do you? If you do locate her, please let me know as I would like to see her again – she may have absconded with something of mine."

The Crow had a most peculiar look on his face, as he digested the seemingly astray comment. The Ferret took the opportunity of silence to mediate.

"Ambassador Kayka, I believe that Ambassadress Quentain and M'Lord Pindlebryth have addressed your concerns. Given that, I would render..."

"A moment, if you please," the Crow interjected, coming back to his senses. "We still haven't heard an explanation why there were a sizable group of Lemmings on board a Beaver ship, most notably among them the Lenland wizard." The Crow sat back and held the two with an inscrutable stare. "One might come to the conclusion that trouble was *expected* that evening, and that they had their own part to play in it." The Crow folded his wings in his lap, obviously quite pleased with himself.

Pindlebryth knew Kayka was attempting to stir him into a rage a second time, using Darothien as a taunt. But Pindlebryth refused to take the bait a second time, and handily maintained his casino face. He brushed off an imaginary mote of dust from the table. "I must confess I was surprised as well, that they were aboard the *Peerless*, Ambassador." Again, an obfuscation. Pindlebryth merely neglected to mention that his surprise occurred several days ago at Elbow Spur.

Quentain held Pindlebryth with a stern look of annoyance, as she retook the reins. "Our wizard arrived in PanGaea to collect a diplomatic package from M'Lord. The other people you refer to were her escort for her voyage."

"Package?" Kayka asked, his eyes suddenly burning with curiosity, dancing between the two Lemmings. He tapped the shoulder of his assistant, who quickly fished another paper from his pile. He pointed to a line of Crow scratch on the sheet as he showed it to Kayka.

"We have heard that it might be an item belonging to my government. That it might have even been..." Kayka paused to glare directly at Pindlebryth. "...a gem?"

It took Pindlebryth's every ounce of concentration not to break a tell. How in the world did Kayka know about the carbonado? Even worse, might the Kyaa know about Selephylin's Crown?

"Ambassador!" Quentain replied with indignant superiority. "We assure you that we have never dealt in any stolen goods. Besides, you know very well that the diplomatic pouch is inviolable, and we are under no obligation to discuss its contents.

"But come, there is nothing sinister here, Ambassador. Unless you agree we should also question every visitor that you receive from your homeland?"

The Crow's temper once again got the better of him, as he stood and his tongue clicked in his beak as he huffed and puffed in exasperation. "I can see we shall make no progress today. You leave me no choice but to present my case to the PanGaean National Council, demanding an official apology from Lenland and M'Lord Pindlebryth's expulsion from PanGaea!"

"That is your prerogative, Ambassador," responded the Ferret with obvious resignation in his voice. "But I am sure you realize such a case would be time consuming. And based on what evidence I have heard, and testimony I have seen here," he said waving the affidavit, "the chances of such a hearing having your desired outcome is minimal at best."

The Crow exhaled, his utter frustration venting through his spiracles with a high pitched whine. "This is not over yet. We Crow have a long memory!" he warned, sweeping his wing threateningly at the Lemmings.

Pindlebryth could not resist one final barb. "Then I pity the Kyaa, for Mrs. BlueHood's mind is quite sharp, and her memory especially long."

The Crow snatched the copy of the affidavit from the Ferret's paw, crumpling it as he foisted it upon his assistant. Kayka stormed away, flinging the door open wildly as he left. A Ferret outside the room reached in to close the door as quietly as possible after Kayka's assistant raced out clutching a jumbled pile of paper.

The Regent President slowly rose out his chair, and addressed his fellow Ferret. "Mr. Ambassador, if I may approach?"

"Yes, Mr. President. If we may impose on M'Lord for one moment more?"

Quentain and Pindlebryth were already gathering themselves together to take their leave as well. But as the Regent rose, they instead remained seated, exchanging puzzled glances.

"Thank you, M'Lord and Ambassadors, for your kind indulgence." He walked slowly as he spoke. His small steps under his robe of office made it seem as if he floated, until he stood behind the seat Ambassador Kayka just vacated. "But I am afraid I bear news the prince will not be pleased to hear." He covered his muzzle as he coughed officiously. He withdrew a document wrapped in a satin ribbon from within the folds of his robe. He undid the ribbon and broke the University seal, then unfolded the paper and began to read aloud.

"It is the decision of the Regents, the governing body of the PanGaean University, to temporarily suspend M'Lord Pindlebryth of Lenland's standing as a member of the student body. This action is taken according to those sections of the University bylaws regarding ethics complaints. All rights and privileges due a student are accordingly hereby revoked from the above mentioned by the Regents, which has sole authority in these situations. These rights and privileges may be reinstated at a later date, pending investigations and resultant decisions rendered by the Regents." The Regent folded the document, and offered it to Pindlebryth. The Ferret ambassador merely stared at the space on the table in front of him. The unmistakable frowns on both their faces showed neither of them took pleasure in this formality.

"Mr. President!" Quentain objected, quite flustered. "I don't understand. You were present during these discussions. You yourself heard that M'Lord Pindlebryth is not at fault, and unlikely to found culpable for the affairs at the Royale and the *Peerless*. Why is the University taking this action?"

"Madame Ambassador, the University holds itself to a higher standard than that proscribed by PanGaean law. Pending the investigation by the authorities, and our own investigation, the Regents are answerable to the University's bylaws. They require us to take these actions to preserve the honor and standing of the University, and to protect it against legal redress. You of course, may petition the Regents to set aside today's decision. But quite frankly, I would estimate the chance of success along those lines to be about the same as Ambassador Kayka's chances in the PanGaean National Council." The Regent President quietly dropped the document on the table in front of Pindlebryth.

"That being said," he continued in a softer tone, "my personal opinion is that M'Lord will be fully reinstated after the dust settles from this whole sordid affair, and both investigations are complete. I counsel patience."

An awkward silence followed. Quentain was about to renew her objection, but she was stayed by Pindlebryth's paw on hers before she could utter a single syllable.

"It is all right, Ambassador," calmly whispered Pindlebryth as he turned to her. "I am familiar with the bylaws of the University, and the Regents' interpretation is correct, and their actions quite proper. Truth be told, I half expected this outcome." Turning to the Regent President, he accepted the document, saying, "Thank you, Regent President. I will be returning to Lenland presently. I look forward to your decision in my favor. Ambassador Quentain will relay your decision during my absence. In the meantime, please be sure to thank Doctor GrayMask for his understanding and infinite patience with me. It is my great hope, if and when I return, that he will continue as my advisor."

The Regent bowed with an expression of sadness mixed with relief. With his robe still imbuing the somewhat unnerving quality of floating, he headed towards the door. He opened the door, but he paused holding the door ajar. He turned and regarded Pindlebryth quizzically. Was this the same irresponsible reprobate so colorfully described to him by DarkMane and GrayMask? He shook his head as he left, considering anew the Regents' decision.

Quentain and Pindlebryth took their leave of their host, after thanking him profusely for his forbearance and hospitality, and complimented him on his performance as moderator. The Ferret asked them to stay, relax and share a drink. They politely declined, citing other pressing appointments they had this day.

A valet assisted them to their own embassy's carriage, and Quentain instructed their driver to take them to Pindlebryth's house.

"Back to my apartments, Quentain? I need to talk to DeepDigger, before he leaves – which could be any day now!"

"A necessary precaution, M'Lord. You heard the Crow – he was quite put out!" She permitted herself a smile as she recalled the Crow's consternation, but it was fleeting. "If you didn't hear a veiled threat in his parting comments, I certainly did. I therefore think it prudent that you are never alone on your travels until you are safely back home in Lenland. I will have the driver fetch Grefdel upon our arrival at your residence. I will take my leave at our embassy, and then you both can be on your way to DeepDigger's. In the meantime, I will instruct my staff that an embassy carriage is at your disposal for the remainder of your stay in PanGaea."

Quentain plopped her valise in her lap as she leaned forward to Pindlebryth. "Now that we are finished, I'm dying to know! Is everything in LogSplitter's affidavit true?"

Pindlebryth nodded, his lips pursed. "Essentially, yes. You were there when he wrote it. I only advised him to stick to what was relevant to the events at the Royale, and the attacks on the *Peerless*."

"What a yarn!" she recoiled back into her seat, looking at the roof of the cabin. She smiled an envious grin as she tried to imagine the events of that night. "Part of me wishes I were there, but the other half is glad I wasn't! I've never been in..." Suddenly, a look of concern flashed across her face. "Wait! What part wasn't true? No, on second thought, don't tell me!" she said, closing her eyes and holding up one paw. She nearly fell out of her seat as the carriage rounded a corner onto a jarring cobblestone street.

"If Kayka is successful in pressing his crusade into the Council, I would most probably be called upon to function as your legal counsel, or possibly even be named as a co-conspirator. Much as it pains me, I can't afford to know the answer. The more I would know, the more I would risk an accusation of suborning perjury if either of us are called to testify."

Quentain closed her eyes and rubbed her forehead thoughtfully, as she reviewed the meeting. "Without compromising either of our positions, what *can* you tell me about what happened after you escaped the *Vortex*?"

"Not knowing what I could tell you until it was too late, that would be an extremely difficult question to answer. I've probably hinted at too much already with my outbursts in front of Kayka."

"Then let us concentrate on what we know does not incriminate anyone. Although he did not write it in his statement, LogSplitter did affirm that someone else stole Hakayaa's inheritance. Who was this third party?"

Pindlebryth struggled with his answer for a moment, but in the end decided Quentain would have to be satisfied with, "No one from Lenland. Mrs. BlueHood has the person's written confession."

Quentain pondered for a moment, then recalled aloud, "It wasn't Hayake, was it? She wasn't with us during the degree ceremony."

"No, it was not. BroadShanks and she were together."

"Oh, the poor dear," Quentain suddenly commented. "Is what you said about her murdering her father true? How horrible!"

"Yes, all of it."

"What will become of her, I wonder?"

"Difficult to say," said Pindlebryth as he watched the outside scenery trundle by. "I'm sure the Dowager BlueHood will see to her care. But whether she goes to prison or a sanitarium depends on what she and GanderLord Ankuu can agree on. He is sworn to uphold the law, despite the BlueHoods' considerable leverage. Then again, this may be a matter for the Lodges or the Maritime Courts to deal with – after all, the deed occurred on the open sea."

"Why was Ambassador Kayka so interested in this gem that the BlueHoods gave you? What was so important about it, that Hayake killed her father, and that it and Darothien had to be rushed back to Lenland?"

Pindlebryth was much more concerned about how the Crow knew about the carbonado and possibly Selephylin's Crown in the first place. But he felt he could not burden Quentain with that just now. He leaned forward with a bump as the carriage rolled to a fitful stop. "I believe you were going to have the driver fetch Grefdel?" Quentain rapped the cabin ceiling and called instructions out to the driver, all the while regarding Pindlebryth with mild displeasure at his avoidance. Pindlebryth crossed his arms and his legs, and stared off in the distance pensively.

"Let us leave it at this – I owe you a very long explanation, but only after I return to PanGaean University." Pindlebryth's shoulders sagged, as if he sloughed off a heavy burden.

"I am grateful that I no longer have to play the fool, and deceive so many. But I still have secrets I must guard, to protect those dear to me. I find that almost as troubling."

"That unfortunately is the burden of a King." Quentain's brow furrowed slightly, as she considered her prince. "So sure are you, that you will return to the University? What if the President is wrong, and the Regents uphold the suspension?"

"Unless DarkMane has some special talent given to him by the Quickening Spirit – that no other Badger has, might I add – I'm quite sure that both you and I will outlive him. I doubt the suspension will last longer than he."

Quentain blinked her eyes at such a sudden dark turn in Pindlebryth's thoughts, spoken so cavalierly.

Grefdel lumbered into the carriage, moving a bit more slowly than his usual vigorous pace. Wearing an overcoat on top of casual clothes, he took his place and sighed with relief. "Thank you for saving me from a day of gardening. After stuffing me 'til I nearly bust, BroadShanks was about to set me to uproot and till the entire back lot."

Looking at Grefdel, Quentain pointed to her mouth, and made a sweeping motion. Grefdel took out a handkerchief and brushed away the crumbs of quickbread from his own muzzle. "Where are we off to, M'Lord?"

"First the embassy, then to DeepDigger's."

"You've been there many times before. Why do you need me this time?"

"The Crow ambassador made a veiled threat," Quentain replied. "I think it wise, that M'Lord have an escort for the duration."

"Ah. The meeting did not go well, then," Grefdel said warily as he patted the sheathed dagger under his coat's forearm.

"No," said Pindlebryth impartially. "Ambassador Kayka is not at all satisfied, and will probably pursue my deportation from PanGaea."

"And to add insult to injury," Quentain grumbled, "the University has suspended M'Lord until further notice."

"I want to try one last time to persuade DeepDigger to

accompany me to Lenland. Given the current situation here, and since the... 'gem'..." Pindlebryth stuttered as he glanced at Quentain, "is in Lenland by now, I see little reason to wear out my welcome in PanGaea. Besides, it will good to be home again," he opined. A calm wistfulness came over him, as they approached an elegant storefront with a centerpiece featuring a lady's long gown of deep emerald.

Quentain studied Pindlebryth for a few moments, and sat erect with a knowing grin, scrutinizing his profile as he peered out the window. "Oh, I've seen that face before. And, I might add, on those with less level heads than yours, M'Lord." She sat back again, and folded her arms, with the fingers of one paw tapping the other elbow. "If I may be so bold, M'Lord, what is the doe's name?"

Pindlebryth was momentarily confused as he returned from his woolgathering. Grefdel slowly turned his head at Quentain, barely trying to hide his amusement at the entertainment unfolding before him. Pindlebryth glanced repeatedly at Quentain and Grefdel in consternation, with an expression that dared either of them to say anything.

But Quentain took the challenge, and sallied forth. "There aren't many eligible does in PanGaea, let alone the University. It's not BlondeStripe, or HazelEye. Beautiful they may be, but I've observed how you found them exceedingly uninteresting – and rightfully so. Tapioca is more fascinating than either of those two! That would leave the comely daughters of Gabaduren – and I *know* you had seen immediately through his ploy of having one of them ensnare you, and associating his family close to the royal line."

Pindlebryth dumbly looked at Quentain in surprise, not quite sure which more confounded him – her temerity at prying into his social life, or that her assessments of it were so accurate.

"So, it's someone back in Lenland. But who – of course! I saw how you came to her defense with the ambassador. An excellent choice!" she tittered.

Pindlebryth found he could not rail indignantly against Quentain, but rather only wryly admonish her. "That's quite enough of that, thank you very much," he tried to say at flatly as possible. "And *you*," he added, turning towards Grefdel, "can wipe that smile off your face. Or on our next daily sparring match, I'm taking the button off the end of my sword!"

They deposited Quentain at the Lenland embassy, and said their farewells, Pindlebryth only adding two requests – to keep him apprised of any legal developments, and to keep his "private life just that." Quentain happily agreed, still giggling to herself as they pulled away.

Pindlebryth and Grefdel could hear Old Pan in the distance clang out the noon chime as they drove down Arbor Drive.

"Quentain doesn't know about Hakayaa, does she?" Grefdel asked as the carriage slowed.

"No," Pindlebryth replied, glad to return to the business at hand. "It's for the best, and for several reasons. The authorities will learn about him soon enough, and I want to give him as much lead time as possible. Also, if Quentain represents me during deportation hearings, she cannot know."

"Expelled and deported," Grefdel growled. "And now we prepare to run away with our tails between our legs!" he said grinding his teeth together.

"Fear not, Grefdel. PanGaea will see me again, one way or another." Pindlebryth could have said more to assuage Grefdel's irritation, but he put it aside as the carriage stopped.

If it was at all possible for DeepDigger's abode to be even more bleak than before, Pindlebryth could not have imagined it. The late autumn wind blew leaves off of poorly trimmed trees, and made some of the house's clapboard shutters bang intermittently against their frames. The neglected grounds about the house had turned grayish brown, and bare windows unadorned by curtains made the whole building seem most uninviting, despite the bright noonday sun.

Grefdel stood in front of the door, which was beginning to show signs of termite or powder beetle infestation. He and Pindlebryth exchanged worried glances. Grefdel took a step forward, and knocked on the door. When no answer was forthcoming, he knocked again more vigorously. He dusted off a small portion of the door with his overcoat's sleeve, then pressed his ear against the grubby panel.

"I hear some movement," he said. A moment later, the door shuddered, then ground slightly ajar with a grating sound as the lower corner of the door scraped along the floor.

"Ah, Pindlebryth! You made it back!" DeepDigger said, having long ago dropped Pindlebryth's formal title at his own request. He tried to heave the door open wider, but could not. "Oh, bother!   Give us a hand, will you?"   Grefdel put his shoulder to the door, and it grudgingly gave way. DeepDigger stepped to the side of the foyer, smiling broadly. "The events of the other night are the talk of the University, if not the whole town!"   The old Ferret was positively giddy as he led them inside.   "Come in, come in, you must tell me all about it! Between the BlueHoods' honorarium and the BlueHoods themselves, how in the world did you pull it all off?"

"You give me too much credit, Professor."

"Pindlebryth, we agreed! I am no longer employed in that capacity."

"I know. But it still does not feel right, Professor. Anyway, I can only claim credit for some of that night's goings-on. Which part I had a hand in orchestrating I leave to your imagination."

As they entered the house, Pindlebryth maneuvered past piles of boxes, crates and trunks lining the walls throughout the entire house. Furniture was corralled into corners in each room and covered with clean sheets.

"I would offer you some refreshment, but the larder is quite bare. Oh, and thank you for your staff's assistance. They have been invaluable since I had to let poor Miss Roan go several days ago."

"I daresay, I've never seen the place this clean!" Grefdel whispered in Pindlebryth's ear.

"Welcome back, M'Lord!" came HighStance's call from the top of the staircase. He labored with a dolly holding another tower of containers.

"Oh, HighStance, take your lunch now, if you please. Pindlebryth and I have some business to attend to upstairs."

"All right, professor. I am a bit peckish! Would you care for anything, M'Lord?   Grefdel?   BroadShanks packed me a truckload of food leftover from this morning."

"No thank you!" they replied in unison.

"I'm still full from this morning," Pindlebryth added, holding his stomach.

"Suit yourself." HighStance shoved the dolly away from the stairs, came down and rounded the newel towards the kitchen, pulling a copy of *The Facade* from his work pants' side pocket. Pindlebryth spied a snippet of a headline about the ongoing mystery of the BlueHoods and the University.

"Professor, have you thought about my offer?"

"Yes I have. But come up to the library first. There is something we both need to see."

The three wended their way to the attic, dodging boxes and trunks, and several crates hastily hammered together, holding trove upon trove of books. Their path became more difficult to negotiate the closer they got to the tiny attic room that had served as DeepDigger's personal library. Outside the room itself, open crates were filled to overflowing with statuary and books, partially wrapped in piles of crumpled newsprint, old draperies and excelsior. The crates and their top panels were scattered covering most of the floor, leaving only a tortuous trail still navigable.

The library itself presented a shocking contrast to the halls outside. The room was almost completely bare, except for empty shelves, a desk and chair, and the strongbox built into the otherwise empty bookcase. DeepDigger stepped over the last crate into the room, and collected the ever-present two pairs of white gloves on the desktop. Handing one of the pair to Pindlebryth, he donned his own pair. He knelt down in front of the box, and as he did so many times before, undid the combination tumblers, and opened the interior lock with his key. He carefully lifted the book out of the safe, and placed it reverently on the desk.

"If you would, Pindlebryth, please open the book."

"But," he stammered, "I can't. You know the book won't let me!"

"Indulge me." He took a pace back from the book, as Pindlebryth hesitantly approached. He eyed DeepDigger questioningly, as he reached out. He lifted the cover, and quickly withdrew his paw by sheer reflex. He cautiously tried again, and opened the book to its title page.

"What!" Pindlebryth exclaimed. "But how?" Barely managing to restrain his excitement, he turned a page of the curious material as gently as he could manage. He turned a second page, as it made a sound only something much larger could make. Pindlebryth tittered uncertainly as still another page fluttered by. Still leaning over the book, he turned towards DeepDigger and asked, "How can this be? I don't understand!"

"If I may," said DeepDigger with a strange, almost pained look on his face. Pindlebryth stood aside as DeepDigger looked at the exposed pages. He reached out to turn the next page, when the book sent an arc of orange dancing across his fingertips. He withdrew his hand as if he had touched a hot stove, and yelped meekly more out of anticipation than actual pain. Pindlebryth stepped back in amazement, not entirely sure if he could trust his eyes.

"When I first showed you this book, I told you the book knows who its owner is. It seems that it is more accurate to say that the book selects its owner. Apparently the book has decided, and it has chosen *you*."

DeepDigger's eyes had a sadness in them, as if he had lost a long dear friend. He drifted to the chair behind the desk, and sat down, defeated and abandoned. It seemed he could weather all the previous losses inflicted on him, but this was too much to bear. He removed his gloves, and started to remove the key from his watch chain.

"You asked if I had thought about your offer. It seems the book has decided for me." He held the strongbox key out to Pindlebryth. "You don't need my assistance anymore to research the codex. It is yours. I wish you success in all your endeavors."

Pindlebryth took the key and regarded its heft for half a minute. "A student of history. A professor of history. Are they not in the end, all one and the same?" He turned the key over in his paw once, then twice. The two sides of the key struck him as poignantly symbolic. On one side, the prospect of being free to peruse and research this ancient and eldritch work was positively tantalizing. On the flip side, he felt, he *knew* that the mysteries buried inside this tome were far too crucial, and the time too critical, to keep it only to himself.

"Have you never wondered, how it would be to have a hand in history? To actually influence its course?"

"Certainly," DeepDigger replied, absently watching the fingers of his paws as he interleaved them together in an arch. "After a lifetime of steeping one's self in the exploits and foibles of others great and small, what scholar of history hasn't entertained such a dream at least once?" Looking Pindlebryth straight in the eye, he continued, "But such ambition is almost immediately tempered by another lesson history teaches us –

how to recognize hubris."

"Oh, come, Professor. Grant me enough wisdom to not be blinded by delusions of grandeur." Pindlebryth held the key up in front of his muzzle, regarding it solemnly. He set it back down on the desk, and with both hands, slowly closed the book. "It is not glory that I seek, or vanity that I serve. After all this time, do you not realize? I am not trying to leave my indelible mark upon the world. I prefer the world just as it is, in all its faults and all its beauty. Do you not understand that I fear, and am trying to prevent, the catastrophe of another placing his stamp on us all, and rearranging the world in his own corrupt image?

"And to that I end, I need your help."

DeepDigger pursed his lips, his hands still knitted together. He was lost in a stare, focused on a point miles behind Pindlebryth.

"My offer still stands, Professor. Please," he beseeched, "*please* come back to Lenland with me?

"Imagine having free run of our archives, and our archivist at your disposal. You could work with me and Lenland's wizard – a most formidable sorceress – who would be glad to count you as a friend. You would have a place and a purpose in Lenland's CityState.

"And you would still be with your friend here," Pindlebryth said as he patted the cover of the codex. "What say you?"

DeepDigger closed his paw into a loose fist, and leaned his head against it, as he turned his stare at the book. The two remained silent for quite a while, until DeepDigger placed his hands into his lap. He sighed wistfully, and finally replied, "There is naught for me elsewhere. I will go where this book goes. I accept."

"Excellent!" Pindlebryth beamed. "Finish your packing, Professor. We have a lot of work ahead of us in Lenland." He handed the key back to DeepDigger, then leaned over to lift the tome. DeepDigger held up his paw.

"No need. I can put it back – it still allows me to hold it. Now off with you!" he stood and sniffed. He waved Pindlebryth away with the back of his hand, as if he were dismissing a class. "HighStance and I have much to do – I have to vacate these premises before tomorrow evening."

"Very well, Professor," he said clasping DeepDigger's

shoulder in congratulation. He left the room with a smile as DeepDigger replaced the codex in its strongbox. Veritably bounding down the stairs, he called for HighStance.

He emerged from the kitchen, munching on a sandwich with several alfalfa sprouts dangling from his lips. A wake of loose pages from *The Facade* swirled behind him on the floor. "Yef, M'Lud?" HighStance sputtered between chews.

"Change of plans! Professor DeepDigger will be joining us. Please see that he and all his belongings are on the next ship to Lenland. And a respectable ship, not just any tramp freighter!" Pindlebryth commanded.

"Absolutely, M'Lord!" he gulped.

"And you, my friend," Pindlebryth added more congenially. "Take care of yourself and BroadShanks while I'm gone. I don't know when I will return to PanGaea, but mind the apartments until I do. Give the Professor the guest room, until he can depart."

"Farewell, then, M'Lord," HighStance said with melancholy echoing down the hall.

The rest of the day seemed a mad dash, as Pindlebryth and Grefdel filled it with all the minutiae of preparing for travel, beginning with packing their necessities for the trip home. It took a bit longer than they planned, as BroadShanks always seemed to have one more item or morsel to add to their already hefty saddlebags. It stopped only when Grefdel's long-suffering finally broke.

"Enough, you dotty doe! Lords Below! Do you want to break my bird's back? Do you want Voyager to spiral into MidSea from exhaustion?"

BroadShanks countered that the poor creature had more to fear from Grefdel's increased weight brought about by laziness. As she began a torrent of grievances against Grefdel starting with his ineptitude as a gardener, Pindlebryth's first impulse was to quiet the brouhaha. But as the two traded insults, he instead folded his arms and leaned against the wall, watching the tirade with a smile. He was in no way going to interpose himself in such an epic battle. Besides, he surmised that the two of them were enjoying themselves thoroughly. The volume and speed of their taunts continued until they spied the broad grin on Pindlebryth's face.

"Oh, please go on! This is *far* better than any play at the

CityState Theatre!" he cajoled. The two combatants dropped their expressions of righteous indignation, and howled with laughter at each other. Pindlebryth left the two to finish their goodbyes, as he returned one last time to his study upstairs. He closed the door, and sat behind his desk. He surveyed the room, feeling more than a bit nostalgic. But as always, his eyes at last rested on the telltale splotch of ink on his desk blotter.

A cascade of memories came again, as it often did when he meditated on that ink stain. He was entirely lost in his thoughts when a polite knock roused him from his reverie.

"We're all packed, M'Lord. We had best be going if we are to make the Archipelago by nightfall."

"Quite right." Pindlebryth replied. He got up from the desk, and closed the room to his study behind him. It seemed to resound with a note of finality as it shut. He changed into his riding clothes in his upstairs room, and after checking that the Talking Gem was in its proper place over his heart, he went downstairs to a waiting Grefdel and BroadShanks.

All business, Grefdel hefted both saddlebags and slung one over each shoulder. He checked the exterior through the small window pane next to the front door. He was about to open it when Pindlebryth paused a moment, and took BroadShanks by the paws.

"Thanks again for all your help – nursing Hakayaa back to health and keeping his secret, helping poor Hayake, and last but not least, putting up with me and Grefdel these past months."

BroadShanks squeaked a tiny "You're more than welcome, M'Lord," but was otherwise speechless as her lower lip trembled. Pindlebryth continued on, lest she start bawling incessantly.

"I hope to come back again soon, to finish my work at University. If for some unforeseen reason I cannot, join us at the CityState castle. You will always be most welcome there."

After a moment, she replied with a strange sad look on her face. "If I had my druthers, M'Lord, I think not. We'd have to learn all sort of new behaviors for the castle, and I and HighStance are just too old to learn new tricks. If I were there, I would have to treat you with all those "Thee's" and "Thou's". And even more so, when you are King – and you *will* be, if the Quickening Spirit has a lick of sense in Him! The castle's just too formal for my taste, M'Lord. And besides, I would never be allowed to do this!"   She lunged at Pindlebryth and squeezed him with a bear hug, like a mother doe would give her pup. Pindlebryth laughed at Grefdel's open-jawed disapproval of BroadShanks impropriety, and with a small shrug of his shoulders, hugged her as well.

She let go, and stepped back.   She wagged a finger at Grefdel, nagging with a mischievous grin, "Now you take good care of him and bring him back safe, or I *will* come to the castle, and give you what for!"

They said their final goodbyes, and went to the awaiting embassy carriage. After loading the saddlebags into the coach, they gave the embassy driver directions to the Double Eagle. As they pulled away, Grefdel leaned out of the cabin and called to BroadShanks as she stood waving goodbye in the front doorway.

"I forgot to tell you – you'll have to cook for a Ferret for the next couple of days!" Grefdel collapsed in his seat with a belly laugh, as Pindlebryth looked out the window at BroadShanks, shaking her fist at him in full bluster.

They approached Lenland's CityState in the middle of the afternoon of the third day of travel. Normally they could span MidSea in two days, or even one in an emergency – but both Pindlebryth and Grefdel agreed that it would be best to spare Voyager. Grefdel's mount, provided by the embassy, was eager and well able to fly back home. But Voyager, having spent far too many idle days in the stable, and getting only a minimal amount of exercise from the stable hands at the Double Eagle or Pindlebryth himself, required an extra day.

They accordingly camped first at the most westerly islands of the Archipelago, then on an atoll along the most easterly group of islands the next night. Even though Voyager was winded at the end of each day, it was easy to see that he preferred sore wing and back muscles in the open skies over a softer existence in the confines of the city. Throughout the voyage, Pindlebryth reflected that he shared the same preference, but for different reasons – he vastly preferred flying over sailing.

Over the course of the second day, the closer they approached Lenland, the more impatient Pindlebryth became. When they finally landed as the sun set over Archipelago, his wish to be home again with family and friends was palpable.

As soon as they landed, Grefdel tied up his tern in a copse of palm trees, and fed him from the foodstuffs provided by the Double Eagle. Voyager was given his usual free range, but he hunted and swam for only a very short while. After catching a few fish, he returned to the beach and wasted no time in nesting. As soon as he half-buried his abdomen in loose sand, he fell fast asleep.

After promising Grefdel he would always remain in sight, Pindlebryth took in a stroll along the inner beach of the small sheltered bay. As moonlight glistened over the relaxing waters, he sorely wanted to go for a swim. However, they had only enough fresh water for drinking, and he did not relish the thought of feeling salt-encrusted fur under his riding clothes for the remainder of the trip. He took out the Talking Gem, and spent a good deal of time talking with Darothien. After hearing that everyone had arrived in Lenland safely, and ensuring that the carbonado was safely hidden in her laboratory, he gave her the good news that DeepDigger would join them soon. Once the important business was taken care of, the two talked for more than an hour. Although he could later recall little of what exactly they conversed about, Pindlebryth found it raised his spirits considerably and only fueled his desire to return home as soon as possible.

The mid-afternoon sun over Lenland was low and not very warming as they circled the castle. Low and fast moving cirrus clouds were a sure sign that autumn was quickly coming to a close. The pilots and their steeds read the weather, and flew slowly into the prevailing westerly winds. They gently glided, hovered and finally landed, like stepping off a well-worn path, next to the stables west of the castle. Pindlebryth gave Voyager a rub with both paws under his wings, before he and Grefdel handed the birds off to the stable grooms. The were barely out of the stable, when they were met by Pendenar.

"Good day, M'Lord. Darothien told us you would be arriving about this time."

"Has she sent you to collect me? A new revelation in her

laboratory perchance?" he asked as they walked between the barracks and the western wall of the castle enclosure.

"No," replied Pendenar as he stopped at the walkway turning to the right into the barracks. "But you're just in time. There is something I thought you might like to see." Pendenar gestured towards the barracks' main doors invitingly. Pindlebryth looked inquiringly at Grefdel who shrugged his shoulders in response.

"It's been a long flight, Pendenar. I could use a bath, an actual meal and a long rest."

"I'm sorry, M'Lord. As you desire, but I really do believe you won't want to miss the goings-on in the gymnasium."

Pindlebryth's shoulders sagged as he resigned himself to Pendenar's urging. "Very well, lead on." The three of them entered the barracks, and turned down the long hall. As they approached the room, they could hear a commotion building. Cheers, applause and the occasional gasp echoed down the corridor. Grefdel opened the doors to the gymnasium, and Pendenar shouldered a way open through a throng that blocked their view. As he pressed past members of the Red and Blue platoons with firm calls of "Make way," the soldiers complained at first, but quickly snapped to silent attention as they realized Pindlebryth was behind him.

They emerged through the innermost ring of the crowd, and Pindlebryth beheld three Lemmings in formal fencing garb. General Vadarog sat on a bench along the dueling court, holding a foil in one paw and his fencing metal mesh mask in the other. He was sitting erect, but he was still breathing heavily from an exhilarating workout. He did not notice that Pindlebryth had entered, instead being fixated on the match unfolding on the court.

Two contestants both wore protective masks, and sported full sets of breeches, plastron and jacket protective gear. Colonel Farthun's batman Gangon sidled nimbly along the side of the court in step with the combatants, watching competition intently and holding red and blue flags in opposite hands. The fencers at first seemed unfairly matched – the one wearing a blue band on his arm was half a head taller and much stronger than his opponent wearing a red band. However, the smaller competitor more than made up for the difference with speed, agility and deftness. Several minutes passed as a blinding flurry of attacks and lunges, and parries answered by ripostes and remises, were accompanied by the near-constant clang of the épées' metal against metal. Only occasionally would a strike be made, and Gangon would raise his flag to the cheers and whoops from the crowd. Each strike was soon answered by a return point, with the pair evenly matched. The crowd reached a fever pitch until a voice in the corner of the room yelled, "Halt! Time!"

A chorus of disappointed voices rang out as the fencers stopped, stepped back and saluted one another with their blades. The chorus quickly hushed as Gangon raised one flag and announced, "Blue, three!" Silent anticipation reigned until Gangon followed with a knowing grin and raised the second flag. "Red, three!"

A tidal wave of hoots and hollers, cheers and jeers, and mixed cries of celebration and rejection erupted in the gymnasium. Several of the crowd groused as money changed hands, into the pockets of those few savvy enough to predict a tie. Tabarem was laughing the loudest in the center of a large knot of griping soldiers. He was easy to spot, with his multicolored patchwork jacket afloat amongst a sea of monochrome uniforms, as he scooped his winnings into his equally vibrant hat.

General Vadarog stood up, and congratulated the pair. "One of the most exciting contests I've seen in ages!" he bellowed above the din as the pair took off their masks. As Vadarog handed the red fencer his familiar eyepatch, Pindlebryth was not disappointed when the red fencer facing him was revealed to be Duke Trevemar. He was however slightly surprised that a warrior of his reputation – and ego – would deign to wear protective gear and a button on the end of his sword.

Pindlebryth had to see who it was, whose puissance with a blade made Trevemar take such precautions. But he could only manage to see the fencer's back as he undid and removed his plastron and helmet. Two blond stripes bordered a mane of black fur that ran down his neck, meeting in the center of his back. He thought he recognized the markings, but could not recall them on such a large athletic frame.

But the throng of soldiers pressed closer to the fencers, clapping their backs in congratulations, as Pindlebryth tried in vain to step closer and sideways to catch sight of the face of Trevemar's opponent. This time, both Pendenar and Grefdel intervened, shoving the madding crowd aside to allow Pindlebryth through.

Pindlebryth froze in disbelief when he caught the blue fencer's profile.

"Selephygur?" Pindlebryth barely whispered, quite thunderstruck. This was not the defenseless infant that Selephylin tortured. Nor the young cub that lay in hospital, a pitiful little thing with his head bloodied and bandaged after the Lens was so cruelly torn from its socket. Nor the sadly outmatched young buck that tried to foolishly stand against a Ravenne at Vulcanis. Nor the angry and directionless young brother he had left in Lenland still mourning for LongBack. And certainly not the uncoordinated neophyte that received a spanking with the flat of Trevemar's blade.

Shattering all of his preconceptions, towered a strapping and rugged Lemming before Pindlebryth. Broad of chest, with powerful arms and thick muscular legs, stood a self-assured Selephygur exuding a confidence that indicated he clearly saw his purpose and destiny. Punctuated by his black obsidian eye, the set of Selephygur's jaw inclined Pindlebryth to believe that his brother would allow very little to get in the way of his achieving that destiny – whatever he chose.

Pindlebryth quickly became aware that Pendenar was laughing. "Much has changed in a few short months, eh, M'Lord?"

Pindlebryth glanced to his other side, and observed that Grefdel was just as surprised as he was. "That is an understatement!" Pindlebryth chided. When he last saw Selephygur, he knew his brother was determined to improve himself, but he never expected to see such a rapid and monumental change. Regardless of what brought about this metamorphosis, be it whatever combination of training, reward and punishment Trevemar could have doled out, or the blessing of the Quickening Spirit, or perhaps – though unlikely – his own heartfelt advice to his brother, Pindlebryth was genuinely proud and happy for Selephygur. In the end, all he could do was shake his head, and join Pendenar in his uncharacteristic mirth.

Pindlebryth trumpeted over the crowd, calling his brother's

name. Selephygur and Trevemar had just handed their fencing masks and épées to Gangon, who struggled to balance his own equipment in addition to the combatants'.

Selephygur's ears twitched, and he turned to search out the source of the voice calling his name. His eyes locked on his brother, and he underwent a startling transformation.

His strong but benign determination became a mask of unadulterated hatred. His lips curled back in a snarl, and his eye seemed to fill with blood lit by naked rage.

"*You*! You meddling bastard! Is there no end to your interference?"

Selephygur swept aside the two soldiers nearest him with one arm, and charged directly at Pindlebryth. Coming in low, he bowled Grefdel over with an elbow solidly planted in his abdomen. Grefdel crumpled to the ground, gasping for air. Shouldering Pendenar aside, he tackled Pindlebryth. All the other soldiers stood in stunned silence, their training for action at terrible odds with their instinct to never lay hands on royalty. The two fell to the floor, with Selephygur's hands scrambling to throttle his brother. Pindlebryth tried to push Selephygur off with his arms and one leg, but could not budge his brother's formidable bulk. Selephygur pivoted his hips to shove Pindlebryth's leg to one side, and planted a knee on his chest, bringing his full weight to bear on his ribs.

At first Pindlebryth was able to block his brother's grip, and roll partially from side to side, but Selephygur's knee kept him essentially pinned. Pindlebryth tried to also brush away the pain in his leg and ribs, but it would not be ignored. His thigh felt like it was being pulled out of its socket, when he felt and heard a pop inside his chest.

Selephygur's hands soon found Pindlebryth's throat. A murderous iron grip clenched shut the blood to his brain, and both thumbs began to crush his windpipe. Pindlebryth gripped one wrist trying to wrestle it away, while solidly punching his brother in his good eye. He struck a second time, but more weakly than the first, as splotches of brown and indigo increasingly obscured his vision and inexorably dulled his consciousness.

Oblivion nearly overtook him as Pendenar, Trevemar and two others grappled with Selephygur. They managed to pull him off Pindlebryth, but could not break his grip. A moment later, General Vadarog stood over Selephygur and unceremoniously grunted, "Forgive me M'Lord." Selephygur went limp as Vadarog clubbed him on the back of his head. Retching for air, Pindlebryth tried to sit up but could barely roll onto his side.

Vadarog threw a small kettlebell back towards its rack, and commanded, "Take them both to the castle infirmary. See that Prince Selephygur is strapped down in his bed – hard. Put a guard on him, and triple it!"

Grefdel managed to find his legs again, and helped Pindlebryth to his feet. He almost toppled over again when

Vadarog shouted next his to ear, "And have Sacalitre take out that damned eye!" He commented aside to Trevemar, "It makes my fur want to fly off."

Vadarog stood in front of Pindlebryth and held up his left hand in front of him. He lightly clapped Pindlebryth's muzzle to get his attention, and said, "How many fingers do you see?"

Pindlebryth tried to answer, but only managed a croak before being overcome by another spasm of coughing. He made a horrible wheezing sound, and he felt like he had swallowed his tongue. Yet Pindlebryth still managed to fixate on Vadarog and hold up three fingers.

"He's out of danger. But Sacalitre should still take a look at M'Lord immediately." He motioned for Grefdel and another to escort Pindlebryth away. Trevemar and Pendenar were binding Selephygur's arms and legs with ropes cut from pulleys of weight stacks next to the kettlebells. Within less than a minute, two appeared with field cots. Trevemar and the three others each took a handle of one and trucked Selephygur off to the infirmary. Trevemar's usual inscrutable expression was overrun by undisguised confusion.

Pindlebryth tried to bravely dismiss the need for a cot, but neither Vadarog nor Pendenar would stand for it. As Pendenar ushered two soldiers and Pindlebryth away on his cot, Vadarog called after him. "Put Prince Pindlebryth in a separate infirmary room, away from Selephygur until we get to the bottom of this!"

✾

Flocks of Crow tore at Pindlebryth's throat and innards. Keeyakawa and two other Ravenne squabbled amongst themselves as they tried to rip out his liver with claw and beak. Another Crow buried his head in his thigh, tearing out and gulping down mouthfuls of muscle and tendon. As its crop bulged to the limit, it turned to look at Pindlebryth. Through the mass of feathers dripping fresh blood stared two eyes filled with malice – one blue and one obsidian.

Pindlebryth woke up with a start, coughing with a hoarse rattle. He rubbed his eyes with paw pads damp with sweat as the last of the nightmarish image left him. The last thing he could remember before the dream was a nurse giving him a small cup of weak tea and blueberry honey, mixed with a strong dose of valerian and chamomile to help him sleep. He propped himself up in bed, and grimaced with pain. His right abdomen stabbed like it was run through with a javelin, and his leg throbbed dully. Both were covered with plasters that smelled of crushed herbs and mint. A large bandage was wound several times around the rib plaster and over the opposite shoulder, and a splint held the leg plaster in place and his leg immobile.

Beside his bed sat Jarjin on one side, and Darothien on the other. The curtains on the window were closed, but he could tell that there was no light behind them.

"What..." he croaked, then coughed agonizingly. "...time now?" he whispered.

Darothien reached over and stroked the top of his head. She frowned slightly, but otherwise her face was unreadable. "It's well after midnight," she said. "You should still be asleep."

Pindlebryth tried to push and shimmy his body towards the head of the bed, so as to sit upright. But the stabbing in his side made him groan. Darothien placed her paw gently on his chest.

"Don't get up. Sacalitre says you have a bruised larynx, a cracked rib, and a small tear in your leg. You'll need at least a couple of days of bedrest."

Pindlebryth knew without his Name, he would be bedridden for at least a week, and forced not to exert himself for an additional two. Even so, two days seemed like an eternity. He looked around, then asked Jarjin slowly, swallowing after each word, "Where's... Grefdel?"

"After you were brought here to the infirmary, both Pendenar and Grefdel had a dressing down by Colonel Farthun," Jarjin explained nervously. "He holds them responsible for not keeping you out of harm's way. He would've laid the blame for Selephygur on them too, if Vadarog hadn't convinced him otherwise. They've drawn cleaning the stables for a week, and are confined to the Royal Guard's floor in the castle when they are not on duty."

"What about Sel..." A rattling wet cough interrupted Pindlebryth, and wracked his rib with another stab.

"He's strapped into bed, two rooms down. He's being watched by three guards, as Vadarog ordered. Sacalitre, however is stumped. He can find nothing physically wrong with Prince Selephygur – other than a black eye, and the lump that Vadarog gave him."

"General Vadarog had me examine his obsidian eye after Sacalitre removed it," Darothien joined in. "There is no magick on it. It's just a stone."

"He's been awake since an hour after the attack. But he's been strangely silent. I checked in on him before I came here. He looked – afraid." From his manner, Pindlebryth knew that Jarjin witnessed something more in Selephygur than just simple fear. And recalling what his brother shouted when they met, Pindlebryth didn't need that familiar itch to tell him that something alien was at work on Selephygur. But the itch did tell him he needed to find out what that something was without delay.

Pindlebryth grimaced anticipating the pain, and forced himself upright in bed. "Take me," he growled and swallowed to clear his throat, "to him."

Both Jarjin and Darothien clamored in unison, "M'Lord!" Then, minding where they were, they continued in hushed tones.

"Sacalitre said you must rest!" insisted Darothien.

"Colonel Farthun will send me to the stables as well!" complained Jarjin. Pindlebryth ignored their protests. He swung one leg over the edge of the bed, then with the arm away from his complaining rib, he lifted the splinted leg over as well.

Pindlebryth fixed Jarjin with a determined stare. "Help... up." Jarjin's shoulders slumped, as he realized he could not find it in himself to disobey. With a fatalistic nod of his head, he put an arm around Pindlebryth and lifted him onto his legs. They slowly made their way to the door, with Darothien by Pindlebryth's other side. She focused on his weak leg as she walked with him, ready to catch him if he faltered badly. She opened the door into the adjoining room, where a nurse stood up with a small peep of surprise.

"What in the world do you think you're doing?" she hissed. "Get right back to bed!"

"Get M'Lord a crutch, or be silent!" ordered Jarjin. The nurse clamped her jaw shut and chewed on her next words. She exhaled theatrically, her arms akimbo. After a moment and another loud puff of disapproval, she went off to a supply room.

But Pindlebryth brooked no delay.   By the time the trio painfully made their way to Selephygur's room, she returned with the crutch and slipped it under Pindlebryth's arm on the side opposite his torn thigh.

Jarjin entered first, and Darothien guided Pindlebryth through the doorway. Two guards, on either side of the solitary bed looked up with surprise and worry. Duke Trevemar sat guard at the foot of the bed, but did not look up. He remained stock still with his arms and legs crossed as he stared at the younger Prince.

Pindlebryth pointed with his crutch to the side of the bed as they approached. Jarjin coughed, and addressed Trevemar. "My Duke. We have need of that," he said as he motioned to the chair. Trevemar looked up at Jarjin, then regarded Pindlebryth with an austere veneer that did not quite fully disguise his turmoil underneath.   Trevemar stood and stepped aside, surrendering the chair.   He folded his arms again while he remained standing, and returned to solemnly staring at Selephygur.

Darothien moved the chair aside of the bed, close to the door. With a groan of relief, Pindlebryth sat down next to his brother and handed the crutch to Jarjin. Next to him was a small table crowded with a carafe of water capped with an upended glass, a few stoppered vials, a muzzle, a lamp and Selephygur's obsidian eye.

He picked up the eye, and examined it. He had never before had the chance to look at it closely. It was a well crafted orb, but did not even approach the level of detail that the Lens of Truth had had. An engraved iris encircled a pupil that was bored into the volcanic glass, but it contained no concentric rings nor any glyphs. He placed the eye back where he found it and studied the prone and restrained Lemming before him.

If ever he witnessed a more noble creature in such a pitiable state, Pindlebryth could not recall it. Selephygur's head was bandaged in three places: one large wad of cotton cushioned the lump behind his right ear; another gauze was taped over the welt under his good eye; and his old eyepatch was fastened back over his empty socket. Selephygur himself was wrapped in a large canvas straitjacket, with his arms crisscrossed over his abdomen. The sleeves were not fastened behind him, as might have usually been done, but instead each sleeve was threaded under his back and buckled to the metal rails on either side under the mattress. Each leg was manacled to metal posts that formed the footboard. So securely was he held, that all he could do was turn his head or at most raise his neck.

"This... necessary?" wheezed Pindlebryth at one of the guards.

The two guards looked at each other nervously, but it was Trevemar who spoke. "Sacalitre took forever to find this... garment. We barely had his arms strapped down in time before he came to. He screamed like a mad spring Hare, swearing oaths to kill us all. It took all three of us and Sacalitre to hold his legs down until they could likewise be secured." He moved to the side of the bed opposite Pindlebryth, and leaned over to look under the mattress. "So yes, M'Lord. It was necessary."

Pindlebryth likewise looked at his side of the bed. Where the heavy canvas sleeve was wrapped and buckled around the bed frame, the metal bar had bent inwards.

"Sacalitre gave him something to calm him down," Trevemar continued, nodding to the vials on the side table, "but he has roused himself a few times since then. When he did so, he seemed much calmer than before, even lucid. Sacalitre removed the muzzle after he quieted down. But he may be playing possum, and I don't think we can take any chances yet." He leaned sideways to more closely examine Selephygur. "He's probably awake right now, listening."

After a moment of deliberation, Pindlebryth stretched forward his arm, and placed his paw on Selephygur's forehead. Jarjin hissed, "M'Lord, no!" He and the two guards nervously shuffled and placed their hands on nightsticks slung through their belts, anticipating the worst.

"Selephygur," Pindlebryth grunted hoarsely.

Selephygur's eyelid snapped open immediately, and his deep blue eye spun and focused on his brother. His face was not filled with unreasoning anger, but the wariness of a wild animal caught in a snare. But as soon as he recognized his brother, he turned his head to face him. A wave of relief washed over his features.

"Pindlebryth," he sighed. "Thank the Quickening Spirit you're alive! Lords Above, I'm so sorry!" Selephygur's head and chest suddenly twitched with a shiver, and a change rapidly overtook him. There was a flash of unbridled hatred as

Selephygur's snout curled in fury, followed by another shiver and the return of wary sanity. It was then Pindlebryth saw the fear that Jarjin spoke of.

"Lords Below, I can feel him. I can *feel* him!" Selephygur breathed rapidly several times, and squeezed his eye shut. "He's in my head!" He began to pant like he had finished a grueling footrace. "Darothien, *please*! " he begged, "Get him out of my *head*!"

"Who?" Pindlebryth coughed.

"I – don't know. I can't see him." He shivered again, his whole body making the bed rattle. "He *knows* I can see what he sees!" Selephygur's entire mien changed again, and his look of abject fear slouched into malice. "You!" he spat at Pindlebryth. "You cannot hide from me! I will see you *dead*!" he shouted, his neck muscles straining apoplectically against his restraints.

A gasp resounded from the doorway. All in the room looked up to see Queen Wenteberei, with the nurse and another of the Royal Guard standing behind her. She covered her mouth with a paw, as she radiated an empathic mix of fear and pity driven by a mother's love.

"And you!" Selephygur slavered like a rabid beast at Wenteberei. "Your husband will pay dearly for what he did to me!" Wenteberei shed tears from unblinking eyes. She began to swoon, but she steadied herself against the doorjamb.

Selephygur grimaced and shut his eye again with a growl. He drove his head down against the pillow, wailing like a frightened child.

Sacalitre pushed his way past Wenteberei and the others in the doorway, holding a bottle and a large gauze cloth. He took a deep breath, unsealed the bottle, and haphazardly poured a copious amount of a clear aromatic liquid onto the gauze as he scampered around the people in the room. He clamped the cloth over Selephygur's muzzle. Selephygur rocked his head from side to side, trying to breathe free of the cloth. Pindlebryth's paw was knocked aside, but Sacalitre held the gauze firm. Selephygur quickly slipped into a stupor.

The room breathed a communal sigh of relief, except for Sacalitre. He beckoned the nurse to join him, as he stoppered the glass bottle. He handed her the cloth, ordering her, "Dispose of that before we all pass out!" The nursed dodged like a mouse through the people between her and the door.

Sacalitre took one of the vials, and filled the dropper that stoppered it. He produced a tongue depressor from a pocket, prized open Selephygur's mouth, and dripped a small amount of the dark amber liquid onto his tongue. He shut Selephygur's mouth and stroked his throat, forcing a swallow response. He was about to repeat the operation, when Pindlebryth uttered a single word.

"Stop." Sacalitre looked inquiringly at Pindlebryth. "Need him to talk." He signaled Jarjin to help him up.

"What is happening? What happened to my child?" bemoaned Wenteberei.

"He needs his rest!" protested Sacalitre. "As do you."

"Need to talk. Not want. *Need*," grumbled Pindlebryth. "See me when done here," he rasped. He swallowed, which brought on another spasm of coughing.

As Jarjin situated Pindlebryth with his crutch, Pindlebryth said curtly, "My room." Assisted by Jarjin, he limped over to his mother and gave her a light hug. "Come," he wheezed, and they both escorted her out of the room. As they passed by the nurse's desk back to his own sickroom, Pindlebryth halted and pointed. Holding his crutch in one hand, he held the other paw open and flat, then made a scribbling motion. Jarjin nodded that he understood, and collected several sheets of paper, a stylus and a small hardcover book from the nurse's desk.

Remaining behind, Darothien approached the bed and knelt next to Selephygur's head. She carefully folded back his eyepatch, closed her eyes, and wordlessly held her open paw over the open socket.

Jarjin carefully assisted Pindlebryth back into his bed, leaning his crutch within reach against the wall and handing him the writing materials. He then frantically bustled to place a chair for Wenteberei next to the bed. She stoically held back her emotions as she took her seat.

"What has become of Selephygur?" she said with measured words. But her demeanor became suddenly fiercer as she demanded, "Who has done this to him?"

Pindlebryth scribbled quietly, using the book as a hard writing surface. He grunted with exasperation, as he discovered even the simple task of writing made his ribs ache. "*Don't know. But his words may give a clue.*"

Wenteberei shifted her chair closer to better see his writing, and to keep him from lifting the book. He wrote furiously, trying to recall verbatim everything Selephygur said in the gymnasium and in his room. When he finished, Wenteberei read aloud, "He said, 'your husband' instead of 'my father'." She looked up to the ceiling and sniffled. "What does it mean?"

"That was the owner of the Lens. Selephygur still sees what the Lens sees," pronounced Darothien sullenly as she entered. "I fear he has been trying to connect to the Lens several times, and has never told any of us."

Pindlebryth rapped the stylus against the papers with a resounding tick. "*I asked him to inform us of visions! And they now know he sees them. He is in more danger than ever.*"

"More dangerous than having his mind torn apart?" Wenteberei cried.

"Ravenne," Pindlebryth croaked. He coughed wetly, wincing against the jab in his side. Jarjin scrambled to pour him a glass of water from the decanter on his own side table. He gulped down a mouthful, and nearly retched. He caught his breath, then sipped carefully once more. Handing back the glass, he wrote, "*Darothien, do they see what Selephygur sees?*"

"No, I don't think so," Darothien responded after she read from his tablet. "The connection is stronger than it was before, but I have to believe it is only in one direction."

"I disagree," Pindlebryth wheezed, sounding only marginally better. He set to writing again. "*The Crow know about Selephylin's Crown and the carbonado. How else could they know?*"

"I'm sorry my Prince, but I just do not sense that. Nor do I think Selephygur is being controlled. Not directly, at least." Darothien rubbed her paws together and blew on them, as if they were freezing cold. "I tried to detect who might be behind the Lens remnants in Selephygur's head, but what I felt was an imprint. Like an echo inside a cave." She folded her arms about herself, like the cold was spreading across her body. "What we witnessed was an afterimage of sorts. Selephygur is not directly controlled, but he is overwhelmed by thoughts and emotions of the Lens' user when he tries to see. In his own mind, Selephygur is fighting against what the Lens leaves behind."

"Get Sacalitre," Pindlebryth gurgled, followed by a round of wet phlegm-filled coughs. He yelped in pain as his ribs reminded him again of their limits.

He yawned as Jarjin returned with the physician. He had written in his absence, "*We need Selephygur to be rational. Is there something you can give him to allow him to be questioned without becoming violent?*"

Sacalitre read it, and scratched his scraggly chin. "Yes, I believe so.　Some valerian, and one or two nightshade derivatives."

"Nightshade? It's not dangerous, is it?" worried Wenteberei out loud.

"Your Majesty!" he replied, sounding hurt.　"I wouldn't suggest it at all if there was a risk to Prince Selephygur." Pindlebryth trusted Sacalitre's expertise, but he couldn't rid himself of the memory of BroadShanks' opinion about the physician. "I'll set it up for first thing tomorrow morning. It's best if it's done on an empty stomach." He took the papers and stylus from Pindlebryth in mid-scribble, and stood at the doorway. "Now if you please, this patient needs his rest as well, or I'll put off your meeting for an additional day."

Pindlebryth held up a finger, to beg one more minute's attention, then showed Wenteberei that he wrote, "*I have my suspicions, and wish I could tell you more. We will know more tomorrow.*" Wenteberei kissed Pindlebryth on the forehead, and left silently, her chest quaking as she quietly sobbed.

Jarjin dimmed the lamp on the side table, and followed Wenteberei and the doctor out. Pindlebryth reached for Darothien's hand, and beckoned her to sit beside him.　They lost themselves in each other's eyes for a time, until Pindlebryth placed her paw on his forehead, then guided it to his heart.　In turn, she leaned over and guided his paw, placing it over her ear.　He sighed slowly, closed his eyes and allowed himself a small smile of contentment.　Darothien likewise closed her eyes and smiled, nuzzling his muzzle with hers.　She quietly held his paw at his side until he fell asleep.

He woke as the pale morning light made the window shade fill the room with an ambiance of gray dishwater.　He reached again for Darothien, but she was not there.　He coughed and sat up in bed, grateful that it hurt far less than the night before.

"Good　morning,　M'Lord,"　said　Jarjin　pleasantly. Pindlebryth simply nodded his head in return. "Water?"

Pindlebryth again nodded, and carefully positioned himself

on the edge of the bed. His ribs and leg still ached considerably, but at least the sensation of being skewered was absent. Still recalling the night before, he sipped the water slowly and deliberately. It was refreshing enough, but he yearned for a good cup of plain Pu'erh tea to snap him fully awake.

"Need nurse. Privacy," Pindlebryth creaked.

"Ah! I see," Jarjin acknowledged knowingly as he draped a dressing robe over the chair. "Your voice sounds a mite better, but it could use more rest." He presently returned with the nurse carrying a toilette pitcher and bowl, then closed the door while he waited outside.

A few minutes later, Sacalitre could be heard bickering with Jarjin. "Nothing I haven't seen before!" he finally quipped, as he opened the door. The nurse had just finished helping Pindlebryth into his robe, and was repositioning his crutch.

"Not so fast, M'Lord!" rebuked Sacalitre. "Please sit." He produced his ceramic dome from a deep side pocket, and undid the top of Pindlebryth's robe. "Breathe deep, mouth open," he said habitually, as he placed the dome over Pindlebryth's chest. He listened to his heart and both lungs, then stood upright with a strangely dissatisfied look on his face. "Still a little congestion, but I don't suppose that will stop you." He signaled the nurse to accompany him, as he sighed resignedly. "Prince Selephygur will be ready for you in a couple of minutes."

Pindlebryth closed his robe, and tightened the sash again. "Fetch Darothien," he commanded Jarjin.

"She's already on her way," he replied as he assisted Pindlebryth out of the room. They stopped a few paces outside of Selephygur's room. Gesturing to the closed door, Jarjin explained, "Sacalitre instructed me that we should wait here until Selephygur is in a more receptive state." He fetched a chair, and motioned for Pindlebryth to rest himself until all was ready.

Darothien soon arrived with her velvet lined case in one hand, and her wand in the other. She did not wear her usual flowing green robes, but a heavy jade colored dress, and thick coat that made her look like she was dressed in moss. The coat was damp, and the last of large clusters of snowflakes were melting into its fabric.

Her state made Pindlebryth curious. Her laboratory was in the same wing as the infirmary, and she would not need to dress so. "Outside?" he ventured.

Darothien looked at him quizzically, then chuckled. "Oh, yes! I promised my aunt that I would write once every season. I always read the first snowfall, and let her know if it's going to be a mild or harsh winter."

"Verdict?" he snickered.

"Cold but not harsh, but very wet." She looked around the waiting room, and cocked her head at Selephygur's closed door. "Am I late?"

"No," he murmured still smiling, shaking his head. He growled away an irritation in his throat, and Jarjin jumped in.

"Sacalitre's administering his concoctions now. He'll let us know when Selephygur is ready."

Pindlebryth signaled the nurse, who was writing at her desk. She was tabulating several columns of data, quite oblivious to the world around her until Jarjin tapped on her desk. "Tea, please?" Pindlebryth punctuated with a small cough.

"Yes, M'Lord," the nurse replied as she stood and straightened her uniform. She quickly disappeared into the room behind her desk.

Pindlebryth pointed a thumb to Selephygur's room and asked Jarjin, "Trevemar?"

"Yes, he stayed with him all night."

"Fetch him," Pindlebryth obeyed the itch of his intuition. "He needs to hear this." Jarjin entered the room, and after trading a softly spoken verbal barb with Sacalitre, he reemerged with the duke. Trevemar looked tired, but still alert and his eyebrows had the tilt of anger. Pindlebryth surmised he was angry at himself for some reason.

"This is what we know," Pindlebryth started. "Selephygur sees what the Lens sees. He might not control when he sees through it, and certainly no control at what he looks at. Otherwise, he would know who wields the Lens." He inhaled deeply with a slight wheeze, grateful he could speak almost normally, and only needed to clear his throat after each sentence. "I believe whoever has the Lens, has had it..." he swallowed, "...implanted."

Darothien and Jarjin shivered with disgust, but Trevemar was unmoved. "Intentionally?" frowned Jarjin.

"It fits what I've seen," commented Darothien thoughtfully.

"The filaments that the Lens left behind in Selephygur have continued to grow. We have observed him struggle against someone attempting to dominate his will. I don't think such a connection would be possible, if the owner just used it casually or simply held it in his hand."

"Agreed.

"Selephygur could move the Lens on his own before.

"It must have been implanted for him to lose that control.

"But I've read nothing in DeepDigger's books that indicate the Lens has this power.

"Then again, it was always assumed there was only one owner."

The nurse returned with a large flask, and handed it to Pindlebryth. He nodded in thanks, and immediately quaffed a healthy portion to ease his parched throat.

Trevemar leaned against the wall, and seemed disinterested, or at best lost in his own dark thoughts. Pindlebryth was irked by this, and decided to engage him directly. "Duke," he said as authoritatively as he could muster. Trevemar looked up, and pushed off the wall to stand at attention, though he still harbored the same fierce expression. "The Crow know Selephygur can see them.

"The Ravenne may come after him.

"Crow shapeshifters cannot impersonate anyone.

"Coordinate with Farthun.

"No one sees Selephygur unless you, Vadarog or Farthun know them personally."

With each sentence and cough, Pindlebryth's voice became more coarse and constricted, until the last sentence sent Pindlebryth into a spasm of hacking. Jarjin lent him an arm of support as he doubled over from a sudden jab in his ribs. Pindlebryth was pushing his healing to its limits, and they both knew it. Pindlebryth downed another gulp of tea, and his voice returned as he exhaled in relief.

The door to Selephygur's room opened and Sacalitre hissed, "Lords Below! You could wake the dead with that cough. Why do my patients never heed their doctor?"

"How is the Prince?" grumbled Trevemar.

"He's calm. He should be responsive for the next several minutes. Be quick about it, if you please."

They filed into the increasingly crowded room. Trevemar

moved to the left side of the bed, standing on Selephygur's blind side, and the darkest part of the room. Darothien entered last, after she removed her prism and lens from their case.

Selephygur lay quietly on the bed, his barrel chest rising and falling calmly. The sleeves tightened with each breath, and the bed frame creaked in response. His eye was only half-open, and rapidly coursing from side to side, as if he were deep in dream.

Pindlebryth commanded the guards, "Leave us." They looked at Trevemar, who nodded but held out one paw. One of the guards handed him his truncheon.

"Is that really necessary?" groused Sacalitre.

"We don't know what other abilities may manifest," Darothien replied, while holding her prism across both her eyes and keeping her attention fixed on Selephygur.

As the guards exited, Pindlebryth added, "You too, Jarjin, Sacalitre."

"What!" hissed Sacalitre.

"This is not for your ears." The itch of his intuition would not leave him be until he said that. The three stood patiently and quietly until Jarjin left and Sacalitre finally closed the door behind them. Pindlebryth sat next to his brother, and took one last swig of tea.

"Selephygur?" He paused, then tried again more forcefully.

"Selephygur.

Do you hear me?"

His eyelid fluttered, as his eye stopped flickering in every direction to rest upon Pindlebryth. His eyelid stopped twitching, but still remained half-closed. "Yesss," he slurred.

"Do you see me? Or do you see him?"

"Never see him."

Pindlebryth quickly realized his mistake – only ask one question at a time. He leaned closer, so that Selephygur looked directly only at him. "Who do you see now?"

"Brother," he intoned dreamily.

"Have you seen any Crow today?"

"Yesh-sh." His cheeks were so relaxed, they puffed as the sibilance trailed off.

"Can you describe them?"

"Yesh-sh."

Pindlebryth shook his head as he quietly snorted at his

continued impatience. "Describe the Crow you see," he meted out slowly.

"Crown. Must be Kyaa." Selephygur inhaled slowly and deeply. "Red. Red robe. Red hat. Funny hat."

"That would be the Vizier," Darothien whispered. "So neither of them has the Lens? Then who?"

Pindlebryth rubbed his chin. "Who has the Lens? Do you see who has the Lens?"

"No."

Pindlebryth realized he had asked his question wrongly. "Can you see yourself?"

"Tried. No mirrors. No windows. No reflections. He stays away. Avoids them. Knows I might see." Saliva began to dribble from the lower side of his jaw.

Pindlebryth sat up with an idea. "What color are your feathers?"

"Black." Selephygur chuckled as his eyelid fluttered again.

"Good, Selephygur, good! Do you have any other colors?"

"Black and... dark..."

Pindlebryth sat back with a slight frown and scratched his throat, disappointed in his answer. He had thought if the BlueHoods had their characteristic blue and gray markings, and Hakayaa had turned all gray, then he hoped other Crow might also have distinguishing marks. But Selephygur's answer frustrated that avenue of thought.

"Black paws," Selephygur rambled. "Dark red fur."

The trio gasped, then fell silent for what seemed an eternity. They looked between each other in consternation, only to be interrupted by Selephygur.

"I won't let you, young pup," he growled weakly. He looked at the ceiling, but seeing nothing. "You're mine."

"He's fading," whispered Darothien. "The other entity is trying to dominate again."

"You?" Selephygur grunted as he peered at Darothien, and tried impotently to exert himself against his bonds. "You escaped me once. Won't... happen... again."

"Hm?" Confusion came over Darothien's face. "Who are we speaking to now?" she ventured in a louder voice.

"Your doom." he muttered slowly. "You all dead."

"Why?" Pindlebryth asked, sounding like a teacher goading a recalcitrant student.

"Interfering bastard.   You mealy-mouthed mongrel," Selephygur slobbered. Trevemar straightened suddenly, as if he had been slapped.

"Whom do you serve?" Pindlebryth coughed.

"Never! They serve *me*. Just don't know it yet."

Trevemar remained on Selephygur's blind side, but retreated farther into the dark corner of the room.   He whispered, "M'Lord, if I may." Pindlebryth nodded quickly.

"Who killed your son?"

"Trevemar slew him," Selephygur snarled with sudden hatred. He suddenly rocked back and forth violently against his restraints, making the feet of the bed hammer against the floor. Sacalitre burst in exclaiming, "Enough!   I will not have my infirmary made into a torture chamber!" He shooed everyone outside as he called for the nurse. The trio obliged, and left silently. Sacalitre was about to close the door, when Jarjin politely reminded him that the two guards were still required to be present.

Outside, Pindlebryth pivoted on his crutch and splinted leg, and sat on the edge of the nurse's desk, and swallowed the last of the tea greedily. Darothien put her prism back in its case, then returned to Pindlebryth's side. Trevemar stood sullenly with his arms folded across his chest, as he looked at the floor and shook his head in disbelief.

"Son!?" hacked Pindlebryth, holding his side. "What son?"

Trevemar raised his head to look at them both, rubbing his temple. An uncharacteristic trembling in his voice betrayed an emotion Pindlebryth could only guess at. "I know who has the Lens," he declared through clenched teeth.

Darothien   and   Pindlebryth   exchanged   glances   of excitement. "Who?" she blurted.

"BrokenTail. The Iron Baron."

A deathly silence blanketed the room like the snow falling outside.   It was finally broken by a low growl.   Jarjin instinctively looked at the closed door to Selephygur's room, but was shocked instead when he realized it was Darothien.

Pindlebryth was the first to recover from the shock of Trevemar's revelation. "Dead. He's *dead*. Washed away in the Archipelago."

Darothien's paws were clenched into fists, and Pindlebryth could swear he could see them begin to faintly glow a sickening green – not the verdant green of life and growth, but instead the fouler shades associated with rot and decay. She stared intently past Trevemar as she mumbled, slowly nodding, "Black paws and feet. Dark copper fur everywhere else."

"And the words Selephygur used," added Trevemar. "'Mealy mouthed mongrel' was a favorite of his. The young prince could not have known that."

"A trick," Pindlebryth wished out loud. "A Crow shapeshifter trying to trick us."

"No," Trevemar contradicted Pindlebryth with steely confidence. "You yourself told me that Crow shapeshifters cannot impersonate. So unless there is a breed of Crow in the Rookeries with all red feathers...?" he trailed off, knowing that Pindlebryth could not refute his conclusion.

"Too old," Pindlebryth protested. "He had no Name. He *couldn't* live this long." Suddenly, the picture of the youthful Selephylin flashed in his mind. The two thoughts collided, and Pindlebryth realized an insight that almost brought him to the edge of panic: both the Iron Baron and Selephylin were in the Archipelago for years; Selephylin through her magick had the secret of longevity. Had the two of them somehow schemed together from the very beginning?

Pindlebryth's mind reeled. The itch in the back of his head told him he was right. He leaned over slightly, feeling dizzy and nauseated. "You're right," he finally capitulated. "The King must be told."

He started to hear the sound of rushing water, as he felt his grip on the crutch loosen. He clutched at it futilely as dark flashes of maroon and umber swarmed over his sight.

IX - The Search for the Orb

"Thank you for the update, Jarjin. When you next see Pendenar, relay my thanks for his information. I think I have a very clear picture of what has been going on in my absence.

"Let him and Grefdel know I'm doing well, and that unlike Colonel Farthun, I do not harbor any – Ouch!"

Sacalitre ignored Pindlebryth, while he calmly and methodically poked and prodded his patient's body. He pressed gently but firmly against Pindlebryth's ribcage where the break occurred, then compressed slowly but with increasing firmness on his sternum and back. In both instances, he increased the pressure until he heard Pindlebryth grunt or groan with discomfort.

"It has to hurt, before it can heal!" quipped Sacalitre, paying much more attention to the condition of his patient's injuries than to what he was saying. Pindlebryth frowned on one side of his muzzle, as he lay on his side in bed and watched Sacalitre with growing impatience. He wondered how many other quaint and vacuous aphorisms the good doctor kept squirreled away to preemptively quiet any complaints from his charges.

"There is one other item that you would be interested in, M'Lord," added Jarjin as he snapped his fingers. "Archivist WagTail pitched a fit with Major Domo Melajen."

"Oh?"

"Everything has since been smoothed between them, but WagTail was initially quite displeased about the prospect of, as he put it, 'an outlander in his sanctuary.' "

"That would be Professor DeepDigger, no doubt." Pindlebryth sat up with interest, but Sacalitre immediately pressed him back into a supine position. Pindlebryth sighed with increasing aggravation at the doctor's high-handed bedside manner. "Has he arrived yet?"

"His ship pulled into Cape Ark this morning, but the amount of his cargo is larger than anyone expected. Transporting it all is slow going, and he refuses to have any of it leave his sight. Melajen expects he will arrive by tonight. He is still fretting about fitting it all in one of the guest rooms of the North Wing."

"Excellent. Tell Colonel Farthun that DeepDigger and my book are to be escorted to the archives the moment he arrives."

"Your book?"

"DeepDigger will know what I mean."

"Yes, M'Lord," Jarjin acknowledged.

"Now, assuming the good doctor here doesn't incapacitate me anew, please fetch Duke Trevemar. I would like to speak with him," Pindlebryth grunted as Sacalitre poked his ribcage one final time. "...while I still can!"

Jarjin bowed quickly, and left his prince's sickroom.

Sacalitre turned his attention to Pindlebryth's thigh, where the plaster and splint had been removed, and kneaded the fur through to the underlying muscle until Pindlebryth again displayed any sign of discomfort.

"Everything's healing quite well, as we might expect."

"As well it should!" Pindlebryth rumbled hoarsely for a moment, before regaining his voice. "I've been cooped up here for two whole days."

"Yes, yes," Sacalitre responded patiently, with an air of stodginess that shouted, 'I've heard it all before.' He shoved his paws in the pockets of his cotton white-coat, and pronounced, "And it seems your voice is in working order to boot!"

Sacalitre stood up, and shuffled towards the closed door. "Well, I shan't keep you here any longer. I'll have the nurse bring you a cane." Sacalitre waited with his paw on the door handle, until Pindlebryth closed his robe. "Remember, you are *not* fully healed! Rest often, even when you feel you don't need to. I'll check up on you regularly, but I don't want to see you back in here anytime soon."

Pindlebryth got the distinct impression that the physician thoroughly enjoyed giving orders to royalty. But Sacalitre's air of superiority evaporated when Pindlebryth asked him about Selephygur's condition.

"I am afraid I have exhausted all of my medical options – not that I have anything that could overcome magick. Darothien and Archivist WagTail have been searching through both of their libraries for any indication how to assuage his condition, but as yet have little to show for it."

"I know," agreed Pindlebryth. "Darothien puts on a brave

face, but I can see she is more upset each time she visits me."

"To make things worse, your brother refuses to eat or drink anything. We have to render him unconscious daily to force feed him." Sacalitre's shoulders sagged signifying defeat. Looking down, he did not see that Pindlebryth was beginning to tremble with anger.

"If we cannot find a solution to Prince Selephygur's condition," the physician continued unawares, "you and your family have a decision to make. This infirmary is simply not equipped to accommodate your brother for any long period of time." He sighed heavily, and looked Pindlebryth squarely in the eye. His usual practical attitude was replaced with glum empathy. "I'm sorry."

Sacalitre opened the door, but before he could exit, Jarjin slipped inside the room. Pindlebryth looked at the young guard expectantly.

"Where is he?" asked Pindlebryth, growing even more irritated.

"I'm sorry, M'Lord. But Duke Trevemar refuses to leave Prince Selephygur's side. He continues to keep a vigil over him."

Pindlebryth fumed, as he struggled to stand. "Tell his Grace to get his tail in here before I annul his ennoblement and bestow a new title of butler upon him!"

Jarjin hesitated, torn between assisting his Prince and carrying out his instructions.

"Never mind me. Go!" Pindlebryth barked, then groaned as he finally stood erect. Jarjin bowed again, and scurried out. The nurse scampered in with a cane as he took his dressing robe draped over a nearby chair, and donned it over his bedclothes. He was familiarizing himself to the cane's heft and walking with it, pacing back and forth in his room, when Trevemar finally entered. Pindlebryth held up his open paw at Jarjin, to signal him to wait outside. Jarjin nodded, and closed the door, leaving the duke and prince alone.

Trevemar, as Pindlebryth expected, was far from cowed and made no effort to conceal his indignant disbelief at Pindlebryth's challenge.

"At your service, *King* Pindlebryth," he said curtly, without even the slightest effort at a bow.

Pindlebryth ceased his lopsided circuit back and forth

across the room. He fixed an unblinking stare at the duke as he spoke.

"Believe me, I do not covet that title and the responsibilities it entails. And if the Quickening Spirit deigns to appoint me to that highest office one day, I sometimes wonder what He would do if I declined.

"In the meantime, Hatheron is still our King, and deserves our last bit of service." Pindlebryth swallowed to quell a cough. "From both of us. No matter the cost. Now, shall I tell him about your blunder, or will you?"

Trevemar squinted fiercely at him, and took a step closer. "I beg your pardon?" The duke clasped his hands behind his back, like General Vadarog often did – only Trevemar made the action look like a threat.

Pindlebryth placed both paws on the head of his cane and leaned forward, bringing his snout within reach of the duke. "You've spent a lot of time with my brother, have you not? Endless hours of lessons, training and practice. The results of which are obvious, even to my untrained eye," Pindlebryth added with a note of sarcasm. "I may not be up to your standards in the finer points of combat, but when your prodigy has me by the throat, I tend to take notice of such things!"

"You're not going blame me for..."

"Lessons, training and practice," Pindlebryth continued, brushing off Trevemar's interruption. "And let us not ignore endless hours of observation inside and outside the classroom.

"How many days, how many weeks has Selephygur spent drilling and sparring under your watchful..." Pindlebryth cocked his head and glanced at Trevemar's eyepatch, as if to mock him. "...eye?

"Then there is all that time you two have spent outside of the field of training."

Trevemar folded his arms in front of himself, and wore a smirk akin to that of an adolescent bracing himself for another lecture from an overbearing parent.

"I am sure you could regale me with several stories about the exploits of revelry, and dozens of nights spent painting the town red. CityState is positively abuzz with tales of you and Selephygur carousing as if there were no tomorrow." Pindlebryth also leaned back with a smile, still balancing himself with both paws on his cane. "Now, I do not hold that against you. I myself have had several festive nights of my own in PanGaea that might even rival my brother's here in CityState. If anything, I envy you – for you've watched my brother grow into adulthood, something I regret having missed.

"But there is one thing I *do* hold against you. After these many months, how could you not see the influence of the Lens on Selephygur?" Pindlebryth pressed harder, intentionally goading Trevemar. "Are you blind in *both* eyes, oblivious to the character of the Iron Baron that lurked all this time in my brother?"

Trevemar's jowls bunched as he clenched and unclenched his teeth several times. He could see what Pindlebryth was trying to do, but not would allow himself to be drawn in. He unfolded his arms, and opened the door. "You will excuse me, M'Lord, but in this matter I do not answer to you."

"Then you *will* answer to me," demanded Wenteberei, as she blocked the doorway.

"Good morning, Mother. I was beginning to wonder if you had forgotten your daily visit."

Trevemar slowly pivoted his head towards Pindlebryth, with a look of unvarnished contempt. Pindlebryth returned his gesture with a flippant grin of satisfaction. Trevemar relented, and pulled back allowing the queen to enter. She stepped into the room, and with an incongruous air of serenity closed the door behind her.

"I believe the Prince is waiting for an answer to his question."

Trevemar bowed and began, "As you wish, Your Majesty. But some things may not be pleasant to hear."

Wenteberei's unwavering gaze made plain her resolve. Trevemar shrugged his shoulders.

"I am not the young Prince's wet-nurse, reporting daily on his comings and goings," Trevemar began, speaking as though it was his turn to lecture.

"Besides, before M'Lord's arrival, there was little clue as to what was brewing in my pupil's head. Certainly nothing as spectacular as his misdeed two days ago. If anything, what I did observe these past months convinced me day by day that Selephygur was indeed worthy to be called a scion of the Enorel dynasty. His drive and determination, his quick familiarity then expertise with almost every weapon, his strength of personality, all put his fellow Lemmings at ease. Even his false eye, which he originally wore intending to instill fear in his opponents on the battlefield, was soon regarded by his comrades as a badge of honor and pride.

"But we shouldn't be surprised that underneath all that was a venomous clandestine behavior. If there was one thing BrokenTail excelled at, it was keeping a secret.

"On the other hand, unlike Prince Selephygur, the Iron Baron was not one to sully his paws with a weapon. He would leave such unpleasantries to his malignant son and the rogue's gallery of villains he surrounded himself with.

"Now you demand of me how I failed to notice the effect of the Iron Baron's corruption on Prince Selephygur? Are you that unaware of what goes on under your own roof?" Trevemar glared with uncensored incrimination as he clasped his paws behind himself again. Pindlebryth rocked from one leg to the other resting his injured thigh, while Wenteberei steeled herself in anticipation against the accusation that was sure to follow.

"From what I've been able to surmise from discussions I've overheard between the sawbones and the sorceress," Trevemar continued as he folded his arms again, "my Prince must have been trying to use the 'Lens', as you call it, in private for a very long time. What he has been able to see, and how long he has been under the Lens' influence is anyone's guess. He certainly did not give *me* any hint before the other day of what he might have seen from the Rookeries.

"And that is not all that has occurred, apparently under your very noses. Do *you* think you know all there is to know about the young Prince? Selephygur has more than once proudly shared with me over several flagons of ale the details of his many... conquests. If his activities as such continued unabated, I would not be surprised if Your Majesties were presented sooner or later with an embarrassing revelation from one of his many dalliances."

"What!" both Wenteberei and Pindlebryth gasped. The queen's arms locked straight at her sides, ending in fists. "You should have told us immediately!"

"No, Your Majesty," Trevemar intoned solemnly, shaking his head. "It is not my place to spread indelicate gossip. *Selephygur* should have told you." He paused, taking a deep breath, anticipating his denouement. "And he should have confided in you – *any of you*! – long before the Iron Baron had such complete domination of him." After a moment, Trevemar unexpectedly blinked. For the first time, the specter of introspection crossed Trevemar's face before he barely murmured, conceding, "Any of *us*."

Wenteberei fought her compelling desire to put this upstart duke in his place, but held her tongue as she reflected for a moment. Perceiving how strong Trevemar's self-doubt must be to affect his towering pride by the slightest measure, she relented.

"Very well, Duke Trevemar. I will discuss with the King how we shall proceed in this matter," she began with some warmth. But there was one point she would not leave unattended, and a sharpness returned to her voice. "But there is one last thing, my dear duke. You *will* treat Prince Pindlebryth with respect, for he has accomplishments to his credit you haven't. At least, one that even *you* might care about – he has killed a Ravenne and a Warder."

Perhaps Trevemar expected her to storm out of the room, but he was mistaken. Wenteberei stood in place, expectantly. The air hung thick with tension. The duke was not intimidated, but instead looked troubled. Seeming as if he were struggling to understand some moral concept that was unfamiliar to him, Trevemar bowed as he murmured, "Yes, Your Majesty." He turned towards Pindlebryth, and bowed again, although only slightly. As he bowed, however, his held Pindlebryth fast in a contemptuous glare.

Satisfied nonetheless, Wenteberei stepped aside clearing the doorway, and without a single emotion looked at the space between Trevemar and the door. "You may leave Us."

After the duke closed the door, Wenteberei breathed a sigh of relief and regarded Pindlebryth with a half-smile, half-frown that he not had seen since Selephygur's childhood. It bespoke of years of the long-suffering that only a parent has endured. Pindlebryth shifted his weight back, evenly between both legs.

"My son, I have enough to worry about. I do not need the extra burden of worrying about another child."

"What have I done, Mother, that would concern you so?" Pindlebryth inquired with feigned innocence and barely hidden playfulness. "I would have thought you rather enjoyed dealing with the duke. I know I did!"

"That," Wenteberei emphasized with a wag of her finger, "is exactly what I'm talking about. You not only expertly manipulated the duke, but myself as well. It would have served you right if I waited outside a bit longer, just to see the two of you stew."

Wenteberei moved the chair away from the bed, and closer to Pindlebryth, motioning for him to sit. "I see now I'm going to have to keep an eye on you, as well as..." Her demeanor softened from a whimsical scolding, to a flash of doubt, until anxiety washed them both away. "...as Selephygur."

Pindlebryth slowly lowered himself into the seat, then hung the cane from one of the chair's arms. He hesitated, and chewed his lip for a moment, hoping he wouldn't sound indelicate. "Did Sacalitre speak to you about Selephygur's prognosis?"

"Yes," Wenteberei answered flatly, a small frown the only indication of her state. "I cannot stand the thought of sending Selephygur away. I will pass the doctor's recommendations on to Hatheron. I daresay all of us have much to think about until we discuss it tonight at dinner."

Pindlebryth hoped against hope that such a radical step as an institution would not be necessary. "I also do not relish the idea of my brother being locked away in some facility." He tried to get up, to reassuringly hold his mother's hand, but his leg warned him it needed to rest. All he could do was lean forward, and muster some promise on the horizon. "Let us hope Darothien can find some solution to the Lens' influence on Selephygur. I place a lot of confidence in her. I and others have witnessed her abilities, and her craft surpasses that of Graymalden."

"I pray she can find an answer soon," Wenteberei fretted. "Farthun and Vadarog have their paws full, trying to ensure that news of Selephygur and the Iron Baron does not leave the castle grounds. That it happened outside of the castle proper is bad enough. Prime Minister Amadan fears that if the general populace finds out, it may generate a crisis of confidence in government."

Pindlebryth leaned back again in his chair. "Darothien is our best hope to stay such an event. She returned with a magickal tool, held by the BlueHoods in the Snow Goose WetLands since the days of Selephylin. If anyone can coax a solution out of it to heal Selephygur, she can." Pindlebryth then looked askance, as his itch tried to tell him something. "And maybe there is something else we need to add to the mix," he added as he rubbed the back of his neck.

"What do the Snow Geese have to do with it?" Wenteberei inquired with mild surprise. "Ambassador Onkyon is with Prime Minister Amadan as we speak."

"He is?" Pindlebryth burst out, as he fumbled for his cane. It slipped out his paw as he tried to stand, and clattered to the floor. He struggled to retrieve it while still seated, but his ribs complained mightily when he tried to bend down.

"Jarjin!" Pindlebryth called between gritted teeth. Aside to Wenteberei he explained, "I've been sending out messages for the past two days that I wanted to see Onkyon! Why was I not told?"

Wenteberei moved to assist Pindlebryth out of the chair, but Jarjin was through the door and at his side almost immediately. "The day you returned from PanGaea," she said as she looked helplessly on, "Onkyon petitioned for an audience. As I said, we cannot let our citizens know that the Iron Baron has returned, let alone a foreigner. For that reason, we have kept Ambassador Onkyon from meeting with you, until things can be explained. Why do you need to see the Ambassador?" she insisted.

Pindlebryth grunted, as Jarjin lifted him up, and handed him his cane. "I don't need to see Onkyon, but his son Unkaar." Wenteberei looked at her son, as confounded as ever. "He has the Gift of the Snow Geese, and I firmly believe we need it to find one more piece of the puzzle of the Artifacts." Wenteberei stood still, as she tried to comprehend Pindlebryth's seemingly random thoughts. Pindlebryth saw that she was lost and troubled, then explained simply, "To help Selephygur, we need Unkaar."

Wenteberei's countenance immediately lit up, not with understanding but instead with satisfaction that she could finally assist in some fashion. "Oh, you don't need to see Onkyon for that. Unkaar's governess and I have become good friends, since that first day that Unkaar 'explored' the castle. I have since entertained her and Unkaar on a regular basis. I'm sure I could have her over for tea tomorrow!"

"If you do convince her to come tomorrow morning, would

you be able to pry Unkaar away from her?"

"Oh my, yes. My two handmaidens simply dote on him, and have taken care of him more than a handful of times. The governess welcomes the break from her routine."

"Excellent. If you can occupy the governess for an hour or so, Darothien and I can set to the task at hand."

Wenteberei placed her paw on Pindlebryth's, and squeezed it fervently as he held the cane with it. "You're not going to do anything to upset Unkaar, are you? He can be very sensitive."

"We will do our utmost to not upset him, and your handmaids can accompany us to ensure that. But it is his sensitivity I am counting on." Pindlebryth set his shoulders, preparing to leave. "Now I suppose I should meet with Onkyon, if only to determine why he wanted to see me."

"You're not going out like that!" Wenteberei declared. She waved in one of her handmaids, bearing a change of clothes for Pindlebryth, and the nurse with a pitcher and washbasin. "Now remember, don't be late for dinner tonight – we will have much to discuss."

"I shan't forget, Mother." Pindlebryth was about to undo his sash, when he paused and realized he needed to say one last thing, for both their sakes. "It was good to see you smile, Mother – if only for a moment. There will come a time again, when we all can."

A few minutes after Wenteberei and the others left, Pindlebryth emerged refreshed. If not for the presence of his cane, he would have looked as well as ever. Jarjin patiently guided Pindlebryth up the flight of stairs in the East Wing to the Prime Minister's offices, where they found Prime Minister Amadan and Ambassador Onkyon sharing a cup of tea. They sat not at the outer anteroom's long table, but in two large stuffed chairs in the waiting room between Amadan's main office, and the office of his undersecretary. Their high-back chairs faced each other across a small table placed in front of the large window facing west over the central courtyard. As Pindlebryth entered the room, Jarjin remained in the anteroom with another Royal Guard already posted at the door. The prince looked around the room, wondering where any others were, until he heard hushed voices and the rustle of documents in the secretary's room.

Amadan and Onkyon rose, both smiling. Before Onkyon

could speak, Amadan preempted him. "M'Lord, so glad to see you up and about again, after your riding accident!"

Pindlebryth graciously nodded, if only to hide his mild surprise and disdain for Amadan's theatrics. He reflected momentarily how quickly deceit infiltrates so many corners of one's existence.

"Thank you, Minister. I'm glad also, if only to be finally free of the prison we so blithely call an infirmary."

Pindlebryth's discomfort only increased in Onkyon's presence, as his conscience was pricked by his clandestine scheme involving Unkaar the next day. He recalled how gratified he was that he no longer had to hide Hakayaa's identity from those it hurt the most. Unfortunately, that selfsame relief only made worse his distaste for Amadan's misdirection hiding Selephygur's condition, and his own plan for the ambassador's son.

"Please, M'Lord," said Amadan as he gestured for Pindlebryth to take his seat. Through the ajar door, Amadan politely asked his secretary to fetch another cup for the prince. Pindlebryth sighed with relief as he lowered himself in the exquisitely comfortable chair, after Amadan formally introduced the ambassador.

"Yes, we have met before," Pindlebryth agreed as Onkyon took his seat, "albeit under less fortuitous circumstances. What brings you here today, Ambassador?"

"My visit is twofold. Our staffs are busy finalizing some trade agreements," Onkyon indicated with a wing pointing to the room behind him. "On a more personal note, I was inquiring as to your health." He paused to sip some tea, as Amadan's secretary brought in a third tea service for Pindlebryth. "I was quite distressed to hear of your misfortune over such a piddling trifle, especially after your escapades on the high seas outside of PanGaea."

"And it was indeed over the silliest of things," interjected Amadan. "M'Lord's cinch somehow came undone, and he was unseated. Fortunately, the mishap occurred close to the ground as he was landing – otherwise the outcome could have been much worse."

"Indeed," observed Onkyon before he noisily slurped his tea. Pindlebryth put his best casino face forward, despite his realization that Onkyon was buying none of Amadan's cover story. "Well, I will be quite happy to pass along to GanderLord Ankuu and the BlueHoods that you are doing well."

"How are they doing? I've already given my condolences to the Dowager BlueHood, but they seem so inadequate at such a time. How fares their daughter?"

"She is better. Normally, decorum would dictate that I not divulge personal matters of such a delicate nature, but Mrs. BlueHood was specific that I inform you. Hayake is almost her normal self, as long as she is alone. Whenever she is visited by her mother, or is reminded in any fashion of her family, or the..." Onkyon paused as he eyed Amadan, who innately understood this was told being in confidence. "...the carbonado, she flies into a violent panic or worse. It has become serious enough that she has been... admitted to the best medical facility in our CityState."

The parallel between Hayake and Selephygur did not escape Pindlebryth. He could not help letting a small frown crack through his mask, while Amadan gulped audibly. "Let us hope that she can be helped, and as quickly as possible. The BlueHood family has had more than their share of misfortune and grief."

Pindlebryth frowned even more, after tasting the tea. The simple skill of brewing was apparently not one of the undersecretary's strong suits.

"Quite," agreed Onkyon, as he sighed and put down his cup. "On the brighter side, I at least can let you know that Mrs. BlueHood and her other relations – a brother or two if I recall correctly – have settled into their new residence, and have already set about reestablishing their businesses in the WetLands."

Onkyon reached into his jacket, and produced an envelope sealed with the BlueHood crest. "Madame BlueHood also asked me to give you this message."

Pindlebryth leaned forward to accept the letter. But when he groaned from the ache in his ribs, Amadan took the letter and passed it to Pindlebryth.

"As for GanderLord Ankuu," Onkyon continued as Pindlebryth read, "he has retired both from public and private service since you last saw him. I am sure he will be glad to hear that you are doing well. As well as can be expected, that is."

Pindlebryth summarized the letter written in Crow after he

finished reading it. "Mrs. BlueHood sends me her warmest regards, along with other news. But she does ask that if I wish to contact her, that I do so through you, Ambassador."

"Ah." Onkyon covered his beak as he coughed. "I expected as much. It seems she was most anxious to hear from you about any developments concerning 'a common interest', as she put it. Though I must confess, it sounded much more ominous when she spoke it! In any event, I would be happy to oblige, M'Lord."

Pindlebryth felt a pang of worry come over him. He would have to reflect long and hard over whether to inform the Dowager BlueHood about the Iron Baron, and how that might affect her vendetta against the Kyaa.

The undersecretary and Onkyon's assistant emerged from the side office, with identical folders of documents. They ceremoniously bowed to the trio in the room, went to the table in the outer anteroom, and prepared the stacks of papers for signing.

"Ah, it seems that the gears of the economy are ready to be greased with ink!" quipped Amadan.

"Very well, Prime Minister," Pindlebryth said as he waved away Amadan's assistance, hooked his cane on the table in front of him, and slowly hefted himself out of the high-back chair. "You both have your business to attend to, and so do I." He collected his cane, and carefully navigated his way into the anteroom, pausing to glance at the mirror-imaged piles of papers on either side of the table.

"Surely this cannot be just another simple trade agreement, to warrant your presence, Ambassador. What is so special about this treaty?" he asked as he slowly leafed through one of the copies.

"Oh, strengthening of economic ties, smoothing of previous financial impediments," proffered Onkyon.

"And...?" insisted Pindlebryth, heading off another itch he felt coming on.

"In the simplest of terms," Amadan acceded, "a revenue sharing agreement between our countries stemming from certain incomes from the BlueHoods' precious and semi-precious stone trade, and the waiving of tariffs on their metallurgical concerns that take place between us, the WetLands, and the Lodges of the WeatherWorn."

"Hah!" Pindlebryth chuckled to himself, as he formed a

mental picture of LogSplitter laughing as he swam in a river of gold coins and steel. Pindlebryth had to resist the temptation to laugh out loud when he spotted Jarjin's bewilderment. He continued to page through the document, to the last paragraph of the executive summary.

"I'd wager the wording of this accord has some interesting acrobatics. It must surely avoid mentioning the BlueHoods by name, or any other Crow for that matter, seeing that the King's edict is still in place.

"Good day to you both!"

Amadan and Onkyon bowed, albeit with smiles of consternation mixed somewhat with admiration, as Pindlebryth and Jarjin left. Pindlebryth paused just outside the Prime Minister's anteroom, realizing he hadn't had anything for breakfast and was quite hungry. He mused aloud to himself, "I think I have just enough energy to make it to my rooms, and take in a quick meal followed by a nap." He maneuvered quite well to the southeast stairwell, and was about to climb it, when he said to Jarjin, "I should speak to Colonel Farthun as long as we're right next to his office and the Royal Guard barracks, but I simply don't have the energy for it."

As they climbed the stairwell to his rooms, Pindlebryth reminded Jarjin of all he needed from Farthun – that Jarjin needed to be assigned to the queen tomorrow morning, and either Pendenar or Grefdel be assigned to Pindlebryth, and that DeepDigger and the book be escorted to the archive posthaste.

"And notify me when DeepDigger arrives. I need to be there when we show the book to WagTail and Darothien." Pindlebryth was about to close the door to his apartments, when he added finally, "And tell Farthun these are requirements, not suggestions."

Pindlebryth pulled the embroidered bell strap hanging next to the door to call for food and service, then slowly limped to his reading chair. He melted into its well-worn upholstery with a sigh of relief. He looked with regret at the bookshelves of his personal library on the opposite wall, as he realized he just could not bring himself to rise again to fetch something to read. Instead, he occupied himself with reviewing his plans and itinerary for the rest of the day and tomorrow. A servant politely knocked at his door, and was admitted by a guard. To his pleasant surprise, she already bore a tray of food and a pot of tea.

"I bumped into Jarjin, who told me you needed breakfast."

"Perfect! Set it on the dining table for me, please. Then give me a hand up from this chair, and fetch me the book..." He trailed off as he scanned the book spines from his seat, then tapped his cane on the floor as an idea struck him. "On second thought, I believe there is a large book in the Royal Study labeled 'Royal Law Transcripts' or something similar. Bring that here for me, or have someone else if it's too heavy."

She helped him up relatively easily, unexpectedly strong for her petite size, and guided him to the table.

"Forgive me! You should have no problem whatsoever bringing the book!" Pindlebryth chortled. She bowed with a beguiling smile and left the room. Pindlebryth watched as she left, wondering where he had seen her before. He lifted the teapot lid to see if it was sufficiently strong, and sniffed – his favorite Pu'erh! He began to pour himself a cup, when he recalled she was a maidservant that usually tended to Selephygur. She had matured quite a bit over the past year, since Pindlebryth last saw her before he left for PanGaea.

However, something about the maidservant began to trouble him as he ate his granola and fruit. Just as the thought that something about her seemed *too* mature, he felt the itch come on again. It wasn't dire or urgent, but it was the smallest of twinges that told him something was off kilter. He was grateful that it wasn't a raging flash of insight that might warn him of danger. Wouldn't it be a perfect pickle if she were a Ravenne shapeshifter and the food were poisoned?

Another knock came at the door, and he bid the caller to enter while his mouth was still half-full of apple. Pindlebryth stopped in mid-chew as Tabarem stepped through the door with the book of transcripts. He strode in wearing a beret, his favorite multicolored patchwork jacket and a pair of pants with thin stripes of white and indigo that almost hurt the eyes to look at. With both paws he plopped the hefty tome on Pindlebryth's table, making the plates, teapot and silver rattle loudly.

"Some light reading during lunch?" Tabarem asked in his accustomed bombastic manner. "I was in my usual perch in the study, when that sweet young thing was about to bring you the wrong book."

Pindlebryth swallowed, and echoed incredulously, "The

wrong book? How..."

"She was going to bring you the most recent volume. This is the volume you really wanted. It includes the transcripts from BrokenTail's trial."

Pindlebryth sat back and blinked at Tabarem in astonishment. Tabarem's knack for sticking his nose into things that didn't concern him at all, yet still yielding the best result never ceased to amaze him.

"As for *that* pretty little bit of tail, keep your eyes on your own doe. *She's* already spoken for!"

It took a couple of heartbeats for Pindlebryth to digest all of what Tabarem was intimating, and begin to sputter an indignant response. But Tabarem wouldn't let him get a whole word out.

"Oh, come now. Don't tell me you haven't noticed?" Tabarem teased as he opened the door and beckoned Pindlebryth to accompany him. "And here I thought you were the brightest of the bunch. Possibly even smarter than me!

"Very well, I guess I have to show you myself, so that your eyes may be opened." Without a further word, he spun out the door and sauntered down the hallway. Pindlebryth, not knowing whether he should be amused, intrigued or flat out insulted, plucked his napkin out of his lap and temperamentally threw it onto his plate. He grabbed his cane and began to lumber after Tabarem.

He looked down the corridor to see the castle gadfly leaning against Selephygur's door, innocently inspecting his nails as he waited. As Pindlebryth approached and was about to demand an explanation of his insinuations, Tabarem shooed away the nearest guard.

"Oh, go be menacing at some other door!" he rattled off smarmily. He waved the guard away with the back of his hand, as if he were ridding himself of a pesky fly. Pindlebryth nodded to let the guard know he could leave, as Tabarem opened Selephygur's door behind him. He stepped backwards, almost looking as if he were about to pratfall into the room. Pindlebryth silently followed, as Tabarem began to ramble anew.

"One thing I liked about Selephygur, is something you share with him. You both prefer to dress yourselves, with none of that butler balderdash."

Tabarem boldly strode into Selephygur's bedroom as if it were his own. He looked about, tapping a finger on his chin, until he settled on an armoire in the corner. He threw open both its doors, and pulled open one drawer, then another below it. He stopped on the third drawer, and stepped aside pointing to its contents with an open palm.

"Selephygur may not have the noodle that you possess, but he at least has enough gray matter to know this is not a proper undergarment for a prince. I don't think it even fits him!"

Pindlebryth eyed Tabarem suspiciously, and began to doubt the raconteur's sanity even more than usual. He sighed with one arm akimbo, and limped over to the open drawer. He picked up a sheer and very slender bundle of material – a maidservant's slip. He suddenly recalled Trevemar's warning about Selephygur's indiscretions earlier this morning, and turned to Tabarem with a look of shock. So this was what his instinct was telling him?

But Tabarem was already out of Selephygur's apartment. Pindlebryth saw only his head poke from around the hallway door, as the madcap Lemming looked up and down the hall, grinning like a demented gossip. Before he disappeared, he whispered into the room as he doffed his beret at Pindlebryth. "I believe congratulations are soon to be in order, *Uncle* Pindlebryth!"

Pindlebryth tossed the slip carelessly back at the drawer, and began to steam after Tabarem, when an avalanche of questions stopped him cold in his tracks.

Who else knew about this? How soon until the servant was visibly and unmistakably pregnant? What if the child was given a Name? The entire nation would know about the scandal then! And how could he face his mother and father at dinner tonight?

He stumbled out of Selephygur's bedroom, and wearily slumped into a nearby velour chaise lounge in the main room. He sat lost in thought for almost an hour, until he unintentionally fell asleep in the deliciously comfortable seat.

Pindlebryth was late for dinner, after a servant roused him

from sleep in Selephygur's lounge. He remained silent for most of the dinner, as Wenteberei updated Hatheron about Selephygur's condition, and their plans for the coming morning – that she would distract Unkaar's governess while Pindlebryth and Darothien would try to find what the young gosling was drawn to in Henejer Hall.

He explained his silence was due to a complaint making him feel rather unwell. He hated to make such a feeble excuse to his parents, but he allayed his conscience with the thought that it wasn't too far from the truth, given the revelations of the day and the continued ache of his ribs and thigh.

It was evident that his father was deeply troubled, especially by the news that the Iron Baron was alive. The additional possibility that Selephygur might need to be shut away somewhere weighed on him heavily. It was soon also clear to Pindlebryth that his parents were still unaware of the situation between Selephygur and the maidservant, and Pindlebryth simply did not have the heart to add Tabarem's accusations to their worries.

Though he was still hungry, he excused himself from the table, and bid his parents a good night. The ill are not supposed to have much of an appetite, are they? Unfortunately, when he opened the door, Colonel Farthun and Grefdel stood outside, waiting for the Royal Family to finish its dinner.

"Yes, what is it?" Pindlebryth inquired, trying to sound tired and annoyed.

"Excuse me, M'Lord. You asked that you be notified when Professor DeepDigger arrived?" hesitated Farthun. Both he and Grefdel looked concerned at Pindlebryth's apparent bedraggled condition. "He and Darothien are with WagTail, and await your help with a book."

Pindlebryth looked over his shoulder with a look of vexed weariness, as if he were being kept awake by an errant sound, like a tree branch tapping against his bedroom window. "No rest for the weary, I suppose. But Selephygur needs this, and I must do what I can." He turned back to Grefdel, still pretending he wanted to hibernate for a month. "Very well, Grefdel. Assist me to the archives. I think I can manage walking, but I may still need help on stairs."

The three of them went to the southeast staircase, with Farthun and Grefdel each holding one of Pindlebryth's arms as they descended to the second floor.   Once there, Farthun returned to the barracks as Pindlebryth and Grefdel took the hallway to the northeast stairs to the archives.   As soon as Farthun was out of earshot, Pindlebryth limped less extravagantly, leaving a flummoxed Grefdel plodding behind.

Grefdel was about to ask what was going on, when he shook his head and merely chased after his charge until he was once again in lockstep with Pindlebryth.   He did, however venture a word of thanks, hoping that it might yield the same result. "Thank you, M'Lord, for getting me away from stable duty."

"You're welcome.   I'm just glad you don't have the smell of the stable about you right now.   By the way, where's Pendenar?"

"Still in the stables, unfortunately.   Colonel Farthun begrudgingly assigned me to you, but felt Pendenar needs to learn a stiffer lesson for masterminding his end of the PanGaean affair behind his back."

"Ooh, bad luck," Pindlebryth grimaced.   When they finished walking down the hall, Pindlebryth added, "As you can tell, I'm not tired or unwell, I was just trying to avoid a lengthy awkward discussion with mother and father.   But I *will* still need some help on the stairs.   One stairwell down from dinner was good exercise, but this second stairwell challenges my mending thigh."   When they finally attained the archives' level, Pindlebryth was in fact looking forward to sitting again.   His hopes for a quick respite were dashed, however, when Grefdel opened the door to the archives' front reading room.   It was festooned with open books, scrolls and charts occupying almost every square foot of furniture, most of the chairs, and even a good portion of the floor.   The only place free of the seemingly random disarray was a place on the central table where DeepDigger's strongbox lay.   It rested on a small rug, which WagTail had placed there to prevent the unwieldy metal box from scratching the antique table.

Darothien and WagTail were both feathering through a pile of documents on the archivist's writing table.   WagTail pressed flat with both paws the documents that had spent ages rolled up, as Darothien read them.   She scanned each page with her prism of green tsavorite for hidden passages, before reading its contents as written.   WagTail kept glancing distrustfully at DeepDigger, as the Ferret stood behind both of them, craning his neck to look over their shoulders at the writings.

They were all so engrossed by their task, that they failed to notice Pindlebryth and Grefdel enter, until WagTail announced their arrival by tapping on his writing table. Darothien looked up and smiled gently, and surreptitiously waved her paw in greeting under the arm holding the prism. WagTail, however, continued to look disapprovingly at Professor DeepDigger.

DeepDigger looked up and erupted in happy surprise. "Ah, m'boy! I mean, M'Lord! It is so good to see you again!"

"I am very glad you are here, Professor. I trust you had a pleasant journey."

DeepDigger jostled over to Pindlebryth, and looked as if he were about to give him a handshake that would tear his paw off, when he stopped and pointed at Pindlebryth's cane. "But what's this?"

"Just a riding..." Pindlebryth began, but stopped as his smile left him. "...a riding accident." He completed the thought with a bad taste in his mouth. It was his resolve against unnecessary duplicity that made him change his mind.

"At least that's what we are telling people for now. However, I am afraid we have some very pressing business ahead of us. It will be almost impossible for us to function efficiently if we have to dance around the truth. So I rely on your discretion, Professor. Do not take this lightly."

Despite his royal station, he still found it discomforting to so order an elder he respected and genuinely liked. But Pindlebryth knew it was required.

"I was injured by my brother, who is suffering from an unexpected effect from the Lens of Truth. We hope to find something in the book that can help my brother.

"Darothien, have you or WagTail found anything in the archive that might help Prince Selephygur?" Pindlebryth ventured.

"No, I'm afraid our search to date has been quite fruitless," Darothien sighed with tired exasperation. "I had great hopes that the writings of Gazelikus might offer some solution, but he has written nothing here about any of the Artifacts, other than what little he could recall about the Orb, and his protective cloth."

"Then where would you like to begin?" Pindlebryth said as he placed his hand on the strongbox.

"Anything about the Lens of Truth, of course."

"That would be towards the back," DeepDigger pronounced.

DeepDigger dialed the four discs of the strongbox, and pulled out the drawer by two of the discs' handles. He took out his key, still on his watch fob, and undid the inner lock, then raised the lid. It was DeepDigger's turn to be the center of attention. WagTail and Darothien vied with unabashed curiosity to gape as DeepDigger carefully raised the book out of its form-fitting recess.

"If someone would be so kind," the professor asked as he continued to hold the book above the open box. Grefdel moved to the other side of the table, closed the box, and hefted it and the rug off the table to lie on the floor. As DeepDigger rested the book on the cleared space on the table, he flipped it over, front down. He glanced at the archivist and the enchantress and admonished, "You may look but you may not touch."

He straightened his white moustache to steel himself, then demonstrated by placing a single finger along the bound pages, as if he was about to open the book. The tell-tale spark of orange arced to his fingertip, and he recoiled with a grimace of pain. He whipped his paw away, trying to shake away the burning sensation that followed.

"Your turn, M'Lord," he said as he stepped aside.

Pindlebryth opened the book, and began to leaf backwards through the pages. Darothien silently and intently watched as he did so, but WagTail muttered an intrigued guttural "Hmph!" Pindlebryth continued leafing backwards, page by page, passing the diagram of the Orb and the protective cloth.

"Wait!" Darothien interjected. "What's that? Is that Gazelikus' Cloth?" She instinctively pointed towards the page, but stopped far enough away not to raise the book's defense.

"Yes, it is."

"We can use this!" she exclaimed. Darothien's face brightened with the prospect of a solution to ease Selephygur's suffering. She fetched her notebook and prism left on WagTail's writing table. Opening it to the first available blank page, she began to sketch the cloth in the journal.

"Just a moment more. We can use this to help Unkaar find the Cloth," she said absent-mindedly as she proceeded to write the few glyphs she could make out on the drawing. Pindlebryth looked with some curiosity as she drew a diagonal stroke through each glyph after she wrote it. Sensing his interest,

Darothien added, "If there is a spell in these writings, we wouldn't want it go off unintentionally, now would we?"

"Wherh? Whooh?" WagTail inquired, pointing at the book.

"I think he wants to know where the book came from, and who wrote it," Pindlebryth interpreted. WagTail nodded in agreement.

"From my mentor," DeepDigger hastily explained. "And it wasn't written by a Lemming. It isn't even written in any language. You see it written in your own language."

"Enh!" WagTail said as he leaned closer to the book. Pindlebryth was about to ward him off, but the book sprang to life. A miniature arc of orange passed from the page to WagTail's snout. The archivist howled in pain, as he covered his nose. Both Pindlebryth and DeepDigger desperately tried to hide their mirth at WagTail's expense.

"There, there! No lasting damage done," DeepDigger said in a consoling tone as he patted him on the back. "But we did warn you!" WagTail shot him an angry look of betrayal.

When Darothien was finished drawing, Pindlebryth turned the pages to the section of the book dealing with the Lens. Darothien set her prism aside, and produced her wand from her sleeve. "Let me try something, unless...?" she said looking inquiringly for permission from DeepDigger.

He shrugged his shoulders in response. "I'm sorry my dear, but I simply have no experience in such things. Just be as careful as you can."

Darothien whispered a word that sounded like a rushing breeze, and pointed her wand at her palm. Just as once before in the archives, a green firefly emerged from the wand, and fluttered towards her open paw. A page began to rustle then rise slightly, but slapped back down as an angry arc jumped out of the book. It obliterated the firefly, and continued the full distance to the tip of her wand with a crackle and the smell of ozone. The bolt coursed down the length of the wand to Darothien's paw. She yelped in pain as the wand flew out of her hand, and clattered on the floor. Soon the smell of burned fur and skin accompanied the scent of charged air. Darothien whimpered as she unfolded her paw to show a blackened stripe where she held the wand.

"Oh my!" commented DeepDigger. "That looks nasty."

"To the infirmary with you!" Pindlebryth said.

"No, it's not that bad. My pride is hurt worse than my paw. But I do need to clean it with some cold water, and wrap it. I'll be in my room." She collected her wand, notebook and prism with her uninjured paw and scurried down the stairs.

"All right, I think we're done for now. I'll see if Darothien is all right, and will be able to continue later tonight. WagTail, if you would, please return those documents that Darothien has finished perusing to the archive. Then fetch all of Henejer's writings you can find on the construction of this castle, including those we read last year – and especially anything about Henejer Hall. I think Darothien and I will concentrate on those when we return."

Grefdel assisted his prince down the stairwell, and down the East Wing corridor to her dwelling. The door to her rooms was open, but Pindlebryth knocked on the doorjamb all the same.

"Come in," Darothien's voice echoed from a side room.

Pindlebryth expected that Darothien's room would be green, just as Graymalden had left it. But he was pleasantly surprised to find that she had almost completely reworked the motif. Her living quarters were rich in earth tones, from light tan throw rugs, a reading chair and a wide divan in a thick weave that resembled pyrite, side tables and a small dining set in dark cherry, to a ceiling paneled with tongue and grooved birch. The room smelled like rich, freshly turned loam. Light came from two solitary globes in opposite corners of the room suspended from the ceiling. They glowed with a luminescence that reminded Pindlebryth of the archive lamp that Graymalden had created. The only hints of green in the entire quarters were the heavy drapes paired with sheer pastel curtains that bordered the window and the double doors leading out to the balcony.

He told Grefdel to remain outside, who closed the door after Pindlebryth entered. He followed her voice, to find her hovering over a washbasin and jug. Next to her were two washcloths, a small opaque glass container and a mitten. She was pouring water over the burn, and dabbing it dry with a washcloth. She repeated the task several times, until she was satisfied it was as clean as it needed to be. She then took the small nacreous jar, and tried to unscrew its lid with one hand without success.

"Here, let me help," Pindlebryth said as gently as he could

muster. He set his cane aside, and handily unscrewed the pearlescent lid, but his snout wrinkled and his whiskers twitched at the scent of the salve within.

"Thank you," Darothien chimed as she dipped a clean corner of the washcloth into the balm. She dabbed the salve over the burn, then gently worked it in after she covered the entire injury. She inhaled sharply at its initial sting, then sighed with relief as it faded. She took the second washcloth, folded it, and pressed it into the injured palm. She was about to fumble with the mitten, when Pindlebryth assisted.

"This is fine for now," he said, as he slipped the mitten over her hand. "But you really should have Sacalitre look at it soon."

"He has his ways, and I have mine," Darothien said with a smile. She lifted the mitten's cuff and whispered into it a sound that Pindlebryth couldn't begin to describe. A dim verdant glow peeked out from under the cuff, and was quickly extinguished.

"It's an ointment I concocted when I was young, to help heal surface wounds – small cuts, burns and the like. One of the first things Graymalden taught me was how to speed up healing." She began to rub the heel of her palm into the cupped mitten. "Now we just have to work in the salve some more."

Pindlebryth offered, "Here, let me." He held her covered hand, and pressing gently but firmly into the mitten, working the underlying balm with both thumbs. "Like this?"

"Mm-hmm," Darothien replied. "Quite nice. Good hands." Pindlebryth smiled along with Darothien as she closed her deep green eyes and hummed in appreciation. Pindlebryth silently drank in Darothien's innocent beauty – he was especially enamored of the blond stripes that ran from both her eyes, over the crown of her head, and a matching blond swath down the front of her neck as it plunged into her gown. The peaceful reflective moment didn't last, as Pindlebryth's stomach grumbled. Darothien's eyes snapped open as her stomach replied.

"Oh my!" she faltered apologetically. "I've forgotten I've spent almost the whole day in the archives, and haven't eaten!"

"I too, have not had much more than a few nibbles all day," Pindlebryth echoed with some chagrin.

They both laughed at themselves, as Darothien guided Pindlebryth to her divan and arranged two throw pillows in the corner between its back and the overstuffed armrest. Darothien broke off and went to a small pantry cupboard in the other room. "I don't have much here, but it is enough to keep spirit and body together. Would you like some?"

"Absolutely!" Pindlebryth sighed in appreciation as he sank in the divan. "Ohh, this feels wonderful," he purred as he reclined fully into the pillows and his aches diminished.

Darothien produced a tea set, and three discs of polished green geode from the cupboard. After she poured water and put a tea infuser into the kettle, she placed it on the largest disc. She thrummed a single syllable that sounded like tinder burning as she scribed a finger around the edge of the disc. The green of the geode began to glow intensely. Pindlebryth could feel warmth emanate from the luminous stone.

Darothien brought and placed two empty mugs onto the cherry side table between the reading chair and the divan. She returned to her cupboard and placed a bar of pressed granola onto each of the smaller geode discs. She touched them to the larger disc, and they too began to glow. The kettle came to a boil, and the granola toasted. She removed the green heat by blowing on the discs, as if she were extinguishing a candle.

One by one in her uninjured hand, she brought the bars and kettle with their geodes and placed them on the side table. After she poured the strong steaming tea, she sat in the chair next to Pindlebryth. She invited Pindlebryth to partake, and began to nibble on her own granola. She stared off into nothingness, but Pindlebryth found he was, for lack of a better word, still spellbound by Darothien's eyes. She glanced at him, and noticing his attention, by force of habit quickly looked away with feigned modesty. But Pindlebryth saw a subtle change in her face, and she turned back to him.

His heart rang in his chest, and echoed happily in his ears. A rush of memories spoke to him in rapid succession: the insipid does that foisted themselves upon him, trying and failing miserably to win his heart; the vacuous and spoiled daughters of privilege who fared none better; all paled against the mind, manner and beauty of the doe now sitting in front of him.

Pindlebryth reveled in the turns that their own relationship had taken as it grew and matured: the tongue-lashing given him on Vulcanis by an upstart novice of humble birth that somehow had received a Name; the playful and intriguing enchantress in the birches of the southern forest; the powerful and inventive wizard in her full glory on the high seas. He knew his heart was lost, and yet he was at peace with the knowledge.

"I missed you all the time I was in PanGaea. So much constantly reminded me of you," Pindlebryth said simply, honestly, earnestly. He put down his half-eaten granola, and looked intently into her countenance, as he put his paw over the Talking Gem always over his heart.

"Every green thing I saw reminded me of your eyes." He held out his paw to her. "Let me hold you?"

Darothien raised herself slightly out of her chair. She dropped the toast onto the geode, and took his paw in hers. She swiveled herself onto the edge of the divan, and reclined gently with her back against him. Folding Pindlebryth's arm over her own waist, she pressed herself against him like two spoons.

Pindlebryth's ribs complained, but he counted it as pleasure as he squeezed her even more firmly against himself.

"Like this?" Darothien said with a playful lilt, as she felt his growing tumescence.

"Mmm, Hmm," Pindlebryth purred unhurriedly. He nibbled on the side of her neck, and quietly added with a gentle smile, "Quite nice."

Darothien reached up her hand to caress his jowl, and turned her head. They pressed the sides of their muzzles together, their velvet nares touching. She slipped her thigh between both of his, and pressed his swollen firmness even more tightly against her back. Pindlebryth moaned, falling into a low growl of desire. Embracing her from behind with both arms, Pindlebryth avoided her mittened hand and stroked her abdomen once then again partaking of its fullness. He stopped, holding her firmly in his grasp. A serene satisfied stillness filled them, as they simply lay peacefully entwined, both content just to feel each other's heartbeats between them.

A full minute passed before Darothien turned in place towards her prince. They smiled generously towards each other, then closed their eyes and breathed each other's scent. Through a subtle touch of fragrant nemesia, Pindlebryth found her scent and knew he would never forget it.

"How I've longed for this," Pindlebryth said, losing himself again in the deep emerald wells of her eyes.

"My heart raced every time I hoped this moment would

come," Darothien replied.

The two pressed the sides of their muzzles firmly together again, as their hands began to search each other through the folds of their clothing.

A soft rapping came at Darothien's door.

They pressed their foreheads together as Pindlebryth exhaled with a prolonged growl of frustration. The rapping occurred a second time, but more urgently. Darothien let escape a small snort of amusement, and the pair softly giggled. Pindlebryth's eyes spoke volumes of chagrin, vexation and finally resignation to Darothien.

"This had better be important," grumbled Pindlebryth softly as his ardor diminished rapidly. He released Darothien, adding, "Grefdel should know better."

Darothien stood up and straightened her gown, as Pindlebryth adjusted himself on the divan. He sat up, and took a swig of warm tea as Darothien answered the door.

A contrite and visibly embarrassed Grefdel stood in the doorway, his head bowed towards the ground. As he spoke, he glanced upwards haltingly, unsure of what he might see. "Begging your pardon, M'Lord. But there is news."

Darothien craned her neck, and Pindlebryth sat up to see Jarjin standing behind Grefdel. Almost immediately, Grefdel observed with obvious relief that nothing seemed improper, and stood aside for Jarjin.

"M'Lord, Prince Selephygur is awake," Jarjin announced. "He is in a rare state of clarity, and requests to see you immediately. Time is of the essence – no one knows how long it will last."

Darothien dashed to the side room to fetch Pindlebryth's cane, as Grefdel entered and lent Pindlebryth a hand out of the divan. Pindlebryth took the cane from Darothien, and with a smile meant only for her, said softly, "Thank you kindly. 'I wish I could stay' sounds so feeble and selfish, but I must see to my brother."

"Don't stand on ceremony. Go!" Darothien whispered.

Despite her protest, Pindlebryth still took her paw, and kissed the top of it. Grefdel had deftly interposed himself between them and Jarjin, who stretched around him only in time to see Pindlebryth grab his bar of granola and pronounce, "Let's be on our way!"

As he shuffled through the doorway, shepherded down the hall by Grefdel and Jarjin on either side, Pindlebryth called one last afterthought to Darothien. "WagTail should have the plans out for Henejer Hall by now for us to study. I'll be up to the archives as soon as I can. If I can't make it back, I'll meet you in Henejer Hall after breakfast tomorrow!"

Pindlebryth knew there was no one to blame, as he gulped down the last of the toast. However, as he hobbled down the stairwell to the ground floor and the infirmary, he was sorely tempted to make a rude observation about Selephygur's and his guards' less than impeccable sense of timing. Such thoughts were chased away as he entered the waiting room, and finally Selephygur's room.

The ever-faithful Trevemar seemed to stalk his own shadow as he paced back and forth along the far wall. King Hatheron stood at the foot of Selephygur's bed huddled over with his arms folded as if he were fending off a cold wind. Selephygur still lay in bed shackled to the frame in his straitjacket, but was at least covered by a rich and warm blanket. Sacalitre stood in the corner next to a table filled with jars of nostrums, as he quietly observed his patient.

Pindlebryth's snout wrinkled slightly as he entered the room. Although the floor was recently washed and the bedding changed, there still hung in the air a whiff of defecation.

"It's about time!" Trevemar scolded as he stopped chasing his shadow, and Hatheron looked up with rheumy eyes. Jarjin glared at the duke, and coughed stentoriously. Trevemar, duly reminded of his admonishment earlier, added curtly, "M'Lord."

"Brother!" Selephygur exclaimed with sincere happiness.

Pindlebryth advanced to clasp Selephygur's shoulder, but he was rebuffed. The legs of the metal bed jounced loudly on the floor, as Selephygur wriggled his head and his huge shoulders back and forth.

"No, stay away! I'm free of BrokenTail for now, but I cannot tell when he will return." Selephygur flashed a voiceless snarl in Pindlebryth's direction, to emphasize the danger. Pindlebryth surveyed the length of the bed, and it seemed the metal frame was deformed even more than before.

"BrokenTail's probably asleep." Trevemar stood in the darkest corner, fuming with his arms folded over his chest, and a large saber glinting like a silver comet's tail at his side. "The rutting pig would often do so after gorging himself on dinner."

"Forgive me, Pindlebryth. I have kept so much from you all these years. At first, I was selfish. I had childish dreams of being the hero, fighting and vanquishing the Crow. Then I jealously resented you, and out of sheer spite I kept to myself the knowledge that the Lens had shown me. But it's a trap – an addiction!

"The more I used the Lens, the more I needed to use it. Then came the day the Iron Baron took the Lens to himself." Selephygur shivered with revulsion. "I used it even more, trying to find out who he was and what he was planning. But he soon learned I watched him, only giving up small crumbs of information. All the while he quietly built himself a fortress in my mind. Then one day I tried to see where he and the Kyaa searched for the Orb, and he..." Selephygur made a sound that was both a growl and a whimper.

"Lords Below," Hatheron champed. "That monster intentionally put out his eye for the Lens?"

"How do I describe it?" Selephygur whinnied.

"Does he control you at those times?" Pindlebryth asked through a grimace.

"No!" he snapped, trying to assert himself. Embattled indecision soon washed it away. "I don't know. It's as if I'm trapped in a prison cell, and BrokenTail is my jailor. From time to time, I can see out and affect the world about me. Other times, I can't see anything but him – and afterwards, I find myself in places where I don't recall how I got there, or what I did. But he's always there in a fashion, holding the door shut, whispering in my ear or shouting at me – wearing me down. It's better when BrokenTail is distracted or asleep. But his voice and his will are never fully gone." Selephygur clamped his eye shut for a moment, then grunted as he tried to stretch his arms. The straitjacket strained, making a sound like a sail about to tear away from its mast.

"He is never quiet!" Selephygur weakly gibbered. "He talks to me when I try to sleep, and is still yammering at me when I awake. He rails at me even when I know the Baron is asleep! He won't... shut... *up*!" he screamed.

"He whispers to me even now," said Selephygur, his voice trembling wretchedly.

"No wonder Vulpinden kept the Lens hidden away in a

vault. It was just too dangerous," declared Hatheron.

"They must have been cognizant of the Lens' hazards, but I doubt even they could predict what would happen if two somehow shared it," Pindlebryth brooded.

"The Fox!" Selephygur gasped feverishly. "They know too!"

"What? What do they know?" pressed in Pindlebryth, as he sat down in a chair less than arm's length from the bed.

"The Fox and the Crow are engaged in a battle of shapeshifters, spying on each other endlessly. Thrust and counter, espionage and deception – I couldn't make heads or tails of it, with what little I managed to see.

"The Fox are trying to find a way to get their Lens back, and trying to find the Orb as well. They've learned the Orb is in Lenland, but is lost to the Crow. They know the Iron Baron together with the Crow are looking to steal it and all the Artifacts. The Fox learned all that when the Crow forced a Snow Goose to steal their own Vessel of Sorrows." Selephygur began to pant, like he was fighting to maintain control.

"Lost?" Pindlebryth leaned in further, placing his weight on his cane in front of him. "But their map – you saw Keeyakawa's map. I thought the Crow knew where it was!"

"Their map was wrong. It indicated the Orb was near the southern forest where you, Pendenar and Darothien were attacked last year. They've long since given up looking there, and have turned their attention elsewhere thrice since then. They don't yet know where the Orb is, but it's only a matter of time. BrokenTail obsesses constantly about the Orb, and refuses to yield."

Selephygur grimaced and growled, as his eye squeezed shut and his whole body tensed. The metal frame of the bed squealed under the strain. He held his breath as his body trembled, then exhaled like an explosion as he relaxed. He chuffed as if he were fighting for his life.

"You have little time, brother. Both the Fox and the Crow are looking. I don't know if they have spies here in CityState, but I wouldn't be surprised."

"We're working on it, little brother. We're also working on finding a way to free you from the Iron Baron."

"No! You have to keep away!" Selephygur looked with determination at his father. "You have to put me away someplace. Anyplace! Anywhere but here! If I escape, there's no telling what I'll do, who I'll hurt!" His powerful torso curled up again, straining the jacket into taut bunches. "Agh! He's coming back!

"Don't you *see*? He wants you dead, and he'll make me kill you all! Quickening Spirit, Father! Put me away! Put me away where I can't get to you!" Hatheron stood immobile, still huddled against the cold, hard words of his son. Selephygur turned his head, peered into the darkness and glared at the sheen of the saber.

"Trevemar, use it! Father won't listen. Kill me, or I'll kill you, too!"

Pindlebryth's muzzle wrinkled again from a familiar but powerful sickeningly sweet odor. He sat back in his chair, aghast at his brother's suffering, just as Sacalitre dove in to slather a damp gauze over Selephygur's snout.

At first he growled and resisted, but Selephygur's hulking frame went limp as he finally inhaled and exhaled, wheezing like a grampus. He then began to breathe normally, almost placidly.

Sacalitre left the gauze in place, then went to the window and opened it slightly. A curling jet of cold night air whistled into the room. "You might as well go," the physician said as he selected the vial of dark amber fluid from the table. "He'll be unconscious for quite a while. We'll let you know if there's any change."

Hatheron and Pindlebryth went out into the waiting room. Hatheron looked desolate as he rubbed his forehead.

"How do I tell Wenteberei? It would kill her."

Pindlebryth stood next to Hatheron, and clasped his shoulder with his free hand. He felt utterly helpless, as he shook his head, unable to do anything to comfort his father. But there was still one thing he could offer him.

"Do not lose hope, Father. Tomorrow, Darothien and I will search for..." But he trailed off, as Hatheron trudged away, his head hung down.

Pindlebryth's brow furrowed in concentrated anger – not at his father or his brother, but at the Fox, the Crow and the Iron Baron. He silently vowed to himself that he would find a way to make Selephygur whole again. Pindlebryth set his shoulders, and gripped his cane so firmly that the skin of white knuckles poked out under his fur.

"Grefdel, help me to the archives. We have work to do," he pronounced with grim finality as he marched out of the infirmary.

"Where are they?" demanded Pindlebryth as he paced back and forth along the wide oaken doors of Henejer Hall. Sunlight beamed down through high stained glass arches on the south wall, filling the floor and northwest corner of the hall with a multicolored chiaroscuro. The tall windows underneath the stained glass were shuttered against the morning sun, in order to protect the pigments of the centuries old paintings that hung in the gallery. Ambient light flowed in from the matching windows along the north wall, filling the chamber with a shadowless winter's light.

Darothien patiently went from stone to stone in the hall, periodically checking notes made the night before. Grefdel, however, watched Pindlebryth with bated breath. Although his prince assured him he was fully healed after a good night's rest, Grefdel still followed Pindlebryth's every move, as if he feared his legs or ribs would shatter like glass with every step.

"Breakfast finished an hour ago! What in the world is keeping them?" Pindlebryth carped. He glanced at the door angrily, then at Grefdel and Darothien. Perhaps he expected sympathy, but he received none. Grefdel remained stock still. Darothien meandered along the walls, inspecting the amount each constituent block jutted out or recessed into the overall surface. In addition, she meticulously checked the inlaid diagram on every block, and made additional notations in her notebook. Occasionally, she flipped pages back and forth and crossed the hall to inspect a block in a different section. She stopped to look behind a sculpture then behind a nearby painting.

Pindlebryth took a respite from his pointless exercise, and walked over to Darothien. As she wrote, he marveled that her paw, so badly burned the night before, bore no scar and the fur between the pads was only slightly discolored.

"What are you looking at?" Pindlebryth asked, as he glanced

over her shoulder into her notebook.

"Hmm?" she mumbled, lost in thought. "Oh! Just toying with an idea I had while going through Henejer's documents last night. I couldn't help wondering if he had hidden some pattern or code in the blocks – which ones jut out, which ones are pushed in, or maybe there's something in the symbols carved in the block faces. Some have carvings of animals – beasts and people – others of tools, plants, bodies of water, constellations, and so on. They run the gamut from the most serene mathematical and geometric shapes, all the way to mundane everyday objects." She pointed at one behind a statue, chuckling, "That one is of a bucket and mop, for goodness' sake!"

"But what does it mean? What is its purpose?" Pindlebryth puzzled.

Darothien sighed with determination, "I don't know – yet." She took a step to the side, then back. She scanned up and down along the wall's length. "The blocks are set in and out unevenly along the entire height of each wall, yet the symbols are only in blocks that we can reach." She sighed again, but in exasperation. "Maybe they were meant for a blind person!"

Darothien and Pindlebryth turned as the southern doors opened.

"At last!" Pindlebryth whispered severely, as two of Wenteberei's attendants entered. They were all smiles, each holding the wingtip of a young gosling between them. They playfully swung his wings back and forth as they walked, almost skipping along. The gosling, dressed in a simple yellow jacket with tan trim, made a strange hacking sound, as if he had no voice but still was doing the closest he could manage to laughter.

"Unkaar!" Darothien erupted, as she walked hastily towards him. She held her paw in front of her mouth, thumb touching fingers. She then opened and closed them several times, as if she were working a puppet. Unkaar let go of the maidens' hands and rushed to her, and coughed excitedly as he ran. He wrapped his wings about her, embracing her legs. Darothien slipped her notebook into her sleeve, and patted his back ever so gently.

Pindlebryth approached the pair. As he did so, Unkaar released Darothien, and took several steps back. He stopped hacking, and his eyes had the look of uncertainty bordering on fearfulness. The maidens caught up to Unkaar, who immediately hid behind one of them and peered at Pindlebryth.

"I'm sorry, M'Lord," the maid explained, "but Unkaar does not handle new acquaintances all that easily."

"Per-haps if you do this?" Darothien said calmly and rhythmically as she held her thumb and fingers in front of her face as before. "Remember, he's deaf and dumb. Apparently, those around him use this as a way to greet him."

Pindlebryth mimicked the gesture. Afterwards, he made to smile and wave, but he stopped himself, reasoning that an otherwise innocent gesture might be misconstrued by this mute Snow Goose. Unkaar saw the greeting, and took a halting step out from behind the maid, nodded his head and hacked. Even so, he stayed behind the maid and eyed Pindlebryth cautiously, his neck snaked into the shape of a question mark.

"He seems to trust you much more than me, Darothien."

"Tabarem and I had met him here in Henejer Hall, when he was lost during his first visit to the castle. Since then, I have from time to time entertained him with Queen Wenteberei by casting some small charms and glamors. Like this!"

She held out her nearly completely healed paw, and blew a word into it that sounded to those around her like a loosely strung drumhead. A dot of green flashed into existence on her palm, and grew to the size of a plum. She closed her hand around it, and tossed it onto the floor towards Unkaar. It bounced with the same light thrumming, and arced over his head. Unkaar coughed with delight, flapped his wings once and caught the translucent green ball a foot in the air. As he clapped his wings together, the ball popped into a shower of emerald sparks all about him. He collapsed on the floor, hacking with innocent glee, rolling in the sparks as they bounced and extinguished themselves.

Under different circumstances, Pindlebryth might have enjoyed such a display. But he was determined to remain focused on the immediate task. "How shall we begin?" he said flatly.

"We need Unkaar to find something," Darothien addressed the handmaids with a note of apology. "Can he do that, when you want?"

"Oh yes!" the second maid giggled. "We play 'hide-and-go-seek' with Master Unkaar all the time! It's one of his favorites. He's not old enough to realize it's his Gift, so he thinks it's just a game he excels at."

"But how do you ask him?" Pindlebryth inquired.

"Like this! We –"

"No. Do not show us," he interrupted firmly. "Tell us."

The maids looked troubled, but complied. The first one began, "We cover our eyes, then uncover them as we show Master Unkaar the item we will hide. He'll cover his own eyes, while we hide it. But watch him – sometimes he peeks! As if he needs to! We tap his shoulder when we're ready and have hidden the object."

The other handmaid jumped in as she remembered one last detail. "Oh! He'll expect a treat when you're done playing."

"Excellent!" Darothien replied. "Tell you what. Go fetch a treat or two for Unkaar, while we play 'hide-and-go-seek' with him. We'll only be a few minutes."

The two shared a concerned glance between themselves, until Pindlebryth reassured them, albeit with a tinge of sarcasm. "Don't worry, he's safe from the Big Bad Prince!" Darothien took Unkaar by the wing, and the maids scurried out the east door. As they turned towards the kitchens, they discussed what treat would be best for Unkaar this time of day. Grefdel quietly closed the doors behind them.

"Swift thinking, keeping them from knowing what we're looking for," Pindlebryth remarked. "Now, how to proceed? We can't show him what we're looking for if we don't have it."

"Ah, but we can," Darothien said as she retrieved her notebook. She opened it to the page where she sketched Gazelikus' Cloth.

Darothien knelt down to Unkaar's height, and covered her eyes with one hand. She snatched away her paw, and flashed a pair of happy eyes at Unkaar. Unkaar hacked as he nodded his head vigorously, and Darothien showed him the book with one hand, while tapping the drawing with the other. Unkaar looked at the drawing, and tilted his head.

Pindlebryth wasn't sure if Unkaar was either studying the picture, or if the mute gosling had simply never seen a book before.

Darothien closed the book, and pointed at Unkaar. He put his wings over his eyes, and when Darothien was satisfied he wasn't peeking, she slipped the book back in her sleeve, stood up and tapped him on the shoulder.

Unkaar craned his neck around, searching while standing still. In the scantest of moments, he looked directly and intently at Darothien's green duvetyn sleeve, and pecked at it. The notebook slid out, and fell on the floor with a slap. Unkaar flapped his wings once, and immediately folded them at his sides. He peered strangely at Darothien, accusing her of being too obvious.

"Un-unh," Darothien said while she shook her head exaggeratedly. She stood up, and deliberated how to instruct Unkaar to substitute a drawing for an actual item.

Pindlebryth snapped his fingers. "Do you have a drawing of the Talking Gem?"

Darothien's eyes lit up immediately as she discerned Pindlebryth's intent. She picked up the notebook, and flipped past several earlier pages, until she found her initial sketches of the gem. Pindlebryth took the Talking Gem out of his breast pocket, glad that he never broke that particular habit. Darothien showed the book and its drawing to Unkaar, who at first seemed bored or uninterested. But Darothien knelt down again to meet him at eye level, and looked at him imploringly.

Unkaar finally acquiesced, and followed where Darothien pointed, and examined the drawing of the Gem. She then pointed to Pindlebryth, who held the Gem out directly in front of himself for Unkaar to see. Darothien repeated pointing alternately between the drawing and the Gem, until she believed Unkaar might understand.

"Put your Gem back, M'Lord," Darothien instructed, not taking her eyes off of Unkaar. She returned to the drawing of Gazelikus' Cloth, and pointed to it as Unkaar watched. She stood up and moved her finger to point in a wide sweeping motion over the entire hall.

Unkaar coughed in excitement, as he understood how to play this new game. Once more, he stood quietly and still, craning his neck and swiveling his head to look over the entire expanse of the hall.

He walked to and fro for a full minute along half the length of the hall, making not a single sound save for the slapping of his webbed feet on the stone floor. He moved calmly and deliberately, periodically looking behind paintings, or snaking his neck around busts on pedestals. He passed a bust of a very young Henejer, and approached a painting on the north wall. He halted in front of the portrait of Enorel III hanging from a block protruding between the northwest corner and the first unshuttered window. He angled his head to one side, then spread wide his wings as if to take flight. He hacked loudly, then began to peck at the painting. Flecks of dried oil pigment flew as he threatened to bore a hole into the canvas.

Grefdel hesitated only for a moment, not expecting an act that would damage the treasures of the gallery. He dashed to the painting, as Darothien protested.

"No! Don't frighten him!"

Instead, Grefdel grabbed the painting's frame and swiveled it up and away from Unkaar. The gosling dodged the moving canvas, and resumed pecking on a block inscribed with a sewing needle and bobbin.

"That must be it!" Darothien exclaimed.

Pindlebryth raced to Grefdel's side, and assisted standing the portrait gently on the floor, leaning it in the corner so as not to tear or puncture the canvas on other blocks. The two then set to testing the block Unkaar had selected. Unkaar hacked and flapped back in a panic, and hid behind Darothien. Darothien patted him consolingly on the head and the shoulders, and he soon calmed down again.

"Careful!" admonished Pindlebryth. "Henejer used neither pointing nor mortar in this hall interior, the tolerances are that exact. So let us not be overly hasty, lest we bring the whole hall down about our heads!"

Grefdel and Pindlebryth alternately tried to shift the block from its position. Gently at first, then with increasing effort – up, down, left and right, in and out. The block refused to budge. Darothien produced her prism from her other sleeve, and examined the block.

"I don't understand. It's just like when I examined this hall with my prism a year ago. Not a whiff of magick! Not on the block, nor behind it, that I can see." She took out her convex lens and reexamined the block with that device also, but to no avail.

A rapid tapping behind them caught Pindlebryth's attention. "Look! Unkaar's onto something."

The gosling waddled slowly with his head down to the

ground, pecking each tile in the floor as he came upon it. Occasionally he would stop and look closely at the tile below him, then to its neighbors as if he were trying to decide something. But each time, he haltingly resumed his plodding towards the opposite wall. The three Lemmings breathlessly watched Unkaar as he finally obtained the opposite wall and looked at the blocks with insignia before him. A moment passed, and Unkaar pecked rapidly on a block nearly out reach for his height.

The group dashed madly to Unkaar's side, and looked at the block's inscription – an inlaid miniature rough map of the Northern Lands. Darothien pulled Unkaar to the side, praising and preening him again. Unkaar, unlike when he found the first block, was not silent. This time he coughed happily in rapid succession, flapping his wings in joyful success. The group said nothing, but Grefdel and Pindlebryth set again to testing this block. With several tries it obstinately remained immobile – until it finally pushed in a single inch.

A series of sounds, the grinding of smooth rock against rock, the metallic clank of locks and levers, resounded inside the walls and under the floors. Pindlebryth tried to anticipate where the sound was leading, but the echoes of each new sound seemed to come from no direction, and every direction simultaneously. The series of sounds terminated with a loud thud of metal on stone from the south wall, and finally the sound of stone sliding against stone as an irregular panel of several jutting and recessed blocks flattened themselves into a contiguous surface, and slowly lowered into the floor.

"A mad genius," whispered Grefdel in awe.

"How in the world did he do this by himself?" Pindlebryth gasped.

Unkaar began to cough rapidly, and started to sway side to side. He was becoming impatient for his treat. Darothien tried to assuage him, but met with only limited success.

The wall stopped at floor level, revealing a small cubicle. In it was a simple stone pedestal, upon which lay several sheets of oddly shaped parchment paper. Pindlebryth gingerly picked them up, afraid they might crumble at his touch. But they were as firm and as crisp as any newly written document. He slowly leafed through them, and a look of confusion and disappointed consternation came over him.

"What is this?" he asked rhetorically. The sheets were maps of the various cantons of Lenland, each drawn on a unique shape of parchment. One sheet was trapezoidal, another an oval, another an asymmetrical rhomboid, and so on. "What is this!" he ranted again, as he thrust the papers toward Darothien and Unkaar.

Unkaar hacked once and hid again behind Darothien. A rapping came from the east door.

"Oh, for pity's sake, let them in. There's nothing of worth to see here," Pindlebryth groused. He made to dash the papers on the floor, but thought better of it. Instead he simply sighed as he lowered his arm, and his shoulders sagged in defeat. Grefdel jogged to the east doors, and opened them to admit the maids. One of them carried small dishes of little treats and candies, while the other greeted Unkaar with her paw opening and closing in front of her mouth.

"Come, Unkaar. You've earned this – you've had a rough day!" said Darothien as she led Unkaar to meet the handmaidens. She looked back at Pindlebryth sternly, upset with him for frightening Unkaar. But Unkaar quickly forgot his dismay. He coughed happily as he tucked into the sweetened paste of seeds, nuts and millet wrapped and baked in crisp young reeds. Darothien thanked the handmaidens and gave Unkaar one last hug, as Grefdel escorted them all out of the hall and closed the doors.

Pindlebryth, however, felt like the world had darkened about him appreciably as he abjectly leaned against the wall next to the cubicle. Thoroughly despondent and demoralized, he felt the specter of utter and abysmal failure revolve around him, mocking him. All of his hopes – to find the Orb, to save his brother, to stop the Iron Baron – that hung on this last piece of the puzzle lay about him ruins, scribed upon pointless pieces of paper.

He pushed away from the wall, absorbed in his own crumbling world as he shambled towards the center of the hall. He was entirely oblivious to the fact he was weeping; that he had dropped the sheets of parchment as he tottered away from the wall; that Darothien was walking beside him, desperately calling his name.

Until he felt an itch run up and down his spine.

"Pindlebryth! What's wrong? Are you all right?" pleaded

Darothien.

"Darothien!" Pindlebryth shouted as he grasped Darothien by the shoulders. "That hidden passage of text – the palimpsest! From the archives!" He shook his head as if to shake a memory loose. "What was it? What *was* it! The writing that Gazelikus had obfuscated! What did it say? 'To set the world aright...' "

Darothien's eyes glinted with recollection. " '...you must turn my world upside down.' But what...?"

"Yes!" Pindlebryth exploded, as he turned and raced back to the second key block. He grasped the block like one possessed, and pulled with all his might. The block slid smoothly back into its original position with a click. Pindlebryth looked over at the cubicle as it began to close and resume its original shape. It sealed itself as cleanly as if it had never moved, and its blocks resumed their seemingly random protrusions.

Pindlebryth then grabbed the corners of the block and tried to twist it. It failed to move in the slightest. He grunted with reckless abandon as he tried to force it – and Lords Below take him if the hall collapsed! He tried one last time, but was thwarted by the obstinate stone. Panting from the exertion, Pindlebryth glared furiously at the block as if he could somehow bend it to his will. Then he took the block one last time, but by the sides. He pulled on the block gently, then ever so more forcefully. When his arms felt like they would pull out of their sockets, the stone finally gave way with a firm click and pulled out an inch, to reveal a recessed seam along all four sides of the block.

With bated breath, he grabbed the corners of the outermost part of the block and twisted. It now easily spun around a full half circle, until the map inscribed on the block was upside down. Pindlebryth pushed the block back into place with a resounding click, then pushed further in.

Again a series of grinding and clanking sounds reverberated throughout the hall, culminating in a section of the north wall, including the inlaid insignia of the sewing needle and bobbin, reshaping itself and lowering itself into the floor.

Eyes wide with anticipation, Pindlebryth ran to the newly uncovered cubicle. He stood staring, and trembling in excitement as Darothien rushed also to his side.

In the cubicle stood two pedestals. One had a square surface, almost fully occupied by a large oddly shaped indentation, with three tiny diamond-shaped flattened nibs of leaded crystal near the pedestal's center.

On the other lay the Cloth of Gazelikus.

Made of a glistening royal purple material, it was embroidered around all its edges with gold lettering. The material was unique in that is looked like satin or velvet, but had a pattern embossed into it not unlike the scales of a serpent. Pindlebryth and Darothien instantly recognized the glyphs that encircled it as magickal including a smattering of the impenetrable tongue that was inscribed in Selephylin's five broken rings.

With a whoop of victory, Pindlebryth picked Darothien up by the waist, and spun her around himself. He laughed as though he had never laughed before, and set Darothien down gently. Darothien squealed with surprise, and began to laugh with her prince. He embraced her fervently and pressed his muzzle against hers. He purred for just a moment, then broke out into infectious laughter again. He was still weeping, but with tears of joy, and of utter relief.

The two of them leaned on each other, still hugging until Pindlebryth happened to glance up and spy Grefdel standing a few paces away. The guard stood simply with his hands clasped in front of him, his head tilted slightly and graced by a whimsical smile. Pindlebryth snorted an embarrassed snigger, and broke into another cascade of unbridled mirth.

They quickly calmed down as Grefdel approached the cubicle, and stuck in his head to more closely investigate the enclosure. He looked up at Pindlebryth, then over where the first cubicle was.

"Pardon me, M'Lord," he said as he hurried over to the south side of the hall, and collected the parchment Pindlebryth had dropped. Darothien quickly insinuated herself into the cubicle opening, and pulled out her prism.

"Lord's Above, the magick is almost blinding!" she blurted in disbelief as she squinted through the tsavorite crystal. "How did it remain hidden?" She turned the prism on the surroundings of the cubicle and gasped. "It's black! It's totally black."

Pindlebryth looked at the cubicle with curiosity. To him it

seemed ordinary stone, exactly like all the walls of the gallery. Darothien touched the surface of the cubicle, hesitantly at first, then steadily as she ran her fingers down one of its walls. "I don't know how Gazelikus did it. It absorbs all magickal emanations. No wonder I could never find it!"

She lowered the prism, and stared at the cloth with trepidation. She cautiously inched her paw towards the cloth to touch it. Pindlebryth grabbed her wrist moments before she could reach the pedestal.

"No, let *me*. If it does anything, you'd be the best able to counter its effects." He slowly reached in, until his paw was directly over the cloth. He held his breath, and grasped the cloth firmly. By instinct, he leaned his head away from the cubicle, and closed his eye closest to the cloth.

But nothing happened. He still held his one eye shut as he withdrew the cloth from the cubicle. It felt strange, almost like skin, as he held it in front of him. He cautiously held the cloth up in both hands by two corners to inspect it, and flipped it over.

"Ah!" exclaimed Darothien, her prism fairly glued to her eye. "The other side is black, too! Just like the cubicle." Again, Pindlebryth looked at the cloth with wonder, as both sides seemed the same shade of purple.

"It seems... harmless," Pindlebryth ventured as he opened his eye.

"Wait a tick," Darothien muttered. She slipped the prism into her sleeve and retrieved her notebook again. She flipped through the pages until she came to her notes on the five rings. Glancing rapidly between her scribblings, and the gold embroidered letters, she uttered a few unintelligible syllables to herself. A wide-eyed Pindlebryth momentarily stiffened, expecting Darothien to cast some magick on the cloth while he still held it. He relaxed as he almost immediately realized that it was just ordinary mumbling, not the strange speech of wizards.

"Ah! Quickly! Bring Gazelikus' Cloth to my laboratory!" Darothien clapped the notebook shut, turned and ran down the hall. Grefdel heaved open the great door as she dashed through the opening. Her voice echoed as she disappeared around the door, "M'Lord! Quickly, I say!"

Pindlebryth snapped out of his distracted state, and ran

after her, the cloth bunched lightly in his hand. He managed to catch up to Darothien just as she well-nigh skipped down the steps. She threw open the door, and circled around the table in the center of the outer room. The wolf statuette howled a greeting, wagged its tail once, and panted with its tongue lolled out to the side. She shouldered open the door to the laboratory, and Pindlebryth followed. The wolf whimpered loudly as Pindlebryth passed holding Gazelikus' Cloth, its head hung down low between its shoulders and tail curled under its haunches as it backed into the pedestal corner farthest from the cloth.

Darothien hastily moved a rack of glass tubes and a nested set of iron tripods to the side of the large table. She began to frantically search behind a workbench on which sat Selephylin's Crown and its cap piece on opposite ends, a set of baskets filled with various apparatus, each for a function Pindlebryth couldn't fathom in the slightest, and a side table piled with large crystals of various minerals. She finally looked behind a slate board half her size, when she exclaimed with satisfaction, and pulled out a thin rectangular metal plate. She set it on the place she had just cleared on the table.

"Set the cloth here, and flatten it out with the letters facing up," she absent-mindedly commanded, as she pulled out her prism and lens. Pindlebryth did as she asked, but making sure he did not touch the lettering as he flattened the cloth.

Darothien placed her crystalline tools and open notebook next to the plate, and began delving thru the baskets of arcane contraptions. She had placed one or two of them on the other side of the plate, when she paused. She looked at Pindlebryth, almost as if she were surprised that he was still there.

"Oh, Pindlebryth!" she burbled, as she hugged him firmly. She held him thus for a few moments, then began to gently push him towards the laboratory door. "There is something I *must* try! If it works..." She stammered, as if she wasn't sure how to complete her thought.

"What is it you are planning to do?" Pindlebryth asked with an incredulous frown.

"I... I don't want to say." She squeezed her eyes shut, waving her hand back and forth in front of her, like she was erasing the writing on a slate. "I don't want to raise any hopes unnecessarily. But the benefits! I myself dare not even hope!"

She urged Pindlebryth out the door, until he was standing next to the panting wolf.

"Give me an hour or two, and we shall see." She put her paw on the door latch, and was about to close it when she turned back to Pindlebryth. "On second thought, there *is* one thing you could do."

"What's that?"

"Wish me luck!" she tittered, as she pecked her muzzle against his. Pindlebryth was left standing dumbly, staring at the grain of the wood inches from his face, after she closed the laboratory door with a resounding thud and the muffled clank of the latch.

When Pindlebryth climbed the stairs from the outer room to the ground floor, Grefdel was running up the hall to him.

"I've alerted Colonel Farthun, and he's sealed off Henejer Hall. What do you want to do now, M'Lord?"

"We wait," he replied as he shrugged his shoulders, and looked behind him.

"Maybe, maybe not," Grefdel proffered. "There's something else in Henejer Hall you should see." The two Lemmings double-timed it to their destination, and passed two new guards stationed outside the hall's closed doors. Grefdel hauled open the nearest ceiling-high door, to find Colonel Farthun and King Hatheron inspecting the cubicle. In a folder, Farthun held the sheets of parchment which were precariously in danger of spilling out onto the floor, as he was fixated by the mystery of the cubicle's workings.

A flurry of activity clattered outside, as pairs of guards could be seen closing the shutters on the northern wall's windows. The ambient light quickly diminished, save for the angled sunlight through the stained glass high above on the southern wall, and four lanterns newly hung on either side of the east and west doors.

As Pindlebryth approached behind his father and Farthun, Grefdel grabbed the folder Farthun held angled carelessly at his hip.

"Excuse me Colonel. M'Lord requires this," Grefdel said perfunctorily. He opened the folder, and thumbed through the sheets of parchment. He stopped and pulled out the trapezoidal sheet, and handed the map to Pindlebryth. "It matches the pedestal."

Pindlebryth's eyes widened at Grefdel's revelation. He held the translucent sheet in front of him, and easily discerned the canton from the map drawn on it. It was the central northern canton from which Farthun's batman Gangon hailed. While the map contained neither writing nor legend, there were various examples of that canton's notable geographical features sketched within the border of the canton – rivers and lakes, mountain ranges, forests and the like.

Pindlebryth slowly stepped towards the pedestal, and the other Lemmings made way for him. He bent over to peer into the cubicle and the top of the pedestal. Looking over the edge of the parchment, he saw the recessed shape was indeed a trapezoid that matched the parchment's outline exactly.

He reverently pressed the parchment into the open form. Through the translucent sheet, he could see the diamond shapes made by the triad of leaded crystal nibs – one each of gray, green and red. It lay under a drawing of a group of mountains that were taller than they were wide.

"Lords Above!" Pindlebryth gasped, not half daring to believe. "The Orb is in the Valley of Giants!" For a heartbeat, not a solitary sound was heard, as if all the air were sucked out of the room.

"Of course!" Pindlebryth shouted. What better place for the master architect and mason to secret away his most prized and dangerous possession? Remote and forbidding, the granite megaliths of that valley were the perfect medium for Henejer's genius.

He started to stand erect in his excitement, but stopped short of whacking his head against the top of the cubicle. He glanced up at the surface of the cubicle above his head and froze.

Inscribed with large block letters, was written the phrase, "I asked the stone to forget."

"Darothien, what do you make of this? Here's another item from the archives," Pindlebryth blurted, before he remembered she was not there. He stood up, and Farthun and Hatheron took his place to view the inscription. They both muttered to themselves, shaking their heads.

Pindlebryth collected the parchment, and took the folder from Grefdel. He ordered it with the other sheets neatly in the folder, pondering their contents. "Now that we alone know where to look, we must hide these again."

Farthun stood up and seized the folder with both hands, turning towards Hatheron. "Your instructions, Your Majesty?"

Hatheron nodded to him, saying, "Take it to the Vestment Room. I'll meet you there presently, and we'll lock it away."

"Begging your pardon, father," Pindlebryth interjected, somewhat affronted by Farthun's actions and subsequent deferral to his father. He motioned back to the southern wall where the first cubicle had opened. "Why don't we just return it to where we found it? It was safe enough there for centuries."

"If Selephygur was correct in his intimation that we still may have a spy, it's safer in a place where he would have to get past the entire Royal Guard," Hatheron explained. "It would draw undue attention if we had a guard detail in this hall for any extended period of time, without a viable public reason."

Both Pindlebryth and Farthun nodded in agreement with Hatheron's logic. Farthun bowed with a functional "Your Majesty," and left, clutching the folder tightly to his side.

"Have the guards assist you, Pindlebryth. Leave this hall as you found it – everything closed, everything hung in its place."

Hatheron leaned against the wall above the cubicle, peering down onto the pedestal one last time. "You are *sure* that's where the Orb is?" Hatheron demanded of Pindlebryth, intently fixing him in a stare.

Pindlebryth searched himself, and finding no itch, no intuitive nay-saying, he responded, "I'm positive." He paused in thought for a moment, then made a request of his father.

"I want to take a small party to the Valley, consisting of myself, Darothien, and the three guards I trust with my life – Pendenar, Grefdel here, and Jarjin. Tell Colonel Farthun I need Pendenar off of his current duty immediately. I want to leave within, say, two hours."

"How does this help Selephygur?" Hatheron said, as his stare softened again into that of a worried father.

"I am not sure." Pindlebryth said sadly. "In fact, once the Iron Baron learns we have prevented him from obtaining the Orb, he may exact an even more terrible retribution on poor Selephygur."

Hatheron hung his head, and rubbed his forehead slowly. He sighed with a trembling voice – painfully exhausting his lungs until it ended almost in a whimper. He inhaled sharply and with determination, standing upright and overflowing with resolve. "If he and the Kyaa harm my son further, it will be *war*," he growled.

Hatheron stormed off through the east doors, leaving a slack-jawed Pindlebryth looking after.

"War," Pindlebryth echoed in an apprehensive whisper. He quickly shivered himself out of his state of surprise, and said to an equally shocked Grefdel, "Back to Darothien's workplace! She needs to prepare for travel."

The pair tramped back down the main hall of the East Wing, and down the stairs to the laboratory. Pindlebryth stepped quickly down, but Grefdel tread carefully, fooled yet once again by the steps that looked slick with dampness but were in fact deceptively powder dry.

The wolf statuette bounded to life as Pindlebryth entered the outer room. He stopped halfway across the room, as the wolf jumped off its pedestal. To Pindlebryth's surprise, it doubled in size as it padded onto the floor. It sat in front of the laboratory entrance and cocked its head, whimpering as it held Pindlebryth in its predatory stare. Pindlebryth cautiously took a step towards it, then another. When he was within arm's reach of the door, the wolf stood up on all fours, and riveted Pindlebryth with its eyes. It started to pace back and forth, closer and closer to Pindlebryth. It did not growl, but it did force him back, shepherding him towards the outer door.

Grefdel came through the door, and uttered in surprise, "What the...?" But he didn't finish the question.

The wolf's hackles rose, as it growled and snapped in this newest intruder's direction. The stone beast redoubled in size, snarling at Grefdel with slavering malice. It pushed Pindlebryth back as it padded menacingly towards the guard. Grefdel instinctively began to draw the sword slung to his belt.

"No!" Pindlebryth commanded firmly. He splayed his paws in front of him, signaling Grefdel to stop. "Just back out!" he barked. More calmly, he continued, "Back the way you came. It knows me, and won't harm me. Just leave – I'll be right behind you!"

Grefdel cautiously slid the hilt of his sword back into its scabbard, and stepped backwards out the doorway, never taking his eyes off the wolf golem. Once Grefdel exited the door's threshold, the wolf shrank to its middling size, and plopped itself in front of Pindlebryth. It grunted at Pindlebryth with a finality accented by its intent and unblinking stare.

Pindlebryth stepped back out of the room, and watched the wolf shrink back to its original size, and leap back onto its pedestal, where it whimpered once, then froze into its usual sitting position. He shook his head, half in wonder, half in relief, as he climbed back up the stairs.

"Maybe we'll leave in three hours?" Pindlebryth quipped.

Three hours came and went.

Beginning at the top of the second hour, when the clock in the CityState square chimed, Pindlebryth visited the laboratory, only to be greeted by the friendly but adamant wolf. Between the second and third hours, he met with Jarjin, Grefdel, and Pendenar, who still had the bouquet of the stable about him. In his quarters, Pindlebryth discussed his plans to launch a recovery party to the Valley of Giants. After nearly a full hour, they agreed that they needed to take several days' provisions for their party of five. They enumerated all their requirements for an extended bivouac – food, gear and weapons, tools, tents and bags to protect them and their mounts during the colder nights of the northern canton. When the bell tolled the third time, Pindlebryth set them about their tasks. Before he left his apartment in the South Wing to revisit the laboratory, he opened a window and gave one additional order to Pendenar.

"Take another bath! If the Fox or Crow are waiting for us, they'll smell you long before we arrive!"

When the CityState square's clock chimed the fourth time, Pindlebryth had finished his lunch, and grew restless in his quarters. He felt the sourness of resentment building, but after a moment he found he could not harbor such a feeling against Darothien for long. His feelings for her notwithstanding, he also reasoned that Darothien would not seclude herself away so completely unless it were absolutely necessary.

He resolved not to leave the laboratory empty handed a fourth time. Gathering the book of transcripts from BrokenTail's trial, he marched down to the laboratory. He was halfway down the stairs when he was met by a short-winded Jarjin.

"Darothien was out of the laboratory a half hour ago!" he squeaked in his tenor voice, stressed even higher from his labored breathing. "She raided the kitchens, and visited the infirmary."

"Where is she now?" demanded Pindlebryth urgently.

"No one has seen her since. I think she's locked herself in her workspace again!"

"Blast!" Pindlebryth blurted with annoyance. "What *is* that doe up to? Doesn't she know we're waiting on her?" He scrambled down the remainder of the stairs, and stamped down the East Wing main hallway with Jarjin in tow.

"What was she doing in the infirmary?" he panted as he quickened his pace.

"She floated into Selephygur's room without a word, and checked him with her prism. Trevemar said she also checked his medication table."

"Well, *that* doesn't make *any* sense!" he champed as he bounded down the laboratory stairs two at a time.

He burst through the outer door, and the wolf obediently sprang to life.

"Darothien?" Pindlebryth shouted. "Darothien!"

He stood across the table from the wolf, who grew as he leapt from his pedestal and sat in front of the laboratory door. The golem beast peered over the edge of the table at Pindlebryth, staring intently at him and Jarjin just outside the doorway. Its head bobbed from side to side, like a predator judging distance to its prey.

Pindlebryth inhaled once deeply to fully catch his breath. He then calmly placed the law book on the table, and sat down. While he held the beast's gaze, he quietly said, "You can go, Jarjin. Report back to Pendenar, and see if he needs help. I'll be fine. You can leave me here – this creature will protect me as well as any guard."

Pindlebryth opened the book and began to settle in to read the trial transcripts. As Jarjin was closing the door, Pindlebryth added with a start, "Oh, one last thing. If I'm still here by the next toll of the clock, bring me a teapot full of Pu'erh. I'm staying put until Darothien comes out!"

He glanced at the wolf, who tilted his head at him with a

soft whine. He looked about the room, to see if there was anything else to be wary of before he delved into the book. He stopped as he noticed the glass case across the table from him was disturbed. The doors were left flung open, and the contents of the case – the broken fragments of Selephylin's rings – were gone. The only thing that remained was one of the two pair of gloves that Darothien also stored in the glass cabinet. He puzzled over this for a full minute, before he rationalized that Darothien must have collected them during her recent jaunt about the castle. He shook his head, returning to the open pages before him.

Pindlebryth read the transcript of BrokenTail's trial for treason from the very beginning, and was almost halfway through, when he came across the section where the child Darothien was in the docket describing her harrowing adventure – how her father obtained the damning contract between the Iron Baron and Vulpinden, how her mother ran to draw the Baron's soldiers away, and her life in seclusion with her aunt's family. He shivered as he recalled their first day trapped together at Vulcanis, when she had told him this very story. He wondered at himself – when she first told him of these events, he listened only slightly more than dispassionately. Now he could easily envision the events as he read them. His heart ached in sympathy for his love as the pages rolled by.

The wolf howled.

Pindlebryth nearly jumped out his seat at the sound. He looked at the beast as it jumped up on all fours and turned towards the laboratory door. The door unlatched with a firm clack, and opened slowly. As the door opened, a thin cloud of blue-gray smoke wafted up under the lintel, and the outer room filled with the pungent odor of charcoal and burnt metal.

With an exhalation of vindication, Darothien emerged with a small box. She closed the door behind her as the wolf panted several times. She patted the golem on the head, and it yipped gleefully as it shrank and jumped back on its pedestal. She turned to walk around the table, and was genuinely surprised to see Pindlebryth rising out of his chair.

"Oh! Pindlebryth!" she put a paw on her chest as he startled her. "Goodness, how long have you been there?" she said with a playful look on her face. It quickly evaporated, changing into a look of uncertainty. "How long have I been gone? Two hours already?"

"Five hours," he replied.

"Oh, dear," Darothien absently apologized.

Part of Pindlebryth tried to be angry that she locked herself away oblivious to the astounding developments in Henejer Hall, but couldn't. Another part of him tried to at least look put out, but it simply wasn't in him – the image of young Darothien bravely weathering the trial was still too fresh in his mind.

Instead, he took a few steps towards her and simply embraced her. Darothien returned the gesture as best as she could, but she still held the box in one paw.

"And what have we here?" Pindlebryth inquired as he released her, holding her slightly away, while he looked at the box with a raised eyebrow.

"A gift for Selephygur. And the sooner he has it, the better!" She disengaged, and wagged her finger at the stone wolf. "Guard!"

The statuette did not move, but Pindlebryth suspected it heard her well enough. "Where's Gazelikus' Cloth? In the box?"

"No, in the laboratory. Hurry, before Selephygur's gone! Time's wasting!"

"Indeed! I was going to say the same thing to you!" He was about to complain that he had been waiting for her since the Orb's location was uncovered, but Darothien dashed up the stairs before Pindlebryth could either complete his thought, or inquire what she meant about Selephygur. He caught up with her and they hastened towards the infirmary.

They arrived at Selephygur's room quite winded, to find Queen Wenteberei sitting next to Selephygur, lovingly stroking his forehead. He was unconscious and unshackled, but still bound in his straitjacket. The last wisps of the noxious liquid used to dose Selephygur asleep faded in the chill air trickling through the barely ajar window. Trevemar stood in the corner, as Hatheron stood behind his wife.

Selephygur's massive chest rose and fell placidly as Sacalitre adjusted and secured the last of the buckles on the side of the canvas garment.

"What's going on?" Pindlebryth hissed.

"We're preparing to move Selephygur," Sacalitre answered

without looking up, as he grabbed the muzzle from the side table.

"Why wasn't I told!" he demanded barely above a whisper.

Hatheron looked sadly at him. "I thought it best to tell you only after you returned. You didn't need an additional distraction."

"No, wait!" Darothien insisted. She placed a paw on Sacalitre's shoulder and stated in a voice somewhere betwixt a question and a command, "I have something to help, if you please?"

She leaned over Selephygur's head, and removed his eyepatch. She opened the box, to reveal three small spheres. The one in the center was Selephygur's obsidian eye. On either side of it were silver spheres of the same size. Each was covered with several lines of glyphs, crisscrossing each other several times at odd angles over the entire surface of the miniature orbs. She extricated one of the silvered curiosities from its hemispherical recess in the box, and held it for a moment above Selephygur's head.

All eyes were fixed on the sphere, and all voices gasped as Darothien suddenly forced the sphere into Selephygur's empty socket. Trevemar jumped forward to restrain Darothien from behind, but was halted when Pindlebryth shouted, "Touch her, Trevemar, and so help me, I'll skin you alive!" The look on Trevemar's face was inscrutable, as he couldn't decide if he took the threat seriously.

Darothien firmly worked the orb into place, then gently turned the orb one final time. She took out her prism, nodded with satisfaction at her work, stood erect and took a step back.

"Doctor," Darothien said without taking her eyes off of the young prince. "If you please, wake up Prince Selephygur now." She closed the box, and laid it by his pillow. She slipped her paw into the opposite sleeve, returning the prism and partially withdrawing her wand. All the while, she remained focused on Selephygur as intently as she might a wild animal.

Sacalitre looked dubiously at Hatheron and Wenteberei. After a moment, the queen stood next to her husband and they held each other. They looked at Selephygur, then regarded the glaring Pindlebryth, and nodded in agreement. "Do as she asks," Hatheron commanded.

The physician delved into one of his side pockets with his

paw, and produced a small vial filled with thin paper packets. "Close the window," he requested of Trevemar. He removed one of the packets, and broke it in half. He placed it under Selephygur's snout, and waved it back and forth. The tang of ammonia smelling salts filled the room. Selephygur continued to breathe peacefully several times, then began to cough and snort. He gagged and rocked his head back and forth, instinctively trying to get away from the pungent stench. Sacalitre followed Selephygur's snout, keeping the packet directly under his nose.

Selephygur's eyelids snapped open. A look of utter confusion washed over his countenance, as he looked at all the faces about him.

"What are you doing?" he snorted with a slur, complaining bitterly. "You have to get me out of here!" He rocked back and forth, and might have fallen out of his bed, had Sacalitre not tried to hold him in place as best as a Lemming of his slight build could.

"Shh," admonished Darothien. "It's all right. All right. Calm down. Peace, my Prince," she warbled in soothing tones as she stroked his black mane and blond stripes. Selephygur lay still and turned his head towards her, but regarded her with a look of fear – not of her, but for her sake.

"Selephygur. Do as I ask." She smiled pleasantly at her old pupil. "Do you trust me?"

"Yes," Selephygur replied slowly, still unsure of what was happening.

"All right. Take a deep breath, and try to see. Try to *see* with the Lens."

"But – BrokenTail will know! He'll take over as soon as he feels me there!"

"Then *let* him!" Darothien replied darkly and loudly, as she gripped her wand firmly and intentionally revealed more of it to Selephygur. "I want to tell the cad something directly!" she growled, displaying a grin filled with gnashing teeth.

Selephygur beheld her curiously, and said in a slow cadence, "I... trust you." He slowly closed his eyes, and exhaled a long and steady breath. His head worked back and forth while it still rested on the pillow. Underneath the eyelid, the bump of his cornea flitted to and fro. His brow furrowed, and he seemed to squint even with his eyes fully shut. He squeezed his eyes shut so hard, that his brow almost touched his cheekbone.

Then his eyelids snapped open again.

"Nothing!" Selephygur was overcome with authentic and transparent shock. "I can't *see* anything!" He closed his eyes again and held his breath. The room was deathly silent. Selephygur released his breath, and exploded, "He's gone! Quickening Spirit, he's *gone!*" He laughed nervously in a single blasting guffaw of disbelief.

"Darothien! Darothien! What did you do? He's gone! I... wait." Selephygur blinked once, then twice. "What is this? What's in my eye?"

Darothien picked up the box, and opened it showing its remaining contents to Selephygur. "I placed one of these in your eye socket," she replied, pointing to the second silvered sphere. "These will stop the Lens. You cannot see through it anymore. BrokenTail cannot influence you.

"You are free from him." Darothien patted his head, as she often did when she tutored him as a pup. "You are free from the Lens, as long as you keep one of these in your head."

Selephygur exhaled with exhaustion, and his eyelids fluttered closed. A weak but grateful smile grew on his lips, as one might when suddenly cured of a chronic debilitating pain.

"Is it true? My baby is safe?" Wenteberei whispered, asking no one in particular, not quite believing what transpired before her.

"This nightmare is over?" intoned Hatheron softly. "My son is... is whole again?"

"Yes," Darothien replied with tired eyes, as she slipped her wand back into her sleeve. "It is as I said. As long as Selephygur wears one of these spheres, the Lens has no hold on him."

Wenteberei blurted out an unintelligible sound, that was something between a laugh and sob wracked with pain, then embraced Darothien wholeheartedly. "Bless you, my dear! Thank you for giving me my son back!" Darothien held her lightly in return, patting her back twice slowly. "I don't know how I'll ever repay you!" Wenteberei effused, as she collapsed back in her chair.

"But why two of them?" Trevemar asked from his corner. Unseen by all in the room, he had drawn his saber. He slid it back in its scabbard as he posed his question.

"Because glass eyes need to be cleaned regularly," Sacalitre replied snidely. "He wears one while the other is cleaned." He looked up at Darothien and winked at her. "Clever child!" he murmured.

"High praise indeed," remarked Pindlebryth.

"I know we'd all like to end this moment happily," the physician resumed entirely ignoring Pindlebryth's barb, "but I would like to keep M'Lord in bed – as is – one more day for observation."

"That would be prudent," Hatheron agreed. "I think Selephygur and..."

Selephygur began to snore quietly, as Wenteberei rolled up a blanket over him.

"...and Duke Trevemar would agree."

The duke nodded in agreement.

"All right," said Sacalitre firmly, yet in a whisper as he made a scooping motion with his arms. "Every one leave my patient be. This is the first time I've seen him rest naturally." He swept the air a second time. "Everybody out!" he hissed, like a librarian enforcing order in his domain.

Hatheron bent down to nuzzle his wife on the cheek, then also tried to herd everyone else out. Trevemar held up his paw to decline, satisfied to stand quietly in his dark corner. Wenteberei kissed Selephygur's forehead, then leaned back in her chair, sobbing quietly to herself with gratitude. Hatheron left with Pindlebryth, Darothien and a guard who positioned himself just outside Selephygur's door.

As soon as they were outside the infirmary, Hatheron asked, "How was this done, Darothien?" He seemed slightly taller, as if a crushing weight were finally removed from his shoulders.

"Something in common with Gazelikus' Cloth and Selephylin's rings... the Mother Tongue, I'd guess?" Pindlebryth speculated.

Hatheron scowled in thought, trying to comprehend what his son meant.

"Quite!" Darothien affirmed. "Gazelikus had woven in his Cloth a spell that could shield against magickal emanations, even those of Artifacts. From the very first time that I laid eyes upon the drawing in DeepDigger's book, I had the idea to compare the actual cloth's glyphs against those in Selephylin's rings. Peppered amongst Gazelikus' magick letters and eldritch symbols were some of the same glyphs of the unknown tongue as we found on the rings. The ones on the cloth specifically involved the Orb of Oblivion. I substituted those glyphs with those other petroglyphs we knew corresponded to the Lens of Truth. I adjusted the inequities and counterbalances in Gazelikus' original spell, wove in new auspices to combine..."

Darothien halted in mid-sentence, as she realized that she had totally lost Hatheron, and that Pindlebryth also showed difficulty in following her explanation. She cleared her throat, and began again as if she were still tutoring Selephygur. "I changed Gazelikus' original spell to block the effect of the Lens. I smelted two eyes of silver and aluminum alloy, and inscribed the new spell on them."

"How did it manage to help Selephygur? I thought magick did not affect those with Names," Pindlebryth postulated.

"There are two reasons. First of all, Gazelikus' original spell on the cloth is by no means a lesser magick. Secondly, my version of the spell is on the spheres – not on the young prince himself. They block the effects of the Lens, much like Gazelikus' Cloth blocks the Orb, and the cubicle hid the cloth."

"Whatever the reasoning, Darothien, your have Our gratitude for restoring Selephygur to Us," Hatheron pronounced. "The Quickening Spirit indeed was wise to bring you to us, and Graymalden to sponsor your apprenticeship."

"But now for the news while you were locked away downstairs," Pindlebryth said, looking quite anxiously at Darothien. "We know the location of the Orb. We will almost certainly need your skills to successfully retrieve it."

"You found it! Where is it?" Darothien said excitedly, her forearms raised slightly with her paws clenched in anticipation.

"But a few hours flight from here," Pindlebryth replied indirectly, his eyes flitting to and fro as if the walls had ears. "We need to leave immediately. We have prepared everything else while you were occupied with Gazelikus' Cloth." Pindlebryth looked Darothien over with concern. "Speaking of which, fetch it and bring it with us. Include any additional magick you will need to assist the search and to ward against the weather, assuming your divination of a cold wet winter is reliable." Despite Darothien's look of mock umbrage, Pindlebryth continued. "We will make a party of five. How soon can you be ready?"

"Within the hour, Pindlebryth."

"Then off with you, while we still have daylight! Meet us at the stables when you are ready, if not sooner!"

Darothien rushed off to the northeast stairs. As Pindlebryth turned to take the southeast stairs to his quarters, Hatheron remarked, "Hmm. 'Pindlebryth' and not 'M'Lord.' And my son willing to take on Duke Trevemar, as well. When did all that change, I wonder, eh?"

Pindlebryth froze at his father's words, and glanced back over his shoulder. Hatheron spun on one foot and went back into the infirmary with a curious grin.

Pindlebryth resumed walking with renewed energy, thinking to himself that he was eminently glad to be flying into potential danger. Rather that, than facing an endless barrage of questions from a curious mother.

Unfortunately, Darothien's forecast from days earlier was remarkably correct. They had left, as Darothien had promised, within the hour. But within an hour following their departure, a strong northwesterly clipper bore down on them, threatening a near-blinding blizzard.

Voyager, a snow petrel, and Pendenar's favorite mount Mariner, a roseate tern, had little trouble with the weather. In fact, the two birds of the far north seemed to revel in the building snowstorm. Grefdel's and Jarjin's shearwaters had a harder time of it, as their long tan and gray wings were better suited to calmer skies.

Before it became too difficult for them, Darothien pulled her wand from her heavy moss-colored overcoat, and wove the phosphorescent sphere that protected them once before against the elements over MidSea. As before, she centered her spell on Voyager. But since they were within the bounds of Lenland this time, she assured them it would remain in effect for the entire voyage, if need be.

As the blizzard enveloped them, they quickly gave up on trying to climb over the storm. Despite the ease of travel that Darothien's globe of protection afforded them, the clouds of the preternaturally strong clipper were simply too high to soar above. Instead, they were forced to fly low and close to the ground, so they could at least navigate and attain their destination as expediently as possible.

As quickly as it beset them, the storm continued past them on its rampage to the southeast, the only evidence of its passing the thick white flocking left behind on the ground and the growing population of coniferous trees. Once free of the raking snow, Darothien dispelled the sphere of pulsating verdigris.

They crossed into the northern canton as the sun was setting, turning the receding wake of the storm a violent red. The early winter night encroached quickly, the gloaming twilight promising a prohibitively gloomy night. With only the merest sliver of a crescent moon just beginning to brighten above the setting sun, the group elected to land and set up camp while they could still select a defensible site in the darkening terrain.

They settled on a long snaking rill that crested higher than most of the surrounding snow-covered countryside. On the leeward side was a sizable hook-shaped granite outcropping.

"We can keep lookout on top," Pendenar called to Pindlebryth, "and set up camp with a fire in there." He pointed to the center of the outcropping. "That ring of boulders will shield us from the wind, and hide the light of our campfire from any prying eyes." Pindlebryth nodded and signaled the rest of the flyers to follow Pendenar.

"Do you really think we must be prepared for an attack?" asked Darothien, as soon they landed.

"This close to our goal, we simply cannot afford to blithely ignore the possibility." Pindlebryth nimbly dismounted, and undid the bindings that held a tent canvas and his bedroll from the back of his saddle. "Especially after Selephygur alluded to a spy somewhere in CityState."

"So *that's* why you didn't tell me we were headed to the Valley of Giants until after we left." Darothien suddenly became quite put out. "Surely you don't suspect *me* of being a spy!"

"Of course not!" Pindlebryth said dropping his roll into the snow, and taking her paw to help her down. "I was merely cautious about who was in earshot. The guard, the nurse, and whoever else was down the hall from the infirmary – the fewer who know our destination, the better."

Darothien set aside her resentment, and squeezed Pindlebryth's paw back in affirmation.

Before the guards were finished unloading the rest of that night's provisions, Darothien rescued her small backpack sandwiched between two larger packs of canvas. Pendenar and the others did quick work of unloading the steeds, taking only those items they needed that night.

As the wind whipped stray bits of their plumage awry, the mounts quickly preened themselves and nestled into the deeper snow drifts. Darothien trudged through the shin-high snow, into the shelter of the granite and basalt cul-de-sac.

Grefdel and Jarjin finished pitching three tents – two smaller ones against the inner wall, and one larger tent to the side. All the canvas tents faced a central area already cleared for a campfire. Pendenar was in the process of collecting rocks strewn along the outcropping, and building a ring with them to hold the fire.

Darothien adjusted her small rucksack on her back, and looked around for Pindlebryth, but did not find him immediately. She finally spied him atop one of the higher boulders, peering over the ridge. Looking northwards, he craned his neck as he scanned up towards the sky, then the entire circumference of the horizon with Grefdel's spyglass. He carefully scaled down the side to rejoin the whole group.

Pendenar finished constructing the stone ring, just as Jarjin returned with two armfuls of small kindling. He poured it into the ring, and set off in search of larger pieces of wood, as Pendenar arranged the kindling and dug out a camp stove from his pack. All the while, Grefdel was digging a pit behind a curtain of granite slabs that had sheared off of the inner wall.

"No sign of being followed," Pindlebryth announced as he alighted on the sloping ground. "There is a cabin southwest of here, but I doubt its owner would have noticed us. Darothien extinguished her spell long before we came over their horizon." He placed the spyglass on top of Grefdel's pack, before he went to his own tent to lay out his groundsheet and bedroll.

Jarjin returned with a small pile of wood, nowhere near sufficient to keep a campfire alive for the whole night. "This wood is no good!" Pendenar complained. "What isn't soaked through is green. It'll smoke like crazy! We'll be seen for miles."

"That's all that can be found," Jarjin responded in his own defense. "We're close to the timber line, and wood is scarce. It must have been snowing before today's storm and melted, because the ground where old wood is available has a thick layer of ice below new snow."

Darothien clicked her tongue in mock annoyance, and unslung her pack. "Must the sorceress do *everything*?" she teased. She pulled out the three green geodes from her apartment, and set them on the rack above the superfluous kindling. After she primed the geodes to heat at a moderate intensity, Pendenar placed pans on top of two of them, and a pot of melting snow on the third. He then set to preparing the evening's meal of plain oats, seeds and millet, and a few other foods that would not have a strong cooking scent. The only thing that truly kept Pendenar busy was a sealed pan warming above the stove, and the chow for the mounts. He tended a series of cured fish and other treats on the stone ring about the stove. He handed the feed to Jarjin as soon as it was warm enough to feed the mounts, but before it started to cook and give off a strong odor.

The rationed portions for their own mess barely made a meal and went quickly. Which was just as well, as it was rather uncomfortable to sit on cold bare rock for extended periods. Pindlebryth found it additionally unsettling that they ate by an unwavering green light, rather than the comforting flicker of real fire. He looked about, but saw none of the guards were distracted thusly. The group was just about to put their mess kits away, when Grefdel told them to wait and pulled the sealed pan from off the stove and opened it.

"Here, M'Lord," he said tersely as he whipped his fingers back and forth to prevent the pan from burning them. "Eat this quickly, or who knows what it'll attract. The last thing we need is a curious bear or some such critter investigating!" Grefdel broke off a piece of the steaming foodstuff, and offered it to Pindlebryth.

"TwitchNose's quickbread!" exclaimed Pindlebryth, before quickly giving thanks for the unexpected boon. He forgot all about the unnatural emerald light as he closed his eyes and inhaled its aroma deeply. Without further ado, he bolted his portion down in two bites. Compared to the bland meal that preceded it, the cinnamon and nutmeg and other spices were exquisite. "Grefdel! How in the world did you manage this?" he mumbled with a small spray of crumbs.

"BroadShanks has been trying to recreate TwitchNose's recipe in secret for your return to PanGaea. I copied BroadShanks' recipe one night," Grefdel said with a wry grin while he passed the remaining pieces to the group, and finally helped himself. "Then one morning I caught her putting in a few things not in the recipe – a pinch of clove and allspice and a jigger of sherry. I had our kitchens whip up a batch while we were waiting for Darothien to finish in her laboratory. For goodness sake, M'Lord – don't tell BroadShanks, or she'll cut my tail off!"

Pendenar, who was also familiar with the rotund housekeeper, nodded his head in sympathy.

"Jarjin, you've got latrine cleanup detail tomorrow morning," Pendenar decided. Jarjin was about to complain, but Pendenar cut him off. "Grefdel did his portion of the detail, and deserves recognition for perilous duty in the face of kitchen utensils!" The entire group chuckled, even Jarjin after a turn.

Pindlebryth at first struggled to restrain a hearty laugh, especially in light that it was Pendenar of all people who made a jest. But his high spirits vanished when his intuition intruded upon him once again. He scowled to himself, torn between conflicting thoughts. One part of him searched for what his instinctive itch was warning him against and how immediate its need was. The other part wished he could somehow free himself of this often inconvenient and sometimes intolerable talent. Darothien also ceased her gaiety as soon as she noticed Pindlebryth's reaction.

She got up and brushed off a scattering of snow on a stone next to him. "What's wrong, Pindlebryth?" she asked earnestly as she sat near his side.

"Something's not right. But I don't know what it is yet." He peered at the black starry sky, wondering if he should expect to see anything other than the twinkling stars and the milky road that spanned the night firmament from horizon to horizon. "Grefdel, fetch your spyglass, and check our surroundings again, including the cabin to the southwest. No surprises tonight, please."

Grefdel sprang to collect his spyglass, leaving Pendenar to

cleanup their mess. "I'll take first watch," Pendenar declared as he scrubbed one of the pans with melted snow. "Then Jarjin, and Grefdel last. Jarjin, check the mounts are safe and covered for the night. I see you've found your tent already, M'Lord. M'lady Darothien, yours is next to his."

Pindlebryth stifled a yawn. "I think I will turn in now, and try to sleep if I can."

Pendenar's gaze followed Pindlebryth until he disappeared behind his tent flap. Darothien observed rhetorically, "You're concerned about him. As am I."

"We all are," said Grefdel with spyglass in hand. "I've seen this look about him before. And it affects him far more than ever it did his father the King. It often starts this way, and I worry if one day it will haunt him into indecision or paralysis when those about him need him most."

"Don't be too hard on him, Grefdel," Darothien said softly.

"Oh, I believe I'm not. As I learned on PanGaea, the right word of trust and encouragement at the right time allows him to see what he needs to do. Once he does, he sees it through."

"We're just at a loss how to help him this time," Pendenar mused.

"That's true of any of us – things are in motion that no one alive has ever witnessed before," she said with a sad look in her eyes. "I wonder if even Enorel the Great had suffered what our dear prince must endure." Darothien collected her pack, and retired to her own tent.

Grefdel shook his head, and climbed the rock wall to scan the countryside. As Pendenar finished his chores, he wondered what Darothien had up her sleeve, as he thought he spied a soft pulse of green leak out from between her tent's stakes.

Pendenar only had to wait until the next morning to make up his mind. The night had passed uneventfully, and he was instantly alert when Grefdel awoke him. As he made his way to the latrine, Pindlebryth was already wide eyed and bushy tailed.

None of the previous night's foreboding weighed on Pindlebryth, as he stood wrapped in his riding clothes and heavy coat, with his warm breath puffing about him. He wondered why his itch had allayed him so the night before, as he let the simple beauty of the sunrise soak in. He gathered the spyglass from Grefdel, and ascended the shield wall.

Pendenar passed Darothien, as she emerged from her

morning toilette. She noted his raised eyebrow, but mistook its significance.

"Oh come now, Pendenar! In the shanty towns of the iron canton, accommodations such as this were quite ordinary."

"No, m'lady!" Pendenar stumbled in a whisper. "I was just wondering what came over our prince since last night."

"Oh, nothing that Graymalden didn't use to help King Enorel III and King Hatheron, when sleep evaded them." She hurried back to her own tent, to collect her things and help break camp, leaving a puzzled Pendenar behind.

Pindlebryth returned from his lookout, and assisted with the last half of the group's packing. "If I read the lay of the land right, the Valley of Giants is about an hour to the northeast. We should continue to fly low, until we attain the Valley itself. Then we should spread out and adopt a search pattern."

"What are we looking for?" asked Jarjin as he cinched his saddle to his shearwater, and tied his bundle to it.

"I'm not exactly sure," Pindlebryth replied as Voyager wheedled his head under his rider's arm. The great bird cooed and whined, in his manner of both greeting Pindlebryth and indicating he wanted to be petted. As Pindlebryth happily obliged, he continued, "Whatever it is we are looking for, the only clue Henejer left us was that it was green, gray and red."

"The Valley is dozens of leagues wide!" complained Grefdel. "That's all we have to go on?"

"Yes," Pendenar scolded. "And the sooner we finish packing, the sooner we can get to it!" Within less than an hour, the mounts were fully loaded, the last item being Jarjin's shovel. Grefdel clambered down from the lookout, and gave the all clear as he mounted his steed.

The troupe took off towards the northeast, with the early winter's morning sun still low to their right. As the hour passed, the terrain grew higher and higher, until no trees could be seen anywhere. The only vegetation were low grasses, shrubs, and the occasional field of heather or moss on acres-wide stone stratum. Their cover all but gone, they flew closer to the inexorably upward sloping landscape. Even higher, the last of anything green disappeared, yielding to seemingly endless leagues of stone and snow. Just as Pindlebryth began to wonder if they would ever achieve their destination, the vista suddenly changed.

The rocky landscape fell into a cyclopean crater surrounded by cliffs half a mile high on all sides. Scattered like fields of stone mushrooms around the floor of the valley were scores of mountains surrounded by thick forests of a variety of conifers. Some were craggy, some were smoothed with ages of erosion; some were naked hulks of granite monoliths, others were graced with thin coatings of lichen or moss or snow, fewer still had a lone scraggly fir clinging to its near-vertical sides. Some peaks stood in groups, others stood alone like forbidding sentinels. All of them shared the same remarkable trait of being at least twice as tall as they were wide. There was no doubt they had finally arrived at the Valley of Giants.

The entire troupe marveled at the stunning beauty of this miracle of nature. Following Pindlebryth's lead, the squadron of flyers banked and dove below the rim of the cliffs, then began to spiral horizontally along the mountaintops towards the center of the basin. One by one, Pendenar signaled his fellow guards to peel off from the group, moving further inward but staying behind the rest. Pendenar and Darothien on Mariner were the last to leave Pindlebryth by himself on Voyager.

Each bird wove about a different quadrant of the valley, hunting for any clue as to the meaning of Henejer's last puzzle, and the whereabouts of the Orb. Every few minutes, Pendenar would verify all their flyers were still airborne and safe, or scan the horizon for intruders.

After about an hour, Pindlebryth landed Voyager on top of a spire near the center of the basin. He dug out a fish treat from his provisions, that Voyager greedily devoured. The others soon gathered on the central mount, joining him to feed and rest their own mounts, while they planned their next move.

They took in a small and hardly filling meal of hardtack and dried fruit before they mounted again. Each advanced clockwise from the quadrant they had previously searched. They barely meandered a league away, when Grefdel sharply pinioned his shearwater and made a straight line towards Pindlebryth. He signaled his prince to follow, as he spun his mount away and landed on a peak of snow-covered basalt. Seeing the commotion, the others abandoned scouring their newly assigned quadrants and joined Grefdel and Pindlebryth.

Pindlebryth sidled Voyager next to Grefdel's mount and breathlessly asked, "What? What do you see?" He peered into the crisp mountain air, following the direction where Grefdel pointed.

"There! See those three peaks to the south clustered together?" he clamored excitedly as the others landed close by, hopping their mounts over to hear Grefdel.

Two leagues off in the distance, Grefdel directed Pindlebryth's gaze towards a threesome of giant peaks. Each of them consisted of a different type of stone. The two farthest megaliths sat on either side behind the nearest one, forming a near-perfect equilateral triangle. The one on the right, though sitting in the shadow of its leftmost sister, was a naked granite hulk. The leftmost, partially eclipsed from their view, was a towering mountain of rust-colored basalt mixed with garnet and rose quartz. The peak closest to them was almost entirely covered by snow on the north side facing them, but it was clear that a black gray basalt lay underneath.

"No, Grefdel. That doesn't match..." Pendenar groused, dismissing the guard's excitement.

"Look more closely, M'Lord." Pindlebryth squinted against the rising sun still hanging low in the southeast. "*Under* the snow!" In the basalt peak's dark umbra was a field of fresh snow from the previous night's clipper, that almost seemed to glow with reflected light. Poking through the snow here and there were dark splotches – hardy patches of holly and bearberry.

"The plants?" Pindlebryth questioned.

"They're ever*greens*, M'Lord. They cover the entire northern face of the mountain. They're old growth, too – they would have been here during Henejer's time," Grefdel proffered hopefully.

Pindlebryth's heart leapt into his throat. "Up!" he yelled to Voyager. The bird keened loudly, surprised at the unusually violent kick to both his sides by his rider. Voyager flapped his powerful wings twice, and boosted off the mountain with a speed the group had not seen before. Within a heartbeat, he was over the edge of the mountain, and dove sharply. Voyager drew his wings close to his body, and flexed his primary feathers straight back. Pindlebryth leaned in close to Voyager's neck, and as one they spiraled into a power dive towards the base of their mountain. Halfway down, they leveled out, and shot speedily directly towards the three sister peaks. Initially stunned at Pindlebryth's reaction, the group gathered themselves together and followed – though not as recklessly as their prince.

Pindlebryth flew over the top of the three mountains, peering down into the valley that formed between the three sister peaks. He then dove to one side and made a tight spiral, circling the outside of the mountains, while descending to the floor below. Seeing nothing extraordinary that attracted his attention, he let his intuition select one of the gorges between the three peaks, and landed near its mouth. He vaulted off his saddle while Voyager still was bobbing on the ground after touchdown. Deftly pulling his sword and scabbard from the saddle, he slung them to his belt.

He ran headlong into the gorge between the black basalt and blended quartz monoliths, slowing down as the passage gradually constricted. The land outside of the peaks flourished with winter grasses that poked through snow that crunched underfoot. As Pindlebryth delved farther into the ravine, he entered a world of gray. Light diminished the further he proceeded, and the winter grass soon gave way to bare rock and scree. The stone on either side of him seemed to be more inhospitable as it closed in, as the rock interior was only subject to erosion by the wind, and not the full arsenal of weathering at nature's command.

As the rock became even more angular and jagged, Pindlebryth plodded slowly and carefully, scouring the ground and the walls for any sign of Henejer's handiwork. Pendenar and Darothien presently caught up with Pindlebryth.

Pendenar breathlessly reported, "I've pulled Voyager and my mount into the mouth of the gorge, where they should be well hidden. Grefdel and Jarjin are settling in to watch the other two entrance ways." Pindlebryth seemed not to hear him as he continued to survey the stone walls, sweeping up and down both sides.

"What is it you expect to find?" Darothien asked.

"I don't know, but we'll know it when we see it. Henejer brought us this far – he *must* have left another clue."

"Given that every morsel of information about the Orb has been obfuscated by him, or intentionally hidden by others and the Orb itself," Darothien countered, "I'm not sure I would agree."

She moved to Pindlebryth's side, and together they walked and examined each section of the walls as they passed by. They proceeded ever more slowly, the closer that the walls encroached. Pendenar lent his eyes to the search only to a certain extent. He periodically checked the path behind them, or stopped momentarily just to listen.

The path constricted even tighter, when Pindlebryth murmured, "Hello, what's this?"

A ragged crack twice the size of a Lemming revealed itself as they rounded a turn in the path. A large diagonal ragged gash cut straight into the heart of the stone, the crevice was barely wide enough to enter. Pindlebryth was forced to turn sideways, and shift his sword to lay flat along his leg as he edged into the fissure.

Darothien uttered "Be careful!" by habit, even though she herself followed Pindlebryth into the crevice a few steps behind. She held her tsavorite prism ahead of her, and every few feet she would peer into the failing light the deeper that they went. A few yards further, Pindlebryth stopped.

"The crevice ends here. It's a dead end."

Darothien had to be satisfied with searching past Pindlebryth, as there was no room to squeeze ahead. Even so, she could affirm Pindlebryth's assessment. "It's so dark, that if there were anything magick hidden, it would shine like a beacon in this crystal. We might as well go back."

They wended their way back tortuously, Darothien rechecking her observations along the way until they exited. Pendenar awaited them at the opening.

"Nothing," Pindlebryth said to him brusquely. They resumed their trek towards the center of the three peaks, but the path became so constrained and choked with rubble they were forced to advance single file. Darothien slipped ahead before Pindlebryth could protest.

They continued until they could see the path ahead widened, and the third peak of granite loomed into a small glade between the three sisters. There were no trees, but only small scrub that eked out an existence with the scant light that was only marginally brighter than in the pathway. As they approached the wide clearing, a constant breeze began to build. The stone about them began to take on a ribbed aspect, with countless horizontal lines scraped and scooped out by millennia of erosion by wind and rain. Just before the path splayed out into the clearing, Darothien found another crevice.

This one was slightly larger, and its outline into the basalt resembled a lightning bolt. Darothien immediately pressed herself into the fissure, with Pindlebryth following behind. The walls of the fractured cleft quickly closed in on them, and Darothien was forced to remove her backpack. She left it behind wedged in the bottom of the angling crevice, as they were forced to shimmy down its remaining length bent backwards.

Darothien glanced into her prism every few feet, but when the last vestiges of daylight almost failed their sight, she gasped.

"I see something!" She slipped sideways further into the crevice, following it as it turned hard to the left. "Pindlebryth! Come quickly!"

Pindlebryth scrambled past the elbow in the fissure as quickly as he could manage, until it opened into a large expanse. He emerged behind Darothien's silhouette limned by a green aura. His spine shivered as he saw the entire crystal luminesced from end to end.

Darothien removed her wand from its sleeve, and uttered a sound akin to tinder burning. A greenish white sphere rose from the tip of the wand and hovered a few feet above their heads, and quickly brightened in intensity, illuminating the entire chamber.

But this was no natural subterranean cavern. The interior was perfectly smooth and cylindrical, with one notable exception.

Above a waist-high dolmen floated the Orb of Oblivion.

With the advent of Darothien's light, it responded and echoed with its own luminescence. But far from a warming light, its sepulchral emanations had an ashen tinge to it, that drained the color from everything it illuminated. Like two wide-eyed sleepwalkers, Pindlebryth and Darothien approached the Artifact, encircling it on either side of the altar. As they came close, the grapefruit-sized globe's uniform gray translucence mottled. Strange patterns of pallid darkness and light began to swirl as they advanced even closer. Pindlebryth truly believed he could sense it was angry.

Darothien secreted away her prism and wand, and in the selfsame motion produced Gazelikus' Cloth from the other sleeve. She held it in both paws, but then stood still as she realized she was reluctant to hazard its use.

Pindlebryth backed away from the sphere a single step, glancing about to make sure he did not trip. He froze as he glanced at the room's entrance. On either side of the craggy opening were pillars carved out of the stone. They arched towards each other, meeting to form a rectangle above the opening. In the oblong stone were inscribed words with the same block letters as he had found in the cubicle in Henejer Hall. The words, though familiar, in the shifting light of green and gray seemed to mock him.

"Ask the stone to forget."

"Well, there is no doubt that this is indeed Henejer's doing. But no record from his day, not a single one of his contemporaries, no one even hinted at the existence of this vault," Pindlebryth said in admiration. "Yet another example of Henejer's mastery of the mason's craft to build this by himself!"

"That is the third time Henejer has told us that, is it not?" Darothien asked, still holding the cloth as she read the inscription. "Why does he keep telling us how he was inspired? Was he really so full of himself? It's almost annoying." Pindlebryth looked askance at the writing. Despite Darothien's comment, he tried to convince himself that Henejer was reaching out across the centuries, trying to explain something important.

Instead, he turned his attention back to the Orb, as Darothien hemmed and hawed. "Well, we can't just stand here forever. How do we proceed?" Pindlebryth approached the Orb again within a few paces. The eddies of opalescence inside the Orb pulsed with renewed energy, swirling faster with each step he took.

Pindlebryth stood next to Darothien, gazing thoughtfully into the depths of the Orb. "Henejer was no sorcerer, and yet he could use the Orb of Oblivion. In fact, he took great pains to keep it away from Gazelikus. Gazelikus never forgave him for that." He paused, as he cocked his head as if he could somehow peer deeply into the heart of the Orb. Or perhaps he expected Darothien to make a counter-argument. Whatever his reason, he continued as a thought struck him.

"What if Gazelikus actually *had* used the Orb? Henejer would have known, but the Orb would make Gazelikus forget.

We know the Orb made the great sorcerer forget almost everything else concerning itself." He edged even closer to Darothien. "Perhaps Henejer kept it from Gazelikus, because they discovered it was safer if a sorcerer *didn't* use it?"

Darothien looked fearfully at Pindlebryth. She silently mouthed, "No," as he took the cloth from her hands.

Holding the cloth so that it covered the entirety of both of his palms, he stood over the dolmen and cradled the sphere into the folds of the cloth. The Orb momentarily pulsed with a muted sickly gray phosphorescence as its eddies spun madly, and hummed with a short low burst. But once Pindlebryth firmly held it within Gazelikus' Cloth, it seemed to acquiesce. He took a step away from the altar, and with it, the Orb. He felt a tug against his arms, as if he were pulling weight out of a shallow depression, but the resistance and the forbidding hum vanished as the Orb finally moved from its resting place in midair.

Pindlebryth looked at Darothien with an expression that bespoke surprise, elation, indecision and apprehension all at once. He rotated the Orb to support its weight in one hand, while he folded the remaining cloth over its top and sides, almost completely covering the sphere. The pallid light of the Orb almost fully extinguished, the room fell once again to the pale green hues thrown off by Darothien's spell.

"Let's get this outside," said Pindlebryth. "I'll feel better when I can store this away with the Cloth in a box, or a rucksack. Anything other than holding it like this!"

The two made their way to the exit, Pindlebryth turning sideways to slide into the crevice. But as he entered the fissure, the Orb pulsed with an angry whirr and a flash of gray that leaked and shone through the folds and around the overlaps of the cloth. In a split second, it grew to twice its size. Pindlebryth let out an involuntary yelp of surprise as the Orb burst out of the cloth, struck the sides of the cleft, and bounced out of his grasp. It landed on the ground with a dull thud and a cloud of dust. Once it hit the ground, it diminished in luminescence and size.

"What! How?" sputtered Pindlebryth in consternation.

After a moment's consideration, Darothien responded, "Ah! Unexpected, but not entirely unprecedented." She tried to sound calm and collected, but her rapid breathing belied that she was just as amazed as Pindlebryth. "We have seen something like this before." Pindlebryth regarded her as if she were not in total control of her faculties. "Remember the Lens of Truth! Selephylin blasted the Lens into Selephygur's head when he was but an infant. But as Selephygur grew into adulthood, the Lens grew with him." Darothien managed to compose herself as she spoke further. "We've often spoke of how the Orb wants to be left alone. It simply resorted to this ability, in its desire to remain hidden away, here in its lair."

The Orb pulsed a hum in response. But this time it was higher in pitch, and somehow far less menacing in timbre. Darothien took a tentative step towards the Orb. Pindlebryth was about to command her to stay away, when the Orb's reaction gave him pause – or more accurately, it's lack of reaction.

It did not hum angrily; the perpetually moving currents inside the Orb did not spin faster nor glow threateningly.

"Maybe..." Darothien began, unsure of the idea that sprung into her head. "Maybe the *Orb* selected Henejer? What if like us, both Gazelikus and Henejer tried to access the Orb, but *it* chose instead of them? You've said the Orb has a will of its own.

"Perhaps it will leave with me?" she suggested as she shrugged her shoulders.

Pindlebryth considered her proposal, but his head began to swim with ideas fighting against their contradictions, and fears conflicting with exigent needs. He took an uncertain step and hesitantly handed the cloth to Darothien, flinching as the Orb hummed intimidatingly at his approach.

"Are you sure you want to do this?" he urged.

She did not bother to answer, but instead wrapped the cloth about the Orb as he had done, and lifted it effortlessly off the ground. Pindlebryth sidled into the fissure, and Darothien likewise turned to slip into the hollows of the cleft.

But once again, the Orb grew and pulsed, flying out of the fissure and Darothien's grasp. Darothien yelped, but not with surprise.

She dashed back into the room, holding her paws in front of her. She ran to the green light, still hanging in the middle of the cylindrical room. Pindlebryth, ignoring the Orb and cloth lying near the entrance, ran after her fearing the worst. She held her hands under the light, and flipped them over and over again, inspecting them. She didn't know what to expect – were they burned, were they damaged?

"I – I touched it!" she whimpered. Pindlebryth grasped her paws, as he examined them too. After several breathless moments, Darothien flexed her digits, and shook her paws like someone whose hands had fallen asleep. "They – they seem none the worse. But I *did* touch the Orb." She drew in a sharp breath and took a few steps away from Pindlebryth and the light. "Am I all right? Do I look the same?"

Pindlebryth looked at her, now that she was not directly under the green illumination, and not unduly disfigured by long distorted vertical shadows. Once he took a step to the side, so that he also shaded her face from the lifeless grey light of the Orb, she looked as beautiful as ever to him. He nodded his head, and managed a brave smile for her.

"There has to be a way to get the Orb out." Pindlebryth swiveled around, looking high and low, searching for some answer. "If we fail today, someone will sooner or later find a way – even if they have to mine a wider opening." Darothien took out her prism, and joined his search, in hopes there might be something to be found. But the prism glowed with such intensity from the proximity of the Orb, that its sympathetic resonance washed out any features that the prism might have otherwise revealed. Disappointed, she slipped the prism back in her sleeve.

Pindlebryth scoured the dolmen, the floor, ceiling and walls, but they were all smooth, polished and featureless – save for the fissure, the pillars and the text. Suddenly, he stopped on the text. His eyebrows arched, and jaw dropped as a moment of clarity broke in upon him.

"It's a command," he barely whispered. "It's an instruction!" he repeated loudly. "Henejer's not telling what he did, he's telling us what to *do*! Darothien! Do you... *Darothien!*"

As he turned, Pindlebryth froze in a rictus of dread. Darothien was holding the Orb in her bare paws, and looked through him as if he did not exist, staring at the crevice.

She uttered a sound that recalled the rush of a strong wind and the scratch of blowing sand across a vast landscape of barren stone. A single heartbeat of gray luminescence pulsed

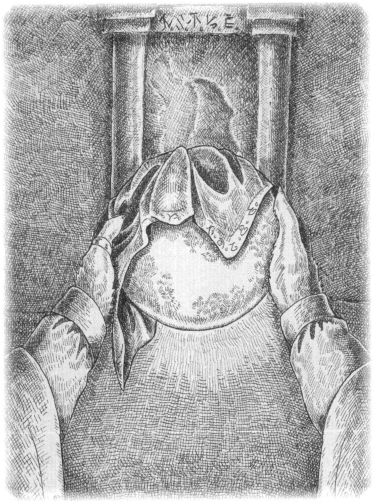

from beneath Darothien's irises, and a gust of wind blew past Pindlebryth's back, towards her and the Orb. Pindlebryth could only stand stock still in shock and trepidation, as Darothien calmly exhaled and closed her eyes with satisfaction. She bent down to collect Gazelikus' Cloth, and wrapped the Orb in it as if nothing out of the ordinary had taken place.

She stood and looked at Pindlebryth with a reassuring smile. "Look. Behind you."

Pindlebryth's hackles shot straight up, as he beheld a rectangular opening, wide enough for both him and Darothien. It went flush into the cylindrical wall between the two pillars, and curved out of sight, following the path of the original fissure. Darothien stood beside him, holding the enshrouded Orb between both her paws.

"What... what did you do?" he asked stiltedly.

"You were right. Henejer was *telling* us all along. I asked the stone to forget." Her voice had a strange quality, as if she were a long-suffering parent explaining a complex idea to a pup in the simplest terms possible.

"But forget what? Where it was? How it came here? How Henejer fashioned it?" he stammered, still marveling at the impossible corridor.

"I – I'm not sure," she replied.

Pindlebryth looked at her in disbelief, and was troubled by what he saw. He had seen this in others, and remembered how it had felt in his own face – she was lying.

He probed her countenance further, but he could not see what he most feared. She did not lie for the sake of deception, for personal gain, or for any number of darker motives. Rather, she seemed to be unsure of how she had manipulated the Orb, or unsure of the reason why she had done so, or that she was simply afraid to face some ominous truth.

"Come," he said pensively, as if he had lost something dear. He held out his paw reflexively to hold hers and lead her out of the repository. But realizing she held the Orb in the cloth, he put his arm around her shoulder and pulled her close as they walked down the snaking hallway.

"After all these centuries," Pindlebryth ruminated with an odd snigger, as he came to a sudden revelation halfway along the corridor.

"What?" Darothien asked flatly.

"For generations, Henejer was regarded as the genius architect, the brilliant mason, the master who single-handedly built such marvelous edifices, often without mortar or pointing.

"He was a *fraud*!" Pindlebryth said with a laugh. "It wasn't he who cunningly built the bridges between Lenland and our neighbors, or the monuments scattered throughout our country. It wasn't he who fashioned the intricacies of the listening hall of the North Wing, the never-changing environment of the archive, nor his eponymous hall, nor this impossible vault.

"It was all the Orb!" he shouted, his voice echoing endlessly in the curving hallway. He ran his free hand along the polished edge of the corridor's cool stone. "The Orb was the tool he used to construct everything he had laid claim to."

They came upon Darothien's backpack, where she left it. Except now, instead of being wedged between the angled walls of the fissure, it simply lay in the center of the corridor.

"If you would, please," Darothien nodded towards her backpack. "My hands are rather occupied just now!" Pindlebryth shouldered the rucksack with a chuckle. Soon the warm glow of the tenuous daylight of the central glade grew in strength, washing out the pallor of the Orb and the pale green light shining in the room left behind.

Suddenly Pindlebryth stopped, holding Darothien closer. "Wait here," he said quietly but urgently. He released Darothien and padded a few steps ahead. He set down her backpack and drew his sword when he heard the shouts of unfamiliar voices. Advancing a few more steps pressed against the smooth wall, he spied Grefdel's back. He was slightly crouched with sword drawn, his head twitching left and right. Another step in the dimness, and he saw Pendenar similarly poised with his back to the corridor. They stood between the corridor and a pack of Arctic Fox.

"Come out, come out, my good Prince! Give up your sword. You and your friends are outnumbered two to one."

Pindlebryth's ears twitched as the smug, obsequious voice issued its challenge and command. He had heard it before.

"Keeyakawa?" Pindlebryth shouted. "What are you doing here, assassin?" he bellowed defiantly.

"Why, looking for the very same thing you are, M'Lord! And by the look of things, it seems you have been successful!" he cawed. He might have sounded congratulatory to another's ears, but Pindlebryth discerned the menace lurking in his tone.

"Forgive me, M'Lord," Grefdel whispered over his shoulder. "The Fox caught us off guard. We failed to see them against the snow outside the mountains until they were almost on top of us. We were forced to retreat..."

"Now, now, you mottled egg!" the Crow interrupted. "Your master and I were already engaged in conversation. Do not be so rude! Especially one in *your* position."

Pindlebryth took a few steps into the light, at the threshold of the corridor. "And what about your position? You could not enlist the ranks of your own Ravenne?"

"Oh, don't worry about my Brethren of the Order. There are several of us scattered about. Some in the Warrening, some in the Lodges of the WeatherWorn, but most of them are all about Lenland, searching for the Orb."

"Yes, since your last map was so accurate," Pindlebryth gibed.

"I just thank my lucky stars that I drew the assignment to this locale. We had started combing this inhospitable pesthole of a crater just two days before, but I knew we were on the right track when we spotted you approaching."

Pindlebryth quickly surveyed the large pack of Arctic Fox that faced their paltry number. They were all nearly completely molted into their white winter coats. Next to Keeyakawa stood a Fox with a few teeth sticking out of his mouth at odd angles, including one grossly oversized canine that protruded down past his jawline. He surmised he was the Ravenne's second in command, the pack leader. Several others in the motley band had series of scars and other healed injuries – whether they were from honest battle, or from bar fights was impossible to tell. One had a bald spot where scalp had been crudely sutured back on, another had striking red fur on his forearms, one had a jagged scar across one eye, and still another had his left ear torn off even though its stub twitched incessantly.

"But *Fox*, Keeyakawa?" said Pindlebryth as he gestured towards them by sweeping his sword point across the pack's feet. Some of the mercenaries grumbled and growled at Pindlebryth's tone.

"Don't your friends know that their lives are forfeit if they are found in Lenland? The squads of the White Ghost platoon regularly patrol this canton, and these mewling cubs wouldn't stand a chance.

"Don't they also know the Kyaa and the Iron Baron have the Lens of Truth, Vulpinden's pride and glory? They are using it as we speak to bring about the downfall of Vulpinden itself! Have you told them how the spies of the Rookeries and Vulpinden are each other's throats, engaged in a war of nerves?"

Keeyakawa held up a crossbow and inspected it laconically, seemingly bored by Pindlebryth's soliloquy. Pindlebryth ground his teeth when he realized it was his very own crossbow taken from Voyager.

"Oh, do not worry about these fine fellows. They are swords for hire, and have been in hostile lands before. As for their allegiances, the only heads of state these soldiers of fortune care about are those stamped on gold coin!

"But come! I do not have all the time in the world. And you *certainly* don't! Your choice is simple – surrender the Orb and live, resist us and die.

"Oh, and don't worry about your precious steeds," the Crow said sardonically as he pointed with the crossbow down the path that Pindlebryth and Darothien came. "We'll put them to good use after you're gone. After all, though I can fly out, these poor land-runners would otherwise have to climb out."

Keeyakawa stepped forward, the oily pleasantry gone from his voice. "So, what shall it be, M'Lord? Surrender or resist? The Orb under my wing, or a sword in your belly? Life or death?"

Suddenly, a shadow darted from behind the wall of the sister peaks behind the crowd of Fox. It grew larger and its outline more distinct, as it swiftly arced tracing the outside of their circle. Whether they noted the Lemmings' attention drawn to the moving shadow, or the shadow itself fell in their periphery, only a few Fox themselves spotted the dark form. They looked up, vainly squinting directly into the sunlight that angled through the two peaks into the clearing. Fewer still made out the silhouettes of two terns bearing riders wearing black lacquered armor.

The first swooped in, and banked hard into the group. The rider flashed out his saber, and swung as the bird pinioned. A Fox's head went flying, as the others cried out, yipping, barking and dispersing in all directions. The second tern spun sideways directly into the Fox pack, bowling over three of them who still had their blades pointing at Pindlebryth and his comrades. A fourth was better prepared for the incoming tackle, and tried to hack at the belly of the bird as it smashed into him. He was not quite fast enough, and succeeded in only slicing off a tuft of feathers from its abdomen as it passed, and a handful of secondary feathers from the lower wing.

The first flyer reined in his steed harshly, stalling the tern a few feet off the ground. He leapt off and continued running a few steps before decelerating and facing the crowd, his longsword drawn.

"Trevemar! How...?" yelled Pindlebryth, dumbfounded that the duke was here at all.

"Not quite the same, fighting close quarters without your crossbow, eh, M'Lord?" the duke taunted, his ego still smarting from the previous day's tongue-lashing. He charged the scattering Fox with a cry that was more akin to laughter.

Pindlebryth shouted at Trevemar, using his sword to indicate Keeyakawa, "Look out! Ravenne!" But the duke was reveling so in the mayhem he caused, he made no indication he heard the prince. Nor was the Crow anywhere to be seen. Pindlebryth's sword pointed at empty air.

The larger tern skidded sideways to a halt, its cut wing dragging on the ground behind it. A bloodless cut, it folded its wing to its side, and hopped away from the fracas as its burly rider dismounted. He brought his leg over with an exaggerated swing, and launched himself into the nearest Fox, brandishing a bastard sword with a blade twice as wide and heavy as the Fox's saber.

Selephygur screamed bloody death at the Fox, who froze in terror at the sight of the behemoth with a silver eye bearing down upon him. Focusing his considerable momentum through his blade, Selephygur easily cleaved first through the feeble defense of the Fox's raised saber followed by the creature's clavicle, caving in the Fox's chest.

Selephygur was rushed by three forms. Jarjin reached him first, and took a position back to back with him. Two Fox rushed in immediately afterwards, one on either side of the duo.

"Glad you could join us, M'Lord! But what are you doing here?" Jarjin said breathlessly, as he deflected a weak feint from his opponent.

"Father begrudgingly informed me where you went, and I knew this was one of the places BrokenTail set a trap!"

Selephygur's opponent lunged, then slashed sideways at his abdomen. Selephygur handily knocked the Fox's saber aside, his bastard sword clanging more like a hardened anvil than a refined blade.

"Trevemar wouldn't let me leave alone."

The Fox swung around, and sliced downwards, the saber whispering as it sliced through the dry winter air. Selephygur's ears twitched, and he anticipated the strike. He spun his steel, driving the Fox's saber point into the dirt, the Fox's own momentum pulling him forward.

"Father will be most displeased with us when we return!"

The Fox tried to recover from the counterstrike, but folded to the ground in a heap with a yelp and a broken jaw, as Selephygur punched him with his other fist. Without a second thought, the young prince launched himself at another pair of Fox charging them.

Jarjin pressed his own attack, alternately lunging and advancing a step at a time. The two circled each other, as his Fox similarly blocked Jarjin's sword with his épée in a circular parry. The sword was unlike the sabers the other Fox possessed, in that the hilt was an ornately domed pommel, a hemisphere of metal layered with a filigree of hardened steel. The Fox jabbed once then again at Jarjin, probing his defenses. Seeing an opening, the Fox slashed, crossed back, then doubled back the blade yet again with an immediate remise. He chuckled as he observed Jarjin's classical technique, obviously yet untried in a true skirmish.

"You fight like a doe!" he ridiculed. Jarjin became flustered, as he countered with an opposition parry. "My bitch wields a rolling pin better than you!"

Jarjin was taken in by the Fox's verbal barbs. He lunged and slashed wildly, which the Fox easily countered and redirected with another wide circular parry. Jarjin fell for the bait, and leaned into the circling, matching it with a spinning moulinet. The edge of his saber skimmed down the Fox's épée. As he did so, the Fox thumbed a release hidden in the pommel. The steel filigree clicked forward away from the pommel, and the Fox pressed the edge of his sword down. Jarjin's saber point drove in between one of the openings in the filigree pattern and became lodged. The Fox leaned in with his full weight and twisted his sword hard, forcing Jarjin down and snapping his saber in two.

The Fox laughed once more, and lifted his arm to plunge his épée down into Jarjin's chest, when the Lemming jumped up with an unexpected abandon that only the young can muster. He drove the splintered crack at the end of his foreshortened saber up into the jaw of the Fox. The mercenary rolled his head back, and stumbled as he gagged on gullets off blood filling his mouth and nostrils. Jarjin forced the Fox's jaw up with his free paw, as he pulled down on his broken saber. He withdrew his sword with a guttural cry and rammed it into the Fox's heart. Leaning on his knees to catch his breath, Jarjin then tore the Fox's épée from his death grip.

He swatted the lifeless Fox across the nose, and acerbically proclaimed, "She *had* to be good with a rolling pin, with a lout like you at home!" and sped off to the next Fox that caught his attention.

Darothien stood silently against the corridor wall, while her friends dealt with Keeyakawa and the Fox mercenaries. But when she heard the chaos of fighting ensue, she quickly crossed over to her backpack. She knelt down, setting the cloth-shrouded Orb next to it. Light from the clearing wavered in brightness as figures dashed past, and others advanced, fought and retreated past the corridor entrance. Looking anxiously around the last curve of the corridor into the daylight, she opened the pack and shoved its contents aside to make room for the Orb. The light and shadow about her ceased changing, even though the sounds of conflict still echoed down the corridor. She looked up with a gasp as the red-armed Fox stood between her and the entrance, dropping the weighted ends of a large bola and slowly spinning them.

Darothien scooped up the Orb haphazardly, one hand on the cloth, the other against the Orb directly. She bounded upwards, and dashed down the corridor away from the Fox and the intensifying whirr of his spinning weapon. Red-arms heaved the bola, and expertly struck his mark. The three weights tangled around Darothien's ankles, sending her sprawling to the floor. The Orb fell on the flat stone next to her with a heavy thump, and rolled out of her reach. With angered determination in her eyes, she pushed herself off the ground, and sat up rolling her knees to the side. She faced the Fox and reached into her sleeve for her wand. As Darothien fumbled past the prism, Red-arms had pulled a second, smaller bola from his satchel, and was already spinning it. He flung it at the center of her body, and it wrapped around her wrists, entangling them in her sleeves, each against her opposite forearm. She struggled for a moment to free her arms and her wand, but her effort made the bola only constrict further. She scowled at Red-arms as he towered over her. She began to utter a sound akin to rushing water, but Red-arms punched her solidly across the snout, sending her reeling into unconsciousness.

Red-arms flipped open his satchel, and removed from it a large bola. He considered using it to bind the sorceress' mouth shut, but her muzzle tapered too smoothly for it to be effective. He instead settled on simply hanging the snare around his belt, and savagely kicking Darothien a second time across her forehead for good measure. Into his emptied satchel he stuffed the cloth and the Orb. It hummed angrily at him, but the Fox ignored it. He trudged back down the corridor towards the clearing, dragging Darothien behind him by her bound forearms.

As he emerged from the corridor, Red-arms was nearly rammed by Scar-eye, who was retreating from a rapid onslaught of lunges and ripostes from Trevemar.

Snaggle-tooth quickly chased after the duke, but spotted Red-Arms and delayed himself for the slightest of moments. He pointed at a large boulder across the clearing, shouting, "Give me that! Cover the archer!" He grabbed the satchel from Red-arms, and slung it over his shoulder.

Red-arms drew his sword and bolted towards Bald-pate, deflecting stray blows with his saber from nearby battles as he ran past them. Snaggle-tooth resumed his sprint, following Trevemar to attack from behind. In addition to his blade, he also drew a dagger with his defense arm.

But he was cut short by Pendenar, who seeing Snaggle-tooth's intention, dashed directly into his path. He clanged his sword against the Fox's saber to get his attention, and smiled in a mocking apology. Snaggle-tooth growled and slashed at him rapidly and repeatedly with both his blades. Pendenar, momentarily unbalanced, was forced to step back. The grin quickly left his face as Torn-ear also rushed in, who with Snaggle-tooth pressed Pendenar's defense viciously.

Trevemar deflected Scar-eye's thrust to his abdomen, and cut upwards, knocking his opponent's shield arm's dagger aside. He pressed the Fox hard, forcing him off balance with a roundhouse kick, and slashed his sword down to cut the inside of the Fox's inner thigh, and the artery underneath. But he abandoned his attack, as he heard an ominous whistling from behind. In a split second, he recognized the sound, and turned to dodge or deflect the cowardly arrow attack from behind.

But he was far too slow – he was shoved forward by the

impact. A pain shot through his back and pierced his heart. He looked down to see the jagged head of a crossbow bolt sticking out of a hole of splinters in his lacquered chestpiece. He instinctively grabbed at the bolt, but his paw slipped on the gore and black oily film that spilled out of the cruel wound. He managed to turn, to look at his craven attacker, as his knees buckled and mouth foamed. The malevolent face of Keeyakawa sneered at him, his eyes nictating like a serpent about to devour its prey.

"A crossb...?" Trevemar spluttered in consternation as he crashed face down in the dust across his blade.

But Keeyakawa's victory was short-lived. The Crow threw down Pindlebryth's crossbow, and drew his saber as a black and blond blur rushed at him. Selephygur saw his mentor fall, and in a fit of rage, easily threw off two sorely wounded Fox that had been bearing down on his sword. He charged, shouting incoherently as he pounced on the Ravenne. A berserk searing bloodlust burned in his eye, and even shone through his silvered eye with a ghostly argent luminescence.

He swung his bastard sword down with all his might on the Crow's head, a juggernaut of blood-stained metallic death. However, the assassin nimbly stepped aside, and held his blade upward at an angle to deflect the blow. But Keeyakawa's puissance was no match for Selephygur's sheer power. The blow forced the Crow's blade downwards, and snapped it out of his grip with a resounding clang. Before the Ravenne could recover, every muscle and cord in Selephygur's hamstrings, back, shoulders and arms bunched and flexed taut, driving the thick sword ripping upwards at a prodigious speed. The sword caught Keeyakawa from the bottom of his loins. Selephygur spatchcocked the Crow, slicing him upwards clean through his breastbone, chest and neck. The Crow's ribcage and innards exploded out of the gaping rip that split open his entire torso, spraying gushers of red blood across Selephygur's face and chest, and grey bowels over his abdomen and legs.

With a final, unreasoning feral howl, Selephygur plunged the bastard sword into Keeyakawa's head with both fists. Imbuing it with every pain he ever suffered from Selephylin, the Lens, the Iron Baron, and the agony of LongBack's and Duke Trevemar's deaths both at the hand of this accursed fowl, he impaled the sword hilt-deep into the ground, crushing the

Ravenne's skull.

Pendenar faded back against his two opponents, until his back was against the face of a boulder. Snaggle-tooth and Torn-ear both slashed down on his shoulder, but Pendenar held the flat of his saber up with both hands to block the attacks. He lowered his arms, but suddenly pushed off the boulder, driving his sword against both Fox's hilts to force them back. Snaggle-tooth had ready his defense arm to drive his dagger into Pendenar's belly, but Torn-ear got in the way as they faded back.

Pendenar wavered his blade threateningly at both of them in alternate turns, ready to stab the first to come at him. Torn-ear chanced to weave and thrust when Pendenar's blade turned away. Snaggle-tooth was ready to follow in, when Pindlebryth tackled him from the side.

The Fox rolled onto his side and continued, using his momentum to find his feet underneath himself and stand, both blades poised for defense.

Pendenar and Pindlebryth cringed as an arrow flew between their heads. Pendenar deflected Torn-ear's blow, sidestepped his follow-through and shoved him past into the flat boulder. Pindlebryth charged Snaggle-tooth with a balestra, then lunged beating against both his opponent's blades, trying to loosen the Fox's grip on one of them.

Bald-pate drew another arrow from his quiver. However, he was forced to fade behind cover, as Grefdel leapt into the Fox's rock blind. The Lemming swung down ferociously, forcing the Fox to dive away, sending him, his bow and the contents of his quiver scattering onto the ground. Grefdel stood to stab the Fox where he lay, when a black wire came across his snout. Red-arms jumped from a covert in the blind, looping two arms of his bola around Grefdel's neck. The central knot of the snare pressed mercilessly against his windpipe, as the Fox used the bola as a garotte. Grefdel dropped his sword, and clutched at the cords tightening around his neck, but he could not manage his fingers around them. He struggled vainly, until with a savage twist the Fox crushed his larynx. Grefdel went limp, his lolling tongue turning blue. Red-arms twisted the knotted cord in the other direction with a sudden jerk, breaking Grefdel's neck with a sickening pop.

Bald-pate scrambled on all fours to retrieve his bow. He

shouted to Red-arms, and pointed him towards Jarjin, who had rushed to engage Scar-eye after Trevemar fell.   Red-arms released one end of his makeshift garotte and kicked Grefdel's body away.   He drew his saber, and ran at Jarjin spinning the bola in his defensive hand.   Bald-pate resumed his position, after he gathered his bow and a scant handful of arrows.   He nocked one arrow and waited for a clear target amongst the various melees around him.

Jarjin swung pell-mell against Scar-eye, a series of rapid blows that forced the Fox backwards.   What Jarjin lacked in finesse with the unfamiliar blade, he more than made up for with adrenalin.   Scar-eye was frantic, turning his blades this way and that, up down and across, blocking some strikes and deflecting others.   One of Jarjin's blows finally found its mark, as his épée knocked Scar-eye's sword so hard it nearly dislocated the Fox's shoulder.   Jarjin riposted immediately avoiding his dagger defense, and hacked deep above Scar-eye's hip.   Scar-eye fell in a gasping heap, and Jarjin turned just in time to accept Red-arms' charge.

Jarjin continued the wild stampede of strikes against his new opponent, but he soon found his battery of attacks was foolhardy.   Red-arms swung forward his shield arm, and hopelessly entangled Jarjin's new épée in the spinning bola. He pulled his bola towards himself, while driving his sword down. Jarjin's attempt to dodge was only partly successful, for the strike meant to cleave his neck instead impaled his shoulder. Red-arms tried to drive the point home, but Jarjin twisted away, causing the saber to tear out sideways.   He then hooked his other arm around Red-arms' neck and wrestled him to the ground.

Pindlebryth slashed upwards, clanging against Snaggle-tooth's dagger, spun around and brought his blade down again. Snaggle-tooth crossed his saber and dagger at the hilts and caught Pindlebryth's sword between the two.   He surged forward, pushing Pindlebryth away.   They faced each other en garde, their blades angled threateningly at each other's eyes. They circled one other looking for an opening.

As he came close to Darothien, still bound at her forearms and ankles, Snaggle-tooth glanced down to assure his footing would not falter.   His feet scraped and scattered small stones, however, spraying Darothien's face.   She twitched and quickly clawed her way back to consciousness. She shook her head, wincing at her eye nearly swollen shut, and spat out several droplets of blood from her aching jaw.

Snaggle-tooth saw the enchantress stir to life, and was momentarily distracted by indecision – continue to engage the prince, or deal with the sorceress before she brought her magick to bear? Pindlebryth took the opening, and leapt forward. He battered Snaggle-tooth's dagger away, and stepped to the Fox's open flank to strike – only to be knocked back by a searing, piercing pain. He looked down in surprise at the arrow sunk deep into his chest.

"No!" Darothien screamed at the top of her lungs. She leapt futilely at Snaggle-tooth, the large bola about her ankles preventing her from doing much more than toppling over again. Like a worm, writhing and exposed, she wriggled towards Pindlebryth. Her forearms, still bound by the smaller bola, scrabbled and scratched at the dusty ground in front of her.

Pindlebryth grimaced with determination against Bald-pate's arrow sticking through his lung, and pushed hard with his legs, ramming Snaggle-tooth with his shoulder. Coiled to bring his sword down on Pindlebryth's unprotected back, the Fox was unbalanced by the impact. Snaggle-tooth stumbled backwards, flailing his arms to maintain his balance. The satchel slid off his shoulder and down his arm, but caught in the crook of his elbow. Fighting against the searing in his ribcage, a gorge of bloody foam clogging his throat and his blurring double vision, Pindlebryth slashed as best he could at Snaggle-tooth. He missed the torso, but sliced the tendon in the Fox's defense arm, and through the strap of his satchel.

The bag bounced off a small boulder behind the Fox and rolled unevenly in front of Darothien. With a grunt that crescendoed into a fevered cry of violent fury, she coiled her legs under her and shoved herself towards the satchel. She twisted her forearms, to force the palms of her paws to face each other. The cord of the bola cut through her fur, and bit into the skin, drawing blood. Disregarding the pain, she thrust both hands into the opened satchel flap, and clamped down on the Orb.

"*Forget!*"

At the word, a pulse of gray malevolence exploded with a low growling hum. Lifeless ashen light streamed out from between the folds of the satchel into Darothien's face. Straining with effort, her face shone like a death's-head wreathed with fur that glowed like funereal cinders. Her eyes at first merely reflected the ghastly light, but within a heartbeat they echoed the cinereal lambency, beaming out a sickening gray light of their own.

Pindlebryth crumpled at the feet of Snaggle-tooth, fighting to remain conscious as blood coursed from his side and frothed in his mouth. As he struggled to raise his blade in defense, he beheld Snaggle-tooth standing at a strange kilter.

He became dimly aware of a sound he had heard before. It grew louder and louder still, until the sound of a sandstorm blowing across an endless wasteland roared throughout his entire being.

Snaggle-tooth and his band of mercenaries stood frozen for an eternal moment, and then they were gone. They seemed to disintegrate like tissue paper torn apart from the inside by a sirocco. Their mouths were arched in silent screams until they too were scrubbed away by the sound of blasting sands.

Selephygur and Pendenar were both left standing like statues, frozen in mid-strike in confused wonder as they watched their adversaries dissolve in front of their very eyes. Jarjin found himself rolling in the dirt, suddenly clutching at thin air.

The sound of raging wind died quickly, leaving a silence broken only by a single voice. Darothien lay writhing face down on the ground, though the snares that bound her limbs were gone, as if they never existed. Her voice started low in volume and pitch, but grew to a size of an unbridled scream as she stared with revulsion at the Orb that lay in front of the empty satchel. Her voice shook the small glade as it reverberated in sympathy with her anguish.

"What have I done!" she shrieked just before her breath gave out. She gasped with several shallow breaths and sobs in succession, sending small clouds of dust flying around her. Her breaths accelerated as she gathered herself to stand, and in one motion stood bolt upright.

Loathing filled her entire being – not only for the Orb, but also more strongly for herself. She had surely injured adversaries before, sometimes severely in the heat of battle. But she had never killed – never before acted with the sole intention of taking a life. And now she had killed so many – *so many*!

She didn't know what to do with this blinding revulsion. She wanted to tear out her tongue, to claw her eyes out, to rend the very hide off her face. But the gray lambency of the Orb filled her vision, and became the focus of her hatred.

Both her visage and her very stance a vision of utter condemnation, she ripped her wand from her sleeve and screamed something that sounded like the shattering of glass. A blinding surge of violent green burst from the wand with a concussion of a cannon volley, striking the Orb.

The sphere received the blast, answering with its own pulse of gray power that knocked Pendenar and Selephygur off their feet. But the Orb was untouched – it absorbed Darothien's fury, subsumed it, spinning and humming like a hundred angry hives before falling silent. Darothien fell to her knees utterly spent.

Selephygur scrambled on all fours over to Pindlebryth, and turned him on his side. He tried to undo his brother's riding jerkin, but could not do so without worsening the wound.

Pindlebryth lay coughing spurts of red foam, as blood drained slowly around the base of the arrow shaft. He turned his head slightly to Selephygur and tried to speak, but panic filled his eyes as he coughed and began to strangle on his own blood.

Selephygur began to mindlessly repeat, "No, no, no!" as he pressed on the wound, fruitlessly attempting to staunch the blood. Jarjin rushed over to assist as best he could, ignoring his own injury. He tried sheathing his sword, but the épée didn't fit his scabbard. He tossed it aside as he knelt down next to Pindlebryth, across from Selephygur.

Pendenar glanced for but a moment of indecision between Darothien and his prince, then sprang into action. He sheathed his sword and knelt next to Pindlebryth, shoving Jarjin aside.

"Take care of your own shoulder. Otherwise you're no good to me here!" Pendenar scolded, as he switched his dagger to his sword hand. He lifted the back section of Pindlebryth's jerkin already loosened by Selephygur, and saw just the tip of the arrow pointing out.

"Hold him down," he ordered Selephygur. He cut a swath off his own jerkin, and jammed it into Pindlebryth's mouth. "Bite down. Hard."

Pendenar hammered the arrow once firmly with the hilt of his dagger. Pindlebryth yowled through the jerkin amid a spray of red froth, as the arrowhead cut through his back. Pendenar grabbed the arrow by the fletching and cut off its tail at an oblique angle along the grain to prevent splintering. He seized the crudely cut jasper arrow head and yanked, deftly removing the arrow shaft with only a single thin stringy trail of blood.

Pindlebryth whimpered once and fainted.

"Keep him on his side and clear his mouth, so he doesn't drown." He clamped down on the entrance and exit wounds, using Pindlebryth's jerkin. "Jarjin! Go to Mariner, and get bandages and alcohol."

"But he's bleeding internally. They're not enough!" Selephygur replied through gritted teeth as he pulled out the strip of heavy cloth dripping with his brother's saliva and clotting blood.

"Just do it, Jarjin!" barked Pendenar, his eyes betraying the desperation he kept from his voice. Jarjin obeyed with a sob of despair and stood, still holding his injured shoulder. He turned to run, when he was surprised by Darothien standing behind him. At her feet lay her backpack, opened and its contents scattered. In one paw was her wand, the other grasped an opalescent jar.

"Stand aside," she ordered Selephygur and Pendenar as she brushed past Jarjin, still rooted to the ground. Her face was a strange mask devoid of emotion. She quickly knelt beside her prince, and scooped out a large portion of unguent from the jar with her wand. She tossed the jar aside, and slathered the ointment along the entire length of her wand. Then with a cry steeped with remorseful exigency, she wielded the wand like a knife, and plunged the wand into Pindlebryth's wound. She drove it deeper into the injury until its salve-covered point emerged out the arrow's exit wound. She twisted the wand as she pulled it out, leaving most of the ointment in Pindlebryth's body.

Selephygur, Pendenar and Jarjin cried with shouts of disbelief and revulsion, but did nothing to stop the enchantress. She bent over, bringing her mouth to just over the wound and whispered into it. She folded the jerkin back over the wound and pressed. A lambent green aura flowed out from under the garment. She whispered a second time, and the emerald glow increased to a wild intensity until it suddenly ceased like a bonfire extinguished by a flood of water.

Darothien sobbed once and collapsed over Pindlebryth's hip, her bloodied wand rolling out of her numb grasp. Pendenar held his breath as he hesitantly pulled Pindlebryth's jerkin aside. His jaw went slack at the sight of the red puckering of a freshly healed wound, and his snout wrinkled at the pungent scent of the remaining traces of ointment. He sat back on his haunches, and sheathed his dagger.

"Lend – lend a paw here," Pendenar's aghast voice trembled, as he pointed Selephygur at Darothien's slumped form. "Jarjin, fetch some water, the bandages and alcohol. The water and bandages are for Pindlebryth. The brandy is for me!" Selephygur revived Darothien as Pendenar continued to examine Pindlebryth. Darothien quickly came to, and wordlessly pushed Selephygur away. She knelt next to Pindlebryth, staring blankly at his unconscious form.

She came out of a dark place. She tasted inside herself a cold hard steel that she hadn't known since she was a pup. She recalled hiding, huddling in a small circle of stones, twigs and grass in the hollow of an enclave of rocks. She replayed the blurred image of her mother running away, trying to lure the Iron Baron's soldiers away. She remembered how she sat motionless like a small bird facing a predator. She recollected how she ran directly away from her mother, not stopping, not reacting in the slightest when she heard the strangled cry for mercy from her mother before the soldiers slew her. She relived in a few instants the endless panic as she loped through fields, crawled through thickets, plowed across streams, and tore through forests. And finally, she remembered how she clawed panic-stricken at the person who found her and held her close, until she recognized the friendly face of her mother's sister. Having traveled blindly across the canton border, she had finally stopped her running. Grief caught up with her, as she collapsed with shrieks of agony into the embrace of her aunt.

Darothien felt like she now stood behind herself, watching some other enchantress struggling against the Fox and Crow. She felt like that tiny urchin, hiding herself while a separate Darothien witnessed Grefdel and Trevemar die, and was helplessly bound as Pindlebryth lay dying before her eyes. The fearful young pup spied from the safety of her stone shelter, as another Darothien used the Orb to kill with unrestrained hatred and vengeance, as some other Lemming drove the wand mercilessly, needfully into the prince. The shivering pup sat quietly by, holding her breath as the other Darothien did everything that needed to be done, but she was too scared to do.

But then the pup pulled on Darothien's gown, wanting to show her something. Darothien looked down with emotionless eyes at the child. The urchin stepped aside, revealing a killdeer hen. It huddled over her clutch of eggs amongst its nest of stones and twigs, chirping madly at the intruder that crouched next to its brood. The pup spoke to it, and petted it. The killdeer suddenly quieted, and began to preen the Lemming pup as if it were one of its own. The waif spoke to the bird, and it flew off several yards away to the blurred image of her mother. It harassed the blurred Lemming doe, flying about it then crying out loudly as it began its instinctual broken-wing display. It continued to hop and keen and flutter noisily, until the blur was surrounded by the Iron Baron's guards.

The cold steel shattered as the guards slew the blur and the killdeer. The flavor of burnt iron dissolved, receding back from whence it came, like a tide of numbness. All that was left was the taste of the Valley's granite in her mouth.

She looked down at Pindlebryth laying in front of her, and she cried. She cried, every fiber of her being writhing in a cathartic release of agony and fear.

Darothien wept even more fiercely, as she realized with horror that something was different – something was shared. The little pup revealed to Darothien something from the enclave she had buried so long ago, and Darothien had shown the scared little waif the ruthless monstrosity she was capable of becoming. And they both knew they were one and the same.

Darothien leaned over and buried her face in the dirt, and screamed.

Jarjin landed his shearwater in the glade. He leapt off and dashed towards Pindlebryth with the medical supplies, but he slowed to barely a trot as he saw Darothien. Selephygur pulled Darothien up, trying to console her – but she threw herself to the ground again. Jarjin first handed most of the supplies to Pendenar, then set to mending his own shoulder.

After Pendenar cleaned Pindlebryth's mouth and verified he no longer ventilated blood, he washed his wounds. He took a gulp of brandy from the metal travel flask, then a second before dousing a gauze with the liqueur. He then only lightly bandaged Pindlebryth's injuries, to keep them clean. His prince breathed more easily, without fresh blood coming out of his mouth.

Pendenar had barely finished wrapping the last swath, when Pindlebryth emerged from unconsciousness. The guard was dumbfounded at the speed of Pindlebryth's recovery brought about by Darothien's magick.

Pindlebryth's eyes fluttered open, and he tried to draw a deep breath. He breathed tentatively at first, but then fully, as he discerned that he could do so without pain. He instinctively reached for his wound expecting to find the arrow, but instead found Pendenar's bandages. He slowly lifted his arm – although a little weak, he still felt no pain. He cupped his palm on Darothien's head, and gently caressed the side of her muzzle.

She painfully pushed herself off the ground, and knelt again, putting her hand under his head.

"I saw her!" she exclaimed suddenly, her eyes wild with disgust. "I *saw* my mother die! And I made it happen. *I caused it*!" Her jaw went slack, and she looked skyward, not being able to face anyone about her. "I was afraid. I was afraid to die. I was afraid, that you, too..." she said, each sentence punctuated by a breathlessly apoplectic sob.

"But I'm here," he replied softly. "I'm *here*. You saved me."

Darothien bowed her head, and touched her forehead to his. She yowled anew in blind horror at her crimes – both the one so long ago in the nest, and the one in the Valley's glade. She clutched at Pindlebryth, hugging him desperately as if to beg his forgiveness.

Pindlebryth reached over with his arm and held her close. He knew he could only dimly understand Darothien's anguish, and just being close was the best thing he could do for her. He stayed that way until her strident cries slowly reduced to soft sobbing.

Selephygur leaned back, and marveled at what Darothien had wrought, when he spied Jarjin's sword.

"Where did you get that?" he asked.

Jarjin, had returned from collecting the épée's scabbard, shrugged his good shoulder and replied, "From a Fox that broke my own sword."

"That's a Vulpinden count's sword," Selephygur said pointing to a crest on the scabbard. "A good trophy."

Pindlebryth sat up with only a little pain, asking with trepidation to anyone who could answer, "What happened? Where are the Fox and Crow? Where's the Orb?"

"I – I made them – *forget.*" Darothien shivered at the word. She looked at the ground in front of Pindlebryth, afraid to meet his gaze, and racked with whimpers and gulps of air, afraid to confess her deed.

"Forget?" Pindlebryth probed her further, cocking his head to try to look at her face to face. "Forget how? Like the stone corridor? Forget where they were? Forget to come at all?"

"No!" she screamed furiously, locking him with a piercing gaze that rung with anger and fear. "I made them forget they *existed.* I *unmade* them!" she shrieked.

"Lords Below take the Orb!" she wailed, clamping her paws over her eyes.

Pindlebryth gathered his legs underneath him and stood. A strange resolve came over him as he began to realize the power of the Orb. "Quickening Spirit help us, if the Kyaa or the Iron Baron got a hold of this! It has to be destroyed."

"We cannot. I tried!" Darothien whimpered as she also stood. "Don't you think Henejer and Gazelikus tried too, and failed? It was made by the Quickening Spirit. We mortals cannot unmake it by our own means. And when I... I used the Orb, I understood it could not – would not – unmake itself."

Pindlebryth found himself staring at the Orb. It lay quiescent on the ground, but he felt it contained every malevolence in the world. "Yes, Lords Below take this hateful thing."

"No, it's not hateful," Darothien said flatly as she stared into the Orb, as if she were recalling something it told her. "It's only a tool. We – the living – are just in its way. Temporary shadows. Things to be endured."

But Pindlebryth could not agree. He stepped towards it, and it hummed to life, pulsing with anathema. Pindlebryth continued to sullenly stare into the lifeless light that exuded wave after wave of enmity against all life. He felt the wraith of despair clawing its way back out of the pit in the darkest recesses of his heart. He had not tasted such anguish and doubt since he sat contemplating his parents' fate – and his own –

when they lay frozen in Selephylin's enchantment of sleeping death. Only this time it somehow felt worse when combined with his intuition to warn him of some nameless terror.

The clamor of the itch had started the first day of this journey, and had been growing incessantly until it now fairly roared up and down the back of his neck. The most egregious part of it all, was although his intuition shouted since the very beginning that their mission to locate and rescue the Orb of Oblivion would have horrific consequences, Pindlebryth nonetheless knew it was still the most favorable of all other outcomes. If the Fox, the Crow, or worst of all the Iron Baron, wrested control of the Orb from Lenland, the future of Lenland if not the entire world would spin into a pit of endless nightmare.

But could he trust himself? Who was he to believe that he could rescue the world? He had already witnessed the ruin that a lesser Artifact, the Lens of Truth, wreaked on his brother. Could he withstand the temptation of the most powerful and dangerous Artifact on himself? – be trusted to deny the hubris that seemed to infect those who had prolonged contact with these blessed and cursed arcane devices? – be trusted to keep the world and himself sane, or at the very least keep the world as it was?

So many depended upon him, his talents and abilities, the authority of his Name – it nearly crushed his psyche. It was only now that Pindlebryth began to appreciate what a gift, what a blessing, it was for the Orb to have the will and power to make one forget.

The despair finally got the better of him, and it found vent as he lashed out at the group. "Don't you understand?" he bellowed, not caring how far his voice carried, or where it echoed. "This cursed Artifact will always be sought after. If not the Iron Baron, then someone else will covet its power.

"We cannot keep it, for it will draw constant attempts from any number of unknown enemies, inflicting devastations upon Lenland and any innocents who happen to be in the way. We cannot hide it, for either our enemies or some other unwitting race will always find a way to uncover it, no matter where on land or sea we hide it. We cannot destroy it, for it cannot be unmade. And no one can be trusted with it, for its temptation will eventually corrupt even the most noble creature – certainly more noble than I!"

Pindlebryth's despair was infectious. As he railed, Pendenar and Darothien's countenances began to melt into sorrow and despondency beyond description. Selephygur and Jarjin stood not knowing what do, or what it all meant.

But railing against Pindlebryth's self-doubt, and his self-denigration, something within Darothien refused surrender.

Something steely within her answered back – not cold like an unforgiving blade, but burning like an ingot waiting to be forged. It answered not for her own safety and protection, nor in response to fear, cowardice, absolution or revenge, but rather to somehow give aid and comfort to her love. She stood directly in front of him, to meet his eyes with her own, so that he could see her earnest belief in him.

"After all we've been through, *My Lord* Pindlebryth, I have faith in you. I pledge everything I can give to you, to overcome whatever may happen. If we cannot trust *you* to prevail against the Artifacts and those who covet them, then no one alive can prevail."

At her words, Pindlebryth inhaled sharply and looked skyward. He clenched his paws, and tensed his whole body as if he were about to scream havoc, to swear blasphemy against the Quickening Spirit Himself.

Instead, he grasped Darothien by the shoulders, and shouted, "That's it! *That's* the solution!" The incessant itch of his compelling intuition finally fell blissfully silent. He drew Darothien into an embrace that squeezed the breath out of her. As he nuzzled her roughly, she felt the gratitude of Pindlebryth's damp eyes trickle down her own cheek and erode the sharpest debilitating pangs of guilt.

"Thank you Darothien! We've found the answer!" She marveled with bewilderment at Pindlebryth, as he almost laughed while releasing her. "And thank you, Tanderra!"

The entire group exchanged looks of utter confusion, at the mention of the deceased previous Prime Minister's name. They also were disoriented at the radical change that overcame their prince – one moment he seemed crushed by despair, the next he became positively euphoric.

"Darothien, you will take Jarjin's shearwater. Jarjin, ride home with Pendenar on Mariner. Selephygur, you and Pendenar each tow one of Trevemar's and Grefdel's steeds, and return our honored fallen home. Darothien and I will follow you partway to CityState. When we are far from here, and are sure we are not followed, we will go our separate ways. I will need Darothien's help to seal away the Orb, hopefully once and for all."

"Wait!" Pendenar spurt. "Darothien, do you know how to take the reins?"

"I've ridden reindeer by the score, but I confess I've never held the reins of a flyer."

"It's not too different," confided Jarjin. "It's just the takeoffs and landings that are touchy."

"Where will you go?" Selephygur asked, as he looked skyward, shielding his eye from a column of sunlight that angled down between two of the mountains.

"Where no one will find the Orb," he answered as he tied the ends of the satchel back together. "And when all is done, neither I nor Darothien will remember where."

Pindlebryth tried to lash the satchel containing the Orb to the pommel of his saddle. But Voyager cried suddenly and bucked, hopping away from the prince. The feathers on his head splayed out in fear, as he turned his head to cast a baleful eye on the satchel.

Darothien interposed herself, and held out an open palm. She trilled softly, combining the sounds of a cooing dove and the lapping of a serene lake on its shore, as a crescendo of emerald glowed about her fingers. Though still feet away from Voyager, she made a motion as if to pet and preen the bird. Voyager immediately calmed down, nestling peacefully on the ground as his feathers lay flat again.

"He'll now accept the Orb," she instructed Pindlebryth.

"What did you do? He'll still be able to fly, won't he?"

"Of course." Darothien glanced sheepishly at Pendenar, then faced Pindlebryth again, though she looked at the ground contritely. "I'm afraid I have another confession to make. I used the same spell on you last night, to help you sleep."

Pindlebryth hooked a finger under her chin and lifted gently until she looked at him directly. "Casting two spells on me in two days? Without my knowledge, nor permission? I will have to think on whether I condone such behavior, or not," he said with a sly grin.

"Now, where were we? Ah, yes – we must be off!"

Pindlebryth jabbered as he slung the satchel to Voyager's pommel.

"Alone?" Pendenar protested, the protective mother hen as always. "Surely I need not convince you the danger of going this alone! And you are not in the best condition to ride, M'Lord!"

"I've ridden Voyager with wounds before, Pendenar. And ones far worse than this," he ruminated introspectively, as he pressed a paw over one of the bandages. "Voyager knows me well enough to ride without reins at all if need be. Besides, I won't be alone." He took Darothien's paw firmly, and held her close. "Darothien has proven time and again that she is a force to be reckoned with. However, just to allay even your fears, Pendenar," he retorted, starting to reach for his breast pocket. "Darothien, where is your Talking Gem?"

"Here," she replied simply, pressing her paw on her thick overcoat, over her heart.

Pindlebryth smiled with modest surprise at her answer. He expected her Gem was somewhere back at the castle.

"Selephygur, take this," he said producing the pouch containing his Gem. "One of these was supposed to be yours to begin with. If we run into trouble, we will let you know."

Pindlebryth led Darothien to Mariner, and helped her to transfer her belongings to Jarjin's mount. "Let's be quick about this.   We don't know if the Fox mercenaries had more accomplices. If they did, they must find us and the Orb gone. And they will have a great mystery on their hands without a single body to tell them what happened."

They made quick work of their preparations for departure, except for cleanup. It took quite a bit more time for Selephygur than the others to collect enough snow to take a field bath to remove the gore of combat.

Pindlebryth was about to mount Voyager, when he realized he needed to attend to one last detail. He went back to Grefdel's mount and opened one of the saddle bags, and retrieved Grefdel's spyglass.

"I have need of this, old friend. I shall return it to you when I return to Lenland," he said reverently with the glass in both hands. He was securing it in his own bags, when Pindlebryth spied Selephygur standing by the flank of his tern. He stood with his back to him, staring over his mount at the draped form of Duke Trevemar. Pindlebryth approached him, and clasped his brother's shoulder from behind.

Selephygur turned to face him, and returned the gesture.

"The duke would be proud of you. As am I." Pindlebryth shook Selephygur's shoulder for emphasis. "It is good to have you back again."

"You were gone before I had a chance to apologize," Selephygur said with earnest penitence. "I'm not sure how I can apologize now, either. I could spend a lifetime trying to understand where I ended and the Iron Baron began over the past several years."

"I understand, and I believe you. I was there in your sickroom, when you spoke of your 'jailor.' I saw the real you, the real Selephygur, my real brother, fight against BrokenTail."

"Then you must also understand that I cannot even be sure of all the ways I might have injured you. How do I apologize for..."

"Apologies are only words," Pindlebryth interrupted. "The fact you are here, and had helped me when I most needed your help, is a deed worth more than a thousand apologies."

Pindlebryth took a step back, and took a moment to consider how to help his brother address another matter that awaited him back home. He looked about himself – although it was nearly certain everyone here would find out sooner or later, there was a certain level of decorum to be observed. That is, if Selephygur's maidservant truly was with child, and this was not some elaborate ruse on the jester Tabarem's part.

"There is someone else back home, however, that also needs more than merely an apology."

"Who?"

"It is a matter of some delicacy. Perhaps you should speak to Tabarem when you return."

"Tabarem? What in the world did I do to him?" Selephygur asked, almost afraid of the answer.

"Nothing. But I will let him explain the situation to you. I think you'll also find he is willing to help you deal with it." He clasped Selephygur's shoulder a second time. "In any event, I will be there to help as well." Selephygur regarded his brother with a look of puzzlement mixed with a strange fearful grin.

They left as the noonday sun hung low in the south. Despite Pendenar's nervous misgivings, Darothien made almost a textbook takeoff, thanks to some prior coaching from Jarjin, or so Jarjin would boast afterwards. He failed to see Darothien lean forward and whisper a few viridian tinged phrases into her shearwater's ear-hole.

Halfway home, near the very geographical center of Lenland, Pindlebryth and Darothien turned due north, as the rest continued southwest to CityState. Pindlebryth and Darothien waved their farewells to Selephygur and the two guards. Pindlebryth aimed a solemn salute to the terns bearing their fallen riders, which Pendenar and Jarjin returned.

The farther they separated, Pindlebryth increasingly reined Voyager back, slowing their progress northward more and more. Darothien paralleled him effortlessly, glancing between Pindlebryth and the squadron shrinking with distance.

"We're not going north, are we?" she asked, even though she knew the answer.

Pindlebryth looked over his shoulder, satisfied that they could no longer be seen without Grefdel's spyglass. He kneed Voyager into a dive, and Jarjin's shearwater followed suit without any urging or reining from Darothien. At half their previous altitude, they leveled off and headed due west.

"Our destination is Vulcanis Major. Where it all began," Pindlebryth finally declared with grim determination.

"Vulcanis? But the Iron Baron knows Selephylin was there! Wouldn't Vulcanis be the most obvious place for him to search for the Orb?" Darothien reasoned.

"He won't be able to disbelieve the lie that is the truth, staring him in the face," Pindlebryth said enigmatically, with a finality that he found oddly pleasurable.

They continued for a little under two hours, until they crossed Lenland's coastline.

Once over MidSea, they dove even further until they were only a few scant yards over the surface of the deep blue water. Pindlebryth and Darothien breathed deep the moist, warmer air of the sea. Pindlebryth snapped his reins, and Voyager keened happily. The birds banked to and fro, gliding on the weak updrafts of air from westward heading waves, frolicking in the winds they always considered their playground. They chased the low hanging sun westward, but soon the prevailing westerlies were impeding the speedy progress they were hoping for.

"How are you feeling?" called Pindlebryth across the speeding wind. "Should we overnight on one of the Archipelago islands, or press on?"

"You'll need me while I can cast effectively," Darothien replied.

Pindlebryth nodded, knowing that her power waned the longer she was away from Lenland. "Onward it is!"

Darothien once again cast about her shearwater the green-veined globe that calmed the air. Pindlebryth reined in the sprightly Voyager, and pulled aside of Darothien. Darothien made a sweeping motion with one arm and the globe instantly expanded to envelope both riders and their mounts. Free of the buffeting headwinds, the steeds easily increased their speed.

"I wonder if you might fold this into a torus, and blow us even faster to Vulcanis?" Pindlebryth ventured, not quite sure if it were a sensible thing to do.

"Tempting, but no!" Darothien chortled. "I'd need my wand, and I don't feel brave enough to fly without reins!"

"It's just as well," agreed Pindlebryth. "I'm not sure myself, how Voyager or your shearwater would take to such a strong tailwind!" In a reassuring tone, he added, "With this glamor alone, we should reach Vulcanis before sunset."

But Pindlebryth's prediction was not quite accurate. Daylight was beginning to wane as they reached the first islands of the Archipelago. As the dimming sun sank closer to the horizon, its comforting yellow light transformed to an all encompassing blood red, casting long horizontal shadows.

"Lords Below, there's nothing for it. Remove your enchantment, Darothien. This close to our goal, we can't afford to attract attention, like some green comet!"

She regretfully complied, but fortunately all was not as bad as it might have been. With the approach of the cooling evening, the blustery headwinds had died down appreciably, and they barely managed to make Vulcanis just after the last dying gasps of sunset.

The island's long-dead caldera had crumbled somewhat since the days of Selephylin. In the rapidly decaying twilight, it looked even more foreboding. The pier that had once harbored Selephylin's great ark was smashed by years of battering from the relentless waves, and great pieces of it lay as bleached bones of driftwood along the beaches of volcanic sands. The road that connected the two landmarks was obscured in many places along the way, covered by years of blowing sands, and crumbling rockslides. They glided over the broken road, Darothien following Pindlebryth's lead until they landed yards away from the forbidding silhouette of the obelisk that marked Selephyrex's grave.

They dismounted, this time Pindlebryth coaxing Voyager to nest on the ground. His wound was already beginning to complain from the long ride, and he appreciated the easy dismount. He dug out from his saddle bag a sealed pan. He opened it and divided all the remaining dried fish among Voyager and Darothien's shearwater, who both hungrily gulped them down. Pindlebryth then untied the satchel from the pommel of Voyager's saddle, and brought it to the side of the grave.

Looking about him, he futilely searched for a digging implement. He then shook his head at his own doltishness – even if there was a shovel or some such implement that was still usable after years of weathering, such heavy labor would surely tear open his newly healed wounds.

He turned to Darothien sheepishly. "Can you manage? I need to unearth Selephygur's casket." Recalling her reaction years ago to Selephyrex's grave, he was somewhat anxious about having asked her to perform such a task now. But his apprehension left him, when he saw the determination in her face.

She wielded her wand one last time, and burbled a sound akin to a flowing stream. Dim green waves exuded from the ground in front of the stone marker, and began pushing the sand and dirt, then pebbles, then larger rocks and finally all the scree away from the obelisk.

As she labored, Pindlebryth's attention was drawn to the writing on the obelisk. This time, he was able to read it for himself by the light of Darothien's spell. It confirmed that this was indeed the final resting place of Selephyrex, son of Selephylin and Enorel III. There was an unflattering adjective before Enorel's name, which he chose to ignore. But as he read the last of the inscription on the black cenotaph, he pondered on the last sentence. It was a phrase of an old variant of Vulpine. Pindlebryth's eyebrows knotted in puzzlement as he translated the phrase, which indicated this was only part of

Selephyrex's remains.

Darothien began to breathe heavily with effort, and her arm began to shake the deeper she dug. But just as her waning power was about to exhaust itself, the sands revealed a polished flat platform only three feet below the surface. In the center of the platen was a square hole, in which rested a black-green obsidian box. Totally spent, Darothien dropped her arm and stepped away from the grave.

"Selephylin must have cremated Selephyrex," she panted. She then gasped, adding, "Must you disturb his remains?" as Pindlebryth sat on the edge of the grave and carefully lowered himself.

"Yes. Believe me, I do not take pleasure in this, but I must – if we are ever to be free of this cursed Orb." He placed the satchel next to square opening, put his hands on the lid of the obsidian cinerary. As he lifted the lid, he was nearly overcome by the stench that wafted out of the box. It took a moment, but he recognized the noxious foetor. He jumped back with an instinctive cry, as his nostrils were assaulted by an impossible mix of acid and lye, of ammonia and bleach, burnt flesh combined with a noisome stink of something not found in nature.

After the surge of adrenalin wore off, Pindlebryth doubled over in pain as he realized he, without even thinking, had jumped clear to the edge of the grave and began to climb out. Darothien rushed over to help him. But Pindlebryth summoned his courage, and stood next to the receptacle.

In the last sputtering of the dying twilight, Darothien and Pindlebryth peered into the obsidian container. It was half-filled with blue white crystals – the same left behind by the Living Moat as it dehydrated and died.

"Lords Below!" Pindlebryth muttered in disbelief. "Selephyrex – the Living Moat!?"

"What kind of monster *was* Selephylin? To turn her own son into that – that *thing*!" Darothien shrieked. She stumbled back in horror at the concept as she gave it utterance, not wanting to believe it.

"We may never know. It may not even have been wholly her doing at all. It may have been the Lens of Truth. After all, it began to invade Selephygur's body and change him. Maybe it was a cumulative effect in Selephyrex's case, or a combination of it and her magick. We shall never know."

"I know. *I* know! *I – Know!*" Darothien spat with complete loathing. "She sacrificed her own son, just so she could continue using magick away from Vulpinden!" She clutched her paws together in front of herself, as she recalled how Selephylin used the Lens to manipulate the life force eaten by the Living Moat. "Monster! Fiend! Abomination!" she wailed.

Pindlebryth held up the satchel, and removed the Orb from within, still wrapped in Gazelikus' Cloth. He threw the satchel at Darothien's feet, and unwrapped the Orb as he held it in his left paw. Its sickly gray fluorescence cast long distorted shadows about him, as it thrummed malignantly. He then dropped the cloth and held the Orb between his hands.

"What are you doing?" hissed Darothien. Her head sank low, and her shoulders squeezed together as she unconsciously tried to hide from the Orb.

"What I must do – to forget." Pindlebryth peered into the heart of the Orb, as it hummed even louder, even more menacingly.

"I give you what you so desire – to be left alone. Take my memory of your resting place, you misbegotten wretch. I and the whole world will be glad to be rid of you."

He bent over and placed the Orb in the obsidian repository, and pushed it down into the crystals, taking care not to touch them. Even though they lay dead for years, he felt he was tempting fate far too much already, this close to the potentially lethal remains. The Orb safely nestled in the azure crystals, he took the obsidian lid and sealed the box.

"Should you not cover it with Gazelikus' Cloth?" Darothien hypothesized.

"No," Pindlebryth replied after a moment's consideration. "Just as Unkaar found the cloth, so can another Snow Goose."

He climbed out of Selephyrex's grave with Darothien's assistance. He faced the grave, solemnly clasped his hands in front of him and bowed his head.

"We commend to rest the body of Selephyrex, son of Selephylin, son of Enorel III, half brother to Hatheron, King of Lenland. I, Prince Pindlebryth of Lenland, give to Selephyrex the item that he and his mother so coveted – the Orb of Oblivion. By the authority of royal birth, I hereby grant to Selephyrex citizenship in the kingdom of Lenland. And in the name of Lenland, I claim this parcel his final resting place."

After observing a moment of silence, Pindlebryth took a step back and collected the satchel. He moved to the piles of displaced dirt, and using the satchel as a scoop, began to throw the sand, dirt and stone into the grave. He winced and grunted with each satchel load, but persevered. Darothien tried to move the aggregate with her wand, but she had completely exhausted her reserves. She laid her wand, lens and prism aside, and rolled up her sleeves to assist Pindlebryth bury Selephyrex's remains and the Orb.

They both remained silent as they labored in the light of the prism, still glowing sympathetically with the Orb. Its light diminished as they filled the grave, until only starlight was left after they finished replacing the last of the ground.

They collected their things – the satchel, Gazelikus' Cloth, and Darothien's implements – leaving no evidence that they were ever on Vulcanis. They mounted their steeds, clapping off any traces of the volcanic soil on their hands, feet and clothing.

As they prepared to finally take off, Darothien asked wearily, "I still don't understand how this hides the Orb. What is this 'lie that is truth' you spoke of?"

"The Orb is buried with Selephyrex who is now legally a citizen of Lenland. Normally, the MidSea Archipelago is sacrosanct and by the first PanGaean Accords, cannot be claimed by any nation. Prime Minister Tanderra found an obscure clause in that very same law, that granted an exception for burial. In that sole case, that land comprising the grave belongs to the deceased citizen's country.

"When we return to Lenland, I intend to display Selephylin's Crown in the CityState museum for all to see, including the Iron Baron's spies, whoever they may be. In fact, now that I think of it, I think I will convince my father to lift his edict expelling citizens of Vulpinden and the Rookeries from Lenland."

He looked up at the stars to get his bearing, and then back at PanGaea. With a sigh he wistfully said, "It would do my heart good to see Hakayaa again." Pindlebryth urged Voyager up from his nesting place, and pointed him eastward. Darothien's shearwater followed Voyager's example, trilling softly.

"In any event, the Kyaa and the Iron Baron will be forced to come to the inescapable conclusion that the Orb is still in Lenland. Let them hatch their little plots and intrigues until they rot. They will never find the Orb, because no one will know where it really is. There is only one last small detail to complete the lie."

Pindlebryth and Darothien lightly snapped their reins, and urged their steeds up with a light kick. Both the birds eagerly leapt into the air and easily flapped away into the calm cool air, keening their delight at finally leaving the blighted island.

We have hidden the Orb, where it will stay until the End of Time. Do not look for it. Display Selephylin's Crown in the museum, but keep the carbonado hidden. Give the Cloth to Tabarem. Rescind Hatheron's edict. Destroy this note when you no longer remember the location of the Orb, but can still remember these instructions. Trust yourselves.

Signed,
Pindlebryth, Prince of Lenland
Darothien, Wizard of Lenland

They sat in the laboratory with the door closed, as they wrote the note to themselves. Next to the note was a crucible, and Selephylin's Crown. Three of its gems glowed a fierce crimson, and a fourth still glowed a deep indigo indicating the Raccoon still had possession of the Ring of Fortitude. The final gem indicating the ownership of the Orb remained Lenland's vibrant emerald color.

Pindlebryth yawned and nodded to himself in satisfaction as Darothien signed her name to the note, and laid it in the crucible.

"We'll destroy this note tomorrow morning, if its conditions are satisfied," Pindlebryth decided.

"I'm sure they will," Darothien replied, her head tilted as she tried to think. "I know the Orb is on Vulcanis, but I'm already having trouble remembering exactly where it is."

Pindlebryth stood still for a moment, then nodded in agreement. "As am I. Hopefully, by tomorrow we won't even remember that much."

Darothien looked at the document, some questions still haunting her. "I understand the need to keep the cap piece to Selephylin's Crown here in the laboratory – no need to tempt fate by putting it on display.

"But Gazelikus' Cloth? Tabarem?"

"Tabarem's patchwork trousers are in constant need of mending. What better use for the cloth? A friend told me several times the wisdom of 'hiding in plain sight.' And I for one, would like to see Unkaar peck at Tabarem's behind!"

They shared an unreserved laugh as they stood up from the table and made for the door. As Darothien was about to open the doorknob, Pindlebryth pulled her back and took her in his arms. He embraced her warmly, and they stood nuzzling for the longest of times.

Finally, Darothien said, "I know of a perfect way to end this adventure, but..."

"As do I!" he said with a knowing grin, which faded into a sympathetic smile. "...but we both have not slept since before the Valley of Giants. Besides, we should give the Orb time to do its work." They left the laboratory and outer room paw in paw, both of them looking forward to the oblivion of sleep and forgetfulness.

Epilogue

Pindlebryth found himself beside Voyager, walking through a fog denser than he could ever remember. Voyager was obviously distraught, walking a few steps, then hopping nervously. Occasionally he stretched his wings then flapped and hovered for a few seconds, thrashing his legs as if he were unsure where the ground was. Once he did clumsily alight again on the invisible ground, he lowered and pivoted his head, trying to sniff the floor and examine it with one eye.

When Pindlebryth reached over to calm his friend down, he noticed that Voyager had no reins, no saddle, nor tack of any kind. He eased over to place his right arm over Voyager's shoulders. The beast quickly calmed down, and rubbed his head against Pindlebryth's chest. Exchanging a glance, the pair resumed walking through the monotonous grayness.

They continued for a short while until a strange glow began to emerge in front of them. It consisted of a handful of washed out colors – a faint yellow, a pallid orange, a feeble blue, and a sickly brown. Closest to them was a greenish pastel that Pindlebryth hoped would resolve itself into Darothien's familiar emerald green.

Voyager also spotted the lights as they steadily grew in intensity. He turned his head to one side then the other, trying to focus on their distance from themselves. He opened his bill, and his thin tongue pointed out between his beak's tomia, as if he were trying to sound a call. But Pindlebryth heard nothing.

As they approached, the hues coalesced and began to take on distinct shapes. Pindlebryth began to perceive they were in a specific order. Indeed, the green luminous shape was closest to him, neighbor to a second distinct green contour, both in the shapes of cylinders. The second one seemed to be less muted than the green cylinder closer to him, and periodically would flash with vivid intensity. As Pindlebryth continued to walk towards the lights, all the shapes' colors bloomed in depth as they formed a row of similar cylinders in the mist.

Straining to see more clearly, Pindlebryth thought he could discern vague silhouettes in most of the cylinders. The closest one was empty, but the second one seemed to have a statue enclosed within it. Almost immediately, he could distinguish that the figure in the cylinder was a Lemming. He initially had a foreboding of who might be trapped inside the cylinder, but within a half-dozen paces he could ultimately tell from his gray outline that the figure was an old shell of a bent-over male. The codger was stooped, and seemed to be in pain. His stance did not belie an excruciatingly debilitating pain, but rather the ever-present dull ache that accompanies old age.

Pindlebryth tried to call out to the old skeleton, but was confounded when he discovered his own voice, like Voyager's, was also silenced. He continued forward to get a better look at the imprisoned stranger, but he found that it became more and more difficult to press forward with each step. It was as if he were walking against a force that became stronger the closer he came to the cylinders. He looked at Voyager who also struggled against the increasing resistance. Voyager bowed his head forward, and began to flap his wings heavily as he tried to muscle his way forward to keep pace with Pindlebryth. Eventually the pair came up against a point where neither of them could proceed further. The force was unyielding, as if they came up against a great glass wall. Pindlebryth moved to the side with little difficulty, and surmised that the impenetrable wall was curved. At first he thought the invisible force also conformed to a large cylinder, but the arch of the wall as he reached overhead indicated it was more akin to a great sphere.

Pindlebryth struck the dome with his fist. It felt almost as if he flailed against a great glass bell. With his left paw he could feel the vibration caused by the impact of his right fist – yet there was no sound. He checked his person, perchance to find some tool that he might test against the wall.

To his surprise, he found he was completely naked. His initial distress at his scandalous state dampened quickly – some part of his reason told him that it was normal, almost necessary in this place.

But his attention was drawn back to movement near the many colored columns. The mist subtly waned as two figures slowly walked towards Pindlebryth, approaching from beyond the farthest of the cylinders. One of the forms seemed normal and almost familiar, but the other was that of a formidable giant.

It towered over the first figure, and walked like nothing he had ever seen before. Pindlebryth could only gape as the creature gradually revealed itself through the attenuating grayness.

Its gait and posture were striking – its two legs were long and straight, bending only slightly at what Pindlebryth presumed were its knees and ankles as it walked. Its feet were impossibly small and colored the same as the rest of its mostly hairless body. The torso broadened at its shoulders, and supported two long arms and five-fingered hands at its sides. Behind its back was what seemed to be two folded wings. Its head sported a long flowing mane, but its face was turned away from him as it looked down at the diminutive creature walking beside him.

The petite figure pulsed a livid green, and he finally heard a voice. The sound reverberated in his head in the most peculiar fashion, almost to the point where he did not recognize it at first. He tore his attention away from the giant, to look at the outline of a gray form limned in flashing green light.

Darothien!

He pressed against the wall and struck it again. He tried to yell her name, but still there was no sound – merely the mute vibration of the impassable clear dome. The pair turned squarely away from him, and faced the cylinder at the edge of his clouded perception. It was then he noticed he could see the figures within all the remaining cylinders.

He could clearly see the old Lemming, standing naked inside his green cylinder. Beyond him, other creatures could be perceived, each more bizarre than the previous.

In a cylinder of ecru tinged with yellow along its edges, stood a reptilian creature. Its scaled skin, mostly beige with splashes of turquoise and fuchsia around its hands, feet, eyes and along the spines of its long horned tail, glistened as though it were moist. Rows of interlocking jagged teeth showed through its scaly lips, and its four-fingered hands ended in cruel talons. Like the Lemming in the neighboring cylinder, the bipedal reptile was naked and frozen in position. Pindlebryth tensed with a start as its two eyes, jutting prominently from its skull, swiveled in their sockets independently and focused on him. Pindlebryth shivered as he could sense an evil intelligence in those eyes. But the moment quickly passed, as the reptile turned his attention away from Pindlebryth and its eyes gimbaled back towards the pair emerging from the fog.

The third cylinder filled with orange light housed what Pindlebryth could only describe as a giant beetle. It had compound eyes, antennae, six limbs, three body segments – except for its size, all the recognizable parts of an insect anatomy. Its most remarkable features were the horns that extended above, below and to either side of its intimidating mandibles.

Beyond it was yet another cylinder filled with aquamarine, and it imprisoned a fish with arms ending in webbed hands. It was buoyed motionless in the cylinder – its arms, tail and dorsal fins never moving. Pindlebryth tried to discern whether the beast was looking at him or the approaching pair of figures, but its eyes were emotionless pools of flat blackness.

The last of the mist seemed to part, and Pindlebryth could finally clearly see Darothien facing the farthest cylinder – but that was not all. He was not abashed that Darothien also stood naked before him. As with his own condition, it somehow seemed proper. However, as he drank in the scene around Darothien and the giant, he also could unmistakably see the horror inside the last cylinder.

The creature in the bilious dark brown cylinder was an abomination. A heavily ridged barreled torso was supported by five thick tentacles. From the upper portion of the torso hung several rope-like appendages of various lengths. At the end of each of them was a different extremity – a blood-red sucker, a chitinous three-pincered claw, a slime-covered yellow-tinged sphere covered with purple spines like a sea urchin, and other organs that defied description. Vestigial leathern wings sprouted from its back. They were far too small to bear the seeming weight of the monster, but perhaps could function in a medium other than air. Upon the top of the torso, a neck with an array of gill slits on either side supported an appendage that could only loosely be called a head. It was a thick pulpy mass crowded over with swollen and squirming papillae. Along its circumference, the head extruded out into five tentacles, giving it the appearance of a distorted starfish. At the end of each protuberance was a three-lobed eye, each with a nictating membrane that would occasionally slide over the entire trifurcated globe. The eyes of three of those tentacles were fixed separately on Darothien, the giant standing in front of it and Pindlebryth.

The hungry intelligence that Pindlebryth had sensed in the reptile paled in comparison to the cold, calculating malevolence emanating in waves from this nightmare made flesh. Pindlebryth feared the hateful and utterly alien intellect from the very pit of his being.

The giant, standing to Darothien's side, had turned his head from Darothien to face the fiendish monstrosity. Pindlebryth spied the giant's profile immediately after he saw the monster. A flowing mane of hair framed its face, and was long enough to touch the top arches of folded feathered wings. Pindlebryth was initially baffled at the uniqueness of a creature that had both hair and wings. But his surprise quickly waned. Added to the panic he barely held at bay, caused by the loathsome freak in the cylinder, came an additional assault on his psyche.

The giant's face was simultaneously beautiful and terrifying to behold. It was filled with an inner light that Pindlebryth thought should burn his eyes, but instead he was held entranced. He lowered his paws from the glass dome, and wondered if he was in the presence of the Quickening Spirit. But he realized his fallacy quickly enough, once he recalled that he had seen this body, this face, this impossible combination of features before. The images of the faces on the scabbard of the Sword of Enorel, and the statuettes in DeepDigger's library all tumbled into his consciousness – this was an Angel.

And between those two diametrically opposed poles of frozen malevolence against unbearably brilliant wonder stood the calm, emotionless, naked Darothien.

As the insanity, the total and utter madness, of this nightmare washed over and threatened to smother him, he silently screamed. It wasn't a simple cry of one being frightened, but the long sustained primal venting of a mind unbalanced perilously at the edge of never-ending delirium. Pindlebryth ran out of breath, held his fevered temples against the crushing lunacy, and screamed again.

In the abyss of silence, Pindlebryth's mind raced out of control. Where was he? Why could he not reach Darothien's side? Who were these creatures, both mundane, fantastic, and horrific?

What made it all even more maddening for Pindlebryth, was that he felt with perfect assurance that he should know *why* this was all happening. But for the life of him, he could not recall what that reason was. His lucidity began to falter even further.

Until he again heard Darothien's voice.

The sound of her soothing and gentle voice brought him back to a semblance of sanity. It was an anchor of stability that he could desperately cling to, amidst the onslaught of mind-rending sights and the rage of hysteria rampaging in his spirit.

But he became confused as he realized that she was speaking in the sounds of magick he had heard her use several times before.

She spoke once again to the horror, as coolly as if she were speaking to one of the castle staff in Lenland. Though Pindlebryth could hear her with crystal clarity, he was transfixed in wonder as he realized her mouth never moved. Instead, the green aura about her pulsed with every syllable. Darothien spoke in green light for only a little more, but he could tell she had asked a question.

Then the thing in the cylinder replied. An aura about it pulsed in a sickly turbid brown, and its voice echoed in Pindlebryth's head. It sounded like flesh rending, like slabs of blood-drenched meat flapping together obscenely as if it were unaccustomed to the task of speech. But its words, as stilted and erratic as they were, he did understand.

"This world was ours. You will all die when we take it back."

In a flash of white brilliance that still did not burn his eyes, Pindlebryth heard the Angel reply.

"Your time is long past, and will not come again. Another Change is coming soon, but your kind will have no part in it."

With the sound akin to a chorus of horn blasts and cymbals shattering, the Angel's voice reverberated in Pindlebryth's mind like an explosion. For the Angel's voice not only assaulted his consciousness with a volume sufficient to tear walls asunder, but it crashed upon him simultaneously in every language he knew. His thoughts crumpled like paper, and his temples and ears felt like they were being crushed by the pressure of an underwater abyss. He turned his head in a feeble attempt to lessen the pain. He saw that Voyager had retreated a few paces behind him, and was flailing flat-stomached on the ground. His wings flapped spasmodically, like a mother fowl drawing a predator away from her chicks. Voyager must have shared in Pindlebryth's agony, as he futilely tried to hide his head under a wing to avoid the Angel's voice.

Pindlebryth's head swam in a pool of pain inflamed by a

myriad of unfocused sensations.   Time broke down as Pindlebryth fell into a cynosure of chaos.   He again heard Darothien speak, and still new voices converse with her.   He attempted raising his head, but could only do so barely.   He tried vainly to focus on the speech that swam around him in a whirlpool of dizzying fury.   Oscillating lights of green, aquamarine, orange, brown and yellow refused to come into focus for him, adding a spinning vertigo to his distraction.   He could sense that Darothien had spoken to the denizens of the other cylinders, but he could still not understand the arcane tongue that Darothien used.   And even though he recognized that the other voices of strange and varying pitches and textures responded in Lemming, he simply could not wrap his mind around the words, nor their meaning.   His mind was so numbed and reeling from the concussion of the Angel's voice, that all the others' words seemed disjointed and nonsensical, like the jumbled pieces of unrelated jigsaw puzzles.   For what seemed like hours on end, he squeezed his eyes shut and reflexively held his hands over his ears, though it did little to stem the cacophonous flood.

At last came blessed silence.

Tentatively he opened his eyes and released his ears, fearing the onslaught might resume at any second.   After a moment, he relaxed ever so slightly, and assessed his position.   He had curled into a fetal ball on the ground.   Laying next to him was Voyager, quaking in fear with his head still tucked under his wing.   When Pindlebryth scratched together the will to look inside the dome again, he saw Darothien standing over him with a most disturbing expression.   It was as if she was attempting to show him a beatific smile of sorrow, compassion, and hope, but that such concepts were alien to her.   Instead of the green aura with which she was limned before, she instead was surrounded by nimbus of white around her.   She knelt down and extended her hand to help.

Pindlebryth reached for her hand, but flinched at the point he expected to touch the dome.   He wasn't fully sure whether he was more afraid of finding his way to Darothien still barred, or what he beheld was mere apparition.

But the barrier was gone.   He gently grasped her paw, and was grateful for simply being able to touch her.   He slowly struggled to his feet as she steadied him.   As he rose, he blinked and leaned away from her when he discovered that the nimbus was not hers. Rather, it was due to her standing between him and the Angel. He diverted his eyes from the Angel's blazing argent, and looked into Darothien's green eyes with a look of gratitude, mixed with a thousand questions.

As if she knew what he thought, she nodded with a curious smile, and led him hand in hand past the vacant cylinder to the occupied green cylinder. Pindlebryth walked unevenly, like a newborn taking his first steps. He shielded his view of the Angel with one paw as they slowly walked – his newly regained grasp on reason in such a place as this was so tenuous, he knew he could not bear to look directly at the Angel. With Darothien's support and patience, they soon found themselves facing the green cylinder and the prisoner within it.

The old Lemming stood crooked and bent over, with a beard that hung down to his chest, and gnarled hands that looked like a laborer's hands. His eyes belied immense weariness, although a glint of awareness could still be found within them.

"Greetings, Grandfather Lemming," pulsed Darothien.

The graybeard's eyes, wavered slowly upward, then focused on Darothien.

"My child, what hast thou wrought?" The green light in the cylinder flickered wanly as he spoke with a thought.

Pindlebryth took some comfort at hearing the language of his home spoken plainly, rather than imitated or approximated by hissing, buzzing or something more obscene. The reassuring sound helped him gain a firmer grasp of himself.

"You have found the Orb. And you have used the Power of Unmaking," the old fossil blinked accusingly.

"Yes," Darothien replied simply. Pindlebryth tried to assert himself and proffer a defense for Darothien – that the action was taken to save their lives. However, he was once again thwarted by the blanketing silence. He tried to imitate the thought-speak he observed Darothien and the others do, but this effort was fruitless as well. Impotent, all he could do was stand by and observe.

"You have sealed your fate, my poor child. Like all of us, you will become a prisoner of the Orb."

Darothien scarcely could bring herself to the conclusion staring her in the face. "Henejer?"

Pindlebryth stared at the old Lemming in disbelief. He turned his head and narrowed his eyes to examine him. There indeed was a resemblance, but all the drawings and portraits of Henejer that Pindlebryth had seen were of a younger more vibrant person.

"I was once known by that Name of Power," he replied wistfully. "But no longer. The Orb has given me a new Name, but it is not for your ears."

Darothien paused, weighing her next question, and fearing what the answer might be. "How is it that you are here with these other... creatures?"

"In each Age, we here all employed the Orb for our own purposes. Some were noble in their intention, others were base and selfish, and some were borne out of madness. But none of us here used the Orb for its true purpose – to bring about The Change."

Pindlebryth desperately wanted to ask a question. He squeezed Darothien's hand, and turned to face her. He used his paws to gently coax her hand into a fist. He then slightly curled his other hand, and waved it back and forth slowly over her fist, then rested his paw and spread his fingers to cover hers. There was a spark of comprehension in Darothien's eyes, and she nodded at Pindlebryth.

"Where is Gazelikus?" she asked Henejer. "Did he not also use the Orb of Oblivion?"

"The Orb of Oblivion is strict. It is the Power of Unmaking that is a trap. I kept that cursed power hidden from Gazelikus.

"Consider the Power of Unmaking as a transgression against the Quickening Spirit if you so desire – such as we were never meant to Unmake so frivolously what He created. Or instead consider it a fitting irony, that we who used the Power of Unmaking unwisely, have ourselves been removed from the world.

"Each of my predecessors here have remained trapped after someone of their own Age used the Orb and the other four Artifacts of Old to effect The Change. Races, lands and oceans – the entire world – were unmade, made and sometimes remade, and so began a new Age. At least until the next great Change after that. And so we are doomed to remain here until the Final Change.

"And when your time comes, my child, you also must rejoin us here. You shall remain with us until the end of the Final Age, and share with us whatever destiny awaits us beyond that."

Darothien squeezed Pindlebryth's paw. He felt her tremble,

and saw her mouth agape with fear at her portended fate. She measured her words, knowing her very being was at stake. Henejer must have been here for hundreds of years. And there was no telling how long the other creatures had already remained here, trapped in their prisons.

"Is there no help for me? Is there no way to escape this doom?"

Henejer's eyes regarded the Angel for a time, then returned to Darothien. "We may not answer."

All the creatures joined in, and in a babel of buzzing, hissing, and humming, they echoed, "We may not answer."

Pindlebryth immediately knew that their reply was hiding something. He looked towards Darothien in an attempt to try to communicate this to her. He badly wanted to let her know of their obfuscation, and somehow help her ask the right next question. But she had already turned to face the Angel. Pindlebryth slowly followed her example, wincing instinctively at anticipated pain. Once again, they beheld this indescribably beautiful and dreadful creature, as he raised his hand in salutation to Darothien.

"The Change is coming soon. May you fare well."

Pindlebryth doubled over with skull-crushing pain at the sound of the Angel's voice. The Angel swept his hand to his side, and Pindlebryth thought he heard Darothien scream.

Pindlebryth sat bolt upright in his bed. His bedsheets and the ends of his sleeves were damp from sweat around his four paw pads. He instinctively reached for his temples with the fresh memory of the Angel's thundering voice, but the pain so calamitous a moment before was gone. In its place was a dull throbbing in his ribs, where he had been wounded at the Valley of Giants. He tried to focus his sight and assure himself he actually was in his room.

The door to his bedroom burst open, and a Royal Guard poised for action entered. His hand was on the hilt of his sword still in its scabbard as he scanned the room for threats. With none found, he sped to Pindlebryth's bedside.

"M'Lord, are you all right? We heard you cry out."

Pindlebryth snapped to full awareness, and scowled at the guard. He tossed his bedding aside, and leapt out of bed. He swept up his dressing robe draped over the chair next to the door, and charged out without a word. Donning his robe as he went, he dashed past a second guard in the outer rooms of his apartment, who stood with a look of alarm changing to confusion. Pindlebryth ran pell-mell down the hallway, ignoring calls and questions from his room as they faded away, and scrambled down the stairs into the East Wing. Racing down the hall, he reached his single-minded destination.

He banged on the door, and tried the handle. It was unyielding, and the door would not open. He tried the door a second time with both hands and called her name loudly, but no answer came. One of the guards came rushing down the corridor, following belatedly after him. With fevered panic, he rammed the door, and forced it open with his shoulder. His chest felt like it was being pierced again. Regaining his balance inside the main room of Darothien's apartment, he started to close the door. "Wait outside!" he commanded the guard, as he strained to fit the door back into its frame.

His eyes quickly adjusted to the diminishing darkness, until the front room's globed lights slowly increased in brightness after he entered. A column of their light spilled into the apartment's bedroom through its open door. Though his heart pounded in his own ears, he could still hear sobbing coming from the bedroom.

A handful of fears flashed in his mind as to what he might find, but he had to see her and to know she was all right. He flew to the doorway, and paused leaning with both arms holding either side of the threshold, heaving for breath as he scanned the room. Blankets and a quilt were thrown off the bed in all directions, and torn sheets lay crumpled in a pile at the footboard.

"Darothien!" he shouted as he darted to the figure sitting on the floor along the side of the bed.

Dressed in a nightgown, she sat curled up with her back to the bedside. With her arms folded around her knees, she rocked back and forth. She looked vacantly over her knees and interlocked arms as she mumbled softly, broken only by intermittent sobs and whimpers.

Pindlebryth knelt beside her, put his arms around her and drew her close to himself. Her pressure changed the pain in his chest from a dull throb to a sharp sting, but it almost felt sweet.

"Darothien," he echoed softly with concern, but she showed no response, no recognition that he was even there. "Darothien! Are you all right?" To his surprise he found he was weeping.

Darothien kept her head down, and her entire body shivered. "I saw them. I heard them. Wanted to run. Scream. He wouldn't let me. The Orb. It has me. Forever. Henejer said so. Can't run. Can't cry. Stay with them. Stay in the Orb. Forever... forever..."

Pindlebryth repeated her name again, gently shaking her. "It's me, Pindlebryth! Come back to me, Darothien."

"Pindlebryth?" her voice cracked, as she stopped rocking, but continued to blindly stare into nothingness. "What have I done? Quickening Spirit, what have I *done?*" She raised her head, and looked plaintively at Pindlebryth. Her tears darkened the fur at the corners of her eyes and where they coursed down the side of her muzzle. Her mouth opened, closed, and opened again. "I... I did it to save you!"

"You saved the *world*," said Pindlebryth painfully.

"Am to be damned for all eternity for it?" She sobbed, then placed her head on her knees again and wept. Pindlebryth was filled with empathy that words could not describe. All he could do was hold her.

She released her knees and reached for Pindlebryth. For a time, they both cried in each other's arms. Pindlebryth shivered at his own memories of the dome, filled with creatures that could drive the strongest of minds mad.

"There were so many things in that vision that confounded me. At first I thought it was just a dream, until the pain. The voice of the Angel drove Voyager and me to our limits. The sights of those creatures nearly drove me to madness. Yet you were as serene as a quiet lake. How could you endure such things?"

Darothien's face went blank, an unemotional mask. "I don't know. The very core of me quelled at those unimaginable sights and sounds. But I felt like that part of me was suppressed, somehow imprisoned just as those creatures in their cylinders." Her back stiffened then shivered violently as she imagined herself in the empty cylinder. "It wasn't until the Angel dismissed us, that all my fear, loathing and panic were released." She clasped her arms around her knees afresh, squeezed her shoulders together, and rolled herself back into a ball at the memory.

"I am lost!" she whimpered in abject surrender.

Then Pindlebryth recalled his flash of intuition before the Angel had dismissed them. He knew, for both their sakes, he could not let her fall in a pit of despair again. He knew he had to do something, anything, to rekindle hope in her – and himself. Pindlebryth stood up, prying Darothien's paw from her knee. She looked up at him with expectant eyes, dark and wet. He raised her arm gently, and helped her up as she falteringly stood.

"Perhaps not. I tried to tell you something inside the dome, but I could not speak.

"There may be a way to get the Orb to release you."

"But how?   Do you remember where the Orb is?" Darothien's eyes flitted back and forth madly as she searched her memory. "I can't! I remember leaving Selephygur and the others, and we flew... north? Or was is south? I... can't! Oh, I am lost!" She began to tremble with fear and panic once more.

Pindlebryth held Darothien firmly by the shoulders and forced her to look at him. "Darothien! I... I cannot remember either. But you are *not* lost!" The itch shouted at him telling him what he said was so, telling him he was right.

"Let's get some air while we reason this out. There is a way – I *know* it!"

Darothien struggled to regain her composure, but still occasionally coughed a sob and sniffled back tears. He led her out of her bedroom slowly, then across the main room to the balcony. He opened both sides of the drapes, and the sheer curtains behind them, then opened the balcony doors. Cold fresh air cascaded in around their bare feet, as they felt the room's warmer air billow out around their heads. They stepped out onto the balcony, and took in deep calming breaths. The crisp winter air quickly cleared their heads. The darkness of the moonless night was marginally held at bay by a smattering of stars, two lamps at the West Gate, and the stray glow of CityState washing over the castle's roofs. They embraced, the simple act of holding each other being sufficient to give solace, and ward off the bitter solitude they both had tasted in the Orb. Darothien gradually stopped her sobbing, and despite the cold ceased her trembling. She buried herself in Pindlebryth's fur, losing herself in the safety of his scent.

The notion of them reasoning out the enigma of the Orb was nearly forgotten, until the echo of a loud crash followed by a great commotion came from the direction of the West Gate. An animal's cry and several indistinct voices sounded and echoed from beyond the outer barracks. A crash of wood, then a clattering of metal tools rang out, and a gray shape rose over the wall to the right of the West Gate.

The two stepped back towards the door, as the shadowy form flew towards them. It darted directly to the balcony and hovered above the balustrade. Pindlebryth and Darothien took another step back into the apartment until it perched on the railing, holding its wings moderately outstretched while it found its balance. The light from Darothien's rooms cast a warm glow onto the agitated and shrilly keening bird.

"Voyager!" Darothien exclaimed.

"Daro! Dot!" he screeched, as he folded his wings. "Dot aw rite!"

Pindlebryth was flabbergasted – Voyager was trying say Darothien's name! "Voyager... you can... *speak*?"

The pair approached the steed. Pindlebryth reached out to him, but instead of his usual greeting, Voyager turned away and tried to nuzzle his head under Darothien's arm.

At first, she was taken aback, but Pindlebryth assured her, "Do not be afraid. This is his way to express affection. He's greeted me thusly often... until now." Though Pindlebryth was awash in astonishment, he found it now was also tinged with disappointment. He easily put down such thoughts – he knew he should not be jealous about Voyager's attentions, but should instead be glad for Darothien having another protector.

The guards of the West Gate opened their doors, allowing a pair of stable hands to enter the courtyard. They rushed over to the East Wing until they were directly in front of Darothien's balcony. They whistled and called Voyager by name, but the snow petrel ignored them. Voyager continued to coo and nuzzle adoringly under Darothien's touch.

"Never in all my days," Pindlebryth mused absently. "It seems that you have won a new friend's loyalty. I guess he, too, was concerned about you." Darothien watched a wrinkle of a grin grow on Pindlebryth. It swelled to an earnest smile as he shook his head in wonder, and paused to assemble his thoughts. "And he can speak! How is this possible?"

The specter of unreasoning panic and desolate solitude forestalled, Darothien was able to turn the question over in her mind.

"You once said the Angels conferred the gift of language to the Five Races. Voyager may have also gained this boon, when the Angel of the Orb spoke to us."

"Yes, he did hear the voice of the Angel. It was as fearful to him as it was painful for me." Pindlebryth instantly knew it was necessary to immediately test Darothien's conjecture.

"Voyager?" The bird continued to nestle its head under Darothien's arm. Pindlebryth repeated his name with a more commanding tone.

"Voyager!" The petrel withdrew its head, and raised it to look at Pindlebryth.

"Do you understand me?" The bird nodded in agreement. Pindlebryth twitched with excitement.

"Say 'yes' if you understand me."

"Yaa!" Voyager keened.

"Astounding," Pindlebryth whispered to himself. "Voyager, can you say 'no'?"

"N-n-naa!" came the reply.

"Why did you leave the stables?"

"Hep." Voyager stretched his wings, then folded them back again. "Hep Dot."

"Help... *me*?" Darothien asked, becoming almost as excited as Pindlebryth.

"Yaa!"

"Incredible," whispered Darothien. "He *does* understand us!"

Pindlebryth was almost giddy with the possibilities. But before he could give voice to them, let alone sort out his rushing thoughts, the stable hands below interrupted. They cried up to the balcony, their voices loud enough to be heard, yet tempered so that they didn't rouse the entire castle.

"Are you all right, M'Lord?" said one of them, his arms waving frantically.

"Forgive the interruption, M'Lord! Voyager somehow undid his stable door. He's been carrying on like this for a while – crying, squeaking and squawking enough to wake all of CityState!"

"Squawking?" Pindlebryth mumbled to himself, his eyebrows angled severely in thought. He turned to Darothien, unsure of the thought that just occurred to him.

"They don't understand him," he said slowly, becoming more skeptical of his conclusion as he spoke it. "...do they?" he added, wondering if his sanity might be slipping again.

"There's one way to find out," Darothien replied. She turned to the stable hands, and called down only loud enough for them to hear. "What will you do with him?" she asked, as she patted Voyager's neck and head, gently coaxing his attention towards the stable hands below.

"Um, put him in a fresh stable, m'lady?" hesitated the first stable hand.

Darothien guided Voyager's head back to her gaze. "Voyager," she began sweetly, "did you hear those Lemmings down there?"

"Yaa!" Voyager peeped.

"Did you understand them?" she probed, tilting her head.

"N-n-naa!" the petrel shook his head.

"I think you're right, Pindlebryth," she agreed as she released Voyager and stepped back. "He understands us, but not them. We must have shared something in the Orb, made some connection, or perhaps it was the Angel's doing. Who can tell?" she shrugged her shoulders in bewilderment.

"But he never used the Orb," Pindlebryth mused as he also took a step back, looking at Voyager inquiringly. He scratched his chin as he pondered for a moment. "He couldn't have. I do remember putting the Orb in a satchel, around his pommel. So he was, however, in proximity of the Orb for a while."

"At least as long as it took for us to reach our destination – wherever that was," Darothien concurred.

Then Pindlebryth saw it – the possible solution that his itch was trying to tell him about. "If he didn't use the Orb, maybe he isn't subject to its effects!" He stepped back towards Voyager, and petted him as calmly as he could, which was quite difficult considering the nervous energy his inspiration imparted to him.

"Now, Voyager, this question is very important. Do you remember where we hid the Orb? Where we hid the gray ball?" Pindlebryth asked soothingly, though a slight tremble of anticipation leaked through.

"Yaa!" Voyager bobbed his head in agreement.

"He does? You do?" blurted Darothien. "Where, Voyager? Whe..."

"No!" commanded Pindlebryth loudly, his hand flashing out to stop her. He looked at her sternly, his eyes reaffirming his order. But his face softened quickly, as he turned back to Voyager.

"No, Voyager, no. Do *not* tell us where the Orb is. Do not! Not yet." He held up a single finger to focus Voyager's attention. "Do not! Not yet."

Voyager looked sullen, like a pet being punished.

"Now, now," Pindlebryth murmured as he first patted Voyager's neck, then hugged it fondly. "You've done well, Voyager. Now, please, go back to your home with your friends, the stable hands. Darothien and I will be all right," said Pindlebryth in a singsong fashion, pointing to the Lemmings below. When the stable hands saw that Pindlebryth gave leave to Voyager, they resumed calling and whistling in a vain attempt to get Voyager's attention.

Voyager looked at Darothien, who also reached out to stroke his neck. "It's all right," she said softly. "I'm glad you came to help."

Voyager dove off the railing to the courtyard below, keening several farewells as he banked and circled once around the two waiting stable hands. Pindlebryth and Darothien both leaned against the balcony railing as he landed between the two of them chirping a simple "Hello! Hello!"

Pindlebryth and Darothien looked at each other with amused wonder and shared a nervous giggle between themselves. They both still could not quite believe their ears nor their eyes, as they observed the stable hands tending to Voyager none the wiser.

Pindlebryth called down to them. "He'll follow you back now. Give him extra food tonight – he's earned it!" They gingerly slipped a bridle over Voyager's head, then bowed to Pindlebryth before leading Voyager back to the stables.

Pindlebryth smiled to himself, his intuitive perception was quiet again, letting him know he had the answer.

Pindlebryth placed his arm around Darothien's waist, and led her inside. Pindlebryth shut the balcony doors, as Darothien dreamily meandered into the room. After he also drew the heavy drapes closed, he turned to face her.

Muted globe light shown through her nightgown, revealing her silhouette. Pindlebryth caught himself, and wondered how such a sight would excite him now, especially after seeing Darothien's naked form in the Orb drew no response. But that momentary carnal flush paled in comparison to the thrill of what Voyager just confirmed. He could barely contain his elation as Darothien returned to the middle of the room with him.

"So, what are we to do about the Orb?" Darothien began.

Pindlebryth took up her paws in his. "Did you notice what Voyager said? What language he spoke in?"

"Why, Lemming of course," she replied, tilting her head with a questioning look.

"Yes. Just like all the other creatures trapped by the Orb. How would those creatures know a language that didn't exist in their own Age? Also, why was there only one Angel? We know there were five, one for each of the Artifacts. I believe the answer is this – the Angel we were with was the one that gave the Lemmings the Orb, gave us the Gift of dreaming the Names of Power, and the Gift of Lemming language."

"And?" Darothien followed slowly.

"For reasons I'm not sure we fully understand, Voyager shared our dream – if a dream was all it was... And now he can understand us. Furthermore, only we two understand his speech. No one else does!"

"I'm not sure I see where you're going with this." A look of lost confusion grew within Darothien. Pindlebryth could sense her climbing panic, the doom Henejer pronounced over her beginning to take root again. But his earnest, guileless smile of hope kept her focused on him.

Pindlebryth guided his love to the wide divan against the wall across from the doors, and they both sat.

"Here's the last part of the puzzle. Voyager can remember where the Orb is. If our failing memory can be trusted, he never touched the Orb! He is therefore not subject to its desire to be left alone and forgotten. That is why he could not join us next to the Angel.

"So, even if we cannot remember where we hid the Orb away from the world, Voyager can still take us there. But this is the most important part – only we know he can do this!"

Darothien swayed forward and back in her seat, her lips pursed as she tried to understand.

"Don't you see? No one will know to ask Voyager to take them to the Orb. No one but *us*!"

"But hiding the Orb is what we wanted to do – what we *had* to do, to keep the world safe. Now you *want* to find the Orb again?" Darothien began to get restless and more perplexed. Worse than that, a new fear dawned on her as she suspected what Pindlebryth was proposing.

"To save you from Henejer's fate – Yes! Only we will know where to find the Orb. With no written record or clues, neither Crow, Fox, Iron Baron, nor anyone else will know where to search for the Orb. And no one would ever think to talk to a petrel! And even if someone else were insane enough to talk to Voyager," he said with a wink, "he couldn't understand them anyway!"

"But why do this? Do you believe I can avoid Henejer's prediction, if I use the Orb again?" Her brows furrowed as she tried to prove to herself this was indeed the solution to her enigma.

"Yes! Don't you recall? Henejer and the other creatures all said that they '*may* not answer.' That implied there was an escape for you, but the Angel did not allow them to tell us."

Darothien's hope was quenched with doubt, as her new fear was proven correct. "Oh, no. No, no, no! You surely can't mean you *want* me to bring about The Change?"

Pindlebryth held her hand over his heart. "Yes! It is the only way I can see for you to escape the Orb. Think of what Henejer told us!" Pindlebryth surged with hope. "Someone other than themselves effected The Change in their Age. Whoever did, would *have* to use the Power of Unmaking to do so. Yet the ones who made The Change escaped the fate of the creatures in the cylinders!

"If you bring about The Change the Angel spoke of, you are free of the Angel's Doom."

Darothien's gaze unfocused as she realized the truth of what he said. She began to cry again, both at the possibility of reprieve from an ineffably terrible fate and the gaping unknown of whatever blessing or damnation would take its place.

"Do you realize what you ask of me?" Darothien pleaded.

Pindlebryth bowed his head for a moment, then gazed into Darothien's deep green eyes. A hundred of his voices rang in his head, the most undeniable one shouting, "She is the one! I would sacrifice the world and myself in it to keep her safe from an eternity of solitude." One by one, he willed all his other voices silent, and resolutely agreed with what the last voice told him.

"The ancient writings tell us The Change need not be a bane – they also promise The Change may be 'an extraordinary boon.' Whatever world you would make in The Change, I am sure it would be beautiful and filled with hope.

"And I would be happy to spend the rest of my days in it, as long as I am with you."

Darothien's heart welled up with a confluence of relief and hope, mixed with the startled exhilaration of what Pindlebryth was finally saying to her. A part of herself that she had long consigned to be silent and alone was transformed to overflowing euphoria.

Pindlebryth leaned closer and rested his head on her shoulder. "Be with me always."

"I will," Darothien replied breathlessly. She pressed against him more firmly, and responded in kind. "Be with me always."

"I will."

They caressed each other's muzzle, face then shoulders. Slowly and delicately they folded back each other's bedclothes, to hold each other closer and know each other's touch and scent. They lay back and took comfort in each other as only two could, sharing in the oldest magic of all.

To be continued in –

Pindlebryth of Lenland - The Race to Change

ABOUT THE AUTHOR

Christopher D. Ochs has far too many interests for his own damn good. Starting out with degrees in physics and math from Moravian College, of course it was only logical that he should pursue careers in computer engineering, integrated circuit design, electrical engineering and software QA at Bell Laboratories and Lattice Semiconductors. Among his current interests are the *grande orgue*, anime, computer animation, an eclectic appreciation of music, music composition, broadcast radio, storytelling... and recently rediscovered, writing.

www.anigrafx.com

www.otakon.com
www.muhlenberg.edu/wmuh   www.wdiy.org
www.lvstorytellers.org
www.greaterlehighvalleywritersgroup.wildapricot.org

Made in the USA
San Bernardino, CA
17 August 2014